RIDMON

RIDMON

LES STONE

PARTRIDGE

ISBN:	Hardcover	978-1-5437-5247-2
	Softcover	978-1-5437-5245-8
	eBook	978-1-5437-5246-5

Scripture quotations marked KJV are from the Holy Bible, King James Version (Authorized Version). First published in 1611. Quoted from the KJV Classic Reference Bible, Copyright © 1983 by The Zondervan Corporation.

Print information available on the last page.

To order additional copies of this book, contact
Toll Free 800 101 2657 (Singapore)
Toll Free 1 800 81 7340 (Malaysia)
orders.singapore@partridgepublishing.com

www.partridgepublishing.com/singapore

This book is dedicated to the men and woman of the former Rhodesia, both black and white, whose efforts to stave off political injustices, cost many their lives, their homes, hopes and aspirations.

———————————————————————————————

CONTENTS

INTRODUCTION

05.00 hrs. Sunrise. Tractors cranked into life and drivers began to worm their way to the fields, hauling farm labourers on flat-bed trailers to the work place for another day of stifling heat beneath acres of plastic hothouses in which various types of vegetable crops were cultivated.

Mike walked out of the west gate, away from the Moshav Naraf, an Israeli farm community, into the surrounding Arava desert. He needed to walk the silent paths, out there where the empty stillness, devoid of people and aggravation, brought peace of mind. For the past 5 years his stay in Israel could not be reconciled with any inner balance. Nor could he accustom himself to the dog eat dog mentality of modern man. Six months of unemployment did not help matters either. The frustrating unemployment lines merely brought about the expected responses to his unsuccessful applications. Angered by the situation, Mike ceased making the weekly bus trips to Eilat, the seaside city on the Gulf of Aqaba. Subsequently any financial support to be had was duly terminated. To add fuel to the fire, his ability to read or write Hebrew left much to be desired, which consequently acted as a catalyst for unscrupulous persons to prey upon his disadvantaged situation. He prided himself in being a man of ethical moral fibre, a man who had achieved a mature level of self-understanding. Achievement in his eyes was measured neither by one's bank balance, nor the ability of confidence tricksters to feather their pockets, but by the goodness of the individual self.

Once the Moshav was out of sight, he felt more at ease alone in the desert. His senses sharpened, closing his mind to the cares of the world. Living in over- populated areas tended to numb the mind to all that is natural and it was at times like these that those senses could be re-tuned. One might consider him as above average and fiercely individual. Brought up as a child during the 1960's and 70's at a time of Africa's most violent political changes, he had fought in its bush wars, witnessing tribal bloodshed, where innocents were brutally butchered in the name of political change. Mike survived those experiences relatively well, yet they left deep, lasting impressions, some that he could not readily shake off. Trained well by the Ian Smith regime in martial arts and guerrilla warfare, Mike was in all respects a very capable combatant, yet presently a very listless civilian.

Pausing from time to time to admire desert plants or interesting rock geometrics, his wandering led him down a twisting, sweltering Wadi, one of the countless ravines or dry river beds that are a feature of the Arava desert. He had learned not to drink much during the heat of the day, a by-product from past experiences. There was nothing overly dramatic about the man. Not the Rambo type most movie hero's depicted, just an ordinary man who, through exposure to unusual circumstances, developed unusual talents. Yet, in

Israel he was unbalanced and lethargic. These were annoying times filled with self-doubt and apathy. In the desert, alone with the silence, his senses came together. Here nature and man could be one. Out in the desert he was free from smothering man-made restrictions.

Deciding to cut across a jagged rocky incline, he made his way down to a fawn coloured sheer walled limestone gully, its sides extending well over thirty metres above his head. The moment he reached its sandy base his senses reeled. Something was disturbing the harmony, made the air static. He trained his eyes from right to left in an arc, taking in everything, until his brain triggered a warning. There it was, a large opening suspended inches off the ground, its edges alive with minute static electrical charges through which he could see into another world, another time and place. His mind raced, weighed and measured, analysed and formulated, then without hesitation, Mike sprang through the hole, a taut, fighting fury.

THE PORTAL

ONE

Mike's personal information specifications drafted as a missing person's report was passed around the community of the Arava desert in the hope that someone might have seen or heard something. No one had seen or heard anything. It read.

Identity Number:	4182 14 8 1949.
Name:	Michael Sinclair-Randall.
Date of Birth:	4 August 1949.
Place:	Kariba, Rhodesia.
Status:	Married.
Children:	None.
Last Known address:	Moshav Naraf, Arava desert, Israel.
Present Location:	Unknown.

Employment:	nemployed.
Citizen of Israel:	Yes.
Religion:	Non-Jew.
Criminal Record:	None.
Status: Missing:	Moshav Naraf, Arava area, Israel. No known explanation.
Action:	Investigate and report.........

"That's odd!"

"Yeah!" Agreed the American.

"According to these Israeli police reports the guy simply disappeared into thin air." Exclaimed a sweating, slightly overweight reporter, fanning his reddened face with a soggy handkerchief.

"What I can't figure is, how?"

"Abducted by aliens." Smirked the grey haired American, blue eyes twinkling, adding, "A chopper picked him up, that's the only explanation I can think of and one which makes the most sense."

"Perhaps you are right, but my gut feeling says something else happened out here, something really strange."

The reporter gazed off over the parched thirsty ground into the hot sweltering heat shimmering across the distance in waves. He thought to himself how odd that a man could just up and disappear as if into thin air. It didn't make sense. There had to be a logical answer to it all. The missing man's wife didn't act overly concerned and this made the reporter raise an eyebrow, sensing things were not good on the matrimonial front between the missing man and the spouse. There was nothing further to report. He could continue investigating the issue, but that would only bring him back to this point, nothing. So his article would be filed under the heading "Unsolved, no explanation."

Both men climbed into the air-conditioned interior of a metallic grey four-wheel drive vehicle and drove back to the Moshav in silence. Their departure didn't go unnoticed by a black crow perched high on a rock, watching with bored indifference. Once again the desert fell back into its usual silence. All was still, all waited for the cool night air to relieve the unrelenting heat of the day.

Far off, a Bedouin tracker sat beneath the shade of a thorny Acacia tree, brooding thoughtfully into the swirling smoke of his cigarette. Yes, he had followed those tracks and read the signs. He disclosed nothing to anyone what the signs conveyed to him. Why should he. They would have only laughed at him and called him a stupid old man. The truth was written in the sand. A man went missing, so Abu Ahmed followed the man's tracks with growing unease, their message rippling down every fibre of his body and vibrating through his sub-conscious. This was no ordinary situation. He had felt the unseen force like sharp needle jabs at the precise point where the footsteps had come to an abrupt end. There he squatted off to one side and lapsed into a very uneasy silence. He did not hear the questions the police fired at him, nor did he care. His job was done, now it remained their problem. Slowly in the stillness, as if an awakening lotus blossom was uncoiling her delicate petals, so the extent and depth of what he had sensed became apparent.

The stranger had simply walked through a doorway into another world. Impossible as it may seem, it had happened and there was no way he was going to even attempt to justify this revelation to anybody. He could still feel the electrifying impulses bouncing off the rocks, the Wadi walls, in the air. For the first time in his life all his senses accelerated to levels never before experienced and an adrenalin surge threatened to explode his pounding heart. In the Wadi was a doorway to another world, another dimension of time and place. The man he had tracked had found it, and had gone through.

In all his years he had never known such clarity, such sharpness of his abilities as tracker until that day. It had started like any other occasion, find what was left of any tracks, identify them as the party to be tracked, then begin to formulate a mental picture of the man you were following and read the signs. You estimated the time, the weight and speed the man was travelling. You built up a profile of the individual from which one could gauge the type of man, his strengths and his weaknesses. You could almost read his mind.

The man Ahmed was following walked with an easy gait, yet it was the footprints that fascinated him. The deliberate outward to inward roll of the step, the equal displacement of balance and weight. The intricate use of gravity on slopes. This man was an athlete and Ahmed sensed a danger, the kind of danger one encounters when tracking a leopard. But, something else pricked at his sub-conscious. Something indescribable. For the first time in a long while he felt alive. In that Wadi where the tracks ended Ahmed's senses took on a new significance and definition. The full extent impacted, leaving him weak and trembling. He could smell it, taste it, almost touch it and the realization frightened him. He wanted, more than anything, to go through the Portal.

That was three weeks ago. Ahmed, the Bedouin tracker, stood in the gully once again; he searched it from beginning to end, yet always coming back to the same spot, the same point where his senses danced. The same place where the stranger's track ended. He had been there going on four days, instinct telling him his wait would soon be over. Throughout the sixty-three years of his life, nothing was more compelling, more irresistible, than this journey into the unknown that he would without hesitation take. There were no answers or explanations. What he understood was that he could not turn his back on the very thing which heightened his nerve ends to such a pitch it was almost unbearable. The master tracker was tracking even if it meant into the unknown and he wasn't about to miss a chance of a lifetime. He would find his man. Slowly, methodically, he broke camp as the evening shadows were beginning to creep into the gully. Nature's beautiful array of colours were displayed as the setting sun reflected against baked rock faces in hues of deep reds and brick tints, streaked by black melting into yellow sandstone, creating shades and patterns too intricate to imagine. Almost imperceptibly the surrounding air became static and alive. The camel jerked its head nervously, frightened eyes focused. Ahmed's spine tingled, it was time. Mounted, he waited, speaking in low tones to calm the jumpy animal beneath him. Tense as a guitar string he sat with an AK-47 assault carbine at the ready. He was not taking any chances. It had been an extremely risky purchase, this instrument of war, for if he was apprehended with it in his possession it would have meant imprisonment for a long time. The risk was worth the taking considering the circumstances. Should he get the last minute jitters, he could always bury the offending object where it would not be found out somewhere in the desert.

Suddenly, off to his right, up against the rock face, the air became alive with flashing static bolts and sharp cracks as electrical charges bounced off each other. The camel became extremely agitated. Then, as if witnessing the birth of a beautiful Garden of Eden, the Portal door opened, throwing rainbows of light into the almost darkened gully. In dazed wonderment Ahmed watched this indescribable transfiguration of nature materialize. The gap through which he gaped in disbelief was awesome. The sheer beauty of what lay in front of him was beyond description. Without hesitation, the Bedouin tracker screamed, "God be praised", and drove his camel through the opening.

Moti Levi woke the following morning feeling very relaxed and energetic. There were three days left of a ten-day pass before his tour of duty in the army would continue for the remainder of the year. Working with his father on the Moshav as Labour Manager, a task he carried out with pride, occupied most of his spare time. One day the business and farm would be his. Today he decided to take another route on his daily cross- country run. He wanted to be ready, strong and fit. His dream to become a Commando in the Israeli Army was a reality. As usual his track gear consisted of heavy boots and weighted day pack. It was early, with the first streaks of daybreak heralding the new day. Birds sang and chirped. Tractors coughed into life. Moti ran out through the south gate and along the two-metre barbed wire fortified fencing surrounding the Moshav and down a pathway between jagged volcanic hills, then cut due west. The going was tough. Many rocks and boulders lay scattered about, with ground levels rising and falling unevenly. Good stuff to get the heart pumping and the body into shape. For an hour or so he ran down Wadi's until he reached a fork at a boulder-strewn cross section of hills, jagged and tortured as the moon's surface. Because today was his day off he could afford to run a longer distance. And so he chose a left split. The sun rose hot and sweltering and Moti was feeling great. Israeli Commandos were expected to cover large distances a day on foot. For two hours he ran, jumped and heaved his body over rock, crevice, rise and fall. The sun was merciless. It drained a man's energy and sucked at the very life blood of one's soul. So engrossed was he in maintaining his footing and regulating his breathing that he did not notice an opening in front of him until he ran straight through a Portal and plummeted into a river.

Inspector Ben-Moshe of the Special Investigations Unit, flew from Tel-Aviv to Moshav Naraf and stood in silent sullen contemplation, mentally cursing the stifling heat. A sequence of very unusual events had unfolded on the Moshav revealing disappearances of two people. His investigation opened with the arrest of a suspected Hamas terrorist in the town of Dimona. After hours of very persuasive interrogation, information was made available concerning the sale of an AK-47 to one Abu Ahmed, a police tracker. This information stirred up a hornet's nest. Immediate action was taken to apprehend the offending party, but when the Police arrived at the given address according to records, all they found was a very distraught elderly woman being comforted by neighbours. After much argument and threats a story unfolded. Police in Sapir confirmed reports of Ahmed's involvement in the missing person's search conducted a month prior in a Wadi five kilometres northwest of Moshav Naraf.

Family members confirmed Ahmed's strange behaviour after the incident which aroused suspicion. The brother finally volunteered information about Ahmed's last days with them and the prognosis offered was one that Inspector Shimon Abaksis could not accept. It just didn't make sense. Why would a respected tracker do such a crazy thing as acquire an AK-47 knowing full well the consequences? Why did he tell his brother he was going to the Wadi and not to expect his return? No, there must be a very good reason behind all this, and it seems to be connected with the Zimbabwean's disappearance. He decided to inform Inspector Ben-Moshe of Special Investigations without delay so as to organize an investigative team. A call came through from Moshav Naraf. Another missing person, this time a young eighteen year old Israeli Commando, who apparently disappeared at the exact place of the previous disappearances. There was something else. They had found the personal documents of one Abu Ahmed and according to trackers, both persons seemingly ran and rode into the side of the rock face and then vanished. Shimon would now have national support in this investigation.

"What do you make of this, Moshe?" Asked Shimon Abaksis.

"I really don't know. With all the forensics and tests performed here there are still no clues as to what occurred here. We must have overlooked something."

"How could we. Every inch of this ground for the surrounding half kilometre in all directions and nothing, absolute nothing. It's a mystery, a complete and utter mystery."

"The Prime Minister is not going to be happy with the report I deliver to the Knesset tomorrow." Remarked Ben-Moshe.

"I would not like to be in your shoes, that's for sure." Hesitated Shimon Abaksis.

"I spoke to Abu Ahmed's brother again this morning. He can offer no more information other than what we already know. We played those interview tapes over and over again, searching for clues and possibilities, but there are none. Abu Ahmed knew something for sure. What, exactly no one knows. Whatever it was it spooked the old man into doing something really drastic or foolish. Why deliberately leave his identity documents behind? It's almost as if he was marking the spot trying to tell us something. But what?"

"You knew him well, didn't you, Moshe?"

"Yes, that's what makes it so difficult to believe. What was the damn fool playing at anyway?" Exclaimed Moshe in disgusted anger. Night was beginning to close in at the mysterious Wadi and with it Military Troops took up positions. Everything was locked down tight and Inspector Ben-Moshe clambered aboard a helicopter which would ferry him to Jerusalem for the early morning Knesset session. As it lifted off the ground he felt a shiver down his spine and he thought to himself,

"Abu Ahmed, you bloody fool. You knew something. You just couldn't leave it alone, could you? What really pisses me off is that you didn't phone me. After all, we have been through much together, yet you couldn't trust me. Why?"

Through the tent flap into the dark pre-dawn gloom Shimon stirred. Sleep had not come. His mind had been over and over the facts of this strange case and still there was no explanation, no tangible evidence. Three men who bore no relationship to each other had simply disappeared in the exact same place, apparently by the exact same method. What had drawn these three men to this particular spot? On into the approaching dawn Shimon pondered. Today the files would be labelled "Case unsolved." It had been a very long two months this case, and Shimon was tired. Those two reporters, the American and the Englishman, were getting on his nerves. Whoever allowed them onto the site in the first place, needed their heads read. Gradually the first streaks of dawn broke over the horizon. Shimon rolled off his camp bed and walked out of the tent.

He died in excruciating agony. The life juices sucked out of him by black, hairy, spider-like tentacles which entrapped him. Shimon Abaksis saw the open Portal and the thing which reached out from it and had taken hold of his body. He saw also the horrified face of the English reporter standing beside three soldiers whose rifles were being brought to bear. Shimon screamed, and then felt the slap of 0.56 calibre bullets as they wrecked living tissue and bone. In the last throes of agony he saw the gap close and envelop him into a darkness of hell. With Shimon's scream echoing the horror he felt, the English reporter tried frantically to control his shaking hands. Just then the American came into his line of vision, his face an ashen mask of disbelief. The Israeli troop commander was barking instructions over a radio, while the fifteen soldiers making up his unit lay sprawled in all round defensive positions, rifles cocked and ready.

"It's impossible, what in the name of heaven was that thing?" Gasped the American.

"That." Stammered the Englishman. "Was our worst nightmare come true?"

Before either of them could gather their tattered senses together, the air became alive with humming rotor blades of a helicopter landing, then both reporters were roughly bundled into an awaiting jeep and driven off, racing across the bumpy ground to the Moshav, where they were ushered very unceremoniously into a room and told to wait. Their wait was short. Army officers came in and sat down at a table, opening writing pads and switching on tape recorders. The officer in charge asked.

"Tell me exactly, what you saw."

Neither of the reporters responded until the officer pointed to the American. Nodding, the American began to relate his account of the events which took place an hour earlier.

"I awoke around 04.45 hours and noticed that my colleague here was not in the tent. It made me curious, so I went looking for him. I found him sitting on a rock about two metres away. So I joined him. Just then something in the air went sort of static. We both looked around but at first saw nothing. It was only when Shimon Abaksis came out of his tent that we saw what looked like a door with live static electricity at its edges, out of which came hairy, spider-like tentacles."

"How long had you been sitting there before Moshe came out of his tent?" The question was asked.

"I don't know, but I guess about 10 minutes."

"Explain what you meant by static." Another question was fired.

"Everything became still and the air literally crackled and sparked where the damn opening appeared."

"Describe the hole to us." Came the next sharp command.

"From the angle we were sitting, all that we could see was a thin sparking line. Both of us jumped up and ran to the spot where we were able to see into the hole. Gentlemen, believe me, there is nothing like this on our planet. What we saw was another world and the creature in there was not from Earth."

"Draw a picture of it on the piece of paper in front of you."

Taking up the pencil the American began to sketch out what he had seen. In like manner the Englishman was prompted to do the same. When both men had completed their allotted tasks the papers were withdrawn and compared. They were identical.

"Now gentlemen, if you please, what happened next?"

This time the Englishman spoke up.

"When that thing grabbed Abaksis we could see its tentacles. They looked like the suckers of an octopus on the under sides. We could also see how Abaksis was being sucked dry. It was like watching a man become mummified before your very eyes. Completely drained dry. He never had a chance and we were in no position to help him. Neither for that matter were the three soldiers. They did what anybody would have done. They opened fire on full automatic at the thing."

"All three at once?"

"Yes."

"And the creature you saw, was it affected by the rifle fire?"

"No, not from what we were able to observe."

There were endless other questions, other answers. Both reporters were grilled for twelve tiring, exhausting hours, then flown to Tel-Aviv under the strictest security.

Back at the Wadi there was a hive of activity. The area was cordoned off within a radius of 5 kilometres. Scientists from all round Israel were being called in. The Portal became a curiosity. Though none could see it, they were aware of its existence and waited, hoping for a re-opening. What exactly they were waiting for none understood. However, what they feared most was if anything could pass through into the hole, probably sooner or later something was going to come out of it. They were taking no chances. The scientific world debated, theorized and speculated. National security sweated and grew impatient, religious groups campaigned more aggressively. Total censorship was imposed on information available to the press, yet the story leaked to every major newspaper and television station across the world. Moshav Naraf was suddenly thrown into the limelight. What was once a quiet farming community had become an attraction? The public's imagination ran wild and for a while life on the farm became extremely disrupted. Days passed into months and months into years. For the families of the three men who had disappeared, their lives changed drastically.

Abu Ahmed's wife died, Moti's family sold up their farm and relocated to the Galilee area and Mike's wife went to live with relatives in America. Soon the incident at Moshav Naraf became a memory. It was now the year 2012. Earth was well on its way into the 21st Century.

Many years later, an ageing English reporter sat quietly on the porch of his Australian home in Perth where he had retired. On his lap lay a communiqué from his old friend and colleague the American. The note simply read.

> Paul Old Buddy,
>
> I fear I have been discovered, so the game is up and therefore we must get the children to the arranged place. I need not remind you of the stakes involved and what must be acted upon in the strictest of secrecy. I expect you will not be hearing from me again, so I will say goodbye. Our little escapade at Moshav Naraf has turned out to be a nightmare, but also offered us an opportunity. As previously agreed, the network has been set up and awaits activation. Timing is of the utmost importance now. I know it is not much to go on and the likelihood of any duplication of events remain very slim. We both know the risks, but also the rewards. You do not have much time, so I suggest operation Cheroma Kadoma be acted upon immediately.
>
> Your friend,
> Hank.

The phone rang breaking the silence and Paul's train of thought with a jolt. Paul stretched out and picked up the receiver. It was a long distance return call from the States. A female voice told him,

"No, Hank was not available. He had been rushed to the hospital in a critical condition. Apparent suicide attempt."

The alarms bells rang in Paul's head. He replaced the receiver, gathered the papers scattered around him, checked the time and drove to his son's home. Hank commit suicide? No ways would he do that? Someone else had come into the picture with sinister clarity. This meant the game was definitely up. Instinctively he knew his time was equally limited. Questions raced through his head as he parked his car. Paul's son, an adventurer and freelance photographer for National Geographic, greeted his father at the doorway and immediately sensed the urgency.

"What's up, Dad?" Smiled David.

"We've got trouble, son, big trouble." Paul responded.

Both men eyed each other and David could see agitation written all over his father's features. He indicated and both men made their way through the interior of the house to the kitchen.

"Remember the Portal episode?" Asked Paul.

David nodded his head and became very attentive.

"Well, Hank wrote me, enclosing some highly confidential documentation. He has come up with some startling revelations and facts that we need to act upon without delay, but there is a problem. Someone else is in the game and Hank now lies in hospital after a so-called suicide attempt. I know Hank, he would never do that. I made a follow up phone call to the States to Hank's sister to verify the situation. She confirmed her brother's plight and agreed, Hank would never try suicide and so there is something more sinister going on. We have a situation now and one which spells major trouble. I need you with me on this one David, it is important."

"Can't you let the police handle this? You're too old to be playing the hero." Inquired the son.

"No." Came the angry response.

"Well then please enlighten me." Quipped David.

Paul took hold of his son's athletic shoulders and with a level of gravity in his voice said.

"My son, you are young and full of bull, sure you made a name for yourself, but now your whole damn future is at stake. Hank worked for the Mossad, the Israeli Intelligence service, and the information in this envelop he sent to me is classified as Top Secret. He must have stolen it. Believe me, they will leave no stone unturned to find this information and take down whoever gets in their way. This means you as well, so cut the bullshit and listen to what I have to say."

Sitting with mind racing, he listened as his Father revealed facts about himself and Hank. The more he heard the more it sounded like something out of a science fiction novel.

"We were reporters to begin with, Hank and I. After the Portal story we were sworn to secrecy. For a short while we went about our business, each in our own way, until the day the full account of the happenings at Moshav Naraf were made public. We did not have a hand in that at all, but as it turned out, one of the Israeli soldiers who had fired into the gap did. We were brought before an Israeli Interrogation unit once again and for two weeks did not know our backsides from our elbows. Sodium pentothal and other more frightening mind drugs cleared us of complicity. But it put us in a rather precarious position, so we were offered an alternative, one we could not refuse. To become agents for the Israeli government. A role we carried out very efficiently, considering we feared for our wives and children's lives. Believe me, in the beginning it was hard to justify the moral issues involved, but as time went by we learned to survive and keep our families intact. Then came the day our usefulness expired and we were given an ultimatum. Hank's wife, as you know, was killed in a hit and run accident. We considered it a freak accident at the time. Your life and Hank's daughters' life came under the control of the Mossad. They very cleverly manipulated your lives to take on occupations which would allow both you children access to places and fame without suspicion. You both subsequently became celebrities in your own rights and unwittingly furnished the Mossad with information they needed. It was ingeniously done. Both Hank and I lived in fear of all our lives, yet knew that as long as you guys did your thing everyone would be safe. We dreaded the day when either one of you would get clever or figure out what was going on. I guess Hank took it upon himself to do something about it and the answer he figured out was using the Portal as an escape route of sorts. We saw the danger lurking in that hole, but we also saw an opportunity. It has taken a long time, frequent travelling, very unusual meetings and a lot of patience to calculate the probable. Our lives are over whereas you two have a lot going for you. We kind of figured to give you guys a break and a fighting chance. Anna is arriving in Sydney this afternoon from the States, where you will join her to catch a connecting flight to Zimbabwe. At Harare airport you will be met by an old friend who will take you directly to Cheroma Kadoma. Whatever you need will be made available. You are going through the Portal son; it's your only hope of survival. Now I suggest you grab what you can and you best get out of here."

There followed a long silence as David studied his father. This was all too far-fetched, too bloody ridiculous. Paul, sensing his son's hesitation, handed him a plastic wallet. Looking at the contents David knew this was no joke, but a deadly serious game of cat and mouse. Inside were flight tickets and US $10,000 in 100 dollar bills, passports for two of American origin in the names of Mr. and Mrs. L. F. Santana. There was a photograph of a black man in his sixties on which was inscribed "From Amos" and an American Express Card, as well as confirmed hotel bookings in Sydney for the couple and paid for in advance. In almost numb fascination he studied the envelope containing the Israeli reports. David could read and speak Hebrew well. An Israeli education had seen to that.

Paul stood up and walked to the curtained window saying, "I will not be going to Sydney with you."

The gravity of the statement brought home to David the significance of the words. His father was buying time for him at the cost of his own. Tears welled up and he was about to wrap his arms around the old man who brushed him aside with a curt.

"There is no time, you must go now."

David hurriedly packed his day pack with a few things, which included cameras and spare film, clambered into his Land Rover and raced off to Sydney. He cried for most of the way. A grown son weeping for the father he loved and knew would never see again.

Three days later the Australian newspapers covered the story of an old man who had been found dead in his bathtub, apparently from heart failure and drowned as a result. By this time David and Anna were deep in the Zambezi Valley of Zimbabwe, away from everything and everybody. The two sat huddled together for warmth against the evening chill. They were at the base of the Cheroma Kadoma Mountain, a single pillar of rock reaching up over a third of a kilometre into the heavens, which they were to scale to the summit and wait. As the twinkling stars dotted the skies David stood up and checked his gear, it was going to be one hell of a climb. They were no strangers to this type of activity, having experienced the Himalayas together on previous climbing expeditions. Because of the nature of their occupations both understood the need to succeed and both were committed to their respective crafts. Anna was an accomplished anthropologist.

The climb began up the rock face. It was hard going and care needed to be taken in the dark not to lose a grip or footing. With practiced ease they inched their way up the granite. After four hours of climbing the sound of vehicles drifted up to them from the dark undergrowth below. Anna's fingers were raw and every muscle in her body ached. The sounds emanating up from the bottom spurred her on knowing they were soon to be discovered. The race was on and time was fast running out. David muttered under his breath and climbed harder. To have come this far and fail, no way, not without a fight. The following two hours were nerve wracking, listening for tell-tale sounds of pursuit, but there were none. Instead they spotted camp fires at the pinnacle's base, which meant whoever was down there was in no hurry. Besides, all escape routes were covered. David did not climb directly upwards, but traversed at an angle looking for specific nooks and crannies where it would be possible to hide. Just before dawn the exhausted pair reached the flat summit. There were sprinklings of waist high bushes that offered minimal cover.

"Now what?" Asked Anna.

"We wait." Answered David and searched for an advantage on the thirty to forty metre diameter surface from where he could monitor any movement.

Their pursuers were down there alright and it was just a matter of time before a helicopter arrived. Anna extracted from her backpack a Static Analyser the size of a small radio and switched it on. Tiredness clawed at her brain, but she knew better than to fall into that tempting trap. She watched David intently and sighed. What a fitting way to end life. Together like this, very romantic and foolish. She was a pretty woman, typical Israeli with dark hair and complexion, a great body which she tortured no end to keep in shape and she loved the adventurous damn photographer. Her thoughts went back to the time they had first met as adults. It had been in Israel when both their fathers were released by the security forces after the Portal event. They all met as friends in Tel Aviv one evening over dinner eight years earlier. She was seventeen then and David the same age. It was love at first sight, though the course of true love did not run smoothly for either of them. The families subsequently kept in contact over the following two years during which time both completed their schooling and were conscripted into the Israeli army to do their national service. They met once again by chance whilst in the army on one of their reprieves down in the City of Eilat, a tourist haven on the Gulf of Aqaba and it was there that love sealed their hearts as one. She was attached to the Historical resources division as an up and coming anthropologist whilst he, in Reconnaissance, was doing both ground and aerial photography. Nothing glamorous in terms of military achievement and no medals to be won on any battlefield. It was a chance occurrence they would be in the same hostel in the same place at the same time. Those were to be five days of sheer bliss for her. She entered womanhood and lost her virginity. He was a good photographer and took many pictures of her. Then the news that her mother had been killed really hurt. Her best pal and confidant was gone and she felt at a total loss. David disappeared somewhere under a blanket of security and was not heard of until she met up with him again in the States.

By now her career had taken off and his was very flamboyant, having made a name for himself covering the Rwanda Urundi genocide in 2004. Their reunion was to be a passionate affair which lasted the best part of 3 months, touring the Himalayas until she was duly summoned back to Israel by her employer. For the next two years they only twice came into contact with each other. She could never quite figure out why both her father and Paul seemed to keep them apart. That's when she began to take notice of what was going on in their lives and soon made some startling discoveries. Her father and Paul were somehow connected to the Israeli government. She did not understand the meaning of anything at first until one evening she stumbled across some papers wedged between the drawers of her father's writing desk. They were Mossad documents. She understood only too well the implications, so took a short vacation to Cyprus from where she phoned David's father. He was very evasive about the whole thing, neither confirming nor denying and told her to let it be for everyone's sake. She could not let it rest and launched a one person investigation into her father's affairs, only to unearth startling facts which shocked her terribly. The Mossad's vice grip on her father was absolute. Her mother's death she suspected was intentional in order to keep the silence. That was it, she confronted both men and the whole sordid story emerged. Thus was born the plan of action of which David was totally unaware. Their meeting in Sydney was heaven sent and she knew in her heart she would rather die up here on this rock with her man than have to go down and be executed like some dumb defenceless dog.

She watched David and understood his anger, but recognized his commitment to purpose and realized how both would need each other in the moments to come. The sun rose and David scouted the pinnacle edge checking for climbers. Not long after that they heard a Helicopter approaching. So also did the Static Analyser go crazy? David grabbed Anna close, searched and listened. With every heartbeat the sound of the rotors grew louder. They both saw the Portal gate open. David kissed Anna hard, swept her up in his arms and leapt into the hole just as the chopper came into view over the lip of the pinnacle. The pilot of the chopper saw them go through the Portal, yet was too late to take evasive action and crashed into the side of the opening. Wreckage flew in all directions and the flaming bodies of those in the ill-fated craft were hurled into an empty sky and down the long drop to the densely wooded floor below.

Zimbabwean Security forces were alerted to the fact that there was unscheduled activity in the vicinity of Cheroma Kadoma and sent troops to investigate. The troops fell upon those foreign armed men and butchered them without mercy. None survived. Their bodies were laid before the Grand Tribunal for the entire world to see. A Presidential press statement was released saying suspected Israeli agents were planning a counter revolution in Zimbabwe and demanded an answer and an apology. Amos smiled to himself. Justice had been done. He thus avenged the deaths of his friends Paul and Hank. Israel was politically embarrassed now and no one dared ask what had become of David and Anna. Up in the skies orbiting the Earth a spy satellite took snapshots of an event which made the members of an American military tribunal, gathered around the developed photos, stare in wide-eyed disbelief.

Amos turned to the Sangoma, the witch doctor, and smiled.

"You have done well, Father. Now if those children of the other world return one day, I shudder to think of the outcome."

"Yes my son, we have done well, only we know the secrets hiding behind the Portal. It is up to those that have walked through to change the course of history on this planet and put an end to the madness."

Mike sank to his haunches like a deflated balloon, mouth agape, taking in the sheer beauty and splendour of this indescribable Paradise with its array of unimaginable colour. It took him a while to regain his senses, perched on an outcrop of pure crystal. All around him were flowers of such rare brilliance and colour, outstripping anything he had ever seen. Three moons hung suspended in a reddish sky and a sun shone as brilliant as Earth's. There were gigantic crystal peaks and mountains reflecting the sun's rays as rainbows of colour in a kaleidoscope of fantasy. The air was fresh, pure and warm. The valley he looked down on was covered in thick forestation, immense trees reaching up well over 100 metres into the air with a river winding its way far into the distance. From where he sat he could see a cascading waterfall falling hundreds of metres into a river below. It was breath-taking. How long he sat there he did not remember. Moving was difficult, as it would disturb the peace and tranquillity, but move he had to. Clambering to his feet he searched for a way down into the valley and to the river.

Instinct kicked in then and Mike became wide awake, searching for a weapon of sorts. Even in this incredible beauty his cynical mind reminded him that danger could lurk anywhere. On his walks he never failed to carry a knife and this was one occasion where that forethought would prove itself very useful. It was very hard to concentrate with so much to distract one's attention. Mike never wore a watch, so time was irrelevant. Halfway through his descent he paused to recheck his bearings then continued, the area becoming denser as he descended. He stepped up sensory awareness and trod extra carefully. On entering the forest he was amazed at the girth of the trees, reaching straight up and crowned by very densely interwoven branches dwarfing everything from view. The undergrowth consisted mainly of colourful plants approximately waist high through which he waded. With extreme caution he picked his way through this wonderland till arriving finally on the banks of the river. Here he checked and rechecked the surrounding woods and peered into the transparent waters. He sensed no danger and heard no sound other than the rushing water and distant cascading falls.

Making his way upstream he followed the course of the river through the vibrant floral décor along its banks to a huge pool into which the waterfall cascaded in a thunderous white churning mass. The sound was deafening. His eyes scaled the crystal cliffs around the falls looking for a cave or crevice which he could use as a refuge. There were none he could see, so he scouted around the pool for a better view of what lay behind the falls on the cliff face which meant having to climb. The idea was good, yet as soon as he started it became very apparent any attempt to scale these cliffs would be met with disaster due to their wetness from spray given off by the falls. Then a dark shadow caught his eye about seven metres up from the pool's surface on a section of the cliff where the crystals jutted out to form what looked like a stairway. Making for that point and a short nervous swim across the pool, he climbed up to a hole in the face about two metres in diameter. Once inside he crouched, waiting for his eyes to become accustomed to the gloom before investigating further. It was indeed a cave of sorts which led off into the deep recesses of the interior. The thunderous roar of the falls suddenly became silent. He crept forward, every fibre in his body tingling in anticipation and readiness. The deeper he penetrated the cave the more he became aware of the fact that he was not engulfed by total darkness, but rather was able to see fairly well. There was a faint fluorescent glow emitting from the cave walls. Mike counted his steps. He was walking, placing his feet lightly and squarely in a semi crouched position that a fighter adopts when facing an enemy. At thirty metres the cave narrowed into a tunnel large enough for a man to pass through. Another thirty metres and Mike found himself in a cavern the size of a football field and as high, in which was a subterranean reservoir. He had found a safe haven.

Retracing his footsteps back to the cave entrance Mike sat down to make a mental study of the surroundings and check out his defences, escape routes and chances of survival. The water looked drinkable, so gingerly he tasted the liquid. Sweet. Then the acid test, a whole mouthful and.....Nothing happened, no stomach pains, no dizziness and no vomiting. The water was drinkable. Another problem solved. He now had a roof over his head and water to drink. So far he saw no sign of life, no insects, birds or animals, only plant species. He went on a foraging search and returned carrying branches and bundles of grass with which he set up house. He found a palm-like tree from which originated not only leaves he could weave, but also almost perfectly straight stems three metres in length that he could fashion weapons out of or use as building materials.

He settled down in his new habitat quite well. All that remained was finding something to eat. This was puzzling, with so many plant species around some of them must be edible, but which ones? There was no wild life foraging the forests that he could study that would give him some indication as to what was and was not edible. It looked as if it was going to be a case of trial and error. The problem was that there were no medicines or doctors, so one had to rely on instinct and gut feeling together with all the luck in the world. At the water's edge on the cliff side of the river he did find a pineapple-looking fruit growing on long, tall, thorny stalks. The stalks were extremely tough to cut, exuding a red sap consisting of the plant's life blood and the fruit had a pinkish potato type interior. Slicing off a piece he sniffed at it, inspected it, tasted it with the tip of his tongue and finally ate a piece. It was delicious, something like a cross between a mango and an apricot flavour. Well, he figured, if that plant had thorns then the plant was protecting itself from being eaten. The thorns of the plant were testimony to the statement. They were long, sickle like protrusions that ended in vicious sharp pointed ends about 12 centimetres long. Another ideal weapon. Having fed himself, he collected his primitive spears and retired to the cave.

Once in the cave he set up an early warning system which would alert him of predators or intruders. He spread crystal sand on the floor of the cave some at its entrance. No one was going to creep up on him without him hearing it that was for sure. There was no way to walk over that sand without the whole cave vibrating to the grinding sound of crystal upon crystal. It made a very loud distinctive sound. Making final checks, he settled down to sleep. He fell into a deep sleep and slept for a very long time. Through the next few days he measured the cycle of night and day and studied the sun's positioning in an attempt to fix some form of time. A primitive calendar was set up. Single palm leaves representing the days and three-plaited leaves the weeks. For three weeks he explored the valley, the river and the forests and studied the plant life. Two more fruits were added to his diet, one of which was lethal if eaten in quantity as he soon found out. The plant bore a yellow fruit the size of an ostrich egg. Inside it contained a green, pulpous substance and one large pip. The taste was exquisite, but the kick terrible. It was the ultimate vodka Martini and whiskey rolled into one. The hangover, a mother of all hangovers. The other fruit in the larder tasted like chewing gum and its properties were much the same. It came in a hard black shell which, when cracked open, revealed a gooey substance. When chewed, it hardened to form a rubbery paste. If left in the sun, it dried rock hard. Here was a basis for cementing things together which became indispensable. What the nutritional value of the fruit was, he did not know except it became a pastime and replacement for the nicotine urges his body went through.

Throughout his searches there was still no sign of life other than himself. It was puzzling to say the least, yet by the same token it was a relief. This afforded him the opportunity to familiarize himself with his new environment without threat. One vine-like plant, once it had dried out and its fibres were plaited, became ropes; strong flexible ropes with a diameter of 2.5 centimetres, which he used to construct a bed, rope ladders and a long climbing rope for the ascent or descent of those huge trees. Scaling the trees to their heights was no easy task and took a lot of effort and nerve, having to trust in the rough bark for hand and footholds. The ropes were invaluable to his needs and gradually he began to feel at home. He soon became master of his little paradise and could sleep in blissful ignorance. He never felt better in all his life and grew stronger, fitter every passing day. At the beginning of the fourth week something woke him abruptly. Creeping to the edge of the cave mouth he cautiously surveyed his domain below. Nothing had changed, but he sensed something down there. For long moments he peered in every direction high and low, until his eyes fixed on a movement. Coming up alongside the river was an Arab mounted on a camel. Mike watched in silent disbelief, totally fascinated, as the figure drew closer, then the alarm bells sounded in his brain. An AK-47. He sprang into action. The hunted become the hunter and Mike was not going to forfeit his valley and comforts without making a stand.

He became the Snake and the Tiger as he slithered down behind the cascading waters into the shrubbery along the pool's banks and stealthily worked his way in an arc leading away from the approaching enemy, then cut in towards him at right angles. The camel suddenly stopped and the turbaned figure on it peered around. The AK-47 was brought up into the ready position as the Tiger Snake stalked its prey. Abu Ahmed did not see or hear a thing. All his senses were alive and pulsing a danger warning. He frantically tried to pinpoint the source of scent or sound which might betray his stalker. He was being hunted and the feeling was as nerve-wracking as anything he had ever experienced. He must remain calm, centred if he were to have a chance. Ahmed never saw it coming. A figure launched itself at him from the side. In spite of the camel's evasive sidestep it was too late. Mike struck Ahmed square and solidly with the impact of a stream train which sent the old man plummeting to the ground with a bone shattering thump and oblivion.

Abu Ahmed slowly opened his eyes to a throbbing, painful reminder he was still alive. Gradually clarity replaced dizziness and his eyes focused. In front of him stood a man who he immediately knew was the one he had been tracking into this paradise. Ahmed had found his man, or rather, the man had found him. He studied his quarry carefully and decided discretion was the better part of valour. From the corner of his eye he could see the camel. She was alright, no harm had befallen her and he breathed a sigh of relief.

"You speak English?" Mike fired the question.

Ahmed heard the words, but didn't understand, so he responded with a string of abusive mutterings in Arabic. The silence of the valley was broken by amused laughter and the Infidel before him grabbed a handful of Ahmed's beard and in a low tone, mocked in Hebrew.

"The old Wolf curses the Lion. Does the old Wolf not know he is in no position to be humorous?"

The Bedouin understood those words very clearly and smiled. The Lion, he thought, has long teeth. It would be better to play this one by the rules.

"Why does the Lion seek to destroy the old Wolf, when the old Wolf has lost its teeth and can't defend itself?" He replied.

"Ha! The old Wolf is as slippery as an eel. Given the chance he would gnaw at the loins of the Lion."

Ahmed laughed.

"I see the Lion is wise in the ways of the Wolf."

"No, old man, the old Wolf and hyena are the same, they attack when the back is turned."

Abu Ahmed considered those words carefully and understood this man was no fool. He had been hunted before and lived to tell the tale, which confirmed his initial fears when he tracked the man back in the Wadi. He was extremely dangerous.

"What does the honourable Lion intend to do with this old Wolf?" He enquired.

"Given the fact that the old Wolf tracked the Lion into this paradise and, given the fact that there is no way either of us can return home, it would be foolish for the Lion or the Wolf not to join company to ensure each other's survival and perhaps try to be friends." Mike answered.

"Well, would the Lion release the old Wolf from his bonds as his bones grow numb and stiff?"

Mike considered the options and decided to give this old Bedouin the benefit of the doubt. Besides, he had hidden the AK-47 and did not believe this Arab to be a man who went against his word.

"The Lion seeks the word of the old Wolf that he will honour it. Will he swear it before Allah to be true?"

"Abu Ahmed swears it before Allah." Came the tired reply.

So began a relationship of two men stranded by circumstance and forced to unite for the common purpose of survival. The following days were busy, with the old Bedouin learning the ins and outs of their environment and setting up lines of communication. They developed a system whereby neither of them would be out of each other's sight at any one given moment and formulated a defensive strategy. Mike developed a healthy respect for this old man during the course of the following weeks. He was very sharp for his age. In turn Ahmed grew to trust this warrior of paradise with his life. They made a good team. Ahmed the shrewd cunning fox and Mike the powerful soldier and defender. Ironically, a Christian and a Bedouin Muslim conversed in the Hebrew language. There was much to do. Food gathering, exploring and building. The two men carved out of nothing a semi civilized existence for themselves. The camel became very useful as a work horse sharing the work load. A ramp had been built up to the cave mouth and every night the camel was brought in. No one was taking chances.

A month went by. Still no sign of life other than their own. Both men decided to extend their area of exploration deeper into the forest and further away from home, which would mean camping over. Preparations were made, the AK-47 cleaned and oiled, lances and Mike's newest addition, a very powerful bow with formidable barbed arrows, flights made from a very thin film of the black nut gum. All traces of their existence around the cave were carefully concealed and camouflaged. With Mike leading the way this odd spectacle made its way down the valley amongst the gigantic trees.

They found Moti on the third day, he was slumped against a crystal rock, burning up with fever. Mike stood over his limp form and for a while did not recognize him. Then it dawned on him. This kid lived next door on the Moshav. The poor fellow was in a state. The trek back to base took longer than expected. For the following week Ahmed nursed Moti back to health. Mike, on the other hand, extended his exploration to cover a wider area deeper and deeper into the forest. He noticed subtle changes in the vegetation and the air was a little more humid. The forest was denser and more difficult to navigate. The thick canopy overhead blocked the sun, making it much darker on the floor. Walking around down there was not wise; there were too many unseen traps. At a slight bend in the river where the huge trees formed a tunnel over the receding water Mike had a brainwave. The canopy extended down to about thirty metres above the ground and from where he stood, he could not see the sky so thickly were the branches interwoven. The tunnel extended for a distance of five kilometres at least. An ideal home from home up in the trees. He went to work. Climbing those trees was no easy feat. After four days he had built a makeshift tree house high up off the ground, invisible between the foliage. Returning to the cave he was greeted by a recovered Moti and a beaming Ahmed.

Moti sighed in relief. Things had been going pretty rough for him. Emerging from the Portal into the river amid a dark frightening forest did not altogether help matters. He ate what looked like edible berries and almost immediately went into spasms of pain and vomiting. Fortunately for Moti he was next to water. He could not remember the journey to the cave. For days he lay in a semi coma, fever burning his already emaciated body. Then it was over. The three men settled down to a fixed daily routine. The calendar of palm leaves told its story. Three months passed by. The weather never altered. Thick early morning mists would shroud the forest, then sunlight would break through to another day of discovery. Mike and Moti penetrated deep into the forest by now, always keeping close to the river and, where possible, travelling from tree to tree like two monkeys in the Amazon rain forest. They scouted the river by raft for five days and found nothing. Still no sign of life. Up till now no fires were necessary as the nights were pleasantly cool, never cold and both Mike and Ahmed had almost lost the craving for nicotine. Mike decided to go on a one-man discovery expedition over the Crystal Mountains. He needed to be sure there were no other life forms and, if there were, what to expect. Last minute preparations were made. Weapons were checked and honed. The course to be followed would be up the cliff face to find the river source. Then, if possible, check out the other side of the mountain range. Paradise had its benefits, but one needed to know of possible threats to existence and make contingency plans to overcome those threats, if any.

Mike's journey of discovery took him high up the mountains following the course of the river which consisted of numerous majestic waterfalls cascading down from level to level. The climate became cooler. There was no lack of caves, so finding shelter did not pose a problem. The journey was uneventful. He found the river source, a raging torrent of water gushing out from a cliff face. It was a spectacular sight. The noise was so deafening it made it impossible to linger to long. Towering above him stood cliffs he estimated to be at least 3 to 5 kilometres high. Impossible to scale. He would have to find a route around this impregnable fortress of crystal. For days he traversed the cliff face and finally reached the conclusion that it was impossible to leave this valley over the mountains. He returned back to camp with the news and the alternative. The only way out of the valley was going to be by river and even then there was no guarantee. A plan was formulated and put into action. They would use the canopy of the Dark Forest as a means of travel. This meant they would have to build staging posts along the way high up in the trees. So began a feat of engineering second to none, giving birth to a network of interconnecting platforms on which the three men could move without once descending to the forest floor. They used the interlaced branches of the trees as gangways by securing them in such a way as to make passing from tree to tree a quick and safe method of travel. The drop would be fatal, so safety became top priority. Securing ropes were put in place, rope ladders and woven safety nets. This became a single-minded effort where time was of little consequence. Each had his allotted task and each performed their tasks without fault. Their lives depended on it.

They became tree people. Human monkeys of the forest. Necessity was the mother of invention and before long ingenious wooden tools appeared. Pulley systems were put in place, drawbridges and defence mechanisms at every kilometre a large tree house was fully equipped. Their little kingdom stretched for five kilometres high up in the trees along the river bank. It took them the best part of three years to accomplish. All the climbing, heaving and pulling turned Mike and Moti into very powerful and athletic men. Old Ahmed never felt better, fitter or more alive. Allah had been kind to him. This was indeed a blessing. Religion or politics never entered the topics of discussion. Everyone was on equal footing. There were the moments of loneliness when thoughts of friends and family came to mind. All three accepted their fate and adapted to it without question. The Dark Forest below, silent and foreboding, remained out of bounds. Not a place any of them liked nor did venture into to investigate. They devised a form of long distance communication using bugles fashioned out of gum from the Black Nut fruit. Moti's musical tendencies had brought melody to their world and a code of sounds through which, when working alone, they could keep in touch with each other.

On the 6th day of the 1st month of their 4th year 2016, Mike and Moti stumbled upon the first signs of life. They were working a stretch of river some six kilometres from base and came upon a make shift lean-to. By now both men were expert trackers thanks to Ahmed. The hunt was on and the warning sounded. There was someone else in the valley. The hunters took to the trees and for the next day and a half followed the course of the river downstream. They were silent aerial predators stalking an unseen prey. On the second day of their hunt they found what they were looking for. Nothing could have prepared them for the sight down below. There were at least thirty people milling about and a smashed red tour bus was wedged between two trees suspended some five metres off the ground. From their appearances it seemed as if they had not been here long. Mike studied the scene below. The group consisted of elderly and middle aged people, some young teenagers, with a few children romping around and a mother with a baby cradled in her arms. He listened to the chatter that emanated upwards and heard both the English and Spanish languages. Both men were silent, taking in this new event with mixed feelings. They noticed something else, shallow graves to the left just off into the forest, twenty in all. An hour passed. A breaking twig gave the warning down on the floor that something was moving around. The sound came from the rear, from within the Dark Forest. Mike and Moti clung poised and ready. Three dark shapes came into view, two men and a woman emerged out into the sunlight to be greeted with yelps of joy from the children and happy smiles of the others. A scouting party obviously had returned. Somehow this discovery provoked feelings of intrusion in the two men clinging high up in the trees. The feeling that their privacy had been invaded was at the same time a welcome sight.

Beckoning to Moti, Mike very stealthily descended to the forest floor and crept to its edge and waited. Hidden beneath the undergrowth unseen by those unsuspecting people and sure enough, a woman moved away from the group and into the forest to relieve herself and that's what Mike was waiting for. He pounced upon her without warning, knocking her senseless, hefted her body across his shoulders and climbed up to a surprised looking Moti. The younger man had learned never to question, many times he found out the hard way that this blond headed fighting machine was not to be trifled with. It did not take long for those down at the bottom to realize one of their party was missing. A warning was shouted and everybody clustered together. The scouting party Mike had seen exit from the forest stepped forward and it was then that the hand guns came into play. All three were armed. Moti whispered, "Interesting." Mike merely grunted. It was time to go. These people would be able to look after themselves for the moment. He needed answers from this still unconscious woman. They retreated back the way they came for about two kilometres to the river bank. Mike placed his now conscious and struggling bundle gently on the ground. She seemed so fragile he almost felt guilty for hitting her so hard. She stared at the two men, frightened out of her wits.

"What's your name?" Was the gentle question from the blond muscular man clothed only in a loincloth like something out of the ancient past? The question was in English and she gaped. Her bright, intelligent blue eyes darting from one to the other.

"Susan." She stammered.

These imposing individuals unnerved her. There was something about them that she instinctively realized cooperation would be the best method of defence.

"Susan, we know how you came to be here and we know this is all very confusing, but we would like to know if there are any others of your group still out in the forest, how many and are they armed?"

"Yes, there is another group of guys and they are armed with rifles." She volunteered.

"How many?"

"Four."

Mike translated what was said to Moti, who scowled with disapproval. Rifles stacked the odds a little and those odds had to be neutralized as quickly as possible.

"What happened to the twenty buried people?"

"They were badly injured or killed when the bus landed between the trees." She replied.

She needed reassurance. The poor girl was petrified.

"OK Susan, Moti here is going to take you to another safe place and please don't be afraid, no harm will come to you, he will leave you there and whatever you do, don't try to escape please for your own good."

With that Mike gave Moti instructions to take her to Ahmed and to return with the other bow. Moti understood and effortlessly hoisted the slim girl over his broad shoulders and swung aloft into the trees. Susan clung on for dear life. This was unbelievable, the power in this man. Her nerves hit an all-time peak when Moti began his aerial trapeze. She clamped her eyes tightly shut and prayed. Meanwhile Mike took off back at high speed in the direction of the bus. Four rifles and three hand guns were more than they could handle and no ways was he going to be subject to that kind of threat hanging over his head, it was too dangerous. If these people were jumpy they would shoot at anything moving regardless. He had to get those guns and bring these people into the trees away from any danger. Things had been too quiet for too long in the valley and he was suspicious something was lurking somewhere. A community was in the making, a safe and controlled community where each individual became responsible to the others for their survival and wellbeing. Bang goes the peace and quiet he thought. Skirting the area of the bus he traversed further downstream. By tacking in a cross-grain fashion he was able at last to locate the four men. Perched high up in a tree, he formulated a plan and went into action. Mike was a formidable opponent. Using cunning, stealth and his powerful body like a well-oiled machine, the Tiger Snake was not one to meddle with. The results could be alarmingly swift and deadly. The four men sat next to the river with their rifles within easy reach. A happy, unperturbed discussion was going on between then. They had been members of a shooting club on their way to a shoot when the bus went through the Portal.

Mike struck with blinding speed and accuracy, rendering all four slumped on the ground in total oblivion. He then stooped, retrieved the rifles and calmly cleared the breaches. Mission successful. Now the long walk back to the bus for these four with Mike in the trees to make sure they arrived safely. Shouldering the weapons, he perched once again in his tree domain and waited. Not long afterwards the four men came around, and for the first time in many years Mike had to stifle his laughter. The scene was comical. Four men milling around desperately searching for their rifles and not finding them, realizing something lurked out there. This spurred their departure back to the bus at a hearty run. Following up above the Tiger Snake planned his next disarming move, the handguns. On arrival back at the bus pandemonium reigned. Frightened children clung to grownups and all did exactly what Mike had predicted. They clustered together in a group facing the forest and an unseen enemy. The handguns were levelled and ready. The tension was electrifying. Mike waited for a while to make sure there were no hidden surprises. From high above his voice boomed down at the group, startling them even more.

"You three with the handguns, place them on the ground with the barrels facing towards you and everybody take a step backwards."

There was hesitation, so Mike sent three arrows in rapid succession into the ground at the feet of the armed trio. The shafts quivered ominously in the ground and that triggered an immediate response from one of the men who levelled his

Smith & Wesson .44 Magnum and fired. The next arrow slammed into the shooter's thigh and he catapulted forward as if hit by a steam train.

"Anybody else wants to be a hero?" The voice boomed.

Two handguns hit the dirt and the group retreated backwards. The wounded man, clutching his right leg with one hand, still held his weapon in the other. His eyes frantically searched the trees and undergrowth for a target. Teeth gritted in pain, he was fighting to regain his composure. Mike admired the fool, he had guts this one. The Tiger Snake lunged out of the undergrowth at the man on the ground and before unbelieving eyes disarmed his quarry with a sharp kick to the head to stand before these people, a forbidding figure of a man in total command on the situation. He stood silent and immobile listening. The shot rang out to echo way up the valley and Moti heard it and bugled three short notes on his horn. The answer came back, "All's well." He smiled to himself. Mike was a dangerous son-of-a-bitch. A very good man to have on your side in any crisis. Ahmed once recounted his own encounter with Mike to Moti weeks before and both agreed this strange man was worth having around.

The group heard the bugle call coming from up-river somewhere and saw the man in front of them respond and they shuddered. In deliberate tones Mike barked out his commands.

"I want all of you to gather what possessions you have and can carry comfortably and head off upstream in the direction of those mountain ranges in the distance. You will need to move fast. If there are any more guns in the bus or on your persons, place them in my basket here very carefully. We do not want anybody else hurt unnecessarily, do we?"

The man on the ground regained his senses and lay staring up at Mike with sheer anger and frustration. Mike crouched down next to him and broke the arrow, then extracted the broken shaft in one quick, painful wrench. Inspecting the wound he found no cause for alarm. The arrow had only pierced through the flesh, missing any vitals, but extremely painful nonetheless. He looked into the eyes of the man and fixed his stare.

"Out here in this foreign place we live by a code of co-existence and mutual survival. If you have any intentions to the contrary forget them. I could have killed you if I wanted to, but did not see the point of it. We are going to need every able bodied person if this community is to hold together. I don't expect your blessing neither your friendship, but I do expect your undivided co-operation. Do I make myself clear?"

The man remained silent and sullen.

"Tough guys do not survive out here alone, so whatever or whoever you are, forget it. We are team players here."

Lifting the injured man effortlessly on to his shoulders, Mike gathered the basket with its three handguns, clamped it shut and watched as the group gathered their belongings. He held the man on his shoulders in a vice-like grip. Trust had to be earned and he needed the trust of this man in order to extend their defences.

Frank hung like a sack of potatoes over the shoulders of the long-haired blond ape. His leg throbbed. He felt the power in those arms and decided it would be better not the invite trouble. Who the hell was this prehistoric human? He spoke English with an accent which, from what he could guess, was of Southern African origin. Damn, the man was fast. Frank had never seen a man move like that before. He was on him in the blink of an eye. Those arrows come out of

nowhere. Frankie Boy, thank your lucky stars, things could
have been worse. Frank himself was no slouch, he played
league football which kept him in shape. By all accounts,
he was a big man, weighing in at a cool 110 kilograms and
as tough as they come. One had to be, in the Seals. You
were the elite of the American armed forces. Under any
other circumstances he would have had a go at this ape, but
somehow deep down he sensed a whole bag full of trouble
and he wasn't about to go one on one with this dude, no Sir.
He would bide his time, watch and wait. Frank was a Seal
Instructor. Thirty nine years of age, he had been on many
missions and considered himself more than capable. When
the bus went through the Portal the shock and reality of the
situation hit home. All his training and preparedness stood
him in good stead. He managed to bring a chaotic situation
under control and formulate some form of discipline into
the group considering the circumstances. Twenty people
had died, of which three were children. What a mess. He
secured the area, set up defensive parameters and posted
sentries. Fortunately there was enough food on the bus to
feed this group for a short while in spite of rationing. As
luck would have it there were eight able-bodied individuals
aboard, of whom four were marksmen with rifles and two
others, a man and a woman, who carried side arms, and
one trained nurse. The rest of the group was made up of
two elderly couples, two teenaged girls and three teenaged
boys. A young mother and her baby and five middle-aged
adults, one a man and four women of Latino origin and
six young children, their ages ranging between two and
ten. Under his leadership they had survived. Mike's words
echoed in his mind. Looking around at the group of people
he had to admit things were beginning to look up in spite of
everything. What puzzled him though, where was this ape

taking them? The group formed up in some form of order waiting for their next instruction, all the while glancing curiously at the apparition before them.

"Which one of you is the leader of this group, if you have one?" Asked Mike.

With that they all indicated to Frank perched precariously across Mike's shoulders. Mike dumped Frank onto the ground unceremoniously. Frank gritted his teeth against a new well of pain.

"Anybody have a first aid kit or something?" Enquired Mike, smiling at Frank.

But Frank did not see a smile behind those eyes, only cold calculating death. Tiger Snake was wary. Beneath the man's clothing he felt the hardness of trained muscle. This was not a civilian; this was a military man of sorts. A woman came forward carrying a white plastic box on which was inscribed the insignia of the Red Cross. Breaking the box open Mike rifled through the contents. Frank was agitated. He wasn't about to let this oaf mess with his body, so he called out,

"Mavis, please get over here and see what you can do."

Out of the corner of his eye he watched the Ape. There was still that half-cocked smile on his face. The man was apparently enjoying himself. Mavis approached and timidly dressed Frank's leg. Just then Moti appeared into view, dressed in similar fashion and just as big and powerful, carrying a bow and quiver of arrows. Both men conferred in a language Frank could not understand. Things were really becoming complicated. Moti came up to Frank and hauled him to his feet. The leg had gone stiff. Mike then disappeared and reappeared a few minutes later with a primitive crutch and handed it to Frank who accepted it thankfully. The march upstream began. Moti took to the trees and for the first time Frank was able to observe the unity between these two men. They were so in tune with each other there was no need for words. As they proceeded Frank became more and more awed by those two. They were incredible athletes and as much as he hated to admit it, he was way out of his depth. There was no way he could get past either of them. That blond ape was everywhere and nowhere. He would come and go like a shadow. The younger one floated through the trees on invisible wings, it was uncanny how he did it. Frank's leg hurt and some of the smaller children in the group showed signs of weariness. It was time to take a break. Those two sentinels forced the pace.

Moti watched carefully. Mike told him he had sensed something in the forest and when Mike said something you had better believe it. That explained the bows. He saw Mike emerge from the undergrowth next to the children and from his body language Moti became all the more alert. Something was up. Mike saw or heard something out there. Mike grabbed two of the small children and took to the trees. Moti held his ground, he knew his task well. Mike then returned and two more children disappeared up into the tree tops. Frank was becoming uneasy. He had been around long enough to be able to smell trouble and trouble was heading their way. That big ape knew it and was taking evasive action. Children first. Don't arouse panic. He was good, this guy. The other ape must be bringing up the rear. A one-man defensive force and suddenly Frank felt naked, exposed and helpless. His mind raced. It must have been the gunshot, that's why the apes were so quick to grab the firearms. A gunshot echoes for long distances in a valley, especially this one and someone or something would be bound to come looking. Frank felt such a fool knowing that he was probably responsible. All the children were safe. Next would be the women. Like a clock Mike worked. His body glistened with sweat. It became a race against time and he knew danger was close at hand.

One by one the group thinned out until only Frank remained, pushing himself to the limit through the undergrowth next to the river. His spine prickled and he felt the eyes focus on his back. He was the bait. Those apes had set him up as bait. For shit sake, what kind of people were these? He thought. He did the unexpected, he dived into the river and swam to the opposite bank and looked back. There it was, a hideous black hairy thing, standing well over two and a half metres tall, with long tentacles waving through the air scenting him. Frank froze. For the moment he was safe. As long as he kept the water between him and that thing he would be OK. Where were those damn apes? Let's see how they resolve this little problem. His mind raced, searching for an escape route in case the creature decided to enter the water.

Mike and Moti surveyed the creature below them very carefully. It used its tentacles as scenting devices. Who knew what other attributes this horrible thing hid up its sleeve? Both men noticed the creature's reluctance to follow Frank through the water. Then it struck them, the water was the possible key. There was an agonizing delay while Frank watched the creature sway from side to side, calculating. What followed next stunned Frank? The two men came down from the trees, each with a cauldron, positioned themselves well out of reach on either side of the creature, filled the cauldrons with water and then rushed the animal from both sides. Before the creature could turn to face either threat, water was thrown onto it and both men hurtled away to refill their cauldrons, then swung back and repeated the exercise.

The creature screamed and twisted, its tentacles beating at the air. Again and again the apes launched themselves at the creature and delivered their watery bombs. The animal burned, white smoke coiling from its body and it died with shuddering death throes until all was still. Frank watched in fascinated horror as the two apes plummeted into the river and from the shallows they hurled cauldron after cauldron of water onto the dying creature until there was nothing left. Water acted as acid on the creature's body. This discovery was the solution to a very nasty situation and by now everyone became acutely aware of a very real danger in this Garden of Eden. Frank cautiously swam back to stand in the shallows next to Mike and Moti and breathed a sigh of relief, not saying a word, just looking at the empty patch of crystal sand where the hideous creature once had stood and thanked his lucky stars.

Before he could gather his thoughts Mike grabbed him and ascended into the tree tops. He pushed the group along the sky walkways high up in those trees until they arrived back at base. Everyone, with the exception of Ahmed, had seen the horrible creature. Nobody was aware exactly what the creature was capable of. Frank had to admit to himself, these three strange men were the answer to their prayers. Without them things could have been a lot different. With the increase in the community it meant there was a greater demand on food supplies, so some form of agriculture was to be established. A communal room was quickly constructed, with everyone lending a hand, where people could congregate, hold discussion groups, schooling, and make community decisions. Ahmed was appointed chairman and domestic crises solver, but needed either Mike or Moti to translate. Frank became responsible for policing and food gathering. Mavis continued her trade as nurse and Susan was appointed school teacher. Mike and Moti kept their distance from the group, going off for days at a time. They constituted the military wing of the group. Life settled down and soon they were one big happy family. For Mike and Moti, however, things were not that simple. They were hungry for adventure and discovery. Many weeks were spent in training the new additions to the community to reach a level of proficiency to be relied on in the event of catastrophe, defence or offence. The skywalks were extended which gave a greater control over their habitation and lines of communication. Frank proved to be an ideal administrator and, as things happen, found love in the arms of Susan. A tree people emerged. Moti, Ahmed and Mike had now been in the valley for seven years, the year 2019. Ahmed was seventy years old and his camel was still alive.

Came the day that Mike and Moti gathered their weapons and disappeared from the tree village. They headed off down the valley and kept going for two months, following the course of the river. Through valleys, crystal ravines and empty crystal plains, until they reached the Red Sea. Not once did they find any life forms. On the shores of this sea they came across the first sign of civilization. It was not a large city, but one of architectural splendour, beautiful lines and very futuristic with its translucent domes and huge pointed spirals. The whole city was built off the ground, supported by an immense pylon half a kilometre high. The entire city was built or fashioned from crystal. From where they sat the sight was awesome in the sunlight. Both men were extremely cautious. Hidden in their forest tree tops at the edge of a wide grassy plain leading down to the city, they studied this vision with keen interest. Here in the trees they were hidden from view, but down on the grassy plain they would stick out like a sore thumb. They watched and waited. Mike estimated the distance to be about two kilometres between them and the very attractive crystal city. Two kilometres of grassy plains to cross would arouse someone's attention. Then there was the problem of scaling the pylon. It appeared awfully smooth. Even if one managed to avoid detection, which was highly unlikely, how on earth were they going to gain access from under the circular platform which must have been at least one kilometre in diameter? Mike cherished his freedom too much to run the risk of capture and confinement. Certainly they would become objects of scientific interest and paraded around as zoo animals. What of the rest of the community? No, the risks were too great and he and Moti decided to return to their valley. Like two skulking monkeys they headed back for home many kilometres away.

Zorak spotted them on his scanner. At first he thought he was imagining things. Pinpointing the exact location, the scanner zoomed in. To his utmost surprise two faces appeared on his large wall-to-wall monitor. They were Human faces. Now he was extremely attentive, yet highly puzzled. What were two Humans doing on this planet of all places? How had those two come to be here? Earth was billions of light years away and they certainly did not possess the technology. Zorak quickly reached a conclusion which would be the best course of action to take to further observe those two. He had to keep his discovery as quiet as possible or the Committee would certainly find out and order their capture. They were more useful to him out there than in some science laboratory. Zorak, the head of the Planetary Research Station on Ridmon had acquired the post as a result of having fallen out of favour with the Committee, and thus was banished along with his sister to carry out studies on this planet. Humans had always held a special place in his heart due to the similarities between them. They were a case study he would have given his left hand for, but such privileges only befell a few favourites. Now here, out of nowhere, his dream mysteriously became a reality. This opportunity would not be missed. He would protect those two with all the resources at his disposal, so he launched one of his specially designed Drones, a spherical-like object the size of an automobile which could track, monitor and analyse anything, anywhere. Its function was multipurpose, destroy or protect. The Drone was undetectable and that's exactly what Zorak wanted. Only he was able to access the control codes via telepathy. The Drone obeyed no command other than Zorak's, its master. The monitor on the wall blinked twice and a face appeared. The face of a stern old man who calmly asked,

"Zorak, your report please."

"Your most high Excellency, we have stabilized the weather patterns on this Planet and are attempting to regenerate life in its seas. The fossil DNA'S have been duplicated and the expected results of all three life forms specified are positive."

"Excellent Zorak, you will keep us informed?"

"Yes indeed."

With that the monitor went dead and Zorak cursed under his breath. He did not agree with genetic manipulation. Especially when it came to recreating monsters of bygone eras just for some over-inflated idiot's personal pleasure. He frequently travelled around Ridmon, but for a very long time did not visit sector 4. There was no reason to do so. If he started to visit sector 4 too often, it would arouse suspicion and subsequently result in an investigation into his activities there. The Drone was the only answer and the safest for the Humans. He would have to come up with a plan which appeared perfectly normal, yet would give him the opportunity to observe the Humans first hand. A woman's face appeared on the screen. It was Penagee, his younger sister and greatest ally. She proved to be his best and only trusted friend. In her he could freely discuss his thoughts and ideals without fear. She was an extremely attractive woman with jet black hair and bottle green eyes, highly athletic and powerful for her sex. She was Ridmon's Security Officer and had earned her stripes. One thing in her favour was that she never lost her sense of humour. He was always pleased to hear her soothing voice.

"Zorak it's time for lunch, you haven't forgotten again brother dear?" She teased.

"No my sweet sister, not at all." He laughed back.

They met under the observation dome so as to view their surroundings whilst having lunch. Today Zorak sat facing Sector 4 and not in his usual seat facing the sea. This action didn't go unnoticed by his sister, who remarked,

"Getting tired of the sea view are we?"

Zorak smiled and replied,

"You are too sharp for your own good, and yes, why not view a different scenario for a change. It makes for a more pleasant sight, don't you agree?"

Penagee laughed. She loved her brother dearly. Somehow today he was different. She knew him too well, he was hiding something. She was curious. There radiated an aura of excitement from him and she doubted it was due to the progress they had made with those ugly primeval monsters. She watched him gazing off into sector 4 and her intuition told her that he had made a discovery of sorts. He always had that look on his face when he was on to something. She could contain herself no longer and asked,

"What is it, what have you found?"

For the first time in her life Penagee saw a shrouding of his eyes and a tensing of the spine.

"Oh nothing, I was just thinking how beautiful sector 4 is?"

Penagee merely offered a confirming. "Yes." Reverting to silent contemplation. So there was something out there. Something he did not want anyone to know about. Whatever it was it certainly brought a reaction from him she did not at all expect. As security officer, any experiments or work in any sectors were first channelled through her for approval. What was he hiding out there? She decided to find out very discreetly, without detection and did not need anyone to authorize her actions. Whatever it was, her brother was very protective and evasive.

The meal finished in silence and Penagee took the initiative by excusing herself and left the dome and her estranged brother. Zorak watched her from the corner of his eyes and smiled to himself. The die had been cast. Now what remained was for her to find the two Humans and come to the same conclusion as he had. He understood her sense of priority and knew beyond a shadow of doubt what her reaction was going to be. Zorak would then be secure in the knowledge that the two Humans out in Sector 4 would, for the time being, remain free.

Penagee checked her roster for the rest of the day and found no pressing schedule. Instead of taking in her usual training session and swim, she locked herself in her office and switched on her personal security monitor. This equipment was not linked to any database, nor was it accessible from any other source, allowing her total freedom of use. Penagee punched in the co-ordinates for sector 4 and began a block by block scan of the zone, starting from the base of the city up towards the far distant crystal mountains. The scanner was very efficient and soon enough it detected movement. Penagee sat mesmerized at what she was seeing. The scanner focused in and she blinked in disbelief. Two Humans. She focused closer and whistled. She watched in sheer fascination as Mike and Moti glided with effortless ease from tree to tree. No wonder Zorak was excited. The scanner did not pick up the Drone, but in Zorak's mind came the message.

"The subjects are being scanned."

Zorak admired his sister's tenacity. By now she would be totally engrossed and how right he was. Penagee could not take her eyes off Mike. Never before had she seen such power and grace. She was enthralled and something deep within began to stir, echoing across aeons of time, beckoning and calling, growing stronger until Penagee felt her pulses racing and her breathing became ragged. Base instincts were taking over and she fought to control the urges. Her palms were sticky and her hands trembled. She shut off the scanner and sat back confused. Still inwardly shaking, she paged Zorak. His face appeared on the monitor screen.

"Would you mind coming to the security room please Zorak?"

The screen blinked off and Penagee cradled her head in her hands. Never before had she experienced such raw passion and animal arousal. It unnerved her and flustered the ice cool composure she had become famous for. A short while later Zorak entered the room to find his sister with her head cradled in her hands. He sat down opposite from her across the table in silence. It was a while before Penagee spoke. She raised her head from behind her hands and Zorak saw the tears. He simply nodded.

"I have to go there Zorak, I have to see the Human, he's so beautiful." She pleaded.

Zorak looked deep into his sister's bottle-green eyes and sighed.

"Penagee, dear Penagee, you know as well as I that any undue attention by us in this area will arouse suspicion. It would be the end of the Human, wouldn't it?"

"I know, but there must be a way to beat the system. Please Zorak, think of something."

In spite of his beloved sister's position on this station, Zorak was still the most powerful person on the planet and whose authority accessed the entire city's facilities, including its computers.

"Penagee, for the time being I urge you to confine this information to yourself until I can come up with a way for us to move freely within Sector 4 without raising eyebrows for whatever reason. We have to have a totally legitimate reason. I will find one."

With that Zorak abruptly left the room. Penagee was left to her own thoughts and self-analysis. She was shaken. She dared not switch the scanner on again just yet until her composure returned. For the next month Zorak was too engulfed in his work to give Penagee much attention and she in turn buried herself in work to dull the aching in her heart. Only Zorak, in the quiet seclusion of his office, followed the Drone's reports and supporting imaging of the two Humans. He could see why Penagee had emotionally crashed at the sight of this almost perfect specimen of humanity. Each day as the reports came in he was able to formulate a prognosis of both Mike and Moti. These two were highly trained and resourceful persons who displayed extraordinary tendencies and abilities for Humans. Why did they not walk on the ground like the rest of their race? The answer to that question came a few days later. The Drone reported,

"Alert, alert, dangerous life forms detected. Threat to subjects."

Now he understood why the Humans kept to the trees. The Drone sensed movement in one section of the very dense and deep forest and had gone to investigate. The images sent back were enough to convince Zorak of a legitimate reason for moving into sector 4. He summoned Penagee. She arrived almost immediately.

"Get ready, we have reason to move into sector 4. A foreign life form has been detected deep in the forests which we need to sample. I could not understand why those Humans used the high trees to move around in instead of on the ground. Then reports came in with these images."

The monitor flashed on. Penagee's heart stopped.

"What are those?" She whispered.

"I don't know, but we are going to find out. Our scanners don't pick them up, which means they give off some form of distortion pattern or electrical impulse."

There was the reason and a good one. All they had to do now was to ensure the Humans stayed in the trees when the collector Drones picked up the samples. Penagee was as excited as a little girl. Zorak felt good. The computers notified Command Centre. Collector Drones where fed the co-ordinates. They were large cylindrical type canisters measuring thirty metres in length and ten metres in diameter. They were self-propelled and computer controlled. There was no escaping once they had targeted their subject. Their retriever arms were virtually indestructible and operated with clinical precision. Zorak and Penagee climbed into a transport shuttle acting as a control centre for the collector Drones. A sleek, streamlined machine capable of inter galactic travel and armed with a devastating arsenal of weaponry. Once in the shuttle, confirmation was given, systems were checked and the Drones were released. Operation Retrieval began.

Moti spotted the cylinders in the far distance when the sunlight reflected off their silvery shapes. He was quick to point them out to Mike and instantly both sought refuge amongst the thick tree foliage. Zorak's Drone reported,

"The subjects are concealed, remain undetected."

The collector Drones swung into position about a kilometre away with Mike and Moti remaining completely motionless. Not a muscle flinched, their breathing shallow, minds focused. They watched as the Drones descended through the tree tops and disappeared from view. Sometime later they reappeared and shot off back towards the City. Only once completely out of sight did the two men move. They were still a long way from base. The Drone reported.

"Subjects on the move again, will monitor."

Zorak was satisfied. The station computers had a new interest to keep them occupied and he had found a reason to be in the area. Mike was far from happy, as the incident proved more than ever if the community were to survive, then they would have to do so very quietly and discreetly. There was no delaying; the others had to be told and fast. How could the two men know their every step, breath and movement was being monitored, analysed and studied?

Zorak decided to share his Drones' reports with his sister and allowed access. She was ecstatic. He was also figuring on a way to preserve their secret. This posed a major obstacle given the technology at the station and its high degree of success in obeying the Committee's will and command. His personal Drone was performing its allocated task extremely well and only two persons knew of its existence. The Drone was undetectable and assigned to the Humans as a shadow protector. Zorak was confident his plan would remain

undiscovered, but realized Penagee needed to be kept in
check, which was vital to the success of his mission.

Four months later two very tired and weary men arrived
back in their tree city. The Drone reported.

"Subjects have multiplied."

Zorak's heart skipped a beat when the images came on
screen. This was indeed a mystery. A Human community
existing in Sector 4. No one was to know of their presence,
so he relayed a command to the Drone.

"Isolate subject number1 and observe."

To Penagee he gave an official instruction to do an
aerial survey of Sector 4. However, unofficially to establish
communication with the Humans. She was to keep in
contact with the Drone via the protected medium and
act accordingly. Mike was off on his usual scouting route
over the Dark Forest. He was looking for signs of the hairy
creature. Alone and unaware of what was about to transpire,
the Drone, unseen, chose a spot well away from any prying
eyes to deliver its paralyzing yet painless sting. A beam of
blue light shot out. Subject number 1 was immobilized.
Mike was frozen. Suspended in mid-air some 100 metres
off the ground and held there by a thin blue ray of light.
He could not move, yet his mind remained active. He
was trapped and knew it. A shuttle manoeuvred beneath
him and very gradually inched its way upward to swallow
Mike into its interior. The Tiger Snake was snared and
strapped down on a table. The securing bands clamped
tightly around his body and all went still. Mike breathed
slowly and methodically, calming the gnawing feeling in
the pit of his stomach. Around him a multitude of lights
flickered and danced. Somewhere behind him there was a
faint hissing and then he was aware of something's presence
behind him. He was still paralyzed by the blue light beam

and the sensation was maddening. Bound and gagged like a pig ready for the slaughter.

Penagee traced her green eyes over his body, taking in every part of him. She was savouring the moment. Preliminary checks made by the computers and scanners confirmed no dangers of disease, parasites or any other oddity which would constitute a danger to the ship or its occupant. Its checks completed, a monotone voice issued the all clear. The Drone released its hold on subject number one and reported,

"Subject successfully in place."

The table swivelled to an upright position and Mike regained control of his body again. His eyebrows rose in surprise, standing close to him was the most beautiful woman he had ever seen. Her torso was covered in a very tight fitting jump suit made of a material the colour of gold with a glass-type sheen. She was a superb figure of a woman, well-structured and proportioned. Her skin looked tanned against the long jet black hair which adorned her head. And those eyes where pools of living green into which he felt himself falling. Penagee stretched out her slender, strong hands and touched Mike's chest. The sensation was both confusing and enticing to Mike. He sucked in air through clenched teeth and forced a smile. Penagee's knees threatened to buckle at any moment. The electrifying feelings this Human was sending up and down her body were almost too much to bear. She needed to be careful not to jeopardize the situation to win his trust. It was frustrating, nerve-racking and difficult to control her urges not to fling herself upon him. Mike watched this apparition before him and was awed. All resistance seemed to drain out of him at her touch. Then in a voice so gentle and soothing she asked in faltering English,

"By what name go you?"

The question took him by surprise and he answered.

"Mike."

"My name is Penagee." She said, pointing to herself.

"To answer any questions, my scanners probed your mind."

That was not good, thought Mike, not good at all. It meant the community was at risk of discovery.

"You are from that city on the sea shore?" Enquired Mike.

"Yes." Came the response.

His voice was nice and strong, she thought. Mike could feel her eyes taking in every part of him and it made him uneasy. He was physically attracted to her in a very strong way. There was chemistry between them and they both knew it. She wanted desperately to untie the bonds which held him, but instinct told her not to until some kind of mutual understanding was arranged between them. The man was like a caged animal and very dangerous.

"You are going to have to trust me, Mike. If I loosen the bonds, do I have your word you will do nothing foolish?"

Mike studied her face. In spite of the electrifying chemistry between them there was still reason and logic.

"Not unless my freedom has been compromised."

"It has not, so do I have your word?" She asked.

"Yes."

Instantly the straps fell free and Mike stepped forward. The unseen Drone positioned itself. Mike sensed it and made a mental picture for later reference. Penagee motioned for him to follow. He followed her through a doorway into a lounge type area with reclining sofas and Penagee turned to face him. Her closeness was all-consuming.

"Your people are in danger from some rather nasty life forms living in the forest and in addition, your greatest threat lies in being rounded up as laboratory specimens if your presence here is detected."

"By whom?" He questioned.

"By my superiors and the computers in the city."

"Then how come you warn us?"

"Because my brother and I do not wish to see you or your people become mere specimens, but would rather protect you and allow you your freedom. We are very much alike in physical structure, except our blood is transparent while yours is red. All of us have green eyes and black hair. For as long as I can remember my brother's secret passion has been Humans and you being here will guarantee your survival. Zorak, my brother, has fallen out of favour with the Committee because he spoke out against their cruelty. The Committee once sent Drones to Earth to collect specimens on a number of occasions and those poor things died on route each time. This is why we are doing everything in our power to protect you." She related.

"Not a very comforting thought is it?" Remarked Mike who was beginning to see the bigger picture.

"No." She responded.

"Tell me, Penagee, how are we supposed to protect ourselves in this case if, from what you tell me, there is nothing to stop you from trying to win back favour by reporting our presence, or turning us into specimens yourselves?"

Penagee smiled, "Rest assured, Mike, it will never happen. For your interest, we have launched twenty specialized Drones into this area whose sole function it is to serve and protect any Human subject anywhere, anytime, against any threat from the City or outer space or those creatures of the forest for as long as you and your people live on this planet."

"What kind of Drones?" Queried Mike

"They are invisible to the naked eye and to the computer scanners of my world. That makes them undetectable and untraceable and believe me, they are devastating to anyone or anything threatening their subjects."

This was all very complicated, thought Mike. Just when one thinks things couldn't be better, something comes along full of surprises and your whole world turns upside down. Who said life was boring? He listened to Penagee's voice, trying to find traces of deception but found none. Yet all appeared to be genuine on the surface, however he would need a lot more proof of her sincerity than just words. He was standing in a spaceship of a very advanced order, what they would care for apes like humanity. Yet this woman had somehow stolen his heart right from under him and he was compelled for the meantime to believe in the credibility of her story. The odds were stacked very heavily against them, so care was needed. Suddenly Penagee produced a pen-like object and pointed it to the left of him. Too late, there was a red flash of light and the women slumped to the floor unconscious. Mike spun, the Tiger Snake went into attack mode. The flash originated from a monitor on the side wall and Mike smashed into it then everything went crazy. The shuttle listed and shook and all the lights in the lounge switched off. In the darkness he found Penagee, lifted her up and searched for an exit. The following moment the side of the shuttle was wrenched asunder, opening like a tin can. In that instant Mike leaped outwards into the trees. The shuttle crashed down on to the Dark Forest floor, exploding on impact and spewing debris everywhere. The protector Drone reported.

"Mission accomplished. Subject No.1 safe. Shuttle destroyed. All other Drones in position."

Zorak had launched his plan to perfection. Now all that remained was for Penagee to be in place. The Protector Drones would see to their safety. He knew the computers had started scanning, which meant the end for him. He could never leave the city, he was sealed off. Everything was in place and his last act would be to destroy the dome. If he did not, all would be lost. He knew the risks and the benefits. He also knew that for the Committee to re-establish itself on Ridmon would take a very long time and many heads would roll as a result of his little act of selfless giving. Penagee would live among the Humans and be safe. Any Committee space vessel coming within thinking distance of Ridmon would be eliminated. His gift to the Committee. His gift to his beloved sister would be life. For him the knowledge that she would pursue his lifelong ambition was reward enough. Standing in the Crystal Dome and gazing out at sector 4 for the last time, Zorak had no regrets. He smiled and gave the command to his protector Drone. It received one response, one confirmation, it then shot off to the seaside city and plunged head long into its infrastructure and self-destructed. The resulting super explosion destroyed the city and everything in it. The ground trembled, trees shook everywhere and from a distance came a deep rumbling sound. The Crystal City detonated, imploding in one massive blast, sending shock waves throughout the Trigon Empire. Once the dust had settled, all that remained of the Dome was a mass of crystallized sand on a desolate seashore.

Light years away a Sangoma chanted in the dark recesses of a cave. The year 2019 found David and Anna in Sector 4, Planet Ridmon.

Mike hurtled through the trees. Penagee was limp and unresponsive. He paused to sound the general alarm. The response came from afar. Moti would be activating Defence mode. But Penagee worried him, so he made for the river to a sheltered section where he bathed her face in the cool waters. All the time his eyes searched the forest, the skies and the surrounding mountains. His ears listened for tell-tale sounds and senses extended outwards, probing. He saw it. So indistinguishable, so subtle. He focused and the image was gone. A Drone was hovering above the ground. Through his peripheral vision he could make out a shape, but not a shape, so he turned his attention back to Penagee. She was breathing shallowly, but the pulse rate was good. Her pupils had not dilated and her body was warm, not that cold, clammy feeling. He decided to continue, but was abruptly stopped by a huge black hairy tentacle creature in front of him. Tiger Snake reacted with lightning speed, so did the Drone. It fired a bright, white stream of light and the creature disintegrated. Mike breathed a sigh of relief and thanked whoever from the bottom of his heart and headed back into the trees.

On hearing the general alarm sound the community dived into their defensive duties with a vengeance. Everyone knew their station. Moti trumpeted the confirming response and stragglers from the outer circles were coming in quick and fast. The water bombs were in place and the lances, the bows and the camouflage nets swung into position. On the forest floor the pits were activated with their array of brutal spikes and impaling rods. Nasty booby traps were set. They were ready. All waited in silence, listening for the second bugle call. Instead Mike swung into view with a strangely dressed woman over his shoulders. Moti sounded the second call. The forests became still and silent. Nothing moved.

Ahmed helped Mike lower Penagee gently onto a plaited rope-bed. His wise old eyes saw the look on Mike's face. Gently his gnarled hands checked the woman's vital signs and gave Mike a reassuring smile.

"So the Lion has found a mate." He whispered.

Mike blushed and replied, "I see the old Wolf is still very perceptive."

Leaving Penagee in Ahmed's capable hands he checked their defences and fortifications. A man could move without being detected either from the ground or the air so effective was their network. Mike knew the Drones would be there and that was a great comfort. Still, he needed answers from Penagee and the sooner the better. He found Moti in his designated place with the children. There was a look of curiosity written all over his face.

"Everything in place?" Mike asked.

"Yes." Responded Moti adding "Beautiful, isn't she?"

Mike merely nodded.

Moti beamed a broad smile and winked at Mike who Retracing his steps to where Frank crouched poised for action, Mike shook the extended hand and whispered into Frank's ear,

"We have taken a step into the future, thousands of light years ahead of our time."

The American nodded acknowledgement, although not quite sure he had heard right. Mike swung off into the trees to do his 360 degree outer patrol. It was strange not having Moti on these rounds. The boy had become a younger brother to him over the years and Ahmed the father. Now additional companions were on the scene, the unseen Drones and the woman Penagee. He was eager to get back to her, but knew the importance of his task. The community relied on him to bring back information in order to prepare last minute strategies for their defences. Mike's 360 degree scout was further out than usual this day and ensured that his field of vision included the skies. He dreaded the thought of those cylinders. His mind raced over the events of the past few hours. Things were beginning to hot up. It was crazy. First the Portal, then the valley, the community and now the space people. He thought back to his wife and realized she must have remarried by now. He would want that. Penagee was another confusing issue. She made his blood boil. He wanted to hold her, feel her close. The question was how long could the community survive. If what Penagee had told him and didn't tell were fact, then their chances of avoiding detection were slim. Drones or no Drones, the community's future hung in the balance. The members of the community meshed very well together and life in the trees was calm and pleasant. There were the disputes and arguments from time to time but those never lasted and good old Ahmed was a fine peacemaker. Frank and Susan were united in a special relationship. He smiled to himself when he thought of Moti, poor shy Moti, having a soft spot for the grieving Ana-Maria. Time heals the wounds and those two seemed to be doing fine on the romance side of things. All in all they were a good bunch of people. Through his peripheral vision he spotted a Protector Drone. Ever present, ever ready to do its duty. He stayed out there in the forest a long time. A bugle sounded the stand down.

Penagee opened her eyes to find Mike's face hovering above her. With a sob she threw her arms around his neck and wept. Ahmed wisely ushered curious onlookers out of the room and closed the door. The old Wolf sighed. "Allah be praised," and went to his camel.

The camel was lowered to the ground by a system of pulleys. The animal, now used to this ungracious ascent and descent, still bellowed its protests. Ahmed never left the animal's side once down on the valley floor and the two were inseparable. Both were old now. As usual Ahmed walked in front and the camel followed, nudging the Bedouin's shoulders. The children loved it and squealed with glee. He headed off to the pool. Not long afterwards Moti joined him, both men sat in silence, each with his own thoughts. Up in the cave two sets of eyes gazed down in amazement. It was Ahmed who very carefully placed his hand on the younger man's thigh and whispered.

"The old Wolf and the Hawk are being watched."

"Where?"

"Behind."

They were sitting in the open. Moti's first priority was to the old man and his safety.

"I think the old Wolf should go to his camel."

Ahmed understood and slowly stood up and walked to where the camel was grazing on grasses along the river bank. Very casually he slapped its rump and followed the retreating animal into the trees, whistling. All understood that whistle. Moti remained seated in a posture of relaxation. Tiger Snake heard and every fibre in his body reacted and instantly he was on the move, hitting the ground running and passing Ahmed on the way who merely mouthed the word, "Cave". The sight of Moti sitting in the open, exposed, spurred his endeavour. The killing mode clicked in and the Human machine sought its prey. David and Anna, oblivious to the oncoming tornado, were too busy watching Moti and not knowing what to do. They had come through the Portal into the cave and had been there for two days, too afraid to venture out. They heard the bugle calls, so they figured the valley was inhabited, but could not see anyone. It was not until Ahmed and Moti appeared that they did relax a little.

The sight of Moti persuaded David against any heroics. Tiger Snake came through the cave entrance and Anna screamed. Moti was up and climbing. It happened so fast, David found himself in the grip of iron talons. Anna was screaming. Moti silenced her with a sharp jab of his fingers. David's eyes bulged. Those bands of iron held him dangling in the air, then promptly released him and he collapsed to the cave floor choking for breath. They were dragged out of the cave down to the river edge. Mike was angry. The warriors gazed down at their fallen captors. David managed to stop the coughing and reach out to Anna. He was afraid. His fear was compounded by Anna's still form. Taking her in his arms he pleaded.

"Please don't hurt her, please don't hurt her."

Mikes anger subsided and he gruffly asked.

"The Portal?"

David's response was a weak nod of the head.

"Come." Mike commanded,

So Moti bent and lifted the limp form of Anna in his arms. David stood up weak at the knees and with Mike in the lead the group made its way to the trees. The community gathered to greet the newcomers. David and Anna, still shaken by their experience, were relieved to be among the crowd. They were greeted with open arms. Their equipment had been retrieved from the cave and in time they too would become settled. For three days Penagee remained closeted in Ahmed's room, grieving for Zorak, refusing food or water and refusing to see anyone. On the fourth day she emerged into the sunlight. Ahmed was there to greet her and they sat together on a bench staring into the sky in silence until Moti passed by and Ahmed was quick to grab him and sit the man down.

"The Hawk will translate for me word for word?"

Moti blinked. "Translate to what?"

"English, you dummy." Mocked Ahmed.

"You must be joking, my English is very bad."

"So, try anyway."

Ahmed spoke and Moti translated in halting English.

"Little Sparrow, do not grieve too long for the dead. Grieving is good, but life must go on. You are alone in this world like the rest of us here. We have all lost loved ones and friends and all dream of the day we might see them again, yet we know that is an impossibility, yet we have found comfort in each other and learned to accept our fate here in this valley."

Penagee sat silent for a few moments, then asked.

"Where is Mike?"

Taking her hands in his he looked long and hard into those beautiful sad eyes and whispered, Moti translating,

"He loves you, although the stupid ape still has to admit it."

Moti promptly fell off his chair in fits of laughter receiving a boot from Ahmed in the process.

The Trigon Committee sat in silence, watching the last recorded images from Ridmon flash across the huge monitor screen. The images came from Zorak, sent at the moment the Crystal City exploded. The voice was saying.

"Men and women of the Committee, hear this, Project Ridmon is no more. You are now warned should you attempt in any way to destroy this planet, any other action on your behalf will be met with devastating consequences. Not only from Ridmon itself, but also in the very heart of your empire. There are infrastructures in place to ensure your undivided attention should you choose to ignore this warning. For too long you have ruled these Galaxies in a shameful manner, a poor example of our advanced culture. Your scanners, monitors and computers are of no use to you now. You are now held in abeyance. As you will see, I have destroyed the Crystal City and with it all connection to yourselves. You may consider this to be an idle threat and you may consider my act of suicide meaningless, but in doing so all of Ridmon's defences are activated and likewise those placed on Thedrah. It's no use, Ridmon remains and will always be, out of your reach. I bid you farewell."

With that the images ended and the monitor went silent. Members of the Committee sat motionless as a computer's monotone voice echoed what they feared.

"Confirmed detonation in Sector 4 on planet Ridmon. All communications severed and the planet blanketed, untraceable."

"What do you mean, untraceable?" Barked the command.

Once again the monotone voice answered.

"Ridmon is no more, the planet does not appear in orbital position. No scanner or monitor detection."

"Computer, was the detonation large enough to have eliminated the planet, and why no interstellar shock waves or readings?" The angry question came.

"No planetary destruction, only total disappearance."

"Impossible." Boomed the voice. "Continue search."

With that followed more silence in the Committee Room. All knew Zorak was a highly intelligent and inventive scientist capable of extraordinary achievements in the field of science. They were also acutely aware of the danger he had posed for them should he have been appointed to the Committee and they collectively saw to his banishment, put out of the way somewhere where he could still be of use and service to the Committee and its needs. One did not kill the goose that laid the golden egg, one kept it in check, under control. It appeared that the scientist, left on his own, came up with a mad plan to go against the Committee, which was intolerable. Ridmon must be located and also Zorak and his sister, together with whatever scientific work Zorak was conducting. Both were to be rendered mindless. The computer's voice echoed its findings.

"Confirmed. Ridmon untraceable."

"Dispatch retriever Drones and Robots to Ridmon's last known orbit and secure," Snarled the order.

"Acknowledged."

The Committee waited, watching the monitor as a fleet of Drones began their ascent into space. Without warning the sky erupted in sudden blinding flashes and the Drones were no more.

"Computer, report." Shouted the Chairman of the Committee.

"Unidentified threat, unidentified threat, searching."

And a moment later.

"Threat not detected, threat not detected."

The alarms sounded throughout the planet of Thedrah. It was confirmed, Zorak had played his masterpiece and Thedrah was under his control even in death. The Committee sweated. Ridmon was out of bounds. Thedrah was stalemated so very efficiently. Computers were humming, scanners and monitors searching, but to no avail. Whatever was out there it was undetectable and very lethal. Thedrah was held captive by unseen forces and she writhed at the thought. The Committee turned on itself and what ensued was exactly as Zorak had predicted. Heads did roll. The whole nation on Thedrah witnessed a new Committee take office. With it came a new and revised policy and once again the people of Thedrah breathed more easily. The threat did not vanish, it would remain in place for eons. Only Zorak had the power to change the status quo. His apparent selfless death ensured the lives of all those on Ridmon and changed the pattern of things on Thedrah. Without his stand down command, the infrastructure he had set up would remain permanent. That command would never come from Zorak. Back on Ridmon, housed in a Protector Drones' memory banks were Zorak's records, his research and his life's work. Above all, there was a new generation technology which he had expanded through the discovery of a strange hairy tentacle creature in the forests of Sector 4. A technology he so cleverly and secretly implemented in his last act as station commander on Planet Ridmon.

For Ana-Maria, life in the valley slowly healed her emotional wounds. The death of her husband left her alone and bewildered in a strange and foreboding place. Her baby girl Carla prevented her from falling into complete depression. Many Hail Mary's and prayers did not dull the ache in her heart. Her husband was a fine man and she loved him dearly. They had travelled to Portugal from Brazil on a holiday and took a bus tour in order to see as much of Portugal as possible at a reasonable price, which included hotel accommodation in various towns and cities. Their roots lay in Portugal so it was only fitting, seeing as they had saved enough money to take the trip. Roberto was as excited about the trip as she was. Amarante, a small town in the north of Portugal was on the list of places they were to visit. Its historical significance and pleasant atmosphere were priorities. She remembered boarding the bus at the bus station with little Carla sound asleep, oblivious to her surroundings, which in Ana-Maria's opinion was the best thing for the baby, as bus travel did tend to play on the nerves when children became restless. The tour guide informed them of the day's schedule, which was to be a trip to Guimaraes to visit the medieval castle there. The bus never arrived. One moment Ana-Maria was watching the countryside whiz past with its small plots and vineyards dotted everywhere there was available land and the next moment the awful crash and confusion. She remembered clutching little Carla to her chest, then nothing. Something struck the side of her head and she passed out. When Ana-Maria came to she found herself lying on the ground. She sat bolt upright, her first thoughts were for her baby and her husband. A man she recognized as being one of the tour group quickly came up to her and sitting down, handed her little Carla. She heard the words, but refused to believe them.

"You must be strong, your husband has been killed."

Ana-Maria screamed, a long heart-rending scream stopping the rest of the group in their tracks.

"Where is he?" She pleaded above little Carla's cries.

The man helped her to her feet and guided her to the spot where 20 bodies had been laid out. Ana-Maria saw Roberto's lifeless, twisted body and collapsed. She felt empty inside. She avoided contact with anyone and sat alone, rocking to and fro with little Carla in her arms, muttering endless incoherent phrases. Someone shook her and told her to feed her baby. Like an automaton she went through the motion of suckling her child. Members of the group rallied round and found diapers with which to change the child. Slowly acceptance and sanity crept in to her mind and she started to be more attentive. Hours passed into days, yet still Ana-Maria hung in suspended animation. Her mind was numb. Then came the day a wild man appeared and everything after that appeared to happen in slow motion, leaving her dazed and withdrawn. It was not until days later, when one on the wild men took Carla from her arms did she recoil and sprang at him with all the fury her slight body could muster,

nails flashing and legs kicking. Her only thought was for
the child's safety. Moti had his hands full and did the only
thing which came to mind. He grabbed Ana-Maria in one
powerful arm and pinioned her to his chest, with the baby
snuggling contentedly in the other. She fought furiously to
free herself and failed, then the tears flowed in great, heaving
sobs of despair. Moti was mortified. Ana-Maria buried her
face in his chest and wept bitterly. He stood there in dumb
stupidity, not knowing what to do. Frank came to his rescue
and together they pacified the distraught woman. From
then on Moti decided to be their self-appointed protector.
Ana-Maria recovered her composure and began to move
about and in the months that ensued she even managed to
smile when she caught Moti romping like a big clown with
Carla securely in his massive arms. She learned to put aside
her grief in a corner of her heart. Carla was too precious to
her and was a living testimony of Ana-Maria and Roberto's
love. Now she had found a friend in Moti and felt safe and
secure once again. Besides everything, she had grown very
fond of the Human ape.

Penagee took stock. She was back and in full swing. Old
Ahmed chuckled to himself. This was going to be interesting.
Two very strong characters, two very competent people and
two hearts not yet woven together. Fireworks. In his old age
Ahmed had many things to keep him occupied and he was
enjoying every moment of it. First off Penagee went in search
of Mike. He kept a distance between them she did not like
and now was the time to sort things out. Locating Mike
was not easy, so she recruited Frank's assistance. She liked
this man, he was sincere and open and above all he could be
trusted. She found Frank sitting with Susan, admiring the
Crystal Mountains. They were discussing something and

were a little surprised by her intrusion. Frank jumped to his feet and smiled.

"Hello Penagee, please join us." Indicating to a bench beside them. Penagee sat down. She studied the two and felt a pang of envy race through her. Thedrarian's were not supposed to show emotion or lose control over them, but circumstances had changed for her when she first caught a glimpse of Mike. All her training and conditioning disappeared out of the window. She was experiencing a whole new spectrum of emotions.

"I need to talk to Mike." She told Frank.

"He is at the pool where he goes often to sit by himself. Crazy man takes a shower in that waterfall, says it's for meditation and conditioning exercises. Tried it once myself and nearly had my head beaten to death." Came the reply.

Penagee was gone in a flash and Frank laughed. Turning to Susan he said.

"Mark my words, there goes Mike's undoing."

Mike sat in a meditation pose beneath a section of the thundering falls. The cascading waters plummeted down onto him with a crushing force, beating at his head and shoulders. There was the pain, but Mike put it out of his mind. For years he did this and its massaging properties were indispensable. In spite of the man's bulk and definition one would normally find on a body builder, his physique came as a result of hours of hard toil, lifting and carrying, swinging from tree to tree, plus exercise routines he remembered from bygone martial arts days. His skill with the lance and bow were exceptional through hours and hours of practice. He was a remarkable athlete for his age. This form of water meditation helped to keep the muscles loose and in tune. He became acutely aware of someone watching him. Across the pool Penagee stood. She drank in the sight of him sitting with legs crossed under the pounding water and her heart raced. By Thedrah, she thought, the man was beautiful. Without hesitation she stripped naked and plunged into the waters. Mike, watching her, could not contain himself any longer, as he loved this goddess from the stars with every fibre of his being and he dived in to meet her. Their bodies locked in an embrace, an act of love so intense, so powerful, electrifying raging passions melted into each other to become one with the universe.

For days Ahmed and Moti watched the forest, for days there was no sign of either Mike or Penagee. There was no cause for alarm, all knew, all waited for the lovers to return. David took his photos in spite of the fact there was no way to develop them at the time. Anna was in her element with new fascinations and discoveries, while Ana-Maria and Carla found comfort in Moti. Frank and Susan became expectant parents. A community took roots and began to flourish. Penagee opened up her heart and found love in the most unlikely of places, with a man light years behind in technological advancement, yet through her he was catapulted into her world. By circumstance she now entered into his. Together they would strive to build a new one. Ridmon was about to become a planet of peace and tranquillity, a Garden of Eden in a vast sea of stars and home to a new breed of people.

Amos sighed, "Now it begins," and the old Sangoma next to him chuckled.

"Yebo."*

*Yebo – African dialect for the word "Yes."

TECHNOLOGY

TWO

It took a while before the newer situation on Ridmon descended on the population there, so life took time to reach a point of semi-normality. Up in the trees people were secure in the knowledge that any threat so far encountered on the forest floor did not or could not reach their habitat. Communication did however, still pose the biggest problem, which in time would sort itself out one way of the other. Relationships between races relaxed into jovial fun-making and much laughter. Freedom to express oneself was encouraged and where such expression complimented the betterment of life in the trees, it was accepted without reserve. Fearing reprisal action from Thedrah, Penagee insisted on establishing communications with the Committee on Thedrah to further emphasize the relationship existing between the two planets. Protector Drone perfectly fitted the task as a go between and so Thedrah was contacted.

On Thedrah, an image of a man and woman appeared on a large wall-mounted monitor screen. The seated Committee members, a little surprised by the unauthorized intrusion, were nevertheless curious; on the screen there appeared the faces of a Thedarian woman and a Human male. The female's voice echoed around the large council chamber with its oval shaped amphitheatre type construction.

"Members of the Thedarian Committee, greetings from Ridmon. As you are aware, to you the Planet Ridmon does not exist and it shall remain so. You are also aware that any acts of aggression against us will result in cataclysmic retribution."

At this point Penagee paused to watch for facial expressions and reactions. The faces remained stern and unmoving, so she continued.

"We threaten neither your sovereignty nor your existence and expect the same in return. This channel of communication will be the first and last between us, after which contact will be terminated permanently. Kindly understand, and take careful note, we are capable of destroying your entire planet should we so choose, reserving the right to do so if our existence is in anyway jeopardized or compromised. You have our guarantee Thedrah will not be subjected to any interferences of any nature, unless, and I repeat unless, you pursue any action deemed to be life threatening on Ridmon. Gentlemen, Ladies of the Committee, we of Ridmon are a peaceful people, yet your survival hangs in the balance depending on your next moves, don't compromise it for yourselves."

Another pause then.

"Therefore, I urge you to consider very carefully your options and make the right choices. You do not have the technology or the ability to prevent your own extinction.

If by definition we appear to be the aggressors and hold Thedrah prisoner, it is due only to your own deceptive manipulation of this and other Galaxies that has placed you at risk. That is all, Ladies and Gentlemen, we on Ridmon wish you all a pleasant evening."

The screen went blank, leaving the Committee sitting in silent contemplation. The exact positioning of Ridmon in the Sixth quadrant was well known in spite of the fact that it could not be traced. What prevented their attack from surrounding quadrants which would make it appear as if someone else acted aggressively?

"No." Came the chairman's reply, gazing about him at the eight council members.

"Do you honestly believe a scientist the calibre of Zorak overlooked such a possibility? Think again. What did his last act of persuasion tell us, no matter what we attempt to do, the reprisal will not come from Ridmon, but here on our own Planet. That, members of the Committee, is Zorak's trump card. Somehow he was able to set up an infrastructure here on Thedrah monitoring anything remotely connected to aggressiveness towards Ridmon. You find the source on Thedrah, you have Ridmon. I am inclined to believe such a source will not be found. We therefore better consider well the threat and for the time being do nothing foolish. Equally, I am of the opinion we forget about Ridmon for the moment and concentrate on our own affairs. Ridmon is of no value to us. It does not support our needs in any way, neither does it bear significance in the overall scheme of things. The only problem facing us is, if those on Ridmon become overly agitated, we could face an immediate situation none of us want. My suggestion therefore calls for patience and prudence. In the meantime, we behave ourselves. After all, it's only a matter of time before our scientists come up with a solution to the problem, then Ridmon will pay for its insubordination."

There were unanimous verbal agreements and a singular decision was made. Thedrah would not react or create ripples which could jeopardize their existence. They were checkmated by a set of circumstances they themselves were to blame for. They would, however, seek ways to neutralize the immediate danger by stepping up technological research into improving monitoring and scanning, and a revised security system to rid themselves of the thorn in their side, Zorak's legacy.

An inter-galactic personnel shuttle took off from Thedrah destined for the fourth quadrant of X-79 where on a planet named Shishon, Thedrah harvested Zumi crystals. The crystals were needed for various propulsion methods. Shishon, a high- level security area, was entirely computer controlled. On board the shuttle an even mixture of men and woman, a relief crew to replace those stationed on Shishon, sat strapped in their seats in sullen silence. Their stay on Shishon was to be semi-permanent, which meant until such time as the authorities deemed otherwise. Everyone knew living on Shishon amounted to extreme unpleasantness and danger. The gaseous climate and atmosphere were lethal, storms raged for hundreds of kilometres, with winds gusting in places at speeds of over 300 kilometres an hour. Shishon was totally alien for all life forms, therefore living underground in specially designed structures constituted the only way by which the Zumi crystals could be extracted. It was a prison sentence and everybody knew it. What they could not understand was the reason behind the new policy proclaimed by the Committee.

All fifty of the relief crew chosen by virtue of their collective skills would form the first of a series of work units that would be sent out to all quadrants where Thedrah's invested interests were located. The so-called reward at the end of their service, an undefined period, would be resettlement back on Thedrah in the beautiful Krazanz corridor. Many had heard of this place, but none actually ever saw it or encountered anyone who lived there. Any refusal to embark was met by swift and decisive action. No one refused a Committee command. To this group the thought of spending the rest of their lives on Shishon held no attraction and some, if not all, would perish before their service terminated. The shuttle, navigated by computer on fixed co-ordinates, allowed no escape or seizure possible, as the group was housed within a sealed self-contained unit on board. Space travel was not without its dangers and pitfalls and the shuttle's journey to the 4th quadrant was no exception. No matter how advanced a technology may be, nature has limitless resources and surprises. This was to be one occasion of such an act of fortune for the fifty people aboard their space shuttle travelling towards Shishon. Through some strange phenomena, nature decided to terminate a solar system in the 4th quadrant. It's Sun simply exploded for no apparent reason. The supernova set off ripples far and wide and the shuttle, caught up in one of those ripples, was hurtled light years off course into the 6th quadrant, straight into the Trigon Universe. Shishon ceased to exist.

Protector Drones intercepted the personnel shuttle's tumbling descent through Ridmon's atmosphere and their retractor beams locked on. Inside the shuttle the on-board computers disintegrated and for the fifty occupants, strapped in their seats in the darkness of the shuttle's interior, death must have seemed imminent. All became still until the side walls of the shuttle crashed open like a peeled banana. One can imagine the thoughts that must have raced through the occupants' minds once their eyes regained focus in the sunlight, to see a bunch of people standing around the opened shuttle, clothed in nothing but the barest essentials. Penagee climbed onto the remains of the shuttle's deck smiling.

"Welcome Thedarian to the Planet of Ridmon. I am Penagee, a Thedarian like yourselves and these." Indicating to those standing on the outside, "Are Humans from the Planet Earth. Now will you all be so kind as to follow me. Do not be afraid and please, you have nowhere to go so be calm, don't become aggressive and we will all be very happy to assist you and try to make you all as comfortable as possible."

Mike and Moti stood behind Penagee their imposing appearance must have triggered a warning. Once the group was at a safe distance, an invisible Protector Drone fired its white beam of destruction and the shuttle wreckage disappeared.

Mike studied these fifty very fortunate Thedarian's while Penagee listened to their story. Their age group he estimated to be between the early and late twenties. Non-military for certain, but one never knew. Moti moved amongst them checking for anything resembling a weapon. One could clearly see that they were intimidated by him.

Ahmed and Frank strolled over, Frank saying.

"Well, well. Our community has expanded a little. This is going to be very interesting, as not only do we have a language problem, but a long road lies ahead trying to teach these people how to be primitive. Poor beggars, what a shock this is going to be!"

Mike translated for Ahmed. Frank eyed Mike. "You three are bad enough, with your Hebrew, now we all have to learn Thedarian."

Mike laughed and, turning to Ahmed, asked.

"What does Old Father see?"

Ahmed beamed. "The Old Wolf sees lots of helpers, perhaps now he can take things easier instead of having to run after his two sons."

"Hmmm! The Old Father is perhaps right and the sight of those Thedarian beauties is enough to make him feel young again and have thoughts of his own harem." Mocked Mike.

The old Bedouin's wrinkled face broke into a broad smile. "The Lion knows the Old Wolf well, does he not?"

Frank listened to the exchange of words passing between the two men and he could just guess what the topic was about. They always conversed in a way distinctly formal to the non-initiated, but he understood the deep bond between these two and realized it was their way of showing their affection without losing face or pride. Since living with the three, Mike, Moti and Ahmed, he had encountered true friendship, a unity like no other. They spoke the same language between themselves, yet were as far removed from each other by nationality and conviction as anyone could be. The fact that they didn't even share the same religion made the relationship even more unique. These three never argued and never got mad at each other. They were a fine example for the rest of the community. What made all the difference was that they cared, and made time for everyone and anyone within the community? They were the accepted leaders and managed their task beyond reproach.

The task of housing the newcomers and seeing to their immediate needs fell on the shoulders of Luisa and Jose

Rodrigues, a middle aged Spanish couple with three children of their own, formerly hotel owners. The Community Room was converted into a dormitory until such time as proper facilities were available. Penagee of course was ecstatic having people of her own kind in the valley, yet had to follow procedure and read them the Riot Act. Moti less enthusiastically posted guards at various strategic points as a safeguard to keep the people in. The Thedarian's found it difficult. Who could blame them? Climbing up and down trees, no computers to act upon their every whim, having to perform basic functions in such a primitive manner, not to mention the diet forced upon them, took some getting used to, yet they were more than grateful considering the alternative.

Among the Thedarian group was a doctor and, for the first time in a long while the community relaxed, knowing there was a qualified person to deal with any major medical crisis. Anna came up with a suggestion that, seeing most of the group were qualified as crystal workers, why not use their talents to build a crystal city on the side of the cliffs above or adjacent to the waterfall, with an interconnecting bridge over to the trees. In this way both the old and new would complement each other to afford greater safety overall. The idea was met with much enthusiasm from all concerned and so began a joint Thedarian, Human venture which was to prove the catalyst in cementing the two sides together. It was a daunting task to be tackled without proper tools. Nonetheless, the Thedarian engineers came up with a plan both ingenious and as simple to apply as one could imagine. Water mixed with a concoction of natural plant juices proved to be the solution to cultivate crystal growth very rapidly, exactly in the shape they wanted it, by applying the solution at boiling point to existing crystal formations, thus expanding on their shape and size. The entire community launched themselves into the art of crystal manipulation with gusto. With a lot of time available and no deadlines to keep, it gave the community something to keep themselves occupied with for a long while.

Penagee became so involved in the project that Mike found himself back in the trees alone with his Protector Drone. For the second time since being in the valley he became restless. What lay on the other side of the valley? The question nagged at him over the years, but getting over those cliffs was an impossible task. He smiled to himself. This time he would go the easy way, he would go by Drone. First off, perhaps Penagee could command them to allow him access and follow instruction.

"Would she do it?" He wondered.

"No! No! No! I can't allow it. As much as I love and trust you, and it pains me to have to do this, no and that's final. The Drones have specific functions and this entire planet's existence hangs on them being able to protect us. You must understand that any break in the Drone's triangulation means Ridmon is at risk. Please, the Drones are highly sophisticated and intricate pieces of technology, both mechanical and biological creations that have the capacity to think and act of their own accord. The Drones of Ridmon can't be terminated by conventional means, they can only self-destruct in specific circumstances and by specific command and this is why I can't let you have what you ask. I am very sorry. Please don't hold it against me."

Mike took her in his arms and held her tight.

"I understand and appreciate your fears. No, I will not hold it against you." He kissed her hard and left her to her duties.

His mind raced. There must be a way to gain access, so he took to the trees. Things were becoming quite dull in the valley for a man of his talents. Perched high up in the trees Mike spotted the Drone through his peripheral vision. You see it but you don't see it, it's always there to protect, so that means it has a profile on its subject, which means it is able to read the subject's thought patterns, which means there is a mental link between the two. He chuckled to himself. He had found a way, all that remained was to tune in to the Drone. Mike drew in deep breaths, crossed his legs and forced himself to relax. Closing his eyes to a point where they were mere slits, he concentrated on the Drone, fixing his stare squarely on the hovering object. Through his slit vision his periphery was extended and the shape of the Drone became more distinct. He sat like that for hours, motionless and relaxed in a state of semi-consciousness which comes with meditation. All the while his mind was focused on the Drone. Nothing happened, but Mike persisted. He repeated this little exercise every day for two weeks until he felt the probe. The Drone became curious of his action. Obviously no one informed it about the benefits of meditation. One could restrict thought activity to an absolute minimum whilst in meditation and, with practice, one could keep it up for hours. Seeing as the Drone was tuned into its subject's thought patterns, it had a basis by which it gauged reactions to given situations. When there was no physical activity and limited brain patterns over an extended period of time, especially when the subject was not in the sleep state, its curiosity was aroused and so it was required to find out more about the reason in order to update its synopsis list. The sensation was weird; he remained immobile allowing the Drone to probe. Stage one of his plan was accomplished, now for stage two. Every day the probing became stronger and Mike repeated one thought over and over in his mind.

"Friend, I am your friend."

A few days later Mike got his response. It came through loud and clear, in a high pitched tone.

"Friend, I am your friend."

Mike had gained access and realized that Penagee controlled these Drones through a form of mental telepathy. She was waiting for him on his return, greeting him as usual, only a smouldering fire burned behind her eyes.

"So Mr. Earthman, you are very smart, aren't you? Imagine that, accessing a Drone and to top it all, the Drone refuses to respond, but keeps telling me, Subject No.1 my friend, respond only to friend."

A pause then.

"Do you realize what you have done?" She yelled.

"Yes Penagee, I know full well. It's called kindness. I have accessed a Drone through kindness and given a biological machine a name, not some number, not some code, but an identity. Protector Friend. Of course it has no attributes which remotely resemble your or my make up, but It has a brain though, a highly developed and progressive brain. We have on Earth an animal with similar characteristics called a Dolphin."

Penagee regarded Mike with renewed interest. She was angry sure, but she had to admit Mike was a man full of surprises. He had accessed a Drone through the only medium possible, the mind. What was she going to do with him? She walked over to the edge of the platform and stood gazing into the sky. She felt a slight pressure inside her head, understanding the words "Love me." It was Mike's voice. She spun around to see his smiling face and open arms. She watched him. His lips were not moving, the throat was not moving, yet she was hearing his voice inside her head.

"Yes, my Thedarian beauty, it's called mental telepathy and thanks to Protector Friend you and I are able to communicate with each other without physically saying a word."

"But how?" She questioned.

"I don't know, but it uses our thought waves channelled via its own brain and amplifies them. It is not a comfortable feeling knowing something monitors your innermost thoughts and whenever one of us thinks of the other or wishes to make contact, those thoughts are sent and received like a two-way radio."

Penagee smiled.

"So, not only have you found a way into my heart, but now into my mind. That could be dangerous."

"Yes and no, however, one thing is for sure, we are going to have to be very honest and open with each other from now on. The other side of the coin though, we have instant contact whenever or wherever we are."

Just then, Moti, Ahmed, David and Anna with a few of the Thedarian engineers arrived to discuss a problem concerning them regarding the interconnecting bridge. In the valley paper or pens with which to record information were non-existent, so the inventive Ahmed had reached down into his ancestral past and came up with a type of parchment based on the same principle of the ancient Egyptians, papyrus paper. For writing materials he devised and fashioned out of young palm stalks dipping pens that, when coated with a very thin film of Black Nut gum, worked perfectly. Writing ink, a deep magenta sap extracted from the thorny pineapple and diluted with water, became the base colour for anything drawn or written. Parchment was unrolled on to the floor and weighted down, on which were drawn plans for the bridge. All gathered around and Moti explained, indicating to the lines and angles.

"This bridge is approximately three-quarters of a kilometre long. It will have to span well over a hundred metres off the ground. What we propose is to lower the height by twenty metres, meeting at the trees where a pylon will be erected supporting a large platform connecting to the bridge, forming a complete unit."

Taking another parchment from Ahmed, he spread it over the first and stepped backward for all to see. The drawings were excellent. The supporting artwork depicted a visual view of the completed construction, very realistic and precise.

"Who's the artist?" Enquired Mike.

Moti pointed at David. Mike transmitted his thoughts at Penagee.

"Please ask him, my beautiful sexy lovebird, if he would mind to be the community's official historian."

Her eyebrows shot up. "And don't look at me like that, it turns me on!"

Penagee blushed.

Ahmed's shrewd eyes caught the silent exchange.

"Will the Lion leave his panting over Little Swallow for some other time and pay attention." He bellowed.

Moti roared with laughter, slapping his thigh. Ahmed was the only one who could put Mike in his place and an exchange such as this rarely happened, but when they did it was sheer enjoyment just to watch Mike squirm. The Thedarian's looked puzzled and Anna's eyes twinkled. David quickly brought the situation back into focus by exclaiming,

"We do not want to harm the trees in any way. By bringing the bridge to the trees in this manner, we still have access to the trees from the platform or to the forest floor by way of the supporting pylon."

One of the Thedarian engineers added.

"The entire upper section of the bridge and platform will be enclosed by a thin transparent crystal covering for pedestrian protection."

Now it was the Humans' turn to look puzzled. Moti questioned.

"What did he say?"

Penagee translated for Mike who translated for Moti and Ahmed. Anna piped up.

"This is no good. We have to find a language that everyone can understand. We can't go on like this, you translate, he translates and they translate business. We can't afford it. What if we have a real crisis on our hands, how are we going to be a cohesive unit when half of us don't know what the other half is saying?"

"Point taken." Replied Mike and added,

"By the way, if no one has any objections, I think David should be our official historian. With his artistic abilities we have both a written and pictorial account of events in the valley."

The idea met with enthusiastic agreement and David was promoted to a position of importance. Mike sounded his bugle. The community gathered in its designated place. Positioning Penagee and Anna next to him as translators, Mike addressed the group in English.

"As you all know, we have amongst us people of all shapes, sizes and languages. This has caused some problems in communication and a few frustrating incidents."

Laughter, murmurs and whistles erupted from the group and Mike waited for them to settle down.

"It has been decided that, strategically, our present forms of communication are lacking, so we put it to you to take a vote as to what medium of communication we are going to use in future, in order for everyone to at least be able to communicate. Now before you all start a war, consider who's who in the zoo and let's try to accommodate each other and come up with a workable solution. Let's say the various representatives of the different language groups will meet with us a week from today and present their ideas, language substitutes and a programme for possible quick learning."

A week later the various representatives met in the community lounge and presented their proposals. The importance of verbal communication was paramount, therefore it was agreed that a language based on lingua franca would be the most appropriate, not only for the present but also for the future, particularly considering the possible influx of additional community members from who knows where. Mike, Penagee, Frank and Ana-Maria became the community's appointed language

Moderators and translators and were tasked to create a simplified spoken language that all could learn very quickly. The building of the Crystal City forged ahead more efficiently and effectively in the following months. Both Humans and Thedarian's worked side by side, beginning to share a common bond and new language vocabulary. There were drawbacks of course, but never serious ones, as most people learned very quickly to shout for help rather than get flustered or angry. It was during that week that Ahmed's camel died. The man was devastated; his only true link to the past was gone forever. Ridmon buried the camel with honour. Ahmed withdrew into himself and for the first time in many years he missed his past, sitting for long hours each day near the waterfall in deep contemplation. The community became concerned.

Mike worried about his adopted father. He did not know what to do to offer the old Bedouin solace, other than sitting with him in silence. He tried humour, which failed. He tried reasoning, but that too had failed. What the old man needed was a distraction, something to take his mind off things, something to take the camel's place. During one of Mike's daily waterfall meditation sessions the Protector Drone offered the answer. By now they shared an interesting relationship and through it Mike understood Ahmed's depression. Penagee, Mike and the Drone had become inseparable, a tightly knit threesome that made up a very strange and complicated understanding, a man, a woman and a biological entity. The Drone's message was loud and clear.

"Subject No.1 and Drone friend. Friend of Friend need friend. Drone know where friend."

An image flashed into Mike's mind. He knew it, there were other life forms on this planet. In his excitement Mike jumped up shouting, slipped outwards cracking the back of his head and plunged headlong into the pool. Penagee went rigid. She bounded down from a construction platform in full flight for the pool. Protector Drone acted with lightning speed. Ahmed heard the shout and turned to see Mike's body smack into the crystal rocks just below the water line and his heart stopped. Gently the Drone beamed Mike's unconscious form from the water into its invisible interior at the same moment as a breathless Penagee sprinted up. She was beside herself, and her mind screamed, "Protect, protect." Frantically she searched. A retriever beam shot out and Penagee was lifted into the Drone's Interior, then they were gone. Someone sounded the general alarm. Moti reacted instinctively, almost knocking the heavily pregnant Susan off her feet in his haste. Frank, with a bunch of people, spilled onto the tree-top platform and Moti spotted Ahmed standing by the pool staring into space. Alarm bells rang in his brain and he charged like a bull out of hell, watching helplessly as Ahmed pitched forward clutching at his heart. Abu Ahmed whispered through clenched teeth.

"The Lion is dead, the Old Wolf goes to meet him in Allah's garden and the Hawk must be strong." He died in Moti's arms.

It took a moment for the words to sink in then a piercing agonized scream rocked the silence, reverberated against the cliffs to echo far down the valley. Moti clutched Ahmed's still form to his chest and wept bitterly. After a while he jumped up, raced for the trees and disappeared. The community laid Ahmed to rest next to his camel. Frank, by order of succession, took over command of the community, imposing stricter vigilance and security. He stepped up work on the Crystal City. He was concerned; without Mike and Moti they were vulnerable. Three weeks went by since Moti took off and both Mike and Penagee within a Drone, to who knows where. Anna proved to be an excellent organizer and together they brought the community back to a level of normality. The Thedarian's adapted well to their new environment and all things considered, seemed happy. He dared not issue the firearms, remembering too well the last incident and wasn't about to take the chance with Susan so near her time. He was sure that once Moti had gotten over his grief he would be back. As for Mike and Penagee, that remained a mystery. Poor Ana-Maria just sat day-in and day-out watching the forest. Frank sincerely hoped for her sake this did not mean a second misfortune for her. The Thedarian doctor was good. The doctor began a research into the vegetation in the valley and as a result came up with alternate menus to their diets which made a change. It was not caviar, but offered a better variety, plus a range of homeopathic remedies. The days were full. Gradually the Crystal City took shape and Frank had to admit it was going to be a work of art and very futuristic in its design, offering much needed security and protection. He would miss the trees though; they grew on one somehow and brought out the primeval instincts. But like all things, people must evolve, and that's just what they were doing. Their chances were very good unless something devastating happened. Two weeks later, Moti returned and Frank breathed a sigh of relief.

Protector Drone observed Subject No.1 Friend fall to the water and felt the pain. It reacted with blinding speed. "Save friend, save friend," and beamed Mike's unconscious form into itself. The diagnostic machinery was set in motion. Mike was hurt, hurt bad, with severe lacerations and a broken neck. Protector Drone groaned within itself and set its healing abilities into an accelerated mode. It heard Penagee's pleading "Protect, protect" and scooped her up, rendering her immobile in a state of suspended animation. Its purpose was to protect and protect it would. Protector Drone's mission was simple, Mike's recovery. All else took second place, not the planet, not the people, not their defence. It left Ridmon's valley of Paradise on a journey that would take it to the farthest reaches of space. Within the Drone's interior Mike and Penagee hung suspended, encased in a life sustaining substance and the healing began. Minute electrical pulses passed through every nerve fibre, bone and muscle. A mauve beam of light tracked from head to foot in a constant cycle. Protector Drone tapped into their brain cells. It slowly and systematically fed into the sub-conscious a technology more advanced than anything in the known worlds, a gift to its friends. Protector Drone was no ordinary biological machine, as at some point in its complicated creation a genetic malfunction occurred. This oversight led to a Drone of immense intelligence and abilities of comprehension, reason and logic. It was an entity housed within a machine.

For six months Protector Drone navigated deep outer space while his subjects' bodies healed, adjusted and their minds developed. Only once all was in place and functioning did he return to Ridmon to deposit Mike and Penagee into the trees, a short distance from the community and then went into a metamorphosis. Protector Drone transformed itself into an entity, a living entity of sheer energy. No longer a simple Drone, but an intellect, an intelligence, that could take on any shape or form at will and transcended itself to become the ultimate Protector. Its discarded shell fell to the forest floor and disintegrated. Mike's brain awoke, something was different, and he opened his eyes. There were the trees, the sky and Penagee. She sat staring past him in deep concentration. He felt good, very good in fact and it all came back to him. The fall into the pool, the pain and then darkness. He sensed someone behind him and turned. A white luminescence the shape of a man hovered and from its eyes beamed a silver light straight into Mike's brain. It was as if the past, the present and the future, all rolled into one, manifested itself. He saw aeons of time flash past and a power surged through his body, down every nerve fibre. Such was the force of it that his body lifted and hung suspended. He was seeing the creation of space, galactic histories, his own life, the Drone's transfiguration and something else. He saw a part of the future. Then it was over.

His brain reeled at the stark reality thumping home like a sledgehammer on an anvil. He and Penagee were alone, facing each other in a silence of mystified disbelief and awe. What they were allowed to witness went far beyond anything imaginable. There was no need for words. Tears cascaded down their cheeks, tears of joy, hope and love. Penagee and Mike had been given a gift, powers few mortals possessed. Theirs was to guard and build on a new evolution in time and space and to be the cornerstones for a greater universal plan. Not all the powers were immediate, but would, through the course of their mortal lives, become manifest. The stepping blocks were put in place, what remained was their growth and through the sequences by which that growth would unfold, came the powers. For the moment, as an infant must first learn to crawl before it can walk, so also Mike and Penagee had to learn to master these unique talents, step by step. Protector Drone evolved on to a higher plane, the biological machine once only a thing, surpassed itself and became a living entity of energy no longer confined by restrictive bonds, but freed to another realm, another dimension. A Messenger had delivered its message and would be rarely seen on Ridmon again, its task there complete. But it would always be close to Mike and Penagee, watching from afar and on standby if they should need.

Moti sat next to Ahmed's grave, speaking to the old man. He came every day for a short while to say hello and keep the gravesite free of unwanted growth. He spoke aloud,

"Old Father, Carla is growing to be a fine child. Ana-Maria is recovering and it will be awhile yet before any of us move into the new city. I miss you and Mike. Life is not the same without you two. But I guess we must carry on and I have much to keep me busy."

He rearranged some flowers he had brought and brushed away debris off the slab of crystal on the grave with its inscribed letters, Abu Ahmed, Father. On his return to the community five months previously, Moti had placed the slab with its headstone onto the grave and bid his farewells in his own way. He was sitting quietly when a gentle voice behind him whispered.

"Shalom, brother."

He spun around and there, as true as life, stood Mike. Penagee retreated into the shadows to allow these men their privacy.

"Mike." He uttered, and the two embraced and danced around like excited children.

Penagee watched this spectacle and smiled warmly. Friendship and love of this nature between men was indeed something she had never actually seen, only heard of. Those two shared between them a very special and unique bond. The romping stopped and Mike knelt down beside the grave in silence, head bowed. He spoke without words, only Penagee heard.

"Old Wolf, you, the Lion and the Hawk lived through much together. The Lion always taking council from the Old Wolf, who at times chastised the Lion when he needed it. Throughout our time together, none of us expressed our feelings, but now, the Lion must tell the Old Wolf that he loved him greatly, like a Father, and to tell the Old Wolf, the Lion shall miss him very much. Go in peace Old Wolf, and may Allah bestow upon you the blessing of eternal life in his Kingdom and may we, by his grace, meet again one day."

Penagee came out of the shadows and together, arm in arm they walked through the beautiful exotic flowers and between the huge magnificent trees to their home. Mike would grieve for Ahmed in his own way, in the quiet stillness of his mind. Penagee never expected he would disappear on her without saying a word. That day Mike quietly vanished.

Ana-Maria never failed to watch the Dark Forest anxiously whenever Moti disappeared into it. She was terribly afraid for him, yet understood that Moti's role in the community called for his unique talents, which contributed to everyone's chances of survival in the valley. Since Ahmed's death and Mike's strange disappearance, Moti had spent endless hours in the forest alone. Less talkative, keeping a distance between himself and the rest of the community, even Ana-Maria. She understood his pain and offered to Moti the only thing she had, herself. Their relationship up to then had been purely platonic, one in which Ana-Maria's memory of her dead husband still carried tremendous influence on matters of the heart. It was not until she heard Moti's anguished scream the day Ahmed died, that her repressed feelings for Moti wrenched open the doors of her heart .She found renewed purpose to escape her self-imposed emotional exile. Things have their own way of working themselves out and it was Ana-Maria who inadvertently initiated events. One day she followed Moti into the forest, finding him beside Ahmed's grave, weeping. Moti was a strong and powerful man, yet the loss of the two men he loved so much broke his spirit. Ana-Maria's emotions took hold of her and she slumped down, cradling Moti's head to her bosom, her tears mingling with his, rocking to and fro. He breathed in her scent, felt the compelling warmth of her and his resistance gave way to an all-consuming need to hold her. He kissed her hungrily, seeking out every part of her face and breasts. The sensations re-kindled in Ana-Maria were too much to bear and she let go with fiery hunger. Suppressed passions boiled over and on the river bank their bodies joined as one beneath the three moons of Ridmon.

A week after Mike had disappeared Penagee, sensing his return, raced down from the Crystal City, her heart pounding with joy and literally threw herself into his waiting arms. There was no need for words between them, she understood only too well. What pandemonium reigned that day, the 4th day of the month December, in the year 2021 the community took to the trees, sealed off all accesses to the tree tops and threw a party? It was a welcome home party Mike would not easily forget. There was dancing, music, plenty of food and drink. Some of the enterprising young teenagers had formed a band, complete with percussion and wind instruments, producing an exquisite collection of haunting melodies. Thedarian's and Humans alike were dressed in the same simple yet comfortable attire which amounted to very little, all bronzed by the sun, all looking fit and healthy. There were mixed couples, new babies, a sense of unity and commitment and, above all, they had all become part of one family. The party raged on for three days. Everyone let their hair down. The community deserved it. All work came to an absolute standstill. A decision was made that on this day, every year, all going well, a week would be set aside for the festivities and celebrations to mark Ridmon Day.

Thedarian females carried their young for a term of six months and, within a space of three months after birth, babies could walk. After a further four months speech, co-ordination and character formation took place. By the time they were three, they were quite capable of all the functions of a Human child the age of ten. This posed a problem for the community and one in which Penagee intervened to bring about a balance. Recruiting the assistance of the doctor, she administered potent potions that changed every woman in the group's pregnancy cycle. The results were astounding. She had altered and realigned the genetics of these women, including her own, to the extent that from the time of conception to the birth of a child, the pregnancy period was reduced to four months. The child's development thereafter was accelerated by a year. All children born were healthy and strong. She went a step further and redirected both DNA and genetic strains in both Humans and Thedarian's alike to a common factor. A woman's monthly period was reduced to once every two months. The men did not escape her attentions either. They too were subjected to genetic modification which strengthened their immune systems, their bodies and above all their reproductive capabilities. Both men and women were thus able to lead healthy, productive lives and produce children well into their later years. Menopause was thus effectively delayed. However, she realized that new blood needed to be added into the community to prevent mutations caused by interrelationships which would occur in the future. That was a definite problem she would have to deal with soon. For the time being, there were no causes for concern. No one questioned the right or validity of her interference with the natural process. On Ridmon it was a case of extreme circumstances having to be met with extreme measures.

In a discussion between David and Frank, the subject had come up and Frank expressed his opinion,

"The moral ethics Humans would bring up in argument against genetic manipulation of this type, considered by many to be highly controversial and against the laws of nature, would be that the evolutionary process had to be given leeway to effect its own changes, at its own pace and time, without intervention from outside forces, whether Human or Alien. On Ridmon it was a case of whatever was necessary to enhance and improve life through a controlled process was acceptable. The bridging of gaps between two races, one Human, the other Alien, was of prime importance and assured the joint survival of all parties concerned. If man has new technology, man takes a step forward in his evolution. Therefore, if man had access to technology so advanced, would it not be safe to assume that he would take ten steps forward, accelerating his evolution? The principle remained the same. The Humans on Ridmon have found out that there is other life in this Universe. A greater intelligence than theirs supported by a technology Humans have not even begun to dream of. So it is only fair to say that for them, their moral and ethical thinking have had to take a dramatic redirection. It does not mean their base beliefs had altered, it meant only an adjustment. They still believed in a God, the Creator of all things. Only now they could fully appreciate that God does exist and not a figment of imagination handed down through the ages by some highly skilled story tellers and manipulators of the truth."

David sighed, then replied, "I never gave it much thought, but none of us here on Ridmon practice, as a group, any given religion."

"No, but if you watch you will see many still carry their beliefs in their hearts and I have come across many of these people in our group, and that includes the Thedarian's, who pray to their God, by whatever name they call him. In this group amongst the Humans, there is a wide range of religious beliefs. Time will tell and I am sure my children and my children's children will adopt a form of religion and ethical policy as a matter of principle. We will leave them Islam, Judaism and Christianity. How that will eventually interact here on Ridmon is anyone's guess. Languages will fall away until we have one group of people, speaking one language and believing in one religion. The Tower of Babel will not be built here, only the tower of hope and progress of a new people." Answered Frank.

"You are really into this, aren't you Frank?" Came the question.

"I guess so, and so should you be, we have a new home, a new life. You are also fortunate to have Anna, she is a fine woman. Never look a gift horse in the mouth, David, and never wish too hard for something or you might end up regretting later."

David smiled and excused himself. Anna was fast becoming a thing of the past for David. His eye had caught sight of a Thedarian beauty, now everything else seemed less important. Moti and Mike navigated the tree tops in their usual manner, Mike knowing every thought in Moti's head if he chose to. Common decency prevented him invading personal privileged information. But it was useful nonetheless and Mike would choose the time and place to communicate with Moti, when or if the situation arose. He could see through Moti's eyes, feel his emotions and know his innermost thoughts. Disconcerting as it was, the values outweighed the morals. No matter where Mike was he could be in direct mental communication with everyone in the community and had the power to control them if he so desired. Then there was Penagee. She was the assurance that Mike did not take his newfound ability to negative extremes. Sometimes her gentle reminder would come through.

"Mike, behave yourself!"

He knew better than to cross swords with her. He had to admit, Penagee was everything and more to him and he loved her with a raging passion. The mere sight of her made his blood boil and he prayed that the feelings would not diminish with time, as was the case with so many relationships when the parties concerned began to identify with different priorities and fall into the trap of losing their partners along the way. There was a library of information housed in his brain spanning aeons of time and a highly advanced technology. He took his time to get used to the idea and to feel the direction which he must travel. He did not have to swing from tree to tree anymore, he could teleport, but tree travel was something he had gotten used to and besides, his muscles didn't feel right without the exercise. The time would come when all things changed. Until then he was a Human tree ape and enjoyed the primitive freedom it offered and the inner mental wrestling to fathom out the awesome powers that he had inherited. He loved the valley with its fantastically beautiful surroundings, feeling at peace and oneness with nature. He missed Ahmed.

Penagee would on occasion join him to ride on his back, clamping her legs around his waist, thick long black hair streaming behind and drinking in the magnetic sensations emanating from his powerful body, until her passions could contain themselves no longer and her aching loins were satisfied. At other times she would follow Mike through his mind. Her eyes became his eyes and often Mike cut short his tree top antics to teleport back into her arms. Everyone observed this relationship with much interest. It was truly a match made in heaven and both Mike and Penagee displayed an open warmth and tenderness towards each other which spilled over and became an example to many couples. Paradise was not without its problems, as is the case in all communities and societies, and there were bound to be disturbances. Social domestic quarrels, disputes of all types, drunken brawls, but never thieving, rape or murder. In that way Ridmon was indeed blessed.

Moti, of course, was puzzled. These days Mike and Penagee hardly uttered a word to each other, yet acted as if they had. To him it was uncanny that two people could be so tuned to each other that words were not necessary. He and Mike shared a bond by which verbal communication was in the end their only medium of understanding. There was definitely something else about those two they kept to themselves. Moti slowly over time through observation figured it out. Telepathy, it had to be, or how else did they know a lot of what was going on in the community and, more disconcertingly, with his own private life. His mind had difficulty accepting that thought. He trusted them with his life, although felt a little peeved his innermost thoughts could be accessed at random. He gradually got over it, knowing they would respect his privacy. His relationship with Mike and Penagee took on a whole new meaning. He knew that they knew what he knew, and that was that. No point in trying to build a mountain out of a molehill. He was not aware of the extent of the powers that Mike had been gifted with and attributed most things out of the ordinary to Penagee. His perceptions were one day shattered. A creature of the Dark Forest inadvertently strayed from its home grounds dangerously close to the community and, to Moti's horror, Mike quite calmly descended to the forest floor, confronting the creature head on.

Moti screamed from the tree tops,

"Mike, in heavens name, get out of there!"

Mike ignored the caution, crouching low as the creature scented, extending its tentacles. Moti couldn't stand it. He launched himself into empty space straight down at the creature. What followed next imprinted deep into Moti's memory. His descent came to an abrupt end, leaving him hanging suspended in mid-air by a force he could feel, but not see. To his dismay the creature slowly began to rise off the ground, up through the trees and soon disappeared from view. Then he was gently lowered to the forest floor to stand next to a smiling Mike. Moti gaped at Mike in total disbelief and it came to him in one massive revelation. But before he could orientate himself, Mike locked him in those massive arms of his, almost squeezing the life out of Moti in a playful gesture of affection.

"The Hawk would give his life for the Lion without concern for his own? This is a gift of friendship that, from this day onwards, shall be worn with much gratitude." Said Mike to which, before either of them could utter another word, came Penagee's harsh rebuke.

"Idiots. What do you think you are both playing at?" Moti quickly gazed around looking for Penagee, but the forest stood dark and silent.

Again Penagee's voice echoed,

"From now on Moti, don't worry so much about Mike, you big ape, he can look after himself far better these days, and thanks, that was a very brave and unselfish thing you did a moment ago and I love you for it."

Moti freed himself from Mike's bear hug and angrily confronted his best friend.

"So, the Lion has new claws and is telepathic?"

Mike became solemn answering.

"Yes, my Brother, very long and dangerous claws. More dangerous than you can imagine."

"How?" Moti questioned.

"I don't know for sure. What I do know is that there is no simple way to explain this to you, so you are going to have to trust me. It is a very serious business, my Brother, and just why and how it happened beats me. In my brain there is a technology and an ability way beyond my comprehension. I have seen the birth of time, seen billions of years of terrestrial evolution, life forms and entities and at the end of it all, I was allowed to see some of the future, Earth's future."

Moti blinked. That last name registered.

"Earth's future?"

"Yes."

To Moti this seemed all too much to swallow, this meant only one thing. Mike was appointed to carry out a task by a higher order of the Universe, to be some sort of a messenger. His mind raced, he was flabbergasted, at a loss for words.

"Come we must return, there is still much to do, and I must ask you to keep what you have both seen and heard locked in your heart." Beckoned Mike.

Moti did not know what to do, whether to kiss Mike's hand, his feet, or what? Once again Penagee's voice came through.

"He is a man, a Human like you and yes, he has been given exceptional gifts, but he is still a man and is to be treated as you have always done in the past, now and in the future. You are not brothers by birth, but have come to be so on this Planet. The reason he saw the future was to remind him of his place in this Universe and not to abuse his powers, otherwise he would be held accountable and have to answer to the Greater powers that be. We can't expect to have such advanced abilities without an advanced watcher. Neither can we take it upon ourselves to act in any way on our own accord and attempt to change the motion of the Universe. Just be happy that you don't carry on your shoulders the same responsibility."

Moti's life took on a new meaning from that day onwards. The new Crystal City of Ridmon, built outwards from the side of a 5 kilometre vertical cliff face, had taken shape in perfect resemblance of the artist's visual impressions and looked like something out of a fantasy world. The

Thedarian excelled themselves beyond all expectation. The city's base was a horizontal half circle protruding 200 metres out from the cliff face, 250 metres off from the valley floor, then extending 600 metres outwards to form the bridge which ended in a fifty metre circular platform. The platform was supported on a single pylon whose circular broad base, 75 metres in diameter, tapered up to a 25 metres diameter to support the bridge and platform. In the centre of the platform stood a vertical shaft of transparent crystal as additional support for the dome's roof. Within the shaft's interior was an elevator with capacity to carry 150 people. The activation mechanism, up or down, was simply very clever. Crystals responded to sound waves or frequencies and, by trial and error, the exact pitch of sound of a crystal gong being struck, propelled the elevator up or down within its housing.

The three metre thick exit or entry door at the foot of the pylon hinged up and outwards, perfectly counter-balanced so that a child could open or close it easily by simply pulling or pushing a lever. Within the pylon base were storage rooms, offices and laboratories. The platform and bridge were domed leading into the Great Hall, the main Community area which could seat five thousand people comfortably. Thin sheets of crystal, twenty metres by eight metres square carefully moulded, shaped and joined together made up the transparent domed roof of the Great Hall which reached a height of 50 metres. Slicing vertically through the centre of the dome was the back-drop of terraced apartments. Each apartment had large concave crystal windows shielding four bedrooms, a lounge, kitchen and bathroom, and all the units were fully furnished. There were outside elevators operating up the entire complex and stopping at each level. A complex mosaic of hidden entrances and facades blended into the surrounding cliff face so as not to appear as one accommodating 5,000 families. There was constant running water, garbage disposal and a very sophisticated sewage system into which all waste product was recycled and fed back to the vegetation on the valley floor. The same vegetation's sap was mixed with other ingredients for the recycling processes. Nothing was left to go to waste. From within the complex there was an escape route leading via an elevator down into the cavern at the end of the cave behind the waterfall. The cave mouth was sealed by a 5 metre thick hinged gate which, when closed, locked into place and was strong enough to withstand almost anything thrown at it. From deep within the cavern a shaft led off for a distance of 3 kilometres exiting at the base of the cliffs into the dense forest, allowing for a concealed escape route.

The community sat back and admired its handiwork from the trees. They had accomplished all this in a space of eight months. Incredible was the only word to describe it. There was excitement buzzing in the air as Mike, Moti, Penagee, Frank and Borz, the Thedarian engineer in charge, stood together on the crystal platform to officiate at the opening of the new City. This day Mike and Penagee would address the community telepathically. Mike's verbal opening address was simple.

"Ladies, Gentlemen and children of Ridmon, what you are about to experience is real, is happening and there is no cause for alarm. Kindly therefore make yourselves comfortable and relax."

They waited for the crowd to settle, and then Penagee transmitted telepathically in every language to the gathered people.

"Friends, it is with great pleasure and pride that we, peoples of Ridmon, declare our Crystal City open. We would like to thank all of you for your efforts in making this possible. You may now officially take up residence in your allocated units. Dinner for everyone will be served in the Great Hall on the third moon rising tonight. Thank you."

There was a silence while the impact of what they had experienced sank in. A tingling sensation, tickling the base of the skull, then a voice inside their heads. The applause began gradually then erupted into full scale shouts, whistles and clapping. The crowd dispersed into the interior of the building to claim their well-earned prizes. Mike took off with Moti to collect beautiful Ridmon orchids for the dinner occasion. A social order had emerged on Ridmon, made up of the most unlikely of races inhabiting a small part of the Universe. The wheels of evolution turned in many different ways. A circumstance sometimes defies explanation. So it was on Ridmon where, by a chance intervention into the order of things, the planet re-adjusted and realigned the balance of its nature. Ridmon was unique. It was a planet whose upper crust consisted entirely of crystal and on which, through aeons of time, there evolved a hospitable life-supporting environment. She boasted three moons and 8 other non- inhabitable planets in her solar system. Ridmon's uniqueness came from the fact that her surface temperatures never altered more than a few degrees in any given time or seasonal period. Its atmosphere had cooling properties that kept an even temperature.

Rain did fall on Ridmon outside the valley's protective mountains and flowed off into vast forests or natural lakes. Underground rivers, such as the one pouring out from the cliffs above the Crystal City, formed the valley's river system which in turn flowed into the Red Sea, aptly named for its reddish colouring. Water covered eighty percent of the planet. The remaining twenty percent consisted of land masses divided into three continents, all of which were situated along an equator line. All the continents were vegetated, with areas ranging from thick dense forests to grasslands to crystal sand deserts, remnants of a bygone error in its evolution. All three continents sustained life forms of some sort or other. Nowhere else on Ridmon though, was there such an unnatural phenomena occurring where an area, the size of Portugal, supported a strange combination of life forms. Its vegetation was home to creatures of three distinctions and a group of people of varied ethnic races not indigenous to the area. The planet was considered of limited commercial value and was therefore ignored. Those who lived on it soon found out just how valuable she indeed was.

The people of Ridmon adapted quickly to their new habitat, realizing that in order to make it their home they would have to first learn her secrets to be able to harness her hidden power. Slowly they began to unravel her mysteries and create for themselves a Garden of Eden. Ridmon would become the envy of many civilizations who, during the course of time, would strive to possess her. Ridmon's main incredible feature was her invisibility. Attributed to her planet's freak magnetic distortion, she orbited in space totally blanketed from visual or electronic view. The nineteen Drones hovering in Ridmon's atmosphere functioned to protect Ridmon and its inhabitants. The planet was therefore, considerably secure. The noise inside the Great Hall grew louder. Ridmonians were having the time of their lives. So they should, considering their achievements. Not once since the people first settled in the valley had any flame been lit. Fires were against the law in the valley. Heat was generated by clever use of crystal lenses and mirrors. A new technology had been invented for cooking, heating, building and agricultural growth. Ridmon was vegetarian. All nutria was derived from plants. There were at that moment no other options, but everyone was happy, healthy and full of hope for the future, determined to make Ridmon their home. One had to be practical and realistic, seeing that the chances of returning to Earth were virtually non-existent.

Food and drink were served. There was much deliberation, debate and laughter. Moti had let his hair down as usual and was totally engrossed with Ana-Maria on the dance floor, swirling, bobbing and jerking their bodies in time to Ridmon's very own dance band. Children were scampering all over the place. Penagee sighed, Mike smiled and both of them, careful to avoid attention, left the Great Hall and teleported themselves to the trees. Days stretched into weeks and the year 2021 had entered its second quarter. Mike was restless again; the Crystal City was fast becoming a thriving small metropolis. He needed some form of additional stimulation, some new adventure. Penagee was pregnant with their first child and busied herself making preparations. She was aware of his needs and so, with her blessing, Mike went on a reconnaissance mission over the crystal cliffs together with an equally happy group consisting of Moti, Anna and Kun, a Thedarian biologist. Their task was to ascertain what life forms existed there, the types of vegetation and what water sources were available. Their intention was to locate other suitable sites to construct new crystal cities. This would prevent over-saturation of the valley. On the appointed day, the reconnaissance group gathered in the Great Hall for their final briefing and equipment checks. The community's growth depended on its ability to achieve, create or invent, succeed or fail within a framework of their own choosing. Values as productive members of a society needed to be upheld and expanded on to bring out the best in each of them.

Frank, the community's administrator, was such a man who gladly shouldered his responsibilities. Susan had given birth to a bouncing, healthy boy named Ivan. A very happy and contented man was Frank. Voted administrator by a resounding majority was reward enough for his persistent efforts. He was one of the foundation stones of Ridmon's first and only Security Unit consisting of a mere twenty highly trained men and woman. Seal training, combined with Mike's martial arts knowledge, had turned this little group into a well-oiled and highly efficient unit. Mike, who had access to many of the more advanced martial arts techniques, set upon them with a training programme so intense and thorough that Frank with his twenty strong force soon became something to be reckoned with. Not only were they in superb physical condition, but also developed their extrasensory perception to uncanny levels. It was a highly effective, lethal fighting machine. The group in its raw form, without the advantage of modern-day weaponry could take on the best there was and give any opponent a nasty headache in the process. All knew they were helpless against spaceships and sophisticated technology, but on the ground it was an entirely different matter. There were also the creatures of the Dark Forest to take into account, as they were more than a handful. Mike had devised a plan to utilize their usefulness in the protection of the valley. Frank had reason to be content. He had everything going for him and, thanks to the Portal, he was able to be the man he always wanted to be. Life was good.

"Frank, all set?" Enquired Mike.

"All set." The immediate response.

"Our progress and whereabouts will be channelled to you via the Drones. Penagee will be in constant contact so, if you need a message passed to anyone of us, you know the drill. If anything crops up that we feel you should be party to, you will be able to follow each and every step as if you were there. I understand that you still have reservations about someone poking around in your mind, but look on the bright side, movies with a difference."

Frank smiled. As much as he disliked his mental thoughts being accessed, he did see the value of this form of communication. It knocked the hell out of anything he had laid hands on. A roving 360 degree camera, complete with audio, plus an instant chat line without wires, buttons or flashing lights and no chance of failure. You saw everything like a chameleon, heard everything and talked without fear of being overheard, all at the same time. Mike took Penagee in his arms and kissed her lovingly. He stepped off the podium, joined hands with Moti, Anna and Kun and promptly disappeared into thin air. Frank heard Penagee giggle playfully. Obviously something had passed between them that she found amusing. Frank loved these two people. They were so natural and easy going in spite of their tremendous abilities. Penagee excused herself, going off to her duties and Frank checked in to see how Susan was doing.

Ana-Maria sat with Carla on her lap waiting patiently for news from Moti. David was too engrossed as the Community's resident historian and artist to bother about what was going on around him. Mavis progressed from mere nurse to a very good homeopathic doctor. Susan taught school from grades to university level in a single classroom with its twenty three students. The Ridmon Army was placed on full alert. Surrounded by a community that went about its business as usual. Drones hovered within Ridmon's atmosphere monitoring and checking, cross-checking and updating as information was fed in. Thedrah, on the other hand, busied itself for an all-out offensive on Ridmon.

They had grown tired of waiting. A week later the Drones reported.

"Thedrah preparing aggressive action. Defence mechanisms activated."

Penagee summoned Mike. It was time. Mike immediately teleported back to the Crystal City with Moti and sounded the general alarm. Everyone took to their stations with well-rehearsed ease down into the underground cavern. Seated on the floor of the Great Hall, Penagee and Mike faced each other, hands clasped. The waiting began. A few hours later the Drones reported.

"Thedrah ships in position, preparing to fire."

Slowly Mike and Penagee bodily rose off the crystal floor and into an electrically charged space of air. Moti could feel the power build-up radiating from the two and shifted expectantly. The air pulsed, and then vibrating streaks of white light began to flow from the two suspended figures into the surrounding crystal walls. A low hum became a high-pitched siren and Frank, for the first time in his life, felt fear grip like hot talons around his throat. To his dismay, each one of his Squad sat in a cross legged lotus position, suspended three feet off the floor, eyes wide, unseeing. The high-pitched siren's sound was deafening, tearing at the brain. Moti sank to the floor for better stability, Frank wasted no time in joining him. The Drones reported.

"Thedrah has fired."

There was a blinding flash of white light, followed by another and another, then silence. A deadly unease ensued. Gradually Mike and Penagee descended to the floor, unlocked their hands and stood up. Moti and Frank sprang to their feet like two sets of springs. The static charged air gradually returned to normal. In a soft voice, hardly audible, Penagee uttered.

"It is done." Then left the Great Hall with tears rolling down her cheeks.

Mike gave the command to stand down and sat facing Moti, Frank and the Squad.

"Today, in response to a threat to our survival and possibly all life on this planet, we have had to take steps to defend ourselves and as a result, a great many Thedarians have lost their lives. Thedrah no longer has any functioning infrastructures or its damn Committee. We have completely neutralized their planet."

Images flashed into their minds as Mike transmitted scenes of devastation on Thedrah. It was a terrible sight, almost every strategic city on the planet lay in ruins, there were people wandering around in shocked dismay, aimless and beaten, many lay where they had fallen. It was a disaster of cataclysmic proportion. Frank gasped.

"Yes Frank, terrible, such a waste of life and property. There was no other choice. Thedrah fired its weapons of mass destruction."

Moti, Mike and the Squad walked out of the Great Hall to oversee the Community's return to their quarters, leaving Frank shaking with rage. In the silence of the hall Susan embraced Frank and slowly the rage subsided.

"Frank." She said softly. "War is never kind to the innocent, we prepare for it under the illusion that we are impervious to its effects and that we will always come out the victors. We give no thought to the countless men, women and children who as a result lose their lives, loved ones and homes. Throughout our own history wars have raged with terrible consequences. We have witnessed the brutality man is capable of and we should hang our heads in shame. But, Earth people have survived and through it better lives and policies have been adapted in an attempt to stop other wars from occurring. Yet man is basically a primitive beast and will not be satisfied, so will continue to wage war on someone somewhere. Thedrah is no exception. With its highly advanced culture it still waged war on the less able. Ridmon has now become an aggressor and will no doubt have to face other warring factions ready to challenge her. It's a never-ending cycle, past and future."

She took Frank's face between her hands.

"Frank, you are a good man and I know whatever it was that you saw must have hurt you deep down inside, but please find perspective within yourself. We are fighting for an entire planet's survival and the odds stacked against us are awesome. If Mike and Penagee did not do what they did you, I and our baby would not be here at this moment. Spare a thought for Penagee. She has had to virtually destroy a planet, on it many friends and possibly family. That must have been an agonizing decision for her to make. I saw the look on Mike's face when I passed him and believe me Frank, the man is hurting."

Frank stared into Susan's blue eyes.

"I know Honey, it still doesn't make it acceptable. I have seen death and war, but I have never seen such devastating destruction over such a wide area. It was horrifying. I am afraid, really afraid for Mike and Penagee. If their powers somehow get out of control, I shudder to think of the consequences."

"I somehow don't think that is possible, not with those two. It's not in their mentality, besides, whoever gave them those powers did so in full knowledge of responsibility." She smiled and hugged him close.

"Come; let's take Ivan for his walk."

In the confines of her heart Penagee wept bitterly. Although Mike was not there, she felt his closeness and comfort. What had to be done was done to stop the tyrant committee on Thedrah, who had taken office with good intentions, but became an avenging heart. Ridmon was free from Thedrah and the Drones could be used to help the survivors on that ill-fated planet. They were going to need all the help they could get because there were many civilizations out there waiting to pounce and completely obliterate Thedrah out of existence for past crimes and atrocities. Penagee would see to it that never happened. Moti followed after Mike like a faithful dog. He too was afraid, very afraid. Mike had become an all-consuming power machine capable of destroying planets and who knows what else. He was afraid for their relationship and what effects all this would have on it. He missed the old Mike, the one who dashed through the trees like an ape. In the past everything was simple and clear cut. Things were becoming too complicated and he was worried. Mike stopped, turned and hugged Moti.

"Listen, you clumsy oaf, the Lion does not desert his brother the Hawk, but will travel with him side by side for many seasons to come. And besides, where would the Lion be without his Hawk to swoop down out of the skies and remind him of his place. Old Wolf did leave some of himself behind in you."

Moti grinned from ear to ear.

"Cut that out Mike, you know it gives me a weird feeling when you dig around in my brain. The Hawk is only concerned for the Lion and feels the pain in his heart."

The powerful arms released their grip, and Mike gave Moti a hearty slap on the back. Laughingly he challenged.

"Last one to the trees has to wrestle one of the creatures from the Dark Forest."

They were off racing between pedestrians for the platform at the end of the bridge, hoping against hope someone had the common sense to have opened the windows of the Dome or else a no-contest would be called when Mike teleported himself through them. They were like two little boys having made a brand new discovery and were racing home to tell their parents. Penagee was sucked into the race without choice by Mike and in her heart the tears ceased. Mike could never outrun Moti, the younger man was not called Hawk without reason. He was fast on his feet and soon the distance between the two became apparent. Suddenly Mike felt Penagee on his back and propelled forward like an express train. From the corner of his eye Moti spotted the horse and its rider. The sight was hilarious and he folded in fits of laughter, clutching at his stomach and shouting,

"That's not fair, come on guys that's really not fair."

Mike hauled Moti to his feet and the three faded into the trees. There were mixed reactions from the Community to the news. Borz for one was distressed and requested a meeting with Frank. The administrator in turn did the next best thing. he summoned all the Thedarian into the Great Hall.

"I guess by now you are all aware of what has happened on Thedrah. I cannot ease your minds by offering you explanations or details. What I can tell you is that everything possible is being done to alleviate the suffering of those unfortunate people. More information will be passed on to you as and when it comes to hand. Borz has come up with a suggestion entailing your return to Thedrah to assist with the reconstruction, restoration and attempt to locate any surviving family members. I know this is a high priority with each of you, so I am going to put it to you this way. Those of you in favour, raise your right hands."

Hands rose into the air and Frank counted. Thirty five out of a total of fifty Thedarian adults. Out of nowhere

Penagee appeared. It startled every one. Frank could see them visibly shrink away from her.

"Would I be permitted to address my people?" She asked Frank.

The man nodded, after all she was boss lady.

"Fellow Thedarian's, right now you dislike me intensely, thinking I am a vile thing. How could I have allowed this to happen? Thirty five of you wish to return. The rest of you are angry, but have roots now on Ridmon with families. I need not recount Thedarian history or spell out its policies to you. This you know all too well. I need not remind you our survival here is extremely high priority. Adding to that, I must remind you of the Thedarian Committee. It is a well-known fact on Thedrah that the Committee was the ultimate power and many outside civilizations have become nearly extinct because of them. If they wanted something they got it, one way or the other. We, the people of Thedrah, are to blame for allowing it to happen in the first place. Because of our complacency and lack of backbone, many suffered. Thedrah decided that, because Ridmon had openly defied them, they would terminate its existence. If Mike and I did not do what we did, Ridmon would no longer have existed. It is within our power to completely eradicate Thedrah. We chose not to. There are survivors, yes. Now it's up to us to pick up the pieces and make sure a better governing body is put in place under Ridmon's scrutiny. My Drones did not completely destroy everything and at this very moment a few shuttles are being brought over to Ridmon for us to transport a team back to Thedrah to commence re-structuring."

Borz stood up to speak, but Penagee silenced him with a wave of her hand.

"As I talk to you, ships from the 5th quadrant are winging their way to Thedrah to complete its destruction, and we can't allow it to happen. Thedrah is completely defenceless. In a moment, Mike will be going to Thedrah with Moti and the Squad. You will follow as soon as the threat is over. In the meantime, I suggest you prepare yourselves for embarkation."

She turned to Frank and murmured.

"You will be joining Mike this time. Your skills will be needed." She turned and left the Hall.

As much as he hated to admit it, Frank was excited. He gathered the Thedarian together and gave instructions. The information already in his mind, implanted by Penagee, he sought out the Humans who were to accompany them. Within two hours the team was seated in the Great Hall waiting to board the newly arrived shuttles which made the journey in record time through full Warp.

Mike, Moti and the Squad had long since arrived on Thedrah. The race was on. Survivors were being shuttled in their hundreds to staging points all around the Earth-sized planet. Food, water and shelter were the main concerns, so the staging points chosen were those closest to their requirements, but in uninhabited areas. The task was awesome and Mike, realizing that time was running out, superseded his authority by ordering the Drones to mutate and increase by 100. There was no time left to collect all the people, an impossible task over such a vast area. Mutation of the Drones a wonder of Nature, occurred within a few hours to reproduce exact replicas of themselves. Mike teleported into one of the Drones and gave his orders and fifty Drones raced to meet the oncoming Space Battleships from Nirque. The Nirquéns were a bloodthirsty nation resembling more the Neanderthal men. In the past they had suffered greatly at the hands of the Thedarian. It was payback time. For too long they had been under the leash, now they were going to give it back once and for all.

"When does Thedrah come into view?" Barked a tall, pot-bellied Fleet Commander.

"Three hours." The curt reply.

"Good, I am itching to chew a Thedarian's heart out."

Alarms suddenly blinked on control panels, signifying the detection of something at very short range.

"Identify."

"No identification."

"Impossible!"

"Confirmed, no identification, no solid objects, nothing."

Alarms continued blinking. Something was out there lurking unseen.

"Fools, try again." Bellowed the Commander.

The monitor screen remained empty save for the blackness of space and countless stars. The Fleet ship requested status reports from the other vessels and the response returned was the same. All three hundred heavily armed fighting ships detected nothing.

"Check your instruments, idiots!"

"Checked and rechecked, still nothing."

Then came the command, "On my mark fire patterns, 2 and 4."

The whole Fleet positioned itself to fire their destructor beams down a plotted corridor. Mike's face appeared on the main communications monitor of the Fleet ship and the Fleet Commander blinked.

"Human." He hissed.

Mike smiled and bowed slightly, enquiring.

"Are you Nirque on a picnic trip or just admiring the view?"

The Commander was outraged. With spittle flying from his mouth he shouted at Mike's face on the screen.

"Why, you indolent Human pup, you challenge the might of Nirque? What are you doing here anyway?"

"Oh! I thought I might take a stroll from Planet Earth just to stand in your way so that you don't finish off the planet Thedrah." Quipped Mike with a dazzling smile.

The eyeballs in that grotesque Nirque head almost fell out, and then the Commander laughed.

"Why, you puny, insignificant Earthling, you don't have the means to stop me. Get out of the way and mind your own business before I finish you off."

"Tut-Tut, touchy aren't we? This puny, insignificant Earthling, as you call me, must first be detected before you can show him anything. But, I see you very well and will show you my teeth after which we will continue our discussion and perhaps then you will return to your own planet."

With that six of the spacecraft to the left of the Command vessel disintegrated in balls of fire. The response was immediate, the Fleet fired. Another six spacecraft erupted in flames and debris on the right. Mike's face on the screen had the look on it, I told you so. The Fleet put down enough fire power to have taken out anything in its path. Still the alarm lights blinked. Still the obstruction was there and the Fleet Commander jumped up and down in sheer frustration. Mike's voice quietly cautioned.

"There will be worse to come if you don't turn around and go home."

The Fleet Commander ordered tactical manoeuvring and random firing. As his command was executed the Fleet dispersed into tactical attack formations, Mike's voice roared.

"You were warned!"

The dark heavens exploded in a massive fire ball. Only one solitary Command vessel remained. The Fleet Commander gazed in disbelief at the Human face on the screen.

"Who are you?" He shrieked.

"Your worst nightmare, now go home and forget about Thedrah." With that the monitor went dead.

The Nirque vessel turned about and headed home with its tail between its legs to face retribution for its failure. With the threat gone, Thedrah was gradually and painstakingly brought back to some form of normality. It was a major effort. New cities were under construction, major clean ups took place, and there was an agricultural and industrial rebirth. Frank had never faced a challenge of such magnitude and applied himself well. Nonetheless, setting up effective administration would take a long time, so Susan and child were brought in take up temporary residence on Thedrah. Shuttles ferried to and fro in a seemingly endless flow. Thedrah was a large planet, with an ocean covering nearly 90 percent of its surface. On its equator line most of the 10 percent land mass was distributed across many large islands and only one continent. It was a beautiful planet with temperate weather patterns and seasons, plus a day, night cycle. Winters were mild at the equator but bitterly cold at the poles. Moti and the Squad had their hands full. Some Thedarian were not so enthused by the idea of Humans barking orders at them and tried on occasions to physically put their point across. The result was a swift and painful reminder. Moti's policy was simple. You tell them, they don't listen, so they feel. Thedarian quickly learned to have a healthy respect for the Squad. The desired results were achieved in the end.

Several months went by, in which time Mike and Moti had not been back to Ridmon. Mike decided on the spur of the moment it was time for a break. The immediate crisis on Thedrah was over and his services were no longer needed. Fifty Drones positioned around the planet could take care of any new threats. Informing Frank, he and Moti teleported back to Ridmon. Penagee was waiting. She still had a bone to pick with Mike over his ordering the Drones to multiply. Mike had somehow found a way to keep things from her and it was infuriating. He walked into the Great Hall where Penagee was seated with their first born twins on her lap, to a cool reception. She was radiant in her new role as a mother. Mike just smiled and lifted her into his arms babies and all.

"So my beautiful fairy, you look especially lovely in this state of affairs. What are we going to name these little bundles of Joy?"

Penagee scowled at him. She was very glad to have him back and feel his closeness. But he needed chastising, so she was playing hard-ball. Of course Mike saw through the bluff and it did not take long before his tickling had the desired effect.

"I think it is time you and I sat down to a serious chat first." Said Penagee, motioning for Mike to sit beside her.

"You and I share almost every thought, emotion and feeling. I understand from your point of view, it must be a little uncomfortable sometimes as we both have come to know each other's strengths and weaknesses. I know that you feel left out of things concerning the Drones, having not been able to utilize their full potential as and when any situation arose. The incident on Thedrah, I have to admit, angered me no end. It is not the fact that you took control, it is the first time in our relationship you did not include me in your decision. I don't know how you managed to keep it from me and it hurts. I guess in a way I am to blame for not trusting you more and perhaps I was being a little selfish myself. My brother's genius created those Drones and I suppose I took it upon myself to protect his creation by not allowing anybody access to them. I realize my mistake and ask you, please, not to shut me out again. You have my unconditional support in all things, not only as a friend and a wife, but as a partner in our journey together."

Mike took her face between his hands and replied.

"If I have, by reason of acting on instinct in a given situation for the preservation of life, exceeded my station, then yes, I am guilty. I asked you once to allow me access and you refused, so I went about questioning that refusal and found a way to gain access. My concern was if something happened to you, all of us would have no chance. Someone else needed to have access to the Drones and I decided it was going to be me. As a result, I probably have accelerated a set of circumstances from which there is no turning back now. Yet, you continued to refuse me and I knew the day would come when I would have to make a choice and override your monopoly of the Drones. I found a way to blanket thought waves so that you could not channel into, and as a result, this conversation. I love you so very much and it too pained me that you could not trust me enough to take on the responsibility of the Drones. I did basically what had to be done for the good of all with much reservation, knowing your reaction. It was a gamble I took. If by this I have angered you and put a wedge between us, then I must sincerely apologize. But Penagee, my love, you of all people know all too well how difficult decisions are sometimes those that go against the heart."

"Yes I do, and that is why I also can kick myself for doubting you. I love you more than life and can't bear the thought of anything happening to you, so I guess I was being a little over protective." Answered Penagee.

Mike smiled and kissed her.

"So, are we going to decide on names for these two little additions to the family?" He asked.

A cheeky grin and sparkling eyes gave him the answer. Moti's cheerful intrusion broke the intimacy and Mike motioned for him to take a seat. The man flopped down with a smile on his face saying,

"You two are cordially invited to little Carla's second year birthday party. Bring lots of love."

Both Mike and Penagee laughed. Penagee teased,

"So Moti, when are you and the lady going to make it official?"

The man's expression flashed momentarily in panic to which Mike quickly added.

"She's only joking, besides you and I are from now on going to have our hands full chasing after twins."

Now it was Moti's turn to laugh.

"Yes, Daddy!" He mocked.

Penagee took Moti's hand in hers.

"Moti, we will be along shortly."

"Come, we will decide on names later, a girl and a boy, wow, I am ecstatic." Said Mike after Moti had left.

"We have a little present for Carla I want you to see and tell me if you think it will make her happy?"

With that the couple made their way down to the fields on the valley floor to a crystal cage. Mike extracted a small, smooth-skinned grey creature with large sea blue eyes and tiny pointed ears. It clung to Mike's wrist with four human-like hands.

"Looks like a mixture of tailless monkey and a cat, but ever so cute." Smiled Penagee clutching the twins.

"It does, and it makes a very good, loving and faithful pet."

Mike and Penagee made their way back to the complex and up to Ana-Maria's apartment. Moti, noticing the little creature, stepped forward for a closer look saying,

"So this is the famous little terror of the forest. Doesn't intimidate me at all."

Mike smirked, held the little creature out at arm's length, saying to Moti,

"Make a threatening move towards Penagee."

Moti complied with the request by pretending to want to hurt Penagee. The next moment an ultra-high-pitched sound emanated from the little creature directed at Moti with an intensity so powerful that it literally flattened the man to the ground as if he had been struck on the head by a 5kg hammer. Moti's head buzzed, his ear drums throbbed painfully and he felt dizzy and sick. He lay there staring up at the creature in amazement. Mike helped him to his feet saying,

"Now extend your hand forward slowly, palm upwards." Moti did what he was told and the small creature transferred itself to his arm and clung on, rubbing its head against him. Gingerly he stroked the thing and it licked his arm.

"Good pet for Carla or not?" Asked Penagee smiling.

"Wow! This little thing certainly knows how to look after itself." Replied Moti enthusiastically.

"Yes and the beauty of it is that it is very clean in its habits, shy, loves people and is highly social. The down side of course, no one better entertain the idea to hurt it or its friends as any act of violence will result in a quick and painful reminder to keep a distance, as you have found out." Explained Mike, to which Penagee added.

"Sorry Moti, but there was no other way to explain to you, so we had to stage this demonstration for you to understand at first-hand what this little thing is capable of. Cute, isn't it?"

"That's for sure. With this little creature, anywhere Carla is she will be safe and that's a relief."

"Just one more thing, those creatures in the Dark Forest in the valley are petrified of it. Which for us is more than a good thing." Mentioned Mike.

"What are you going to call it, Moti?" Asked Penagee.

"Male or female?" he asked.

"Female." Penagee's reply.

"Well, then let's call it,Nuchi."

Carla entered the room then and her dark eyes immediately noticed the little creature clinging to Moti's arm and she instantly fell in love with it.

As was the custom with Thedarian women, when Penagee went into labour in the privacy of her quarters alone to deliver her babies. Mike was on Thedrah so Protector Friend appeared in the room with Penagee and was there when the twins were born. Now that Mike was back and in the privacy of their own quarters Penagee introduced the twins formally to her husband. Mike knelt down beside Penagee and kissed her tenderly, "Thank you," was all he could say. Four days later Mike and Penagee presented the twins to the Community in the Great Hall. It was an auspicious moment for them. Mike held the little girl and Penagee the boy. Standing before the assembled people Mike bellowed.

"Friends, we would very much like to present to you two more additions to Ridmon. Here are Zakrose, named after our benefactor, Zorak and Wolf, named after a true friend and father, Abu Ahmed."

Both parents lifted the infants into the air for all too clearly see. Any excuse for a party on Ridmon and you were on and this was the ideal event in which to have one. While the women gathered around Penagee and the twins, Moti and the males bustled Mike to the Bar area and insisted on "Down Downs". Twenty Crystal glasses filled with Ridmon whiskey were lined up on a table, Mike had to climb onto the table, assume a kneeling position, hands behind his back, and bend forward, clench a glass between his teeth, throw his head backwards and swallow the contents. This was done in quick succession without falling off the table. Then he had to stand up and turn three full circles, get off the table unassisted and down one beer. Penagee observed this with much interest. She had never seen Mike actually get inebriated, only slightly happy. Moti shouted,

"Ready!"

Mike knelt, poised. Ridmon whiskey was explosive; under normal conditions one sipped it carefully at lengthy intervals. This was no normal condition, the menfolk wanted blood and they were determined to get it.

"Ready." Responded Mike.

"Go!" Everyone barked in unison.

Mike dived into the glasses like a man possessed, anything less would have been met with boo's and whistles of disapproval. One glass after another, then finally the three circular turns and to everyone's amused amazement, Mike floated from the table through the air across to Penagee and collapsed at her feet, dead drunk. The party kicked off with gusto and Mike was soon forgotten, sprawled at Penagee's feet. Everyone else drank Ridmon beer, it was safer. The Squad arrived and lifted Mike's limp form and, together with a laughing Penagee, left the Hall.

Mike awoke with a hangover to beat all hangovers. He did not mind making a fool of himself, it made him more human to the others seeing him fall down from grace. But, that was something he was not going to try again in a hurry. Half a year later the Drones reported.

"One thousand Nirque battleships class1 heading for Thedrah. What are our orders?"

Penagee's heart skipped a beat. Class 1 type battleships were the most powerful craft in the Trubian sector of the Universe. They were formidable vessels purchased from the warmongers on Polarim who made a living out of destruction for a price, a high price and she turned to Mike and saw the gleam in his eyes as he felt the ancient call to battle coursing through his veins.

"Be careful, those ships are not easy to get rid of." She cautioned.

"I know, but neither are our Drones and there is me and something else."

She laughed out loud, "What?"

"Protector Friend."

"Are you keeping secrets from me again?" She demanded.

"No, only surprises, and that's a secret, so forget it, OK!"

Before she could respond Mike had vanished.

"Why, that infuriating man!" She shouted out aloud after him and David who had been recording in his journal a few metres away couldn't contain his laughter.

The sound of it stopped Penagee in her tracks and instantly David was hanging upside down in the air. Anna came into the library and, seeing everything, calmly walked over to Penagee, linked arms with her favourite woman friend and stood looking up at the wriggling David suspended in the air and said to Penagee.

"That's my girl, don't let him down until he has learned some manners." Both women burst out laughing and left the room, leaving David dangling.

Mike positioned himself with the fifty Drones and waited. Next to him sat Moti, eyes mere slits. Mike didn't like to leave his friend out of things, especially this kind of action. Moti was after all his right hand man, his second in command as it were on these occasions. Protector Friend had come through with a plan, and what a plan it was. Nobody wanted to eradicate life, or get involved in a full scale war of this magnitude so, in order to persuade the Nirquens that their attempts to attack Thedrah again would only lead to total annihilation, Protector Friend positioned himself over the planet Nirque. Nirque's entire Star Fleet of class1 battleships were engaged on this mission. Failure was not acceptable. With confrontation imminent, Mike locked on to the Fleet Commander's Monitor screen and his image appeared on its surface. His broadcast would be transmitted to the entire Fleet.

"Warriors of Nirque, I must say that you are persistent, perhaps brave and courageous men and women, but what you are attempting to do, well, just doesn't go down well with me and I am forced to inform you that unless you return to your planet forthwith, there will be no more planet to return to." He waited for a response. A short, chubby, elderly individual shook his head and then responded.

"You address the might of Nirque, Human?"

"Oh! Forgive me, mighty Excellency, but this Human does not like it when people try to disturb the peace. So before you go any further with this useless conversation, perhaps you would be so kind as to contact your planet. Please, be a good man for everyone's sake."

The Nirquéns face flushed in anger, knowing the Human was toying with him, yet what he had said needed to be confirmed and if it proved to be a ruse, he would blow the interfering Human out of the Universe. He gave the order and all waited. A minute later the reply came back and the chubby individual's face went ashen. He looked at Mike's face on the screen before him, silently studying the man. Long moments passed in which Mike smiled pleasantly.

"Who are you?" Came the question. Mike remained silent for a few seconds allowing the full impact of the news from Nirque to sink in then replied.

"I am Mike, formerly of the planet Earth, now protector of Thedrah and its peoples, a peaceful person until someone like you comes along to try to change things. You see, that really pisses me off and I become very upset and well, you don't want to know the result. So, as you have heard, Nirque is surrounded by over 100,000 battleships class 1A, which means you are outgunned, outmanoeuvred and outclassed, and on the brink of seeing your planet disintegrated. I suggest therefore that you exercise extreme caution with your next move, because Nirque and your fleet of 1000 vessels will be no more."

The chubby Nirquen understood all too well the consequences of any false move. They were trapped in a grip from which there was no escape. One wrong move on his part would spell instant and final destruction of an entire nation of peoples.

A message from Nirque's Council came through.

"Break off, return to Nirque."

"I trust you will not be attempting any other stupid moves in the future. We shall not be so accommodating the next time." Mike broke off the communication.

Moti watched as the Fleet about faced and disappeared. Protector Friend held his position until the Fleet had docked, then withdrew his perfect illusion from the skies above Nirque. Another threat had been neutralized without a single shot being fired.

His message to Mike was simple.

"Situation defused, see you soon."

Frank achieved the impossible in such a short space of time. He rebuilt a once shattered nation and in gratitude was offered the position of Thedrah's Governor. He accepted and took to his new responsibly very efficiently. His original Squad returned to Ridmon and were assigned to Moti. A new Army was formed on Thedrah with access to all the latest technology. Thedrah became a thriving planet once more. His duties as joint leader of Ridmon and Thedrah kept him busy. Six months passed by and, as usual, Mike became restless. His daily sessions in the trees and water meditation kept him in excellent shape, in spite of things being very peaceful on Ridmon and Thedrah. What he craved was another challenge. Mike for his age was in more than excellent condition. He by now had put all thoughts of returning to Earth out of his mind. Earth was a contentious issue, seeing as every Human on Ridmon still had living parents or relatives on the planet. Mike approached Penagee on the subject one day and for long hours they debated the ins and outs of it. The question in the end amounted to whether or not it would be possible in the first place and secondly, whether or not the Humans of Ridmon with their families should remain on Ridmon or be given the choice return to Earth. If such a possibility existed then many factors would have to be taken into account. Factors such as would the Humans survive the journey and how long would it take. How would a return to Earth impact on their lives after Ridmon. Mike suggested using one of the Drones for a test run. His argument was founded upon the fact the Drones could travel well beyond the speed of light. The journey would have to be made from Ridmon to Earth and back by a few volunteers who understood that it could be a one way journey or possible death. Penagee had watched Mike and sensed his need for something challenging to do. She understood that he was bored with the easy slow life on Ridmon and, although she did not altogether agree with his theories on the subject, she did have to admit to herself the validity of the effort. She did not relish the thought of Mike going off and not returning at all.

"It looks as if you are determined to see this through, aren't you?" Quizzed Penagee.

Mike studied her face, looking for tell-tale signs of amusement, but found none.

"I am positive it will work. Besides, what do we have to lose?" Emphasized Mike. To which Penagee responded.

"Only your life."

Neither of them understood the full extent of Mike's teleportation strengths. Extending that far from Ridmon or using a Drone was a risk which would have to be tested. Penagee did not feel too happy about the concept of Mike finding himself stranded in mid-space because it would surely mean certain death. New blood was needed on Ridmon and if Earth was reachable, then the much needed injection of people would neutralize the risks of genetic corruption. The twins came bounding into the room breaking the chain of discussion.

"Mama, Mama. Carla and her Mama are here to visit."

Mike swooped the two up into his arms.

"So, what have you two cherubs been up to?"

"Playing with Carla." Zakrose's matter-of-fact reply.

"And you, Wolfie?"

"Kung-Fu." He shouted, then promptly whacked Mike on his arm.

He carried them over to Penagee who muttered,

"Like father, like son."

Mike just smiled, he was a proud Father. Ana-Maria and Carla stepped into the room and for a while Mike listened to the small talk then made his excuses and left. A few hours later, after briefing Moti and Anna, Mike returned home with a 5-man Squad fully equipped.

"You want to go now?" She asked in stark dismay.

"Yup, now." Was all Mike replied, hastily kissing her hard before teleporting into Drone No.3 with his team?

They were taking a gamble and knew it, but as one of the team had said, "Nothing ventured, nothing gained." All knew the risks. The team consisted of the best on Ridmon and Thedrah. Mike had their absolute loyalty and commitment to purpose. All were Thedarian. Along for the ride was a little blue creature with blue eyes clinging to Mike's side. Niki was its name. Moti had insisted it be brought along as added protection. The Squad was placed in a kind of suspended animation, totally encased in a life supporting gel in which they could breathe and from which they could extract much needed nutrients via intravenous insertion. The Drone sped through the Universe well beyond the speed of light and seemed to fly through a vortex of swirling colours. The Drone had estimated the distance as about 800 billion light years, which would need to be travelled over a three month period, Six months in all including the return flight. The twins would then be one Ridmon year old.

In a dark cave at the foot of the Cheroma Kadoma pinnacle a Sangoma chanted and cast the bones. His wrinkled old hands were shaking. Watched by another set of bloodshot eyes in the darkness, his gnarled fingers picked at the bones, then poured a brown powder over an open flame burned hot like magnesium, out of which the vision of a man appeared.

The Sangoma shivered declaring.

"White Matabele. He returns. Manje indaba buya"

* [Big trouble comes]

EARTH

THREE

In the year 2023, an invisible Drone manoeuvred into stationary orbit around Planet Earth. Below lay the continents of Europe, Asia and the upper section of Africa. Mike made his telepathic report to Penagee.

"We are in position."

After a slight delay, then her response.

"I love you."

A lot of changes had taken place over the past years during Mike's absence. The planet seemed burdened somehow. Pollution resulted in increased global warming and there was a definite difference in climatic conditions due to the heavier carbon dioxide in the atmosphere. Out in Earth's orbit hung debris of past space programmes scattered like a garbage dump. Amongst this silent, motionless debris passed satellites of every description and to Mike's surprise, manned military space stations which obviously no one was supposed to know about.

"Target area located." Reported the Drone.

"Destination: Bournemouth Hospital, South England."

Mike teleported down into an intensive care ward. His subject, a young boy dying of leukaemia, lay on a bed with tubes protruding out of him connected to life support systems. A nurse sat next to the bed reading a magazine, completely immersed in its contents. She was gently immobilized, placing her unconscious body carefully onto an adjoining empty bed. Carefully he unplugged all the tubes, then teleported the boy up to the Drone and immersed him into a life sustaining liquid gel container. A miracle of technology based on the fact that most female species carried their young inside their wombs prior to giving birth. Within those wombs, immersed in liquid, a child developed and obtained nutrient support through an umbilical tube. So it only stood to reason that advanced technology came up with a simulated effect into which life forms could be housed and life sustained, wounds healed and even illnesses cured. The gel, in addition, served as a form of suspended animation enclosure for space travel at speeds too dangerous for normal life forms to withstand. The Drone was equipped with a honeycomb network of cells such as these in which life forms could survive the rigors of space travel in a semi-sleep state.

The next phase in the plan was Cape Town, South Africa. Most of Mike's family had resettled there from Zimbabwe. He last saw his sister years ago when she had visited him on the Moshav in Israel. Finding her was not difficult, seeing that her DNA patterns were very similar to those of Mike and were scanned and located from the Drone. Her small, but picturesque house with its white-washed Dutch gabling and quaint cottage windows, had a well-kept, neat, colourful garden with Table Mountain as the perfect backdrop. Walking up the granite tiled pathway leading to a dark stained stinkwood door, Mike felt on top of the world. A dog barked inside when he knocked. Moments later, an attractive, middle aged blonde haired woman in her late thirties opened the door. She stood there studying the imposing image of a powerful man, taking a few seconds to comprehend, then her lovely blue eyes widened, her jaw dropped as full recognition hit her.

"Mike." She shrieked and jumped into his arms.

"Well, well. Have we grown up or what?" Mike held her at arms length off the ground studying her. Jane was ecstatic.

"You big oaf. Where have you been? Everybody thinks you are dead or something."

"Not likely Jane, it's a long story and one you probably won't believe."

"Put me down first." Laughed Jane.

Mike promptly obliged. She looped her arm around his waist and felt something soft and alive. Instinctively she jerked away,

"What's that?"

Mike smiled, "Not now, Jane, not now. Let's get inside first, OK?" With that he shut the door behind them.

She was very happy to see her big brother again and had never believed for a moment that he had died somewhere. Not her brother. The two walked into a very warm and well-furnished Cape Dutch lounge where Jane motioned him to sit.

"Where have you been? Geez! I have been so worried about you. What's this all about anyway?" She questioned.

Mike gently reached into his jacket and extracted Niki. Jane sucked in her breath. As a zoologist she knew almost all there was to know about animals, but this one she had never seen before.

"This is Niki, he is from the Planet Ridmon, eight hundred billion light years from here." Mike explained lifting the creature up and twisting it around for better perspective. Jane stared at the creature. The little thing was fascinating and mysterious, staring back at her with its unblinking large blue eyes.

"You're joking, it can't be!" She stammered.

"No jokes, it's real," He confirmed.

"This here is a very interesting little fellow. For example, Niki is a very loving, sociable chap who hurts no one. But if you attempt to hurt it or its friends, it has a very effective way of immobilizing whatever the threat is, no matter what the size. By emitting ultra-high-pitched sound frequencies this little fellow is capable of knocking the hell out of anything, yet never kills, only renders temporarily immobility."

"How come you have it then?" She questioned, her frowning face etched in disbelief.

Mike considered the question and chose his words carefully.

"For the moment, let's just say I have a story you might think is too far-fetched to be possible. So, I brought little Niki along for the ride as proof."

Jane looked from Mike to the creature and blinked. Mike always was a straight-forward man and never in all the time she knew him did he try to pull a fast one on her. Yet now he was sitting here, out of the blue as large as life, spinning a story and presenting her with a strange live creature as proof. It left her a little off balance, yet an intense curiosity was building up within her. Just then the phone rang, breaking her chain of thought. Getting up, she moved over to an oak sideboard and lifted the receiver.

The dog began barking again. There was a quick exchange of words then the receiver was replaced. Jane opened an interconnecting door and out bounded a large, fierce looking Rottweiler dog, the size of a mini tank, making straight for Mike, its vicious teeth bared, snarling. Niki reacted instantly. Jane could not believe what she saw. The dog twisted as if someone had yanked its neck from behind with such a tremendous force that it flipped the animal head over heels. The dog was out of it, immobilized by a force Jane could not see. She was mortified and gingerly bent down to check on the dog. Niki was jumping up and down on Mike's lap, very pleased with itself and kept pointing at the stricken dog as if to say, Want some more Dude?

"The dog will be back on its feet in about 15 minutes or so. But, any other peep out of it and Niki here will give it another dose." Cautioned Mike.

He stood up and gently retrieved the unconscious dog and placed it on the kitchen floor, then walked back, closing the door behind him and returned to his seat. Jane stared at the little creature in disbelief. With such a pet she could walk around anywhere in Cape Town and not fear being mugged or raped. Niki clung to Mike with its deep, sea-blue eyes fixed, waiting. Jane moved back to her chair gathering herself. Mike leaned forward, taking her hands in his with a bemused grin on his face. Jane blurted out.

"You tell me this little thing is from another world, you bring it into my home and it flattens my dog. As if that's not all, you come back from the dead looking like some muscle-bound ape from the jungle and you expect me to sit here and take it all in my stride!"

"No," Mike laughed. "I understand this must seem way out to you, but I didn't come here to frighten you, but to make you an offer. It's a long story and what I tell you is the gospel truth, so please bear with me. I have travelled billions of light years to ask you to join me in a world one can only describe as a paradise, equipped with a whole different ecology and with a technology so advanced it will blow your mind. I would like you to share in this peaceful and safe environment as our resident zoologist. Your expertise could be very beneficial to us in our world. You will never have to worry about mortgages and debts or where you are going to find next month's rent, traffic jams, and all those city fears. The air is so pure you can almost taste it. We, that is to say all the people of Ridmon, only 150 of us, are made up of Humans and Thedarian. Our children grow up in an almost perfect world and having you there with me, would make me very happy indeed."

Jane looked deep into her brother's eyes trying to read behind them. This all seemed so far-fetched that she had every reason not to believe him. Yet, the little creature, it definitely was not from Mother Earth. How in heavens name did Mike get involved in all this? The idea of going to another world was extremely attractive. How real was it? So many questions. She thought, then said.

"It's not that I doubt you or anything, it's just, if what you say is true, I would need more proof before I can make any decision at all. My mind tells me to question the authenticity of it all."

"I realize and ask you to trust me. It is a very complicated story and, believe me, very real. If you would permit me I would like to make a small demonstration here in the lounge for you and seeing as its Niki's feeding time, I think this would be the appropriate moment."

"Sure." Agreed Jane, curling her feet up under her on the sofa.

"The mind is a very intricate piece of matter, most people use only 10 percent of its full capacity. This means the other 90 percent is inactive. My brain has been brought together in such a way that a full 100 percent is utilized. In addition, a very advanced technology was programmed into my memory cells, making me a walking reference library; I have some extraordinary mental abilities. I am telepathic, am able to teleport myself anywhere and I have the ability to save or destroy life. There is much more that I am not aware of as yet, because the entities from whom I inherited these abilities are releasing them as and when I am able to fully understand and appreciate their applications and exercise proper responsibility in their usage. To further ensure that the powers are not misused by me, I have a partner, my wife on Ridmon, who acts as a sort of safety mechanism which unites us both in mind. It is therefore not possible to exceed one's authority. I control her, she controls me, but jointly we are a force of immense strength and power which collectively can wipe out Earth and its entire solar system if we wanted to."

The room was silent for long moments while Jane digested Mike's words. Incredible as it sounded, she still felt it was a bit far-fetched. Mike cleared the coffee table of all trinkets and ornaments, leaving a cleared surface.

"Observe." He said to her.

Slowly, the most beautifully flowered plant she had ever seen materialized onto the table, growing out of the wood's surface. Its rainbow of colours cascaded in intricate patterns to reveal multi coloured blossoms only possible to visualize in fantasy. She watched mesmerized as the cycle of birth, life and death of the plant was completed within the space of ten minutes, leaving only one perfect blossom as proof of its existence. Jane picked up the delicate blossom and sniffed its exquisite perfumed aroma.

"It's a trick, you hypnotized me or something?"

Mike laughed, "Oh yeah, then how come the blossom is real and you can feel it and smell it, smart Alec?"

Jane sniffed the large blossom once again just to reconfirm its authenticity.

"Beautiful." Was all she could say.

Niki popped his head out of Mike's shirt to where it had retreated, saw the blossom, jumped onto the table, snatched it from Jane's hand and promptly ate it.

"Niki's supper."

Jane had seen many species of animal and plant life, studied literature of extinct species and the most unusual of all on Earth, but never had she seen anything to the likes which Mike presented her with. She looked up at Mike, having to admit that her brother was telling some truth. Yet her mind could still not be convinced that all this was not some kind of elaborate hoax. Mike, sensing her hesitation, decided it was time to bring in a couple of the Thedarians.

Holding her hands Mike softly said.

"Don't be alarmed at what you are about to see, they are my friends from Ridmon."

Two of his Squad teleported into the lounge in full battle dress, face masks off. Jane sat bolt upright, and Mike saw fear flash across her eyes, followed by total disbelief. He stood up, lifted her to her feet and softly propelled her forward towards the two Thedarian's. One stretched out his hand to Jane and she shook it. In a flash pictures of Ridmon passed before her eyes then were gone. The man smiled and bowed his head politely. She stepped backwards and covered her face with her hands then dropped her arms to her sides, mouth agape. Mike gently put his arm around her shoulders and kissed her cheek.

"Ridmon is beautiful, is she not?"

"Yes, yes." She stammered.

She knew then what her choice was going to be. Without hesitation she went to the phone, paused for a few moments to gather her thoughts and then dialled a number.

"Hello Erika, it's me, Jane. You still want my house?" A pause, then, "OK, I will leave the key you know where and Erika, Max my dog goes with the deal," another pause." I can't explain, so you are going to have to trust me. I will leave a signed power of attorney together with all the deeds of the house, papers for my car and will ask you to make sure my policies are cancelled. Could you be here within the next thirty minutes, and Erika, tell that stingy boss of mine its goodbye bozo. Thanks."

With that she replaced the receiver, grabbed a pen and scribbled a lot of lines down on a note pad and signed at the bottom. She then went to a chest of drawers, extracted a folder and pinned the notes to it together with her car keys, went into the kitchen, fluffed her still unconscious dog's fur, turned to Mike and sighed.

"I am all yours big brother."

Mike took Jane by the hand and teleported to the Drone. The house mysteriously shut and locked itself and the front door key ended up under the potted fern.

The return trip to Ridmon cured the boy of his leukaemia. After a three month trip immersed in gel, Jane emerged a new woman and promptly found herself on Ridmon in the Great Hall, facing a very charming and exceptionally beautiful woman.

"Welcome to Ridmon Jane, glad to have you with us. I am Penagee, Mike's wife."

Graciously she extended her hand towards Jane with a warm smile. Jane liked her instantly. Just then, Mike reappeared with two children in his arms.

"I see you have met Penagee, and these two little monkeys are our children, Zakrose and Wolf." So saying he placed the kids down and gently shoved their behinds propelling them forward.

"Hello Aunt Jane." They shyly chanted in unison.

"Hello you two, nice to meet you."

Mike took Penagee in his arms and gave her a passionate kiss. Then turning to Jane he smiled.

"You will have to excuse me for the moment Jane, affairs of State and all that, but you are in good hands for a guided tour of the little miracle we call home. See you in a while."

Penagee put her arm around Jane's waist and they walked, with the twins romping around them, on a tour of the Crystal City.

"Mike has some business to attend to and will join us shortly. You have made him very happy by coming here, and at the moment your head is probably way up in the clouds with all you see around you, the trip here and your brother of course."

Jane was trembling. This place was beyond her wildest dreams and all real, all of it, no fantasy. Her mind marvelled at the technology around her, the Crystal City, the view. Ridmon captured her heart and she fell instantly in love with it. She could not help thinking how nice it would have been if Mike had returned a little earlier. Then both she and their father could have made the journey together. Dad would have been happy on Ridmon. When she told Mike about their father, he didn't seem to display any emotion, but she sensed sorrow in him. Her head spun with all that she saw and heard. Penagee wisely showed her to her quarters and left Jane alone to sort things out for herself. Jane sat on her balcony overlooking the valley and for the first time in a long while felt very happy inside. The next few weeks were filled by a voyage to discovery for her, she literally walked in the clouds. Mike gave Niki to her which resulted in an amazing relationship. She spoke to the little creature that listened intently to the sound of her voice and would cock its head to one side as if it understood every word. Penagee and the twins went out of their way to make her feel at home and Jane inherited two pairs of ears that lapped up every description of the animals on Earth. The twins were like information vacuum cleaners wanting to know all there was to know and more. Anna showed Jane the fauna and flora in the valley and gradually set the scene for Jane's participation in the community's activities. An office and laboratory was set up for Jane in Anna's anthropology rooms for zoological research of all animal life forms on the planet housed within the supporting pylon of the platform. Jane was ecstatic, soon she would be given her first assignment.

A few days later, Mike, Moti, Anna and Penagee sat around the conference table in the Great Hall, having convened a meeting to discuss the next step in Operation Earth. The test run went better than expected and their first subject, a dying boy, was given a new lease on life. The boy adapted well to Ridmon, his newfound friends and his foster parents.

"The list numbers 3,000 homeless street kids on the initial resettlement programme, all of whom are equally divided between girls and boys from Rio Janeiro, Brazil. Ana-Maria will be handling their absorption into the community with foster parents here and on Thedrah." Explained Penagee. As Ridmon's Chief Executive, the overall responsibility for Operation Earth fell on her shoulders. The concept was simple. Orphaned children from all parts of earth were the subjects for relocation to Ridmon and Thedrah.

"Comments please." Queried Penagee. A moment's silence followed then Mike remarked.

"We need to create a Mother Drone for these missions, a Drone capable of at least a 4000 person capacity. Unfortunately we do not have the technology yet to increase the speed of the Drones, so the journey time we estimate the same as the test run. We will also require new recruits into the Squad, additionally trained for long range escort and protection units."

All heads nodded acknowledgement which signalled agreement. Moti suddenly had a brain wave and blurted out.

"I was thinking; why not develop two-man fighter craft." He paused, watching for a reaction then, seeing none, continued.

"Ideal quick deployment units from the Mother Drone which offers us a wider offensive and defensive capability, allowing for the Mother Drone to concentrate on her immediate task, the children."

Mike smiled, Penagee frowned and Anna responded.

"That would make us more effective. I agree."

"No." Responded a defiant Penagee.

"There is no need for another type of Drone, only a more advanced one, a lot of smaller ones only complicates the issue."

Mike stood up, leaned over across the table towards Penagee and flatly stated.

"I agree with Moti. In case you didn't realize it yet, we have entered into the big leagues now and are up against very sophisticated opponents who will stop at nothing to undermine our right of existence."

Penagee glared at him, eyes flashing, but remained silent.

With that Anna intervened.

"I suggest that this meeting be reconvened a month from now. During which time, people, we come up with concrete, feasible alternatives, suggestions and or workable examples. In the meantime, I suggest Moti and Mike see to the support units and their contingent of crews, and the developing of the Mother Drone as a primary directive. I will in the meantime make preparations here and on Thedrah to house and foster the first batch of kids. Borz, Jane and their team are building another Crystal City in Sector 3 where eventually some of the children and foster parents will live as Ridmon's second community. If there is nothing else to add, I recommend this meeting be adjourned before we all begin to kill each other!"

Penagee slowly stood up, walked around the table to Mike, punched him solidly in the chest, flicked her head sideways as a sign of contempt and walked proudly out of the Hall.

Moti sat with Mike in the trees away from the community in peaceful silence.

"Is it possible to make smaller and different versions of the Drones?" Asked Moti.

"Technically, yes. Though the basic principle of the Drone is so highly advanced they are able to mutate independently. We could expand on their ability and have a fleet of Drones specifically geared for military use. Our Drones are more than capable of handling most things, but their function is more defensive. Zorak did make one Drone slightly different, calling it a Warrior Drone, but it died with him when the City exploded. I could reproduce something similar, only far more advanced and more powerful, functioning as a pure strike force. With these Drones we don't need a large Squad. I reckon 100 highly trained men and women would be enough. I feel we need more survival training in all conditions and Earth offers us a viable alternative to do just that. Both of us could take a few months off on Earth with the Squad and get some exercise in the jungles, deserts and at the Poles where there are dangers not found on either Ridmon or Thedrah. I like it, in the meantime I want you to pick out the Squad. Make it a very tough selection. We need above average soldiers. I will develop the Mother Drone and her warriors. This should keep us both busy for a while." Concluded Mike.

"Well, let's get too It." Exclaimed an excited Moti who raced off through the trees back to the Crystal City, with Mike hard on his heels.

In the uneasy silence Penagee studied the two men. What they proposed was acceptable with the exception of the Earth part for an extended period. The two naughty boys were again itching for mischief. She had to smile though in spite of it. Mike broke the silence by saying.

"Why don't you and Ana-Maria come with us?"

Penagee thought about it and began to see some merits in the idea, especially for the twin's ongoing education. It also gave her the opportunity to be close to Mike. Both of them could effectively maintain long range control on Ridmon without any problem. The more she thought about it the more she liked the idea. She and Ana-Maria could involve themselves in more constructive scenarios while the men attended to their war games. Yes, she liked the idea a lot.

"In principle I will accept the idea. Ana-Maria and I will come along to make sure you two clowns don't get up to mischief." Smiled Penagee.

Moti breathed a sigh of relief. Penagee was not a person you wished to get into a boxing match with. Her bite was far more deadly than her bark. Mike smiled to himself, Penagee was playing the role to perfection and besides, he needed her and the twins with him. Call it what you want, but a man was more relaxed with his family beside him.

"Right." Beamed Moti.

So saying he and Mike beat a hasty retreat. Women, how the hell did you deal with them, it beat him how his Zimbabwean brother knew just how to play with Penagee, but allow her so much power over things?

"Moti, she and I are one. That's the way it is and that's the way it's going to stay. She and I are joined at the hip."

"Can't you at least tell her to leave things to their natural process?" Moti asked.

"No Moti, there is no other way. You accept me and you must in turn accept her. She will protect you; keep you safe, because she is very fond of you."

"I would hate to be her enemy." Exclaimed Moti.

"You better believe it." Confirmed Mike, then teleported to Thedrah.

He appeared in Frank's office just as Frank was sending his municipal members on a variety of daily chores. Frank had grown used to Mike's unscheduled appearances and was not flustered by the man's intrusion.

"Hello Mike."

"Hello Frank, how is everything?"

"The usual, ever so smooth."

"Bullshit Frank, admit it, you are bored and need a change." Mike responded.

"Well, Mike, putting it that way, what can I do, you appointed me to this job."

"Yes I did and now I am offering you a chance to join Moti and me on a mission to Earth. Are you by any chance interested?"

A wry grin creased Frank's mouth. The man's eyes flashed.

"Mike, the thing I love most about you is that you can be a real son-of a-bitch. Of course I am interested."

"Bring your family with you. Ten days from now, be on Ridmon." So saying Mike promptly vanished.

Frank sat back in his chair and laughed. One thing was for sure, with Mike life was full of surprises.

Mike did more than vanish. He re-surfaced in Protector Friend's realm of space to confer with his unusual friend for an entire month. Moti began his selection. 300 Potential applicants, mostly from Thedrah, out of which 100 very able-bodied recruits emerged. Jane was brought in to familiarize them on what to expect from Mother Nature on Earth and, for that month, Frank never felt more alive. Penagee was not amused by Mike's absence, especially with Protector Friend, because she was unable to communicate with her husband at all. Nada, Nada. Everything was blank.

Frank and Moti began the initial six months intensive training programme subjecting their recruits to a blistering non-stop schedule. They worked around the clock, time was of the essence in which they needed to produce an effective force. Finally, Mike returned to Ridmon and positioned a Mother Drone and her thirty-four Warriors plus sixteen Protectors in its atmosphere. An immensely powerful defensive and offensive war machine. Mother Drone's credentials were impressive. No one in their right mind, no matter how potent they thought they might be, would be advised to take on the Mother Drone. Only two persons could destroy it, Mike or Protector Friend.

"So the prodigal son decided to come home at last?" Penagee's sharp cutting question. She was angrier than he had ever seen her.

"It is done." Was all Mike was going to say.

He stood there facing his Tigress in silence until she began to slowly smile, her pulse rate increased, her physical animal urges took over and she pounced on her man.

Mike, Moti and Frank watched the recruits going through their paces. Moti had chosen well. They were tough, hard, intelligent, working well as a team or as individuals. All were superb athletes, highly motivated and dangerous. Six months of intensive training welded the group together into a cohesive, well-disciplined unit. The structure of the unit was based on much the same principle as any armed Force, with a 100 strong company split into 4 combat groups of 25 persons each. Overall logistics and administrative functions were controlled by Frank from the Mother Drone, ground troops were under Moti's command and the Warrior Drones were Mike's Task Force. The original Squad made up a special strike unit under Mike's direct command. Ridmon and Thedrah's defences were allocated to the remaining modified 16 Protector Drones. They were ready. A week of frantic preparation followed, then on the given command Penagee teleported in to stand next to Mike in front of the assembled Task Force and delivered her official confirmation speech.

"Well gentlemen, ladies, it seems you all have performed your tasks to perfection and I am impressed. Now I can safely give the go-ahead for Operation Earth. Our combined efforts are in place, all that remains is the execution of Plan A. So, if there are no objections, I suggest we all take a well-deserved 48 hours stand down and regroup at 24.00 hrs on Sunday in the Great Hall for embarkation. But before you all disperse, there is a party being held in the Great Hall within the hour which we would like all to attend. Thank you."

There was a thunderous roar of applause. People dashed off to prepare for the occasion. Tables were set and kitchen staff made last minute preparations. Ridmon's entertainment groups were warming up their instruments. Within the hour Ridmon's community filed in to take their allocated places in hushed silence. Once everyone was seated, Anna stood up and addressed the crowd.

"Welcome ladies, gentlemen and children. Today we have Ridmon's First Tactical Fighting Force. The Unit will be named Matabele. A name taken from an African tribe living in Zimbabwe who in their day were fearsome warriors. Their units were called Impi's. Today however, the Matabele's proud yet infamous past remains only a legend. Mike was born In Bulawayo, a city whose roots stem from the ancient Matabele Kingdom's capital. It is therefore natural to assume Mike is a White Matabele. The name Matabele is also given to a large fearsome ant whose reputation for painful stings is well known in the region. So all things considered, Matabele is the official name given to our armed forces. We have designed new uniforms with emblems which we take great pleasure in handing out to our men and women of the force."

With that Anna stepped down to a table in front of her where lay neatly folded items of apparel. There followed a loud applause. Section leaders came forward to accept their troop's new uniforms, emblems of rank and achievement. The uniforms were of a Thedarian material extracted by chemical process from the Zumi crystals which consisted of four basic colours, black, grey and a deep olive green or gold. The process could either produce a shiny, glassy or a matt, non-reflective finish. Green was the chosen colour for all ranks with exception of Mike, Moti and Frank, whose identifying colour was black. All had only three insignias, name, rank, and the Force. What made the material unique was its elasticity and strength. Once on, it moulded itself around the wearer's body in a snug tight fit. It was impervious to fire, knife slashes and completely bullet proof. The body was covered from head to foot in a protective stocking from which no part was left exposed. The material breathed, allowing for the dissipation of excessive body heat and sweat, maintaining an even temperature, no matter the conditions on the outside. Special pads of the same material formed contours along each muscle group the length and breadth of the entire body from the top of the head to the soles of the feet for additional protection. It gave the impression that the wearer was indeed extremely athletically built. Waiters dashed about serving Ridmon's exotic gourmet delicacies and glasses filled with beer. Penagee took the stand to make a short toast. Raising her glass into the air, she shouted.

"Matabele! Matabele!"

The effect was thunderous; everyone sprang to their feet and shouted the return salute.

"Matabele! Ridmon!"

The Great Hall shook with the vibration and an old Sangoma, seated in his dark, damp cave on Earth, shivered.

"The Matabele are on the march once again and will soon be here, Bulalah Enkosi!"

At midnight, Sunday September the 18th in the Year 2024, a single Mother Drone with her contingent of Warrior Drones, company of troops and administrative personnel, set course for Planet Earth. If Earth had been aware of the approaching force, she would have trembled in fear. Matabele was death and destruction personified of a magnitude too frightening to contemplate. But its mission was peaceful. Orphaned children that no one wanted or gave a damn about were the Task Force's objectives. Mother Drone reported to Mike and Penagee.

"Course set, estimated time of arrival 30 days, location Rio de Janeiro, Brazil."

Protector Friend increased the speed of the Drones to warp factor 30, eight hundred billion light years in only 30 days. Those thirty days were like a long night's sleep for the men and women within the Mother Drone. In a state of suspended animation immersed in life supporting gel, the Humans and Thedarian's could survive the trip unaffected. Mother Drone monitored her precious cargo like a brooding hen. After 30 days her cargo was awakened and released from their gel casings, a maze of honeycombed compartments into which four thousand people could be immersed and housed for the journey. Within her interior were other chambers and rooms to accommodate people, whilst in orbit, in their conscious state.

She reported, "Retrieval force in position. Warrior Drones activated. Retrieval commencing."

The Warrior Drones, released from their Mother carrier, swarmed down on to the city. Rio de Janeiro was oblivious, too busy living it up. Within an hour all 3,000 children were safely aboard, housed within their cocoons of gel, blissfully unaware of what had happened to them and would remain so until their arrival on Ridmon. Mike, Frank, Moti and the entire Matabele force, under the veil of darkness, were deposited into the heart of the Amazon jungle in three separate groups. The object of the exercise was for each group to travel from its drop-off point inwards for a distance of 300 kilometres through the dense jungle to a central regroup point. They were given no food or water or weapons, other than a survival knife each and combat uniforms. Each unit would follow its own pre-determined co-ordinates, navigating only by the sun and the stars. There would be no communication between groups until the regrouping area had been successfully reached. The order was simple; make it, or else be left behind. They would be totally cut off from the Mother Drone. Mike shook Moti's and Frank's hands. "Good hunting, gentlemen," and disappeared with his group, consisting of 29 men, into the dense jungle below to wait for the start signal. Ten minutes after landing in the dark, dense and humid jungle the message came through, the race was on. All felt the electrifying tension of anticipation. Mike's additional powers were neutralized by Protector Friend. Penagee would monitor and be operational Commander. Everyone was placed on an equal footing.

Mike took to the trees like a well-oiled machine with his unit in close pursuit. They would traverse the jungle's canopy where possible, only coming down for food and water. Moti and Frank opted for the same method. The first day passed without incident, covering a lot of distance. At sunset, all groups broke off for a well-deserved respite and something to eat. The groups descended to the thick jungle floor and fanned out in search of something edible, senses alert. Within the space of a few minutes the hungry teams were feasting on berries and grubs to the screech of warning calls coming from monkeys perched high up in the trees. The jungle was alive with sound. Water was not difficult to find within the joints of wide leaves which formed natural small reservoirs. Darkness crept in so the teams once again took to the trees like apes, searching for nesting places amongst the high branches, seventy metres above the ground. The night was black, making travel almost impossible and very dangerous. Mike checked his bearings from the constellation of stars in the night sky, fixed his direction and estimated the time then settled down to sleep. Moti made good headway. He too checked his bearings and settled for the night.

Frank was not so fortunate due to an encounter with a Black Panther which sprung out of the undergrowth on to one of his men, causing a rough and tumble involving everyone. Fortunately their uniforms prevented injury from flashing razor claws and crushing teeth, but the wearer nonetheless was bruised and a little sore as a result of the ensuing rugby match to beat all matches. The Panther was a lithe, agile killing machine and trying to pin it down was no easy feat. Now it seemed as if the panther had the upper hand, then the group. The animal gave as much as it got until it decided these green clad morsels were not playing the game and disappeared into the undergrowth. The laughter and jokes following left the group in good spirits. No harm had been done, but everyone had learned a valuable lesson, developing a healthy respect for the Panther and thanking their lucky stars for their uniforms. Dawn broke on the second day, revealing the new intruder into the jungle dressed in green, bouncing and flying from tree to tree with remarkable agility and speed. The creatures of the jungle cried out their warnings and made way for these strange apparitions in their backyard. On the jungle floor the message passed from hidden village to hidden village by way of drumbeats or runners. Something strange has come into the jungle. Hunters with their blow pipes and poisoned arrows laid in wait for this oncoming prey. They were a lost tribe of Amazonian Indians who had so successfully avoided detection over the years that one had to admire them. They were a remnant of the old ways and the taking of heads was still practiced. They ran through the undergrowth to intercept whatever it was, but found themselves peering up into empty trees.

There were ten men in the group with their blow pipes positioned upwards for the fatal darts to strike home with deadly accuracy. They were standing that way when from out of the surrounding undergrowth Mike and two Squad members struck. It was over in seconds. Ten Indians lay sprawled where they had fallen, senseless. Mike broke the blow pipes and scattered the arrows into the surrounding undergrowth, then regrouped back up in the trees heading off just as the first of the Indians was regaining consciousness. For the rest of the day Mike pushed hard, all the while drums sounded. There was sure to be pandemonium when the ten Indians returned to their village empty-handed, with broken blow pipes and confusion. Mike knew his progress was being monitored, but could not afford a confrontation, or deviate from his course because of the time factor. Directly in his path on the third day lay a village concealed beneath the dense canopy. One of his men on the outer flank was netted and hung upside down in fresh air, frantically trying to free his knife to cut himself loose while all the villagers were gathering in for the kill. Mike had no option, he signalled the attack and it came with lightning speed. 28 men unleashed their talons on those unfortunate Indians and hit hard. They freed their comrade from the nets and faded once again back into the trees. The village chief, who lay concealed under his thatched house, had watched the whole proceeding with wide-eyed fascination. What kind of apes were these that looked like men and women and who in the blink of an eye took out his entire village, every man jack of them. He watched as the apes took to the trees and vanished, then he crawled out from under the house to check on his people. They were all alive, but were going to have sore heads when they woke up. He went to the drum and beat a message,

"Human green apes in trees, very dangerous. Do not attempt anything, Leave them be."

Over and over again to emphasize the instruction. On and on into the setting sun of the third day the groups travelled. Moti and Frank did not encounter any problems on their third day. Four more days remained and the groups were making excellent time. Frank experienced a near miss on the fourth day. His group had to cross one of the streams feeding the mighty Amazon River and Frank was grabbed by a very large anaconda. It took all his men to prize him out of its wrenching grip. Progress that day for Frank was slower, He felt as if every part of his arms and torso had been crushed. Moti's group fared very well. Day five. Moti was well on his way as the hot sun rose into the sky above. The canopy thinned out which meant the going was more difficult and hazardous. No matter how careful one is, most times something is bound to happen and this was to be one of those occasions when Murphy's Law dictated events. He lost two of his men that day. They plummeted to their deaths from over 70 metres when the branch from which they were swinging broke. It was a freak accident. The branch was rotten and snapped under their collective weight. There was nothing anyone could do, so they buried their comrades deep in the base of a hollow tree and sealed the hole to prevent scavengers. It was not pleasant the rest of the day and the pace slowed to prevent any recurrences. The following two days were uneventful and all groups made very good time, arriving at the check point within minutes of each other. Mike, Moti and Frank took stock, two dead and one with a broken leg, a lot of bumps and bruises. Mission accomplished. For the rest of the day they lounged around on the jungle floor next to a river, relaxing and unwinding from their physical ordeal. They were all very weary but satisfied with themselves. In the evening the Warrior Drones came for them. Back in the Mother Drone Mike, Moti and Frank briefed Penagee and the Company took a very well deserved stand down.

"We are extremely sad at the loss of two of your team and their remains are aboard waiting burial on Thedrah. As far as we can ascertain your jungle exercise went very well indeed. The next step in your training programme will be the Sahara desert. This test will be a little more difficult, so we have decided to issue each man with five litres of water initially to cover a distance of 200 kilometres in 48 hours and your route this time will bring you to an oasis which is held by an Islamic rebel faction. Your combined mission will be to overrun their positions and release control to the Bedouin tribes in the area. You are to do this without firing a shot as you will be unarmed except for the knives. How does that sound?"

Mike, Moti and Frank looked at each other and smiled. Penagee was being a hard task master that's for sure. The meeting was concluded and the men stood down. The Mother Drone positioned herself above Mozambique at a place called Pemba. The entire contingent was to be landed at the Nautilus Hotel on the outskirts of the town for some relaxation and recreation. The site was chosen for its isolation, plus the fact that the small garrison of Government troops offered no threat. Its communications with the rest of the country would be terminated for the duration. It was party time and an experience the locals would not soon forget. Pemba was an age-old slave traders' shipping point in the north of the country, a short hop from the Comoros Island and Kenya on its most northern border, with Malawi and Zambia to the west and the Indian Ocean as its eastern border. The poverty- stricken town was no match for the visitors from outer space, but would benefit from the visit through Penagee's intervention. She, Ana-Maria and Susan would be responsible for the humane medical aid and food distribution that was planned. Mike and Moti with thirty troop's teleported into the town's army garrison and took the place apart. The African soldiers did not know what hit them and all communication links out of Pemba were neutralized. Mike held the Garrison Commander one-handed by the scruff of his neck, legs dangling in the air and walked around the assembled, demoralized group of misfit soldiers. He barked out in fluent Portuguese.

"I have never seen such a bunch of unruly people and you call yourself soldiers, you are a bunch of idiots."

Frightened eyes were riveted on his imposing frame with its dangling figure in tow.

"I could have killed every last one of you miserable wretches, but it's not worth it for me to dirty my hands. Instead, I am going to let you go and warn you that for the next four days if I so much as hear a peep out of you, you will be left for the hyenas to feed on. Do I make myself clear?"

His voice boomed across the courtyard and the poor fellows visibly trembled. Dumping the man he had been holding, Mike turned around to his men and teleported to the hotel. The hotel proprietor found himself gazing into eyes of a man with death written all over his face and wet himself. The Thedarian bodily lifted the squirming Pakistani off his feet, carried him into the dining room and plunked him very unceremoniously onto a chair. Mike walked in from the beach and approached him.

"You have an empty hotel with enough room to accommodate 125 persons, so I want to stay here for four days. Food will only be eaten fresh from the sea and the drink we will supply. The kitchen will be supervised to ensure you don't try to poison us and at the end of our stay you will be paid for your services. I expect freshly baked bread first thing every morning for breakfast and chilled South African wine for dinner which we shall provide. Do I make myself clear?"

He pushed his face right up against the Pakistani's to make his point adding,

"You will be safe as long as you do exactly what you are told and don't try any heroics. There is no garrison here in Pemba and all outgoing lines are down. You can try radioing for help from one of the ships anchored in port, but I don't think that will do you any good somehow. Do we have your co-operation or not."

The petrified Pakistani nodded his head and Mike motioned to one of the Squad who came forward and yanked the man to his feet.

"Now let's get some service if you please." With that the Pakistani nervously barked commands at his staff in the room and the effect was immediate. Mike strolled along the white sandy beach beside Penagee, while the twins romped around in the hot summer sun next to the gentle ripple of the tide. The twins were all over the place, checking into every nook and cranny while Mike and Penagee were content to be together, arm in arm in this peaceful setting. Dinner that night was a very special affair for Mike. He had been to Pemba before in the distant past. Candles were lit and the 125 people from another planet took their seats to dine on freshly cooked lobster and prawns, washed down with South African Autumn Harvest semi-sweet wine and Castle beer. It was a dinner all would remember. These people from another planet so far away from home, a people with a technology so advanced, were sitting down to a meal boiled and fried on actual gas stoves, something most of them had never seen and those that did had long forgotten. The Pakistani hotel manager and his wife sat next to Penagee. All the hotel staff were also seated, dining as one big happy family. No one answered questions and, as far as the hotel manager was concerned, they were a group of people from Europe on a holiday visiting for a few days. Moti was a little hesitant to sample the gourmet delights on account of his religious beliefs, but in the end all were feeding their faces to capacity. After dinner everyone lent a hand in the clean-up. Frank and Susan joined Moti and Ana-Maria for a romantic moonlight stroll along the beach. Mike and Penagee teleported the twins back to the Mother Drone and spent the rest of the evening in their bungalow making passionate love. Four days passed very quickly. On the evening of the fourth day, the Pakistani was paid in US dollars an amount exceeding his expectations. The whole company was assembled on the beach in the moonlight and Mother Drone teleported the entire group into herself. Pemba would not be returning to normal for a long time after their visit and many questions would remain unanswered there. In the warehouses there was an abundance of food parcels and the local hospital and clinic were replenished with much needed medicines. Penagee had been very busy.

Mother Drone reported." Confirm position Sahara, await instruction."

The teams were assembled. Mike, Moti and Frank discussed last minute details with Penagee concerning the whereabouts of the Bedouin tribes in the region and of their target, an Oasis. Their task was clear. Secure the Oasis regardless. This in effect meant any opposition was to be crushed permanently. A rather harsh decree coming from Penagee, but no one questioned the wisdom behind it. All was set, so the teams were teleported down to their starting

points, 48 hours to cover 200 kilometres in one of the
hottest climates in the world with temperatures exceeding
48 degrees centigrade. The distance was to be covered on
foot with water rationed per person. Each man and woman
carried two and a half litres of water per 24 hours. If anyone
exceeded their quota, they would have to face the thirst on
their own. The only other water was at the Oasis. The next
48 gruelling hours were a test for even the most stout-hearted.
The course was not easy going, but pitted with sand dunes
and jagged volcanic hills. At 05.00 hrs the signal was given
and the running began. It was murderous going against the
searing heat, sand and rocks. It taxed a person to the limits
of endurance and the temptation to drink grew stronger with
very step. On and on, kilometre after sweltering kilometre,
until the mind went blank and the body operated on its
own. The chest burned from constant breathing in hot air.
The ankles bruised by constant unevenness of the terrain.
Throats and the mouths went dry and lips became chapped.
Kilometre after torturous kilometre the three groups ran
towards their appointed destination. Well into the cooling
night, stopping only every four hours to drink sparingly
and check on their physical condition. On into the dawn
and another day of the climbing sun's fury. By midday the
run began to take its toll. The pace slowed down to a slow
shuffling trot and then sand storms raged, adding fuel to the
already blazing fire. Navigation became near impossible, so
three very weary and heat-fatigued groups limped into the
checkpoint well after sunset. Mike, Moti and Frank made
a reconnaissance of the Oasis by the light of the moon and
planned their strategy. From their vantage point they could
see the darkened shapes of a grove of palm trees in amongst
which stood six low-level mud dwellings. Soft light flickered
from frameless windows. All was quiet. Once in a while

passing shadows indicated prowling guards. The wells lay to the south of the Oasis where most of the rebels slumbered on sleeping mats.

"At least 700-800 men there." Whispered Moti.

Mike nudged him and indicated withdrawal. The three men returned to their units who were sprawled out in sheer exhaustion. Their water supplies were almost depleted and they could not stand another day of running without a long rest. Some men and women were in fairly bad shape, yet were still able to function. Mike decided to give them all a few hours rest before laying out his battle plan. He checked the time by the stars to be approximately, 22.00 hrs. At 04.00 hrs a full moon still high above, he assembled his units and gave them their orders, using a sketched diagram of the target in the sand to assign the assault groups. The attack would be launched in a three-pronged pincer movement. It was to be fast, merciless and, once the momentum was set in motion, it was to be followed through with maximum effect. Mike telepathically would synchronize the groups when in place. The groups dispersed into the surrounding terrain to take up their allotted positions. No dogs barked and no camels or horses shifted uneasily. Telepathically Mike launched his silent, brutal attack. The Islamic rebels were taken completely off guard. The rebels were dealt with by merciless clinical precision. By the first streaks of dawn the Oasis had been secured. One thousand rebels lay bound or dead. Totally and utterly demoralized, the survivors studied their attackers. Not a shot had been fired. The Matabele were rewarded with cool, refreshing water. They had triumphed over the run, themselves and taken on an armed group empty-handed and had won with not a single casualty. A sentry's low whistle saw the Matabele fade from view like ghosts. A laden camel train trudged into view through the trees and came to an abrupt halt, its lead riders staring in disbelief at the hundreds of men lying or sitting on the hot sand. Mike stepped out of a mud bricked building, raising a hand in greeting. He was eyed with extreme suspicion and heads turned left to right seeking out hidden guns. Mike spoke to the black- turbaned figure in Arabic.

"Salaam, greetings brother."

The rider responded carefully. "Salaam."

"It would be wise for the weary travellers to dismount and water their thirsty animals. Then we can discuss what you can do with these captives here."

The Bedouin eyed Mike for long moments. Something about the man's self-assuredness warned him to act with extreme caution. He glanced around seeing no one else, yet his keen senses tingled. There were others. Slowly the Bedouin dismounted, keeping his horse between Mike and himself. Mike remained motionless with a friendly smile on his face. He added.

"These prisoners have a reward on their heads, dead or alive. I think good fortune smiles on you today as we have decided that you should claim the prize money."

The turbaned figure grunted and surveying the prisoners, he calculated the financial remuneration he would gain from such a transaction. A broad grin creased his weather-beaten face as it dawned on him the amount involved. Turning to his still mounted comrades he excitedly barked out orders. The caravan hastily dismounted and rushed forward to ensure their investment was secure. Mike watched the Bedouins looting anything of worth from the dead bodies and from those scowling survivors. Mike then teleported the Matabele back to Mother Drone. There were to be no more stand downs. Gathered together within the Drone, they were confronted by Penagee, who smiled innocently saying.

"Ladies, gentlemen, well, that certainly was a very interesting demonstration of the sheer animal of man. But, I suppose all the same, congratulations are in order. You have 24 hours to rest up and prepare your teams. Destination will be the South Pole. Thank you."

With that she proudly walked out, fully enjoying her role as Commander of these cut-throats. The Squad, unceremoniously dismissed, were puzzled. Everyone parted company to take a well-earned rest. Mike decided against confronting Penagee concerning her actions, so joined his team instead. He checked on the Warrior Drones, all was well. He still had control. The Mother Drone reported all systems in place, nothing out of the normal. There was only the problem with his Lady Love. He did not have the time to argue with her neither did he have the energy at that point besides, he had to prepare his team. Mike was concerned though, Penagee's actions were out of character. To top it all, she blanketed her thought transmissions, so she must have been hiding something from him. 24 hours later the teams were teleported down into the South Pole's frozen wastelands. Penagee made a choice. She would make the return trip to Ridmon leaving Mike and his Matabele stranded on that frozen wasteland for the next two months. This was, she felt, to be their final test, a physiological one. The Warrior Drones refused to obey and would remain. Mike's powers would only be re-instated when the Mother Drone was too far out of reach for him to attempt to board her. It was on the twentieth blizzard wrenching, freezing day that Mike's powers were restored to him and he immediately became aware of their situation. The nature of Penagee's actions angered Mike. Test or no test, leaving them like that was not part of the agreed agenda. Teleporting the teams together he abruptly ended the exercise, relocating his

Matabele to a more hospitable location. His Warrior Drones checked in and Mike ordered them down. His Matabele needed food and shelter to regain their strength. So Mike embarked them onto the Drones and made for the Cheroma Kadoma Mountain in Zimbabwe. There was still some unfinished business at the base of that mountain.

On arrival, Mike stealthily crept out of the dense undergrowth and into a large dark cave like a silent, deadly panther. Two old and withered men sat way back in its dark interior listening for his approach. Mike floated above the floor away from the cave's entrance so as not to silhouette himself. It was very dark within the interior of the cave, but he knew exactly where the two men were sitting, so moved with slow calculated ease. The Sangoma's hardly breathed, sitting rigid, waiting. They knew the predator was close; they felt it, sensed its powers and shivered. A hand closed around one's throat and a voice whispered out of the darkness,

"Old wise men of the mountain, I know you, I have tracked you from worlds beyond worlds and have heeded your call. The white Matabele is here to claim your secret." Mike released his grip and stepped backwards.

Amos heard the words. He could still feel those steel talons around his throat and shuddered. This white man was a nightmare come true and Amos was terribly afraid. An eerie phosphorescent light slowly lit the cave and the two Sangoma's saw their predator standing before them in his black body suit.

"Does the White Matabele come to send the old men to their graves?" Stammered Amos.

"No, the white Matabele wants to learn of the secret to the Portal and will then depart to his own world and leave the old men in peace and a time of their own dying." Replied Mike.

"Then look into my mind, therein you will find the secret, then go in peace and with the blessings of an old Sangoma." Said the old man. In an instant Mike locked into the old man's mind and understood the Portal's secrets.

"Farewell Old Men, go in peace." Mike then teleported to the top of the mountain where all his men were standing waiting.

"Ladies, gentlemen, please board the Drones." He command.

With the Drones poised, Mike telepathically activated a Portal. Thirty-four Warrior Drones carrying 103 men and women of the Matabele Regiment, passed through into Ridmon's atmosphere. Below in the dark cave of Cheroma Kadoma the older Sangoma sighed and then took his final journey into the spirit world, task completed. Amos did not weep, but carried the frail body deeper into the cave and buried it amongst the relics of a past, a Matabele past. Their sudden arrival on Ridmon caused quite a stir. The Protector Drones transmitted a message to Penagee on board the approaching Mother Drone only ten day's journey out of Ridmon.

"Matabele Regiment back on Ridmon."

She was astounded. How in Thedrah's name had that man of hers managed to pull this off? Shaking her head, she laughed. He was full of surprises that one. The news was greeted warmly though and Penagee felt relieved. Operation Earth Phase 1 was almost complete.

Meanwhile Moti and Frank, having dismissed their troops, sat on the bridge walkway at one of the little refreshment kiosks sipping Ridmon whiskey.

"You can pat yourself on the back, Frank, a man of your age to have finished that desert run needs a medal. I am very impressed and you have certainly won my respect."

Frank eyed Moti and smiled.

"Did any of us have any choice? To fail would have meant being left behind and that, my friend, would not have been very wise."

"You said it. But, I tell you Mike would not have deserted us even if it had meant he would never see Ridmon again." Remarked Moti.

Frank did not answer him, noticing the approaching Anna.

"Well, well. So the boys of the Matabele Regiment are back from playing their little games I see."

"Hello Anna. Nice to see you too and yes, things did go pretty well, considering we lost five men." Replied Frank.

"What, some weak links in your super perfect chain?" Quipped Anna.

"No, two fell to their deaths and three were freeze dried." Angrily answered Moti.

"Freeze dried?" Sarcastically muttered Anna.

"Yes, their uniforms had flaws in them around the arm pit areas and back of the neck and the results were instantaneous. The same uniforms you were responsible for performing quality control on." Confirmed Frank.

"Oh! I am sorry to hear that."

"Damn right, you silly woman. Now get the hell away from us." Spat Moti.

Anna stared at him in silence and then turned to walk away, but Moti was on a roll and added.

"Next time you foul up like that I will personally see to it that you pay."

She marched off fuming. After a few moments Moti asked Frank.

"Know where Mike is?"

"Yeah! Doing his meditation thing. I asked him to join us here. Shouldn't be long now." Responded Frank.

Moti sat up straight and stared. Heading towards them, marching in perfect precision, were his 95 Matabele soldiers. Frank whistled. They looked good. The Company came to a halt abreast of the seated Moti and Frank. A command was barked and the entire body did a left face. A Sergeant marched forward up to their table, halted and saluted. Frank and Moti stood up and returned the salute. Then the Sergeant said.

"Sirs, on behalf of the men and women of this Regiment, we wish to thank you and invite you to have drinks with us at the Regimental Bar."

"Thank you Sergeant, we accept, but are waiting for our other fellow officer to join us and will meet you there." Replied Frank.

"That's quite alright sir, we will wait."

With that the man briskly about turned, marched to his Company and barked an order.

"Company……company, stand at ease."

The order was carried out with perfect military precision. Frank muttered under his breath to Moti.

"Hope Mike arrives soon, this kind of situation makes me feel uncomfortable."

Moti was proud of his men and women of the Matabele Regiment. Very proud. They were more than just fine soldiers, but family also. He cast his mind back to his Commando days in the Israeli Army and had to admit that it was nothing compared to this group. Shortly afterwards Mike arrived. He saw the assembled Company and quickly donned his uniform, he carried in his back pack, then appeared in front of the Sergeant who jumped to attention.

"Stand easy." Ordered Mike, stepping forward to shake each individual's hand. Returning to stand beside Moti and Frank, he shouted.

"Matabele!"

The response was thunderous, "Matabele! Ridmon!"

To Moti and Frank he said, "Fall in. We have a party on our hands and I don't want to see any of you holding back."

Moti and Frank took up their positions at the head of the company waiting for Mike's order. By this time there were a lot of spectators curious to see what was going on and Mike saw the opportunity to show off a little. After all, this was a unique Regiment having proved themselves beyond a shadow of doubt to be well-oiled and professional. To be one of its members was not for the faint-hearted.

"Battalion, battalion... shun." Boomed his voice down the valley.

"Right turn." With that the entire body turned right in perfect unison.

"By the centre, quick... march."

The citizens of Ridmon watched their proud Matabele Regiment march off and felt very secure. What a party it turned out to be. For seven days Anna fumed, ranted and raved. The regiment doors were sealed off. She did not know it, but for seven days Mike and his regiment were officially on a stand-down, fall-down party and good old Earth style in a small out of the way place situated in the Namib Desert on the deserted Skeleton Coast. Fishing, drinking, swimming and exploring, but mostly, sleeping it off. Their presence went undetected until the second last day when a light aircraft belonging to the Namibian Parks Board landed on a strip of beach nearby and an irate Game Ranger marched up to them demanding an explanation.

"What the hell are you bloody people doing out here? I have a mind to have you all arrested."

Mike laughed and replied.

"Sir, we know you are only doing your job and do not hold it against you. But, as you see it would be very difficult to try and arrest this lot of drunken bums as I don't think they would take too kindly to having their party stopped. Take a closer look, and then tell me you are going to arrest us."

The Game Ranger took a much closer look at this wild bunch of people, all wearing only the scantiest of clothing in the hot sun. They were mad he thought and then it hit him like a sledgehammer. It was a mixed group of men and women of superb physical form and definition. The women were beautiful, like bronzed goddesses. He watched as a group of them started a game of Catch, the likes he had never seen before. Two opposing sides were required to get a large rock from one side of an area about 25 metres in length to the other side and the opposing team was to prevent them and attempt to do the same. The whole game was played by gymnastics. One picked up the rock and had to flick flack with it and then pass it to another member of the team who was not allowed to stand upright or walk. They were using somersaults, flying cartwheels and every conceivable gymnastic movement in the book to keep the rock in possession. The game was fast, with bodies flying all over the place. He noticed the features, the hair colour and the eyes, the bottle green eyes. Mike placed a restraining hand on the Ranger's shoulder, feeling the man's tension.

"Relax, when do you have to report in?"

Without taking his eyes off the scene in front of him, he stammered.

"Not until tomorrow."

"Good, then you would not mind joining us, a cold beer perhaps?"

"Yes, yes thanks that would be fine."

Mike walked with the Ranger to a large tent, pulled out a chair and motioned for the man to sit and gave him an ice cold beer. The man cracked open the can and took a deep gulp of cold Hansa beer. Mike was amused, the sight of the girls had transfixed the man and rightly so. They were goddesses out of some mythology.

"What is your name?" Asked Mike.

"Koos Le Roux." Was the reply.

The beer can was empty, so Mike gave him another. Moti and Frank ambled up and sat down.

"Beer you two." Asked Mike casually? Both nodded and three more beers appeared.

"This is Koos Le Roux, a Game Ranger."

The three exchanged greetings and Moti winked at Frank who smiled, understanding what Mike was up too. Mike gently put the Ranger into a deep sleep and wiped all memory of their meeting from the man's mind. He teleported the fellow into his aircraft and then teleported the aircraft to its destination in Swakopmond. The party continued. The last day dawned with sadness for having to leave, but happiness for having had such a fantastic time. The beaches were very thoroughly cleaned of debris, leaving no trace whatsoever of their presence there and the Battalion disappeared through the Portal into the Regimental Barracks on Ridmon. When the doors of the Barracks were re-opened, Moti walked straight into a very angry Anna. Mike and Frank beat a hasty retreat, leaving poor Moti to face the music alone. Anna's tongue was as sharp and as vicious as a doubled-bladed sword and she knew how to use it. The two of them stood toe to toe and argued heatedly in Hebrew.

"You bloody idiots," Anna screamed," What the hell are you lot playing at?"

"Nothing, Why? What's up? You miss me?" Replied Moti innocently.

"What's up? You have the cheek to stand there and ask me what's up! What is up is that I, as administrator of Ridmon, cannot find any responsible people to do their jobs because they have locked their doors and degraded to a wild party, completely unconcerned about the rest of this community and I won't stand for it. No sir, you will be hearing more about this and let me assure you, I will have you lot running up and down doing chores around here instead of your silly war games." Anna fumed.

Moti had enough, time to end the conversation. He hefted the angry, spitting and biting she-wolf Anna onto his shoulder and walked out onto the walkway, dumping her into the centre pool, then casually walked off to the bar and ordered a beer. He was calmly sipping his beer when Anna lunged at him with a knife. Moti quickly disarmed her and this time carried her under-arm wriggling and squirming, dripping wet, to a storage closet inside the complex, entered and slammed the door shut behind him. He ripped her clothing off and stepped back to admire her lovely, well-developed body with its full firm breasts. She shrieked obscenities at him, but did not attempt to cover her nudity. Moti waited for the steam to run out of her and then said.

"Anna, you are lovely. Any man would not think twice to penetrate that well of ecstasy between your thighs. To fondle those enticing breasts and kiss that soft warm body of yours. Yet your tongue is so damn vicious it puts men off, so if you are having problems in your bed, don't take it out on the rest of us. It won't solve the problem, it will only make matters worse."

Anna stood there in her nakedness under Moti's penetrating gaze and her loins ached, she wanted to be taken, she wanted to be possessed by him. She hated David for betraying their love and it left her angry and frustrated. She couldn't help herself, her animal cravings were at bursting point and she instinctively took her breasts in her hands and began massaging them so that the nipples stood out like arrows. Her thighs rubbed together uncontrollably. Moti's pent-up desires unfolded and he fought desperately to suppress the feelings. He reached out, took Anna roughly and penetrated her. Pure animal lust drove the two together in a dance of pain and ecstasy. A carnal craving that would not be satisfied until both had reached their peaks. Once, twice, three times their bodies joined. There was no limit, nor holding back, no place sacred. He took her like a man possessed and Anna reached heights never experienced before. Her nails tore furrows down his back and chest, bit into his flesh and thumped her body against his, sweat mingling and finally their passions exploding into one another. Anna clawed, screamed and climaxed, her body shuddering like a leaf in the breeze and both collapsed to the floor exhausted.

Mike waited until the Mother Drone was within range and then teleported aboard. All was still. He stood gazing at Penagee encased within the gel and smiled to himself, knowing what her reaction was going to be when she confronted him about how the Regiment had beaten her back. Another surprise for her would be the news that the second Crystal City, built in record time, had been completed. A community had already been established there with Jane as their Administrator. Mike had not seen Jane since his return, but there would be time for that. He was more concerned for Moti though. Sending the couple out of the valley would leave Mike with a problem dealing with Ana-Maria, a rather delicate matter and one that needed to be addressed with utmost sensitivity. Anna had become radiant, and smiled all the time. She was so pleasant and happy, heads turned in disbelief. David either didn't notice or was not concerned about the fact that Anna had moved out. Mike could only shake his head. Summoning Moti and Anna to a private place in the trees away from listening ears, he then asked them straight out.

"I guess you two more than enjoy your little tumbles in the hay?"

Anna blushed scarlet and Moti hung his head.

"This is a complicated business and believe me, I understand how this happened. But both of you have to now sit back and take stock. My question to you both is, does this continue to satisfy physical lust or does this continue because there is a bond of love between you?"

Anna and Moti glanced at each other, but said nothing.

"What is it then?" Demanded Mike.

The woman had tears in her eyes and reached out to take Moti's hand, answering.

"Mike, we are in terrible trouble, we love each other. Yet are faced with an emotional problem neither of us are able to solve. We are both Israeli and Jewish and we relate to one another in spite of our differences. Our act of betrayal to others will not change the way we feel for one another."

"Moti?" Queried Mike.

"She is right. What we have done may be unforgivable in some people's eyes, but we will not be separated even if it means leaving Ridmon forever."

Mike studied the pair in front of him and sighed. A third Crystal City was to be built on Sector 9 and these two would make ideal leaders there.

"You realize this puts me in a somewhat of an awkward position, so I am transferring you both out to Sector 9 to take charge of operations there until this whole thing blows over. There you will both have enough time to consider your choices. I could separate you, but that would defeat the object. I am buying you time and I need a confirmed yes or no in six months' time when you both have had the opportunity to live and work with each other on an equal footing."

The couple nodded their approval and Mike teleported them to the Sector 9 construction camp in a dense forest wilderness where they were to work and live alone in very primitive living conditions. If, after six months of that, the two still felt so strongly about each other then it would have proved a point to him that he would have to accept. He found Ana-Maria on one of her usual daily walk-about with little Carla trundling alongside humming to herself. He felt very cheap and dirty at what he was about to do, seeing as he liked the woman very much and the thought of her going through another heart-breaking episode would unsettle him. He was mad at Moti for sure, but the ways of the heart are and always will be, a mystery. Gently he accessed Ana-Maria's mind and blocked all emotional memory of Moti, holding it in limbo until the six months lapsed and Moti's final choices were made. Mike hated himself for doing this, but Ana-Maria's emotional wellbeing was at stake. Taking a confirming look into her smiling eyes Mike returned to Ridmon heavy hearted.

The Mother Drone positioned herself above the Second City and deposited her cargo of Human children into the care of the waiting foster parents. 3,000 children, ages ranging from infant to twelve years were given a new lease on life and Ana-Maria would be their community tutor and guide. Originating from Brazil herself, she fitted into the role perfectly, so communication with the kids was made that much easier. The children were all ushered into the city's Great Hall where Ana-Maria made formal introductions and read them the riot act. Street kids had grown up under very adverse conditions and stealing was one of the tricks they had learned well in order to survive. Here on Ridmon one did not have to steal, there was plenty for everyone, yet stopping an instinctive habit would not be easy.

"Boas Dias Criances, good day children. My name is Ana-Maria and these adults around you are your new parents. You are no longer in Brazil, but in a place far away. Here you will not have to be afraid of the police killing you, or being forced into prostitution, nor will you have to go hungry. Here you will all be treated with kindness and given a second chance in life."

Jane listened to the speech, but could not understand a word of it so let her gaze focus upon this dirty, bedraggled, hungry bunch of kids and her heart went out to them. It was not going to be an easy task, but Ridmon was prepared for it. Jane adapted well to her new lifestyle and enjoyed it immensely.

"Next time I see that brother of mine I am going to give him a juicy fat kiss on that mouth of his." She thought to herself. She watched the kids being led off with their appointed foster parents. Ana-Maria walked over to Jane and hugged her.

"Well, it is done, now starts the real work. Turning those little monkeys into civilized Human beings."

"You thrive on this kind of thing, don't you?" Remarked Jane.

"Ah yes, I grew up in a convent and later as a young girl worked with the Catholic Sisters in an orphanage until I met

Roberto. I always wanted to look after destitute children and now I have my chance."

"You certainly will have your hands full with this lot." Smiled Jane.

"Yes, but I am looking forward to It." Added Ana-Maria.

"Will Moti be joining you here?"

A puzzled frown creased Annemarie's forehead.

"No, Moti is only a friend, his work is not here and besides, why would he want to come here to be with these children. He is a fighter, not a kindergarten teacher."

Now it was Jane's turn to be puzzled. Something had happened between those two, she guessed. It was none of her business so she left it.

"If you will excuse me, Jane, little Carla is hungry and I must feed her before we all hear what good lungs she has."

Jane laughed and waved goodbye.

Penagee stepped onto the walkway, her eyes flashing. There, as cool as a cucumber, sat Mike with a cold beer in his hand, smiling like a cat having caught a mouse. The twins spotted him and raced towards him squealing with glee and Mike stood up arms outstretched. The twins jumped into his open arms and were swept up and twirled around with lots of hugs and kisses. Penagee was in no hurry, she would get to the bottom of this soon enough, but for the moment needed to feel him close, so she walked slowly, allowing the kids to have their moment. Mike put them down and said.

"Go on, Uncle Frank and Ivan over there want to say hello." With that the twins scampered off to where Frank sat. Penagee took her time; Mike never ceased to amaze her at his ability to stir in her such wanton passions. Try as she may, she could not escape her emotions and why should she, he was an absolute hunk and she loved him madly. The last few steps were undignified and they both flung themselves at each other. Frank smiled, watching from the corner of his eye. How Mike was going to get out of this one beat him, but he was sure the man had a plan, he always did. Mike danced around the walkway with Penagee in his arms.

"So my Queen Bee returns home to her waiting lover at last?"

"Your Queen Bee is more than happy to be in her lover's arms, but curious to know how he got here before her!"

Mike could hide things from her in a little corner of his mind and no matter how much she probed, she could never manage to find out things if Mike didn't want them found. It used to anger her no end, but after a while she accepted it as it did not do any real harm and besides, the man needed some privacy.

"In good time my Love, all shall be revealed. In the meantime you and I and the twins need to spend some time together, alone."

"Yes my darling, but I have to check on Anna and make sure everything is in order."

"No need, she and Moti are in Sector 9 and will be for six months on a project there."

Penagee stiffened. The cat was out of the bag.

"You're joking." She gasped, and then added," Poor Ana-Maria."

Mike put Penagee down into a chair and sat next to her.

"I have interfered a little there until such time Moti and Anna decide they really want each other and it's not just a lusting of the hormones."

"What do you mean by interfered?" Penagee questioned suspiciously.

"Let's just say I blanked some memory of her and Moti, to avoid any emotional breakdown. Later, once things have sorted themselves out one way or the other, we can always undo."

Penagee went silent. What Mike had done was not right, but under the circumstances it was the wisest move he could have made. 3,000 children were better off for it and any emotional trauma in Ana-Maria's life right now would not be beneficial to those kids. Sometimes one had to be cruel to be kind. Penagee was very fond of Ana-Maria and felt for her.

"Moti and Anna. What about David?" She questioned.

"That's a strange one, he does not seem to be bothered. I spoke to him very indirectly and his response was, if she was away or here it did not concern him. So I dug into his brain and found out the reason. Some time ago when the Thedarians first came here, David had an affair with one of the women. The affair did not last long due to Anna coming in between, but the experience left him at a loose end and now he won't look at another Human female, let alone make love to one. In a way I don't blame him, but on the other hand I think he's nuts for giving Anna up like that. It's to be expected that something would happen as a result and Moti got into the act. Moti's reasons are that although he loved Ana-Maria, it was a different kind of love, with Anna there is the fiery passion plus they both share common denominators."

"I am going to send David to Thedrah to live, perhaps there he will find what he is looking for, what do you think ?" Asked Penagee.

"I have it on good authority that the Thedarian female in question bore David a son and is still unattached, waiting for the day that David may come looking for her."

"Then that settles that. Anything else I should know?" Giving Mike a helpless female look.

He knew the game well and simply said.

"Patience, that's a surprise."

Penagee smiled.

Moti felt bad. Somehow he had betrayed Mike's friendship and it hurt. He admired the man more than anything, loved him like an older brother. Anna stirred the devil in him and he had fallen for her like a ton of bricks many months ago. He managed to keep his feelings very secret and protected. The day she came at him with a knife was the breaking point from which there would be no return. Both were banished to this forsaken place as a form of punishment. He understood Mike's reasoning, but all he could feel was the shame. He wanted Anna so bad it hurt, now they were here together alone. One way or another, both of them would have to rely on each other in order to survive the scandal and come to know each other far more intimately, physically, emotionally and spiritually. She would have to be by his side day in and day out. This was going to be their test. Each other. Mike was no fool. For six months they would neither see nor hear from anyone. Anna watched Moti and could sense his feelings, so she wisely let him be. She would have to do a lot of growing up to face the hardships and was going to have to love a man on an equal footing. In the past she was the spoilt brat, getting men to chase after her every whim. Not anymore. She came down to earth with a big bump here on Ridmon. David proved to be a wimp in her eyes and Moti, the strong powerful protector, would be the one to look after her and see to her every need. How wrong she had been to think and act that way. Now she faced six months of hardship with a man she wanted, craved for, but who would not chase after her like a lovesick animal. The Prima Donna fell from grace right into the lap of an alien planet and into the arms of man she would not have given a second glance on Earth. He was a barbarian, rough, ill-mannered and the only man who could drive her sexually insane just by the scent of him. Their days were busy and hard, the forest needed to be carefully uprooted and replanted elsewhere to make way for the City. An area of five kilometres in diameter was to be cleared in order for the foundations of a single pylon one kilometre in diameter to be grown from crystal at a depth of half a kilometre in the ground. The task was to be completed in six months. Massive drilling machinery was brought in from Thedrah and so the days passed into weeks and the weeks into months. Anna toughened up to a lithe, nubile, sun-bronzed forest woman who could take on any job a man could do, and do it just as well. The two indeed became one through the hardship and Moti taught her all he knew. Each day he worked on her until Anna could swing through the trees with ease, handle a lance and bow like a professional and grapple with Moti on a one-on-one basis and give a good account of herself. They made a perfect team, as co-workers, as lovers and as partners. Mike's plan worked.

At the end of the six months the construction crews moved in. Moti and Anna were summoned to the Great Hall by Penagee. Their entrance caused a stir. Dressed in only the skimpiest of garb and armed with primitive weapons, they looked like two figures emerging from the caveman age. Moti and Anna held their heads high standing before Penagee. Mike teleported in to stand behind the two as a token of support, dressed in his regimental colours. Besides, he missed Moti's face around the place and if Penagee was to get rough about this he would have to, for the first time, go against her. The Hall was still. From somewhere in the building a shout echoed "Matabele!" and the answering call "Matabele! Ridmon!" Then Frank marched in at the head of the 100 strong Matabele Regiment. Penagee waited for the disturbance to quieten down and stood up slowly.

"I see, by the look of things, that the both of you have come through your experience pretty well."

She watched Mike closely and knew that any wrong word would lead to an explosive situation. Since Mike had banished Moti to Sector 9, he spent days at a time out in the forest, or completely disappeared off the planet. She could never find out how he managed it. The Drones monitored his every move, yet somehow he managed to vanish into thin air. Their relationship took a turn for the worse during those last few months and she did not like it at all. Penagee missed her man terribly.

"You are both welcome back into the community, but your positions within it will be reserved for military purposes only."

The Hall rocked, "Matabele! Matabele!"

Mike moved forward to face Moti and his voice boomed through the Hall.

"The Tiger greets the Hawk, his brother."

Again the Hall shook with the chant "Matabele! Matabele!"

Penagee looked at Mike and felt a strange power emanating from him, her heart sank and she was on the verge of excusing herself when the man lifted her into his arms. She was not in the mood for further melodramatics so attempted to teleport out. Nothing happened. Tried again, and nothing happened. Mike was blocking her. He then carried her on to the walkway to where the twins were seated. Turning to face the crowd he spoke, his voice carrying to echo against the crystal cliffs.

"People of Ridmon, the time has come for you to stand alone. You are now going to be left to determine your own future through a democratic process and federal type of government. You have the technology and the infrastructure to do so. In addition, your defences are such that no attackers of your right to exist will succeed in any action against you. Thedrah and Ridmon are joined as one and a new nation has been born. There are now 3,000 Human children on Ridmon and Thedrah who, with Thedarians, constitute the future of these two planets. At this very moment, delegates from Thedrah and our own outer continents are meeting to determine the processes of democracy and law to take effect immediately through electoral voting and new legislation is being drafted to ensure a just and fair implementation. You will have the opportunity to vote for a person or persons within your constituency as leader and representative. The Crystal City here in the valley is to become the Legislative capital and seat of power." A moment's pause then continued.

"Penagee and I step down from office as of this moment. There is no monarch, no single controlling figure or dictatorship, neither chieftainship nor any form of socialistic party government. You are free to vote for whomever you please and your nominees will be decided by bi-electoral vote today. The nominated candidates from both planets will be flashed onto screens in the Great Hall by the end of the Ridmon day for the next seven days and then the entire eligible population on Ridmon and Thedrah will be called to cast their votes. Let it be understood that this is a democratic election which allows for only two official parties in a 100-seat parliament. Each constituency will submit two candidates and from those collective candidates a president and vice president will be elected."

There was a stunned silence. No one spoke or moved. Mike continued.

"You will find touch computers in the Hall which will not only identify you, but give you a pictorial choice of candidates from your own constituencies. Everybody qualifies. No person is allowed to vote for themselves. All you have to do is scroll through the pictures of faces, choose the one you want and touch the screen with your right index finger confirming your choice. The computers will then filter the information and produce two names at the end of the day whose faces will be flashed across the overhead monitor screens. The computers will be clinical. There will be no electoral fraud in these elections. I suggest therefore that you all make your choices now. Good luck, ladies and gentlemen."

With that Mike teleported out with his family to a place in the Dark Forest where he had built a new home up in the trees, not far from the Crystal City. Penagee was quiet as she watched her man romping around playfully with the twins. He had successfully brought their reign of singular power to an end and given the people the opportunity to govern themselves, with leaders of their own choice. She did not quite know how she felt about it, but one thing was for sure, deep down she felt relieved. Now she could concentrate on other more pressing matters closer to home and rebuild bridges between herself and Mike. Their positions on the planet would be determined by the people, the effects of which would only become apparent in the months to come. One thing was certain, she and Mike controlled the Drones, and nothing could change that. It was not a negotiating factor, only an assurance that, as long as she and Mike had a vested interest in the planets, both worlds retained the Drones protection. They could not be duplicated or replaced, so in affect her and Mike's standing was guaranteed, whether in office or not. Penagee smiled to herself, this man of hers was crafty, but in a humane way. She shuddered to think if he was otherwise. Their new home, very quaint, gave off a very warm feeling. It was built entirely of wood, with three bedrooms, two bathrooms, a study, lounge cum kitchen and a sundeck, twenty metres wide, completely surrounding the house. No trees or branches were removed, but formed part of the house that was secured 100 metres off the ground, with interlocking walkways going off in six directions. It was completely self-contained and nothing went to waste. Everything was recycled. All fittings and fixtures throughout the house were hardened crystal and there was running water on tap. That intrigued her.

What fascinated her even more was the fact that the wood that was used to build the house was not from Ridmon or Thedrah. She touched the smooth logs and a picture formed in her mind. Knysna, South Africa. Planet Earth. For every tree that had been felled to build the house, two were planted in its place. The entire house and furnishings were coated with a very thin layer of transparent Black Nut gum, emphasizing its natural colouring and preserving the wood for an extremely long time. Penagee was impressed with the simplicity of it all. She loved it. Attached to the sundeck was a cute two roomed cottage.

Elections were taking place across the two planets and nominees from each constituency would be known by the end of the day. Computers were working at full capacity, documenting, recording and sorting. It also gave them the opportunity to conduct a census, confirming population figures. Ridmon and Thedrah would be launched into a new era of their political history, Democracy. Every person rallied wholeheartedly, creating a festive atmosphere. For the first time in their lives Thedarians and Ridmonians alike felt a sense of nationalistic pride. The two million light

years separating the two planets, was of no consequence.
Frank sat with Susan on their balcony overlooking the
valley in growing anticipation. Mike was somewhere out
there right now with his family, probably doing the same.
He had last seen Moti and Anna physically carried off by
the Regiment and he imagined what a party they must be
having. Jane and Ana-Maria came in together with twenty
mixed delegates from Thedrah who were sitting at this very
moment drafting a constitution and planetary policy. Mike
insisted that he, Penagee, Moti and Frank be excluded from
the proceedings so that none of their past involvements in
governing matters could or would be construed as having
had a hand in influencing any new constitution. It was to
be a people's choice as to who would take overall leadership
and leadership of the various constituencies would be by
popular vote. He cast his mind back to the day that he first
landed with a bump on Ridmon and the course of events
which had transpired since then. He was a very fortunate
man indeed. Back in the USA he would be an insignificant
statistic within a large military establishment, biding his
time until he reached retirement age and qualified for a
state pension. Ridmon was an adventure and a challenge
he had faced to come through with flying colours and a life
more meaningful than he could ever have imagined. He was
blessed with a lovely wife and son and Frank was indeed a
happy man, content with his lot in life.

There was no need to worry about pensions, mortgages
and debts, there were no such things on Ridmon. He
was Commander of its Army with Moti as his second in
command. Susan was an excellent teacher and took great
pride in her work and Frank's son would grow up in a safe
and protected environment, free from pollution, degradation
and crime. On Ridmon there was honour, and a man's word

was his bond. Yes, he had every reason to be happy, no matter the outcome of the vote. By close of day the computers shut down and everybody waited, watching the overhead monitor screens. A message flashed across the screens.

"Results to be published within the hour."

The people waited across the entire planetary group. It was to be a very long hour for all. At last the results came through.

"Ridmon.	Sector 9.......Borz and Mark	Result	Borz
	Sector 5.......Ana-Maria and Zebor	Result	Ana-Maria
	Sector 4.......Frank and Tzanud	Result	Frank
Thedrah	Sector 1.......Jose and Thram	Result	Thram
	Sector 2.......Zadas and Buk	Result	Zadas
	Sector 3.......Udras and Tara	Result	Tara

"That concludes the names of constituent leaders. Thank you."

The Hall erupted in shouts, whistling and dancing. Frank won his seat on Ridmon and in parliament. There was jubilation amongst the community. Ridmon retained its favourites and they were happy. A Matabele Sergeant knocked on Frank's door. When Susan opened the door, the soldier asked to see his officer. She called through and Frank appeared in the doorway to be met with a brisk, smiling salute.

"Yes Sergeant, what is it?"

"Begging your pardon Sir, but you are the official leader of Sector 4, you are now a Member of Parliament. Congratulations."

The soldier saluted once again, did an about turn and departed, leaving an ecstatic Frank clutching Susan in his arms and dancing around the room. Ana-Maria was beside herself. How was it possible that the people voted for her, she was no politician? Jane embraced her and said.

"Well done, you deserved it."

"But how?" Stammered the woman.

"Because you are a wonderful person who cares, it's as simple as that."

Ana-Maria could not contain the tears and muttered." Oh Roberto, I am so happy."

In Sector 9. The news was greeted with equal excitement from all there. Borz was the only man able to take on the responsibility there and was well liked. Three hours later the victorious candidates gathered in the Great Hall. The Regiment, in full ceremonial dress, escorted Frank in from the walkway. He looked very dashing in his new gold Uniform of Office. Taking his designated place on the podium, Frank delivered his short speech.

"Men and women of a united Thedrimon, we thank you, the people, for having chosen us as your various Sector leaders. You have given us a mandate, and that mandate is to govern these united planets as a federal system of democratic government. In a week's time you will be returning to the polling stations to cast your votes for a President. The first ever. All candidates nominated to run for Presidential Office will be displayed on the screens throughout the week. During the week, there will be no active campaigning by any candidates. The people will have to make a choice based on the facts and information they already know. In my capacity as leader of Sector 4 and host to these elections, I hereby declare Crystal City the official legislative capitol of Thedrimon. Furthermore, ladies and gentlemen, we give the freedom of the city... to both Mike and Penagee, as a small token of our gratitude for making this day possible. Enjoy the party."

To a tremendous roar of applause Frank stepped down from the podium to congratulate the other five new members of Parliament. Moti dismissed his Regiment with a week's leave. He and Anna walked to the end of the walkway onto the domed platform. For him there was no celebration. Mike did not come, he was out there somewhere in the trees with his family.

"Anna, I think it's time you and I went looking for the Lion. There can be no celebration without him. Ridmon would never have got to where it is today without those two."

"You are right, but they chose to be out of it for their own reasons and we must respect that. Perhaps they don't want to be found." She exclaimed.

"Perhaps they don't. We have a week to find them and if we don't the effort would be well worth it, instead of being cooped up here with all the noise. "Commented the man.

"Well, what are you waiting for?" Challenged Anna, diving into the trees.

Jane watched Moti and Anna from the interior of the elevator where she had been sitting. She heard their conversation and was about to dive after them when she realized it would be impossible. She just did not have the strength or ability in the trees as those two. She felt disappointed yet understood her limitations, which meant knowing Mike's whereabouts would be delayed for the time being. The news that Mike had moved out of the City to a location no one knew where was in itself upsetting. Knowing her brother, he could be anywhere on or off the planet. This was all very complicated, she thought. For a man who had spent the last eleven years of his life building up an empire like this one, then giving it over to a people who might just as well destroy it, puzzled her. No, there had to be more to it than that. Mike had always been a loner right from very young and preferred to be in a situation with as few people as possible. Yet she sensed that he was up to something and that she would have to exercise patience to find out the answers. Jane was still sitting in the elevator when it suddenly descended to the ground 250 metres below. An impish grin greeted her at the bottom.

"Wolf," Jane laughed, standing up.

"Shhhh!!!!" indicated Wolf with an index finger to his lips to emphasize the point. Little Wolf took her hand and led Jane into the forest to a waiting Mike.

"Good." Whispered Mike.

Wolf's face beamed. He had passed the test and was chuffed with himself. Mike hugged Jane, hefted her and Wolf onto his shoulders and climbed up into the trees. Once inside its protective covering Mike took off like a rocket through the branches and Jane nervously closed her eyes.

"Oh shit," she groaned, to which a voice in her head said, "Chicken."

Jane gulped, it was little Wolf's voice. The imp was a telepath.

"I am not an imp; I am an Impi, a Matabele warrior."

Mike's voice. "Yes you little Imp, I mean Impi, keep quiet, I can't hear myself think."

The little guy just laughed and kissed his father's cheek. Jane was astounded. This meant the whole family communicated telepathically, there was no need for speech between them. Her thoughts were interrupted,

"I wouldn't think anything incriminating if I were you, the twins don't respect a person's privacy as us grownups do."

Now it was Jane's turn to laugh. "That's universal."

Her arms were beginning to ache from hanging on.

"By the way, Moti and Anna are out looking for you." She directed her thought at Mike.

"Yes I know, I passed them a while back and they were definitely not looking for anybody at that stage." Answered Mike.

"Oh! I understand"

Little Wolf piped up, "Will we be visited by Uncle Moti, Dada?"

"I guess so, eventually he will figure out where we are and pay us a visit. But, we don't want to make it easy for him, do we?"

"No."

Jane's arms were really tired now and Mike teleported home. Penagee greeted them with smiles and hugs.

"Ok, Wolf and Zakrose, this is grown ups' time, so off with you, and Wolf, don't you go wandering off too far. You understand?" Instructed Penagee.

"Yes Mama." Echoed their joint response as they scampered off together onto the sun deck.

It was strange communicating without sounding the words, merely think them and viola, everybody heard you. It took a while for Jane to get used to it, but it also was unnerving in that you were exposed to your very core.

"Jane, we want you to live with us for a while in the cottage and become more part of the family. You won't be bored, Mike has decided to make a monkey out of you" smiled Penagee.

"I would like that very much, but what about my duties in Sector 5?" Jane replied.

"I have taken care of that, Zebor will fill in for you while you are absent." Confirmed Mike.

Mike got up and excused himself, leaving the two women to catch up on news and went out to the twins. He estimated that it would be another three days and then Moti would locate him. In the meantime Jane could get settled in before he started turning her into a Human ape. On the planet it was highly recommended to be a tree freak and learn to handle oneself with primitive weapons. He enjoyed his children; both were very supple and agile and took to martial arts training like ducks to water. The twins' sense of humour was sharp and both had very pleasant dispositions, so life was made a little easier raising them.

"This is how Dada does it." Wolf said, demonstrating a side kick.

"No, no, like this." Zakrose's leg lashed out sideways and upwards, higher than her head.

Wolf was not going to be outdone by his sister, no ways. Straddling one of the training weights, Wolf strained to lift the 30kgs dumbbell. She packed up laughing at the sight of his contorted face.

"That's enough you two, save your energy for later." Smiled Mike.

Penagee called out.

"Come and get it." Supper was ready and the twins raced into the house followed by their father.

"The hands, don't forget to wash the hands, you two." Mike cautioned.

Seated at the table with its spread of Ridmonian dishes, Jane felt at home. She was acutely aware that these two people possessed powers beyond her comprehension, yet the simplicity and homeliness of the family was compelling. There was a lot of laughter in this house and it was very catching. Soon Jane was in the midst of jibes and jokes, forgetting all else. After supper all helped to clear the table and while Mike did the washing up, Penagee and Jane bathed the twins and prepared them for bed. The twins dashed into the kitchen to kiss their Father and ran back to their bedrooms and dived into bed. Penagee closed the shutters to darken the room, kissed the twins and closed the door. Jane heard the two whispers.

"Sleep tight, Aunt Jane."

"Sleep tight, you two." She whispered back.

Penagee and Jane joined Mike out on the sundeck.

"Beer anyone." He asked.

"Thanks." Replied Jane and Mike handed her and Penagee an ice cold crystal bottle of Deep Red Ridmon beer, breaking open their sealing caps. Jane admitted that this was not your regular beer, but a very nice fruity flavour with 15 percent alcohol content. A few of these bottles and it was Happy, Happy. They sat, sipping their beers and relaxing, making small talk until Jane began to feel light-headed and excused herself. After a while Penagee also retired, leaving Mike to his thoughts. Early the next day Mike and the twins were going through their daily martial arts lessons when Jane emerged from the cottage to stand watching. Penagee came out to join her.

"One way to burn off steam." Commented Jane.

"Don't bet on it, those two little live wires have more energy than the three of us put together." Replied Penagee. "Sleep well?"

"Yes thanks, very well."

"Breakfast time you lot." She added and both women went into the house.

Mike had installed an outside shower unit for these training occasions and before long the twins were spick and span. Breakfast, they were famished.

Moti sat thinking, he had scouted all the known routes out and into the Crystal City, the old tree village, its surroundings and still no Mike. Where could the man be? He dug back into the past searching his memory until it dawned on him. Grabbing Anna and smiling like a Cheshire cat he shouted.

"Of course, no wonder no one can find him, it's about half a day's journey from here."

"What is?" Questioned Anna.

"Mike's new tree home." He replied, making off in a north-easterly direction with Anna in tow.

Moti had to admit Mike was sneaky, only two people on this planet knew the location and he was the only other one with the exception of Mike's family and now Anna. Years ago they had found the place on their return from the Red Sea and Mike had mentioned it in passing. Moti was excited; maybe, just maybe Mike would allow him to set up home there. He sincerely thought so. Anna was finding it hard to keep up with Moti and shouted,

"Hey, slow down."

Moti slowed down, but not too much. Anna sweated buckets that day and learned some of what it meant to be a soldier in the Matabele. Moti was a hard task master and pressed Anna until she thought her arms and legs would fall off. Just when she was about to give up Mike struck. He struck out of nowhere on to Moti who frantically tried to retain his equilibrium, but Mike had him in an iron hold there was no escaping from. Like a mantis snaring its prey, suspended upside down and hanging only from the insteps of his feet, Mike immobilized Moti. Anna, seeing only the blur, now watched the spectacle with mouth agape. She could not believe her eyes. No Human was able to do that, yet this man had. Moti was pinned and it took him a few seconds to realize what had happened, then he breathed a sigh of relief.

"The Lion snares the Hawk who is getting careless these days." Whispered Mike.

"The Hawk bows before the superiority of the Lion and humbly asks him to release the Hawk before he crushes the Hawk's rib cage."

Mike effortlessly flipped himself and Moti on to the branch from which he had hung suspended. The two embraced and laughed, slapping each other on the back. Anna was trembling, her heart had almost stopped on seeing Moti get taken out like that.

"Come Anna, it's only a few more trees ahead and you will be home and dry."

Anna forced her aching body through those last branches and collapsed onto the sundeck in sheer exhaustion.

"Pushing her hard, I see." Smiled Mike. Moti merely grunted and accepted a beer from Penagee who advised him.

"Shower my boy and then relax." Pointing at the outside shower, at which Moti hefted Anna and both took a long, refreshing shower totally naked. Penagee and Jane beat it back inside, slightly embarrassed. Mike could not care less and admired Anna's physique. No wonder Moti had flipped his lid over her, he thought.

"Watch it, watch it, Mr. Husband!" Interrupted Penagee's thought waves.

"I am yours body and soul my love, but my eyes are flexible." He replied.

Penagee's high pitched laughter filled the area and Mike smiled. Dressed and presentable, Moti and Anna accepted more beers which were brought out by Jane and Penagee cautioned her.

"This is going to be a fall down, so watch yourself."

The children dashed out and both hurled themselves at Moti, who caught them up in his arms dancing about like a mad man to their excited laughter. Moti stopped his antics and released them to which Penagee said.

"Kiss everyone goodnight and off to bed with you."

Once the twins were away she took up her position as self-appointed watchdog on occasions like these when these two men decided to go on a binge. Grabbing Anna, Penagee took her into the kitchen to put some food into her stomach before any more beers went down, otherwise the woman would soon pass out. She didn't bother about Moti, that idiot was made of cast iron and could drink a fish under the table. And as for that husband of hers, he was no slouch in the drinking department either. But Anna was not going anywhere. She had fallen asleep at the table. Penagee teleported her onto the couch and went out to join the party for a while. For the first time in many years Jane got absolutely blotto and passed out. Mike carried his sister to the cottage and kissed her forehead.

"I love you Jane, and I am very glad you are here with us. Sleep tight."

Back in Crystal City things were no better. The Regiment locked themselves behind closed doors and were swinging. Many people milled and danced about the walkway and the barmen were hard pressed to keep the beer flowing. Most reasonable people retired to their homes. Susan was asleep with Ivan nestled in her arms. Frank sat brooding on the balcony. His victory seemed empty without his friends. Cupping his hands to his mouth he shouted at the forest.

"Mike, you son-of-a-bitch, where the hell are you?"

His voice echoed down the valley into emptiness. Pouring himself another shot of Ridmon whiskey he sipped it slowly. He sat that way for another hour. Then standing up, cursed Mike and Moti and turned to go inside to find his way blocked. Sitting there was Mike holding a beer out to him smiling.

"Geez, but you have lousy timing." He accused, snatching the beer out of Mike's hand.

"No, not really, waiting for the right moment for you to pull your head out of the clouds."

"Well it's about bloody time you showed." Muttered Frank.

Mike looked in on Susan and the boy and saw that they were sound asleep, closed the balcony door and asked Frank.

"You free for two days?"

"Sure, why?"

"Well, I was thinking, seeing as you are Sector 4 leader by popular vote, and a well-deserved promotion it is, you and your family need to be rewarded in some way. So I have decided that two days free hotel accommodation, an unlimited expense account and of course Moti and I with my family to keep you company, on the Gulf of Aqaba, Eilat, Planet Earth, would be appropriate."

"You're joking?" Replied Frank.

"Dead serious, my good buddy, a 10/4."

"Well don't just sit there, get your butt into gear." Laughed Frank.

Mike teleported back to Penagee with Frank and the sleeping wife and child. Susan and the boy were placed in the spare room. Mike and Frank joined Moti outside and dived into more beers. Penagee tapped Mike on his shoulder and asked,

"Anybody else coming?"

"No, my Love."

"Well, in that case I am going to bed." She said kissing him goodnight then retired. Mike waited for two hours to make sure she was asleep and then focused his mind.

Penagee stretched and yawned, reached out her arm and felt Mike lying next to her, then curled in alongside his body. She heard the sound of something different, a chirping sound which at first didn't register and then when it did she sat bolt upright, wide awake. The morning sun came streaming in through an open doorway into a strange room. The twins burst excitedly through the doorway and jumped onto the bed, their excited faces beaming.

"Mama, Mama, come quickly and look." Tugging at her hands. Penagee got off the equally strange bed and walked out onto the balcony.

"Huh, Earth!!"

She spun around and charged through to Mike. He sat with a broad grin on his face.

"Good morning my darling, the view OK?" He teased.

"Mike, you are without a doubt, the most infuriating man I have ever met. But I love you to death." With that Penagee pounced on her man.

Moti was kicked awake by Anna," Wake up you big oaf, wake up."

"What is it now?" He moaned.

"We are on Earth, Eilat," She said excitedly.

Moti opened his eyes and the few moments it took for them to focus through the hangover brought a reaction out of him like a springboard. He was up and onto the balcony.

"Shalom, shalom Israel," He shouted at the top of his voice.

Frank heard the shout and smiled. Peering over his balcony he looked down on Moti locked in Ann's embrace with tears cascading down their cheeks.

"Moti, keep the noise down, you will wake the neighbourhood," Frank shouted down.

Moti looked up at him and shouted back,

"Where is Mike?"

Frank indicated to the balcony next to his on the right. Moti ascended those walls and iron railings like a demon and disappeared into Mike's room. Frank waited. The next moment Moti was dangling upside down over the balcony by an ankle secured in one of Mike's hands and being bounced up and down like a rag doll. Frank smiled, those two had a very funny way of showing their affection for one another. Penagee soon put a stop to the antics with a stern reprimand. Both men came off the balcony down to Anna the same way Moti had come up. Mike jumped across into the next balcony and went through the door to find Jane in a blissful sleep and gently nibbled her ear lobe. Jane slapped at the offending irritation and hit Mike. That woke her up in a hurry, clutching at her chest to protect herself.

"You know, one of these days I am really going to belt you one." She laughed.

Mike tickled her. She roared with hysterics. Tickling had always been her weak point and her brother knew it. He gave her the works until tears rolled down her cheeks and her sides felt like they were going to crack. She threw her arms around his neck and held him close, whispering.

"Don't leave me behind, ever."

They were in a 5-star hotel on the 9th and 10th floors overlooking the sea, with Aqaba on their left and Eilat on their right. It was time to hit the beach for some fun in the sun. A telepathic message conveyed instructions and everybody assembled down in the foyer.

"OK Guys, Dolls and kiddies, Uncle Mike is taking you on the town, so follow me."

The strangely garbed group lifted eyebrows as they stepped into the street. Mike with the twins securely in his arms. To all intents and purposes they looked like a bunch of tourists on holiday. There was activity everywhere, with people of all shapes and sizes dressed in arrays of colours heading for the beaches. Mike eventually located a sports shop where bathing suits, towels, sunglasses and footwear were on sale down in the Mall on the beach front. Mike handed out money in the form of bank notes to Moti and Frank, a lot of notes, and joked,

"Buy the town, have fun, but when we leave, everything remains behind."

Frank understood all too well, but didn't mind, he would spoil himself and his family for two days. It was worth it. Moti and Anna were in their element.

"We all meet back here at the stroke of 11 unless some of you have other ideas?" Mike requested, eyeing Moti and Anna and then added,

"Oh, by the way, I forgot to mention, the Regiment is here."

Frank and Moti looked at each other and grinned. The group went their separate ways in the Mall to do some shopping. Penagee stopped Mike in his tracks when the others had left and confronted him,

"Why is the Regiment here?"

"Just for some R&R, nothing more." He answered.

"If I didn't know better I would think you were up to something." She stated in mock anger.

Holding her close with both twins on one arm he said. "My darling woman, since when have I been a deceptive and calculating person?"

"Since the day I met you." She answered. Mike just laughed.

By 11 o'clock the group were all accounted for at the rendezvous point with all their bundles and packages. They walked out of the Mall into a sweltering 48 degrees centigrade heat and Penagee choked.

"Mike, it's too hot for me and the twins, so I am going back to the hotel until it cools down."

Susan agreed with Penagee and Mike turned to the other two women, but they were staying. So it was settled and Penagee teleported back to the hotel with Susan and the children.

Frank blurted out, "I am thirsty, and who's for a beer?"

There was no need to say another word and all walked along the Esplanade to a circular building named the Spiral where they found a restaurant and ordered cold beers. From the restaurant the beach was easily accessible, so Mike and Jane took the first swim in the cool sea. The two romped around like little children. For the following two hours everyone swam, drank, ate and swam some more. By now a lot of female admirers seemed to have gathered nearby. Jane chuckled to herself thinking if only they knew. Moti suggested moving to another location, so everyone jumped into a taxi heading for the Dolphin Reef where the attraction was to swim with live dolphins. What an experience it was for Jane. Mike had to drag her out of the water before she became a permanent fixture. Back in the hotel room Penagee received her daily check in from Mother Drone.

"Nirque delegation wishes to establish diplomatic channels."

Penagee knew what that meant, trouble in capital letters. "Refuse communication until I return."

"Affirmative," came the response.

"Mike, I need to get back to Ridmon, Nirque is trying access again."

"OK." Mike teleported into the room. "You want me to return with you?"

"No, the Drones can handle things." She replied. Penagee closed her eyes, hugged the twins to her and Mike activated the Portal and teleported Penagee through into the Great Hall, then closed the Gate after her.

Mike was peeved, but what could one do, so he re-joined his group. Turning to Jane he said.

"I am a free man. Penagee has gone back to Ridmon, Nirque problems, nothing to worry about. She knows how to handle those people pretty well."

"I must not worry, you had better, as there is me to contend with if you step out of line." Replied Jane.

Frank decided that it was time for him to return to Susan and have an early night so he was teleported back to the hotel which left the foursome to amuse themselves for the evening. Firstly, there was dinner to see to, so Moti once again suggested a restaurant. After all these years away from Eilat, the El Gaucho Argentinean Restaurant was still operating, so Mike and Moti dined on grilled steaks. After eleven years as vegetarians, meat proved to be a little too much. From there their next stop was the Yacht Pub for Happy Hour. Buy one beer, get one free. Anna and Jane were starting to get wobbly, so Mike called it a night and teleported all back to the hotel. Moti and Anna immediately retired to their room, leaving Mike and Jane in the hotel coffee shop drinking coffee.

"Want to go somewhere Jane? "Asked Mike.

"No, not really. I am kind of tired and need a shower and some sleep."

"As you wish, but I will come and tuck you in all the same if you don't mind.

"That I don't mind at all, thank you." Replied Jane.

Together they took the elevator to the 9th floor and Jane's room. Mike sat down on the bed and watched his sister undress. She did not have a stunning figure, but was well shaped all the same, with large, but firm breasts.

She needed to work on her buttocks and thighs to harden the muscles, other than that she was not bad at all. Jane disappeared into the bathroom and Mike lay back on the covers and relaxed. Mentally he checked in on Frank and Moti, all were asleep. Jane came out from the shower naked drying her hair she sat next to Mike. There were no secrets between them and nakedness was something neither had any inhibitions about. They talked into the early hours of the morning and snuggled together until Jane fell asleep. Mike awoke, dressed and took the elevator down to the foyer instead of teleporting. Waiting in anticipation were Moti, Frank and the girls. The rest of the day was spent basking in the sun. Towards late afternoon Mike told Moti and Frank that he would meet them back at the hotel around about seven and, hoisting Jane to her feet, went looking for a cab which took them to the Taba border post bordering the Sinai Desert. From there Mike teleported deep into the Sinai to a natural spring bubbling up under a rocky outcrop to form a large concealed pool. The rock was cold around the pool, protected from the wind and sun. Mike undressed and dived into the cold water followed by Jane. For a while they frolicked around like small children just enjoying each other's company. At seven, the group met again in the foyer where Mike informed them.

"We are cutting our visit short. Reasons being that the Nirques are making sounds of war again and we need to be back on Ridmon, but before we go there is something we have to do and that is pay a visit to the Moshav where Moti, Ahmed and my journey to the stars first took place. I must apologize for cutting the holiday short, but we have no choice."

Everyone nodded and filed out of the hotel into a dark corner away from public notice. Mike teleported them to the Moshav Naraf. In the shadow of darkness, at the exact spot the Portal had first opened, stood four commemorative plaques with Moti's, Mike's, Ahmed's and Shimon Moshe's names inscribed on them. It was a touching moment, standing looking at one's own tombstones.

"Moti, your parents are in the Golan now. Perhaps you would like to see them?"

"Not this trip." He answered.

Nobody said anything more, but stood in silence. In the darkness the sound of marching feet reached their ears and Mike assured them it was nothing to be concerned about. A few moments later the Regiment appeared. Mike activated the Portal and the entire party passed through onto the walkway in Crystal city. Mike dismissed his Troops. Turning to Jane he said.

"Thanks Sis, you make a fine companion."

Jane smiled. Mike teleported her back to the cabin. Moti, Frank, Susan, together with the Regiment, moved into the Barracks on full alert, then Mike teleported himself to his home. Penagee was sleeping so he gently slid in next to her. She instinctively snuggled closer.

The Nirque threat turned out to be a false alarm. The end of the week had come and today was the day Thedrimon cast its vote for their new President. The ballot computers came on-line to begin the vote. The candidates were.

From Ridmon: Frank, Borz.

From Thedrah: Tara, Zadas.

All day people flowed in and out of the Great Hall casting their votes and by the end of the day when the results were published on a huge overhead screen, Frank emerged a clear winner. Frank was stunned. He became the first President of Thedrimon. The most powerful politician on the planet. His head spun. Turning to Susan he gently wiped the tears from her eyes. She took Frank in her arms and kissed him saying.

"Well Sir, Mr. President, your first act of Parliament will be to make passionate love to your wife." Frank needed no second invitation.

Thedrimon had come of age. It was the year 2026, Earth time. Mike and Moti had been on the planet Ridmon for 13 years. Moti was promoted to Commander-in-Chief of the Regiment and relocated with Anna to live next door to Mike. Jane met and married a Thedarian biologist and was expecting their first child. Ana-Maria never remarried, but dedicated herself to her work. Frank performed his Presidential duties to perfection and he and Susan were blessed with another addition to the family, a little girl whom they named Margret after Frank's mother. Penagee was not offered another official post and resigned herself to raising her children and preparing for Mike's next escapade she knew was coming. Mike still had a lot of negotiating power on Ridmon and although a Member of Parliament, he rarely attended. The Mother and Warrior Drones were his trump card and everybody knew it and could do nothing about it. He was the Minister of Defence and that was that. He spent more time in training the Regiment, Anna, Moti and the twins. Only he knew the secret to the Portal, which he guarded very closely. His mental powers grew stronger and wider-ranging. A rumour circulated that there were life forms in the Red Sea and Penagee remained silent, so the unconfirmed reports were ignored. She did not want anyone prying into her deceased brother's underwater laboratories, if anything remained of them. However, it was Mike who one day brought the subject up with Penagee.

"I heard the rumours about the Red Sea so I did a little investigating, and guess what?"

Penagee innocently answered. "What?"

"There are life forms under the water and nasties at that. Best left alone where they belong. There was something else though, an underwater city completely intact."

Her heart skipped a beat.

"Impossible, everything was destroyed when Zorak sacrificed himself for me, you and everyone else on this planet."

"Maybe you're right, it must be only ruins by now. Anyway, it's not serious so don't worry." Agreed Mike.

But Penagee knew him better than that. He must have been down there, inside the water and seen something. Mike was not telling the whole truth. Two weeks later while they were chatting with Moti and Anna, Mike popped a question,

"Who would like to have a picnic on the shores of the Red Sea?"

Everyone in the group raised their hands and the twins became excited.

"You mean it, Dada?" Enquired Wolf.

"Sure Son, it's no bluff." Mike looked directly into Penagee's eyes and she saw the challenge.

"When do we go?" Questioned Moti.

"Oh! I guess right now would be fine. Besides, especially for the twins, it will be their first time, why not make it a treat?"

Penagee was beginning to feel a little uncomfortable under Mike's penetrating gaze, so before the twins started up on her she agreed, went into the kitchen to prepare a picnic hamper and fumed. For this little outing Mike called in two Warrior Drones and loaded everyone aboard. Penagee instinctively knew he was up to something because of the Drones. She became more and more tense. Warrior Drones could submerge and Mike was definitely not on a picnic trip, but on a witch hunt. She was about to protest when Mike, through their own private thought wave channel said,

"I have a surprise for you, so don't go screwing it up for me, please."

He had her full attention. The Drones hovered above the shoreline, searching for a suitable spot to deposit their precious cargo. Mike chipped in and requested the Drones to level the huge crystal mound that once was a City. The Drones promptly complied, scattering the crystal debris over a wide surface area with their repeller beams.

"Task completed." Confirmed the Drones.

"Now land in the centre of what used to be the city." He instructed.

The Drones complied and Mike cautioned everyone to stay where they were whilst he checked the surface out. Penagee saw it coming. Mike had found the entrance to the submerged laboratories. He stood there atop a set of very large pressurized doors then, in mock surprise, he looked straight up at Penagee who would have kicked him if he had been in range. The cogs in Moti's brain began to turn and a light bulb flashed on.

"Wow! If that does not beat all." He exclaimed.

Mike wasted no time, boarded then gave the order.

"Blast the doors."

The Drones reversed to a safe distance. White hot beams shot out, completely disintegrating their target.

"Engage." He commanded.

The two Drones dived down into the opening like pack hounds after a scent. Their brains calculating millions of minute details. Trajectories, possibilities, variants, compositions and threats in less time it takes to blink. All except Mike were mesmerized by the complexity and size of the tunnel which gradually levelled off 12 kilometres down, emerging into a huge Dome. Instrument readings indicated it was 50 kilometres in diameter and at least 5 kilometres high. The Drones were on full battle alert. Suspended in the middle of the Dome was a Crystal City, 2 kilometres high and 3 kilometres wide. The Drones raced towards it, warning lights flashing.

"Life form in City, Thedarian male, age 78, height 1, 8 metres, mass 72kgs. Identification Name ... Zorak."

Penagee nearly fainted. Zorak was alive. Her heart soared and tears rolled down her cheeks. Mike positioned the Drones, then mentally probed and locked on to his subject and struck like an Anaconda. Zorak was held totally imprisoned in Mike's mental grip.

"Well, well, Zorak, you certainly had everyone convinced, didn't you?"

Before the response came Warrior Drone 2 wheeled about blasting and both Mike and Penagee heard a terrible dying scream.

"Threat neutralized." Confirmed the Drone."

"Zorak, whatever you have in here with us, you had better keep under control or my Drones will take this place apart."

"No further threats, but please don't harm any more of my friends, they are very sensitive and protective."

"It's your call Zorak, Penagee with our two children are in this Drone watching and I don't want to have to take you out in front of them."

There was a long silence and then Zorak spoke.

"Penagee!"

"Yes, my beloved brother, it's me Penagee, please do what Mike asks for all our sakes."

Another few moments of silence.

"Ah! The Human Ape Subject 1, as I recall. It appears you are a man with very unusual talents, very impressive." Smirked Zorak.

"Please Zorak." Screamed Penagee, "Mike's too powerful, you can't beat him, and I am begging you for my sake and my children's sakes."

Some more silence and Mike knew Zorak was stalling for some reason, so he encased the Drones in protective shields of pure energy that glowed white and were impenetrable to anything in the known universe. Mike squeezed deeper into Zorak's mind until the man screamed in agony. Penagee pleaded and wept. She knew Mike. He was a terrible predator when angered and with her and the twins on board he would stop at nothing.

"Zorak is trying to isolate me as a target, he has these mind creatures homing in on me through the contact and grip I have on him, that's why he's stalling for time. I am going to have to take his friends out. Any loss of concentration means Zorak escapes."

Penagee was almost hysterical watching the two men she loved more than anything try to destroy each other. She was bitterly torn by opposing loyalties and Mike sensed the probe into Penagee's mind and he unleashed his fury. The entire Dome erupted in one massive planet-shaking explosion, sending water and debris rocketing upwards for kilometres into the atmosphere. Penagee heard Zorak's screams and watched as his spent body went limp. The Drones shot out of the explosion into Ridmon's atmosphere with the limp body of Zorak securely encased between them by retriever beams.

Penagee passed out. It was too much for her. Moti and Anna sat dumbfounded and terribly afraid. They had witnessed a power to the magnitude of a mini super nova. Every Drone on Ridmon rushed to Mike's aid to quell the seismic reaction and still the seas in order to save the planet from destruction. It had worked. Zorak was now just an imprisoned and defenceless old man of genius and Mike sucked his brain dry of any information regarding the mind creatures that had been totally annihilated, Ridmon would not soon forget the day Mike got angry and the news spread like wildfire. The Drones returned to their stations and delivered Mike and his group plus old man Zorak to the Tree House. Mike still had him in a mental vice-grip from which there was no escape. The twins were visibly shaking and Moti took them into his arms and held them close. Anna was petrified of Mike now after seeing what he could do and her brain felt numb and disorientated. Penagee was still out cold, so Mike lifted her gently and laid her on their bed. Going to where the old man hung suspended in fresh air, he pulled up a chair and gradually released his stranglehold. Zorak opened his eyes and stared at Mike.

"The Ape man is a Universal Messenger?"

"Yes." Confirmed Mike.

"I should have guessed it, but I was too determined to teach you a lesson by turning you into a mindless zombie. How is Penagee, is she all right?"

"She will recover. You lost control, old man. Those mind creatures were going to take Penagee out to get at me."

"I know, and there was nothing I could have done to stop them." Sighed the old man.

"If it had not been for Penagee you would have disintegrated along with your Dome of nasty tricks. I took the liberty of wiping your brain clean of the technology that went into making those creatures. This will ensure that you will never be able to duplicate them."

Zorak hung in silence, searching frantically through his memory. The Ape was right; he had indeed erased all traces.

"Yes Zorak, nada, zero. But you have a remarkable brain and it would be a shame to see it go to waste, so in spite of everything, you will be allowed to continue work of a more peaceful and constructive nature. Believe me, you will be monitored every step of the way. Too many lives depend on you being neutralized and although we owe you gratitude, it has been paid in full today. Your deception has forfeited you your rights."

Mike finally released his hold on the old man and lowered him on to the sundeck. Zorak wobbled on his unsteady feet, so Mike gave him a chair to sit on.

"Would you like something to drink?" Asked Mike.

"Yes, water if you have, thanks." Replied Zorak in a muffled voice.

For the next hour Mike watched the old man gather his wits and strength and in that time Penagee slowly came around. When she opened her eyes and realized where she was she leaped up and dashed outside, to see Zorak sitting on a chair staring at the decking. She did not hesitate, but threw herself at him and embraced the old man, their tears mingling against their cheeks. There was no threat anymore and Mike gave the twins reassurances, however the two would have none of it and regarded the old man with suspicion.

"Moti, I have to go and make a report as an emergency meeting has been convened. I want you to keep an eye on the crafty devil and don't be taken in by any stories. There is a Warrior Drone positioned directly above as an added precaution."

"OK, Mike."

An emergency meeting had been convened and Frank was pacing up and down wringing his hands. Everyone in the room was afraid. All had seen and heard the tremendous explosion from a thousand kilometres away and felt the planet tremble. Parts of the Crystal City had collapsed, luckily without loss of life, but the waterfall was redirected by the enormous seismic forces and now thundered down onto the walkway. Elsewhere there were damages to a lesser degree.

Mike walked into the Great Hall to address the gathered body of men and women. There was a hushed silence, no one breathed.

"Mr. President, fellow members of the council, ladies and gentlemen. Please rest at ease. The crisis is over. Ridmon can carry on as normal."

Frank blurted out.

"What in heavens name was that?"

Mike stood studying all their faces and then answered.

"That, Sir, was the result of a combined operation to neutralize and completely destroy a hornets' breeding nest under the surface of the sea. Mission accomplished."

One of the members stood and waving a finger at Mike, shouted.

"Well, you nearly got us all killed in the process."

Mike laughed out loud.

"It's over, the responsible party has been rendered ineffective and all his mind creatures destroyed. That's all I have to say. Good day." Mike teleported out back to his home.

The Great Hall went into an uproar. Frank had enough and called for silence, when that didn't work he gave the signal and the Regiment marched in to enforce silence.

"Thank you." Grumbled Frank," Now, can we get on with this meeting in an orderly fashion?"

Nobody said a word, not with the Regiment breathing down their necks. These were Mike's unit of hand-picked utterly ruthless men.

"You all heard what Mike had to say, not much, I admit, but you can rest assured that whatever he did out there it was for a damn good reason and I am tired of hearing you bunch of idiots constantly bickering. Next time there is a crisis, I am going to send you out there to sort it out by yourselves."

"Hear here." A female voice rang out. Everybody swivelled around to see who had phrased those words. Tara stood up, bowed, then smiled and added.

"I must say, I was very impressed by your reactions immediately after the blast. Makes me wonder how many of you pissed your pants. You want Mike out, you prove to Thedrimon that you are better men than him in every way. My opinion is that you are just a bunch of farts that could not blow their way out of a wet paper bag."

She marched out of the Hall with her head held high. Frank chuckled, Tara was a fighter alright and a good friend to have. She came from Thedrah and was to his mind, a solid down to earth kind of person who had adapted herself extremely well, succeeding in making a name for herself on Thedrah as a good, resourceful, no-nonsense go-getter. Finally the meeting got under way with Tara's return and most of the urgent matters on the agenda were dealt with. Engineers were called in to move the waterfall to its original place as a first priority. A damage assessment was underway and discussions continued on improving issues concerning agriculture on the plains in Sector 6, as an ongoing project to cope with demand. Engineers completed the redirecting the Water Fall back to its original place with the help of the Drones thus freeing up the walk way once again.

"We will have to clear sections of the forest to make way for more arable areas closer to home." A member commented.

"No way Hombre, the trees stand where they are, there will be no felling of trees whatsoever and no disruption of either planet's ecologies." Enforced Tara.

"I agree with her. We start messing with the nature of these planets and we are going to have an Earth scenario on our hands. The nature of present conditions stays. We either build around it, with it or leave it. It's that simple," said Borz, standing to make his point clear.

Zebor stood up and glancing at all the members assembled, stated.

"These planets will, in my opinion, support all life for generations to come. We have the technology to build massive Crystal Cities both above and below ground. We have therefore the duty to preserve all life no matter what the cost and do not need to sacrifice one for the other just because we suddenly get greedy, consider ourselves superior and or suffer from the usual demented lust for power and control over all dominion. I have studied Earth's history and one thing is painfully clear, their road to progress through industrialization and modernization, plus the overwhelming population explosions, brought about their own self-destruction from which there is no recovery. At the moment their situation is so bad that Mother Nature is sure to intervene and eradicate vast populated areas through increased massive natural disasters, diseases and war. There are lessons we can learn from their mistakes and we would be very foolish indeed not to protect our own environments from the people who would ultimately destroy it. And that, Ladies and Gentlemen, means us."

"Sounds a little farfetched, my good friend, but we are talking of survival and progress, so if a few small insignificant ecological life forms happen to get lost along the way, what difference does it make to the overall picture. In twenty years from now we are going to have doubled, even trebled, our population. All these people have to eat and live somewhere. They have to be able to find jobs, which means new industry, which means having to open up more land. If by eradicating the creatures of the Dark Forest for instance, what difference does it make? We will have rid ourselves of a very nasty threat and be able to carry on with our lives."

Tara butted in.

"Now that's typical, we have a Judas in our midst who considers we rid ourselves of those nasties in the Dark Forest thinking they are a threat to our security and suddenly find ourselves far worse off. Because, then we might find that those nasties were controlling the source of an even more frightening life form that we know nothing about. Our lives would therefore be jeopardized because of it. Until we can safely assume reasonability for all life forms on these planets and set up correct management programmes through proper research and understanding, we need to exercise extreme caution in implementing any so-called progressive actions which will impact negatively on any one life form of this planet. I support Minister Jane from Sector 5, who has set up a research facility, where she and her husband are doing exceptional work in uncovering these planets' secrets. Their research will pave the way for us, the policy makers, to act wisely and in the best interests of the whole, not just a privileged few."

Frank stood and cleared his throat,

"Fellow members, we are into overtime and I am famished, so I hereby call this session closed until 09.00hrs tomorrow as usual. Good night." Frank walked out of the Hall.

Tara sat in her usual chair on the walkway sipping a beer. This was not getting anywhere she thought. We need someone powerful enough to enforce the law to prevent fortune seekers and greedy politicians from manipulating the system. But to do that would require very precise definitions of the law, billed through Parliament with clear mandates to protect the entire system against fraudulent exploitation. The concept of individual rights as interpreted by the American judicial system is not without merit, but it leaves no room for prompt and quick action. Everything is bottled up in official red tape which stifles a whole system. On Ridmon, before the slimy hot shots got a foot into the doorway, they had to have their nails clipped. She always considered Mike and Penagee the only true leaders of this planet and was surprised when both of them refrained from participating in any electoral campaign. No, it was not possible that neither of them were chosen by the people. The more she thought of it the more she became very suspicious. She smiled to herself thinking about Mike. Having a father like that would have been a major blast in any girl's life. The first time she set eyes on him Tara knew she would be his most avid supporter. She had often wished Penagee had not left the political arena, but rather stayed and made those short-sighted bastards' heads spin and knocked the puffed up crap out of them. Next time Mike was in town, she would ask him if it were possible to chat privately. Yes Sirree, Mike and Penagee needed to be back to take over things. Frank was a good guy and she respected him, even liked him, still at the end of the day he didn't have quite what it took. She was going to see to it that both Penagee and Mike were brought back. Their leadership and guidance was very important at this stage to set the scene for the democratic progress and to take a more meaningful and clear stance. Democracy had its advantages over many tried and tested systems of government, an Iron hand was needed within the context of democracy to ensure for generations to come, that Thedrimon would not fall on its face through official complacency and lethargy. Stamp out the disease in its infancy and you have a healthy society, do nothing about it then the cancer creeps in and there is nothing anyone can do afterwards to cure it, except by completely cutting out the offending parts. Nobody wanted to have to make that choice; it was tantamount to Fascism. One bad egg being replaced by another. People were so fickle it was unbelievable.

Tara saw Moti and Anna come trotting up the walkway and she waved, beckoning them to join her.

"Hi." She said when they sat down.

Moti smiled and Anna kissed her cheek.

"Where's the beer." Moti shouted to the kiosk barman.

"So how are things in the Hall of Bullshit?" Asked Anna, eyes twinkling.

"Usual crap." Replied Tara laughing.

Moti accepted the three beers, said thanks and broke the caps. He liked Tara. She had been a genuine friend to him since the beginning.

"Moti, I need to speak to Mike, can you arrange it?"

"Yup! No problem. You leave it to Moti."

The conversation revolved around the incident on the sea shore and what exactly had transpired and Tara's eyes grew bigger as Moti recounted the events until the explosion.

"I tell you, I almost crapped myself." He was saying. Coming from Moti that was something, because Tara knew him to be fearless and could really put his money where his mouth was.

"I was petrified. I still can't, after seeing that lot, stand next to him. He frightens the hell out of me." Exclaimed Anna.

Tara changed the subject by asking, "So how are you two love birds?"

Moti answered," Sexually in the next world."

"You big Ape?" Joked Anna.

"Yup," Said Moti turning, shouted to the barman, "Beers please."

Tara watched the two. She was happy for them. They made an ideal couple now that Anna had lost her snobbishness. Moti would never change though, still full of it, a typical male macho character, but down in that powerful chest of his lay a sensitive and giving heart. They sat there until late getting very blotto, eventually ending up on Tara's apartment floor, sleeping it off.

They came for Amos the Sangoma that night, the soldiers of a dictator's regime of Zimbabwe and found only an empty cave with its single grave. They were confused, no tracks led out and only a single set led in, fresh ones at that. So where was the offending party? The cave was checked and re-checked, but to no avail. The man had simply disappeared into thin air. The soldiers became afraid, after all, this was a Sangoma's cave and who knew what kind of magical surprises lay in wait for them and they withdrew from Cheroma Kadoma in haste.

Mike stood on the Pinnacle of the mountain with Amos next to him smiling. Amos bowed his head saying.

"The White Matabele has saved Amos from a fate worse than death and I am very grateful indeed."

"No need old man, because you will be rewarded for your part in this whole saga in the only way we know that will make you a very happy and contented man to live out your life in peace without fear."

Mike placed his hands on those frail shoulders, looked Amos straight in the eye and said.

"You old Father, are coming with me to Ridmon."

THANU
FOUR

Out in the farthest reaches of space, Empires rise and fall. Planets and Galaxies come and go. Life forms evolve or die over aeons of time. It is a cycle that has been repeated since the creation of time. Wars are fought, won or lost. In a never-ending cycle of life and death the Universe continues its existence, entity against entity, struggling for supremacy. The universe cleans and nurtures, gives and takes. The united Thedrimon was no exception. A world where both Human and Alien alike were thrown into a melting pot of evolution. Harmony can never be guaranteed as long as there is someone or something wanting to change the natural order of things. On its own, evolution works perfectly where time and space hold no significance. Mother Nature experiments with her subjects to create or destroy at her will. When civilized life presumes to be part of the chain and takes it upon themselves to act as creators or destroyers, Mother Nature will in the end invariably have the last say. So it was with Thedrimon. There are events which take place beyond reasonable explanation, justification, or understanding. Most times such events are initiated by so-called intelligent life bent on delusion leading to ultimate self-destruction.

During Earth year 2025 when Thedrimon celebrated National Day on the first of June, it became apparent that something was not well with the people of Ridmon. Three members of parliament, the Minister of Mining and Mineral Resources and his two deputies, were on their routine visitation to the most remote settlement on Ridmon, aptly named Siberia. The most unfriendly, inhospitable place on the planet, a crystal sand desert the size of Earth's Sahara. Nothing grew, no water or life form of any kind, except the Thedrimon crystal workers. These hardy people lived under very trying conditions, doing the best they could under the circumstances to meet quotas. It was a purely voluntary opportunity through which they could qualify for land grants in the agricultural belt along the seashore of Sector 4 as reward. The three politicians were on an agenda of their own which called for the exploitation and manipulation of these people in a most foul way imaginable. Support for the workers' existence whilst on contract in Siberia depended on certain concessions being met. Those concessions entailed delivering filled quotas on a tonnage basis and the shipment manifests required accuracy to the last quarter ton. What in actual fact happened was that the quarter ton discrepancy at weigh-in simply found re-direction elsewhere onto an unofficial stockpile belonging to the three members of parliament, who in turn employed their own transport shuttles to quietly ship the crystal off the planet at a profit to themselves. In order to enforce silence and guarantee profits, a private so-called security team worked alongside the crystal workers to ensure that all were fully compliant.

One day the shuttle arrived as usual and a general assembly was called. The gathered workers were duly informed that unless they stepped up illicit production they would be dealt with accordingly. Their contract entailed that they did hard manual labour for five years of their lives. The three-man delegation from Ridmon's Crystal City informed them that, unless they were obliging, it would be very easy to arrange it that none of them ever leave Siberia alive. What followed next was an immediate explosive reaction. The workers, using the excavating machinery, crushed the transport shuttle, attacked the three members and their hired henchmen, killing them and then burying their remains in the shuttle under thousands of tons of crystal sand.

Unfortunately, computers immediately reported a shuttle missing in Siberia and mounted an investigation, sending in the Regiment. After a more intense investigation by the Drones the exact whereabouts of the shuttle was located, together with its gruesome contents. The whole sordid case blew wide open. Eighty families from Siberia were brought back to the holding cells in the Crystal City pending their trial for murder. The news hit Ridmonians with mixed reactions. Tara interviewed the accused and almost wept. Without any hesitation she passed on a message to find Mike or Moti who had disappeared with their families and had not been seen in nearly a year. She was worried, things were definitely wrong with people on Ridmon. The judicial system on Ridmon was falling apart. The eighty families were tried, convicted and put to death man, women and child.

The news hit Thedrah and the shock of it sickened Frank to his core and he immediately declared martial law and placed the Regiment on full alert to quell demonstrations and disturbances. Frank had been unaware of the trial and executions, now it was too late, so he ordered the arrest of all the persons responsible for the execution, without exception. His return to Ridmon became a turning point in his career. So angry was he by the incident and the subsequent unfolding story of corruption within his cabinet that he dissolved parliament. The Regiment, loyal to its core, went about their business with clinical precision and before long both Ridmon and Thedrah were under tight security, with many prominent persons imprisoned or under house arrest. There was no escape from Frank's determined effort to clean up his backyard. So effective were his troops that no one was overlooked. In a national broadcast to the peoples of Thedrimon he advised them that those responsible had now forfeited their rights as citizens of Thedrimon and all properties, assets or holdings belonging to the offenders were confiscated and placed under state control. The offenders were banished to Siberia as punishment and would remain there until they had paid their debt to society. For those who ordered the execution and those who carried it out, Frank publicly mind-altered them. It was a sickening sight to see men and women reduced to mindless robots. The effect on Thedrimon was electric, but achieved the desired results. Life would never be the same again and a dark cloud began to form over Thedrimon. Fearing reprisals, Frank called in his most trusted allies to the Crystal City as added protection.

"Jane, we need to find Mike and Penagee. If you know where they are, this is a good time to have them come in." Requested Frank.

"Sorry Frank, but I am just as much in the dark as you as to where they are." She replied.

"This has really gotten out of hand and I am afraid we have not heard the last of it. I suspect there is more behind all this, but I have not been able to put a finger on it." Continued Frank, to which Tara stated.

"Ridmon has become vulnerable. I would not be surprised if the Nirques or someone else has not had a hand in it somehow."

Frank nodded and added.

"You might have a point there, how else to bring down a nation if not from within itself, leaving the door wide open for takeover or destruction. It's a classic way of achieving results. You know what, I suggest we intensify our monitoring activities in that direction and keep an eye on all shuttle traffic coming or going between our two planets. That is our weak link I believe."

Borz agreed, saying, "The two planets are protected by the Drones, but the corridor between them is definitely a weak link and the more I think of it the more I tend to suspect that we will find our answer out there. We are going to have to alter movement through the corridor and send only specially equipped computer-controlled shuttles that appear to be normal daily traffic, but are Tracker units capable of picking up any kind of interference in the sector."

One way or the other, if there is something or someone out there undermining our defences by subverting our people through mind control, then the shuttles should pick it up. Excellent idea, Borz." Confirmed Frank,

Activating a monitor and issuing instructions by coded numbers. Within an hour thirty shuttles were converted and would replace the normal ferry service which ran on the hour every hour to and from Ridmon and Thedrah. Only cargoes would fill their holds on these scheduled flights. For the following 48 hours no person would be allowed to leave either planet. The first shuttle launched into space following regular flight paths monitored by Borz, Frank and Tara. Nothing untoward happened in that 48 hour period. Borz was not concerned; he understood that unless there were actual people on those shuttles then what they were hoping to find would not be found. Turning to Frank he said.

"We need people on those shuttles, we have broken the routine and whoever is out there knows it. I suggest we allow the normal traffic of persons onto the Tracker shuttles and see what happens."

"Perhaps you are right." Agreed Frank and gave the go-ahead to board passengers. After the fourth shuttle launched the Tracker shuttle sent a coded message to Frank's monitor.

"Being scanned and probed. Occupants of shuttle are in a trance-state."

They had found it. Broz's plan had worked. Someone was messing with people's minds on the way to and from Ridmon. Frank sent back a message to the shuttle. "Resume flight as usual. Pin-point source."

"Source pin-pointed and location fixed." A set of numbers appeared on the monitors. Frank wasted no time sending another coded message.

Four Warrior Drones responded to the given co-ordinates and intercepted a single immense spacecraft of unidentified origin and mercilessly pounced. Whoever they were they did not detect the Warrior Drones until it was too late. The ship's evasive action was not enough to stop the Drones' destroyer beams from completely disintegrating it.

A message appeared on Frank's monitor. "Unidentified subject destroyed. All units on full alert, adopt tactical positions."

Frank sat back and sighed with relief, then sounded general quarters on Thedrimon. Everyone sensed that this was only the beginning. The enemy ship was not there by chance, but came for purposes of mischief and had paid the price. However, where there is one there are perhaps many more and Frank was taking no chances.

"So, we are up against a very cunning adversary who messes with our brains. I need a full scan of every person on these planets, man woman and child. Can you set up the scanners, Borz and give me a time frame as to how long it would take?"

"Yes, no problem. It will take approximately 24 hours." With that Borz began messaging the entire planetary scanner units with specific details obtained from the Tracker shuttle as to the exact nature of the mind viruses. Any citizen on Thedrimon bearing the same signature pattern as the sample would be isolated and have the virus removed.

Frank was edgy sitting studying the images on the monitor showing the unidentified spacecraft just before it was destroyed and the technical details the Drones had sent back to him. There had been 8,000 life forms on that vessel. It was huge. A flying, fortified Battle Starship doubling up as a space city with an awesome array of weapons. Just as well the Drones were invisible to most systems, yet this one detected them at the last moment. This meant they had some form of detector shield around the ship which was extremely advanced. The Drones were like sponges when it came to information and technology absorption. By now every detail of the enemy vessel would be in their memory banks. Counter measures would be in place. If Mike requested a replica, an exact replica down to the smallest microbe would be presented to him. The computers were humming, downloading updates from the Drones. Ridmon and Thedrah became shielded by an invisible dome. Drones searched out far into space with their scanners. 24 hours later, 50 000 people on both planets were cleared of the mind viruses.

Still no new information was coming in from the Drones. Frank was very relieved to have them on his side. Any attack by an enemy was going to be almost like Armageddon for the poor souls. Once a Drone homed in on you it was fatal, it would strike right into the very heart of your planet, destroying everything in its wake and leaving nothing alive. Mother Drone was the controller, the Warrior Drones were the fighters and the killing machines and the Protector Drones were the planet's defences through which almost nothing could penetrate. Additional invisible shields were set in place over every city and outpost just in case. This enemy obviously was bent on destruction coming from within, which would then allow them free access to invade with little or no opposition. What Frank could not figure out was why the Protector Drones were not aware of the intruder's presence in the first place. He needed answers very quickly and sent another coded message to Mother Drone. Her response was immediate.

"Intruder equipped with very advanced cloaking technology. Drones were unable to locate. Now situation rectified by copying their cloaking technology into ourselves and made additional modifications. Drones have supremacy."

Jane and Borz shook their heads in dismay. Tara voiced everyone's sentiment out loud.

"Thank you, Mike, for those shape shifters."

"It's not over yet, that was only one ship, what other tricks they have up their sleeves we have yet to encounter, so I am sounding the Red Alert Class 1." Said Frank and a sequence of codes were fed into the computers. Almost immediately Thedrimon was placed at full battle stations.

Frank, Jane, Borz and Tara stared at the message on the monitor.

"Fleet of thirty unidentified ships fitting sample description entering Ridmon universe. Range still too far to be cause for alarm. Will inform of any changes."

There was a moment's silence and Borz muttered, "A million people, this definitely has to be an intended take over and settlement force. Unbelievable."

Frank's mind whirled. They were facing a massive invasion force. Someone wanted Thedrimon very badly.

The computer's monotone voice broke the silence.

"Drones reporting probes directed this way. Mother Drone instructs negative action to be taken. Will notify."

"What is she playing at?" Asked Jane.

"The spider web and the fly." Smiled Frank. "She's allowing the probes to see only what she wants them to see and when they report back the flies will head for the web."

The large screen came on. It was Mother Drone giving them a bird's eye view of the proceedings. The group watched in fascination as the scene unfolded before their eyes. The probes arrived at the edge of Thedrimon's International boundary line and stopped. The massive fleet following behind broke out of warp, then advanced taking up battle stations. It took 30 minutes until the fleet had positioned itself in tactical formation. Mother Drone's voice echoed.

"Enemy fleet wanting to open communications channel. Strongly advise not to."

The scene was tense and Frank felt every nerve in his body vibrating. Something was up. No communication meant whoever were out there had the ability to mind-control by visual application. Another twenty minutes went by and again Mother Drone's voice.

"Enemy preparing to attack. Drone's undetected and ready."

"Oh shit!" whispered Tara, "This is going to be a blood bath."

Frank watched the huge monitor screen on the wall on which Mother Drone opened visual contact of proceedings as ten of the enemy ships broke formation and came storming down at Thedrah. They never saw what hit them. Neither did Frank or Tara. The ten ships just disintegrated before their eyes. There were no beams, no explosions, nothing. It was as if all the vessels had flown straight into an invisible wall and smashed themselves to pieces.

"Drones still undetected. Ten targets eliminated." Confirmed Mother Drone's voice.

The rest of the fleet hung motionless. One could almost see inside their heads right then. Shock and dismay and nothing to indicate what it was that took out their ships.

"Bet you they are one hell of a ticked off right now." Chuckled Borz.

"Fleet scanning, Drones undetected. Will terminate enemy."

Everyone in Frank's war room watched sickened as all these beings in their ships were methodically disintegrated. This was total annihilation and Frank's heart went out to those beings, but this was war and the strangers had come with the intent to destroy. Three ships remained. Mother Drone struck a paralyzing blow and left witnesses who no doubt would be completely demoralized. The surviving ships hung there, resigned to their fate. The Drones were poised for a further 30 minutes then slowly the three Battleships turned about and warped out of Thedrimon air space. 24 hours later two Warrior Drones returned from a long range stop-group position and reported that Nirque was no more. The retreating fleet of 3 ships, in a fit of frustrated anger, attacked the unsuspecting Nirque planet, firing salvo after salvo of instant death until Nirque was left in total ruins. Ridmon's Drones responded by terminating the three Battleships. Tara and Jane almost wept. Such a loss of life was unthinkable, yet it had happened. One million beings in thirty ships plus the entire population of Nirque, estimated to have numbered in the region of 48 million people. Thedrimon was fast earning a lethal reputation for itself. Frank sat brooding. The destruction of Nirque was totally uncalled for. Ridmon's Drones reacted in the only way possible. Whoever those beings were, they had paid an extremely heavy price. He hoped their masters would take heed and not venture anywhere near Thedrimon again. There was of course no guarantee of that whatsoever.

Mother Drone's voice came through again.

"Invasion Force's origin documented. Identification possible."

Frank sat bolt upright.

"Planet Trafodj, size ten times Earth. Distance 300 billion light years from Ridmon. Population: 4 billion. Technology highly advanced. Area of expertise: Space invaders." There was a pause.

"80,000 Nirque survivors monitored on route. Permission granted to dock on Thedrah. Suggest appropriate measures taken to secure. No brain virus detection. Nirques unarmed."

Frank leapt to the monitor, issuing instructions. He wanted a full interrogation report the moment it was available.

"I wonder how those poor buggers managed to escape." Commented Jane.

"Well, we will soon find out, won't we? In the meantime I am hitting the sack so will see you all later then." Yawned Tara standing and, pulling Jane by the arm, the two walked out of the control centre. A while later Borz also retired, leaving Frank alone with his thoughts.

"This is not over; we need to know where Mike is. Please Jane, you must know how important it is. Could you take Frank or me to the place in the forest where you say Mike lived?" Asked Tara.

"I can't do that Tara, he made me promise. But perhaps there is a way to get hold of him. Let me try and I'll get back to you." Answered Jane.

"Well, we have to do something and fast." Remarked Tara.

Jane went to her bunk and flopped down. She was too dog tired and promptly fell asleep.

Three hundred billion light years away the Planet of Trafodj mourned its dead. They were in a state of shock. How was it possible a crack fleet of 30 Battleships were totally destroyed by an opponent they could not see or detect or defend themselves against? It was inconceivable that a technology greater than theirs existed in this region of space. Not only that, how did those Thedarians escape the mind viruses? The images and data transmitted back showed nothing to indicate the extent of the planet's defences or weapons capable of such swift and devastating retribution. The images from Nirque showed very clearly how powerful Trafodj fighting ships were. Yet at Thedrah the Battleships were taken out systematically in extremely quick succession. There would be no reprisal action against an enemy you could not see, so Trafodj would go after easier pickings and stay well clear of Thedrah. Back on Ridmon, Frank was taking stock. Thedrimon had been lucky this time. Those mind viruses would have eventually led to Thedrimon's own self-destruction and Trafodj would probably have been able to walk right into the front door without firing a shot, but for one minor detail, the Drones. They would have destroyed the Trafodj, but lost Thedrimon. Frank could not understand why Mike did not show his face in over a year. Surely he must be aware of developments on Thedrimon. Perhaps it was some sort of test to see how the people coped with crises without intervention. He certainly hoped so because if Mike had gone then they were in a little bit of a fix.

Two months later the Red Alert was lifted and Thedrimon continued its existence as usual under continued Martial Law. Not until it was completely certain that all brain viruses had been eradicated did the situation revert back to normality and Parliament was re-instated. Intensive screening of members prior to taking office became the order of the day. No one wanted a repeat performance. The Thedrimon Army now numbered 3,200 troops split into four groups. Two units on Thedrah, the balance on Ridmon. Mike's Regiment consisting of two hundred men and women were a unit unto themselves. In all of Earth's history there was never a fighting force of such comparison ever. Not even the famous Ninja could be compared man for man. Their loyalty to Frank was limited as they were Mike's disciples of war and to that end they pledged their allegiance with their lives. It was very unsettling knowing that, if the Regiment wanted to, it could take over control of Thedrimon in the twinkling of an eye and nothing could stop them. Frank, no slouch by any means, could give and take, yet up against any member of the Matabele Regiment he or his Troops were useless.

A few days later, whilst Frank was going through his daily routines of office, the Matabele Regiment vanished into thin air. Tara came running into the control centre and breathlessly declared.

"Frank, the Regiment has gone."

He jumped to the monitor and its confirming response was, "Regiment not located, 200 personnel untraceable."

Tara laughed, "Its Mike, he's back," and danced around the room like a school girl.

To Frank it was wait and see. The screen above him flickered on and Mike's smiling face appeared.

"Hello Frank, a few more grey hairs I see!"

"You bloody son of a gun, where the hell have you been?" Bellowed Frank.

"Oh, here and there. You have an hour to get the people of Crystal City into the Great Hall. We are coming in."

The screen flicked off and Frank sounded the General Assembly.

Exactly an hour later the Community assembled in the Great Hall and Mike made his grand entrance from the walkway. First appeared a group of 50 Africans in full ancient battle dress of cowhide shields and stabbing spears. Their headdresses were white ostrich plumes and animal skins were draped across their shoulders. They chanted.

"Matabele! Matabele!"

Behind them advanced the Regiment in full ceremonial dress, all 200 men and women marching in perfect unison. At the end of the procession came Mike and Moti in their Regimental colours and behind them Penagee, the twins, Anna, old Amos and Zorak. The parade formed up in the Great Hall and total silence descended within. A single black warrior sprang forward and raced left then right in front of the Community wielding his stabbing spear, stopped dead in his tracks, turned to face the assembled Regiment, raised the spear above his head and shouted,

"Bayete Enkosi, Bayete Matabele."

The Hall shook with an ear shattering response as 250 soldiers shouted, "Matabele, Matabele"

The community of Ridmon almost jumped out of their seats. It was a spectacle alright and Mike made the most of it. Frank was not amused. Mike had resurrected some original Matabele warriors from Earth and brought them to Ridmon for this demonstration which was to his mind a little too extreme and excessive. Mike's voice boomed through the Hall.

"People of Ridmon, Frank thinks this little entrance of mine is excessive, maybe so, but we have to break the tension of the last few months in a show of solidarity. The Trafodj tried and failed thanks to Borz, Tara and Frank and, of course, the Drones, without whom these planets would not have survived. The mind viruses were a subtle touch, causing some painful incidents here on Ridmon as a reminder that we as people are susceptible to failure from our own mistakes. All in all, I must commend the leadership of Ridmon, they have done a fine job. A new race has been born on Thedrimon and with it new technologies. You people now face the future on your own to grow, develop and prosper. Ridmon will always be home to me and I shall return to it many times."

Mike moved through the Troops to the Podium. He raised his arms into the air. There was a hushed silence in the Hall and Mike continued.

"As you know, Moti and I with our families have been away for a while and, although I would like to stand here a chat about it, I do think it would be out of place. However, suffice to say I did miss all your ugly mugs and especially the beer. So if it will please the powers that be here on Ridmon, I propose the following, and......correct me if I am wrong, we deserve a party. So let's have a party, what say you? Party time."

It took a few seconds for the words to sink in and when they did the Hall erupted in jubilant shouts and cheers. Frank shook his head and smiled. Trust Mike to pull a stunt like that. He watched the big man dancing around with Penagee like they didn't have a care in the world. Spotting Moti he walked over to him through the mingling crowd.

"Hello Moti"

Moti turned and smiled, "Hello Frank. How are you doing?"

"As you can see, doing my job and wondering what the hell you lot are getting up to. A year and not a beep out of you, then you come back marching in style, swaggering as if you did not have a care in the world. I demand an explanation."

Frank saw an instant steel coldness in Moti eyes and his stomach tightened.

"Well Frank, like you, I only follow orders and if Mike tells me to keep my mouth shut, I keep it shut, no offence. You will have to ask him. Personally, I am very glad to see you and be back on Ridmon, so for the sake of our friendship, don't cross the line."

Moti's massive arm shot out and a hand like a steel vice clamped around Franks throat, lifting him bodily off the ground. Frank inwardly shivered watching Moti's eyes, seeing the bottomless black holes Moti's slow harsh whisper said it all.

"You are President of Thedrimon, but in this room today you are just another man. You are our friend and buddy, not our keeper. We know you are pissed off and want answers, but do not presume your authority allows you to demand anything."

Moti released Frank and only then did both men realize there was a deathly silence in the Hall. Mike walked up to Moti and bear-hugged him saying.

"Easy Hawk, easy." Then turning to Frank he smiled, "Grab a beer Frank, we will have our chat soon, and Frank, you are looking good."

Extending his hand to Frank in a gesture of friendship. Frank shook the extended hand and breathed deeply. That had been close, too close. Susan, frightened by the incident, came to Frank and gently guided him to a table. Mike ruffled Moti's hair and together they walked off to the bar. Penagee quickly moved in and sat down next to Frank, taking his hands in hers. She could see Frank was visibly shaken.

"Frank, a year changes a man in many ways. Those two have changed from the time you last saw them. In this year those two have fought many battles side by side against overwhelming odds. As a result it has bonded them far closer together than can be imagined. Moti meant you no harm, only in his way to put a point across, he is not very tactful I will admit, but that's Moti."

Frank managed a smile. He was not so convinced after seeing what lay in the depths of Moti's eyes. Pure bloody death. Whatever it was those two had been fighting changed both of them into cold, clinical, killing machines. Frank shuddered. Heaven help us if those two ever got really ticked off with Thedrimon he thought. Penagee continued.

"Protector Friend transported Mike and Moti onto a terrible world, without any powers other than their natural physical abilities. A world of terrible existence where kill or be killed was the only known law. As a result, both men now bear the scars of their experience etched in their hearts and on their bodies, it was a raw and bloodthirsty test for both men. They survived in spite of the scars and won back their prize. Life. Frank, please try to understand, there are forces out there far beyond your or my comprehension which have come into play with the intention of using Mike and Moti as Universal Messengers."

Frank looked over at Mike and Moti standing next to the bar and asked Penagee,

"What did they have to survive against in that world?"

Penagee's eyes clouded with tears, reliving some frightening memories and replied,

"Intelligent cannibalistic Reptilian type beings whose only motivation was to kill. Whether for food or sport it did not matter, killing was like an addictive drug. Mike and Moti were outmatched both in physical strength and size and were hunted incessantly. It became a question of adapt or die, Adapt they did. Both men became more vicious and deadly than their hunters and were forced to eat the flesh of their enemy. There was nothing else edible. Both were reduced to such low primitive levels I was afraid there would be permanent psychological damage. For a year they were hunted like dogs and for a year they killed and ate their hunters."

Penagee touched Frank's forehead with an index finger and an image appeared in Frank's mind of the Reptilian beings. His breath sucked in. The image was of Reptilian beings about 2.3 metres in height with skins a light tanned colour, finely scaled like a snake. Their bodies were superbly defined and bulged with powerful muscles on which were Human skull-shaped heads with reptilian yellow eyes and panther-like razor sharp teeth, signalling their ferocious character. The fingers on their hands were equipped with short talon-like claws and the wrists and forearms bore witness to the terrible power with which those lethal talons could be wielded. Frank jumped up and shook his head violently until the image disappeared and he looked down at Penagee,

"Shit, Penagee, and they had to eat...?" Frank gulped.

Susan was beside herself, whatever it was that Frank had seen must have been awful and she turned on Penagee, only to find tears streaming down the woman's face and Susan's heart went out to her. How the poor woman must have suffered in that year, being utterly helpless to help her man in any way. Frank regained his composure, stripped naked to the waist, ran down into the crowd and shouted.

"Game."

He needed the brutality of a game of Catch to clear his head.

"Game," He shouted again.

Slowly members of the Regiment took up positions on the Hall floor to shouts of delight, two 3-man teams of Matabele's squared off. Frank in the middle was the Catch. The rules were simple. Each team had to physically carry the Catch on to a touch line, no holds barred and the Catch was to prevent himself being taken by either team. The Catch's mission was to drink both beers placed on either touch line or both teams were to prevent the Catch from drinking those beers. If he succeeded in doing so, he would be declared the winner. This was a particularly brutal game. At all times there were to be three men a side and one catch. If any one player was knocked out of the game, another took his place until the beers were drunk by a Catch, or the Catch was touched down in a conscious or otherwise state on either line.

The community watched in anticipation as Frank downed a beer and took his stance. A referee came forward and checked each individual for hidden weapons as a formality. This was an empty-handed game. Satisfied that all was in order, the referee stepped onto the invisible side-line, raised his hand.

"Ready?"

A moment's pause then.

"Play!"

The Hall shook from the shouting and chanting and Frank sprung. Six men charged forward, each trying to get a hold on the Catch. The crunching impact of kicks, fists and heads flattened four of the players in the initial contact and Frank somersaulted out of the rough and tumble to take the first beer, but was promptly stopped dead in his tracks. Flattened by a spinning Dragon kick as he steadied himself on landing, Frank was out of it, knocked unconscious. Bodies were dragged off and replacements went into action. Body after body, catcher after catcher, all two hundred of Mike's Guards, until only six of them remained standing and no Catcher. The referee walked over to Moti and nominated him as Catcher, as he was the second in command of the Regiment. Moti moved into position and a recovered Frank, nursing a pulsing head, watched intently. The six men were the Regiment's finest. Frank smiled to himself, this time Moti might meet his match. The referee raised his hand and shouted.

"Proceed."

The onlookers watched in total disbelief, Moti moved with lightning precision, blinding speed and split seconds later six men lay sprawled on the floor. Very calmly Moti drank the first beer and walked humbly to the other touch line, stepping over the unconscious forms to drink the other. Then bowing to the crowd, he re-joined Mike at the bar. With the game over, the community dived into a party spirit which left many victims of alcohol intoxication sleeping it off where they had fallen.

Up in his apartment, whilst the party raged, Frank sat deep in thought. Susan had been all over him about the game. But he felt good. It was a long time since someone had flattened him and Frank realized he had become soft. A result of too much sitting around and not enough hard physical training. Seated opposite him Susan fumed.

"For a President you certainly fell on your face tonight."

"Perhaps you are right." The instinctive reply.

More silence followed, then she blurted out.

"If you want to make a spectacle of yourself, please try not to do it while I am around. I hate it when I see you get hurt like that."

"I am sorry my Love, I didn't think you would get so upset about it. Besides I needed that thump to bring me back to reality." He confessed.

"Some reality, you are the President, for heaven's sake."

"The reality that I am a man as well, can very easily be forgotten."

"Maybe it's time you took a holiday Frank."

"Maybe you're right."

Susan got up and came over to him, kissing his forehead,

"Don't forget, no one stays young forever, my darling, and I still want you in one piece for a long time to come. Sleep tight." With that she retired to the bedroom.

She made a point he thought, the part about the holiday. It would give him a chance to take in some much needed training. Borz was more than qualified to handle things during his absence and Tara would second him. Two people he could trust. Frank processed his immediate notification of leave through the system and left messages for both Borz and Tara to meet with him first thing, for their official appointments. Frank then slipped out of the door and down to the bar where some of the Regiment were drowning their aches and pains in beer. He joined in and after a few hours he too passed out dead drunk onto the floor.

Three days later the Regiment formed up on the walkway. Thirty-four Warrior Drones hovered above. Mike signalled to Moti, who opened the elevator door on the platform and two Reptilian figures emerged into the sunlight. The sight of them was enough to make even the hardiest person shrink with fear.

Tara swore out loud, "Shite. Where did Mike find those nightmares?"

The twins came out of the elevator, followed by Penagee and a Reptilian child. The Reptilians dwarfed every person around them by their sheer brute size. One of the Reptilians bent forward and picked up the twins, then both Reptilians, their tan coloured scaled and powerfully muscled bodies moved effortlessly towards Mike. As they approached it became apparent they were a male and female. Tara studied these creatures intently. They looked like very large Humans in costume, except for the hands, feet and heads which were anything but. The cold yellow King Cobra eyes seemed to penetrate everywhere. She watched as the one creature put the twins down and what looked like a smile revealed vicious ripping fangs, top and bottom of the jaws. But it was the talons on the hands and feet that sent shivers up her spine. The ripping, wrenching and gauging they were capable of to shred their victims to pieces was horrific. The Reptilians turned to face the Regiment and stood motionless. Moti escorted Penagee and the Reptilian child to their places behind Mike.

Frank felt sick thinking of how Mike and Moti ate the flesh of these creatures in order to stay alive. Seeing the teeth and talons he was mighty glad he was not at the receiving end of any of them. At Mike's signal, Frank marched forward and presented to the male Reptilian a beautiful sky blue crystal drinking goblet which, when exposed to sunlight, gave off an aura of every imaginable colour. An extremely valuable and rare gift. The Reptilian bowed slightly, but did not accept the gift until Frank had replaced it back into its special protective container. The Reptilian child joined its parents and Mike teleported them back to their planet. Throughout the entire solemn proceeding not a sound was heard until Frank's voice boomed a command to the Regiment to left face. He turned to Mike and said.

"Troops ready for stand down."

"Carry on." Mike's reply and Frank marched the Regiment off.

Tara edged herself closer to Penagee and whispered.

"Excuse the ignorance, but what was this little ceremony about?"

"Mike's new friend." Explained Penagee.

Tara shook her head. "Some friend." She said aloud, looking across at Mike and Moti, itching to hear the story. Just then Jane came running up and threw herself into Mike's arms, tears of happiness streaking down her cheeks.

"You big Ape, Frank has just filled me in with some of the details. Am I glad you made it back?"

"And I am glad to see your lovely face, believe me." Smiled Mike.

Moti came over and hugged the two saying,

"Beer time."

Mike took Penagee's hand in his and, with the twins chasing each other around, walked to an open-air kiosk and sat down, ordering beers for the adults and fruit juice for the children. Frank, Tara and Borz joined them. Anna came bounding up to sit on Moti's, lap giving him a wet, sloppy kiss. The mood was very relaxed, with laughter and a lot of small talk. After an hour Mike, Penagee and the twins left for their home. More beers and more jokes, then both Tara and Jane prompted Moti.

"Tell us about those Reptilians and how you two guys managed to stay alive."

Everyone pushed and pleaded until Moti gave in. He began to recount their experience.

"A year ago Protector Friend appeared out of the blue and told us we were to face a test instrumental to our advancement. We of course did not know what he was on about and were not particularly concerned either when we were told that we would not have any of Mike's unusual powers to help us, only our own strengths and fighting abilities. We were allowed to take lances and bows. I remember we took about fifty arrows apiece, thinking it would be enough. How wrong we were. Anyway, we were teleported onto a planet virtually devoid of any plant life and those that did exist were not edible. The planet we landed on was in every sense a desolate volcanic mountainous place with peaks and cliffs more than 10 kilometres high. Hot during the day and freezing at night. We almost immediately found a cave to live in and checked out our surroundings, looking for water. It took a week to locate some and by this time we were not happy chappies and very hungry ones at that, chasing down small rock, lizard-like creatures to eat. The problem was to catch this food supply as those damn little fellows could move like greased lightning. We ranged out further and further in search of food and during our second week we encountered the Reptilian beings for the first time. A group of them were chasing down one of their own kind and when finally they caught up with him, they shredded it to bits. We waited until they had left and then came down from our high perch in a cliff face to check out what was left of the corpse. You must remember, we needed to observe our potential enemy close up in order to evaluate them. Considering the fact that we were starving, it was only natural to regard the corpse as edible, so we roasted and ate pieces of that thing. Tasted a lot like grilled snake and it did give us our strength back."

He paused to take a swig of beer then continued.

"Now we had a confirmed food source, so we decided to hunt it down. Well, you can imagine how we must have felt when we eventually did find their community. The Reptilians have a social order and are intelligent beings living in fortified rock fortresses. The idea of approaching them directly was cut very short when we saw a raiding party attack. From our hiding place we could see the whole thing and let me tell you, it was bloodthirsty. Give no quarter, take no quarter. Eventually though, those in the fortress repulsed their attackers, leaving the dead, ripped apart bodies where they had fallen to be eaten later. They were cannibalistic, surviving on each other's flesh. We, under the cover of darkness, grabbed one of the bodies and high-tailed it out of there back to our cave kilometres away. But like everything else, sooner or later one is bound to be found out. Three Reptilians a few days later were hunting us. There was no way we were going to end up as sushi, so we killed them with arrows, moved our location to another cave well away from the first and covered our tracks all the way by scaling horizontally across cliff faces and over huge fallen boulders."

Another pause, another swig.

"We lived like that for months, constantly moving, striking and moving. Our arrow stock dwindled. There was nothing to replace them with, so we resorted to our lances, which meant that we had to get in close to ensure kills and still keep possession of our lances. The lances in time were also either broken or carried off still in the bodies of our intended victims. We became hunted like dogs. Without any weapons, it left us no alternative, but to kill with our bare hands. This of course meant hand-to-hand combat which, by anyone's standards those creatures out-matched us in physical power and size. So inevitably we had a few nasty scratches of our own. The only way to successfully gain the upper hand was to catch them unawares, which meant Mike and I worked as a team and only under the cover of darkness."

Moti paused to take a long swig of beer and those around the table sat glued to their chairs, listening intently. He continued.

"We hit them everywhere, never in one place twice and always at night. During the day they would chase us in packs and we would run for kilometres, criss-crossing every which way. Those hunting packs would cross each other's paths during their searches and battle each other to the death, so we always had enough to eat one way or the other. Came the day though when Mike came face to face with one of those creatures in broad daylight and it became a one on one situation. Let me tell you, if Mike and I had not been so fit and strong and through our martial arts training developed excellent mind and body control, we would not have survived. We knew their fighting styles, having had plenty of opportunity to observe. So we had built up a strategy and trained hard between us to perfect extremely fast and deadly attacking manoeuvres. We used rocks as weights to build up muscle strength in our arms and legs and hardened our hands and feet. We made body armour from dried Reptilian hide to give us some protection against those talons and teeth. We were ready for them. The last thing we wanted was direct confrontation, but we were prepared for the day it would inevitably come and such a day came for Mike. I was too high up in the rocks to be able to get down to him in time to help and all I could do was watch as the two squared off. Mike's size was the creature's downfall; it must have figured Mike as an easy push-over and got careless. It paid the price dearly. Mike broke that thing. He steam-rolled into to it with everything he had, breaking one of its legs and smashing one side of its rib cage in before the creature realized what had happened. It stood there on one leg, blood oozing out its mouth from a punctured lung and the look on its face was one of total disbelief. Mike lunged in for the kill and the creature tried desperately to defend itself but was useless. From where I watched I could hear the thing's spine snap, then it was over."

"We trained even harder, hours and hours of it, paying special attention to flexibility and internal energies. Over the next few months both Mike and I took out many more Reptilians on a one on one basis, swiftly and effectively. Not once did we underestimate our opponents, as it would have been a fatal mistake. Their hunting stepped up, at times we ran full out for long distances, sometimes climbed up sheer cliff faces, other times fought our way out by attacking our pursuers when they least expected it. Make no mistake; we got our fair share of wounds and injuries from those fights. The only time there was a few days' peace was when it rained. The lightning bolts hit ground level and being caught out in a storm meant sooner or later you would get fried from those bolts. We saw a group of ten Reptilians get taken out by a single bolt of lightning after being caught out in the open when a storm suddenly hit. This was the extent of our existence, killing to live and living to kill."

"We were reduced to Reptilian level and after a while it got to us. We needed to stay alive as a team; if not we would be hunted down and killed far quicker. We must have really pissed them off because none of their settlements was safe and I guess we somehow were responsible, the first time in Reptilian history, for them uniting with one singular, uneasy truce and purpose, our extinction. It became harder to find isolated targets, so we were forced to initiate attacks by ambushing small groups, selecting a target and taking it out from under their noses, then high-tailing it out of there carrying our prize. This system worked fine until they stopped coming after us in small groups. There was no other option, so we hit their settlements in broad daylight once the hunting parties had left and then we pounced with all the speed we could muster, then got out equally fast."

"It didn't take long before settlements joined together and pooled resources. Groups would go out, but a strong defence team remained behind. We would follow the groups, hoping to pick up stragglers or let them spot us and keep the chase going all day well away from any settlement. In the darkness it was easier to pick them off. The game of cat and mouse continued for another few months until the day a very large group ambushed us. It was the worst moment of my life. They had managed to separate Mike and me and boxed me into a blind gully. There was no way out and they knew it. I stood my ground. No ways was I going down without a fight, no ways. But sheer weight of numbers eventually had me nicely tied up and carried to their settlement and thrown into a pit. I did not know where Mike was or what had become of him."

"The rest of the day I was being stared at like some caged animal in a zoo. When night fell torches were lit in the arena and I was roughly thrown into its centre, my bonds loosened and my body armour removed. I made a mental note of my surroundings, looking for an escape route, but all exits were very heavily guarded. The walls of the arena were at least six metres high, fashioned out of smooth rock. The floor was approximately thirty metres in diameter and filled with soft sand. I was trapped and being set up for blood sports. There was nothing else to do so I sat down and forced myself to meditate."

A moment of silence then.

"Perhaps twenty minutes went by then I felt someone else in the arena and calmly turned to find myself face to face with a fearsome looking creature. He was big and powerful. Well Moti, I thought, give it your best shot. The creature attacked. He was fast, raking the air with his talons. It took less than 10 seconds to smash its windpipe, leaving the creature writhing in the dust, then dying from suffocation. The hissing from the audience stopped and their yellow eyes stared at me. I stood calming myself, conserving energy and strength. Another candidate entered the arena. It was more cautious than the first and circled around, making the odd feint to get me to move. I stood my ground, watching and anticipating. The crowd's hissing grew stronger; they were impatient and wanted blood. The creature came in low and fast, talons at the ready. I moved sideways, delivering a sweeping outer Dragon kick which broke its elbow, and continued the momentum to bring me in from behind it and smashed my fist into the base of its skull, simultaneously stamping down hard on the back of one of its legs, breaking it. The creature pitched forward, dead before it hit the ground. I felt loose and relaxed and concentrated on my internal energies, the energy of Chi, and waited for the next one. Then two creatures entered the arena from opposite ends."

"Now things were warming up. I wasted no time and attacked with all the speed and force I had, taking out the one without difficulty and bounced off the wall in a high arc to face the other. It did not move, but bowed slightly and turned its back on me, looking up into the crowd. At first I could not understand what its problem was, then it hit me, he refused to fight. What happened next was a blur. Bodies started falling into the arena, smashed and broken and Mike somersaulted down next to me. I could see he was badly injured with deep gashes across his chest and back. He was functioning on pure adrenalin and willpower. The creature that had refused to fight turned to face the two Humans. Mike stepped forward and with sign language indicated to himself, then pointed to the crowd motioning with his hands for them to send in their biggest and strongest fighter."

"The sight of Mike's blood-smeared chest and back made them hiss. Mike then indicated that if he won, he and I would go free. If he lost, then the creatures could eat us. The crowd hissed even louder. A huge, massively powerful creature stepped into the arena. He was a mean and ugly all-killing machine. Their champion had taken up the challenge and Mike whispered to me,

"When I engage you take off, do you understand?"

"I told him flatly no ways, we came into it together and we were going out of it together. He backed me up against the wall and walked into the centre to face his opponent. The creature stood there, hands on hips and a deep rumbling, hissing laughter came out of its throat. Mike smacked him on the chest with an open palm heel strike so hard and so fast it lifted the creature off the ground with a smashed sternum. It crashed to the ground with a sickening thump and lay there for a few seconds and then slowly, painfully it got to its feet. It took a lot of guts and raw determination after bodily

damage like that to sit up, let alone stand. The creature stood
there wheezing, facing Mike, and trying to bring its arms
into a defensive position. Mike had no choice; he ended it
swiftly, allowing the creature some final moments of dignity.
He struck like a demon possessed, smashing into the huge
body with such power, he drove his fingers clean through
the abdomen up into the chest cavity and ripped out its heart
and bodily lifted the creature above his head and shouted
"Bayete, Matabele!" then brought the huge body crashing
down onto a knee, breaking the creature's back like a twig."

Moti paused for a moment, staring at the transfixed
Human faces around him. He continued,

"The funny thing though, was the creature that refused
to fight. He beckoned to me and Mike to follow him at
once and we went out of the arena fighting like mad men,
including our new friend. We kept going, but Mike was
losing a lot of blood, so the creature picked him up and
ran with me close on its heels. We ran all night and Mike
finally lost consciousness. The creature took us to a water
hole where it bathed Mike's wounds and dressed them with
the chewed bark from those plants I mentioned. If it had
not been for that creature Mike would have died. Well, here
we are today, alive and very much relieved to be back on
Ridmon with the people we love."

Tara's eyes were dancing.

"What made the creature do that?"

"We don't exactly know, but let me assure you I am very
glad it did, because he is one very dangerous Reptilian. I
guess something must have triggered in its brain and, being a
group leader, he did have some intelligence, which we found
out later to be quite a lot. It told Mike that, after seeing him
jump into the arena and whispering to me and my shaking
head, he put two and two together and realized Mike was

willing to give up his life for a friend and that I was refusing to leave, no matter what, and it seemed to awaken something in its cold heart. But we still had to get out of there and it knew unless it helped, we would be torn to pieces and for reasons of its own it did not want that."

"And Mike, how come he was injured like that?" Questioned Jane.

"When I was captured Mike ended up in a similar situation, only he went nuts thinking they had killed me and he fought his way out. There were ten of them and believe me when those odds and those talons are stacked against you he managed and escaped. He spotted me, then followed waiting for an opportunity and when that did not present itself, he did what any brother and friend would have done, joined in the fight, to the death."

"And you became friends with that thing?" Quizzed Frank.

"Yes."

"Didn't either of you want to eat each other at some point," Queried Borz.

"No. There is an edible bulbous plant on the planet which grows underground in abundance in specific places. It is very tasty and very nutritious and a damn side better than eating Reptilians. Our creature friend really is a clued-up character and Mike's wounds healed well."

Anna continued the story excitedly, holding Moti close.

"They were still hunted, all three of them for a few months afterwards, until Mike got fed up and all three of them just walked into the main settlement one day in broad daylight, marched straight up to the seated chief and Mike killed it and its bodyguard on the spot, threw their bodies into the dust, spat on them, then turned and sat his creature friend on the empty seat of office and hissed like a snake."

Moti laughed loudly continuing with the story.

"You should have seen their faces, it was like they had been hit by a sledge hammer. I don't know if Mike's hissing meant anything to him, but it certainly changed the whole order of things for us. Suddenly we were the good guys. Our friend sent messengers out all over the place and soon the settlement was packed with creatures. We just stood, not understanding anything that was hissed nor the hand signals, until a while later the crowd opened up and we walked out of there into the mountains and neither we nor they bothered each other again. A week later Protector Friend teleported us back into the settlement and took our hands and joined them with the creatures in a token of friendship, then teleported both of us back to Ridmon."

The group on the walkway sat in awed silence recounting the story in their minds until Borz leapt up and declared.

"Oops, come on Tara, we have duties of State to attend to."

With that the two dashed off into the Great Hall. Frank looked long and hard into his beer bottle then downed its contents and ordered another.

Zorak watched his Human brother-in-law showering after a workout; seeing the horrible scars made him shiver. The memory of the visiting Reptilian still haunted him. How those two had managed to survive was beyond him and the scars were proof enough of the deadly efficiency of those Reptilian talons. This human Ape had come a long way since arriving on Ridmon and, admittedly, was an ideal mate for Penagee. Zorak loved the twins as if they were his own. They were bright, highly intelligent little imps who kept him on his toes. Yes, he was a fool in the past, but that was over now and he was glad things worked out the way they did. Penagee's immense capacity for love brought him back from the edge of hell into a warm cosy family environment like it used to be back in the days of the original Crystal City. He loved his sister dearly and from now on would make it up to her for the hurt he had caused. He understood Mike would never fully trust him and didn't blame the man, resigning himself to the fact that Mike could have crushed him like an egg, but didn't. At first he thought it was because of Penagee, however he soon realized it was more of a humane act than anything else. Once he tried to mentally probe a Drone and nearly had his brain fried for his efforts. No, his brother-in-law had everything sewed up just nicely and he wasn't going to interfere, or try to, in any way. The price would be too high, besides it was nice just to relax in the sun and entertain the twins. Penagee made sure his brilliant mind was kept busy with various projects and inventions which were of an entirely peaceful and productive nature.

"Nasty scars Mike." He casually mentioned.

Mike's penetrating gaze said it all.

"A reminder to keep your place in the order of things."

Zorak nodded, ending the one-sided conversation. That's how it was between them, everything short, sweet and to the point. Just then the twins came bounding out breaking the tension in the air.

"Come Uncle Zorak, come and see our new crystal farm."

Zakrose grabbed at his arm and tugged.

"OK, I am coming." He laughed and went inside the house with Zakrose clinging on to make sure that he obliged.

Mike smiled to himself, finished dressing and was about to go inside when a voice in his head said.

"The Trafodj are heading for the Reptilian planet." It was Protector Friend.

Mike sprang into action. No ways were those bastards going to wipe out his newfound friends.

"Penagee." His voice boomed. She heard the urgency in it and came running.

"There's no time to explain, I want you to take over Thedrimon, Now! Trafodj is going to attack the Reptiles." Mike teleported out to Crystal City.

Within minutes of his arrival the Regiment was assembled, fully armed and equipped all 3,250 fighting men and women. The Warrior Drones came in to embark them and Mike's mind worked like lightning, immunizing everyone on the mission against the mind virus. Moti raced up and the two men watched their troops embark. Mother Drone was already on her way to the Reptilian Planet to take up a defensive position. Once everyone was aboard and on their way, Mike and Moti teleported onto the Mother Drone. Within hours they were hovering above the Reptilian Planet and Mike teleported down. Zi greeted him and immediately Mike transmitted images into the Reptilian's brain. Zi hissed and turned to a large gathering and issued orders.

"Moti, how we doing for time?" He asked telepathically.

"48 hours to get into position around Trafodj. ETA Trafodj forces 52 hours." Was the reply.

"Thanks, stand by." Confirmed Mike.

An hour later 10,000 Reptilians gathered and Mike ordered the strongest fighters forward. Three thousand Reptilian warriors stepped forward. The only way to communicate with these creatures was through imagery and he sent pictures into their minds. Every one of them shifted uneasily. Ushering the remaining 7,000 creatures into the settlement, he immunized all 10,000 against the brain virus. Mike teleported the first three thousand Reptilians onto Mother Drone, then repeated the exercise time and time again until he had built up an army of 10,000 Reptilians. Not many, considering the odds against them, but sufficient for what he had in mind. The warrior Drones arrived and 3,250 Ridmon troops disembarked onto the planet. Mike's Army now consisted of 13,250 ground troops, 34 Warrior Drones and a Mother Drone. He ordered Moti down and cloned Mother Drone into three identical replicas which took the better part of twenty four hours to complete then deployed his troops into two sister Drones. Leaving half the warrior Drones to protect the Reptilian planet, he then catapulted his attack Force to intercept through the Portal. One Mother Drone and the remainder of the Warrior Drones were to advance to contact and obliterate the invaders, whilst Mike with the other two Sister Drones would head straight for Trafodj.

Zi sat with Mike and Moti inside Sister Drone and his Reptilian eyes shot about in confusion. Mike smiled at him as a reassurance. It was time to teach Trafodj a lesson they would not forget. Frank was in the other Sister Drone feeling a little uncomfortable with the Reptilians breathing down his neck. But he was glad to be on a mission again and looked forward to it. Mike teleported aboard Mother.

"Open communication, Mother." He ordered.

A face appeared on the screen. It was the face of a beautiful woman. Her red hair and brick coloured skin could not conceal the pitch black eyes of hate.

"Mind virus." Warned Mother Drone.

"Send it back doubled." Ordered Mike.

He watched as the woman's face contorted, fingers tearing at her hair and her mouth opened in a tortured scream, then the face was gone and the screen blanked.

"Enemy fleet preparing to fire."

"Give them what they deserve." Was the order and 100 Trafodj ships disintegrated?

"Confirm enemy obliterated."

"Thanks, Mother, and by the way, did I hear you laugh when you sent the mind virus back?"

"Affirmative."

"Why?"

"Mother Drone added a twist of her own." She confirmed.

"Oh! Explain?"

"Call it Mother Drone's Antivirus. They transmit, I pick up the transmission, alter it, sent it back as a mind cleaning agent. Bingo, no more."

"Whatever it was, it looked extremely painful."

"It was designed to be." Came the matter of fact voice.

Mike laughed, "Glad you are on my side."

"You are my Master and I serve."

"Thanks, Mother."

"It's a pleasure."

Mike sat in silence for a while and then advised.

"Pass that on to the rest of the Drones, it will come in handy."

"Already done so."

Mike smiled. These Drones were good.

"Let's join the party." He ordered. Mother Drone laughed again.

"What's so funny now?" Mike asked.

"Mother Drone amused at Master's terminology."

"You are becoming more human every day, Mother."

"The Master's good influence."

Mike laughed aloud. For the next hour he scanned his men's minds, feeding in Mother Drone's "Anti-Virus".

Perhaps this war could be resolved without too much bloodshed.

Penagee interrupted, "How are things going?"

"So far, 100 enemy ships obliterated, Zi's planet secured and I have 13,050 troops in two Sister Drones plus the rest of us just outside of Trafodj."

"Who are us?"

"Mother Drone, some of her Warriors and yours truly."

"Just checking." Laughed Penagee.

"I love you too." Mike broke the contact, they were on the outskirts of the Trafodj planet.

On Trafodj, a War Council was convened in an emergency session. The Council leader of a 133 million strong population was furious.

"You can't explain to me, you simple minded idiot, how 100 of our ships just disappeared. I find that every difficult to comprehend."

The Military representative shifted uneasily under the Leader's stare.

"Well, I am waiting." The man barked.

"No logical answer and our locator probe has not reported in either. It too, has simply vanished."

"You blithering numbskull, we must be under attack for that to happen."

"No Sir, there is nothing out there for a billion light years."

The leader shook his head in anger and bellowed.

"Will someone please enlighten me, our computers tell us all is well out there, yet now a locator probe has also vanished. Sound the alarm. Sound the bloody alarm."

Trafodj's attempt to go to full alert was thwarted by the first Thedrimon salvos. Strategic military installations, the council chambers and communication centres were the first to go. The concentrated grids in which the salvos wreaked their destruction within hours homed in on all targets that constituted life-supporting installations; Trafodj was paralyzed, so Mike unleashed his ground forces into their capital city. It was pure carnage. The Reptilians with their Thedarian comrades in arms, backed up by three Warrior Drones, were murderous and unstoppable. Whatever resistance there might have been had no chance to organize itself or regroup and within six hours Mike's men had taken the capital, leaving a trail of destruction and disaster of unprecedented proportion.

Six million people were killed and millions were captured, herded into stockades like rats into a trap. The Drones continued their salvoes across the entire planet, knocking any resistance into oblivion. Within 24 hours the entire planet was on its knees and the Drones began their "Anti-Virus" transmissions. A further 12 hours and Trafodj unconditionally surrendered. In less than 48 hours Mike had crushed a civilization, bringing it to its knees. The final death toll was staggering; 12 million people lost their lives. Most of whom were from the capital and surrounding cities. Mike withdrew his Reptilian force, not stomaching any more unnecessary killing. The bloodlust affected all his men that day, the Reptilians of course were the worst of the lot, which was exactly why Mike wanted them on this mission.

The news by now filtered out to other galaxies of an unknown and unseen force that had been monitored taking Trafodj. Mike also wanted the brigade exposed to wholesale slaughter on a scale which would live with them for the rest of their lives. All brain viruses were completely eradicated from the Trafodj peoples and so it was safe for relief workers to come in from Thedrimon for the long rehabilitation process. The Regiment remained with Frank to oversee the restoration process and act as police units together with one Sister and six Warrior Drones. The Drones on the Reptilian Planet returned to base. Mike took the Reptilian force back to their planet and left a Sister Drone watchdog in its orbit. Mother Drone shuttled relief parties to and fro, leaving 28 Warrior Drones as reserve on Ridmon. Thedrimon groaned, knowing that the price of victory carried a heavy toll and to that end did everything she could to make retribution to Trafodj through humanitarian aid and assistance to gather a shattered nation together once again. This was the second time that Thedrimon had used maximum force and her reputation began to spread far and wide. Months later Mother Drone intercepted an interstellar message which read.

"To the unknown Force which has clipped the Trafodj fingernails, tamed the Reptilian Planet and brought peace to Thedrah, we salute you. Beware; you have aroused negative interest from superior forces."

Mike, Penagee and Moti sat cross-legged inside Mother Drone, locked hands forming a triangle and then reached out with their minds in a concentrated effort to home in on the repeating message originating from very deep space, billions of light years away. The message ended before they could trace its source. All three looked at each other with a single realization that their superiority in their own neighbourhood was restricted to just that. Out there somewhere, a friend had chosen a very simple way of reminding them not to become too confident in themselves, as it would certainly attract more attention than they had bargained for. Mike's concern carried the possibility that they were being targeted for a showdown by a greater force, which would undo the good already achieved and put everyone at risk, unless the existing technological infrastructures and defensive mechanisms were greatly improved upon. As it stood, with what they had it was obviously only scratching the surface. It was time to rethink, redesign and implement their offensive and defensive capabilities. The only question remaining was how much time they had. In reality, Thedrimon had over extended herself, leaving the door open for attack on her weakest links.

"Moti, if we look back on Earth's history to the time of the ancient Egyptians, Greeks, Romans and many others, we see how they conquered, expanded and lost their empires. Nearly all of them fell from within or were completely crushed by opposing armies. We take a look at modern day empires and also notice similar patterns occurring, where super powers are reduced to nothing, not always by the causes of war, but by economic or political changes. What are the weaknesses in our part of the universe? One singular factor sustaining life on all our inhabited planets is our unique solar systems. If anyone planet within that solar system is removed, it creates an imbalance and the resultant realignment of the remaining planets to their sun would wipe out all or most life forms. Alternatively, should the planet on which those life forms exist be moved slightly by degrees out of its original orbit, slowed or speeded up, then the results would be the same. All life therefore revolves around the sun and an unchanged planetary speed, a consistent revolving orbit to sustain itself. Block the sun, you destroy life."

Penagee smiled, Mike was thinking out loud again and she prodded his mind saying.

"Can we be part of this train of thought?"

"Sorry, I wandered off again." To which Moti joked.

"Careful, first sign of old age."

Mike laughed and slapped him on the back.

"Wise guy."

"So what you are trying to say is....let me get this right, you don't need an army to take out life forms on other planets, merely interfere with the natural order of their solar system."

"In effect… yes."

"That's unthinkable, you're not suggesting someone might do that?" She questioned hotly.

"It is one possibility we have to look at as a means of persuading others to fall in line." Replied Mike to which Moti added.

"All you have to do is threaten any civilization with the destruction of their sun or parts of their solar system and you will get the desired results."

"We have in the past applied some heavy duty methods of persuasion causing loss of life simply because our primitive applications limit our minds to basic technology. If someone wanted to take us out and possessed the technology to do it, we would be sitting where Trafodj sits now. Yes, we have the technology to prevent most military invasions, but what we don't have is the technology to protect our entire solar system. The Drones are a marvel of engineering however, are not capable of the vast and highly complicated task of safeguarding an entire galaxy. We need to come up with a method of saving millions of lives in the event there comes the day we face a threat to our existence of the magnitude we speak of and figure out a means to defend ourselves."

"You are not asking much, are you Mike?" Reflected Moti.

"You guys talk about it as much as you like, but at the end of the day, we have to look to the future. We do this now, our children and their children will at least have inherited a safe infrastructure. There is no such thing as a perfect society or system, neither can we, with all our technology, avoid the march of time and natural process of the universe's evolution." Declared Penagee.

"You are right again, my Love, as usual and I agree with you. Whatever we decide to do has to be done with a full understanding of those factors and strive to make allowances for it."

To everyone's surprise Mother Drone's silky female voice broke into the discussion,

"Why not create a world within a world, a sun within a sun in perfectly balanced harmony, protected and self-nurturing. A living, growing organism with its own personalized identity capable of sustaining limitless life, and virtually indestructible."

Three people sat looking at each other in astonishment.

"Define." Requested Mike.

"By simply duplicating Nature." She replied.

"We are not capable of that kind of duplication." Declared Penagee.

"No, you are not, but you have the tools which can."

Again the three looked at each other somewhat puzzled.

"Explain?" Asked Mike.

There was a moment's silence.

"Zorak and the Drones."

Mike was about to say something when Penagee restrained him, asking,

"How can these two separate entities possibly be able to achieve such an intricate and diversely complicated programme?"

Another silence, then.

"In Zorak's mind lies the key, we the Drones are the locks to the door and the door is Protector Friend. With the key, the locks can be opened on the door and you will have your new world right down to the last detail, but you will have to sacrifice something to get something. You will have to give up Zorak and all the Drones, including myself."

Mike's mind raced. The Drones were vital to their survival. A new world? There were so many ifs and buts, contradictions and doubts. Yet there was the burning question, was it not going a little too far and inviting a whole bunch of trouble if the attempt failed. Millions of lives depended on its success. Once the Drones were out of the picture those same people were vulnerable to total annihilation.

"The survival of the peoples from four worlds depend on us. We can't just leave the doors wide open for every Tom, Dick and Harry to come marching straight in." Stated Mike.

"Master, you are just going to have to trust me."

There was a long silence. Moti, who had not said very much listened intently saw the potential, understood the risks then concluded.

"I go with it, after all, what have we to lose. One way or the other, if someone bigger than us comes attacking; we are in major trouble anyway and will suffer a whole lot more."

Penagee smiled at Mike, "I have to agree for the sake of my children, all those millions of people, and you, my Love."

Mike struggled bitterly within himself in those ensuing long moments. Then cast his fate to the winds and made the decision.

"Mother Drone, you asked me to trust you, I give you my trust and pray to the Higher Power we all succeed."

"Thank you Master. Now I must ask you to teleport Zorak aboard." Mother Drone requested.

Penagee complied and Zorak stood before them, looking very happy with himself.

"Master, I am a biological machine created by you. In return, I will give you a new world and every time you touch any part of your new world you will touch part of me and it's that part which will protect all of you long into the future. It is time, farewell for now."

Mike, Penagee and Moti teleported down to Ridmon, unaware of what was about to transpire. Mother Drone summoned all her biological children, absorbing them into herself, tapped into Zorak's mind and slowly a transfiguration began to take shape. Protector Friend focused his energies with her and gradually she grew in size, larger and larger. The beginnings of a living artificial galaxy was born within her womb and shone bright and hot as any sun with a single planet and solitary moon. Slowly, intricately and delicately, a new world materialized. A world of water and of land masses, complete with plant life. A world within a world and a sun within a sun, totally protected from outside interference. Ten nerve-wracking years went by without news and life on Ridmon became tenser. The absence of the Drones worried those who knew. Mike and Moti were ever vigilant, scanning the vastness of space with their minds or shuttling people to and from Trafodj via the Portals. Penagee took over control of the planet which gave Frank more time to gather together relief workers on Trafodj from among its own peoples and set up functioning infrastructures once again, with Jane and Tara assisting him. Borz was relocated to Thedrah as its Governor, with Zephor seeing to matters on Ridmon in his place. The whole Regiment was on Trafodj, which left Mike and Moti as the only defence on Thedrimon. It did not concern them as they were more than able to protect it. Men are not machines capable of endless hours of work without pause for rest or sleep, nor were their minds able to filter billions of bytes of information over extended periods, so absolute vigilance was impossible. Both Mike and Moti therefore were compelled to upgrade the computers; the scanners took over much of the workload.

This gave the two men much needed time to range outwards across billions of light years of space, searching and watching. Their mind journeys took them across the vastness of space, gathering information and new technologies from civilizations who knew not of the men's existence, until one day their passage was intercepted far from Trafodj by a large and technically highly advanced attack force. Penagee and Moti reacted. In an unprecedented effort, they teleported and moved the people of Thedrah, the Reptilians and the peoples of Trafodj through the Portals. The operation was into its fourth week when the attack came. The enemy struck on all three planets simultaneously. It was murderous and systematic. Mike and Moti went crazy. They linked hands and the whole of Ridmon shook as the crystals of the planet hummed and unleashed their accumulated energies hurtling across space into the attacking forces. The effect was devastating. The energy ploughed through the unsuspecting mass of ships like a hot knife through butter and pulsed wave after wave, smashing anything in its wake. The awesome power of it caused the remaining attacking force to pull back and regroup.

Penagee worked frantically, bringing survivors in from the planets, desperately praying for time, but alas as the next salvoes hit and all three planets surfaces became nuked and radiated, void of life rendering those planets uninhabitable. For the first time in her life Penagee became an avenging angel and teleported to Mike and Moti. The three joined hands, formed a triangle and concentrated their energies into a single powerful source and directed its energy into the crystal mountain behind the city which in turn magnified the energy one billion-fold, then channelled the energy down the entrance of the opened Portal above Ridmon's atmosphere into the invading fleet.

Thousands of ships were destroyed and those that managed to escape, fled for all their worth, sending a simple message to their superiors.

"Mission aborted due to massive casualties. Three targets destroyed, unable to locate the fourth. Unseen force of unknown origin, far more powerful than anything we know, intercepted fleet and virtually destroyed it. Returning to base."

Ridmon took stock. The full impact of their losses became known. Only 10 million people were saved from the three planets. Amongst those lost were Frank and his family, Jane, David, Tara, Borz, Zephor and Zi. The list went on, the entire Regiment, and millions more. Penagee tried desperately to prevent Mike from following the retreating fleet, but to no avail. He was like a man possessed and Moti would not listen to reason either. She wept, feeling the full depth of their anger, for her dear dead friends and for all the people who had lost their lives. In the deep depths of her grief a soft gentle voice echoed in her mind.

"Prepare your people, Mother awaits." Penagee understood.

On a planet, billions of light years from Ridmon, a computer registered a small ripple in the atmosphere. It could not decipher the disturbance, so it scanned again, but the ripple had gone, everything appeared normal. It filed its report to the central data banks detailing the ripple, its location and substance. The banks passed on the information to the central controller who analysed it, cross- referenced it to any known descriptions and came up with a negative. No known cause, a cross pattern search commenced probing for the ripple's fingerprints. Still there was nothing. The computers searched again and again, then finally detected something tangible, but unidentified.

"What do you think, Zam?"

"I don't know. There is definitely something out there. What form, pattern or distinguishing identification, there is no way of knowing? Probably an atmospheric hiccup of sorts."

"So I notice." The sarcastic response.

"Keep checking. Extend into long range scan as a precaution. On second thoughts, keep it short. One never knows."

Ten minutes of silence followed until Zam almost jumped out of his skin when the computer's monotone voice reported,

"Security breached, security breached!"

"Where, damn you, where?" Screamed Zam. This was impossible, it could not be happening.

"Unable to locate exact source."

Then, "Warning, warning, unidentified energy source generating."

Razu, ruler of the Vimusi Federation, watched his monitor in disbelief. A Human face peered at him from the screen with an impish grin on its face.

"Who are you and what do you want?" He barked at the image on the screen.

The grin broadened into a smile,

"Who I am is not important, what I want is your unconditional surrender." Responded the voice.

Razu roared with laughter.

"My unconditional surrender, now that's very funny."

"Yeah it is, isn't it?" A moment's pause then.

"Perhaps you need to examine your situation a little closer before making any rash decisions. It would be in your best interests to switch to your main screens." Advised Mike, still smiling.

Razu impatiently flicked his hand and the main screens opened, showing various strategic sectors of the planet, including Razu's home. What he saw jolted him upright. Reptilians in his living room brutally holding his wife and daughter whose faces were etched in pain from the merciless grips. Razu sat down, his mind racing, his home, why his home? Mike's silky voice interrupted once again.

"As you see Razu, not a very nice picture, especially seeing as that beautiful little girl looks so appetizing to those Reptilians."

"So what" Razu's forced smile challenged.

Another image appeared on the screen, an image of Trafodj's last seconds of life.

"You have violated Intergalactic Law by your actions and therefore you must be held responsible for those actions which cost millions of innocent people their lives." Calmly answered Mike.

"What do I care about Intergalactic Law or you?" Roared Razu defiantly at the monitor.

The next instant Razu's sister was standing next to him screaming in absolute hysterical fear, oblivious to her surroundings. Razu felt the cold hand of finality grip his heart at the sight of her. The voice from the screen taunted.

"As you see Razu, your sister is only the beginning."

"You can't frighten me, you impetuous imbecile. You expect me to be impressed by cosmetic effects on an insignificant woman. You must be crazy or stupid Bellowed Razu.

"Well, look behind you." Advised Mike.

Razu turned to face Moti flanked by three of the meanest Reptilians on the Force who between them were holding a little girl strung out by her arms and legs in those vicious talons. Her screams and petrified face triggered panic in Razu who screamed, "Guards," but no guards came. Mike teleported into the sealed room with Razu's wife.

"Watch the screen, Razu." He advised.

When Razu did not oblige Moti telepathically clamped a vice grip on Razu's brain and began to squeeze, lifting the man off the ground. His writhing body and silent screams gave testimony to the terrible pain. The entire Vimusi nation watched their leader's tortured suffering on screens across the planet. Zam tried desperately to gain access to the room with every technology at his disposal, but the room remained sealed. Mike gave the order and his Army struck into the very heart of the planet's security and communications systems and installations. Explosions rocked the planet of 55 million people, causing widespread structural damage and panic, yet very little loss of life. Vimusi's military might were at a loss. Their Council ordered them to destroy the Control Centre and fired salvo after destructive salvo without effect. The building remained standing shrouded in an energy field. Mike struck back with unerring effect and took out military targets on the ground as well as in the air. Clinically and methodically he reduced Vimusi's armed forces to virtually nothing. The Council, in a last bid to salvage itself ordered their people into underground emergency cities. The masses were already in a state of panic and were unable to respond rationally. Mike took out the Council in its protected underground fortifications. Inside the Control Room, Moti released his hold on Razu to let the man watch in horror as his planet was systematically annihilated. Razu could see his planet going up in flames, his armies' crushed and even the underground cities destroyed before the people could get into them. He frantically watched Mike and Moti for some signs of mercy, but found none. Realizing the full extent of their intent he fell apart. How could all this methodical devastation have taken place by only two men who possessed a power he could not believe existed. They seemed to stand like two stone statues and from the depths of their eyes he saw death itself. He felt weak, sick to the stomach and understood unless he put an end to it, Vimusi would perish. Finally he shouted at Mike,

"We surrender." Then collapsed onto the floor, weeping out of sheer frustration. Instantly the destruction ended. Vimusi was silent and still. For long moments the nation were riveted motionless, frightened and trembling. Mike lifted Razu from the ground and stood him in front of the broadcast console and hissed through his teeth,

"Tell your people."

Razu was no coward. He gathered himself with as much dignity as he could muster and stood tall.

"Vimusi surrenders unconditionally."

Mike allowed a few moments for the words to sink in then he spoke in the Vimusi dialect.

"People of Vimusi, this time you are fortunate my vengeance has not obliterated you all. You have destroyed three planets and their millions of inhabitants in an act of aggression. I therefore give you this warning, unless you turn your efforts and intelligence to more peaceful applications, instead of destruction, rebuild friendship and peace in your regions of space, I shall return and wipe you from this Universe."

Mike turned to the terrified little girl, took her in his arms and held her up to the screen for the entire world to see and added,

"This little girl is your future. Many more children like her will be the next generation of this planet, make sure she and the others do not have to relive the horror of destruction on this planet. You rebuild your cities and armed forces, but remember, go in the wrong direction again and this time it will be final."

He gave the petrified little girl to her father, then both he and Moti teleported through the opened Portal into the Crystal City on Ridmon.

Razu silently took his family into his arms, holding them close. Vimusi would lick its wounds for a long time to come. Penagee sat alone in the Great Hall waiting for Mike's return. She had felt the vibrations emanating from space and prayed Mike and Moti would show compassion in spite of their anger and craving for revenge. Ridmon was deserted, not a single soul remained. In the silence of the Great Hall she recounted the years they had lived on this planet and smiled. They would leave it now as they had found it, only there would remain the man-made monuments of the Crystal Cities, to anyone who might one day pass by, as a testimony to a race that once lived there and since left. Housed in a large Crystal sphere were the images of Ridmon's short history. On its surface were the names of deceased loved ones, all 28 million of them. She felt the Portal's static and stood up as it opened. Mike and Moti stepped into the Hall and walked up to her, took her in his arms, kissed her and whispered.

"They live."

Penagee hugged him tightly and answered, "Thank you."

Both men walked to the domed platform and stood looking down at the forested valley and Penagee heard the words spoken,

"Farewell Old Wolf, the Lion and the Hawk salute you."

Both men turned and walked back to where Penagee stood, then teleported into the new world which awaited them.

Ridmon lay silent and still, save for the creatures which inhabited her and, gradually through time, nature removed all trace of anyone having been there. She remained unseen in a vast cosmos and for many years was only visited from time to time by two Humans who sat aloft in her gigantic trees and talked to an invisible long dead old Bedouin named Abu Ahmed.

Ridmon did not stand alone; next to her solar system another came into being with its own sun, a single planet, a moon and numerous stars. An almost perfect replica of Ridmon, only larger, with more land mass and a population of ten million mixed race people, Trafodj, Nirque, Thedarian, Ridmonians, Reptilian and Human. The system was sealed, shielded and protected by an immensely powerful outer magnetic field, repulsing anything attempting to enter it. Solar systems don't just appear out of nowhere. They evolve over billions of years and Thanu's sudden appearance in the universe did arouse much interest due to the nature of its sudden appearance given the fact it did not impact adversely on the ebb and flow of its surrounding Universe. It became known to space travellers as the 'Lovely Round Lady' because of its spherical structure and beautiful opal luminescence when viewed from afar. Spacecraft from many parts came with their scientific crews to observe this phenomenon, only to find access impossible. Every time a vessel attempted to enter, it was deflected away. Salvos were fired bounced back, resulting in many ships falling foul. The new Solar system baffled and frustrated scientists no end not being able to find out more about it. Hence the message circulated, leave the Lady alone, she is harmless and only responds when attacked with very quick and fatal results. No one knew what lay inside her and after so many failed attempts she was observed and monitored, then marked down on intergalactic charts as No. 4/27, a number signifying, the 4th quadrant, System 27. An inaccessible infant cosmos with no known life forms. But 4/27 had a name. She was affectionately called Thanu, meaning Mother. There was only one way in or out of Thanu that was via Portals.

One man suspected 4/27 of being more than she appeared to be. Razu, from the Planet Vimusi, kept his suspicions to himself, remembering all too well past experiences with two very strange Humans. Vimusi lived up to its commitment and became an example of diplomacy between nations and all but wiped clean from its history the tarnishing memories of the past. Life on Thanu was a Garden of Eden, with the most beautiful Crystal Cities imaginable blended into scenic surroundings to create a masterpiece of nature's perfection. Each City accommodating one million people. The constructions were an architectural genius of crystal culture engineering. By comparison, it made surrounding, highly developed civilizations look primitive. Thanu's secret lay in her ability to harness the simplicity of special crystal cultures and expand on their sensitivity to brain waves, enabling the creation of personalized thought signatures for each individual on the planet. As long as a person wore a specialized crystal armlet around the wrist then that person would be able to go to any particular place in the City by just picturing it in their mind. They could physically travel along invisible thought beams to their destinations.

The Cities' construction, carved out of crystal with their Domes and sharp pointed towers, were the generators for thought wave transmission. Every facet of life was fashioned around this concept with such effective precision that even the Cities' garbage was sent directly to central recycling, simply by looking at it. Each City was also the link in a defensive or offensive chain which did not utilize any laser beams or anti-matter or any other known applications. Theirs were thought waves generated collectively and pulsed out through a central tower of crystal from each City with such incredible power it completely destroyed any target it wished. If a citizen of Thanu was on another planet, he or she had instant communication and an instant weapon. Mother Drone fashioned a world to protect her children and given them the tools with which to do it. Life became a collective purpose with one single goal. Maintaining their unique world in which every person actively played a part. The people were held accountable for their survival and could only do so through harmony with one another. Every person on Thanu had something to contribute and did so in ways that enhanced their own particular talents. It was a veritable Garden of Eden and living on Thanu was an absolute joy. Thanuians travelled the universe incognito on educational and technological tours, even to the remotest of places and began documenting a central universal library in which scientific, historical, geological and social up to date information could be stored and studied. Thanu became a power house of learning and technological research and silently went about its business as the Good Samaritan.

She also had an army, her military wing, which was formidable and could be deployed wherever and whenever required. So was born a Universal Peacekeeping Force and it wasn't long before other nations began to sit up and pay attention. Nobody knew where they came from or who they were. What they did know was not to get on the receiving end of this force as it was swift, deadly and highly effective. Should two nations revert to war then the Thanuians Force would step in offering diplomatic alternatives. If that failed, then military action would be taken against both parties with very quick results. Thanu was a mystery to everyone and gradually it became apparent that System No.4/27 was more than just a pretty face. Penagee, Mike and Moti, constituted Thanu's Supreme Council. Each City had its own representative seats on that Council. The system functioned extremely well, holding Council meetings once a week to resolve or implement issues. On Thanu things got done and were not bogged down by time-wasting officialdom. When a decision was made, it was implemented there and then and carried out all the way down the line. In short, Thanu embodied integrity, high moral and ethical fibre. The Universe is a very large celestial body with no end or beginning and within it lives many diverse cultures and civilizations, both highly evolved and primitive. Space travel was restricted only by technological ability, therefore, as technology advanced, so nations were able to move further and further away from home. War was no exception, a normality to some while others preferred diplomacy. There will always be those who consider themselves over and above all else and will attempt to impose themselves or their philosophies on others. Religion and politics will always be the catalyst for division, not only amongst creatures of the same biological identification but also different civilizations.

Thanu was a self-appointed Peace Maker, yet remained aloof, attending to its own affairs. Thanu's Charter was simple:

"We do not interfere in the domestic disputes of any nation, as those nations have to evolve through natural processes. Thanu would only intervene if the rights of any nation's peaceful existence are at risk from outside forces or if any nation or nations became aggressors towards others without probable cause."

Thanuians all knew what it was like to be displaced by the ravages of war and it forced together four different races of beings into one singular coexistence. Unless commonality was found, co-existence would therefore impact negatively making such an existence extremely difficult. This was enough incentive to motivate their ideals into one singular purpose. Without a doubt there were the disputes, grumblings and differences of opinion, however in the end reality has a way of opening the mind to a higher level of consciousness. Thirty six thousand Reptilians found it extremely difficult adapting to their new life style and environment, yet managed to set an example to others in their community of what could be achieved when all put their minds to it. They formed a major part of Mike's attacking ground forces which numbered twenty thousand men and women, Reptilians making up the largest contingent of forty percent. Mike had trained his Army of front line Storm Troopers to the highest and toughest calibre. They took no quarter and gave none. He split the unit into two equal groups, one he commanded, the other commanded by Moti. In addition, a more purposeful unit was established which consisted mainly of relief workers, such as doctors, engineers, agriculturists, teachers and volunteers from every walk of life. Where Mike and Moti were the destroyers, Penagee was the builder. The rule was, we have, we give, we destroy, we rebuild. All the time Thanu, being mindful of her own vulnerability, never shared her own highly developed technology, rather re-developed technologies already in place on other planets. There is a limit to power and control and those who wield it. Positively utilized, such power within individual planetary environments reaped rewards and maintained a harmonious balance. Nonetheless, such technology did from time to time fall into the wrong hands and tyrants preyed on their weaker neighbours. It was Thanu's responsibility to police such occurrences to maintain law and order.

KARAGAN

FIVE

The unexpected call came through from an unidentified source channelled directly at Thanu. It simply pleaded.

"Help, a friend needs you."

Mike called an emergency Council meeting and within minutes all representatives were present and seated around a large crystal table. Standing, Mike addressed the meeting.

"Gentlemen, ladies, we have received a call for help from a so called friend, a friend who once warned us in the past of impending danger and now seeks our assistance. We are at this moment following up on that call's origin and will know shortly who or what our friend is and where he or she comes from. I need everyone in place on immediate standby, ready to go within 3 hours. I must emphasis caution, so those of you who are responsible for Thanu's defences in our absence, be alert and vigilant for subtle approaches to breach our security. Games of cat and mouse are played upon the emotions of goodwill, so consider this as a possible incoming attack situation and stand by your stations no matter what."

The table's transparency took on a bluish shade indicating a message coming through and Mike placed his hand on it.

"Call traced to a world situated in the thirteenth quadrant, named Karagan. Looks like a sister planet of Earth."

Mike activated the Portal and Moti on board one of the Warrior Drones was channelled to Karagan. Everyone waited as the minutes ticked by, then finally.

"We find no apparent life at all which is very strange, something definitely suspicious here and advise foregoing detailed scanning and suggest sending in attack force without further delay. Suspect negative forces at work here, planet feels too eerie." Moti's thought transmission ended.

"Come back in Moti. Check your tail, we don't want unwanted hitch-hikers." Ordered Mike.

"Affirmative." The response.

Thanu, the Mother Drone's voice echoed in their minds, Moti has picked up a tail, will eradicate."

Penagee smiled.

"Gentlemen, ladies, it looks as if our so-called friend has worms feeding from it. I suggest this meeting be adjourned and sound general quarters. Moti is coming in with a tail which means someone wants access to Thanu and is using Moti's slipstream to try it. The Mother is taking care of our little inquisitive adventurer, so before Moti comes in we go on full alert."

Hands touched the table and messages were transmitted across Thanu. The nation was ordered on immediate full alert. Mike closed the meeting and everyone moved to take up tactical positions. Just outside Thanu's universe Mike teleported the Drone out of the Portal leaving Moti inside. Moments later there was a slight tremble in the Council Room then Moti appeared, at which a white light emanating from the crystal table passed right through him and into the opened Gateway. Whatever was behind Moti would have ceased to exist. An invisible shadow was hurtled back at Karagan and impacted into the place from which it originated like a self-multiplying atom bomb. The table blinked and all three placed their hands onto it. Mother reported.

"Interesting probe made up of an energy source controlled from Karagan. Whatever or whoever sent the probe is at this moment very sorry they did so. If you will observe."

With that a hologram type image of the planet Karagan appeared over the table on which could be seen massive explosions chain-reacting around it. Mother's voice concluded,

"It's safe to go down there now and pick up the pieces. However, you need to attack primary targets. I will give co-ordinates on approach. Have your captains be prepared for strong resistance and a fairly long campaign."

Mike sent out his orders and four hours later the Regiments assembled with their contingents of Drones and support personnel. Twenty thousand combat troops, each armed with Sai's made from crystal. When held in a soldier's hands, each Sai was capable of unleashing pure white beams of destructive light, eliminating anything in their path. All wore dark blue crystal helmets completely encasing the wearer's head. Day or night, in whatever conditions of visibility, the troops were able to maintain a 360 degree view in normal, infra-red or heat-sensing mode. This meant the wearer could see in the darkest places and straight through walls. Their uniforms were moulded from a black matt crystal fibre-layered fabric totally encasing the entire body. A vast improvement on the original issue redesigned by Borz and proved to be highly effective in protecting a wearer against small-arms fire. A soldier could take a direct hit from any modern laser or ray gun and survive unscathed. Fully energy absorbent meant the suit could absorb tremendous amounts of energy, neutralize it or redirect it back at the originating source. It took some getting used to learning how to breathe the oxygen that the suit filtered out from even the worst of atmospheres. The suit's greatest attribute was its resistance to high levels of radiation.

Moti gave the order and captains carried out last minute inspections then formed up to wait.

Penagee and Anna came to see them off, saying their farewells, Mike activated the Portals. Immediately a white ball of light preceded them and twenty thousand troops hurtled through the opening onto Karagan in two separate groups. One up to the north, the other down to the south of the largest land mass on Karagan and landed under the cover of darkness, almost immediately meeting resistance. Mother fed in the co-ordinates and the assault began. The defenders fought like demons, but were up against an incredibly efficient and brutal opponent whose momentum, once started, was almost impossible to stop. The crystal helmets came into their own in this kind of situation and transmitted fields of vision of every Trooper on the ground so that not one person was isolated or suffered from a communications breakdown, everybody was able to see and be seen, plus hear each other at all times. Mike and Moti were the controllers and charted into the troop's minds the entire battle scenario so that everyone knew exactly what was going on and could move troops very effectively and speedily where and how they were needed before the enemy knew what hit them. Thanu's troops advanced on an enemy identified only as Humanoids, which posed an additional problem for Mike's forces on a one to one basis, but his troops soon got the message and actually preferred hand to hand combat until Mike reminded them that they were to complete their mission as quick as possible in order to secure the planet. He had to admit to himself though it was good to get into a scrap once again on a one-to-one basis. Moti passed on a message.

"Co-ordinates south side achieved, moving to the next grid sectors."

That's how it was for that first week. By now the enemy had dug in its heels and set up extremely strong defences. Persistent grid scanning enabled Mike to locate the enemy's command centres which he obliterated using the Drones. It was only the tip of the iceberg and his forces met with heavy resistance. Take no quarter, give no quarter. After a month of continuous battle, Mike and Moti re-grouped, took stock, then combined their forces and struck out eastwards where reports of the enemy massing for a counter-attack filtered in from the Drones. At a prearranged position the Matabele's split into small groups of 100 men apiece to cover a larger area and attacked their opponents with well-orchestrated guerrilla tactics, allowing them access into the very heart of the large enemy force, then delivered their fatal blows. Enemy casualties were massive with very few prisoners being taken. There seemed to be no question of surrender so battles were fought tooth and nail every millimetre of the way. Mike's forces suffered their limited casualties, but his losses were minor in comparison.

A further month of extreme combat elapsed until finally the enemy ground forces were forced into submission. Scanners continued to scan above and below ground and soon found the locations where the real residents of the planet were being held captive. Deep down in underground vaults, these poor people had been herded in their thousands and sealed off from above. Mother gave other co-ordinate locations and the scanners located more underground holding cells. Mike's forces concentrated their methodical grid by grid annihilation of enemy forces below ground in an attempt to save the hostages before they were possibly executed. Due to the nature of the underground holding cells it became apparent that a more radical offensive was required. Continent after continent was swept using the opposition's spacecraft to carry various groups of soldiers to various pinpointed locations from where they were able to collectively use their crystal weapons into one single destructive force with far greater effect. This enabled Mike to make better use of the Drones by deploying them as search and destroy units above ground to cover vast stretches of land very quickly. Thousands upon thousands of people had been interned underground and the primary concern was for their safety.

Mother was brought into the fight as time was running out, so she requested Mike to pull out all his troops and the Drones then sent in her avenging light which killed any living humanoid above ground. Like a cloud of death her tentacles encircled Karagan. The enemy never knew what hit them. She marked every holding cell and directed troops in to free the people of Karagan. Underground there were still remnant elements of the enemy who had to be eliminated and as a result each holding cell became another battlefield. Lives were lost in those confined spaces. There were no other alternatives. It took Mike and Moti eight months to clear the Humanoids off the planet and lost five thousand of his own troops in the process. Mother sought out and found the Humanoid control fleet way out in the cosmos and dealt them a fatal blow, sending them reeling for home completely demoralized. It had been a costly exercise and many lessons were subsequently learnt from it. One thing was for sure, Mike's need for sophisticated air support was a prerequisite, so he wasted no time in requesting Mother's co-operation. She obliged with only ten Warrior Drones, but twenty times more powerful and larger than the originals from Ridmon. The new Drones, with the remaining Regiment, scoured the planet, finding the odd isolated underground enemy groups which they destroyed. It took a total of two years to ferret out the Humanoids. The people of Karagan came back into the sunlight free once more, which prompted Mike to remove his troops off the planet. Karagan was not a warring nation, but a peaceful people. Humanoids had invaded this planet knowing full well its peoples were unable to offer any resistance. Like watchdogs Mike's forces orbited out in space within their Warrior Drones, watching as Karagan picked itself up and attempted to start its life over once again. A message was sent from the planet and intercepted by the Drones. It read.

"From the people of Karagan, we thank our friends and would like to arrange a meeting."

Mike replied, "No meetings, not at this time."

The voice responded.

"We understand and are very grateful, yet would be most happy if you were to accept a token of our sincerity which is of great significance to you."

"It is not necessary, you asked for help, we gave it willingly." Replied Mike.

A single space vessel took off from Karagan into inner space where some of the Drones were on it like a pack of wild dogs. The Drones scanned the vessel reporting,

"Two life forms on board, both female Thedrimonians."

"Image." Ordered Mike, whose curiosity was more than aroused?

An image appeared and to Mike's dismay he saw the faces of Tara and a girl child.

"Identification authenticated." the Drone reported.

Mike teleported aboard the vessel and when Tara saw him she flung herself into his arms, weeping with joy. Taking her beautiful face in his hands he asked her.

"How?"

Tara wiped the tears from her eyes with the back of her hand and answered,

"Just before Thedrah was destroyed many of us were teleported to Karagan. There was not enough time so, as you know, everyone else died. Those that did survive have lived here on Karagan hoping for the day you would find and fetch us."

Mike's mind raced and he probed Tara's mind and the verification was there. He held her tight and looked at the little girl standing shyly behind them. Then it hit him, she was Jane's child, the splitting image of her mother and Mike swept her up in his arms asking.

"What's your name?"

"Nina." The timid reply. Mike smiled, taking hold of Tara and teleported back to the Drone.

Opening communication.

"Karagan, as Commander of the Thanu Armed Forces I wish to extend my sincerest gratitude to you for your unselfish acts of saving the lives of many of our peoples and agree to meet with your representatives on Karagan in the presence of my people."

The message came back.

"Agreed, within the hour then, looking forward to meeting with you."

Mike teleported Moti aboard who, on seeing Tara, bodily lifted her up and they danced around like children at a funfair. Nina clung to Mike, not wanting to let him go, her little arms wrapped around his neck.

"Moti, we go on full alert just in case and maintain absolute security. We can't afford to take chances as this might be elaborate bait for a trap, if it is, you have your orders, destroy Karagan."

Moti nodded and teleported back to his Drone with Tara and Nina.

"You know what to do, Drone." Reconfirmed Mike.

"Yes, Master Mike."

"Good, then if all is in place we wait."

The Drone sent its coded communiqué to Thanu

"Master Mike teleporting down to Karagan to retrieve Thedrah survivors, could be trap. Request immediate class 1 security link activation."

Almost at once the link was activated and every City on Thanu channelled their thought energies through space into the Drone who amplified those energies, sending them down on to Karagan and the planet became encircled by an energy source which absorbed every detail of Karagan right down to its microbes, then tuned into the thought patterns of the Karagan peoples, monitored, analysed and probed. Within the hour every detail of Karagan was known to Thanu and Mike was given the go-ahead to teleport down to the location specified. Mike opened his mind and Thanu reached in and became one with him. This procedure had only been done once before. The down side was that he became a living, walking mega bomb. A pulsing bluish light emitted outwards from his body, which was sufficient warning to anyone with ulterior motives. He then teleported down to Karagan into a huge domed enclosure where thousands of Thedrimonians were assembled together with the Karagan Supreme Council consisting of ten men and a woman. Karagan were identical to their Earth counterparts in physical characteristics, but were by far more highly advanced. When Mike appeared there was a thunderous roar of applause yet the Karagan council, seeing Mike's countenance, knew full well its implications. Mike waited motionless until an uneasy silence settled on the crowd, then approached to where the Council were seated, bowed slightly and voiced his greeting.

"Members of the Karagan Council, Thanu greets you and thanks you for your act of kindness to these, her people."

The elderly Karagan woman member of the Council raised her hand in acknowledgement and replied.

"Welcome Thanu to Karagan and to you Mike, we extend our thanks for the lives of the Karagan people. You are probably wondering why the Humanoids put up such a fight?"

Mike remained quiet, allowing her to continue.

"Well, your people are the reason. They wanted your people in order to persuade you into giving them your technology. We, of course, could not stand by and watch that happen. Thanu's technology in the wrong hands would be disastrous for everyone in this quadrant."

The woman stood, walked over to Mike, continuing her narration.

"When the Humanoids landed, it was in force. We are not a warring nation and never have been, so consequently we could not defend ourselves against them. Your people here saved this Council from certain death. If it had not been for their prompt and effective actions, our lives would have been lost. Some of them died during the fighting, yet managed to hide us plus themselves from the Humanoids until you arrived."

She turned to face the crowd who slowly parted their ranks, allowing Frank and Borz to walk forward. In Mike's mind a message echoed.

"Identification confirmed, all are our people, no clones or mind controls."

"Activate teleportation now," confirmed Mike. The next instant all of the Thedrimonians were gone, leaving Mike alone with a very a surprised Council.

"Members of the Council, I regret this hasty and perhaps ill-mannered action, but our people come first above all else and their safety is paramount. As a token of our gratitude to you, we have activated a defensive mechanism around Karagan to protect you and your peoples from outside interference. Now you are able to go about your business and lives without the threat of another surprise attack. Please understand that we retain control of that defensive bridge as it entails sensitive technology we can't afford to divulge for our own security reasons."

The elderly woman smiled at Mike and answered.

"We understand all too well and thank you. There is just one other thing which we have saved for last and we understand that it is of a very personal nature for you, so if you will excuse us, we will take our leave and re-establish communication a week from today, if possible, to discuss mutual treaties and agreements between Karagan and Thanu."

With that, the Council left Mike standing alone in the domed enclosure. Moments ticked by, then the floor opened and slowly a table rose out from its hiding place with a person lying on it attached to what looked like life support systems. Mike's heart almost jumped out of his chest. It was Jane.

"Scan." He ordered.

Jane's tear-filled eyes watched her brother with mounting concern, recognizing the strange light emanating from him. Her body was broken and crippled. A miracle had saved her from the crushing forces of the explosion on Thedrah. She had been pulled from the brink of death just in time, but it had left her paralyzed from the neck down. Karagan doctors pieced her together again, giving her a life back and that of her unborn child. Both survived the ordeal, but the incident had left Jane dependant on machines to keep her alive for the rest of her life.

"Scan completed, damage extensive, but repairable. Subject will have to be incubated for procedure."

"Understood, stand by." Mike teleported Jane directly through a Portal into Thanu's medical centre where she was placed in a special incubator suspended in a liquid gel. The intricate healing and damage rebuilding began. Her body would be restored through ingenious cell and nerve fibre reproduction. It was a slow and highly successful process.

Mike stood alone on the Dome floor until a confirming message came through.

"All subjects relocated to Thanu, Karagan defences in place."

He was about to teleport out when a very old and frail looking woman hobbled into view.

"What's the hurry, young man?" Asked the woman.

Mike recognized her instantly as another Messenger and became cautious.

"I have responsibilities to attend to." He answered.

"So you are the mighty Mike as they call you here on Karagan and I must say I am impressed with your technology and sense of good neighbourliness. I have been watching you, young man, for a long time, since the time you first set foot on Ridmon with your two friends, Moti and that crazy old Bedouin, Ahmed."

"Who are you?" Demanded Mike, suddenly feeling uncomfortable.

"A friend." Ventured the response.

Mike studied her wrinkled face and realized it was she who had sent messages of warning, then later sent a plea for help.

"So friend, do you have a name?" He asked.

The old woman watched Mike for a while then answered.

"A Messenger like you."

Standing there in front of this frail old woman he felt awkward, knowing she probably read his mind as easily as if it were written down on a blackboard. He felt no threat coming from the woman and began to wonder where all this was leading when her crackling laugh broke the silence.

"I must say that little episode on the Reptilian Planet had you two boys hopping? Can't say I would have relished the gourmet delights on offer, not to my taste buds, but then you had no choice in the matter and as Protector Friend assured me, you two were more than capable of surviving. You certainly have come a long way since then although I don't agree with some of your methods, they do achieve the desired results at the end of the day."

Mike was now feeling more and more uneasy with the knowledge that this woman and Protector Friend were somehow involved with the chain of events over the past few years and he was about to speak when she silenced him with a gesturing hand. The air became disturbed and Mike tensed, ready for action. A white, bright shimmering light appeared, and then took form. Mike breathed a sigh of relief. Messenger against Messenger would not be advisable, as the results would be catastrophic. Protector Friend hovered above the ground. He smiled at Mike, then the next moment Moti appeared looking totally bewildered. Both men stood like two naughty little boys about to be reprimanded. The old woman shuffled forward and smiled.

"Easy boys, no need for the tension, relax and tell those Drones of yours to back off. No harm is coming to you."

"Not until you tell us what's going on here." Replied Mike.

"My, my, still so sceptical aren't you, Mike?"

"Well, you can't really blame us now, can you? After all the things we have been through we have the right to be sceptical." He answered.

"Enough!" Commanded Protector Friend.

"Listen up you two, Earth is heading for a disaster of gigantic proportions and there is nothing anyone is allowed to do about it. We have, however, been advised to relocate one third of every living thing on Earth to Karagan the moment a comet strikes it. We have been given an estimated two Earth years to prepare ourselves for the event and to have all the necessary infrastructures in place by that time, and gentlemen, one third means only from those areas judged to be most likely at risk of total extermination. We have three weeks' grace to prepare ourselves, at the end of which a meeting will be held here on Karagan to designate a task force. Until then, farewell friends."

Mike and Moti felt a sudden surge and found themselves back on the Drones heading for Thanu via a Portal. The Drones burst into Thanu's atmosphere and began offloading their tired and weary troops. Mike and Moti teleported into the Council chambers. After delivering their report to the gathered members Mike added.

"So gentlemen, ladies, we have three weeks to decide on our Task Force, then we return to Karagan for a full-scale project strategy. Moti and I will not be present at the meeting, but will be journeying to Planet Earth to conduct preliminary checks and balances. We return in a fortnight from tomorrow accompanied by two other Universal representatives to a joint sitting of the Thanu and Karagan Councils. So if there is nothing more, I would like some much deserved time with my family prior to departure. Over the next 24 hours I will only be available in cases of extreme emergency. Thank you."

The room cleared leaving Mike, Moti and Penagee alone.

"How is she?" Asked Mike.

"She will be fine, it takes time, but she will walk again and lead a normal life with the exception that she will never be able to bear more children. Her daughter Nina is really a cute little thing and our children love her to bits already."

Turning to Moti, Mike smiled and said, "It is time the Hawk went to his nest." Moti laughed, replying.

"Don't look for me, I am gone." With that he teleported out.

Penagee got to her feet and came around the table and fell into Mike's arms hungrily, seeking his body warmth. He teleported Penagee out to his favourite secluded place amongst the trees. During the course of that 24 hour reprieve Mike was in and out of the Medical Centre, checking in on Jane and watching his sister's progress with keen interest. He spoke to her through her mind and would tell her how things were doing with little Nina and everyone else. Ana-Maria also came in to be with her friend and sit quietly next to the incubator to play Brazilian music on a Thanuian guitar. She had a lovely, soothing singing voice. Mike's family of four children had grown. The twins were in their teens, Ridmon was five and little Gnee was four years old and a little lady, who had taken it upon herself to be Nina's friend and protector. Mike had always been close to his children and they enjoyed his company immensely. The twins were very much like their mother, sensitive and gentle, not like Mike at all. He did feel a little remorse over that, but soon put it out of his mind. Ridmon was Mike's double and he copied his father right down to the body language. Penagee would never be too lonely during Mike's absences with Ridmon around to remind her of him. He was a tough child and gave as much as he got at school, which sometimes was a lot more than the other children bargained for. Parents and teachers complaints would force Penagee to reprimand her child whose eyes would twinkle in response saying.

"Just like Dada taught me."

Also during those hours Anna fell pregnant with her first child and Frank met Zara. Borz spent most of his spare time in the library studying up on the latest technologies and getting used to Thanu's unique systems. As for the rest of the survivors, they were made to feel at home and everybody rallied to their aid with advice and help. That evening Mike called a meeting with all his old surviving friends in a warm restaurant overlooking a forest below.

Once everyone had gathered, he stood up with a beer in one hand and announced.

"Friends, we welcome you to Thanu and hope this incredible world has not confused you too much. We are very glad to have you with us because for some, it is not the time to bring up sad memories, we won't delve into that, we are here to have a party and that's just what we are going to do. If Frank would be so kind as to call up his new friend to join us, we can get this show on the road."

Frank flushed protesting.

"Is nothing sacred on this planet?" Then called Zara from a console who appeared a few minutes later to wolf whistles from the men in the group. She was a gorgeous blonde with bright blue eyes, a human.

"Now, now guys, leave the poor lady alone will you?" Demanded Penagee, at which everyone laughed. Zara sat down next to Frank and it was obvious from the way their bodies sought each other out that romance was in full swing. It took a few beers before the mood began to relax and the group became more jovial. Borz let his hair down, it had been a long time since he had tasted good beer and he was going to make the most of it. When Frank got up to go and relieve himself, Mike joined him. When out of earshot from the rest of the group, Mike gently said.

"Sorry about your family Frank, sorry we could not have been there for you sooner."

Frank looked deep into Mike's eyes.

"Yep, I miss them terribly and don't blame yourself; there just was not enough time."

There followed a few moments' silence between them then Mike remarked.

"We have a mission to planet Earth and I would like you to be on it."

"Yes, I would like that very much."

"Bring Zara with you, Frank."

"Thanks," He replied.

Mike returned to the group grabbing another beer on route and dived into the party with gusto. An hour later he teleported them all into the Regiment's Barracks where a party was already in full swing. The party ended the next morning with most of the participants nursing hangovers and many still lying sprawled out on the floor. So much for military discipline, no one cared as Mike had given them a week off. It was fall down time. Mike gathered together a nucleus of twenty prominent scientists, men and women, into the council chamber and introduced Frank.

"Some of you will remember Frank, others will not, so for the benefit of all, Frank is the Regiment's Adjutant. Time is short. We need admin and logistics on this mission for which Frank is more than qualified. If any of you have any objections, please voice them now and let's get everything out into the open before we leave this room."

He looked at all the faces, no one objected and time would prove to them Frank's indispensable worth.

"Right, now that is cleared away, I suggest we get down to business. Our mission is a non-aggressive one, yet calls for cold, clinical selection. We have to remain impartial at all times; this must be understood from the outset. Planet Earth is our target and the aim of our mission is to select a third of all living things on that planet for transportation and relocation to Karagan at an appointed time. It is a massive undertaking and one which we could never do alone in spite of our technology. Accompanying us on this mission will be twenty scientists, plus many other biologists, zoologists, botanists, Marine biologists, and medical research staff whose job it will be to determine, with the help of the Drones, the nearest possible site the comet will strike Earth. Our job will be to determine what life forms exist in those areas and to prepare our evacuation strategy on very precise and exact timing. To help us in this endeavour we shall have two other Messengers to assist us. I need not remind you we are possibly looking at over two billion people, thousands of species of bird, animal, reptile, fish and mammal. For those of you not aware, Earth has supposedly experienced a similar incident, minor by comparison, during which the name Noah's Ark was given to the vessel that carried and saved a family and many creatures of the wild. For purposes of this mission it shall be code-named Operation Karajan's Ark. Timing will be of utmost importance, so your allotted tasks need to be synchronized to the last second if this mission is to succeed. To transport these massive numbers, four Portals will be opened directly onto Karagan through which everyone and everything will be teleported into their respective habitats. Karagan is at this moment making the necessary preparations which should be completed within the time scale allotted. We have two Earth years to set this whole thing up. I need not remind you of the significance of this mission and to answer your question, why only a third? Powers greater than ours have set the rules by which we have to play."

Frank lifted his hand indicating a question.

"Yes, Frank?" Asked Mike.

"Level with us on this one Mike, you are asking a tall order and I for one would like to know why?"

"All I am able to tell you at this stage is that the powers that be know of a comet heading for Earth on an impact course and do not want anyone to interfere, but have allowed us the option of lifting a third just before the impact. They have their reasons and ours is not to question, but to do and do to our utmost abilities."

A silence hung over the room as each person began to understand the complexity of their task and the sheer numbers involved. One scientist whistled out loud and everybody nodded in agreement. Mike touched the table and a holographic image of Earth appeared. All eyes focused on the simulation of a comet as it came into the picture and impacted on the model Earth, sending shock waves and ripples as if the real thing. All the people in the room watched in awed fascination at the reality of it all. Massive tidal waves washed over the continents and the Earth rocked out of its orbit by a margin of two degrees, tilted on its axis, shifting its poles and melting the polar caps. Islands and continents disappeared under billions of tons of water. Volcanic eruptions of gigantic proportions and earthquakes added to the planet's agony. Clouds of ash and debris filled the skies, blocking out the sun. Through all the horrific damages it was a wonder that the entire population of Earth was not destroyed.

"As you can see, our task is an immense one." Commented Mike.

"Shyte." Was all that Frank could utter.

"Well, one thing is for sure, we are going to be very busy men and women for the next two years and Mike is right. From what we have just seen, we will have only one shot at this, so we had better get it right the first time. No second chances." Exclaimed Moti.

One of the scientists asked.

"How are we going to teleport so many things through the Gates at once?"

"The plan is to blanket our designated areas a few hours before impact with generated energies through four Mother Drones via Thanu, which will give us the leeway we need for the actual teleportation into much enlarged Portals. It also leaves us open for intrusion from the elements we don't need, so split-second timing is critical."

Mike touched the table again and the hologram reappeared.

"We will repeat this exercise until everyone is familiar with the sequence of events and familiarized themselves with which land masses and which seas are affected by the simulation. We will now do our preliminary checks and balances on Earth. For the next twelve hours the hologram worked repeatedly until everyone knew their designated areas then the meeting was adjourned with orders to regroup at 16.00 hrs the next day with full contingents of personnel and effects. Moti and Frank went down to the central lounge for a beer while Mike went to the Medical Centre to check on Jane. He sat down watching her naked body immersed in the gel and marvelled at the sciences that were able to repair bodies in this way and thought back to his own experience in Protector Friend and thanked his lucky stars. The Karagan doctors had stabilized Jane's condition and so the repair work needed would not take that long to accomplish. He was sitting there thinking things over when Jane's voice inside his mind asked.

"Is Nina alright?"

"Yes, she's fine and don't worry, she's in good hands. Just get well. OK?" He replied.

"Thanks Mike, kind of funny you sitting there watching me like this."

"Not funny at all. I will be gone for a week, so don't worry. I promise to bring you back a present. Now get some rest."

"See you then Mike."

"Bye for now." Mike teleported to Penagee and the children.

Just before 16.00 hrs on the following day he checked in on Jane once again. A critical part of the process was being introduced, the re-joining of torn nerve tissues in her spine which called for absolute immobilization. At the assembly point, three thousand people were gathered. Operation

Karagan Ark had begun and four Drones positioned themselves for boarding. Frank came up to Mike confirming everything was in place to which Mike gave the order.

"Mount up." Moti laughed out loud, then muttered.

"Cowboys, he thinks we are cowboys or something."

Within two hours, four Drones hung invisible within Earth's atmosphere. Last minute instructions from the various group Commanders and the Drones relocated to their allotted positions at various points of the globe where the anticipated catastrophe was to occur. For two weeks the scientists worked around the clock making their initial selections and calculations while Mike and the remainder of his contingent worked out their strategies and timings and rehearsed repeatedly. Test trial runs were set up to ensure that all the areas were adequately covered. By the end of the second week the selections had been made and co-ordinates fixed. It was agreed other trips were necessary every three months for the first year to recheck facts and figures and thereafter every month until a month before impact was scheduled, when a 24 hour around the clock surveillance and monitoring would be conducted for last minute adjustments. As an incentive for their hard work, Mike teleported his 3,000 strong team down onto Earth in various groups. The Trafodj were teleported into Brazil for a night of Rio carnival festivities. No one would think to question their skin and hair colour, nor their method of dress. Moti, Anna and a number of Humans teleported into Jerusalem, Israel and the remainder of the Thedrimonians into Acapulco, Mexico, wearing dark brown contact lenses to hide their green eyes. Frank and a large group of others were teleported into Miami, Florida, Frank's home town, to have some fun in the sun. Mike teleported himself and Tara into a deep, dark cave at the base of Cheroma Kadoma in Zimbabwe where an old Matabele Sangoma sat chanting into a small fire.

"Greetings, Amos," he gently whispered so as not to startle the old man.

"Ah! The Lion returns with a stranger from another world." The knowing reply.

Mike squatted down next to the fire and extended his hands to catch some of its heat,

While Tara stood behind him, wide-eyed and watchful.

"How fares the Sangoma these days?" Questioned Mike.

"Not well, not well. Troubling times are coming and many will die."

"Yes we know, that is why we are here."

The old man's eyes flashed and he studied Mike's face.

"I see the Lion has seen many strange things and carries a heavy burden on his shoulders and I am thankful you returned me to this place as I could not live in your world. This is my place where I will die in peace of mind."

"Yes, I understand you Amos and have come to say goodbye for we shall not meet again."

"This old man will not leave the cave of his ancestors, but will be buried alongside them when the mountain falls. He does not wish it any other way. Go in peace, son of this Earth, son of the Matabele and do what the Great Enkosi in the heavens bids you. My heart is glad you have come to visit me this last time, now go, go."

"Shala gashle, Baba." Whispered Mike.

"Hamba gashle, Enkosi." Answered the old Sangoma bending his head down so that Mike could not see the sadness in his eyes.

Mike teleported deep into the Zimbabwean bush and found what he was looking for. Two perfectly preserved ancient Zimbabwe Bird carvings in soapstone, standing a metre high apiece, the same bird that is depicted on the Zimbabwean national flag. Sending the two carvings straight to Thanu through the Gate into his living room, Mike teleported with Tara to Paradise Island, also known as Santa Carolina, off the coast of Mozambique. The island was once, many years ago, a penitentiary, until an outbreak of typhus almost wiped out the garrison and prisoners alike. Many years later it had boasted a hotel until the Frelimo Regime converted it into a military base and secure zone for its President Samora Michael. Now it lay deserted, its buildings in ruin. Mike and Tara spent part of the day basking in the sun and enjoying the quiet solitude and undisturbed peace and tranquillity. In the late afternoon Mike teleported to the Drakensberg mountains in South Africa where they ate a light supper in a small mountain hotel and savoured the good wines. It was time to return, so Mike took a last look around, then teleported back to the Drones. With him he brought some bottles of wine for Jane, the kind she liked from the Cape wine lands. A very happy group of people passed through the Gate into Thanu and many continued their festivities way into the next day.

Three days later Jane emerged from her cocoon of gel into Mike's welcoming arms and stood in his embrace for long moments until little Nina demanded her mother's attention and Mike left the room a very happy man. Jane was fine and able to walk once again, to lead a normal life. Thanu returned to normal with the daily comings and goings and Mike spent most of his time in heavy training, tuning his body and mind alone out in the trees where he felt most comfortable. Penagee was bogged down by her administrative duties and endless meetings, which gave her little or no time to spend with Mike or the children. She

rarely went into the forest with Mike these days and so it
appeared that the two had become a normal, dull married
couple, each doing their own thing. Frank had his hands
full what with his own responsibilities and with Zara.
Moti became the attentive expectant father and most of
his time, apart from his allocated duties, revolved around
Anna. After two months of this Mike needed a distraction.
One day, whilst sitting under the daily waterfall routine and
meditation session, Tara approached and watched him until
he had finished. Mike sensed her presence and felt her eyes
on him. Without turning he asked,

"Do you want to try this?"

Tara laughed. "You must be joking."

"So you came here to ask me if an unscheduled visit back
to Earth would be possible."

"Cut that out Mike, it makes me nervous the way you
read people's minds."

"Oh! Do you or don't you want to go?"

"Yes, of course I do." She eagerly replied.

"OK, I will see what I can do."

"Thanks." She jogged off to finish her run.

Mike stood there watching her go and smiled to himself.
The old Sangoma had frightened the wits out of her and Tara
didn't frighten easily. Back in his apartment Mike looked
around the silent rooms and for the first time in many years
felt emptiness inside. His life had been one of adventure and
excitement every step of the way and Penagee had filled a great
part of that life. Then the children, he loved them dearly,
but this life of high technology sometimes got to one and a
person yearned sometimes for the primitive ways where life
had another form of challenge which depended on instincts
for survival. The experience on Reptilia had affected both

him and Moti in a strange way. The raw beast of man had surfaced and it was hard to find reconciliation with oneself thereafter within an existence such as that on Thanu where everything was clinical and controlled. Mike's brand of expertise was not needed on Thanu anymore, which put him in a rather precarious position. In spite of herself, Penagee did not approve of his primitive methods and, although he knew she loved him, something had come between them and he guessed it was Zorak. Sitting on the balcony looking down across the valley, an idea formed in his mind. He would take a year's extended leave to rejuvenate himself. Whether it was a mid-life crisis or not he did not know, but what he needed was some hard-hitting action and adventure to pit his wits and skills against. The question was where and what would the effects be to his relationship with Penagee. Mike was a soldier, expert in the art of war, while on Thanu his talents were not needed. The likes of him would always be needed to carry out certain tasks, but when those tasks became few and far between it did something to a man, leaving him with a sense of unfulfilled self-achievement and loss of worth. He touched the command Pad and sent a message to Tara and the Reptilian Commander to meet him at the waterfall later that day. The waterfall was the only place on Thanu where communication and thought transmission was for some reason distorted. He had stumbled across this phenomenon on Thanu some time back and kept quiet about it as it did have tactical potential. Next, he teleported into the Council Chambers to find Penagee in deep discussion with a few of the scientists over the planned relocation programme on Karagan.

"Excuse the intrusion, but could I have a word with you, Penagee, in private?"

Penagee excused herself from the room and Mike teleported them into the trees. Sitting there, Penagee watched Mike's face and knew he was restless again. She had never forgiven him for his treatment of her brother. In spite of everything and to top it all she had unwittingly agreed to him using Zorak to help Mother Drone, not realizing it would be the last time she would ever see her brother again. In a way she was to blame for the rift between them, but she needed time to come to trust him again. The times that Mike was absent from Thanu, for her, were a relief. She loved him, this she could not deny, but lately his whole being seemed to irritate her no end. They needed time apart to sort themselves out and that was not good for the children and she knew it. Penagee felt cheated and betrayed and took it out on Mike in subtle ways.

Mike took Penagee's hand in his and gazed long and hard into her eyes. She steeled herself, not allowing him to read what lay behind.

"I am going away for a while as I think it's best for both of us."

Penagee simply nodded, concealing the ache in her heart and suppressing the anger that threatened to well up from within her.

"When?" She asked, returning his gaze.

Mike leaned forward and kissed her hard on the lips and was gone. Penagee sat there in the trees with an overwhelming sense of loss, wrestling with her feelings. She was losing Mike and it hurt terribly, but her anger and stubbornness did not waver. Teleporting herself back to the Council Chamber she closed the meeting, then sought out her children and wept bitterly. Mike reappeared at the waterfall to find Mis, the Reptilian Commander, and Tara already there. He addressed Mis directly,

"Mis, I will be needing ten of your people, five couples, to come with me for a year's extended leave. It is purely voluntary, so ask around."

The Reptilian eyed Mike and his instincts told him that there was a fight to be had which would break the boredom of Thanu and his mind was already made up. Mis pointed at Tara and asked,

"What about her?"

Mike looked directly at Tara and replied.

"She is coming as my concubine."

Mis rolled his eyes and hissed loudly. Tara froze and went numb, not able to look Mike in the eye and Mis hissed even louder.

"You have an hour, Mis, in full battle dress and armed."

"Now we are talking."

Mis was gone along the activated Gate, leaving Tara standing with head bowed, feeling extremely uncomfortable. Mike came up to her and Tara's knees went weak on her. Mike gently lifted her chin and looked into her eyes.

"Any objections?" He challenged.

"None." Was all she could whisper?

Mike stepped back and held her at arm's length.

"Go collect your things, think about it on the way, if you still want to come with me, be back here within the hour."

The incident left her shaking inside and when Mike touched her she thought her heart would explode in her chest. It was all wrong and she knew it, but to spend time with him alone was worth the risk, even if at the end of the day she knew it would end. She accepted that. An hour later the group gathered in the water close to the waterfall and then Mike teleported his small army out through a Portal down to Earth. In Penagee's study the console blinked. She acknowledged.

"Penagee here, report."

"Unidentified ripples, suspect Thanu residents activated Gate."

Penagee quickly responded.

"Run status check on all inhabitants in this City and cross reference."

Within moments the report came back.

"No known references, unidentified not from Thanu."

Penagee sat back in her chair and wondered what Mike was up to. If anything, it was a certainty he was out looking for trouble and a fight, but who was he taking with him.

"Report Armlet Status subject Mike."

A few more moments and the voice cautioned.

"No status, armlet inactive."

"Thank you, that's all." She ended the communication.

That's as far as it would go because if Mike did not want anyone to find him no one would. He was a master at this game and knew all the tricks and not even Penagee with all her technology would find him unless he wanted to be found. Who were the others that was the question and so Penagee went about the next few days checking out all Mike's known friends and none of them knew anything. Jane was the last resort and so she found the woman playing with her daughter in the park and asked her a direct question.

"Jane, where's Mike?"

Jane looked at Penagee and shook her head.

"I don't know."

Penagee watched her and could see she was telling the truth, but she had to confront this woman on another issue and now was as good a time as any.

"You and Mike are very close and share secrets with one another, am I not right?"

Anger flashed in Jane's eyes and she turned on Penagee.

"Listen you, whatever my brother and I have between us is our concern and none of your damn business."

Penagee saw the fire in Jane's eyes and her own anger erupted.

"Where has your brother gone and who is with him?"

Jane slapped her hard across the face with enough force to send Penagee reeling, then she was on her like a cat.

"You stuffed up tart, there are some things you don't know and probably would not understand. My brother loves you and whatever happened to Zorak, happened. Maybe it was a mistake, yes! You feel betrayed and cheated and perhaps a little defiled, well, wake up and smell the roses, you are not so perfect yourself and you are going to lose him for sure and I, his sister, is all he has got in this perfect garden of Eden of yours. I lost a husband on Thedrah, a man I loved with all my heart and a man who knew me and my shortcomings. But I tell you here and now, you will leave my brother and I will be there to pick up his emotional pieces and there is nothing, nothing I will not do to hold those pieces together, even if it means trying to kill you."

Jane got off Penagee, swooped Nina into her arms and left, leaving Penagee fuming with rage. Sometime later Penagee knocked on Jane's door and when the door opened Penagee pleaded.

"Don't shut the door, please, we need to talk."

Jane saw the sincerity in her eyes and allowed her in. They both sat down and Penagee asked.

"Forgive me, in my selfishness I had forgotten your own personal loss.

Jane sat silent for a moment then replied.

"One thing I do know is that Mike loves you very much. But you are going to leave him aren't you?"

Penagee suddenly fell silent. Jane had hit a sore spot alright. Jane pursued her advantage.

"Admit it, Mike's an animal of the wild and you prefer the more cultured type of person to fit in with your life as it stands now."

A knock on the door interrupted Penagee before she could reply and Jane got up to see who it was. Opening the door Zara walked through and hugged Nina. Penagee saw her chance and took it. Excusing herself, she left the room. Jane had been right. Her very perceptive discovery of the truth made Penagee realize that at this time of her life she needed a more cultured and sensitive relationship and one that meant her loved one was home every night and not off on some murderous mission somewhere for months on end. It was not good for her or the children either. Mike could no longer fulfil her emotional security and right now she needed that badly. She needed to make the break.

Mike and the eleven Thanuians re-appeared into the dark jungles of Colombia, immediately melting into the undergrowth. All was silent, all was still. For half an hour no one moved. Mike scanned the undergrowth for signs of life and picked up only animal movements. His senses were fine-tuned and alert. He scanned the trees, nothing. For a kilometre nothing showed, no Human, so he ordered stand down, but no noise. The five pairs of Reptilians were happy and the thought of action heightened their natural blood craving. Mike turned to Tara and smiled in the dark and pulled her tense body closer to his for comfort. She smelled good, which was a problem in the jungle. Somebody could sniff her out. He passed the order; sleep in turns, two awake every two hours until 04.30 move out time, he would take the last watch. The night passed without incident, Tara cradled in his arms. At 02.00 hrs. Mike took his watch, scanning further out and located what he was looking for about 20kms south of their position. A drug trafficker's hideout with fifty armed men in it and a stash of cocaine ready for transport. 04.30 wakeup call and the group made their way south through the tree tops, Mike carrying Tara on his back like a baby ape. He had trained the Reptilians well and they had adapted to the trees with ease. The going was good and before long they were within range of their target when Mike called a halt in order to scan ahead. There were guards posted up in the trees about 100 metres from the camp, armed with M16 automatic rifles. There was one other piece of equipment Mike noticed, night vision glasses. No problem, these guys were going to wish they had never sold cocaine to innocent, unsuspecting children. Tara clung to Mike, breathing in the closeness of him and feeling the sheer power of those muscles and her body ached, hungered for him like a wild animal.

"Whatever goes down Tara, you hang on." Mike whispered.

He gave the positions and the Reptiles moved in silently, stealthily, with cold-blooded efficiency. Four Colombian guards died, ripped to shreds, still hanging from their securing belts and not knowing what had hit them. Mike's attack force slithered down the trees and crept through the undergrowth into the middle of the camp where all hell broke loose as the Sai's delivered their beams of death. Within seconds the whole camp was ablaze, destroying the cocaine cache. Mike retreated with his army back deep into the jungle and located another base to the east. He could teleport anywhere, but then the hunt would lose its appeal. There had to be the stalking, then the kill to make it worth the while for the Reptilians. For months they ranged through the jungles and after each attack the cocaine camps were additionally fortified and each time Mike hit them harder, until the message got through. It was not safe in the jungles, someone had a personal vendetta against the drug lords and business was being very negatively affected by it. No one could volunteer information because no one knew who or what it was that had destroyed the camps. The drug lords united their forces and spent millions of dollars on sophisticated armaments and defences, yet still the cocaine was not getting through. American spy satellites tracked from outer space, trying to pin-point this phenomenon that was achieving more results than the Drug Enforcing Agency's squads and the Pentagon's curiosity was aroused. Agents were sent into the area to infiltrate the gangs and they too suffered the consequences. It was impossible to achieve such success unless a whole army was employed to do the task, yet the satellites could detect nothing, nothing at all. Like an invisible killing machine Mike methodically and systematically eliminated camp after camp and the anguished cry for help went out from Colombia's president.

The Pentagon sent in its troops to investigate. What they found caused ripples of fear and the autopsies conducted on the bodies extracted from those camps painted a horrific picture. Mike was undeterred and continued to strike, even in the cities where no drug lord was safe. Cocaine trafficking came to a sudden halt with dire consequences to the drug networks. Many heads rolled. American and Colombian troops searched in vain, combing the jungles on foot, from the air and from space with the same results, nothing. The Pentagon was alarmed. By now it had become apparent whatever it was out there was not from planet Earth. Then in one act of ultimate defiance, Mike took out the drug lords in their fortified stockades and fortresses across Colombia. To add insult to injury, he dumped the bodies at the front gates of the US embassy in Bogotá, then re-located into neighbouring Peru and promptly decimated their drug cartels. The news from Peru was received by the Pentagon with mounting concern. Increased surveillance and troop movements were deployed in those areas to attempt to isolate the threat. Mike hit Panama. By now the news headlines were causing panic. Thousands of troops were flown in, but were unable to halt Mike's personal vendetta. Tara had become one of the group and did what was expected of her with unflinching and unerring effect. By night she lay with Mike and by day she killed. Her body became lithe, supple and hardened, a panther of the jungle. Mike refined his team into absolute terrors on two legs and left his trade mark wherever he went. They earned the reputation of Muerto Preto, Black Death, and all over the world the news media proclaimed,

"No drug baron is safe. It seems that somewhere out there is an unseen force believed not to be from this planet, wreaking havoc on an unprecedented scale throughout the drug trafficking world and the killings continue unabated. United States Home Office refuses to comment as more troops are sent in."

Far away in a dark cave, an old Sangoma chuckled,

"The white Matabele is showing his fangs."

The entire South American drug route was smashed within the space of six months, in spite of the area swarming with troops and satellite surveillance, Mike's group remained undetected. He relocated to the Far East, into the Myanmar jungles and once again struck with frightening effect. The world was perplexed and speculation ran rife as to who or what was responsible for taking out the drug lords and their entire infrastructures. It took three months for Mike to clean out the Myanmar, Malaya and Thailand opium dealers. He hit the big boys, destroyed their crops and Asia trembled. By now the world was paying attention and decided that it was time to concentrate all their resources against this unseen angel of Death. Not because of the drugs, but because whoever it was, was as the newspapers reported.

"In contravention of International Law and committing murder most foul, irrespective whether the offending parties were guilty or not."

Mike called a temporary halt to his activities as a ruse and took a well-deserved break. He teleported the Reptilians far out into space to a planet similar to Reptilia, then he and Tara teleported into South Africa where he intended to backpack along the beautiful Garden Route. He timed it well. Thanu recalled the Drones for their new upgrades and checks in preparation for "Operation Karajan's Ark".

Stopping off firstly in the City of Johannesburg to equip themselves with the latest hiking gear, Mike and Tara boarded a bus destined for the small coastal town of Knysna and, on arrival, booked into a very pleasant hotel situated at the famous "Heads" for a few days. Acting normal after months of living and killing like animals of prey in the jungles was not easy and frequently they both caused a stir when momentarily forgetting themselves in public. The couple wined and dined, toured the town, visited the sites, pub-crawled and had a very pleasant few days. Every evening under cover of darkness Mike and Tara teleported deep into the Knysna forest with its majestic stinkwood and yellowwood trees to train hard. As far as anyone was concerned, they were a newlywed couple on honeymoon. On the fourth day Mike booked out of the hotel and the two hitch-hiked to the town of George, some 60kms away, then headed off into the Outeniqua mountains with their backpacks full for the eight day hike which would bring them back to Knysna. The scenery was breath-taking and each nightly stop at a log cabin, constructed at a strategic location overlooking panoramic view points, was well worth the effort. The two were fortunate to be the only ones on the hike, which suited them fine. For those eight days the tensions of the past months faded into the simplistic harmony of their surroundings. At the end of the trail, back in Knysna, Mike teleported to a place further up the north coast called Nature's Valley where the Tsitsikama Hiking Trail began and for the following five days they walked the forested mountain trails, ending up at the Storm's River Bridge. Trail end. This part of South Africa is very picturesque, with the sea on the one side and mountains on the other, with pine trees and natural indigenous forests covering the landscape. For those who liked the outdoors it was the place to be.

The two ambled down along mountain trails following the Storm's River gorge to the sea where a holiday resort was been built out of natural timber logs, making it a very pleasant addition to the backdrop of trees. Here they spent a few days relaxing, before walking the Otter Trail back to Nature's Valley. Tara loved it there and spent many hours alone in the forests. Living and breathing in the same confines of jungle space with a bunch of Reptilians was not for the faint-hearted, especially a woman. It had taken Tara a while to accustom herself to that fact. Her feminine side had been sorely neglected, having to co-exist with a mad bunch of killers from outer space. Mike was constantly vigilant and protected her moments of hard fought-for privacy and never questioned her nightly separation to sleep away from the group. So the two found ways to relax during the daylight hours away from each other and by night came together for hard training sessions. On the last day of their stay at the Storms River Resort Tara asked him.

"I see everybody pays for things around here and you just sign a piece of paper?"

Mike laughed and replied.

"That's because whatever we eat or drink is charged to my account which, when we leave, I settle in full with cash."

"That's the point, where do you get the cash?"

"Ah, trade secret."

She was silent for a while then asked.

"You know that I have a sister, don't you?"

"Yes of course." Answered Mike.

"Would you mind her being here with us?"

Mike considered the question for long moments then replied.

"Come, let's take a walk into the forest, perhaps it will be easier for you."

With that they both wandered off into the thick pine trees amongst the tree ferns and found a secluded spot where Mike turned to Tara saying.

"Let her out."

Tara almost fainted. He knew her secret. Of course, how stupid she had been to think she could hide it from him, so she asked him.

"How long have you known?"

"Since you first came to Ridmon." Was the reply.

Tara was dumbfounded, not knowing what to say, so released her sister. A perfect duplicate of Tara emerged out of her body totally naked. Mike stepped back and observed this phenomenon. Mara stood before him, an exact replica down to the last detail, a perfect copy. These were two freaks of Nature, the ultimate Siamese twins. Incredible was the only way to describe it. The two kept their secret so well hidden that it was only by chance that Mike had stumbled on to it on Ridmon, otherwise they would never have been detected. He kept their secret, knowing its advantage was indispensable and would one day come in handy. The two women embraced and Mike said.

"Come on, you two, let's get some lunch"

With that Tara handed Mara a body stocking to change into. At the restaurant they caused quite a sensation. Mara was still dressed in her Thanu body stocking. For the rest of that afternoon the trio swam and sunbathed. As the shadows of evening crept in, Mike built a fire and did what everyone else in the resort favoured doing, barbecuing and drinking beers. The women could not eat meat, so stuck to a vegetarian diet, while Mike dived into some healthy sized T-bone steaks with relish. One thing about the twins, whatever happened to the one happened to the other and Tara's physical development over the months duplicated itself in Mara. Mike shook his head and laughed at their antics after a few beers began to take its effect on them. The moon rose into the night sky, illuminating the millions of stars and all around the resort's enclosure the mood was relaxed and peaceful.

Bright and early the next day Mike settled their account with the resort manager and made preparations for the hike. When he got back to the cabin the two girls were still sound asleep, so he quickly teleported himself into a shop in Johannesburg and collected another set of hiking gear for Mara and a few other odds and ends, carefully noted the items on a piece of paper and left cash in payment, then returned to the cabin in time to catch the awakening Tara, who stretched lazily and yawned while watching Mike gather their things. It was maddening for her to lie alone high up in dark trees every night knowing Mike was close by and could not cuddle up to him for warmth or comfort. She had fallen madly in love with him over these last months, so much so that it hurt. The thought of being away from him was unthinkable, so she tolerated the brutality of their recent existence and fought to maintain her place in the group next to the man she loved. Tara was infinitely patient, she knew her day would come. Her instincts had never been wrong. Her thoughts were interrupted by Mara's nudge and knowing smile. After a hearty breakfast the trio set off on their five-day hike along the coast. Mike was not going on this trip empty-handed and intended to enjoy every minute of it to its fullest, so he carried an extremely heavy backpack filled to capacity with beers and steaks. Those five days were the most enjoyable five days of the two women's lives. They did not have to fear detection and for those five days merged in and out of each other at will. Mike was totally relaxed and carefree, although keeping vigilant at all times. To the other ten people accompanying them on the hike they were just another happy threesome who spoke a strange language. When asked where they were from, they replied that they were from the northern countries up around Finland and spoke a dialect of Finnish.

Their Human companions were a group of young students from a University in Cape Town, full of fun and laughter. Little did they know with whom they were sharing their hike? The five days of fun came to an end, though mixed with feelings of regret. Mike suggested to the group that they have a farewell party at Nature's Valley and everyone jumped at the opportunity as Mike was picking up the bill. What a party it was. Very early the next morning, before the sun came up, Mike teleported out of South Africa into the Zambezi Valley of Zimbabwe to a remote place on the banks of the Zambezi River known as Mapata Gorge.

This was wild country. A hundred metres in from the water line, beneath the thick undergrowth, Mike made camp. The women were still sleeping and unaware of where they were. Scanning the area to make sure that no Humans or other dangers lurked unseen, he settled down to wait for the rising sun. Amos, the old Sangoma, felt Mike's presence and smiled to himself. Someone was going to learn a hard lesson in the next few days.

The sun rose hot and humid into the blue cloudless sky. An elephant herd wandered down to the river bank to drink before going off to forage in the thick undergrowth. The matriarch elephant scented the air; all was clear and hung back while her herd of twenty females and three calves moved towards the water. A few large crocodiles slithered into the water at their approach, keeping well out of the way, drifting downstream to safer havens. Somewhere a leopard crouched, perched high in a fork of a tree, surveying its hunting grounds. Another day of struggle, of life and death in the African bushveld began. Across the river on the Zambian side, six dark shadows sat waiting to cross the Zambezi under cover of darkness. Dugout canoes lay camouflaged under tree branches, the men were making final checks of their automatic weapons and equipment. They would sleep the rest of the day, conserving their energies for the task that lay ahead.

Mara was the first to stir from her slumber and opened her eyes, to find herself in a strange, quiet place and sat upright. Mike's broad back signalled all was fine and she prodded Tara in the side to wake her up.

"Oooh!" Echoed the response, "My head."

Mike got up and came over to her, offering her a mug filled with something she did not recognize.

"Drink this," He ordered firmly.

She took a deep gulp and nearly puked.

"Drink it all," He commanded and she gulped the foul stuff down.

"What is that?" Queried Mara.

"Something to take away hangovers, made from herbs and other things. Works quickly, trust me."

Within minutes Tara was feeling much better, but with a raging thirst to quench, so Mike handed her a water bottle which she emptied as fast as she could swallow. Mara stood up, looked around puzzled, then at Mike who laughed.

"The Zambezi Valley."

Both women shrugged their shoulders, they did not have a clue where they were, not that it mattered anyway.

"May I ask what we are doing here?" Tara's question.

"I am going on a hunting safari with a difference," Responded Mike.

"With a difference?" Echoed Mara.

"Yup, I am hunting people, people who kill animals for their teeth and horns."

"Will the Reptilians be coming in?" Asked Tara.

"Not on this trip, no. So relax, I know you don't feel comfortable with them around, but none of them would harm you."

Mara managed a faint smile, those creatures turned her stomach. The heat of the day began to tell and humidity levels rose and the three began to sweat. Mike beckoned and they followed him down to the river bank. The flowing water looked so inviting and tempting, but he cautioned Mara, pointing out the skulking crocodiles. Mike laughed and projected an invisible barrier into the water so that the women could swim in safety. Without hesitation the women stripped naked and dived in. The sound of their bodies hitting the water brought about a reaction from nearby crocodiles that immediately swam in for the kill. The invisible barrier put a stop to it, but it did highly agitate the crocs not having access to the tasty morsels frolicking in the water. One adventurous croc got it figured out. If he could not get at the meal from the water, he would try it from the land and slithered out of the water, only to be imprisoned in Mike's powerful hands and being very unceremoniously hurled like a rag doll back into the water. While the girls swam around Mike scanned the surrounding countryside. He detected the six armed men. He would wait, allow them to cross, and then hunt them down one by one so that fear would creep into their hearts and know what it felt like to become hunted by an unseen predator. There was time, lots of time. Meanwhile he would enjoy the rest of the day with the two Siamese twins, women whom he found very pleasing to the eye in their nakedness. He dared not look too closely, otherwise he would be sorely tempted. He had to concentrate on the task ahead. After about an hour the women emerged from the water and dressed. They then came over to Mike, sat down and Tara asked,

"Anything to eat around here?"

"Well if you two are into something different and natural, there is a whole host of things to munch on, so if you will follow me, let's find our breakfast."

The three strolled off into the thick bush and Mike led them to various edible plants, then to a baobab tree and cracked open it's hard shelled fruit and gave them the cream-coloured, powdery covered pips to suck on. It had a tangy sweetish flavour, but left the mouth dry. Next stop a Marula tree in which a whole troop of blue monkeys were feasting. At the three's approach, the monkeys scampered off amid warning shrieks and Mike collected handfuls of the yellow pigeon egg-sized fruit, then returned to their camp. The sun was relentlessly beating down on the earth, sucking at one's life energies. The trio lay in the shade and snoozed through the midday heat till late afternoon. Nature had its ways and the intruders adapted to those ways and in the late afternoon the bush became alive again with foraging wildlife. With the coming of the evening cool came the hordes of flies and Mike had taken the precaution of erecting camouflaged mosquito netting covers for them to avoid the aggravation from the various pests. Huddled together under the netting and chewing on marula fruit Tara became fidgety and crept into Mike's arms to feel the closeness of him. Mike thought nothing of it and accepted her body against him as a matter of course.

That evening six silhouettes silently crossed the river in their canoes. Creating an invisible dome over the sleeping women to protect them from prowling predators, Mike teleported upstream and waited silently in the undergrowth next to the water. Six silent, darkened silhouettes glided their canoes onto the embankment, hastily dragged them into the thick undergrowth, and then headed off into the night. They were totally unaware of the awesome predator stalking them. Through the night they walked, on into the rising sun of the new day. Mike struck with deadly stealth. The sixth man at the end of the line was crushed as if he were a toy; the shattered body was left hanging in a tree, out of reach of scavengers, but in clear view of anyone passing by. It had been so fast and silent that the remainder of the group were blissfully unaware of it until a half a kilometre further on. Mike waited, hidden. Sure enough, two black men dressed only in loin cloths and carrying automatic rifles came back down the trail looking for their mate. When they saw his mangled body suspended upside down from the trees they dived for cover. Nothing moved, even the crickets fell silent, all was deathly quiet.

After a while the two emerged and cautiously advanced, rifles at the ready, to the tree where the body was hanging. They were nervous and kept glancing about. Satisfied that there was nothing they could do, they ran back the way they had come to report and Mike followed. He found them huddled in discussion, while all the time glancing down the trail the way they had come. Fearing the unseen they raced off down an animal trail, throwing caution to the wind. Mike followed, waiting for the right opportunity amongst thick brush, then struck again. However, this time the poachers were more alert and within seconds realized another one of their group had gone and they instantly hit the ground, rifles at the ready. Long agonizing moments followed. The silence was almost unbearable. Nothing moved, nothing made a sound, until terrible inhuman screams shattered the stillness. Mike drove his fingers into the man's throat to end his victim's agonized suffering, He had no sympathy. These were poachers who had killed defenceless Game Wardens and a group of tourists for no apparent reason. He felt no compulsion, no remorse. The four remaining men lying concealed in the undergrowth froze, the screaming piercing through their minds like a red hot knife, echoing mockingly on across the wide expanse of bushveld. They knew then, without a shadow of a doubt, that they were being systematically hunted down. Absolute fear struck into their hearts. They had neither seen nor heard the predator stalking them. Mike waited, throughout the hot day and into the late afternoon, still the remaining four lay concealed in the undergrowth, listening and watching. Gradually the shadows gathered and night descended once again and the four made their move. They ran in a semi-circle away from their last position towards the river and Mike gave them leeway. The distance towards the river decreased and the four began to see hope until Mike struck yet again. The third man screamed long and tortured and Nature went silent, listening to the screams carrying far out into the night. A camped Game Warden and his crew patrolling the area heard and shivered. The screams said everything and the Warden shuddered, moving closer to his cooking fire. For a man to scream like that meant something out there had got hold of him and it was not animal, otherwise the screams would have ended quickly. No, something lurked out there which was a powerful Muti (medicine). The Warden made a mental note of the direction and would go to investigate in the morning. Tara and Mara heard it and they too huddled in the darkness, thankful for their protective dome. Mara whispered,

"What do you think it is?"

"Don't ask, sister, you would not like to know," She replied.

Three black figures were now sprinting through the undergrowth with stark fear urging their legs to push harder and faster. They could smell the river and another scream rent the night, piercing into the darkness. Again and again the Lion struck. Finally a solitary figure hurtled through the undergrowth onto the river bank, grabbing hold of the canoe to drag it into the water, when Mike stepped out from the dark undergrowth into the moonlight. The poacher felt the presence, whirled about then froze. The sight of Mike in the moonlight was enough. He stared at the white man and saw what he held in one hand and the man shook with terror. The white man's hand and forearm were buried deep into the chest of one of the poachers who was still just barely alive, blood frothing from his mouth. Mike stared at his prey and

smiled, a vicious cruel smile and the poacher saw death worse
than he could imagine. He sank to his knees, all the fight
gone out of him, and waited. His eyes watched as the white
man gave a flick of his wrist and the body hanging from his
arm convulsed and fell to the ground, its spine ripped out
of its shell by the hand that held it. Mike was going to leave
one alive, this one, for the Game Warden to find. He strung
the man from the trees by his wrists and ankles horizontal
to the ground, but high enough to prevent him being eaten
alive by hyenas. Then taking the lifeless form slumped on
the ground he hurled it into the river, teleported back to his
camp and into the river for a cleansing swim. Tara heard
the faint splashing of water and gingerly came down to
investigate, to find Mike bathing She sat down on the bank
and watched in the moonlight. After a while Mike came out
of the water, walked over to her and sat down.

"That was you out there, wasn't it?" She queried.

He sat quietly contemplating, then answered,

"In the morning we need to break camp and move. This
place is going to be swarming with Zimbabwean troops
soon."

Tara understood that he did not want to talk about it so
got up and returned to the camp and the protective dome,
away from the biting mosquitoes. Mike followed in after her
and she snuggled into his arms and fell fast asleep. In the
darkness Mike scanned outwards. The Warden had alerted
the troops by radio and trackers were on their way. As the
sun rose once again into the skies, the trackers came across
the first body. There was much debating and deliberation,
360 degree searches and Mike's footprints were found as
he knew they would be. The trackers informed the soldiers
that they were tracking a big man who moved very fast,
sometimes on the ground, other times it seemed through

the air. The soldiers smirked, the Warden became puzzled and the search continued, unearthing the second and third bodies. By now the soldiers were becoming nervous, realizing the signs spelt much trouble. A pattern began to emerge and from the state of the bodies, the person who killed like that was merciless and cunning. To the trackers, it meant that they were tracking a very unusual and highly dangerous individual, a person who had systematically hunted down his prey and eliminated them one by one. Then, on the river bank, they found the sixth one suspended in the air, still alive. They cut him down and could see the absolute fear in the man. The Warden listened to the man's ravings and stepped backwards in shock. The troop commander listened and became instantly aware of the danger, barked a command and his thirty men all dived for cover, rifles at the ready, facing outwards. A mocking call from a distant a Go-away bird (the Grey Lourie) signalled the futility of it all.

"Relax, whoever it is, is long gone." Muttered the Warden.

"White man, terrible white man, big like lion and strong like elephant. He kill so quick and easy." Repeated their prisoner over and over again.

The Warden raised his eyebrows and summoned the trackers.

"Find this white man." He ordered, but they shrank away and refused, knowing it would not be wise.

The Warden was furious. The captured poacher pleaded.

"Kill me first. If you look for white man you are all dead. He is like a ghost and you can't smell or hear him. He not normal, he walk in the air."

That last phase echoed in the Warden's mind, sounding the alarm bells. Just then one of the soldiers noticed a folded piece of paper tucked into the fork of a branch and called the officer, who retrieved and opened it to find a written message,

"By the time you find this note I shall be long gone. You have five dead poachers, one still alive, their rifles and canoes. Ask the live one about the Warden and tourists in Luangwa who were murdered a month ago. I am sure he will have lots to say about it. I am a White Matabele warrior. Do not try to find me, you will die."

The officer blurted out, "White Matabele! What does he mean? There are no such things as White Matabele".

"There are." The elderly tracker replied who had fixed his eyes into the distance.

The officer grabbed him by the shoulders and shook him, demanding an explanation, but the man shook his head and walked off into the bush, his fellow trackers in silent pursuit.

"Where the hell are you lot going?" Shouted the Warden.

To which one tracker answered.

"Getting the hell out of here. You would be wise to do the same."

The officer radioed for choppers to come in to uplift the prisoner, the bodies and his troops back to base. Mike, well concealed, watched them until they had all gone. The hum of nature continued, forgetting the saga that had been played out. The trackers were uneasy. All the way back to their camp they had sensed Mike's presence. Once in the camp, the trackers turned to face the bush, seated in a semi-circle and waited. The Warden watched, feeling their anticipation and strained his eyes and ears seeking out any tell-tale signs of an intruder.

"This is crazy." Thought the Warden, "What the hell has got into them."

Suddenly a paralyzing force gripped him, raising him bodily off the ground. Then from out of the bush walked a man and two women dressed in strange black outfits which clung to their powerful bodies, hiding their faces. The Warden could not move and stared in disbelief at the man who squatted down in front of the trackers, the women standing directly behind him.

Mike raised his hand in traditional greeting to which all five trackers responded.

"It has been a long night dealing with the hyenas." The deep authoritative voice.

"Yes, the Lion has fed their carcasses to the jackals." Answered the lead tracker.

"Does your white Induna, your Warden, treat you well?" The next question.

There was a burst of spontaneous laughter and one tracker replied.

"He is like the young cub that stumbles around, but his bite is tame."

"I see the Elephant and Rooster people work together." Commented Mike.

"Yes, the Matabele march no more, we are peaceful now," Answered the elderly tracker.

Mike looked up at the Warden suspended in the air and addressed him.

"I suppose you are wondering about the White Matabele, if it's true? Well, Warden Harding, see for yourself."

Tara stepped forward and removed the headwear from Mike's head and the Warden sucked in his breath. Mike lowered the man to the ground and removed the paralyzing clamp.

Paul Harding stood riveted to the spot, speechless.

"Nice to see you again, Paul."

"You bloody son of a bitch, I might have guessed, that was a classic Mike stunt back there, but the damages were too grotesque," Replied Paul, taking a step forward.

"Stay where you are Paul, not a good idea to move right now for your own safety." Cautioned Mike.

The man stopped dead in his tracks and eyed his bygone army buddy and could not understand.

"No offence Paul, it's just my partners behind me will tear you apart."

Paul looked at the two female forms and saw the lithe panther-like quality of their bodies and stayed put. The damage inflicted on those dead poachers was enough to deter anyone from making a wrong move.

"How would you like to do the same job elsewhere, let's say, in a game park far bigger than this one?"

Paul, taken aback by the question, hesitated, then replied.

"What's that got to do with what you did out there. You bloody well murdered those men. They stood no chance?"

"Oh! Still the champion of Justice I see." The casual response.

Paul blinked, the man was toying with him and he began to feel nervous and blurted out.

"Listen Mike, if you are going to kill me, get it over with, don't play games."

"Easy friend, easy. It's a genuine, legitimate question."

Something about the whole situation was absurd. What did this man hope to gain and what had he become. Those dead bodies bore testimony to a vicious and callous butchering of Human life. He had better play this by ear if he was ever to see his wife and two kids again.

"I know the events of the last few hours have probably thrown you, Paul, and made me out to be an absolute monster, but given your present circumstances and the fact that you have been considering leaving your job anyway, why not answer the question."

Paul eyed Mike with suspicion and distrust. How could he have known that? Thoughts raced through his mind seeing Mike's knowing smile. He gathered himself and answered.

"Where is this so-called game park?"

"On another planet in another Galaxy, billions of light years from here." Was the quick response.

Paul could not restrain the mocking laugh, at which Tara took off her head mask and the bottle green eyes burned with an ice cold fire. The trackers recoiled and Paul's jaw sagged open.

"Well, I am waiting." Goaded Mike.

Paul squatted down muttering, his legs weak and shaking.

"Geez Mike, don't play games."

"It's no game. What you see here comes from another planet, what you saw out there is the result of living on other planets and having to survive against things you can only imagine in your wildest dreams. We would very much like to have you and your family join us in our world."

"I don't know if I want to, Mike. It seems your world has no place for compassion".

A woman and three children suddenly appeared in front of Paul. The man jumped up and stepped in front of his family facing Mike.

"I don't know how you did that and I don't particularly care, but leave my family out of it."

"Paul, Paul. Relax, everything is cool. Hi kids, Hi Sally, my name is Mike and these two lovely ladies are Tara and Mara." Mike introducing himself.

The trackers continued their silent observation of the strange events happening before their very eyes. They were not afraid anymore knowing their lives would not be taken by this white Induna, this White Matabele.

"Who is this man, Paul, and how did we get here. What's going on?" The woman demanded.

Mike approached and Paul watched the man's body move, swallowing hard. Here was danger personified. The two black clad women held their ground.

"Sally, your husband has been offered a job as Game Warden on another planet, so in order to short circuit the whole story I have brought you all together so that you can hear me out as a family. It's unfortunately not the right way to do things, but there is not much time and, seeing as Paul is good at his job and knows the wildlife habits and traits etc, etc, he is needed for a very special assignment. There is a down side of course; you would be thrown into a super advanced society with technology light years ahead of Earth's."

Sally looked at Paul in confusion and the man shook his head. Turning to the trackers, Mike teleported them to their village, then facing Paul, whose eyes couldn't believe what he saw, Mike gently said.

"It's OK; they are back in their village with a lot of money to keep them happy for a long while. As for you, it's time to make your decision. Stay here or come with us to a place beyond your wildest dreams."

With that Mike activated the Portal into Thanu. Through the Portal the full splendour of Thanu could be seen. Mike watched Paul's face and saw the light of understanding glow behind the man's intelligent eyes. Without hesitation, Paul gathered his family to him and walked through the gate onto Moti's balcony.

Moti shouted back at him through the closing gate.

"Penagee has decided to dump you, sorry my brother."

In the African sunlight Mike bent his head. He stood there for long moments, then walked over to Tara and Mara and teleported them into the steaming Amazon jungles to a rendezvous with the waiting Reptilians. For two days Mike sat alone in the trees, neither eating nor drinking till finally he came down and gave the order.

"Move out."

For the next three months Mike rained terror on greedy land developers, destroying millions of dollars' worth of equipment. Brazilian Armed Forces mounted a campaign against this unseen "Muerto Preto" and sent in its troops to rid the jungles of the threat, but the destroyers remained elusive and undetected. Forest clearing came to a total standstill, so Mike looked to wage his personal war in other areas. Time was running out for him as another year was rapidly drawing to a close. It was time to go home. Moti waited for them and when Mike did not appear he questioned Mis.

"Where is Mike?"

The Reptilian Commander replied.

"He is not coming and sends you his greetings. Tell Hawk the Lion will see him again one day."

Moti stood silent and brooding. The console in Penagee's study advised her that ten Reptilians had come in from Earth, Subject Mike did not return. She jumped up and teleported straight to Moti who was standing alone and very unhappy.

"You told him, didn't you?" She shouted.

"Yes I told him, now leave me alone, he is not coming back Penagee, not for a long time."

She walked away from Moti, returning to her study where she sat down and touched the console, its light blinked and Penagee requested.

"Call subject Jane to my office."

"Done." Penagee waited for the knock. When it came she opened the door and ushered Jane in, indicating to a chair. Jane sat down.

"Mike will not be returning to Thanu. What you told me before, that should I make this choice then that is what would probably happen, well it has."

Jane looked at Penagee, tears filling her eyes. She stood up, kissed Penagee on the cheek then said.

"I hope you will be happy with yourself and I wish you all the best." Jane walked out of Penagee's life that day and never spoke to her again until years later.

The news circulated throughout Thanu, Mike was gone and the planet groaned. Penagee called her children to her and informed them that their father had gone away for a long time and she didn't know when he would be back. The news upset them no end and for days little Ridmon refused to go back to school. Moti searched and searched, spending hours looking for Mike, but the man had vanished into thin air. When Tara did not return from Karagan an investigation was launched. When no trace of her could be found, except the last reported sighting of her in the dangerous mountain regions, the conclusion was drawn, only after an exhaustive search, that she had been killed by the creatures there.

Two years were up and operation "Karajan's Ark" got under way in earnest. Seconds before the comet impacted Earth, Thanu teleported a third of all living things on to Karagan through four Gates. Earth reeled heavily under the impact. A catastrophe of indescribable proportions took place as was predicted. Parts of the Americas, Africa, Europe and Asia and many islands, including parts of Australia, disappeared under water. Massive earthquakes and volcanic eruptions caused surface changes and the sun was shut out over greater parts of the planet. From a 24 hour day Earth was transformed into only a 16 hour day and global changes took place on a scale that altered Earth forever. On Karagan the transformation was equally tremendous with the arrival of two billion Humans and thousands of Earth life forms. With all the activities going on over the following years on Karagan and Thanu, no one thought about Mike or Tara, except their closest friends. Penagee had been so wrapped up in her work during that period she hardly noticed the time fly by. Frank married Zara, Moti and Anna were very happy with their new position on Karagan and befriended Paul and his family. Borz and Ana-Maria were both relocated to Karagan as Thanu's diplomatic representatives and life settled down to normality. The Reptilians were not too happy and wished for their own resettlement to another planet which was under consideration. Mike's children had grown but missed their father terribly. Earth's problems had slowly begun to subside and those who had survived adapted and readjusted themselves to their new environment.

No one paid the planet Ridmon the slightest attention. She hung invisible in her orbit and to all intents and purposes never existed. To three people on her, however, it had become home again and the tree city once more came to life. By anyone's standards Mike seemed to be an unbalanced and dangerous individual considering his behaviour patterns. But to Tara he was a blessing. Nobody would accept her knowing about Mara, and her chances at a normal relationship were very slim in spite of the attraction it may hold to some, eventually two identical women would become a problem and any long term arrangement would undoubtedly wear thin, one always being favoured over the other. So their lives had become intermingled in a strange yet acceptable way to their situation, but would have been frowned upon elsewhere and condemned outright. Mike was back on Ridmon where it all began. Two more years passed, then one day a Portal opened and Moti stepped through next to Abu Ahmed's grave. To his surprise the grave was well kept and tidy. He spun around sensing something behind him and Mike stood there like a statue, with Tara and her double watching him. He blinked, making sure he was not seeing things and heard Mike's low voice.

"Shalom brother, welcome to Ridmon."

Moti advanced slowly and noticed Tara and her double, tense and crouched into fighting stances and he frowned.

"Why do the cats show their claws?" He asked.

"Because the Cats are wary of the Hawk and fear the Hawk may want to take the Lion's eyes." Answered Mike.

"Ha! Does the Lion need Cats to protect him these days?" Moti mocked.

Before Moti could blink Mike had him in a crushing hold. He never even saw it coming and the steel bands that held him were more powerful than he could believe. He gasped.

"Easy bother, I still need my ribs."

Mike slowly released his hold and embraced Moti, then stepped back holding him at arm's length.

"So, the Hawk looks well and married life seems to agree with him."

"That it does, but I see you have improved a lot, I take my last statement back about the Lion needing the Cats. Damn it, Mike, where did you find the speed and power?"

"Training brother, training and lots of it. Perhaps you would like to see how good my Cats are or don't you think you can take them?"

Moti sized the women up. Pound for pound he was bigger than both of them put together, but it was something in their manner which drew his attention. They were too calm and the cold stares told him that these two were experienced fighters and if Mike had anything to do with it, they were way above average. What the hell, he thought, why not give it a shot, what could he lose by it. Perhaps it was time to show them a few new tricks of his own.

He nodded and squared off and Mike stepped to the side saying,

"Start off with one and after that, if you feel up to it, take on both of them."

Moti laughed and agreed and Tara faced him.

"Ready." Cautioned Mike then, waiting a few seconds, shouted. "Fight."

Man against woman and Moti pounced like greased lightning and struck empty air, he spun round looking for his opponent, viciously sweeping with his leg. His head exploded in a flash of blinding pain and he moved with the strike, coming up underneath it and struck air and immediately somersaulted out, landing in his classic fighting stance. His head still rang from the impact and he searched for Tara. She stood in front of him, hands on hips smiling and slowly Moti, his head spinning, sank to the ground, his arms and legs as heavy as lead and sat there unable to move. Mike walked forward and touched a nerve in his neck and gradually life came back into his limbs and he stood up shaking.

"What was that?" He asked.

"One of the Cat's claws." Remarked Mike.

Moti was still feeling groggy and looked at the women with new respect.

"The Cats are panthers after all."

Mike checked Moti's eyes and all focused.

"You were lucky brother, she only touched you lightly, if she had wanted to you would be dead by now."

"How does she do that?"

"Concentrated energy through her hands and it comes out like a steamroller, the harder she hits the bigger the steamroller." Smiled Mike.

"And the other one can also do that?" Queried Moti.

"You bet, but they work better as a team."

Moti was impressed, he wanted to find out from Mike what he was doing on Ridmon and why he was not returning to Thanu.

"Why are you here and not on Thanu?"

"Because this has always been my home, not Thanu. We can't breathe there. Here we are free to do as we please and when we please."

"What about your children?"

Mike was silent for a while then answered.

"Ridmon will come here when he is ready."

"Come." Motioned Tara and took off into the trees with Mara.

Mike bounded after them in a game of Catch and they literally flew up the tree trunks. Moti watched them and understood why Mike wanted to be here and felt a pang of envy. Maybe it was time he came back as well. Now he knew where Mike was the idea appealed to him even more. He scaled the tree trunk and found himself a little out of practice. Up in the heights he walked around his old home and strong emotions gripped him. He was coming back, Thanu didn't need him, neither did Karagan, this was where he belonged. Moving over to Mike's house he entered the door to a cold Ridmon beer being pushed into his hand. Tara and Mara were good hostesses and soon a full scale Ridmon speciality dish was on the table. Local fruits and berries. Moti watched the interaction between Mike and the women, understanding at once the intimacy existing between them.

"Would you mind if I came back with my family?" He suddenly asked.

There was a long silence, then Mike looked at the two women who nodded agreement.

"No we don't mind, but you have to understand our circumstances are a little complicated and we need your assurance that you will fully accept it, otherwise it will not work."

"I understand and there's no need to explain and I do accept. When can I move in?"

"Right now and bring Paul and Frank with you. Discretion is needed, we want to keep this as quiet as possible, you understand."

Moti needed no prompting and disappeared through the Portal, leaving Mike, Tara and Mara smiling. For the first time in a long while Moti felt alive as he arrived into his home on Karagan and contacted Paul.

"Paul, I need to speak to you urgently, would you mind coming over."

"Not at all, will be over in about thirty minutes. Is that OK?"

"Fine, see you then and bring the family."

Next he contacted Frank. The man answered his console,

"Hello Moti, what's up?"

"Need to talk to you here on Karagan, can you make it?"

There was a pause and Frank answered.

"Yes. Zara and I wanted to see how the Earthlings were doing, so we were going to come out anyway. Bring us in and do you mind putting us up?"

"Anytime pal, anytime." With that Moti activated a Portal and Frank with Zara stepped into the room.

Half an hour later Paul arrived and Moti quickly scribbled a message on a piece of paper and handed it to Paul.

It read." There is no time to explain, you have to trust me on this. I am leaving Karagan for another planet, a beautiful place. Mike is there. You interested?"

Paul took the pen and wrote,

"Yes."

Moti took the paper stuffed it into his mouth, chewed and swallowed. Watching his actions Paul realized what was going on and said aloud.

"So where's the Beer?"

"Coming right up, sir."

Just then Anna came into the room.

"Hello Paul, how are things?" She enquired.

"Great thanks, couldn't be better."

"Where are Sally and the children?" She asked.

"Out on the balcony."

Moti came back with some beers and handed them out. Moti raised his bottle and softly murmured,

"Matabele Ridmon."

Frank looked from Moti to Paul and back to Moti and seeing the look on the man's face it hit home.

"Mike," thought Frank. The man has surfaced on Ridmon, otherwise why would Moti be so excited. It had to be. He raised his bottle and saluted,

"Matabele," a pause, "When?"

"Now."

Frank nodded. The three men stood up and walked into the kitchen where Moti teleported everyone firstly to the great desert, then out into the open sea and activated the Portal on the sea surface, then stepped into the trees on Ridmon to a smiling welcome from Mike.

"Any problems?"

"No, I took the roundabout way and walked into the sea. It will be virtually impossible to track us down." Confirmed Moti.

"Good, now let's get this lot sorted out and nice to have you aboard Paul and Frank, thanks."

Tara and Mara took the new families to their respective homes and settled them in, advising them that dinner would be served in an hour on the sundeck at Mike's home.

On Karagan the computers reported the disappearance of two families and a couple and listed the names. The list was patched through to the Thanu delegation and Ana-Maria, seeing the names, called Borz in urgently. Both looked at each other and smiled.

"Mike," Whispered Ana-Maria and Borz nodded. It was obvious, Frank, Moti and the new one Paul, an ex-army buddy of Mike's. Borz laughed aloud and hugged Ana-Maria, whispering in her ear. "He is collecting."

The news reached Thanu and the list was patched through to Penagee. She scanned through the list and sat back in her chair. Moti would not just disappear unless there was probable cause and that cause could only mean one thing. Mike, damn the man. She touched her console and requested the records for the last six months of Moti's Portal activation. The report came back negative, no record of usage.

"Report on last known active trace, Subject Moti."

A pause.

"Last known activity to Karagan Great Desert and subject vanished beneath the sand. Unable to track."

Penagee fumed. They had beaten the system and could be anywhere in the universe by now. Well it was no great loss, not now anyway. Why they didn't take Jane with them she did not know. The console blinked.

"Yes," She answered irritably.

"Incoming message from Karagan."

"Patch it through."

"Message reads. Congratulations, Operation Karagan a confirmed success. Reptilians from Thanu no longer on Karagan. Unable to trace whereabouts. Unknown Subject reported entry on to Karagan briefly and traced to location, subject Ras then exited Karagan. Untraceable.

Message ends."

"Patch me to Subject Ras on Karagan," She ordered.

The console blinked and a man's voice answered,

"Ras here."

"I see you had a visitor?"

"Yes, would you believe it, your ex-husband? He knows about us." Ras answered.

Penagee was shocked. How could he possibly know? If there were any secrets on the planet, that was one of them and she had been so careful to cover her tracks.

"What did he want?" She queried.

"I don't really know. He was very pleasant and asked after the children, and then left. One thing is for sure though, don't ever underestimate the man. He did not come alone, there were two women with him in uniform, but I could not see their faces, nor identify them."

"I will see you later at the usual place, bye." Penagee closed the link.

How come her security network was unable to pick up the two women? There were holes in her system and people were using them. She would have to make that her next priority and rectify. A few days later Thanu went into Red Alert, there had been a security breach and six persons had vanished without trace. Penagee was agitated. Her highly sophisticated system was being walked all over. She suspected by whom, as the names of the missing persons were too obvious. They were Ana-Maria and her daughter Carla, Borz and his wife Ju, Jane and Nina.

Penagee called a Council meeting and requested the members to alienate Subject Mike and he was to be considered persona non grata on Thanu and Karagan. Her request was met with a definite no by unanimous vote. She was afraid, afraid her children would also mysteriously vanish, and that she would not stand for. The motion was denied as the request was based on personal rather than global motives. The recent loss of individuals from Thanu and Karagan did not constitute a threat as their participation in matters on either planet was minimal. Penagee abruptly left the room and returned to her study where the console blinked.

She sat down and opened the link.

"Penagee here."

A very familiar voice answered.

"Penagee, don't turn this into a war between us. You have your life and I have mine and there are four children caught up in the middle. Let's at least give them a reason to be proud of themselves and not force them to take sides, as it will hurt them more in the long run."

"You think you can come in here and take whoever you want and expect me to believe you won't take the children as well. That I will not have." She angrily replied.

"Relax, here's the deal, the children stay with you, I get to see them every six months for a period of two weeks in a neutral place."

Penagee considered the suggestion carefully and it sounded reasonable, but she had to be sure.

"How can I trust you to keep your word?"

"Protector Friend will act as guarantor." He responded.

With that she could not argue. Protector Friend would ensure the agreement was upheld and she breathed a sigh of relief.

"Agreed. When and where?" She asked.

"The answer to that is in six months and the where I can't tell you as it will be up to Protector Friend who will discuss the agreement with you himself." Replied Mike.

"Fair enough." She closed the link between them.

"Call not traced, unknown origin, unknown energy source," Reported the console. Penagee understood the call had come via Protector Friend. This was madness she thought, why it had to end this way. It could have been so perfect for them both. Karagan became a reality, another Earth away from Earth and for the thousands of men and women who had made it possible came a feeling of pride of having achieved the almost impossible. They had been able to do it only through the talents of five very unique people to which honour was duly given. Five names appeared in the Great Hall of Karagan, inscribed for all to see.

Mike of Thanu
Penagee of Thanu
Moti of Thanu
Jaranah of Karagan
Protector Friend

Thus began a new chapter in the life of Karagan in which Thanu played a vital role. A new Federation of Planets was established with many signatories. Evolution had taken a step forward in those outer reaches of space. Yet, on a forgotten planet where it all began so many years before, life continued to thrive. Where once only the wind whistled through the empty Great Hall, now the happy laughter of children echoed against its walls.

REVIVAL

SIX

The planet Ridmon orbited invisible and ignored in a vast universe. Yet, down on its surface there existed Humans, Thedarians and Karaganda's. Should the Federation have been more attentive they would have discovered a small thriving civilization growing right under their noses. Ridmon in actual fact was officially written off the charts, non-existent. A very industrious group of people were assembled there and prospered secretly, silently. Gradually new additions came in from Earth and Karagan, boosting the population to five thousand, mostly made up of complete family units. The Crystal City reopened with extensive redesigning, taking on a new look with crystal pathways standing 100 metres off the ground and extending to various parts of the valley, serving as communication, water distribution and refuse collection conduits and access to private homes of the Tree Dwellers. Crystal City itself was further extended along the cliff faces with an additional maze of waterfalls, pools and plant gardens landscaping all levels. Borz was an accomplished landscape artist and was allowed free reign to express his creative talents, assisted by very talented helpers who combined their skills to create an incredibly beautiful city. Those who lived within its walls were accommodated in large spacious and very comfortable apartments.

Jane and Paul jointly worked on wildlife enclosures down on the valley floor as part of the children's educational programme, with various types of non-carnivorous wildlife found on Earth and reproducing eco systems matching natural self-contained and self-sustaining environments. Although consensus was against the keeping of caged animals in captivity, especially those that would suffer most by being incarcerated in cages, the animals were limited to the lesser types on the food chain such as Hare, Meerkat, rock rabbits, domestic cats and a certain breed of dog, the Rhodesian Ridgeback who were free to roam within the confines of the city. Above Crystal City a 'Lover's Lane' came into existence, which soon earned a reputation as the most congested place at sunset on the planet, so much so that it inspired a bar and an open air dance floor with live band accompaniment twice a week.

Everybody was allocated to a work detail which operated on a rotation basis, which in effect meant that for two weeks a detail would wait tables, then the following two weeks the detail would be in the kitchens and so on. Work hours were flexible, as it was expected of each individual to put in a seven hour work day, five days a week. Children attended school in which music, art, dance, gymnastics and athletics were encouraged. Teachers accessed mountains of information through the Crystal Libraries and the educational system took on a highly advanced adaptation. From a child's early life, school became a fantastic voyage into learning. Ridmon was a technological masterpiece, yet kept things simple and natural. Technology of a very high order remained in the background and was hardly noticed. Most people preferred the old ways of doing things, to sit at a restaurant and be served by people, not computers, to go into the various lounges and pubs and have a homely atmosphere where one could still read a book or the local paper in spite of the fact that it came in the form of a daily newspaper printed on papyrus paper. Generally people came and went as they pleased, maintained their personal freedoms and were not subjected to monitoring or eavesdropping as on Thanu or Karagan. A sophisticated security system existed and was activated in times of emergency or global threat. If such a threat occurred, Ridmon would lock down and become indestructible. Mike and Moti between them created highly specialized Drones for Ridmon's protection. The process took almost three years to complete.

Most of the new settlers on Ridmon came to the planet via the Drones through Portals that opened and closed anywhere and anytime on any planet without detection. In addition, as a result of technological innovation, new body stockings came into existence and were worn by everyone as part of their daily dress code. The stockings came in all colours and patterns, from plain transparent to highly colourful designs and a new industry was born on Ridmon, called The Body Beautiful. Together with normal crystal fabric outer garment fashions, clothes designers were given total freedom to fully express themselves. In essence it meant that, should anyone scan Ridmon, no life forms other than the creatures that inhabited the planet would be detected. No one left Crystal City or the Tree dwellings without the stockings on; in the confines of their homes or in the city they were not necessary, as the same body stocking technology was incorporated into every superstructure on the planet. It was a major breakthrough for Mike and Moti, offering unlimited potential. With those stockings the two men and their small Ridmon army of fifty men and women could come and go about the universe at will, as the stockings were the ultimate stealth and body cloaking device. Physical education on Ridmon was a big issue and everyone did their daily exercises, from simple jogging to Mike's brand of martial arts. Mike, Tara and Mara would sometimes go off for days on end and come back with new things of interest to science and additional snippets of information. The three worked as a team and often Moti and Frank would join them on their visits to the New Reptilia or other planets.

One day whilst Mike and Moti were drinking a few social beers, Moti mentioned the twins.

"Those two women puzzle me. It's as if they are joined at the hip somehow."

Mike smiled and watched Moti's face as he answered.

"They are Siamese twins with a difference."

Moti stared at Mike, puzzled.

"They are joined only by energy and must merge into one another for a few hours out of a 24 hour cycle. Mara always merges into Tara. They can never be two, it would kill them."

"That must be dangerous for them if ever they were separated." Commented Moti.

"Yes, it would under normal circumstances, but thank heavens for the Portals, in this way a situation like that could be easily neutralized. However, their highly developed sense of survival will not allow them to be far from each other at any one time. That is why I have trained them to perfect a fighting art very unique in their case and enhanced their mental capacities to allow them to teleport to each other so fast anyone or any machine trying to separate them would not succeed. Now, let's say you take on one of them, as you have done, and you try to capture her and she feels unable to protect herself against such a capture, then the two join as one and their combined strengths and abilities are channelled into one and believe me, you would not like to be on the receiving end." Smiled Mike.

"You really look after them, don't you?" Moti's summation.

"Yes I do, they are freaks of nature. People would only exploit them. I have given them a chance to lead normal productive lives and to find acceptance for who they are and not what they are. I love them to bits."

"Don't you find it difficult, I mean, not favouring the one over the other or wishing they were one instead of two?" Asked Moti.

"No, and I can guess where this is leading, so drop it," Growled Mike.

Moti drank his beer in silence and thought to himself. Talk about bodyguards with a difference. As long as Mike lived, those two would stand behind him and take on anything that threatened their relationship. They loved him; there was no doubt about that. Jeepers, not even Anna had that kind of fire in her. How did Mike do it, train them like that.

"The only training, for your information, was their bodies. Their minds are their own and it's their love, not their gratefulness, that bonds us and you best remember that. Subject closed," Concluded Mike, leaning forward and staring Moti right in the eye.

Moti flinched, how easy it was to forget Mike was telepathic. The women came out of the house carrying trays of healthy snacks and more beers and joined the men.

"We spoke to Anna today, she wants to train with us, says it's easier training with women than with men. We told her that we agreed in certain cases when the macho male ego tended to descend to the crotch," Teased Tara.

Mike burst out laughing and slapped Moti on the back.

"Trouble in Paradise, my bro?"

Moti muttered something undecipherable under his breath, then snapped.

"So, my hormones tend to get a little carried away at times. I can't help it."

"It might help matters if you waited until the training session was over before you bonked your wife." joked Mara.

Moti's eyes flashed. "Are you two discussing private matters with my wife?"

"No, trying to say something to you in a nice pleasant way without being offensive. Anna wants to look good for you and we can help her, that's all." Responded Tara.

Mike passed Moti a beer and teleported Anna to the table. She looked surprised, then kissed Moti hard.

The man melted and smiled, "Hi baby."

"So, what's the occasion?" Anna asked.

"Oh, nothing really, we were just discussing your training with the girls here." Mike replied.

Anna's face creased into a broad smile and the three women got up and went inside. Moti looked cheated and Mike thumped him on the chest,

"Last one to the pool drinks doubles." He challenged and both men raced off towards Crystal City, sprinting for all their worth.

Tara watched them go and giggled. That Mike, she thought, was something else.

Neither man won the challenge due to Frank stepping into their path.

"What's the rush?" He challenged.

"Doubles." Breathed Moti.

"Ah, in that case I will join you, if I may?"

"The more the merrier." Confirmed Mike and the three jogged to Crystal City at a leisurely pace.

Tara was having none of that. Grabbing Anna and Mara, they also jogged to the City in search of their men, Zara joining in along the way. It was going to be a "fall down" and the girls wanted in on it. They did not have far to look to find their men sitting at the first kiosk with beers in their hands. Trotting up they plonked themselves down and ordered.

"You guys think you can drink alone, forget it" Zara's terse remark.

"You're on." Challenged Frank and the party began. Anna arranged a baby sitter, then dived onto Moti's lap, saying.

"Ok, you big lug, let's see what you're made of."

Everyone laughed, they were good for each other these two, and it was nice to see their openness. Mike sighed, remembering days gone by when he and Penagee used to do the same. He had to admit it, he missed her. But that was that and life must go on one way or the other. It was not long before Ana-Maria, Borz and Paul with their wives joined the party. Two hours passed and Tara whispered in Mike's ear.

"Mara and I have to merge, be back now." Making their excuses they trotted off home.

"Where are they going?" Enquired Anna.

"Tara will be back, Mara has things to do." Replied Mike and Moti nodded acknowledgment.

Ten minutes later Tara re-joined the group and Mike suggested that they go to the Ridmon Beer Hall to which everyone agreed. This was new on Ridmon. The old army barracks had been converted into a large beer and dance hall and already people were making full use of the facilities. A live band called the Ridmonians was playing. Everyone let their hair down and enjoyed themselves, dancing, singing, drinking, until finally it was time to close the Hall and Mike excused himself, wishing everyone "Good Night," teleported back home with Tara, who was by now well inebriated, and carried her into the bedroom. She promptly passed out on him, so Mike pulled a blanket over her and walked out to sit down on the sundeck.

On Thanu, a young boy stirred and mumbled something in his sleep. His sister Gnee softly said. "Goodnight Dada." Closed her eyes, falling into a happy sleep.

Zakrose was babysitting the little ones as their mother had gone out on a date. Wolf would only come home later from Karagan. In the silence of the room Mike appeared and Zakrose dived into his arms. Mike hugged his daughter and cautioned with his gloved hand, she understood and a telepathic communication between the two began.

"How's my girl?"

"Missing you lots."

"I miss you all very much as well, but we must keep this our little secret, otherwise we will only be able to see each other every six months."

"I know, Dada."

"It's your birthday soon and I have arranged a surprise for you, but I need you to promise me you won't tell anyone. It's extremely important and many people will depend on you. Your mother must never know, if she finds out there will most probably be a war and none of us want that."

"I promise."

"OK, your birthday is in three months time and you are going to have to spend the day here with your Mom. Two days after your birthday I want you to take the little ones and go with Wolf to Karagan to the new Oceanic Centre. Your mother will not stop you from going as the trip is really very good and lasts three days. She will probably want to speak with you once a day to see how things are going and the rest of the time she will have monitors following your every movement. Don't worry, when you arrive you will be given rooms to stay in for the three days? When you get into the rooms you will have one hour to settle in before you are fetched for the tour. Wait for me in the rooms and I will fetch you all and we will have a three-day birthday party."

"Mama will find out we are not there."

"I know, but she will not know where you are, trust me."

"OK, Dada."

Mike took her in his arms.

"You will be seventeen years old. Wow! A young lady already."

"Just be careful, Dada, Mother hates you."

"No, my love, just angry." He corrected her.

Zakrose held tightly onto her father, then Mike gently kissed her forehead and was gone as Wolf walked through the door. The boy stood watching his sister standing hugging an invisible lover and asked.

"Are you practicing a love scene?"

Zakrose spun around and lashed out at him.

"Yeah, at least it will be better than your effort the other day at school."

Wolf laughed. "Funny Ha! Ha!"

Back on Ridmon, Mike sank into his chair and sighed. He had made an agreement with Penagee which he had in a sense broken. His children missed him and Mike had defied Penagee's fears and had seen his children often. It placed the children in a very difficult position and he steeled their minds against her mental probing, thus preserving their individual rights to privacy. He and Penagee had failed their children by creating divisions, which was not a good example of parenthood. Mike knew the so-called abduction of the children for three days was going to stir up a hornets nest and Penagee would be on the warpath looking to take his head. The confrontation was coming and he was prepared for it.

The months passed with the usual events and on the 4th of August Mike and his two Shadows entered specific rooms at the Karagan Oceanarium. The children were dressed in body stockings and teleported back to Ridmon. On Karagan the alarm did not sound until Penagee called in to find out how her children were doing, instead of one of the children answering the console, she received the following message.

"The children are OK, they are with me for Zakrose's birthday party. They will be returned to you in three days. Do not make an issue out of this please."

Penagee slowly paced her study, this was war. She was going to clip the man's nails once and for all. For three days the children were entertained on Ridmon, having the time of their lives and for three days Mike was a very happy man. But the time had come again to return them to their mother and Mike was sure she would be setting up a trap for him, so he did the unexpected. Like a silent predator stalking his prey, Mike activated his special Portal into the waterfall on Thanu and teleported up its length to Penagee's penthouse where he scanned the interior. Sure enough, it was rigged with the most sensitive sensory devices on Thanu and equipped with very powerful paralyzing beams. She sat at her console looking relaxed and innocent. Mike knew her mind was extended and covered all the rooms.

There was something else, body magnetic grids, unseen, whose function was to take hold of a body and play havoc with the central nervous system, which had the effect of rendering a person disoriented and unable to control motor functions. Nice little set up, nice indeed. No doubt the grids had his DNA recognition so that the children would not be affected and the sensors would only zap him. Behind him he sensed the retriever Drones. So, Penagee was playing hard ball. Time for surprises and two Shadows joined him in the water where they joined hands, combining their internal energies, then lashed out with invisible streams, destroying the retriever Drones in massive explosions which rocked the city. When the alarms sounded, Penagee did exactly what Mike wanted. She came running to the window to see what the commotion was about. Mike reached through the opened window and locked her in his mental grip and teleported her out. The diversion had been very effective.

On the far away planet of New Reptilia, mother and children were united. Penagee, freed from her shackles, stood next to her children who danced around happily and faced a man and two women she could not identify until Mike took off the face mask

"Nice little traps you set for me there on Thanu. I am a little surprised that you planned to spring it in front of the children. Sorry about the retriever Drones, never did like those things."

Penagee stared at her ex-husband and had to admit the man was full of surprises. Her trap was perfect and she was so sure he would come in with the children. Instead he came in and took her right from inside her own trap. She felt his power and realized that she was way out of his league. She scanned the two women only to find nothing. They were visible but invisible, with no signature patterns, nothing. Penagee realized with alarm that Mike could be a shadow on the wall and no technology on Thanu would detect him, neither her nor her very sophisticated security system, fear gripped her heart. If he ever got mad enough he could create havoc on Thanu or Karagan and there was nothing she could do about it.

"Penagee, we are reasonable people, we don't need a war between us, as many lives are at stake. I suggest we call a truce to the animosity and agree that the children's well-being is far more important than your or my little squabble."

She refused to answer and gathered her children to her and looked at Mike angrily and requested.

"Please send us home."

"Sorry, your Drones are on the way to collect you. We shall not be here when they arrive, you will be alright here, you are amongst friends." With that Mike signalled with his hand and a few Reptilians came into view with Ras. Penagee sucked in her breath and turned on Mike.

"You bastard!"

"No sweetness, just security, and the kind you like so much."

Mike walked over to the children and kissed them all, then turned to Penagee and smiled.

"There are powers beyond powers, Penagee, forget your personal vendetta and live your life. Your children love you, they love me. We don't have to love each other, but can at least be civil."

Penagee spat in his face and before Mike could stop them the Shadows had Penagee in a grip so tortuous she could not scream. Mike reacted and touched the Shadows lightly, to which they reluctantly obeyed. He picked Penagee up into his arms and held her until she gained control of herself, then gently placed her on her feet. Still holding her close he whispered.

"I warned you there was power beyond power. Take care Penagee, you try to hurt me again, they will kill you."

He stepped backwards and a strange luminescent ring of light joined him to the Shadows and then they were gone. Ras ran over to Penagee and held her. The children had been frightened by the incident, but refused to come near their mother while she was in Ras arms, so they clung to each other. More Reptilians came into view. Penagee was shaken. "Those two women." She thought out loud and a cold shiver ran down her spine.

"Please Penagee, leave it alone." Begged Ras.

Penagee nodded curtly at him, but in her heart she heard the plea, realizing only too well that a direct confrontation with Mike would have devastating results. She walked over to her children and took them in her arms.

"I am so sorry, please forgive me. I promise it's over. If you want to see your Father, its fine by me. I will not stop you."

Little Gnee smiled and pulled Penagee's arm until she was forced to bend down and the little girl whispered in her ear.

"Dada loves you."

Penagee smiled and ruffled her hair and stood up. Tears filled her eyes and Zakrose hugged her.

"It's true, Mama."

The Drones arrived and teleported the group up and then returned to Thanu.

Karagan sounded the alarm. The Humanoids were back. Thanu activated defence mechanisms on Karagan and the waiting began. Messages were sent out to the Federation's member planets, advising them of the situation and to go on defensive alert. Drones reported in, giving constant feedback of strengths and numbers and Karagan braced itself. Razu shook his head, the odds were staggering and if Thanu's defences failed, then Karagan was doomed into captivity and all rebuilding efforts on the part of the Humans would have been in vain. He felt insecure and uneasy with the knowledge that Mike and Moti were nowhere to be found. "Damn that woman Penagee," he thought. If only she had not allowed her personal feelings to get in the way of common sense, then this whole catastrophe would be more acceptable. Penagee was not a soldier, but a politician and what Karagan needed now were soldiers. Thanu's armed forces did not have the morale without their leaders and he seriously doubted that their effectiveness without the Reptilians was going to be of much significance. Sure, there were the Drones, but they could not be everywhere and the 3,000 strong invading fleet were highly sophisticated ships. Penagee was stretching herself a bit thin on this one. The Council on Thanu reviewed the incoming reports and made their decision. It was a foregone conclusion with a unanimous vote. Penagee had no option, she had to find Mike and Moti fast or they would be in trouble. Returning to her study she confronted her children.

"One of you knows where your Father is, this is not the time to be holding back, because we need him. You have heard the news and unless your father comes in, we are going to have a lot of trouble on our hands."

The children looked at each other, remaining silent for a moment, then Wolf stepped forward and faced his mother.

"No tricks, Mom, not now. You want Father, then turn around and look out the window."

Penagee did as she was told. The children joined hands, forming a circle and concentrated just as Mike had taught them. The strangest thing happened, a pulsating blue light emanated from them, enclosing their bodies in a sphere, causing Penagee to spin around and stand in disbelief watching her children. Her mind raced, it was impossible, yet it was happening. Mike appeared into the centre of the sphere and hung there for a few moments, then his image faded and was gone and the children released their hold and broke the circle. Wolf turned to his mother and unemotionally said.

"He is on the way to Karagan."

Penagee stared at her children. The realization that they were capable of such energies shocked her and she understood the implications all too well. She could never come between them and their Father. Wolf turned and walked out, with the other children following him. They had made a statement, now she had to keep her side of the bargain or risk losing them.

Mike and his force located the incoming fleet, checked the statistics and formulated a battle plan. They were up against a formidable opponent and it was all too clear that they had to get at them before the enemy had a chance to take up positions. 3,000 ships were no mean feat and Mike swooped into the attack from the rear. His six Drones were split into three groups attacking in formation, one group forward and two to the sides and slightly to the rear, with arcs for fire spread in a semi-circle. They were to engage the enemy and penetrate as deep as possible, then break off and attack from the front when the fleet reeled about face. Speed and surprise was the key and they had to take out as many as possible before the enemy had time to regroup. From then on it would be an all-out confrontation from all angles, drawing the enemy away from Karagan. Mike locked his mind into Moti and Frank so an all-seeing all-knowing scenario was established. The Drones positioned themselves then dived into the attack.

The Humanoid fleet did not suspect or pick them up and Mike's attacking forces ploughed into their rear. It was a murderous field of fire and the enemy suffered heavily. As the fleet reeled to face their attackers Mike swung out and back into the front, repeating the strategy and inflicting many casualties, then broke away and ordered random attacking, all the while moving the conflict away from Karagan. The enemy tried desperately to regroup, still the hornets kept stinging and stinging from everywhere. It was hopeless, the Humanoids were at a loss and could not counter an unseen opponent, they could only try to fight their way out and many of their ships were destroyed by their own blind firing. Humanoid vessels, in their attempt to break free, lost formation and scattered themselves. Mike's Drones were relentless and individually hunted down their targets and the surviving enemy made a dash for it, only to be cut down. The battle raged for two hours, in which time the Humanoid fleet was decimated. Mike lost two Drones caught in a blind cross-fire and he fought even harder until eventually the remaining enemy fleet of 100 ships formed a sphere facing outwards and waited for the inevitable. Mike hit them with everything he had in one huge rain of fire power. The fleet disintegrated and space became silent.

Karagan watched in awe the murderous decimation and Razu shivered, touched his console asking.

"Patch me through to Thanu, Subject Penagee."

"Penagee here."

"Razu speaking. It's done, I don't know how, but it's done."

"Thanks," was the reply and the console blinked off.

Penagee breathed deeply. Once again her ex-husband had saved the day and she replayed the battle on the hologram. The computers had recreated the events which took place and Penagee was looking for Mike's attack force. There was nothing showing, only the Humanoid vessels. She played the scenes over and over and eventually made out two flashes that bore unidentified patterns. The computer could not identify the flashes, however confirmed two objects of unknown origin had been eliminated. Enemy forces' statistics came through and they were awesome. Their spacecraft were the most advanced in this part of the Cosmos and Penagee's Drones would have had a nasty time defending Karagan. The question was therefore, what Mike's forces consisted of which could outgun and out manoeuvre the enemy and remain undetected, even in death. From what the computer was able to determine through calculations, a total of between eight to ten craft of some sort were involved, as to their exact positioning it was impossible to estimate due to the speed and erratic attack patterns. There had been no communication with Karagan or Thanu from the attack force, so no one knew who or what its losses were.

Out in space Mike took stock, he had lost two Drones and it angered him. He felt their deaths and it was like losing a buddy. The remaining four Drones formed up in battle formation and streaked back to Ridmon. They had been successful only because of the stealth and cloaking abilities of the Drones. But victory left a sour taste in the mouth at so much carnage. Frank was silently recounting the events as they happened so fast and furious; he barely had time to focus on one target when the Drone had taken out three. He was looking forward to a beer to settle the nerves and slowly the adrenalin high subsided.

"Sorry about the Drones," Said Moti.

"Back to the drawing board, those Humanoids have potent weaponry and we need to find a counter measure." Replied Mike peeved as all hell.

"Do we follow up and attack them on their planet?" Questioned Moti.

"No, let's leave things as they are, that way they will be the aggressors and we the defenders and let the Federation deal with it on a political basis. If not, then we have nothing to lose."

"Good idea, gives us time to rethink our Drones. They are too valuable to be snuffed out like that." Agreed Frank.

Mike's Drones were special. Not the spherical type of their predecessors, sleek aerodynamic swallow-shaped living organisms capable of Warp 40 Alpha speeds, meaning they could travel one billion light years in under 30 minutes and were highly agile, flipping, turning, diving and rolling with tremendous dexterity. The Drones' built-in systems protected the occupants from gravity and centrifugal forces which would otherwise instantly kill anyone inside. The organisms were thousands of times faster in calculations than any computers or Drones on Thanu and were designed specifically as full on strike units. Their cloaking and stealth came from re-analysing the creatures of the Dark Forest and expanding on their unique natural abilities to incorporate the self-same abilities into the Drones. Their armoury of weapons included a similar technique as that of the little blue cat-like creature found on Ridmon which, when magnified millions of times, shattered anything in its path. The Drones were close combat craft and, if one was able to observe them in an attack, it was like watching a flock of tiny, fast moving birds weaving and diving, changing direction in perfect unison with each other at ultra-high speed, a simulation of Nature, sleek and very deadly.

Each Drone was named according to the phonetic alphabet to make them more personalized. Charlie and Foxtrot were the ones that did not make it back to Ridmon and Mike would have to redesign, using existing Drones by controlled mutation of two, then merge the four as one, after which further genetic mutations and tests had to be done before cloning. This procedure would take at least six months to accomplish, so if Karagan or Thanu came under attack again during that period they would have to fight their own battles. The minute Mike's forces arrived back on Ridmon he called a meeting with Jane and Paul. Meetings on Ridmon were casual affairs and were conducted in the open over bottles of beer. Jane and Paul arrived to find Mike, Moti and Frank in deep discussion. The two sat down and Mike asked Jane.

"You know those little insect-like creatures we have here on Ridmon, the ones that eat those small opal berries?"

Jane nodded.

"You have seen how they crawl up to the plants and from their heads shoot out an orange beam that draws the tiny branches down to them so that they can eat the berries."

Jane nodded again and replied.

"I get the point, cut to the chase."

Mike smiled.

"We need a genetic breakdown on the mechanism that creates that beam and I want to incorporate it into the Drones. Do you think you could do that?"

"You give me one of the Drones for the next few weeks and I will duplicate everything." Confirmed Jane.

"Great, you have your Drone Echo, and Paul, we need you to catch those tricky little fellows."

"No problem. I will need Broz's engineering talents." Replied Paul.

"You have got it. Now let's say we set a deadline for three weeks from tomorrow. Will that suit everyone?"

All nodded and Mike ordered beers all round. The Shadows came bounding up and sat down.

"Did we miss anything?" Asked Tara.

"Oh, a little, we lost two Drones killed. Charlie and Foxtrot." Answered Mike.

"Damn, Charlie was my favourite." Whispered Mara.

The group changed the subject to more humorous events and after a while disbanded to go to their various homes. Moti walked with Mike and the Shadows deep in thought.

"What's up, Doc?" Mike asked him.

"This thing you have between you three, this energy. Could you teach Anna and me?"

"Yes we could, although Anna has to reach a certain level and you have to improve on some aspects before the link between you is right for meshing and it will take a lot of hard training and mind conditioning," Confirmed Mike.

"We are willing to give it a try." acknowledged Moti.

"It won't be easy, if you persist then both of you will succeed and seeing as we don't have a full agenda for the next three weeks, we can start tomorrow."

Moti smiled and turned off to his house. The next day cycle Mike gathered his pupils together. Moti and Anna, Frank and Zara.

"There is a down-side, folks, so consider well and take your time to answer. By creating this link between you it cannot be undone and will be with you for the rest of your natural lives. If any of you have any doubts about your relationship with each other then I strongly suggest you walk away. By this link you are joined in energy, kind of like a wedding ring and, like being married into the catholic faith, there is no divorce. If one dies the other dies immediately. If after a few years you have a parting of the ways, you will never be able to lead normal lives again because you will always need each other's energy to live on. Think about it carefully."

Mike walked off with the Shadows following. He was a fool in that he had succumbed to a physical desire and in the process had lost any chance of ever reconciling with Penagee. Now he and the twins were joined and Mike did not know if he had the power to end it and survive. He had made his bed, now would have to lie in it. He watched the couples and wondered if it had been wise. One thing was for sure, out of it came the guarantee that each couple would have to do heavy self-analysis within the next thirty minutes. If no consensus had been reached by that time then the teaching was off. Otherwise, the couples would be stuck to each other for life and there was no way out. Perhaps Moti would survive, but still the cost would be great. After thirty minutes he walked back to the group.

"Well?" He questioned.

"You don't give us much time, do you?" Replied Zara.

The other three nodded in agreement.

"No," answered Mike.

"Why?" asked Frank.

"Because what I will give you will make sure you stay as couples for the rest of your lives or until death do you part. Take it or leave it;" Then, after a pause,

"Moti, Anna?"

"We take it," Answered Anna.

"Frank, Zara?"

"We take it as well," Responded Zara.

"You are all very certain, once we start there is no turning back whatsoever." So saying Mike studied their faces and minds for the last time and found no negativity.

"Good, now if you will each hold your partners tightly, we will make a circle around you and, whatever happens, don't let go of each other." Cautioned Mike.

Mike and the Shadows linked hands encircling the two couples within. He nodded and the three of them concentrated. Along their arms flowed a mauve luminescent light which pulsed inwards and encircled the two couples. The ground began to vibrate within the circle, then a light shot up in a shaft above the group, becoming a bright orange and both couples rose off the ground. First Tara broke the circle, and then Mara, leaving Mike standing under the couples, then the light changed to bright white. Mike raised his arms above his head, then slowly down to his sides and the couples sank to the ground, the light sucking back into Mike and all was still. The couples lay on the ground senseless and Mike turned around to the Shadows who caught his falling body. Together they placed their hands on his chest and slowly Mike raised himself up to a standing position and held the two women to him.

"Come," He beckoned and walked over to the couples and touched their foreheads and they too stood up, looking dazed and confused.

They had become one, yet not one, they were joined for life in a union beyond mere matrimony. Out of Mike's indiscretion and failure as a man to honour the sanctity of marriage had come the ability to join. His punishment became the guarantee for others, however a guarantee not to be entered into lightly.

"Tomorrow we meet again at this same place. It is better we call it a day as our energies are sapped and need to be recharged," Declared Mike and with that he teleported to his home and sat on the sundeck, very tired and weary. Mara came to him and sat on his lap, holding him close and transmitted her energy. Mara was the quiet one, yet the stronger of the two in spite of the fact she merged into Tara who seemed to be the dominant one. It was Mara's quite strength that balanced the two. Whatever Mike had got himself into, one thing was certain, the freaks loved him. For the next three weeks Mike and the Shadows worked their students hard in an unrelenting programme that by the end of the day left them all exhausted. Throughout the years Moti had known Mike and the hours of training the two had put in together, nothing compared to those three weeks. His body felt as if a steamroller had rolled over him. Anna fared even worse and would come home to collapse. Frank and Zara were finding it extremely difficult, but managed to struggle through, showing great courage and fortitude.

Jane called Mike to witness Drone Echo's new ability employing the assistance of the other Drones, she demonstrated her genetic break-through. The other Drones were ordered to resist and Echo beamed her invisible light onto them from a distance and locked on, pulling the three resisting Drones towards her without any effort. Mike ordered a greater distance between them of a hundred kilometres and by the command the three Drones were to activate full reverse thrust. Jane smiled and happily waltzed around and Mike gave the order. Echo locked on to them and pulled them in so easily it was like taking candy from a kid. Frank and Moti were very impressed and Mike nodded. He took his sister in his arms and kissed her forehead.

"That's what I call right on."

Jane was proud of herself and had earned it through hours and hours of hard work.

"Better thank Paul as well, without him and his ingenious plan we would never have achieved it."

Paul laughed,

"No need, it was a challenge and we succeeded by a very simple and old method called electricity. We just dangled the carrot and when the little blighters came to feast we shocked them into submission. The rest is history."

Everyone agreed that sometimes simplicity was after all the best and safest method. With the mutation complete, Mike merged Echo with Alpha and then began the slow processes of adjustment to the genetic manipulations, increasing the survival and awareness instincts of the organisms. Between the Drones and his training classes Mike was kept pretty busy and the following four months saw a remarkable change, not only in the Drones but also in his students. He merged all the Drones into one and the metamorphosis began, lasting two months. Mike chewed his nails for those two months, not knowing exactly how the Drones would come out of their cocoon. It was so easy to make mistakes and end up with a very undesirable problem that could backfire. But as fate would have it, the Drones emerged perfectly adjusted. Everyone breathed a sigh of relief.

Testing the Drones posed a problem. Moti came up with a wild suggestion which at first seemed crazy, yet the more it was considered the more attractive it became and with that the four Drones were commissioned to capture and deliver two of Karagan's Drones back to Ridmon in one piece and this was to be achieved all by themselves. Mike gave the order and the Drones took off.

"Let's place a bet you lot, beers they don't succeed or double whiskeys they do," Shouted Paul.

Frank jumped in and shook hands.

"I bet they make it."

"Come on Mike, what about you?" Prompted Jane.

"Abstain, abstain."

"Geez Mike, be sporting." Laughed Frank.

"No, I don't think so, not this time, but I will say that if they do we had better watch out. Mother will be looking for her children.

"Aw, come on Mike, don't spoil it." Muttered Paul.

Moti had remained silent throughout and declared.

"Why wait, we can start practicing right now."

"Trust Moti to think like that." Laughed Jane and all but Mike, moved to the nearest kiosk.

Mike teleported home, collected the Shadows and moved deep into the forest and waited. He did not have to wait long before the report came in.

"Two Karagan Drones captured."

He teleported into Alpha and all four Drones moved out into deep space and released their captives. The Universe is full of strange mysteries and riddles that are either natural occurring phenomena or that result from a superior life's intervention into the order of things. The two captured Drones were an exception to the rule. The Karagan Drones never returned to their planet, they remained on Ridmon, merging with the others, then cloning as a new Charlie and Foxtrot. Mike was taken totally by surprise. The Drones had done it on their own.

"Razu here."

Penagee touched her console and answered.

"Hello, Razu."

"We have reports from two of your Drones a few minutes ago that they will not be returning to Karagan. Listen to this, out of their own free will." Commented Razu.

"That's very strange." Remarked Penagee.

"Funny thing about it, they have been missing for over two months and well, we didn't report to you thinking you had ordered them back to Thanu for some reason."

"Are the other Drones in place?"

"Yes, everything is OK. Looks as if you have deserters on your hands. We tried to trace the reports, could not get a fix. What do you make of this?"

"Which Drones were they?" She questioned.

"No.13 and 14." The reply.

Penagee was puzzled, there was no way Drones would leave their station no matter who or what. They had to take her or Mother's direct orders. These two had broken the rules and gone off by themselves, not likely. Drones didn't suddenly become independent unless there had been a genetic malfunction or unless Mother had intervened and there was no way she could find that out. Mother had to be involved somehow for some reason.

"I will look into it Razu, in the meantime don't concern yourself."

"OK Penagee, bye."

The console blinked, ending the communiqué. Perhaps Mother needed the Drones for some reason on Thanu. It was the only logical answer. Ras came into the study to fetch her and the children for a dinner treat. Ras and Penagee were now married for six months and she was a relatively contented woman. Ras was a kind, considerate man. Penagee locked her feelings for Mike away deep in a special place of her heart and shut the door. The children saw their father often. Where they went to she could never find out and gave up trying in the end. The children were happy, she was happy and that was all that mattered. As for Mike, well, his happiness didn't concern her now. She often wondered though where the rest of her old friends were, she missed them sometimes. The Federation of Planets was well on the way to becoming a reality and every six months delegates would come into Karagan to hold discussions of mutual interest. There were now twenty members making up the Federation and it was decided at one of these discussions to establish a unified Force to police their part of the Cosmos. Scientists and design engineers got together to design a new spacecraft capable of extended periods of travel in space for dual purposes, as a police enforcement unit as well as an ongoing scientific research project. The first academies were opened for Space Cadets and both Wolf and Zakrose made their applications well in advance. It was a chance to travel and offered excitement and adventure.

However, it did not take long before Thanu was called into question about accessibility and her delegates at a Shared Resources conference were hard pressed to give satisfactory answers as to why Thanu was off limits and they withdrew from the conference, returning to Thanu looking like the bad guys. This had repercussions throughout the Federation and all applications for Space Cadets from Thanu were refused. The twins were bitterly disappointed and at the next meeting with their father the subject came up. Mike listened to their story and told them not to worry, but to wait until their eighteenth birthday which was coming up shortly when they would be legally free to come and go as they pleased and Mike had a plan. They reckoned if their father had a plan it was worth the wait and were sure that, whatever it was, they would get all the excitement and adventure they hoped for.

He asked them how many applications had been submitted from Thanu and they told him four hundred.

"Could you arrange to get a list of the names?" Requested Mike.

"No problem." Smiled Zakrose.

"OK, this is what I want you to do. Make a short list of both boys and girls of all those candidates who are between the ages of eighteen and twenty four. I need people with high average physical and academic achievement. Think you can do that?"

Wolf smiled. "Easy, we already know the best ones and can give you a list right now."

Mike nodded and waited for the twins to patch into their console and within minutes the list of 180 names was given to him. He scanned down the names, sending the information to Alpha, who began to cross reference and check the people on that list from birth date to present time, compiling dossiers on each one, with complete and extensive detail right down to body scans and brain wave patterns. There was nothing the Drone left out. Each individual's emotional, temperamental and mental behaviour patterns were recorded and analysed. From the 180 names it chose 110 candidates fitting Mike's requirements and the twins both qualified. Mike received the confirmation and on the twins' console a new list of names appeared.

"Right, you have a list of 110 names, including your own, of candidates that are eighteen and above or will be in the next three months. Three months from now all of you will be attending an Academy with a difference and, for the next three years, you will be given specialist training and, believe me, when you qualify you will make the Federation Cadets look mild by comparison. So, are you two happy chappies now?"

The twins were ecstatic and Mike cautioned them to keep it highly confidential. Bidding them farewell he teleported through his Gate to Ridmon and called a group meeting.

"We have an opportunity to revive the Regiment with its first intake of 110 candidates in three months' time, which gives us the opportunity to set things up and have in place the necessary infrastructures. All of you will be part of the training programme, so from that time your duties will change. We have three years to turn that lot into an efficient and intelligent fighting unit. In addition will come fifty Reptilians for specialist training who will be responsible for the first Reptilian military wing, trained and managed by their own people for their own defence purposes and, of course, they will be available as usual for any of our missions in the future." Explained Mike.

Moti, Frank and Borz sat back in their chairs and smiled while Mike patched the list of names with each name's supporting personal information through to their personal consoles. The men scanned down the list and Frank's eyebrows raised at two names.

"The twins?"

"Yes, they want in, so I gave them the chance."

"This is not going to go down well with Penagee." Muttered Moti.

Borz laughed and leaned forward.

"Gentlemen, let's not look a gift horse in the mouth. We are growing old and who will take our place here on Ridmon? The way I see it the twins are a blessing and will one day, I am sure, be part of Ridmon's future."

All looked at him and agreed. It was worth Penagee's wrath to ensure Ridmon's continuation. Everybody knew the twins had exceptional talents and what better place for

them to be than on Ridmon, instead of on some floating
Federation junk heap. It was agreed and for the next three
months the course instructors prepared themselves and
Frank was in his element. He loved teaching, having had its
merits rubbed off on him through his deceased wife Susan.
Mike did not attend the twins' birthday party and when
Penagee confronted them about it they simply said he was on
a mission and could not make it and he would be back soon
to be with them. Two days after the birthday the official
status of adulthood and new armlets were issued. The twins
were now free to pursue the careers in their chosen fields
of endeavour and had two weeks to consider their options
before the Thanu Tribunal expected their answers to the
proposals submitted to them concerning areas of function
within the society. The twins waited patiently, knowing
that those answers would never be given and for a week they
kept close to Ridmon and Gnee and spent a lot of time with
Penagee. Mike sent the pre-warning, giving them a day to
finalize any outstanding personal issues.

Twenty minutes before they were due to leave the
twins went to their mother and hugged her, telling her how
much they loved her and Penagee was taken aback, never
suspecting for one moment what was about to happen and
that for the next three years she would not see them or
know of their whereabouts. The twins had left a message
on their console and instructed Ridmon to give the console
to Penagee after they had left. Moving casually into Gnee's
room where Ridmon and Gnee waited, the twins kissed
them goodbye and Mike teleported both through his Portal
to Ridmon.

As instructed, Ridmon, who was fifteen years old by
then, marched defiantly up to Penagee and handed her the

console. She took it from him and read the message with a very heavy heart. The message read.

"We love you, Mama, very much, we have to follow our destinies where they take us. We asked our Father to accept us into his world out of our own free will and he will keep us safe and look after us for the next three years. Bye for now. We love you."

Penagee wept and pulled Ridmon to her.

"Take good care of my children, Mike." She said aloud to herself and instantly felt a hand on her shoulder and spun around to find Mike standing there and he answered.

"I will. Keep well, Penagee." Then he vanished.

It shook her, and in spite of herself she was glad it had been him to take the twins under his wing and not some Federation system where the twins would be lost in some obscure out of way place for them to exploit the twins' talents. Ridmon stood staring at her with a smile on his face.

"What's so funny?" She blurted out,

"You still love Dada, don't you?" Came the very perceptive reply.

"You are too clever for your own good young man, now off with you, Mama has work to do." So saying she turned to her console, hiding the tears in her eyes. Her son was right, she still loved that damn man and it hurt.

Ras came charging in breathless.

"Turn on your console, something's going on." He advised.

Penagee touched her console and the news flashed.

"Thanu mysteriously lost 110 of its young people today. It is not known how or who is responsible, but all the young people have one common denominator, they were all turned down by the Federation's Academy for Space Cadets." A list of the names appeared.

Penagee smiled.

"What do you find so amusing?" Asked Ras.

"The children are in good hands and I know exactly who they are with and why." She replied.

"Mike?" Ras demanded.

"Yes, Mike. The twins are with him as well. They all wanted to go to the Academy and, seeing as they were turned down, Mike in his usual unconventional way gave them a solution and one that I know for a fact will be far better for them in the long run. I have to hand it to him, he has given 110 youngsters a chance. Believe me, the Matabele Regiment will be reborn and those youngsters will learn more than the Federation will ever be able to teach them." She replied.

"And you agree with all this?" Quizzed Ras.

"Considering the alternatives, I would much rather have my children with their Father and not on some far distant part of the Universe where I might not get to see them very often. In fact I will recommend the other two when they come of age to do the same."

"You've got to be joking." The angry response.

Penagee angrily hit back.

"Whatever Mike is or isn't, one thing you can be sure of and that is for my children he is the best thing that could happen to put them on the right road and keep them there. Don't ever forget that he is a Universal Messenger, which means he has an obligation to fulfil, and that, my friend, is that."

Ras looked at Penagee for long moments, wondering at the change of heart in the woman and was about to tell her he could not accept that, when the look on her face changed his mind very quickly and so he left the room instead.

108 new recruits suddenly found themselves in the Great Hall of the Crystal City on a planet they did not

know, facing a group of people they had never seen before and were very concerned. A man in the group facing them stood up and walked forward.

"Welcome to the planet Ridmon and to the Matabele Academy. We apologize for the suddenness and inconvenience this might have caused some of you, however as young Wolf advised you when you accepted his offer, things might happen very quickly, you now have an opportunity to become more than mere cadets, but soldiers, very highly advanced soldiers, which no Federation Academy will ever be able to match."

Frank walked up and down in front of the group watching their faces. They looked like a good bunch of young people.

"My name is Frank. I am your training officer."

Frank gave the signal and the fifty man Ridmon Army marched in with Moti in the lead. They were dressed in thick, black, body stocking battle fatigues and carried stout crystal shafts in their right hands. The troops marched up, came to a halt, turned to face the recruits and let out a bloodcurdling shout which made many a young recruit jump.

"Matabele!"

Frank nodded to Moti, who broke ranks and shouted.

"Your attention please, you are in the Army now, so form up as these men behind me, now."

The young men and women sprang into three ranks as fast as they could and stood waiting.

"My name is Moti; I am going to be one of your training instructors for the next three years, so we had better get one thing straight here and now. I do not tolerate nonsense. You work hard, I reward you, you slack off and I see to it that you remember your place. Don't test me. Do you understand?"

There was some low mumbling, so Moti shouted at them,

"I can't hear you, I repeat, do you understand?"

There was an instant loud "Yes," and Moti rubbed it in further,

"Yes, who?"

"Yes, Sir." The responding shout.

Moti returned to his position and Frank stepped up to the dais. It was then Mike's turn to address the assembled cadets.

"Well, well. The young chickens want to become hens and roosters. I just have one problem with that, you see. Hens and roosters in the Academy, not a good idea. We want tigers. You have all been to the game parks on Karagan, so you know what I am talking about. Your training will be hard physically and mentally and there will be the times you will want to quit, so hang in there and you will make it to the end. I intend to make men and women out of you who will be proud of the Regiment and of yourselves."

He walked slowly along the length of the formed up group then retraced his steps then informed them.

"Ana-Maria will be your Barracks Mother, Borz your Barracks Father and, of course, we your Instructors. You will pay them the respect and courtesy they deserve. My name is Mike, the Father of Wolf and Zakrose, let me tell you, there is no favouritism here. Every one of you is on an equal footing until you prove otherwise. After six months some of you who show the right kind of leadership qualities will receive rank. For all of you that is a goal to work towards. The next two days will be off days for you in order for you to familiarize yourselves with this environment. You will be housed in the barracks as of now and issued with your training uniforms and gear, which you are not allowed to wear outside the barracks until you start official training."

Mike stepped back to allow Frank to walk the recruits to the barracks. Moti marched his men out and dismissed them, then returned to stand beside Mike watching Frank walk his recruits into the new barracks with Ana-Maria and Borz following.

"Beer, Mike?" Suggested Moti.

"Yeah, why not." Responded Mike and both moved to an outside kiosk. Sitting down with their beers, Moti asked quietly.

"Are you going soft on me?"

Mike laughed.

"Not on your life, one thing I have learned over the years is that if you want the best out of someone you must give a little in that way you end up with very loyal and efficient people who take pride in themselves and pride in what they do. They will wish they were back on Thanu soon enough, believe me. You know my methods well, don't you, my brother?"

Moti smiled and slapped Mike on the shoulder.

"Yes, you bloody devil."

Just then Jane came up.

"Will you two cut out that Hebrew and speak a language we all understand."

Mike grabbed her arm and sat her down on his lap, thrusting a bottle of beer into her hand.

"That's the language some of us understand around here."

Jane smiled. "You are such a brutish ignoramus, brother dear, I wonder sometimes how we managed to come from the same mother."

Moti shrieked with laughter and nearly fell off his chair. Mike had to smile back at her and raised his beer in a salute.

"And I love you too, sister of mine."

Jane took one of his hands in hers and held it. The three sat there discussing various things until Frank joined them.

"Everything is in place and systems are all go."

"Great, grab a beer. How are my children?"

"They will be fine. I told them to come over here as soon as they were finished sorting themselves out." Stated Frank.

"Thanks. Jane was telling us she found another breakthrough with that little insect we call the "Bug". Apparently it can detect other creatures from a long way off by a very clever method. Better let her explain."

Frank turned to Jane, who picked up on the story.

"Yup, those little buggers have an almost identical sensing system to that of a shark. They can detect vibrations giving off signature patterns of prey or pick out hidden enemy through detecting the minutest electrical charges emitting from an enemy's body. In other words, our nervous system emits electrical impulses and it's those impulses that the Bug feels. Paul and I ran some tests and it's possible to incorporate a synthetic duplication of this ability into our body stockings."

Frank immediately realized the potential behind it and nodded his head.

"You can't play hide and seek because I am going to get you," He joked.

"Exactly." Confirmed Jane. "And what's more, you can accurately judge the distance, whether it be a few millimetres or 500 metres."

Mike's eyes twinkled,

"And to test our new body stockings we are going for a stroll into the Dark Forest to see how it works."

"You have just made that up now, right?" Questioned Moti.

"Yup, so gentlemen, as soon as the new stockings are ready, Ridmon Army goes for a route march." Mike declared.

"Bloody hell!" Exclaimed Frank. "Daniel into the Lion's den."

Jane chuckled to herself at the thought, as Mike had once recounted to her the incident many years ago when Frank experienced his first confrontation with the creatures of the Dark Forest and the look on his face at that moment meant he was having a flash back.

"Never mind Frank, at least this time you won't have an arrow poking out of your leg." Laughed Jane, patting him on the arm. Tara was busy preparing a meal for her guests who were due to arrive shortly. The twins knew her of course, but had never seen her with their father so intimately like this and she was a little apprehensive. Mara set the table out on the sundeck and hummed to herself contentedly. Their reputation as Mike's Shadows was in itself a compliment and she was not complaining. To her Mike was the kindest and gentlest man she had ever met and she loved him with a passion. She never was jealous of Mara's involvement in their relationship and enjoyed him paying her equal attention. It was a different experience feeling the sensations through Mara and not she and her thoughts sometimes got a little kinky at the prospect. Mike always insisted that they be one in any lovemaking. Between them they decided Mike would have them both and looked forward to the experience. It was time. Tara wanted a child of her own, but with Mara inside of her that was impossible. Mara could never have children and it was a shame, because she would make the better mother. The two could not share the pregnancy, so their merging had to be limited and Mike would not be able to touch her during that four month period, so Mara would have to fill in as the lover and Tara be the carrier until it was over. She was fertile and pleaded with Mara, who against her better judgment agreed. She wanted to have Mike's child, yet it was so dangerous she and Mara knew it. Both of them considered the options; the benefits and the risks were great, so were the rewards. They knew and understood that it would probably kill them, but they would have at least given Mike a token of their love for him, a child or, if the fates decreed, children.

At the kiosk the twins joined the happy group of people and Moti took Wolf under his wing by thrusting a beer into his hand saying.

"Now you drink with the big boys!"

"Oooooh, the big boys. Don't pay Moti any attention Wolf. If he doesn't drink at least twenty beers a day something is wrong with him." Advised Jane.

Moti gave her a look of contempt and ignored her. Jane turned her attention to Zakrose and the two began their own conversation. Frank leaned back in his chair and quietly drank his beer while Mike watched silently, his mind working on the new body stockings and their military potential. Eventually Mara arrived and invited everyone, including their families, to dinner.

Wolf jumped up excitedly. "Tara."

Mara shook her head and smiled. "No my love, her sister, Mara."

Wolf and Zakrose could not believe it.

"Tara is at home at the moment and you will see her shortly. In the meantime, Zakrose, do you want to come with me and help me with a few things?"

Zakrose nodded agreement and the two walked off into Crystal City.

Wolf watched them go and his questioning glance at Mike said it all.

"Sit down son, there are a few things you need to know."

Moti, Frank and Jane excused themselves and beat a hasty retreat to go home and get ready for the dinner. Wolf sat down and Mike explained.

"There is something you must know and it will probably offend you, but what is done is done and nothing can change that. You like Tara very much, don't you?"

Wolf nodded his head.

"Well, Tara lives with me and her sister Mara now. It's a very complicated story, simply put, Tara and I are joined by an energy source that can't be broken. If one of us dies, so will the other. I have always loved your mother and still do very much. It is impossible even if I wanted to have her back because of the situation being as it is."

"What do you mean, Dada?"

Mike considered the question and decided to be open with his son.

"Tara is not a normal person like everyone else. She is a freak of nature and I took her under my wing and gave her a chance she would not have had otherwise, in spite of what she was before here on Ridmon as a Member of Parliament. If people found out her secret they would have cut her off and cast her aside. You see my son, she is what is called a Siamese twin, only in her case she and Mara are separate people, but are joined by energy patterns and can't be separated. They can't live apart or they will die. Sometimes you will see both of them and sometimes only one because Mara is inside her."

Mike watched Wolf's expression and could see the boy's mind working trying to picture what he had told him.

"Promise me one thing my son, that you will not treat this as something grotesque, as Tara is very fond of you two and it would hurt her so if you do have a problem with it. Keep it to yourself for the time being to give yourself time to understand more of what it's all about? You can ask her and I am sure she will explain, but don't turn your back on her."

Wolf replied.

"I have always liked Tara and whatever she is it does not matter."

"Thanks, son, it means a lot to me. Come, let's go home."

With that they walked slowly back home along the walkway, Wolf asking questions about the training and Mike explaining. The two had a good relationship with each other and spoke easily about things. They arrived home and Tara came out to greet them. She kissed Mike and stood looking at Wolf with a smile on her face.

"My, my, you have grown. Nice to see you again, Wolf."

The boy stepped forward and embraced Tara and asked.

"Are you looking after my Dad?"

"Like an old nagging woman, yes." Responded Tara and laughed.

Mike sat Wolf down and fetched two beers, offering one to Wolf. Tara sat with them for a while until Mara and Zakrose arrived. The guests came in shortly after that and the meal and subsequent welcome party went very well. The mood was relaxed and jovial. Zakrose and Wolf got up to excuse themselves, saying they wanted to take a stroll and not to worry, they would see them the next day. Mike offered to accompany them to the barracks, but they said no and left. Not long after, the other guests departed leaving the three alone. They sat on the sundeck and talked for a while about this and that then cleared and washed up the plates and dishes. Mara took a shower and retired to the bedroom, her heart pounding in her chest. What they were about to do was deceitful to Mike, but it was the only way. Tara was next into the shower while Mike sat quietly, his mind extended to Thanu and the two younger children. Ridmon and Gnee said goodnight. Tara darkened the room as usual and she snuggled up to her sister and the two waited. Mike came into the room shortly after and stretched out on the bed. Tara began to kiss him and work her hands until Mike became fully aroused and in the darkness Mara slipped out of Tara just as Mike thrust into her and lay to one side. Throughout the night Tara repeatedly worked on Mike and finally when Mike seemed all done in Mara joined in and between them they made love to Mike. The experience was new for him and it had its desired effect. That night Tara fell pregnant and Mara took on the role as lover.

When Mike awoke the next day the two women were sitting next to him. Tara silenced him by placing her forefinger across his lips.

"I am pregnant, Mike!"

The man sat bolt upright, alarmed. He was about to ask how when it suddenly dawned on him and he swore.

"Tara, my sweet Tara, do you know what this could mean?"

"Yes my love, we have considered the options and are more than willing to take the risk. And Mike, nothing will happen to you, last night we made sure of that."

"What do you mean, made sure of it?"

"We have learned a thing or two and you are not joined to us anymore."

Mike stood up and took the women into his arms and held them tightly. It was suicide, if it worked then Tara would have her baby, but if it failed then both of them would die. Why now, he thought, why now.

"I will fix the spare room for you and make it as comfortable as possible."

"Thanks my Love." Whispered Tara.

Mike was perplexed, when the Thedarian women came on heat it was a foregone conclusion and a guaranteed pregnancy would ensue through sexual intercourse and the results of that fertilization was immediate and the women knew it.

For the next four months Tara remained inside and would not see anyone. Mara was beside herself, watching Tara swell and swell and fretted around her like an old hen. Mike was worried, but there was nothing he could do but to let nature take its course. When Tara went into labour he held her and passed his energy into her. For hours she struggled and pushed, until finally a bouncing baby boy was born. Tara had given all she could and the effort cost her and she lay dying. Mike placed his new-born son on to her chest, then lay down next to her. Mara, knowing it was the end, kissed Mike then merged into her sister for the last time. Tara held her baby and whispered.

"We took the chance, my love, and have paid the price. We leave you our gift of life in this little boy and remember, always remember to tell him his mother loves him."

Tara gasped and forced herself closer to Mike and barely whispered.

"We love you, Mike." Promptly died in his arms.

In his mind, Moti heard the anguished scream and raced into Mike's home to find him with Tara's body in his arms. Moti immediately teleported Jane in, who gently took the baby into her arms and was teleported back to her rooms, then Moti walked out and shut the doors of the house, leaving Mike to grieve alone. Mike buried Tara a day later next to Abu Ahmed and took to the trees. After two months Mike reached a point of no return and in a last act of self-preservation reached out with his mind to Penagee.

"Penagee, I am dying and must see you. I am on Ridmon. Step through the Portal."

Penagee reeled in disbelief, called her children to her and stepped through the Portal to the place where Mike lay high up in the branches and at the sight of him her heart almost stopped beating. She looked into Mike's sunken eyes and saw the terrible pain. The man was suffering. Something had taken a lot out of him, drained him and although she could not understand what, sensed that the man needed her help now more than anything. She took him into her arms and held him tight.

He whispered. "Teleport the children to the twins in Crystal City, Wolf is waiting for them."

She did what he asked then held him to her.

"Mike." She whispered and passed her energies into his body. She frantically probed his mind to find no resistance and slowly a picture unfolded. Tara had tried to block the process which had joined her to Mike, but all she had managed to do was prolong the inevitable. Penagee was shocked, realizing unless she could put a stop to his energy drain, Mike would die. The man had sat in the trees for two months waging a struggle against time and fought with everything he had to stay alive, his energies were being sapped, leaving him weak and susceptible and unless she did something and fast, he would succumb to death. All her suppressed feelings of love welled up and Penagee opened the locked doors of her heart. She extended her mind into his and reached out into space.

Protector Friend felt the desperate call he knew would come and responded, drawing Mike and Penagee into his enveloping form. For a second time in their lives two people who had come together in a desperate struggle for life were given back that one life. For a second time Penagee's energies

passed between her and the man she loved and Protector
Friend became the healer once again. He healed her hurt and
showed her Mike's innermost thoughts and she wept with
joy. A week later Protector friend left Mike and Penagee in
the tree where he had found them. Perhaps this time these
two people would fulfil their destinies as they were intended
to and Protector Friend cautioned them.

"There will be no next time. Mike will not return to you
again, Penagee, so I strongly suggest that both of you make
up your minds and fulfil your destinies."

Then he was gone, leaving the two high up in the trees.
Mike was still weak and would need time to recover fully.
But he was back with a determination and so his recovery
would be fast.

"Penagee, there is something you must know about
Tara."

She silenced him by raising her hand and touching his
mouth with her fingers saying.

"I know all about it, the baby and everything else that
has being going on and if you don't mind, I will be returning
to Thanu to work things out for myself."

"I understand." He smiled.

"Right now though, we need to see the children. Poor
things must be so worried."

They teleported to Crystal City to their children.

The twins were out on a training session, so Mike
sat down at one of the kiosks with Penagee and their two
younger children and waited. The children were ecstatic and
their faces shone with happiness to at last see their Mother
and Father together like this and Gnee sheepishly declared.

"You see Mama, Dada still loves you."

Penagee swept Gnee into her arms and replied.

"I know, my baby, I know."

Gnee was not letting it go and wanted to hear the words for herself.

"Does that mean we are staying?"

"Perhaps one day, we still have things to sort out on Thanu which will take time." Whispered Penagee and Gnee hugged her.

Mike and Penagee both knew that it would take a little time for them to readjust to each other again. The road ahead was clear and apart for a few obstacles here and there it looked promising. Mike secretly telepathically contacted Sally, Paul's wife and asked her to bring over her latest fashion designs if she didn't mind.

"Crystal City is beautiful, who redesigned it?" Commented Penagee.

"Borz and his very creative assistants/" Replied Mike.

"That man is full of surprises, it's a work of art." She marvelled being highly impressed.

"How do you like our fashions on Ridmon?" Queried Mike.

Penagee smiled and glanced around at the people coming and going.

"I am enthralled."

Just then Sally came up with a few of her co-workers with arms full of clothing designs and Mike stood up.

"Hello Sally, you remember Penagee don't you?"

Sally smiled and replied.

"Yes, and it's good to have you back Mike, you had us going there for a while. Hello Penagee, Mike asked me to bring some things over and I guess they are for you to look at and perhaps we have something which appeals to you?"

Another table was quickly pushed into place and the items of clothing placed on to it. Penagee laughed.

"You people really look after your potential clients, a travelling boutique and from what I can see I am not moving from here until I choose something."

Mike turned to her and mentioned.

"I have a few things that need sorting out which can't wait. You understand?"

Penagee nodded, knowing Mike was going to see Jane and the baby and she understood.

"We are fine and I am sure the twins will be here soon."

"Thanks." Mike was gone.

He found Jane sitting with a tiny baby in her arms, singing a lullaby. Tenderly he placed a hand on her shoulder and Jane turned to see who it was and found Mike standing there. Carefully, she placed the baby in his special travelling cot, then dived into Mike's arms. No words were spoken as they clung to each other, then Jane handed Mike's little baby son to him. Mike held the infant, tears filling his eyes and declared.

"This is Tamu, the son of Tara," and kissed the little sleeping face.

"Mike, I would like to raise him as my own, if that's not a problem."

He studied his sister for long moments and realized that at that moment he had no other option and she was the best solution under the circumstances.

"I don't want to land this little cherub on your doorstep, but if you are willing then it will be fine by me."

Jane took the infant from him and placed him into the cot saying,

"I have grown attached to this little fellow over the past two months and, believe it or not, I am breast feeding. Don't ask how my body suddenly became maternal because I can't answer that."

Mike folded his arms around her and held her close.

"Thanks, my love, it means a lot to me and the child. At least the poor thing has a foster mother and one that I am very proud of, bless you."

"Listen, you big ape, go and sort out your life and when you are ready your son will still be here with me."

"I had to bring Penagee into this, without her I would be dead today and she knows everything. Perhaps she will return one day to Ridmon, who knows. In the meantime we carry on as usual."

Jane considered the fact that Penagee was in the know and asked,

"Will she interfere?"

"No I don't think so, the twins are here and she must realize it's the best for them, so I don't think she will spill the beans and, even if she does, there is nothing she could do about it. Ridmon can protect itself and fortunately does not have to rely on anybody for anything." Verified Mike.

"What about our Drones and technology."

"Relax, that's one thing she was not able to find out. I made sure of it."

"That's a relief." Breathed Jane.

"I will see you in a while, Have to see to Penagee and look for another place to stay."

"Why another place?"

"Too many sad memories there now. Without the Shadows it will be too empty and I will miss them too much." He explained.

Jane jumped at the chance and without hesitation suggested.

"I have a nice little house built in the trees, should be completed by now if I know Borz. A bit out of the way, there will be plenty of room for you and that gives you a chance to be with your son."

He accepted and left her with the child and teleported to Alpha Drone. The twins had come in from the trees and when they saw Penagee they dived into her embrace. They were happy and could not stop talking and Penagee listened intently.

In the Drone Mike sat and spoke to it. He often did that. The Drone never answered him although he knew that Alpha had stayed with him those two months, never leaving his side. He carefully opened his mind and his memory banks began to transfer in from the Drone all the information he had passed on to it two months prior. He had taken the step as a precaution and transferred most of what he knew into the Drone, thus preventing anyone from digging into his brain when he became too weak and disorientated. The transfer complete, Mike felt rejuvenated and began to feel the old power return through his body. He was going to be whole again very soon and breathed a sigh of relief.

"Come." He said to the Drone, let's take a spin around the Solar System of Ridmon and thank you, thank you very much for hanging in there with me."

The Drone never responded but took off like a playful puppy and Mike knew it understood. The other five Drones joined in and a game of Chase ensued with Alpha the fox and the others the hounds. In that hour Mike's laughter had a therapeutic effect on him and it bonded the Drones closer to him and themselves than he could ever have imagined. Eventually he returned to the valley and teleported down into Crystal City. Alpha never let him out of its sight, becoming Mike's new shadow.

"Well, I see we are all having a great time."

He called and the twins jumped at him. Mike swooped them up in his arms and back flipped. There was a lot of excitement and the news was out that Mike was back. Everyone kept their distance, waiting for the right moment when Penagee was off the scene. Mike took Penagee to one side and sat her down and spoke earnestly to her.

"Penagee, I need your promise what we have here on Ridmon will not be interfered with and will remain confidential between us."

There was no hesitation and she responded.

"I promise, but I need to have access to the twins, so I ask you to allow me to visit freely. Ridmon is a very beautiful place now and I don't think I can keep away."

"You're welcome anytime, you know that. I must ask you to advise us of your intention so we may take the necessary steps to bring you in for everyone's security and peace of mind." He requested.

"Yes, of course and Mike, Ridmon is safe, I will see to it."

"Thanks, now you must return or else you will have stirred up a hornets' nest and your Drones will come looking and I am afraid it will be the end of them."

Penagee studied Mike and asked.

"You have Drones here on Ridmon?"

"Yes, very special ones, as you no doubt witnessed against the Humanoids."

"That figures, and if I am not mistaken you lost two in that battle didn't you?" She queried.

"Yup. Very unfortunate. They have been replaced."

Penagee laughed.

"You borrowed two of mine for their replacement I take it." She teased, her eyes twinkling.

"Actually no, they refused to return to Karagan, so what was I supposed to do, let them loose into the Universe?"

"It's OK, Mike, consider it as repayment for helping Karagan."

"Why, thank you, kind lady, you're most generous."

Penagee walked over to the twins who were about to leave for their next lessons and kissed them goodbye then, taking Ridmon and Gnee's hands in hers, turned to Mike and nodded. He activated his Portal and they stepped through into Gnee's bedroom on Thanu.

For the next year Mike did not see Penagee or the younger children. He devoted himself to the new recruits and rebuilding himself to come back into circulation with a vengeance. Moti and Frank hardly knew he was there and Mike did not socialize. Jane looked after him and his son and kept people away, telling them that Mike needed to heal in his own time. The recruits, of course, saw him every day at the designated spot in the forest where Mike set up a training camp where most of his time was divided between students, himself and the Drones. Wolf and Zakrose would fill in the blanks when Penagee came to visit and Zakrose told her that Mike lived like a hermit in spite of Jane's insistence not to. Moti and Frank were patient and waited. They understood that their buddy was having a rough time, but kept their distance and respected his silence.

Life for Penagee was an endless battle with the Federation and Ras was fast beginning to be a pain in the butt. He was appointed as Thanu's new representative to the Federation and spent most of his time on Karagan. Whenever they did meet it always resulted in a row and Penagee put a tail on him one day and soon the tail reported infidelity and Penagee sued for divorce. For the remainder of the year she stayed on Thanu and on Ridmon's sixteenth birthday she contacted Planet Ridmon, advising them that she was coming in to stay. Moti activated the Portal and Penagee with her two children closed the door to Thanu behind them. Her reception was cool, but in general most accepted her and were prepared to give her the benefit of the doubt.

She asked Moti.

"Where is Jane?"

He of course went on the defensive and replied.

"Jane stays out of your fight Penagee, and I insist you don't haunt Mike by creating problems with Jane. She will tear your eyes out if you so much as think of hurting him or the baby and then there is me. As much as I love and respect you, this thing between you and Mike has to end right here and right now."

Penagee saw the anger in Moti's eyes and saw deep down that he would, if he had to, take her out. She shivered at the thought and realized she could not defend herself against Moti and answered.

"Moti please, I have no intention of hurting anyone. I merely want to apologize to Jane and help her in any way I can."

"I will ask Jane, but remember what I say."

Penagee nodded and walked off to her apartment. There would be no friction on her part and all she wanted was a quiet, peaceful few months with her children and forget about Thanu and the Federation. Later that day Jane passed by Penagee's apartment, bringing the baby with her. She was open and friendly and sat with Penagee for a few hours talking.

Only when Jane had left and Penagee was alone did she break down and weep bitterly. So many wasted years, so much anger and bitterness had passed between her and Mike and in the end they had nearly destroyed each other.

She went about her life from that day on with one single-minded purpose, to heal the wounds between her and Mike. Ridmon's sixteenth birthday was spent without his Father and, although the boy was disappointed, he was happy and glad that his Mother and Father might get back together again and he prayed for it with all his heart.

Frank bumped into Moti between classes and asked.

"Does Mike know Penagee is here?"

"Affirmative." Came the reply.

"Think they will get together again?" The next question.

"I sincerely hope so for all our sakes."

"You bet, see you later at recess for those beers you promised me." Reminded Frank and both men went off to their respective classes. A few more days passed and there was still no word from Mike. Penagee pulled Zakrose to one side and pleaded with her.

"Where's your Father?"

Zakrose had grown up in that year and developed into a strong beautiful woman.

"Don't you dare hurt Father?" She advised.

"My sweet Zakrose, all I want is to be his friend again, so please, where is he?"

Zakrose gave Penagee directions how to get to the training grounds and Penagee teleported out. She found Mike in deep meditation, elevated off the ground and quietly sat down to watch him. He had fully recovered from his almost fatal episode and although he had lost some of his bulk, he was extremely finely chiselled and defined. His body adapted a new tempering to it which spelled trouble, big trouble. She let her gaze wander around the camp with its ropes, stakes and training apparatus, both modern and some of which she could not make out the origins. Ancient, she guessed, by their primitiveness. There were bows, lances and instruments of war she had never seen before. She did not notice Mike sink slowly to the ground and turn to face her.

She was so busy looking at her surroundings she almost jumped when he spoke.

"Hello, Penagee."

He was still sitting in his meditation cross legged pose and a faint smile etched his face.

"Hello, thought I would come down here and see where the twins spend some of their time."

Mike was silent for a while, then got up and, going to a cupboard, took out two beers, offering her one which she accepted and he sat down next to her.

"The twins are doing well and I am proud of them."

They sat in silence for some time then Penagee mentioned matter of fact.

"I left Ras and now live on Ridmon."

Mike drank slowly, then answered.

"I know, sorry."

"Nothing to be sorry about. Can we be friends, no attachments?" She asked.

"I would like that."

Penagee came every day and watched her children train. They never knew she was there, which Mike had insisted on. Afterwards Mike would meditate for an hour then do his own training and Penagee was awed. He had developed a refined grace and split his training into two parts, one very demanding physically and the other she could not comprehend, it was slow rhythmic movements like a dance, but so slow and controlled that she could feel the energy flowing from him where she sat. Then he would pile solid blocks of hardened crystal on top of each other and smash them with the downward thrust of his hands. A month passed, Penagee settled into a routine. Then one day Frank and Moti came in with the Army instead of the students and Penagee witnessed things of Humans that day she never thought were possible. Mike and Moti took on the fifty-one strong Army in a no holds barred empty-handed fight. At a signal the men and women attacked and Penagee could not follow and within minutes fifty-one people lay strewn all over the ground. Mike and Moti slapped hands then walked in amongst the fallen and touched them on their necks and gradually all stood up a little dazed.

Mike clapped his hands and the Army fell in to ranks.

"Not bad guys, you are getting better, so don't feel despondent, next time perhaps."

They all laughed and continued their training while Mike walked over to Penagee's hideaway.

"Fancy a beer?" He asked.

She came out of hiding.

"What was that?" She enquired.

"Oh, just a kind of test to gauge their improvement."

"You are going to do that to the twins?" Penagee asked, very concerned.

"It's part of the training and no, not for a while yet. Only once they have completed their three years training."

Penagee accepted a beer from him and Mike sat down on a bench next to her and they watched the proceedings.

"What's that slow motion exercise they are doing?"

"Tai Chi, an ancient Chinese exercise that blends physical and mental harmony and promotes health and internal energies called Chi." He explained.

"Looks interesting."

"Come, I will show what can be achieved by it."

With that he got up and called out a halt to the training and huge crystal blocks were brought forward and positioned. Ten on top of each other. Each block was 50 centimetres thick and as wide. Mike stood on a single pillar balanced on one foot above a mound of black sand and asked Penagee which block she wanted broken. She took up the challenge and asked.

"OK, this is all you physically, no tricks, no use of your powers?"

Mike nodded.

"The bottom one."

With that Mike slammed his palm down on the top block. With a loud bang the bottom block shattered into pieces. She was stunned, it was inconceivable that a Human with limited physical power could generate such energies exactly where it was wanted. Mike jumped down and the students cleared the blocks.

"That's the power of Chi."

She was still shaking her head when Moti attacked Mike. He never moved a muscle and too Penagee's utter amazement, Moti struck at Mike with a solid crystal bar that would have crushed any person's skull, but the bar splintered and Mike smiled at her.

"That's the other advantage of Chi."

Penagee understood one thing. These men could decimate any Federation Forces hands down, as they had proved on Reptilia. It was not the size or the strength, but the high level of specialized training of this nature which in the end, whichever way one looked at it, was lethal.

For weeks she watched and memorized the movements and in her apartment she practiced. Ridmon saw her the one day and showed her how to do things properly and Penagee questioned him,

"You too?"

"Yes Mama and Gnee as well, everybody on Ridmon practices Tai Chi."

"Would you mind helping me?" She asked.

"OK Mama, no problem." He replied matter of fact and from then on Penagee and her two younger children practiced together every day.

Another year went by and Ridmon was expanding slowly, with new people coming in from the outer planets and Borz turned his attention to the two Crystal Cities on Ridmon which had stood unoccupied for years and took his team in to redesign and upgrade them. Paul and Jane came together in that group and between them started a venture that would complement Ridmon in the finest way possible. The marriage of all life into one harmonious living environment. In that year the students reached an astounding proficiency, both physically and technologically and were fast becoming excellent Shadows that could move in and out of the forest or Crystal City undetected and silent. More and more exposure was given to them by pitting them against Ridmon's small Army and gradually the 160 soldiers meshed and welded into a crack fighting force. They had another year to go before they qualified and so far there were no drop outs. Each one of them pulled their weight as team players as well as individuals. During that year Mike and Penagee began to reach closer to each other and a deeper, more mature love developed between them. Frank and Moti pushed relentlessly and shaped their terrestrial gladiators to their limits and busied themselves for the final test. At the end of the third year Ridmon watched and waited. The day had come for the student's final test and Frank assembled them in the Great Hall.

"Today you start your final test which will run for a period of a week. The first two days will be theoretical and the last five days, well, you will receive your orders at that time. I, on behalf of all of Ridmon, wish you luck." He stepped down from the dais and walked up to the students and let out a mighty shout,

"Matabele!"

All 160 assembled bodies responded in an ear shattering response. "Matabele!"

Frank smiled then shouted.

"Take to your test rooms, now."

The students broke ranks and ran to their various rooms. It was a hard two days and their brains worked until it seemed smoke would come out of their ears and then it was over. Exhausted, they were stood down for eighteen hours and told to report to the training camp in battle fatigues after their rest at 10.00 hrs. Sharp. All instructors worked those 18 hours marking papers and the results were more than satisfactory, not one student achieved less than eighty percent.

Mike and Moti hardly slept. They were concerned, but confident and called in the Drones. The students were going to face a test of fire and perhaps a few would not return. A test they had to complete in order to win their badges of honour.

Penagee came down to the training camp as usual and whilst the students prepared their equipment and made last minute checks, she asked Mike what their test would be and Mike had to lie to her. If he told her the truth she would have panicked. So he answered.

"We are off to a distant planet that is thick with jungles, deserts and biting cold and there they will be tested in a similar way we did years ago, remember."

"Ah yes, well good luck and see you back in five days."

"Take care, Penagee." Said Mike and abruptly shouted. "Mount up."

The Drones retrieved the force into themselves. Mike was in Alpha with Wolf, Zakrose and 18 others. Each Drone carried 18 students. Bravo was under command of Moti and Charlie was commanded by Frank. Once they were in space their orders came through, a full on strike into the Humanoid empire to capture their latest battleship. Frank froze, poor kids he thought. This was really going to be an eye opener. Mike did not forget his friends and from Reptilia came 46 Reptilians under the command of Mis to join in with the 50 Reptilian students.

"Welcome aboard Mis, long time no see." Saluted Mike and the Reptilian hissed.

"You have your orders." He continued and Mis nodded. The Reptilians were split into equal groups of eighteen on each of the Drones and Mike gave the command. Six Drones sped off in attack formation destination, the Planet Ra-azak through activated Portals.

Like shadows within shadows the Matabele attack force crept into Ra-azak's atmosphere and broke formation into three groups. Mike would go for the capture and board while Moti and Frank would be the harassment and support units to ward off the hordes of defenders that were sure to follow after them. Orders were to create as much damage as possible in and around the battleships land moorings and disrupt communications and control, as well as destroy any war cruisers on the ground. Mike was to teleport into the battleship and secure and Alpha would retrieve it, cloak it and head for Karagan through a Portal, with the others bringing up the rear. Just before dusk Mike's forces moved into position and waited. The Drones were scanning, so far they had not been detected.

At precisely 19.00hrs the command came through and Mike's forces attacked, striking terrible blows against their targets. Mike teleported his troops into the battleship at predetermined levels and what followed was a bloody hand to hand merciless slaughter. His forces in their special body stockings had the advantage in the ship, ferreting out and killing. The other groups on the ground were also involved in bloody hand to hand actions and struck with lightning speed, keeping the momentum and surprise in their favour, in spite of alarms ringing out all over the planet.

Reinforcements were being flown in, only to be cut down by the murderous fire from the Drones. Mike seized control of the battleship and it rose off the ground into space. Ground forces were hastily retrieved, the Drones attacking anything that moved on the ground or air. So quick and fast had been the attack that the Ra-azak's were still struggling to organize themselves to implement a defensive position, by the time they had managed to launch a counter strike Mike's forces were long gone, leaving a trail of death and destruction in their wake. The Matabele had secured their prize, without a single loss of life. Moti shook his head and laughed. Unbelievable as it was, they had done it.

"Message to Karagan, Razu."

"Razu here, who is this?"

"We have a present for you, thought you might like to have it."

"Who is this?"

"Let's just say an old friend and defender."

Razu turned on every scanner on Karagan and sure enough out of deep space came an enormous Ra-azak battleship, the most modern of all the vessels in their quadrant. Razu whistled and asked.

"How the hell did you manage that?"

"Thought this would get your attention. Study it, make others and you will have your own defences and Razu, please act with caution with this new technology."

"Thank you, my Friend."

The battleship hovered in Karagan's atmosphere and Razu with his engineers and technicians were beamed up. The Matabele Force's return to Ridmon was a triumphant one and the 160 students marched proudly into the Great Hall to receive their badges.

No one on Ridmon knew where they had been or what they had achieved. Each one of those students was tested in battle and each one came through with flying colours and Mike, Moti and Frank breathed a sigh of relief. Their training methods worked and more than prepared the rookies for actual combat. It was a proud moment for them; they had taken a massive risk and won through. Karagan got a very advanced battleship and could take on its own cadets from Thanu and Karagan. No doubt the Humanoids would be searching for it, but would never think to look on Karagan for a while anyway.

Frank did the honours and stepped forward onto the dais to a thunderous shout of "Matabele!" Ridmon's Army marched in smartly, carrying the Regimental colours and came to a halt, right faced and waited. Frank addressed the assembly.

"Ladies and Gentlemen of Ridmon, our first students have passed their final test and at this moment a very sorry Ra-azak are licking their wounds. Karagan now has in its possession one of the most sophisticated Ra-azak battleships in this entire quadrant, thanks to the efforts of these 160 Matabele soldiers of Ridmon for stealing it from them."

The Hall shook again with the chant, "Matabele! Matabele!" Frank waited for the noise to die down then continued.

"It gives me great pleasure therefore to present to each soldier their badges and official uniforms. I shall call out the names and each person called please come forward to receive your well-earned trophies."

Ana-Maria and Borz were the ones appointed to officiate. Frank called out the names and one after another the men and woman marched forward.

Penagee sat riveted to her seat, Ridmon and Gnee next to her. The last two names were called and Wolf with Zakrose proudly marched forward to accept their badges. They saluted Frank, accepted their badges and uniforms, stepped back, saluted, about turned and marched off to their place in the ranks. Frank raised his arm above his head and bellowed," Matabele!"

The Hall erupted once again with the chant and when all was quiet, Moti stepped forward and barked the order.

"Party time, Regiment, dismiss."

The men and woman of the Regiment raced to their barracks to put their precious prizes away and returned for the banquet. Penagee hugged her twins to her and danced around in circles. They had made it thanks to a lot of people's efforts and dedication. She pushed them away from her and told them to go and enjoy themselves, then went looking for Mike. He was nowhere to be found. She walked out of the Hall and down into the forest to the training camp and found Mike sitting alone at the base of one of the massive trees drinking a beer. She went over to the beer cupboard and helped herself then sat down beside him. They sat that way in silence and then Penagee quietly asked.

"You took a risk with our children, why?"

"Because they wanted it, because they had trained three years for it."

Another few minutes of silence then.

"Did they do well?" She asked.

"Yup, they did their share. They have grown up Penagee. At 21 they have the universe ahead of them and, believe me, those two will go far."

"Was it terrible, the killing?"

Mike sat in silence and simply stated.

"Both of our children killed with cat-like ferocity and gentle Zakrose was a little tigress."

"You have spoiled their innocence?"

"No, I had to teach them the horror of their abilities and hopefully they will think twice about killing next time."

"You're a hard man, Mike, and I don't know if I appreciate your methods or not, but I guess in a way you are right."

Mike got up and fetched two more beers and they sat against the tree and Mike asked.

"Why are you here and not there?"

Penagee smiled and sipped her beer then answered.

"I have been on Ridmon now for two years and find the quietness of the forest more peaceful these days and of course, there is you."

Mike didn't say a word.

"Don't shut me out Mike, I know I hurt you as you hurt me, but we have to put that behind us as we have both changed and have suffered each in our own ways. I love you Mike, I love you so much it hurts, but I feel I have lost you and that is difficult for me."

"You haven't lost me Penagee, I watch you every day and see how beautiful you are and I remember the hurt I caused you and I can't let myself hurt again. Yes, we have both changed and much water has flowed under the bridge and I have grown to love you more than ever, but I seem to be poison for you."

"Not poison Mike, only you and I have been at each other's throats these last years. It seems as if we just wanted to hurt each other out of love." She persisted. Penagee got up and fetched two more beers. She sat down and leaned forward, clasping her knees to her chest. Her neck was stiff and she shook her head from side to side trying to relieve the pressure. Mike stretched out his hand and gently massaged the back of her neck and she felt electricity pass through her body, surrendering to its soothing affect and her pulse raced and she found herself wanting him so badly it hurt. Mike stopped his massaging and withdrew his hand, but Penagee caught it and placed it on her breast. She felt Mike's body stiffen and she turned and fell into his arms. Mike held her for a moment then got up and vanished.

When she got home, she found her four children sprawled out on the lounge floor fast asleep, with beer bottles strewn everywhere. She smiled to herself and wondered how the younger ones were going to feel when they woke up. This was one time she would not reprimand them. Finishing her shower, she darkened the rooms then retired to her bedroom. In the darkness she flopped down onto her bed and fell straight into a pair of arms that were so familiar and so welcome and she melted into them willingly.

"So, this is how you take advantage of a woman." She whispered into the darkness.

"Shssssh." Came the response and Mike kissed her hard, both surrendering in a passionate union of pent-up longing.

Moti crawled out of a wet bed with a head that told him not to move too fast. Anna threw more water over him and fumed. He continued crawling to the beer chest and flattened a beer, then a second and his head stopped spinning. Anna poured more water over him and shouted, but Moti did not hear. He lunged to his feet and disappeared out of the door with Anna close on his heels. She was mad at him, this time he had overdone the drinking thing and had left her high and dry and so sexually aroused, then he had the nerve to pass out and she could have killed him. Well, he was not getting away with it that easy, because she was going to make sure she was going to have him even if she had to chase him around the planet, hangover or not. Frank had come out of his front gate and watched the hilarious spectacle and collapsed onto the ground in fits of laughter, holding himself in case he busted a rib or something. He was still laughing when Zara came out to begin her daily jog and, seeing Frank, she asked puzzled.

"What's so funny, Frank?"

Between gasps of air and laughter Frank replied.

"Don't go that way, you might just catch Moti and Anna doing something out in the open."

"Doing what?" She insisted.

He stood up and put his arms around her and pressed hard into her and replied,

"That."

Zara flushed. "Oh, in that case I had better go the other way, you coming?" They both jogged off.

Penagee awoke to an empty bed. Mike had gone. She climbed into the shower and after a refreshing wash, dressed and moved to the lounge. The children were still out for the count, so she prepared her special hangover cure of plant concoctions. Humming, she felt as if a great weight had been lifted off her shoulders. Going back into the lounge she shook everyone awake and forced them to drink her pick-me-up. Within minutes all four were looking a lot better and not so bleary-eyed. The twins were 21 years old, so they could do as the pleased, but the other two were still too young for this kind of thing. However, seeing as it was a very special occasion all round she did not get angry.

"Come on guys, let's clean up around here and then go find your Father."

Zakrose was very perceptive and she watched her mother for a few moments and turned to Wolf and whispered, "Looks as if Mama and Dada had a very good time together!"

Wolf merely grunted and replied. "About time."

The apartment cleaned, Penagee and her four children went in search of Mike and found him in his usual place training hard. They waited for him to finish then she marched up to Mike, threw her arms around him and kissed him passionately. The children wowed and whistled and Penagee turned to them and still holding on to Mike made a declaration.

"I love your Father and want him back, if that's OK with you guys?" The children looked from one parent to the other, then responded unanimously, except for Wolf, who asked.

"What about you Dada, do you want us all back as a family, including Mama?"

Mike stood with tears of joy rolling down his cheeks and shouted.

"More than anything."

High above on the walkway, Frank and Zara watched as the family stood together arm in arm and smiled. Zara whispered as they quietly walked away.

"The planet Ridmon has its ways and one thing is for sure, it's her immense capacity of love that makes her such a beautiful place."

RETURN

SEVEN

Jaranah's return to Karagan was with a great sense of fulfilment. Amazingly, the two billion Humans had adapted well to their new very high tech home. The collective efforts at relocating such a vast assortment of creatures and Humans alike was, to put it mildly, nothing less than a miracle in which Jaranah had played a vital role. She moved into her new apartment, settling down to a quiet, yet lonely life out of preference. In her late seventies, she did not have too much she could do by herself except visit parks and chat to people, especially the children, or go to the library. It would have been far easier from her apartment to tap into the records with her mind, but the walk did her good and got her out into the fresh air. She was in no hurry, officially retired and with lots of time to kill before her final act as a Universal Messenger would be played out which, at that point, was still an uncertainty, so in the meantime she would enjoy her life as she saw fit. Jaranah was an exceptionally powerful woman in the sense that her abilities as a Messenger were highly developed and in spite of her age, she was very astute. Sifting through the news records on a console she came across mention of Thanu's previous administrator, accompanied by her children, vanishing without trace after a divorce settlement. The article did not have much to say on the topic and merely put the incident down to "Self-deportation to destination unknown."

She smiled knowingly. The two love birds had finally reconciled themselves and had joined hands once again. Jaranah was happy for them. Other news items going further back revealed that Karagan had suddenly come into possession of a space battleship from Ra-azak.

"I know who was responsible for that one, yes I do." She chuckled out loud.

A few hours later she made the return trip to her apartment, sat down out on the balcony amongst its array of beautiful pot plants and a breath-taking view of the surrounding landscape, with its rolling hills dressed in green lush forests and beautiful flower gardens. The Elders, the seat of ultimate Universal Power, had summoned her a few weeks previously, instructing her to prepare herself for a return to Planet Earth for a very specific task which would be revealed to her on Earth, the result would be her brutal death and her resurrection after three days and re-location to Ridmon to live out her life to its natural end. Two other Messengers were to accompany her, but no names were given. She wondered about that and found it somewhat strange, but seeing as they held the reins it was not her place to question. She considered the dying aspect. But, it did not perturb her, not now anyway. Perhaps had they told her years before, there would have been a lot of reservations. Now she understood all too well that in death, life is reborn. If one is summoned before the 24 Elders then something major was going down and, to be considered worthy to participate, meant that she had made the grade. Jaranah was a happy woman and took what life she had left day by day.

Back to Earth after a fifty year absence was for her something to look forward to, although she had no living relatives, having grown up in an orphanage as a child when both her parents were killed in a bomb blast. A bomb that her father had made to strike back at the Israeli peoples for their intolerance of Arabic cries for a voice in that country. Her father had enlisted into the Hamas terrorist group to commit acts of sabotage and was responsible for the deaths of many innocent civilians. When he had boasted about his achievements, Jaranah felt sick at heart and condemned him in her mind. The Israeli authorities placed her in an orphanage where she lived until her early twenties. She graduated as a language teacher and pursued her occupation until the day a spaceship took her away. Sadly, she was the sole survivor out of a group of fifteen other men and women who had been shipped to Thedrah. On Thedrah she became a curiosity, both medically and otherwise and, once they had finished with her, they carted her off to some other obscure planet until eventually she ended up on Karagan, where she was given her freedom to teach once again and so Jaranah taught languages to diplomats and politicians. During this period she met a wise old diplomat from another world who took her under his wing and as a result, Jaranah became a Universal Messenger in his place. She never married nor involved herself in any relationship. Thedarian scientists saw to it by removing any chance of her having sexual intercourse. They didn't want cross-bred bastards being born from a Human being.

When Thedrah fell as a result of Mike's military intervention, she was content, becoming more sensitive to this fellow Earthling, following his career with keen interest. Amongst all the Messengers Mike was by far the most aggressive, employing techniques and tactics frowned upon by terrestrial agencies. Jaranah insisted that his methods were after all achieving a lot of good, in spite of the fact that she hated violence. She realized that sometimes it was necessary and therefore Mike proved to be a very unique Messenger as a man of war, a soldier. When Moti was nominated, many raised their eyebrows, protesting against it because two of the same kind was really pushing it a bit. The Elders reminded them that the choices were theirs to make for universal reasons and that was that.

Jaranah saw the irony of it all, here were three people from Earth given the title of Messenger with its supporting powers and how ironic that the three represented earth's three major religions, Christianity, Judaism and Muslim. This was going to be a very exciting period watching the Elders' plans unravel. What she could not figure out was Mike and Moti's role in this whole thing. They were military men who would not hesitate to kill if the need arose. It went against all profiles regarded as qualifying factors of any would-be Messenger. Yet she sensed she would not have long to wait.

Ra-azak collected itself and prepared technology for a new, more advanced fleet of ships to be used in the destruction of Earth. Much planning and re-building required to be undertaken and Natas, the leader of Ra-azak, an evil, vengeful man who wanted retribution for his failure to take Thanu, was not interested in the Galaxies of the so-called Federation on the basis of their merits; he wanted to eradicate the people who lived in them just to satisfy his own warped, sadistic mind. Thanu, however, proved to be more than he could handle and it frustrated him no end. He was further enraged by the attack on Ra-azak by forces as yet unidentified who, to add salt to the festering wound, had the audacity to steal one of his new era battleships. Then to add insult to injury the same battleship was cloned and thirty patrolled outer space as part of the Federation Police Force. Earth was somehow indirectly connected to the whole thing and he was going to make sure those Humans paid.

So Natas started to gather his forces and build his ships, planning his invasion. Hundreds of thousands of men and ships were to be deployed and split into three groups. One group would take Earth, one would take Thanu and Karagan and the other would wipe out the Federation and its pathetic unity. Natas was going to rule this quadrant, whatever it took. He would destroy anyone who stood in his way. He ordered the immediate production of Humanoids to start and did not mind the wait, he had time. What Natas in his blind thirst for satisfaction failed to take into account was that for every action there would surely be a counter action and destroying planets would cause ripples of immense magnitude which slowly but surely would take their toll in the years to come. This meant Ra-azak would be obliterated through sheer cause and effect by natural processes of nature.

Alpha reported back to Mike after completing a routine reconnaissance of Ra-azak which Mike had instigated as a precaution.

"Unusual activity on Ra-azak. Massing of forces. New technology instituted."

"Patch in details," requested Mike and the information came through onto the console. Mike whistled and immediately called in Moti and Frank

"It looks as if Ra-azak is massing for a major invasion, Alpha has reported in and from the look of things this is one gigantic force building up." Said Mike, opening the console so that the two men could see the details and statistics. Moti and Frank sat in silence as the figures were displayed.

At the end of the report Frank shook his head and summed up the situation.

"Do you realize that with those figures Ra-azak can take this quadrant and destroy it piece by piece?"

"How many ships did Alpha count so far?"

"One hundred thousand. They have, as you can see, improved their technology and we are in for a rough ride my friends, unless we can counter with something far larger and better than we currently have at our disposal." Commented Mike.

"How much time do you reckon we have?" Asked Moti.

"Not much by the look of things." Blurted out Frank.

"Thanu Drones are not going to be able to cope with the sheer mass of an attack like that and our six Drones alone are no match against such odds. We are looking at a very dismal situation, unless we can come up with a solution and very quickly, otherwise we will find ourselves in the soup." Exclaimed Mike.

"Run those ships' statistics again and let's see what it will take to destroy just one ship, then we multiply our requirements to suit." Recommended Moti.

The statistics of one Ra-azak vessel were relayed and the three men studied the information with growing concern. Ra-azak had developed a battleship almost equal to Mike's Drones in ability, in spite of the fact that they were pure machines.

"Well gentlemen, we have a problem. It is time, I think, for a few long overdue modifications to our Drones. I am not worried about Thanu. Mother can take care of herself. It's Karagan I am worried about. I suggest we attack Ra-azak in spite of the fact they will be more prepared this time. If we can catch their fleet in one group we might stand a chance, but if they split and come in from different directions, it means our forces would have to be split and Ra-azak would, by sheer weight of numbers penetrate our defences."

Mike sat back and considered the alternatives. Time was the key to the whole problem. Ra-azak needed to be monitored day and night and delayed as long as possible by attacking them at random, forcing them to go on the defensive, which meant that the Drones would have to be deployed full time near the planet, leaving no defences on any of the other planets should Ra-azak's ships break through the blockade. Karagan and Thanu Drones needed to be modified, a process taking months, during which time the Federation would be obliterated. What Mike needed was a swarm of wasps. The self-same wasps Moti had mentioned far back in the past. Small, very powerful Drones capable of only carrying six people and streamlined down to pure attack capabilities. These could be turned out by the hundreds using only three of his Drones. Touching the console in front of him Mike asked for Penagee.

"Penagee here."

"Listen my Love, could you come over to the War Room right away, please?"

"Be there now." She answered and teleported in.

Mike motioned for her to sit down and replayed Alpha's report. Penagee watched and at the end of the report looked at Mike with a very concerned expression.

"We need four Thanu Drones here on Ridmon immediately, is that possible?" Asked Mike

"Yes, no problem."

"Bring them in and allow our access, it's very important" requested Mike.

Penagee extended her mind and gave the order and four Thanu Drones headed through a Portal for Ridmon.

"They are here." Advised Penagee.

"Instruct them to merge."

She gave the command and the four Drones merged into each other. Thirty hours later the procedure was complete and one large menacing Drone waited. Mike patched into Delta, Echo and Foxtrot and instructed them to merge with the Thanu Drone, then sat on the floor in a meditation pose and opened his mind. He reached out far and requested Protector Friend to assist. A few minutes later he simply asked.

"Moti, Penagee, come. We need to join hands."

Moti and Penagee sat on the floor forming a circle with joined hands. Penagee's body stiffened as energies flowed like electricity through her, then into Moti, who almost stood upright from the force of it and Mike concentrated until the three lifted off the ground and a mauve light encompassed their bodies to reveal a fourth shape without distinctive form. Frank sat watching with mouth agape, feeling the pulsating energies in the room and was sorely tempted to leave, but forced himself to remain. The combined energies flowed from them straight into the now merged Thanu Drone. A strange light filled the skies, then Crystal City began to vibrate very gently. Citizens of Ridmon watched and waited fearfully, not knowing what the cause was. For six hours the vibrations and light pulsed, then the single huge Drone hovered above the Crystal cliffs. Rays of light beamed out from her and bored hundreds of openings into the cliff face into which the Drone distributed herself.

The vibrations stopped, the light faded and all became still again. In the War Room three people collapsed from sheer exhaustion and Frank jumped up to check their vital signs and Mike whispered.

"We have done it. Give us a few moments and we will be alright."

Frank stood waiting until the three got up and sat down, then he questioned.

"Done what?"

"Created some very nasty wasps with ultra-lethal stings incubating in the crystal cliffs. Frank, our Drones Alpha, Bravo and Charlie have been modified and I hope and pray we never have to go up against them ourselves. We had to give a little to get a lot and the price was that the Drones have become their own masters on Protector Friend's insistence. We now have a new member on our council, The Drone Alpha."

Frank gulped.

"Geez, you must be joking?"

"No, seriously. The Wasps will be their adopted children so to speak and will protect this planet and all its inhabitants as before, only this time I shudder to think what the consequences will be if anyone attacks us." Smiled Mike.

A monotone voice cut into their conversation,

"You have nothing to fear from us, you made us and we in return give you our full and unconditional protection. I will only communicate directly with Mike and no one else. Is that therefore agreed?"

"Agreed." Echoed Frank's, Moti's and Penagee's collective replies.

Penagee stood up and faced the men declaring.

"You have your attacking and defending forces which are without match in this quadrant and of most others and

I suggest you act wisely and with much forethought before you unleash the Wasps. They are a terrible weapon and once activated are merciless. They respond to nobody except either Alpha or Mike. Should any outside force engage in any act which the Drones and the Wasps consider as life or environmental threatening, the consequences are going to be so brutal and horrific you will question why we created such tools of destruction in the first place."

With that she walked out of the War Room, leaving the men sitting by themselves. Moti glanced over at Mike and breathed out loudly.

"Perhaps we overdid it this time, brother?"

Mike nodded in agreement. Frank was confused. He still did not know what had been devised and from Penagee's tone of voice he deducted that whatever the Wasps were, they were going to be someone's worst nightmare. Both Mike and Moti sat in silence, neither of them offering further explanation. Whatever it was, thought Frank, Ra-azak was going to come face to face with a huge and deadly headache.

Jaranah felt the vibrations and her senses tingled, somewhere Messengers had joined hands and were transmitting their energies out into space in a powerful and concentrated force. She identified two Messengers by their signature patterns and instinctively knew who they were.

Something really big was going down for such powerful energy transmittance and she reached out with her mind, searching until she found the source, then reeled back in shock. Someone else was in the energy circle, someone she did not recognize and neither was she able to gain access into the circle, but was obstructed by something or persons of immense power. Whatever Mike was up to it was of a magnitude that just about every Messenger in space would detect and home in on her to investigate. She did not have long to wait before the probes started. The needle pricks inside the brain which she was powerless to prevent. Jaranah sat down and waited patiently until the room lit up and four Messengers appeared.

"What's the meaning of this?" One asked her.

"I don't know. Like you I have been denied access by something and whatever it is it emanates from outside of our fields. Two I am able to identify, the other two are not Messengers."

The four men looked at her. A tall lanky one known as Jorat stated.

"Impossible, such energy can only come from two or more Messengers joining hands."

Jaranah laughed,

"You pompous man, do you think that Mike is an ordinary Messenger? Not on your life. Through the years he has trained his mind in other ways and his body is able to generate forces you know nothing about. Of course you would not understand the complexities that go into the moulding of that man, but what I can tell is that he has made a union with his Messenger abilities and those other lesser-known abilities from an ancient Chinese fighting art and such a union gives him strengths you lot only dream about. There is also one other factor you all have to consider and consider very well. It is his relationship with an entity he calls Protector Friend whom none of us are privileged to associate with and who has been nominated by higher power as overall guardian of Ridmon and its peoples."

"That's absurd, I have never heard anything so ridiculous." Defended Jorat.

"Well then Mr. Jorat, in that case you pompous ass, how come none of us is able to obtain answers or find explanations to the energy forces emanating out of Ridmon, you moron?"

The four men stood silent and Jorat fumed. There was nothing further to say, so they teleported out of Jaranah's room, leaving her laughing at them. She had enjoyed the little exchange immensely and felt refreshed by it. At least two out of three of them, the so-called Earthling Messengers were one up on the rest of the bunch and that gave her a lot of satisfaction.

"What now?" asked Frank?

"We send in two Drones to continue monitoring Ra-azak and prepare our battle plan. We will need the Regiment on full alert and all leave is cancelled. Moti, you put Reptilia on alert and inform Mis we will probably require his services again. I will in the meantime monitor the situation from here and as soon as the Wasps are ready, which should be in about two days, we go on a raid, a drawing out raid just to gauge the Wasp's stings. Penagee will keep Thanu and Karagan informed via the Federation to advise them to restrict their activities closer to home in a defensive role until we can figure out what Ra-azak is up to."

Moti wasted no time activating his Portal, then stepped onto Reptilia. Throughout the next two days Drones came and went, reporting in to Alpha and a pattern emerged. Ra-azak had assembled a huge Army consisting of more than 150,000 attack ships with their contingents of crews numbering 12,000 per ship. These ships were ready to go and many others were on the assembly line. Mike studied intergalactic charts and marked Ra-azak, Karagan and Thanu, then all the 25 Federation member planets. All Solar Systems lined up and continued through to Earth. He pondered and then it hit him. Ra-azak was on an elimination invasion and Earth was last on the list. The first in the line was the small Galaxy of Un and Mike cursed.

"Alpha, you there?" He questioned.

"Alpha."

"What do you think of this?" Mike patched through his findings.

There was a moment's silence, then Alpha's voice echoed Mike's fears.

"Affirmative."

"Thanks, be in touch." Mike teleported to Penagee in the Central lounge. Moti had not returned from Reptilia yet, so Mike called Frank and told him to meet in the lounge and bring the twins with him. He then recalled Borz and Jane in from the outer Sectors. Two hours later Mike gave the assembled group the disturbing news. They all looked at him in disbelief.

"Not good, I must admit, but we need to hold thumbs that Ra-azak doesn't launch within the next two days so that we have no option, we have to strike one good blow and hopefully it will stall them for that time period we need."

"I will get the troops ready." Remarked Frank.

"Not this time Frank, the Drones do it alone. We have to build up the trust and this is the time to do it."

"A bit risky, don't you think?" Questioned Jane.

"No, on the contrary, this might be the breakthrough we need, because when Ra-azak launches we are going to need those Drones' support."

"I don't like it." Muttered Frank.

"None of us do, Frank, but what choice do we have, either we play by the rules or die? You want to call that shot?" Penagee exclaimed.

"No I guess not, but I still don't like it."

Mike leaned over to Wolf and asked him to order beers all round at which Wolf jumped up and joined by Zakrose, did their Father's bidding. Moti returned from Reptilia to join them.

"How did it go?" Questioned Mike.

"This time a lot more want in." He answered and Mike filled him in with the latest details and Moti shook his head, then shouted on top of his voice.

"Yeah, we do it again."

People stopped to stare, but the group ignored them, they had bigger problems on their plates right now without worrying about offending some people. Mike gave an order to Alpha telepathically.

"Attack. One very decisive blow to keep Ra-azak on the ground for at least two days and Alpha, no heroics. We need you buddy, for the big battle."

"Affirmative."

Mike smiled and Penagee dug him in the ribs with her elbow.

"What?" He asked.

"Jane was talking to you, what are you smiling for anyway?"

Mike looked at Jane and apologized.

"Sorry Jane. I am smiling because of Alpha. He makes me laugh, that Drone."

"Why, Dada?" Asked Zakrose.

"Because, my sweet child, he is incapable of emotion and does not quite know how to deal with emotional issues." Mike answered.

"Don't worry, Zakrose; your Dad is teasing the Drone again. Thinks he can make a Human out of him." Joked Moti.

Everybody laughed at the thought, but in their hearts they hoped and prayed that was not a possibility, as the Drones were clinical in their effectiveness and being void of emotion made them to be more feared. Alpha's Drones exited through the Portals in attack formation and joined up with the two already there then, without hesitation swooped down on Ra-azak with all guns blazing. The attack was so vicious and so sudden it caught Ra-azak completely off guard and before they could respond the Drones were gone. Natas called for a situation report and within minutes it became apparent that the damages were excessive and would delay Ra-azak's launch by four days. He fumed and raved and screamed for identification and when his computers told him there was none, he screamed like a mad man and all of Ra-azak trembled with fear. Natas called his generals to him and on the spot executed those who were responsible for the planet's security. To the remaining generals he shouted.

"I want to launch in four days or else you will suffer a worse fate by my own hand. Is that understood?"

His generals nodded and very quickly left the room to comply with his orders, still, heads rolled on Ra-azak during those four days. Alpha returned to Ridmon and reported.

"Mission accomplished, you have your two days."

"Thanks, my good buddy, well done. Stand by for Portal activation and the Wasps."

Mike breathed a sigh of relief. They had gained two days before the battle began. One day to be with his family and one day to make final preparations. Mike gave his forces a 24-hour Stand Down, then teleported to Ridmon's outer Sector where Jane lived with his son Tamu. After an hour of Father, Son interaction he teleported back to the Crystal City.

Moti and Frank sat in the Central Lounge where their wives joined them for their usual social, but the mood was sombre. Wolf and Zakrose went to the training ground to put in a few hours of hard training to calm the anticipation. For those 48 hours the general population of Ridmon was blissfully unaware of the situation until suddenly the crystal

cliffs began to vibrate and hundreds of Wasps swarmed
into the sunlight to hover above the valley in full view.
Ridmon froze at the sight of those beautifully sculptured war
machines, knowing the formidable fighting power that they
possessed. Mike linked his mind with Alpha to transmit last-
minute tactical information to the Wasps. Ridmon's three
Warrior Drones and the 15,000 Wasps were outnumbered
a thousand to one by their opponents, but such staggering
odds did not perturb Mike who had the upper hand when
it came to striking power and speed.

To engage in a full on confrontation was not tactically
advisable, so the strategy was to systematically destroy Ra-
azak's forces by adopting a guerrilla approach of hit and
disappear, using the Portals as hideaways, then re-appear
and strike again to disorient the enemy and thus gain time to
inflict as much damage as possible. Mike could do very little
for the planet Unn, due to time factors and distance which
prevented him from deploying his forces in that Sector on
time. Splitting his forces would also constitute losing the
advantage of the first major concentrated strike, enabling
him to take out many enemy craft. Should he not achieve
his objective in the initial strike, it meant that his forces
would be split into smaller groups and would be hard pressed
to contain the inevitable enemy overflow, which would
spill out with a vengeance and destroy planet after planet.
Weighing up probable's it was estimated that at least five
planets in neighbouring Solar Systems would be lost before
the balance would swing in Mike's favour. In the event that
their primary objective failed, then the only alternative was
to kill the Ra-azak Sun and then deal with the stranded
ships. Since Ra-azak was on a murderous mission of wanton
destruction, it would not be unethical to reciprocate in kind.
Mike would deliver that fatal blow personally, which for him

meant certain death. Alpha reported Ra-azak forces were launching. Mike walked through the forest to the old Arab's grave and knelt down.

"Well, old Wolf, the time has come. If the Lion makes it out of this one in one piece it's going to be a miracle. Wherever you are, wait for me."

Then turning, he touched the other grave, bowing his head for a few moments then said,

"Tara, our son is doing fine, he is going to be a strong man one of these days. Jane makes a fine substitute mother, he will be alright."

Standing up, Mike sensed a presence behind him and whirled around. Jaranah stepped out of the shadows to extend her hands to him and Mike recognized the old woman instantly.

She came forward and looked down on the old Bedouin's grave and after a few moments turned to Mike and took his hands in hers.

"It is time for both of us now my friend, the Elders have asked me to break the news to you." She whispered. Mike stared at her for long moments, letting the words digest. Then took her frail body into his embrace and gently hugged her.

"Yes it is time for both of us and my heart is exceedingly heavy, yet thankful, and so we must both fulfil one final act as Messengers of the Universe."

"You have the option not to do this, you know." She gently said, looking deep into Mike's troubled eyes.

"Yes I do, Jaranah, but if I do not do this, then when the next time comes, it will be that much more difficult. Believe me this is not easy and it pains me a great deal. I have lived by the sword, now will die by it."

Jaranah leaned her frail head against his chest and after a while looked up into his face and Mike kissed her forehead.

"The Almighty be with you, Mother Jaranah." He said to which Jaranah replied.

"And may Allah be with you, Son of Africa." she teleported off Ridmon through Mike's Portal to Earth.

With a heavy heart Mike returned to Crystal City and up to the heights. Looking down across the valley below, he remembered so many years ago the first time he had seen this planet. Over those years he grew to love Ridmon and its serenity and gave his all to protect it. Now he faced the greatest challenge of his life and the knowledge that he would not see Ridmon, its people nor his loved ones again, weighed heavy on his soul. Mike raised his arms into the air and for the last time he looked up into the heavens and prayed.

Penagee felt the pain, went rigid and desperately scanned with her mind to find Mike. She teleported to him up on the heights and flung herself into his arms, tears streaming down her cheeks.

"Why Mike, Why you?"

Mike held her tightly.

"Thank you for coming back into my life and making it all worthwhile again. Always remember, I love you so very much. Tell our children their Father is very proud of them."

"I love you so very much," she sobbed.

Mike teleported out of Penagee's arms into Alpha and gave the command. Three Drones and thousands of Wasps streaked through the Portals towards the planet Unn and for the first time since Mike sat in the Drone, Alpha spoke.

"Sadness of parting is painful with the knowledge that a reunion may never be again."

"Yes, my friend, there is sadness and pain, but there is also hope." Answered Mike.

"How so?" Questioned the Drone.

"Hope in the children and in the future," Responded Mike.

The Drone did not respond and remained silent until the enemy fleet came into range, then he said.

"Whatever happens, friend Mike, thank you?"

Mike smiled and replied.

"Let's kick some butt."

To which Alpha answered.

"Mount up!"

Mike went into attack mode and extended his mind to become one with the Drones and Wasps.

"Promise me Alpha, you will kill Ra-azak and you will save Planet Earth above all else when my energies fail Me." whispered Mike.

"It will be done, Mike, it will be done."

Mike then made his ultimate sacrifice by giving himself up and merged his mind into that of Alpha. The Drone sent a message back to Ridmon for Penagee and it echoed through her mind.

"Mike is one with us. We are one with Ridmon and he shall live on through us and his children."

Penagee screamed from the top of the walkway above the Crystal City and all of Ridmon stood still. The crystal cliffs began to vibrate as if in weeping and all Mike's children teleported to their mother and she held them to her, weeping bitterly.

Jaranah felt the vibration and her heart leapt, Mike had passed over and was no longer with them. He had done it, he had given his life so that many might live and soon it would be her turn. Moti would soon face his challenge. She found a florist, purchased a single white rose, then teleported to the old City of Jerusalem and stood near the place where the Wailing Wall had once been after the terrible earthquake, then placed the rose on the ground and whispered.

"Go with God, Son of Africa." She turned to meet her destiny, accompanied by two other Universal Messengers. The gathered crowds were baying for blood, they wanted explanations why the disaster had occurred, so when Jaranah and her two companions began to shout God's message to them, they were filled with bloodlust and stoned the three to death, leaving their crushed and twisted bodies where they had fallen for all to see.

Moti was on Reptilia at the time Mike merged and in his mind he heard the words,

"Farewell Hawk, perhaps the Lion and the old Wolf will meet you once again on Ridmon. Have courage brother and take care."

He activated his Portal and stepped into the War Room, extending his mind. Alpha reported in.

"Ra-azak in range, we are deploying."

Moti sat back and steeled himself. There was too much to do. His grief would come later. Right now he needed to keep track of things and a level head. Frank arrived and together they placed their hands on the console before them on which a hologram appeared showing the Ra-azak fleet heading towards Ridmon's forces.

"Where is Penagee?" He asked Frank.

"Still up on the heights with her children." Was the reply.

Both men watched the hologram and reports came flooding in, giving details and statistics. The next moment Penagee teleported into the room and from the look of her was taking it badly. She watched the hologram for a few moments then asked Frank.

"Will you take care of the children, will you care for them, and will you love them as your own?"

Frank frowned, he could not understand the question and replied.

"Of course, always, you know that. We are family."

"Thanks." Was all she said and kissed Frank on the cheek, stretched out her hand and touched Moti's shoulder, then teleported out and into Drone Alpha?

Neither men realized what she was up to until Penagee teleported into Alpha and merged. Moments later Alpha broke the silence in the War Room, in a low voice he advised Moti to standby to receive the bodies of Mike and Penagee on their way back to Ridmon in one of the Wasps.

Moti teleported to the forest where a Wasp gently lowered two bodies down to him. He could not see properly through his tears as the Wasp cut a single hole in the ground and placed the two bodies side by side into it, then retrieved a large heavy slab of crystal and placed it over the two bodies, sealing the grave. It then streaked off back to the battle through a Portal, leaving Moti beside himself with grief.

Protector Friend's voice echoed in his brain.

"Snap out of it, you have work to do and when this is all over you can grieve. Right now those two people need you to be there for them."

Moti teleported back to the War Room and studied the hologram. Frank watched his face and saw the tears.

"What is it Moti?" he gently asked.

Moti clasped his head in his arms and wept bitterly. Frank got up and went around the table and held Moti in his arms and Moti blurted out.

"They are both in the ground next to Ahmed." Frank understood, walked out of the War Room to Crystal City in search of Mike's children. He found them on the heights, took them in his arms and held them close.

Alpha waited for the fleet to come into range and observed. It then dispatched the Wasps to the rear of the fleet and launched an all-out attack. To Moti watching from his console it was like seeing a scythe cutting wheat stalks in fast and deliberate strokes. Alpha quickly withdrew his forces into the Portals and watched. The Ra-azak fleet closed its ranks and began random firing in all directions. Gradually the firing subsided, then Alpha launched its forces, carefully calculating its force's arcs of fire and trajectories. The Wasps swooped into position and every Drone, every Wasp opened fire, moving with lightning speed to their new positions and firing again and again. The sequences were repeated with terrible and murderous precision. The Ra-azak fleet was cut to shreds. Ships tried to break out but were cut down, then Alpha released the Wasps into the staggering fleet to attack at random. The enemy fleet was in total disarray, firing blindly hitting each other in the process. The Wasps fired salvo after salvo until not one Ra-azak vessel remained unscathed. Without hesitation, Alpha dispatched Two Drones back through a Portal to Ridmon, accompanied by one thousand Wasps, then with the balance of his forces it streaked across space for the Ra-azak Sun and Ridmon's final act of retribution came with the Drones and Wasps diving straight into Ra-azak's sun and nuking it. Moti was in the War Room when Bravo reported,

"Ra-azak forces terminated." There was a pause then.

"Alpha, Charlie and Foxtrot, together with five hundred Wasps, self-terminated into Ra-azak's sun. Ra-azak Solar System is no longer in existence. All life and military attack forces have been terminated. We have orders to carry three people from Ridmon back to earth, stand by for pick-up in 12 hours and Portal activation."

"Whose orders." Moti challenged.

The Drone's voice echoed.

"The White Matabele, Mike."

Moti stood up slowly and asked.

"Who are the three people?"

"Subject Moti, his wife and child." Replied the Drone.

"Why?" Moti shouted.

"Because your friend has freed you from your bonds and debts and requested you to take your proper place in the land of your birth, Moti Levi, and to tell you, blessings Rabbi, the Ark awaits to take its place in the New Temple and now you will be able to fulfil your destiny as Messenger."

Moti sank down into his chair, visibly shaking.

Jerusalem, Israel 2040 CE. No matter the circumstances, religious groups strive to maintain their traditions and despite the fact that wars or disasters may disrupt the pattern of things, some of those traditions will not be forgotten. So it is with the annual Jewish Passover, which happens to coincide with Christianity's Easter celebrations, and many religious pilgrims from across the globe gather in the Holy City during this period. Here Jew and Christian alike come together for a single cause. On the other side of the Wailing Wall, remnants of a by gone error during the year 70 CE. When the Roman occupation forces ran amok destroying the Jewish temple and slaughtering hundreds of Jews, stands the Great Mosque with its golden Dome where Muslim pilgrims gather to pay homage to Allah. Jerusalem still remains divided in spite of global changes, in spite of continued international intervention. It was a political stalemate, with opposing factions battling with each other for over 5,000 years of Earth's history.

The City of Jerusalem was divided by three groups, each claiming historical rights, but only Israel in possession of the sole mandate. On the one side were the Jews with their ancient history and strong belief that God gave them the land of Israel to possess and built Jerusalem as a symbol of their faith, the Zion, centre of the Judaism. History comes and goes and one power is replaced by another and the land of Israel fell to the sword and its peoples were scattered amongst the nations, because a covenant they had made with the Creator was broken. Other powers moved in and for 500 years Islam ruled when the so-called Byzantine liberation failed to deliver Jerusalem's freedom from Mohammedan dominance.

During this time many occupations took place in the city. Empires rose and fell, until the Jews in 1948 at last won back their rights to their historical land. Alas, the transition was not all easy going and the price of freedom sometimes is extremely heavy. Israel was divided in its agenda and over the ensuing years many divisions occurred which called into question the authenticity of its religious leaders, who in themselves were divided. In spite of Israeli successes there were the blunders as is common with any growing nation. Pressure was brought to bear on this small middle eastern country by Arab states who embarked on terrorist campaigns in order to attempt to force Israel to comply with Islamic demands that Jerusalem was not the sole right of Israel, but of two other religions as well, which meant that the city should be administered and populated by all three groups as a free internationally controlled area. Israel had fought hard in the past to reclaim Jerusalem from Arab hands, many lives were lost and they were not under any circumstances going to give it up to anyone. The Palestinians declared Jerusalem as their capitol and charged that their rights of admission to the city were being subverted and violated by Israel's arrogant and patronizing political attitudes.

The sadness of religion is that it persuades and manipulates the political minds of men to such an extent that they are no longer able or willing to accept that the two elements, the physical and the spiritual have never been successfully interwoven, and cannot feed off each other in the quest for control and power. Politicians revert to using religion as a springboard to gain access to men's ethnic nationalistic hearts and minds and win national support. Many men of learning speculate and theorize and before long originality is put aside for the more easily explainable and understood philosophies of the day.

Moti activated a Portal above the City of Jerusalem for the last time and a scene of a group of Orthodox Jews, gathering at the Wailing Wall to pray. There was nothing unusual about it. Paper messages were being inserted into the cracks of the blocks of sandstone, messages bearing requests to the higher order in heaven. It was a very pleasant day indeed and a day in which one could, for a moment, forget the tragedies of life. Christian pilgrims milled about or walked to and fro, having been to their own places of worship. The Mosque in the background was no different, with men coming and going and all was calm in Jerusalem, or so it seemed. Without warning, the ground began to shake and tremble; people panicked and ran in all directions. The shaking grew more violent, then the quake hit like an atom bomb, opening the ground with multiple fissures, swallowing up everything in its wake. It was so intense that the Mount of Olives split in two and rent a gorge straight through the Wailing Wall, the Mosque and the Churches and on through the city, destroying as it went. Moti sat in awed disbelief, watching the events unfolding before his eyes. Then suddenly the Portal closed and Protector Friend appeared in the war room.

"Moti dear friend it is time, you must embark now. Your wife and child are already aboard, sorry it has to be this way, but time is of the essence and you are needed on your home planet to take charge of the Church there in your new capacity as Chief Rabbi."

Moti was teleported aboard a Wasp, through a Portal and deposited on the streets of the old City of Jerusalem among the chaos and confusion. The people of Jerusalem sprang into action to care for the injured and set up shelter centres for the many homeless and displaced persons. Fear mounted, because the usual aftershocks were just as lethal as the quake, now that many infrastructures had been undermined by the force of the quake. The aftershocks, however, did not come, instead a rushing tide of water spilled out from the gaping hole in the side of the Mount of Olives and flowed through the gorge made by the quake and kept on going through valleys and fields, on and on until it found the Dead Sea. Some relief workers, working the area where the Wailing Wall once stood, were sifting through the twisted up-heaved boulders and blocks looking for survivors, when they came across a partially exposed stone wall and doorway thirty metres below ground level.

Realizing the quake had unearthed an ancient part of the city, they immediately radioed the information in to the Antiquities Central who informed them to guard the find, no matter what. Within the hour archaeologists and religious representatives were on the scene and preliminary excavations began. Police cordoned the area off and placed it under heavy armed guard. Carefully and painstakingly the archaeologists worked to clear rubble from the doorway. The doorway was rectangular and measured 2.6 metres in height and 1.9 metres wide, constructed of granite stones, each block approximately one cubic metre and fitting perfectly into the other. Portable generators were started up to provide light and the archaeologists stepped through the doorway into a short passage, then down a long flight of steps to another sealed doorway. Working amidst growing excitement they removed the small granite blocks forming the seal from the doorway which led into a chamber four metres square and high and another doorway led off to the right. Following that they came into another room twice the size of the first.

On the floor stood ancient baked earthen urns sealed shut. In the centre of the room stood what looked like a very large tomb made out of solid granite, complete with its closing lid. The tomb stood higher than a man and wider than his outstretched arms. There were no inscriptions on it at all, so it was decided to open the tomb and see what was inside. Crowbars were forced between the lid and the lip of the tomb and lifted. It was hard work as the lid weighed at least two tons. Gradually, centimetre by centimetre, the lid moved until it was possible to shine a light into the interior. The leading archaeologist peered into the tomb and his face turned an ashen white and he sank to the floor speechless. One of the religious representatives snatched the torch, pushed his arm through the gap with the torch and before he saw what lay inside, his body became a human torch. The kneeling archaeologist screamed.

"Don't go near the tomb, whatever you do, don't go near the tomb. Everybody out, out. This is a holy place."

Someone had the sense to throw a blanket over the burning man to smother the flames. A police sergeant grabbed the archaeologist and shook him, shouting,

"What is it, what's in there?"

All the poor man could whisper was.

"The Ark."

The sergeant's mind reeled and he mouthed the words "Ark? The Ark?" and it struck home. The Ark of the Covenant. By now all those in the room understood and sank to the floor and crawled out of there backwards. Within minutes the news circulated and the entire world heard it, Israel had recovered the Ark of the Covenant. There was dancing and rejoicing in the streets and for a moment the quake was forgotten, until someone at the Ark site suddenly realized the danger of aftershock and the possibility of losing the Ark again. It had to be moved to a safer place immediately. The President of Israel having been informed acted with determination and mobilized the Army with its tanks and troops to cordon off the entire area.

Israeli's were ecstatic and the search for the purest one amongst them to be appointed as caretaker of the Ark was on in earnest. In accordance with ancient laws, only members of the Levi tribe were allowed to handle the Ark and they had to be holy men, otherwise to touch the Ark meant certain death. Engineers assessed possibilities, made recommendations and called for equipment and transportation for the Ark. They then decided which route they were going to take to move the Ark and police cleared those areas of people and obstructions. The Ark had to be protected and kept somewhere, so the obvious choice was the main military base in Jerusalem, until a more appropriate place could be built. Everything was under tight security and nobody was taking any chances, particularly the Zionist religious groups.

The task was a mammoth one, calling for many people of varying professions. A bridge, strong enough to handle the transport and supporting tanks, needed to be spanned across the gorge with its flowing river. Tons of rubble needed to be moved in order to get access to the chamber's roof which lay forty metres beneath. A large mobile gantry was brought in to do the lifting. Everything was in place and the race was on. Crews worked around the clock, not only at the site, but across the whole city where people and equipment were pouring in to give assistance to the quake struck city. The Orthodox Jews went on demonstration, demanding access to the site, as it was their Holy right and the Army stepped in to contain them.

The world watched and waited. Finally the chamber roof was reached by a shaft sank wide enough to be able to pass the granite casing through. Holes were drilled through the ceiling blocks into which were anchored securing cables. The area around the Ark inside the chamber was supported by scaffolding to prevent the ceiling from collapsing, then slowly the masonry saws cut through the blocks in a circle until the cut away piece was hauled out of the shaft. Next the granite casing in which the Ark was housed was jacked up and secured for lift. The crane hoisted the Ark up and out of the shaft onto a flatbed trailer, strapped down on shock absorbent material and the convoy of tanks and trotting troops headed off over the newly constructed bridge towards their military base some distance away. Helicopters hovered close by and Israeli fighter jets kept vigilance up in the skies. No one was taking chances. After four hours the Ark was safely housed in an underground bunker.

Moti with his family hastened to part of the old city they knew where some of their family lived all the while Mike's last message to him played over and over in his mind.

"Take your place Moti Levi, let the Hawk find the peace for his soul with the God he loves. Farewell brother, the Lion and the old Wolf salute you. Shalom, shalom. Remember Ridmon, remember your friends."

Finally they found the address they were looking for and entered the front door into a passage which led to a set of stairs. At the top of the stairs they were greeted by a young boy who guided them to another passage and an open door into which they entered to find a whole group of Church Elders gathered. His appearance into the room caused quite a stir among those gathered there. Moti spoke loudly for all to hear.

"Shalom, I come in peace, fear not my brothers. I am not some devil out of hell, but one of you, a child of Israel who has been for many years in another time and place."

The gathered men just sat and gaped, so Moti turned to the Chief Rabbi.

"Only you and a selected few members of the military know the exact location of the Ark, and you are waiting for one to emerge among you who is worthy to be keeper of the Ark. Is that not correct?"

The white-bearded old man surveyed Moti with contempt and refused to respond, to which Moti responded.

"So, will you sit and contemplate and decide and argue? While nothing has been done about the new Temple, because you are all caught up in your own indecision and waiting for some word from our Creator through a man, a prophet here on earth. There are no such men any more among you. The only reason you knew of this room was because an Angel, or what appeared to be one informed you all to gather here, so please don't patronize me by acting indifferent."

Moti looked at the faces watching him and he smiled. This was not going to work with words so action was needed and one action that would seal his stamp on this assembly and ensure that his future destiny would be fulfilled as it was intended.

"My Name is Moti Levi, high priest of the Ark."

He watched as eyebrows were raised and, before a response was forthcoming, he pinioned everyone to the side walls off the ground, then walked to each one and removed their shoes. Moti teleported the Ark into the room, in its exposed true form. The men pinned against the walls gasped, visibly shaking as they watched Moti, barefooted, his head covered by a white prayer shawl, walk forward and place both his hands onto the Ark. Tears streaming down his face he shouted.

"I am your humble servant, my Lord Almighty, Creator of this entire Universe."

He then stepped back and turned to the men pinned against the walls.

"So, if anybody here still thinks they are the chosen one, then please step forward and place your hands on the Ark."

All averted their faces in shame and Moti released them from his hold and indicated for them to leave. He then teleported the Ark to a safe place pending the rebuilding of the temple.

Many, many years later, a very old grey-haired man laid wreaths of flowers on one new grave in the forest of Ridmon. The headstone was engraved with two names,

"Moti and Anna."

Tamu, a strong young man, the splitting image of his deceased Father, stood next to his elder half-brothers Ridmon and Wolf and they placed their arms around the old man, steadying him.

"Stand tall, Uncle Frank." Smiled Ridmon and together they shouted at the top of their voices,

"Bayete Enkosi! Bayete Matabele!" Wolf sighed deeply then, taking Gnee gently into his arms, spoke softly.

"Come little sister, we have much to do." The group moved off back to Crystal City, leaving the Dark Forest to its own silence and memories.

Two lost Warriors were returned in death to their final resting place on Ridmon, to be laid beside their fallen comrades with honour and dignity. There was an engraved plaque above the entrance to the walled off cemetery on which was inscribed the names of those laid to rest. The names were, Mike, Penagee, Moti, Anna, Abu Ahmed, Jaranah, Borz, Mis, Tara, Mara, Amos, Ana-Maria and Jane. High up in the trees those same spirits gathered to fetch their friend Moti and his dear Anna to take them to a place somewhere in time and space.

Zakrose, sitting beside Protector Friend amongst the branches, bore witness to the strange phenomenon. She watched in fascination, then slowly one by one the ghosts of the past faded until Mike looked up into the trees and smiled. Zakrose's heart leapt and in that instant she knew that when her time came her Father would be there for her and she smiled through the tears and whispered,

"Farewell for now, Dada."

"Go in peace Human." Saluted Protector Friend, gently lifting Zakrose up and teleporting her into the Crystal City.

He stood there for long moments in deep reflection, remembering the moments, he shared with his Human friend Mike, then teleported out to take his rightful seat as the Universe's 24th Elder. Deep in his heart was reserved a special place for Ridmon and all her inhabitants, past and present.

NEW GENERATION

EIGHT

Swiftly, methodically, meter by meter, a shadow scaled fifteen stories up a concrete building's façade above Washington's dark city streets. Secured to its back was a pregnant woman. Reaching the top the shadow stepped through a portal and vanished just as four policemen burst onto the building's roof top. Down below in the buildings foyer behind a security desk, an irate bald heavy set Police Captain was shouting orders in frustration and anger into a communications console. For the life of him, he could not accept how anybody could have managed to get passed his security network purposely located to trap any uninvited intruders by triggering containment doors and shutters. Yet in spite of this, security was breeched and he could not find explanations as to how and by what. All he knew, his prisoner was extracted out of a maximum security cell with as much ease as a walk in the park. Something did not add up. Who was the woman and what was the significance of her rescue by some freak of nature with capabilities beyond understanding? Near the empty cell with its twisted steel door cradled against the corridor wall, lay the bodies of eight men, some of the finest in the force whose responsibility was to guard the prisoner. How wrong had they been in assuming the prisoners vulnerability. Strange one she was, where she came from could not be established, yet her attitude was extremely self-confident, no signs of fear, discomfort or otherwise. Apart from her intense penetrating gaze she uttered no word nor gave any indication of perception to questions asked of her. They knew she was neither deaf nor dumb. Considering where she had been arrested three days prior in a maximum security facility of the Atomic Energy Commission in Washington, she did seem somewhat bewildered when arrested as if confused about where she was. The puzzling question was how she gained access into the building without tripping parameter alarms or be observed in any live video feeds on screen in the Security Office. Her discovery came when she tried to exit a room and set off an alarm at the Security Console which led to her apprehension and subsequent detention. She offered no resistance, merely surrendered herself to be handcuffed and transported. The Captain retraced his steps back up to the cell and gazed down at his fallen men, their blood spattered everywhere and on the corridor floor near the cell was covered in pools of blood which made the man shudder.

"What in heaven's name could do such a thing, it is inhuman." he muttered out loud.

Just then a uniformed policeman rushed up and gave his report.

"Sorry Sir, no sign. It's as if they vanished into thin air."

The Captain was perplexed by this news as he had hoped the roof top would be the one place to find answers being thirty stories high, with no conceivable way to land a helicopter. If that thing was there his men could have had the possibility to get a glimpse or kill it.

"Call the Pathologist to come here will you, and constable, two things, make sure to collect the video tape for this floor and send it over to the Commissioner's Office, and keep your mouth shut about what you have seen here. Do you understand?" Commanded the Captain.

"Right away and yes Sir" The affirmation.

Quarter of an hour later the Pathologist arrived and began to examine the dead bodies with interest inspecting each corpse slowly his eyes widened until he muttered out loud.

"Lord forbid, this was no human doing…this was some beast of immense power and callousness. Those deep gashes were made by talons, razor sharp talons. What in heaven's name did this?"

"Have no idea Doc, whatever it was certainly butchered these poor men. Still, I can't figure out what the girl's affiliation to this, whatever rescuer was." He growled then added,

"You understand this is classified information and all persons will be required to sign documents of non-disclosure that have had access to this floor including yourself Doc."

"Understood" Nodded the Doc.

Whoever had come for the girl did not simply march through the front door, rather somehow materialized right there in the corridor in front of the cell door and took out the eight guards as if they were made of paper. What's more, no human was capable of wrenching a steel cell door completely off its frame like that. His men, their stricken bodies bore the proof as to the sheer brutality of the attack. Ambulance crews arrived to take the bodies to the morgue where autopsies would be carried out to determine the nature of their wounds more thoroughly. The Captain sealed off the 15th floor then descended to the foyer, exited from the elevator to be greeted by cameras flashing and a barrage of questions being asked by over excited pushing and shoving media personnel. This was all he needed and wondered how in heavens name did the media crews arrive on the scene so damn fast, so immediately took the initiative and announced,

"Gentlemen, Ladies of the press, please, there will be no formal release until the full extent of what has occurred here is known."

With that he shouldered his way through the throng and out into the cool night air to where his driver was waiting.

"Take me to the Police Commissioners office."

He climbed into the rear seat of a black sedan. On his arrival was met by a smartly dressed attractive brunette secretary who informed him the FBI was in the office. She ushered him into the room with its plush oak furnishings and shelves laden with law books, pictures of family on the desk top and three FBI agents sitting waiting in their black suits and black ties looking more like funeral parlor attendants.

"Sit down Hank." Beckoned the Commissioner to an empty chair. Hank surveyed the scene before him with mild curiosity then took to his seat and faced the four men.

"These are agents Williams, Miller and Hernandez" Introduced the Commissioner.

Hank merely tilted his head slightly to one side and waited.

"We would like to hear your account of events." Demanded Williams.

A moment's pause then Hank responded.

"Well, the suspect was apprehended by in-house security who then called us and we secured the female in question in an interrogation room and attempted to extract information from her. She was heavily pregnant which further added to the puzzlement. She never uttered a word. We began to assume she had no clue what we were talking about and there was no flicker of recognition in her eyes either. After three days with a Doctor on standby we realized this was not getting us anywhere so transferred her to a maximum security cell on the fifteenth floor and had eight of my best men guard her."

Williams interrupted by asking.

"Why eight men. Why not just one?"

"Something about the woman's demeanor made me feel uneasy and I suspected there was more to her than meets the eye. Then there was her clothing, strange fabric, definitely nothing I have ever seen anywhere. When we secured her in the cell she spoke for the first time. She looked me straight in the eye and said I would regret this day. I could not believe it, what I saw in her eyes was a wisdom beyond its years and I felt a chill run up my spine. Now I understand her words with eight of my men paying the price. What kind of monster protected her? We will all have to wait for the pathologist's official report to try to ascertain what inflicted such wounds."

"Can you describe the woman." Asked Miller flipping pages of his note book.

"She was petite, roughly about four foot nine to five in height, weight roughly one hundred pounds, pitch black long hair with hazel eyes. Age I put as middle to late thirties, did not wear makeup, was not necessary as she was a pretty thing and yes, the strange part, she was bare foot."

Another moments silence while Miller scribbled the information down then looked up at Hank and suggested.

"Alien perhaps?"

All four men watched Hank for a reaction, then.

"That thing that broke her out of her cell was no human being and judging by the wounds on the bodies I would conclude an affirmative yes. My security cameras would have picked up that monster entering any part of the building so the only possible explanation is that it must have materialized right there at the cell door. We should have footage of what went down shortly when a video tape arrives." Responded Hank.

"Question is how she came to be in the section of the Atomic Energy building especially considering there is nothing of intrinsic value in that room at all other than some junk parts of no use to man or beast. My guess she somehow materialized in the wrong place at the wrong time." Commented Hernandez.

The commissioner pressed a button on his console and spoke to his secretary.

"Elsa, be a honey and get me the Pathologist on the line a sap." With that he replaced the receiver and all waited in silence. A couple of minutes passed before the console beeped. Pressing the receive button the Commissioner asked.

"Is that you Doc? A pause then.

"What can you tell me?" another moment of silence then the diagnosis.

"These wounds are from talons of a prehistoric creature no longer in existence on this planet since the Cretaceous Period. It is very puzzling how this creature could have manifested itself, and I tell you this is not from our planet."

"OK, send your official report to me, and Doc, keep a lid on this will you, thanks." With that the receiver was placed once again onto its cradle. Four sets of eyes starred at the Commissioner.

"Gentlemen, the report is in, a prehistoric creature inflicted those wounds and we have no way of understanding how this creature was able to manifest itself here on earth and for that matter how the woman's role in this saga compelled that creature to appear here to rescue her. Those poor men died by something that is not of this world. Hank I will leave it to you to oversee the burial arrangements and the men's family affairs. What a tragedy, such a sad tragedy."

The secretary entered the room with a video cassette and handed it to the Commissioner who thanked her and waited till she was out of the room before inserting it into a video player in a Monitor cabinet and switching it on. The scene on the monitor was of eight men, some leaning against the opposite wall to the cell while others were either sitting on the floor facing the cell or crouched on their haunches. It was obvious there was a discussion going on about the woman. Then, everybody in the Commissioner's room froze. There, on the screen they saw a creature materialize and shock and revulsion made Hank gasp. Never in all their imaginings, had either man conceived such a grotesque creature as appeared on the screen. What transpired next made each man in the room feel sickened to the stomach by the speed and ferocity of the creatures attack on those unfortunate persons? Without effort, wrenched the steel cell door completely out of its frame then gently lifted the girl onto its back and smashed through a window and was gone. The camera continued to record the sequence of events occurring simultaneously, as the security team in the foyer saw the horror of the attack, so an elevator door opened and four police constables stepped out seeing a creature smash through a window they ran to look out down then up and saw a shadow climbing upwards so they dashed for the elevator and punched the loft key communicating on a mobile console to the foyer advising them of the situation. The camera took in the scene of the carnage and seemed to freeze it in time until the Captain entered the level the camera was activated by motion detection, when the Captain arrived and subsequent scenes until the man exited the floor. Five men sat dazed and confused. They watched the tape over and over again until Williams stood up and stopped the video and took possession of it. Hernandez blurted out crossing himself being a Catholic.

"Impossible, that thing is a lizard looking almost human. The size of it must be a good seven foot tall and built like a tank and those talons on its hands and feet, Hijo de puta"

Miller still unsteady, turned to the other men and requested,

"Gentlemen, this stays here, this never happened, are we clear on this? We write this up as a gang related incident and let it rest there. We will file our report accordingly. And Hank, make sure the camera on that floor becomes non-functional, you get my drift."

All nodded in agreement, so it was agreed to suffocate the whole incident and destroy the video tape as the only solid evidence that an extra-terrestrial life form actually existed which, if made know, would have been smothered anyway. Williams shredded the contents of the tape and burned its pieces in a trash can. Hank still had one final job to do and that was to bury his men and make sure the personnel who saw the bodies and that creature signed a non-disclosure forms thus preventing them from telling anyone about the incident. Hernandez and Williams immediately sent in their reports while Miller brought in a cleanup crew to remove all traces and make the cell area in question look as if nothing had ever happened. Hank did his part and a video camera was reported faulty and replaced. He buried his men with honors, saw to the diseased family's needs, handed in his resignation and then disappeared off the grid.

On a far distant planet a pregnant woman was hastily brought to a Clinic facility for observation and possible child birth. Gnee turned to a huge Reptilian standing next to the pregnant girls bed and smiled.

"Thank you, Ki, you have done well."

The Reptile bowed slightly and exited the room leaving Gnee alone with the young girl.

"Nina you silly woman, what were you thinking? Lucky for you Ki found you and was able to rescue you."

"Sorry Gnee, something went wrong with my attempt to teleport." She protested.

"Yeah! Well next time when someone tells you to stay put, you stay put. No doubt Wolf is going to be mighty angry with you so be prepared and besides whatever gave you the idea you could teleport." Rebuked Gnee.

With that Gnee exited the room and walked over to a balcony overlooking the valley with its array of trees stretching far off into the distance flanked by sheer crystal cliffs and sighed.

"Oh, Mama, Papa, if only you were here, we miss you so much."

Naya, daughter of Boaz and Petua, had always been a tomboy, a mischief maker, yet in spite of her antics was madly in love with Tamu who regarded her as a mischievous little imp who needed to grow up. It was on one uneventful day when Tamu was engrossed with physical training in the dark forest that Naya crept up on him and what transpired next forever changed the relationship between them. She was a beautiful girl with long straight black hair and hazel eyes with a figure to knock the breath out of any man. She was almost a perfect as a human specimen one could get yet it was her mind, so fiercely independent, making sure everyone knew of her brashness. Yet with Tamu, her heart raced threatening to explode in her chest at the mere sight of the man who seemed unaware of her existence. Watching Tamu in his training routine something began to stir deep within her and she became acutely aware of a throbbing pulsating need for copulation and her loins ached like never before. This new emotion was confusing and far from understood, yet the fatal attraction gripping her was too much to bear. Tamu concluded his training and was wiping down the sweat from his body when Naya stepped up close and stood stark naked silently in front of him, her chest heaving, nipples ridged. His reaction at first glance did not register, but the second glance drove home the reality of it all and his breath sucked in. She was magnificent, a goddess and all self-control evaporated in her demanding embrace and passionate kisses. Tamu for the first time in his life experienced sexual intimacy and it drove him crazy with hot lusting passion. They could hardly contain themselves and two bodies joined as one in sheer over whelming ecstasy and wild hunger.

Back in the Crystal city Wolf, Ridmon and Zakrose sat together at one of the side walk kiosks sipping beers when Frank, aged and heavily wrinkled with an unruly mop of snow white hair was shuffling by when Wolfe beckoned for him to join them.

"Hello Uncle Frank, how are things with you?" Asked Zakrose.

"Humph!! Old age sucks sweet girl, yet thanks to the powers that be I still have my beloved Zara." Replied Frank.

"Oh, Uncle Frank you amaze me, how old are you now?" The girl asked.

Frank chuckled out aloud, "As old as my tongue and a little older than my teeth."

"OK Uncle Frank, you win." Zakrose fondly joked holding his hand.

Turning to Wolf he asked." So Wolf what's up, what's new?"

"Well if you must know, it's that brother of mine Tamu."

"What's he done now? "Frank demanded.

"He has screwed Naya, and the two of them have taken off somewhere."

Frank contemplated the news, shook his head chuckling and replied.

"I knew Naya was soft on Tamu and expected her to make a play at some time and now it looks as if she did. Great, this makes me happy indeed."

So saying Frank stood up, excused himself and made off to look for Zara leaving Wolf glaring and Zakrose reeling with laughter.

"What's wrong Wolf? You had dabs on Naya or something? "She giggled.

"Aw, shut up, you giving me a pain Sis." Blurted out Wolf.

"Cool it. Naya is way out of your league and besides your sensitive nature would clash with her over robust independence. Its Tamu's headache now because that female is like a predator and you dear brother, would be eaten alive emotionally. Besides you are betrothed to Nina who by the way you made pregnant. Now you have to do the honorable thing and marry her. And by the way brother, I think you had better go and see where she is because Gnee told me she ended up in trouble down on earth and fortunately Ki rescued her." Commented Zakrose.

Wolf studied his sister closely. She of course was right and went in search of Gnee. Finding her was not difficult as all of Mikes offspring were telepaths.

"Hi, Gnee what's cooking sweetheart?"

Gnee watched his expression then very gently said.

"Wolf, I love you to bits, but now you have to take responsibility. We don't have Mom and Dad anymore to guide us and it hurts, so we have to get on with it and solve our own problems as best we can. Your problem is right here in the clinic with Nina, so please do the honest thing and take care of her, she is about to give birth to your child?"

"Your right I guess, and besides it's the honorable thing to do." Wolf answered. With that he walked away to find his future pregnant wife.

Two weeks later Frank and Zara passed away in their sleep. It was indeed a sad day for Mike's children who buried their beloved adopted Uncle and his wife with honor and laid their bodies in the cemetery down in the dark forest. Mike's children gathered together on the heights overlooking the valley and gave their final salute to one of the last of a generation knowing from now on they would be alone to solve their own problems and make their own successes and mistakes. Wolf, Zakrose, Ridmon, Gnee and Tamu linked arms and concentrated, long moments later in their midst manifested Protector Friend saying.

"Tamu, you and Ridmon will be the fortress for this planet as your father was, Wolf, Zakrose and Gnee you will be the brains behind this planet's existence. Make sure you do it well and remember Thanu will always be your ally in times of need. You are on your own now friends, make me proud."

With that he was gone leaving the young men and women with feelings of emptiness and sadness. The planet had a fully functional community spread over three crystal cities with more than fifty five thousand civilian inhabitants made up of differing nationalities. A contingent of twenty thousand highly trained combat troops with all support units and above all, the protective Drones and warrior Wasps numbering three thousands. The planet was no push over, still remaining undetected in her universe and was a silent policeman of her quadrant. Thanu continued to be the center of the Inter-galactic peace keeping force with Karagan the overall legislative center of the combined Inter-galactic federation.

The Reptilian community on planet Ridmon was purely military and every two years new contingents would come in as new recruits and undergo extensive training. In this way Ridmon maintained a global security network right under the noses of the Federation. She was in effect a quick response unit capable of mass destruction if need be. There was one difference on Ridmon, it comprised of young innovative people at its helm who more than proved their worth and leadership potential. Ridmon had accumulated a vast library of information covering almost everything there was to know about anything from the simplest to the most awe inspiring technologies. Then there were the warrior Wasps. A legacy handed down by Mike to his children and the future of Ridmon. These were the eyes and ears and protectors of Ridmon, a formidable force of organic matter capable of death and destruction on a level so advanced it was frightening. Yet one thing that stood in their stead was their thought process. Either collectively or individually, their clinical calculative brains were like super computers void of emotion yet loyal beyond reproach to Ridmon. The Drones fulfilled their role as mass transport vessels and support for battle as well as for the planets defensive strategy planning. The greatest asset possessed by the five brothers and sisters was the ability to activate portals. This gave them a huge edge in inter-galactic travel and was indispensable. Non-the-less, it was a closely guarded secret.

Tamu and brother Ridmon, like their Father before them enjoyed the freedom of the trees and like their Father, practiced hour upon hour to achieve a high level of proficiency traversing tree tops like an ape. The other three family members were less inclined to follow in their Father's footsteps in this manner considering the aspect as too primitive to indulge in. Yes, Tamu and Ridmon were true chips off the old block in every way. With Frank gone things were not the same on the planet for a while and Gnee was most affected by his parting. But, life must go on so she pushed his memory to the side and concentrated on her work.

Thousands of light years away on Karagan, Senate member Klara Weis had her own agenda and one she was to pursue to its limit. She was a highly intelligent woman yet vicious and uncompromising and used to getting what she wanted. In her employ were an array of "specialized individuals" to further her aims legally or otherwise and her web spread to all corners of the Federation. She was outwardly very charming and gracious with a figure and looks to match. Extremely ambitious and domineering she hungered for power and control and was determined to get it at any cost. Yet she had a thorn in her side, and that thorn was the planet Thanu. Try as she may she could never infiltrate Thanu's security to place any form of monitoring devise or actual person or persons with in the planets infrastructure. This infuriated her no end so decided to take the gloves off and do the nasty and use one of Thanu's own to do the job for her. She needed information, the kind of information she could use was a weapon against Thanu at a time and place of her choosing.

Klara Weis waited for an opportunity to penetrate Thanu defenses by employing the services of someone from within. So she began to canvas possible candidates from out of the Thanu delegation stationed on Karagan. What she did not know was that Thanu had foreseen such an event and made adequate preparation for it many years prior knowing full well this type of espionage was certain to take place. All members of the Thanu delegation on Karagan and anywhere else for that matter were monitored and screened without the person ever being aware of it.

She targeted one such person, a junior female clerk of the delegation and made her introduction.

"What's your name young lady?" she asked the shy petite girl with brown hair combed neatly back into a bun at the back of her head. The shy green eyes were down cast, feet fidgeting a little.

"Alua." She replied.

Klara perceived this timid creature was the most likely subject and congratulated herself on finding the perfect specimen to manipulate to her will. All she had to do was win over the girl's confidence and to do that she figured her best bet was to play the role of the mother figure full of sympathy and sensitivity.

"Don't be shy sweet thing, I won't bite you. Come, I'll buy you a cup of delicious sweet Jaripa tea and we can get to know each other better"

With that Klara took the girls hand in hers and steered her to a Kiosk not far off and ordered two hot Jaripa drinks, a hot brew derived from the leaves of the Jaripa plant. Sitting down next to each other Klara rested her hand on Alua's knee and smiled her flashing award winning smile. She could see that Alua was gradually beginning to relax.

"How long have you been working for the delegation?" She asked.

"Just three months." Replied Alua.

"Hmmm! Not very long is it. Are you enjoying your work and being away from home."

"I enjoy my work as I like the kind of work I do and I suppose being away from home and family is no fun and I miss them." Stated Alua.

"Yes I can imagine a young girl like you here on Karagan alone without friends can be quite daunting. I see the Thanu delegation is housed in secured accommodation where no visitors are allowed at all. Must be boring for you?" Queried Klara.

"No, I have my books and there is the home entertainment console plus I can speak to my parents from time to time. I can't call them, they call Me." Answered Alua.

"Wow, security must be tight with you and the delegation."

Klara watched the girls face and instantly saw the flash of wariness cross her eyes. She was about to ask a more direct question when felt the weight of a hand on her shoulder and looked up to be confronted by one of Thanu's security personnel.

"My apologies Senator, but this girl is needed at her post."

With that the Security Guard took Alua by the arm and escorted her into another section of the building where she was met by other security personnel and ushered into a room and made to sit down and was asked what her conversation with the Senator was all about. Alua recounted her conversation word for word and the Chief security Officer pushed his face close up to hers and whispered.

"Alua, you will not speak to that woman again and as from now on you will be accompanied by a security detail where ever you go, even to the ladies toilet. Do I make myself clear?"

She nodded her head and asked." May I at least know the reason why?"

"We have been suspicious of her motives for a long while now, so be warned, she is trying to get to someone on the inside in Thanu and will go to a lot of trouble to do so. I advise you to be careful at all times and don't be caught alone without your security chaperone."

Turning to one of the Guards he said, "As of now Zor, you will crawl up her rear end if need be to be her constant companion. She goes to sleep, you stay in the same room. You are her shadow. Don't hesitate to use force because I don't trust that Klara not one bit and she will be sure to try something, understood."

"Yes Sir."

With that the security team left the room and Alua shuddered outwardly. Zor being a young man of twenty seven, an excellent athlete and security guard was not an overly handsome man. but did project much self-confidence. Blond with bottle green eyes, trade mark of a Thedarian, he took his responsibilities very seriously.

"Where do you need to get to now?" He asked Alua.

"I am off duty until tomorrow morning and I would like to retire to my chamber if you don't mind." She replied.

"Sure, come. Just remember my obligation is to be with you 24/7 so we are going to have to make some adjustments in our living arrangements."

With that they both walked out towards the exit. Klara saw them go and realized Thanu delegation had figured her out and she inwardly fumed. Her day would come she was sure of that, so getting up she walked to the elevators and ascended to her chambers. That was the last thing she did. Her unconscious form was hurtled out of a five story window down to her death. It was done to make it look like a suicide and so ended the short reign of Klara Weis and her conniving, manipulating ways. Within the Thanu Delegations complex a Reptile reported to the Officer in charge of Security and merely nodded his head, turned and left the room. The Officer activated his console and patched a coded message back to Thanu. It simply read,

"Accomplished"

Klara's resultant death saw the collapse of her network throughout the Federation as fear spread of reprisal. Alua remained on Karagan for another six months in which time Zor had become quite attached to her so when she was recalled back to Thanu he requested a transfer back as well just to be with her. A year later Zor and Alua married. During that year things were happening on planet Ridmon. Wolf was a proud Father of a healthy baby boy and was ecstatic. They named him Miteke, the Thedrah equivalent of the name Mike after his father. Both Zakrose and Gnee were very engrossed in their work and rarely took time off to unwind. Tamu on the other hand was as usual up to his antics and caused both his sisters grey hairs with his jovial interference. Ridmon was off in Bruni City chasing after one of the girls he fancied. One day Tamu was in Zakrose's office fooling around when she lost her temper and shouted.

"Haven't you got something better to do, why not go and irritate Naya for a change?"

Tamu stopped dead in his tracks and eyed his sister.

"Oh, so you think I am a pest do you, well we will see about that and don't call me I will call you. See you around Sis."

With that he teleported out to the nearest Kiosk and ordered a beer.

"Damn sister, why doesn't she just get a boyfriend or something?" He grumbled.

He sat there fuming when Naya arrived and stood facing him with hands on hips and demanded,

"Where have you been lover boy? I've been searching all over for you."

"Not you as well." Pleaded Tamu. "I've just about had it with women today."

"So buster, don't expect to come crawling into my bed tonight, the door is closed and anyway it's my period time so keep away." With that she waltzed off with nose in the air.

Tamu sat there brooding when Gnee arrived and sat down.

"Hi Tamu, what's up?"

"Aw, nothing. Did you manage to decipher Aunt Jane's notes?" He asked changing the subject and taking a swig of his beer.

"Yes and no. Some of her writing was encoded so it will take a bit of time to work out but, I did manage to understand her proposed modifications to the Wasps. Pity neither of us can implement those changes by ourselves. We are not Mom or Dad."

"Yeah I know. Yet here we are the five of us so there is no reason why we can't put our heads together and come up with a solution. After all the Wasps are amazingly adaptive and we do communicate with them. I am sure Protector Friend would help us if we asked."

"What exactly are you thinking of changing in the Wasps. Aren't they frightening enough?" She queried.

"The way I see it we have to remain always one step ahead of any opposition and you as well as I know what happened to Dad, could quite easily raise its ugly head somewhere else and this time it may be an even worse threat. Then how do we defend ourselves, it would be a disaster."

"You are right yet it bothers me all those Wasps may turn on us, their very creators, and that would be fatal for the entire federation." She exclaimed.

"No! That won't happen. Remember Dad made sure there were adequate safe guards to prevent such a thing happening and besides, don't we treat them like equals as was agreed upon. We have Drones on Reptilia, Karagan, Thanu and Ridmon amounting to thirty each which gives us one hundred and fifty all told. Then there are the Wasps which we control from here numbering three thousand and they are our front line defense, behind them the Drones then us. In terms of interstellar possible threats, outside our Federation's range we don't know what's out there and that worries me. Now you understand why I want to upgrade the Wasps. We travel through portals to various locations on recognized and fixed co-ordinates or to places we know from memory. We currently don't have long range exploratory probes out there reporting back. The portal activation is only known to the four of us and that's how it might remain which basically means we are stretched a little in our own capabilities if all hell breaks loose."

Gnee listened intently then added, "OK, I will work on the notes and if I am successful will let you know immediately then we can know what direction to take and how to take it."

With that she returned to her office leaving Tamu day dreaming about the Wasps. As they stood, the Wasps were equipped with a formidable range of abilities from cloaking to extremely powerful retractor beams to two types of weapons. One, Ridmon called White Lightning, the other was projected sound vibration of a magnitude so intense it shattered targets in front of it for long distances ahead. Super computers on steroids, a flexible maneuverability second to none accompanied by phenomenal speed. They could comfortably house six occupants, with a squeeze ten, as troop carriers to designated battle areas and beam them down or up. In short, these Wasps were the crème da la crème of any defensive arsenal and were not mechanical, but living organisms. To engage in long skirmishes out in space where games of hide and seek were fairly common place, troops on board the Wasps had to be able to survive perhaps long periods of time within the Wasps. This posed a problem which needed to be addressed as soon as possible due to the problem of human body gases such as carbon dioxide, ammonia, acetone, carbon monoxide and other gases which affected the Wasps in negative ways in spite of the fact they were capable of producing oxygen from hydrogen and other combination of chemicals, their skins became irritated by those gases and even with venting did not improve matters.

A week later while dark shadows began to creep over the valley. Tamu sat at a Kiosk drinking. Wolf appeared with his new son Miteke and joined Tamu.

"Congrates Bro, fine looking boy."

"Thanks. Hear you been giving Zakrose a hard time, something wrong?" Asked Wolf.

"No, just a little frustrated I guess about the Wasps which Gnee is working on so I hope she is able to come up with something positive."

"If I know Gnee you will get you answers soon I am sure" Replied Wolf.

"Want a Beer?"

"No, I had better not."

They sat that way in silence for a long while then Tamu jumped up and dived into the trees where he was at home. Wolf watched him go and just shook his head. Naya was angry. The nerve of the man. No sir, she was not taking this lying down. On the way to the crystal platform she bumped into Wolfe who told her Tamu was somewhere in the trees. He knew exactly where Tamu was but refrained from saying. Let them sort themselves out he thought. Naya was no chicken female, but the dark forest petrified her and the thought of entering into it at night was very discomforting even if she was on tree top level. She guessed Tamu would be at his mother's old home and headed in that direction along the gangway system. A little while later she found him, sitting in the dark brooding and breathed a sigh of relief. Tamu felt her presence and was glad for the company even if it meant a little negative verbal exchange. She sat down on his lap and entwined her arms around his neck kissing him on the cheek.

"Ah! My darling man, I love you. You know that? She whispered.

Tamu remained silent entwining an arm around her waist and resting his head on her ample chest. They sat like that for a while until Tamu stood up with her in his arms and teleported onto the Wasp Echo. Echo was one of the wasps that brought the bodies of his Dad and Penagee back for burial and to Tamu this was a very special Wasp.

"Hello Tamu." The monotone voice welcomed.

"Your orders?"

"Hello Echo, pleased to be with you once again. I have a question which I want you to pass on to all the others Wasps and I will expect an answer when you are ready in your own time."

"Yes Tamu, we will attempt to answer your question as best we can."

"Right, the question is, what you would consider the most important upgrade to yourselves to improve on your capabilities? No rush, discuss it among yourselves and report to me tomorrow."

Tamu teleported back down into the crystal city still clutching Naya in his arms. Inside the Crystal Dome night life was beginning to emerge so Tamu sought out friends and family with Naya in tow. Gnee sat with Zakrose and a couple of their female friends chatting so Tamu asked Naya if she wanted to join them but she declined. Finding an empty table they sat down making small talk until interrupted by sounds of music. Ridmon's home grown live band was kicking off the evening and gradually couples merged onto the dance floor. A short while later some of the Matabele Regiment officers walked in straight to the bar. Since the death of his Father the Regiment had deteriorated a little with their mentor gone the spirit of Matabele seemed to wane. They were still a force to be reckoned with and now it was up to Tamu to bring them back into line once more. This was one job he did not relish due to the fact that some of the soldiers were miles ahead of him when it came to martial arts. What stood in his favor was his rank and only that.

"Come I will teach you to dance." And dragging Naya after him got on to the dance floor lifted her up in his arms and swayed in time to the music. She held him tight and let the music flow over her and snuggled her head into the nape of his neck and swooned.

With Moti, Frank and his Father out of the picture the battalion was under the command of a ruthless yet fair Ridmonian who had come up the ranks before the time of Thanu's creation. He attempted to carry on where Mike left off but did not quite have what it took. He was a fine leader and administrator all the same and demanded perfection from his troops many of whom fell foul from time to time and suffered rather harsh punishments. Bordred was the man's name. A huge and powerful man, who bore the scars of combat to prove it. He did not tolerate Tamu to well thinking the young man was too unsettled and did not have direction, yet was powerless to do anything about it except give the man a hard time. Tamu bore the man no love and bided his time with patience and tolerance knowing the day would come when he and Bordred would have a confrontation. Later that evening both Tamu and Naya called it a night and retired to their room in the crystal city. Naya bathed then went to bed promptly falling asleep. Sleep did not come to Tamu who waited anxiously for news from the Wasps. The hours passed and then Echo broke the silence.

"We have decided."

He teleported into Echo to hear their recommendations and waited.

Echo's monotone voice sounded.

"Our abilities are a tribute to Jane and seeing as Jane is no longer with us we have decided to wait for Gnee to find solutions in Jane's notes. However, this may take time so we request you teleport Gnee with the notes into me and allow us to work together to decipher the documents."

Gnee was not going to be happy about her beauty sleep being disturbed not one bit. Tamu woke Gnee from her dreamland telepathically and informed her of the Wasps request. She was far from pleased, but collected the notes all the same and teleported into Echo to sit next to Tamu. Word for word she verbally transmitted to Echo who opened his lines of communication and three thousand Wasps began a collective deciphering of Jane's notes. Within minutes the results were made known.

"We have broken the code and this is what we have found."

Both Tamu and Gnee were all ears.

"We have the schematics and procedures to perform all modifications as is suggested by Jane ourselves. We only request that this be done in two stages. Half of our number will incubate while the other half adopts battle positions for the duration of a month or so. Once the procedure is complete the other half will incubate and so on. We feel we do not wish to disclose at this moment what Jane has revealed and will only do so once all Wasps are modified out of respect for Jane. Are you in agreement?"

"Fine by us then, we accept" replied Tamu and together he and Gnee teleported down to their respective rooms.

This was going to be a long two months. Life on Ridmon passed as usual day to day and people came and went between crystal cities. Zakrose recollected a message from Bruri City on her console which read, "Anna-Maria, calling for you. Please respond post haste. In a flash, Zakrose teleported into Bruri City, to a room where Anna-Maria's frail body lay lifeless accept for her eyes housed in sunken sockets shone with a glowing light. Zakrose held her hand gently and Anna-Maria smiled.

"My child, my life has been a wonderful one full of hope and giving and I leave it with no regrets. I just have one request and that is you lay me to rest next to my dear friends in the dark forest."

"It will be done, I promise you." Replied Zakrose with tearful eyes.

"Ah, dear child, we had some good times and some bad, but look at you how pretty you are and all grown up. Your Dad and Mom would be so proud."

Anna Maria coughed then just like that the light went out of her eyes and she passed away. Zakrose could not contain herself and broke down, tears streaming down her cheeks. The next instant Ridmon, Gnee and Tamu arrived in the room and together they lifted the frail body and teleported to the dark forest and laid Anna-Maria to rest with her dear friends. Another name was added to the plaque at the entrance to the cemetery.

Sadly two friends passing away in a space of a year of each other was the last of the original settlers on planet Ridmon. The rest of the month passed without any change except for one. Bordred decided to put his Regiment through its passes which included Tamu. His plan was twofold. First stage would be ground exercises in full battle readiness where he would divide his troops into groups and give them missions to accomplish by a certain time scale and difficulty level. The second would be a joint exercise on Reptilia to hone the two forces together as a single fighting unit. This called for massive logistics especially on Reptilia. Landing a combined force of twenty thousand troops with support gear was not going to be walk a in the park. Housing and feeding on a barren desolate and mountainous terrain was going to be an exercise on its own. Bordred summoned Tamu to his office and demanded he make available all the Wasps for this exercise and a number of Drones on Reptilia.

"Sorry, the Wasps are undergoing transformation at this moment and will be so for the following two months." Tamu Declared.

"On whose orders." Demanded the man?

Tamu went on the defensive.

"Mine, and excuse me, you have no jurisdiction over those Wasps what so ever. Their deployment rests entirely on my say so ultimately and no one else's and that includes the Drones as a standing order passed down by my Father, your Commander in Chief. And should I be perished then that order belays to Wolf, then to Zakrose, Ridmon and Gnee."

Bordred eyed Tamu with growing anger and wanted to ring the young man's neck.

Tamu smiled saying.

"Bordred, I advise you to be cautious in what you think. I am a telepath so can read your mind and teleport you off world to a very unpleasant place."

The man's head jolted backwards in shock. Never in his born days did he suspect Tamu to be like the other four. He knew the brother and sisters were weird now this young wiper snapper just revealed himself. His thoughts raced and was about to say something when Tamu intervened.

"Perhaps if you would like to postpone the exercises until the end of two months then the full contingent of Wasps will be battle ready and deployable."

Bordred thought about what Tamu had just said and it made sense. This would give him time to fully work out the logistic nightmare involved.

"Yes I agree and you will inform me as to the Wasps progress?"

"Indeed." Tamu teleported out.

Bordred sat down on his chair contemplating. That young man would not surprise anyone if he emulated his Father to the letter. In future he had better work with rather than against that young man because who knows what else he hides beneath the surface. So it was for those two months, while the Wasps incubated. One day Wolfe brought up the subject concerning Moti's son.

"Wouldn't we like to know where he is and what is he doing? Hey Guys come on, lighten up, give me some slack here after all its Uncle Moti's son for heaven sake."

Wolf glanced around waiting for some reaction and seeing none muttered.

"Guess what, you guys are the pits."

A moment's dead silence then Tamu, Zakrose, Ridmon and Gnee erupted in fits of laughter rolling on the ground in exaggerated hysteria. Wolfe was not impressed and teleported out.

"Might have a point, but can't imagine his son to be anything like his father. Wow, those are big shoes to fill." Gnee Commented.

"But you know, maybe we should bring him here. Makes a lot of sense otherwise how is the guy going to know his old man's past. Especially here on the planet." Protested Zakrose to which Tamu piped up with his contribution to the conversation.

"Man, he's probably some fanatic Jewish zealot by now, seeing his old man was chief Rabbi in Israel."

"Tamu, sometimes you are a real twat." Reprimanded Zakrose.

"Let's take a vote, let's bring him here." Challenged Gnee.

"I know." Interrupted Ridmon, "We'll send Ki to fetch him, he would have a small cadenza seeing that reptile."

"Rubbish, we will go and fetch him, all four of us and that's final." Declared Zakrose.

"Excuse me girls, but we are not exactly Dad remember, so Ki comes for protection otherwise mission off, understood." Reminded Tamu.

"Agreed, when and where?" Zakrose asked.

"After Bordred's exercise program." Tamu responded.

Jokes over, the four separated company to their own duties and not far away Wolf smiled to himself.

"Those four are not as stupid as they look."

Two months passed and it was time for the remainder of the Wasps to emerge from their hibernation so Echo sent a message to Tamu to convene.

"We have completed our task very successfully and now advise you we are in possession of the portal secrets which Jane left for us. In addition, something we were so worried about was the ability to regenerate ourselves and this was the single most important factor concerning us. We do not need more weapons or abilities, we need longevity and survival. Jane has given that to us and we are content."

Silence, whilst the information was absorbed into the minds of the five. Wolfe realized then that Jane had given the Wasps their freedom and a greater degree of independence making him feel uneasy.

"We are now a cohesive unit, we are now part of Planet Ridmon's community as functional intelligent beings." Echo's voice declared.

Bordred received the news that the Wasps were in readiness and initiated what he called.

"Operation Lizard."

The planet went into lock down, complete shut off from the outside universe and the exercises began in earnest lasting five months. Bordred was under no illusion and spared nothing to make sure all his troops performed to capacity. He was quick to realize Tamu and Ridmon's worth as an outright leader and motivator of men and women. The Wasps were Tamu's, no question of that and only obeyed his command no matter what. It dawned on him those Wasps were different yet still so effectively clinical. Something had changed with those entities which made them less robotic. After six months the Regiment began relocation to Reptilia. The Drones came in to board the troops and all the support needed to sustain a lengthy exercise. Two thousand Wasps and twenty Drones embarked twenty thousand troops and deposited them on Reptilia. What turmoil. People running to and fro like crazy ants trying to get themselves organized and set up a camp large enough to accommodate such an enormous troop contingent from scratch was not easy. Ki approached Tamu and hissed. His message was simple; come to our camp there is someone you must meet. Tamu jumped on Ki's back and teleported to a Reptilian village far from the action. There he met for the first time an old Reptile called Zi.

"So, you are the son of Mike. Did you know, your Father and I were good friends? Ah yes, we saw many things so terrible it's amazing we stayed sane. But, I respected your Father as a man of this word. Now I give to you Ki, my son, and he will be by your side to protect you and your family. He will die for you if need be."

Tamu knelt before Zi and bowed his head in humble submission.

"Son of Mike, your Father was a great man, try to walk in his footsteps and become a great man yourself."

"It will be my life's mission Sir, and humbly accept Ki as my partner."

"Well said Son of Ridmon, now go and fulfill your destiny."

With that Tamu exited with Ki tagging alongside.

"Really Tamu, what's this, a Reptilian side kick?" Protested Gnee.

"Yes you noggins and why not. After all, like I said before, we are not Dad, we don't have his abilities and damn it, we have use for Ki's muscle power and besides we are all in this together including the Reptiles."

So ended that conversation abruptly and Ki was elevated to a member of the group howbeit a grim and grotesque entity. Throughout the following weeks everyone was put to the maximum test of their abilities and Bordred became the most hated individual on Reptilia, yet achieved to bind everyone into a cohesive and highly efficient battle ready brigade. The Wasps finally found place among the community and recognition as intelligent beings and not just some robotic creations. With the exercises over, Bordred concluded by awarding rank to those who showed above average potential and so the Matabele Regiment regained its vigor and drive and returned to home planet with renewed purpose. Planet Ridmon's committee held session in the Great Hall where Bordred's achievements were acknowledged publicly. There were mixed feelings about the affair, but most had to admit he had succeeded in brushing the cobwebs from the regiment. Ridmon gained a new respect for their army's commander in chief. However, this did not meet with equal enthusiasm from the five who preferred to reserve their judgment. With the exercises over gave the four more freedom to act on their plan to find the son of Moti.

The five descendants of Mike and a reptilian teleported into Echo, launched through an activated portal to earth.

Destination Israel where they hovered in orbit while Echo ran DNA scans of the country's population. Soon Echo found a match located in the city of Jerusalem, two matches in fact of a male and female. The five were excited by this news. Without considering other factors like possible children or partners Tamu instructed Echo to beam them up. He knew it was going to be a shock for the pair but they had to know and that's all that mattered. Whether they wanted to pursue the situation after this meeting was up to them entirely. Gnee asked Ki to wear his full body stocking hiding himself from view until they knew which way things worked out.

The next instant a bearded man and a young woman materialized into Echo. Their faces were etched in shocked surprise and clung to each other.

"Do either of you speak English?" Asked Zakrose.

Both nodded.

"Zakrose, my name is Zakrose, and these are my brothers Wolf, Ridmon and Tamu. This young lady is Gnee my sister. We are the children of parents who many years ago colonized a planet out in space. Your father, our Uncle Moti was one of those people along with your mother Anna who helped to develop our home out there."

She paused to watch the couple's reaction. They still did not register what she had told them and looked very confused. So Wolf spoke up in Hebrew.

"Didn't your Father ever tell you of his adventures?"

No reaction.

"Guess not. Well in truth your Father was a Universal Messenger together with our Father and later your Dad returned to earth to become the Chief Rabbi of Israel."

The expression on the man's face changed. Slowly, the part of the Chief Rabbi dawned on him and he looked at his sister the back to the four and asked.

"You knew our Father and Mother, but how is that possible? He never mentioned anything about having non-Jewish friends anywhere. Where are we anyway?"

Now it was Tamu's turn to speak up.

"What are your names?"

"I am Amnon and this is my sister Ruth." The man answered.

"OK Amnon and Ruth, I think it's time you sat down because what we are about to tell you will come as a shock." Tamu waited for the couple to be seated.

"You are both on board a space ship in earth's orbit."

With that Echo opened a portal so that the couple could see earth.

"This must be some kind of trick or something." Shouted Amnon clutching his frightened sister to him.

"No trick, no illusion. If you would kindly tell us where your Mother and Father are buried?"

"In a Jerusalem Cemetery." Blurted out Ruth.

With that Echo closed one portal and opened another into the dark forest where Moti and Anna's grave stones stood with inscriptions in both English and Hebrew.

Gradually reality began to dawn on Amnon's face and he shook his head in disbelief not wanting to accept what he saw. Ruth began to cry so hid her face in Amnon's chest.

"This can't be, it's impossible. How can it be? Amnon stammered.

Next Echo opened a portal to a rock in a desert where a brass plaque hung and on it was inscribed the names of Mike, Moti and Ahmed. It went on further to read, these three persons disappeared here in the most strangest of circumstances and have never been found. Gnee moved over to Ruth and embraced her.

"It's all true, every last piece of it and I know this comes as a shock to you and your brother, but we came here to meet you because we loved your father very much and he played such an important role in our lives we just had to see you."

While Gnee was consoling Ruth, Tamu approached Amnon who back stepped fear written all over his face because of the huge imposing black clad figure also stepped forward towards him.

"Easy there, no one is going to hurt either of you. We have a question, will you both be willing to journey back with us to our home and see for yourself the legacy your Mom and Dad left behind?"

Amnon was fearful, this was all too much. He needed time to digest everything. Then Ruth spoke up with an expression of determination etched on her face.

"Yes, we will come with you as long as you guarantee our return."

"Of course Ruth that is a promise, but allow me to say that if you wish to stay on our world you will be most welcome."

Ruth turned to her brother, took him by the hand and spoke to him.

"Amnon please, we both knew that Papa was no ordinary man especially his physique which he trained every day saying it was for healthy purposes, but we knew his body didn't come from time in a gymnasium. Ask yourself why the other men in the Church group feared him and how come he was the only one able to open the Ark. We need to find answers and this is an opportunity for us. Why have we been so miserable since our parent's deaths?"

Amnon nodded his head, so Tamu activated a portal and the next moment Echo deposited them on the heights. Both Amnon and Ruth stood in awe surveying their surroundings.

The view was spell binding for any new comers. Zakrose gave them a few more minutes to take in the splendor of Ridmon then ushered the couple into the crystal cities Great Hall. On one wall were minute photos and inscriptions of all those from Ridmon who had fallen and they numbered in their hundreds. At the top of the list of names were just four, those of Mike, Penagee, Ahmed and Moti. Ruth and Amnon stood looking at the photo imprint of their Father and the truth finally hit home leaving them stunned.

"Come." Beckoned Gnee and led them down the external platform to the elevator then down into the Dark Forest and on to the cemetery. The five stood back allowing the brother and sister time with their deceased parents. Half an hour later Tamu asked the couple to spend a few days then make choices about what to do next.

"We would like to stay more but we have families back home and can't just disappear like that." Answered Ruth.

"Ok, I tell you what we will do, we will take you back and at any time you want to, you will be welcome to come for a holiday or to stay. To be able to contact us wear this bracelet Ruth, it's a homing device and activates the moment you call any of us by name. In that way you are protected as well. We only ask is that you never speak about this to anyone. Do we have your word?"

"Yes you have it and thank you for bringing us here and showing us our Fathers resting place. He must have been very happy here to be brought back and buried." She acknowledged.

Zakrose put her arm around Ruth and kissed her cheek.

"Don't forget you two, you are family to us as well."

With that a portal was activated and both Ruth and Amnon stepped out into the streets of Jerusalem. The couple sat on a park bench and slowly came down to reality.

"Do you realize our parents were amazing people? They must have hated it here after leaving Ridmon. Can you imagine what Papa was? It's hard to believe he was a Universal Messenger, a real holy man. Those people on Ridmon lived and died knowing Mama and Papa like their own family yet there were a lot of things they did not tell us. We need to know, yes Amnon, we need to know."

"I am still in shock, but you are right. Life here now will be meaningless, not after this. I think it would be Papa's wish for us to go to Ridmon." Reflected Amnon.

"How are we going to convince our families we are moving to a better place without telling them where and why? My husband is very religious as you know and will not understand and my three kids, I can't bear the thought of losing them. Your wife would probably go for it and your son is still a baby so change will not affect him."

"I am going home to speak to my wife and I'll contact you later." With that Amnon got up and headed for the nearest bus stop.

Ruth walked slowly with heavy heart to catch her bus knowing she would have to make a very hard choice. She knew then what she had to do and it was not going to be easy. For the next few days both Ruth and Amnon fought inward battles with themselves then Ruth received a call on her new fancy Como1. It was Amnon.

"Hello Amnon."

"Hi Ruth, listen I have decided, I am going with my family. Michal knows we moving, but does not know where to."

"I have made a decision as well. My husband will never agree, so, I am going with my three kids."

"Right, come to my place and bring the kids with you this afternoon. Your husband will be at religious studies and Ruth, bring as little as you can so as to not arouse suspicion."

"I will be there." Answered Ruth and signed off.

What she was about to do pained her no end, but the truth about her parents was too much to ignore and wanted above all for her kids to know who their grandfather was and for her to find closure and live on Ridmon close to her parents graves. As usual she prepared lunch for her family and acted as normal as possible announcing that in the afternoon she and the kids were going to visit Amnon to which the husband told her to make sure she was back by seven that evening. Ruth just smiled. After her chores were completed she sat down to write a note to her husband. It was probably the most difficult thing she ever had to do in her life, but it had to be done. Her husband came to say goodbye and left for his studies. Ruth quickly gathered her kids and packed a small travel case with the barest of necessities and headed out for Amnon's place. On arrival Ruth concentrated hard repeating the name Tamu, Tamu over and over again and the bracelet on her arm began to pulse light. The next instant a portal opened in the lounge and before anyone could blink Tamu and Wolfe yanked everyone in and the portal closed. It took a few moments for the kids to realize what had just transpired and seeing their mother in another woman's embrace and their uncle Amnon hugging a strange man they gazed around them in dumb struck amazement. Michal clinging on to her baby stood with her mouth agape in shock. Gnee noticing her shocked expression went to her and hugged the woman.

"Welcome Michal to our planet and the rest of your life."

"Where, where is this?" She stammered in Hebrew.

"You are on a planet millions of miles from Earth, a planet Amnon and Ruth's father lived on before he became Chief Rabbi. We were like family to him, all of us. Right now just take your time to get accustomed to your surroundings." Replied Wolf in Hebrew.

Amnon came over and took Michal in his arms. The three boys could not believe their eyes, yet stayed close to Ruth. The youngest of the boys, Uval, asked his mother.

"Imma, who are these people?"

"They are family, my family, a long lost family." She replied.

Tamu came over and kissed Ruth on the cheek.

"I know this must have been difficult for you and believe me we appreciate it. Gnee will take you all to your new accommodations and we will meet up later."

Tamu activated a portal and slipped into Ruth's lounge on Earth with Ki and waited. At 19.00 hours precisely, Ruth's husband opened the door to his home and walked straight into Tamu.

"Who are you?" He shouted angrily.

Tamu took his time, a definite Language problem here. A medium sized man, paunchy with a white complexion and a face full of brown beard dressed in an all-black suit with black hat on his head and the word penguin came to his mind.

"I don't know how to put this, but Ruth and the boys are no longer here or for that matter on the planet." Answering the man and telepathically projecting an image into the man's mind.

The man became enraged spluttering something about police and waving his finger in Tamu's face. Tamu smiled and beckoned to Ki who appeared behind the man and tapped him on the shoulder. He spun around and abruptly pissed his pants at the sight of Ki and fell to his knees paralyzed with fear. Tamu confronted him and handed him the letter he had found earlier where Ruth had left it for her husband. With shaking hands he fumbled to open the envelope. Reading her words he sank to his haunches defeated. Tamu activated a portal and both he and Ki left the man trembling with fear. After a while the man re-read the letter and understanding dawned on him. Then the pieces began to fall into place, the pieces concerning the past Chief Rabbi and he realized what Ruth meant in her letter about her father having been a Universal Messenger.

Back in the Crystal City, Tamu joined his brothers and sisters in the Great Hall where they were entertaining the new arrivals. On his approach Zakrose stood up and telepathically rebuked him for what he did to Ruth's husband. Tamu just shrugged his shoulders and sat down. He was not finished yet, so asked.

"Ruth, what are your son's names?"

"This little one is Uval, the middle brother is Ariel and the oldest is Jacov." She replied.

"Here on Ridmon we have different origin of people from other planets all living and working together and sooner or later you will be meeting these people here in the city. We have also some creatures living here and these creatures are our friends and I have to warn you that when you see one you are going to be frightened at first because believe me they are ugly, fierce and look like human lizards without tails."

Tamu waited for Ruth to translate in Hebrew for the Kids, then continued.

"I know all this will take time to digest and the sooner we get our creatures into the open the better for you if you should bump into any of them while here in the city or outside and haven't seen one before you will freak out. Ruth, hug your boys, and Amnon hold your wife. I will now introduce you to my friend Ki."

Everyone braced themselves watching for the reaction that was to come from the new residents.

Ki ambled into the Great Hall and very tactfully kept his distance by having a beer at the bar. Tamu joined him and together stood for a while drinking. Other people who passed stopped to talk to Tamu who cracked jokes and created an atmosphere around Ki. The newbies, eyes wide, studied Ki and although his imposing form was frightening, seeing him interacting with other people in a relaxed manner seemed to lessen their fears slightly. Ki grabbed Tamu onto his shoulders and started to horse around playfully then he and Tamu would take turns in a game of catch with hilarious results. The kids could not resist and soon they were all laughing out aloud. Gradually Tamu and Ki worked their way closer to the group. When they were four meters from the group Tamu leaned against Ki's large frame and crossed his feet folding his arms and smiled a flashing smile. The kids instinctively moved closer to their Mother who did a surprising thing by getting up and approaching Ki with extended hand out to him. Well, you could have knocked the group flat by her action. Ki gently took her hand in his, dwarfing it completely then bowed slightly. Tamu translated Ki's hiss.

"He greets you and your family in the name of his Father Zi who was one of your Father's friends."

"Thank you." Turning to her kids she beckoned for them to come closer. With timid halting steps the boys approached Ki who squatted to his haunches to lessen his imposing form. Bright cookie this lizard thought Wolf. Ki and the boys faced off.

"Ask them Ruth if they want to go and see Ki's little Ridmon pet. He will bring it on to the walkway just outside. The pet is very affectionate and we will go to sit at one of the kiosks out there while they get acquainted." Enquired Gnee.

Ruth asked the boys who were a little hesitant, but she soon persuaded them and followed Tamu out onto the walkway while Ki dashed off to retrieve his pet. The group sat at one of the kiosks and ordered drinks. Ridmon had come a long way since the old days and now had a wide range of soft and alcoholic drinks on the menu. Ki returned with a small bundle under his arm and came to stand a short distance away from the group. Gently he extracted something fluffy and grey from a bag which clung to his arm its big blue eyes darting about taking in everything. The boy's interest was awakened and came forward to see what was on Ki's arm.

"What is that?" Asked Jacov addressing Wolf in Hebrew.

"That my boy is a Moncat, well that's the name we gave it here as we don't know exactly what it is and found only in this valley. It looks half monkey and half cat but of course it's not, but makes the best pet ever. Go on, touch it." Prodded Wolf.

Jacov gingerly stretched out his hand and all at once the Moncat locked onto his arm and was in his shirt before he blinked, it's little face peeking out quite content to just hang in there. This of course sparked a reaction from his brothers who crowded around him in excited banter. Ruth understood what Tamu and that Lizard were doing and smiled, yes, she had made the right decision to come to Ridmon. Darkness began to descend and Gnee ushered her guests back into the Crystal building informing them that she had arranged super for them in the restaurant and a surprise of new clothing for everyone. The Moncat was back with Ki and replaced in its special abode and fed. Zakrose and Ridmon cornered Tamu and sat him down.

"So little brother, you are quite a comedian it seems with your side kick Lizard Ki. Yet we have to agree you pulled off an amazing performance and sorted out a thorny problem for us. Well done and you are not as stupid as you look you scoundrel." Commented Ridmon.

"Geez guys, I though stupid looks ran in the family." Mocked Tamu to which Zakrose responded.

"Yeah, wise guy."

Ridmon laughed and was about to say something when Tamu pounced. Like a tiger on hot coals he grappled his brother before the man could respond and pinned him through a chair in a much undignified way making Zakrose collapse with laughter. Ridmon was taken completely by surprise and Tamu knew if it was a one on one he would get a hiding big time. So, before Ridmon could retaliate, Tamu teleported out leaving Zakrose still screeching with laughter. Ridmon disengaged himself from the chair in mock pouting seeing the funny side of things and laughed with Zakrose. Still, they loved Tamu because of his jovial nature and knew in a pinch he would be there for them at any cost. They didn't quite feel comfortable with Ki hanging around like he did, but realized the Lizard was part of their life and that was that, after all, Ki and Tamu were inseparable.

Ki became a celebrity with the three boys. Yet they had to attend school where Ruth took charge of their education. In their spare time Ki would take them on tours of the city and surrounding valley and escorted them up in the tree tops and between them developed a sign language only they understood. After a few months Ruth spoke to Zakrose and asked her if she could return to Earth one more time to speak to her husband and try to explain the situation to him and perhaps he would agree to come back with her. If not, nothing ventured, nothing gained. Zakrose summoned Tamu who arrived with Ki.

"Listen you two, Ruth wants to go to Earth to speak to her husband and maybe convince him to come to Ridmon, so you two behave."

"Why of course dear sister, we will be as placid as little mice." Smiled Tamu.

"You had better be brother or else." Advised Zakrose.

"Ready Ruth?" Asked Zakrose.

"Yes" she replied to which Tamu stepped through a portal into her husband's living room and found the man sitting at a table with his head in his hands. Ruth moved through the room and touched his shoulder saying.

"Isaac, it's me, Ruth."

The man lifted his head to show a tormented face with black rings round sunken eyes.

"My sweet Ruth. What have I done to you by refusing to believe in you and care more for my selfish self than my own family?"

"Isaac, the boys are happy where they are and told me to tell you they love you and wish you could be with us in this wonderful place. Come look into the portal and see this truly amazing world where we now live."

The man turned to the portal opening and sucked in his breath. Ruth linked her arm into his and said,

"You see Isaac, how beautiful it is and the people are very special. Come back with us please my husband, we miss you so much."

Just then the boys bounced into the room and embraced their Father begging him to go with them.

"Isaac, this is Tamu. He is our friend and protector and he explained to me what happened the last time you met and he asks for forgiveness for being too aggressive."

Isaac stepped through the open portal onto Ridmon soil, saw its splendor and heard his boy's excitement, looked into Ruth's smiling face and to top it all, watched as his boys ran off to hug a massive lizard creature he recognized from their first encounter, who gathered the boys up in his powerful arms.

"You see Isaac how happy the boys are, don't disappoint them. Come with us." She pleaded.

The man walked forward with his family and never looked back and so Ridmon had achieved yet another victory and brought a family back into its fold. The days passed into months and two years had flown by. Isaac's family was well settled and speaking broken Ridmonian. During this time Tamu and Ridmon spent his days training with the help of Ki and began to develop into powerful men physically. Their brother and sisters hardly saw them and on the rare occasions it was a fleeting glimpse. Naya they did not see at all either and then one day she emerged out of the forest into the Great Hall accompanied by Tamu, Ridmon and Ki. Gnee's jaw dropped. Here were her brothers and Naya as large as life and looking absolutely phenomenal. She rushed forward to embrace them.

"Geez brothers, what's with the muscles?" Hugging them tight. Tamu kissed her cheek and ruffled her hair.

"Miss me." He asked.

"You bet you big oaf." Turning, she hugged Naya.

"Looking great babe."

"Thanks, it was hard work, but worth it." Came the reply.

Gnee was so beside herself she even gave Ki a hug. This single action meant everything to him as it in more ways than one, confirmed his acceptance. Moving to the bar the four sat down to a few drinks while Gnee teleported out to Zakrose and Wolfe in their office.

"Guess what guys, Ridmon, Tamu and Naya are at the bar in the Great Hall and you won't believe the changes in them. They look absolutely physically gorgeous."

"I have to see this for myself, you coming Wolf?" She queried.

Wolf stood watching his two brothers admiring their physiques and knowing the hard work that went into developing them. There was something else there, a message of danger, of beware. Cautiously he approached Tamu from behind only to be cautioned.

"You looking for a beating brother of mine." Asked Tamu.

Wolf stopped in his tracks thinking. Well, well so the brother has sharpened his wits, good, now he will have no excuse to enter into a little wager of combat at some time with me to test his skills and asked.

"Ha! Still think you can take me Bro?"

"No problem." Mocked Tamu.

Wolf laughed. Well the boastful ass will learn a new lesson or two from his older brother one of these days.

"Now, now you two cut that out and let's enjoy ourselves for a change as a family without this macho goings on between you boys." Gnee pleaded.

Both men nodded and shook hands. Wolf was startled, he felt the power in that grip and the energy flowing from it and realized Tamu had somehow mastered the power of Chi. The question was just how developed was it? This was a different set of circumstances and he had to watch himself around his brother. Turning to Naya took her hand and kissed her on the cheek. She whispered into his ear.

"Be careful Wolf, Tamu and Ridmon are very dangerous now and get better day by day. Watch out also for Ki, that Lizard is a walking slaughter machine and damn fast." She smiled and turned to Zakrose and the two started small talk about the events in the city with Gnee filling in bits and pieces.

"Sit down Wolf and have a drink with us." Tamu prompted slapping a bar stool next to him. The man obliged and ordered a beer.

"What's going on Tamu? Why are you suddenly into martial arts? You have never really been that enthusiastic about it."

"Times change Wolf, and so we must change with it and besides someone has to follow in Dads footsteps don't you think?" Answered Tamu sipping his beer.

"Perhaps, but times have changed and we live in a peaceful Federation without major threat to our existence and besides, the Federation is well equipped to deal with any contingency which might arise."

"Ha! What Federation? Those knuckle heads couldn't knock their way out of a wet sack if they tried."

Wolf chuckled, Tamu was dead right on that point. Although he and Zakrose visited Karagan since their Father's death no one dared to venture off Ridmon and even then, exits were very limited. Planet Ridmon remained off the charts completely to the outside world and none knew of the bustling community on her surface. Tamu, Ridmon and Gnee only visited Reptilia and never Karagan or Thanu. Perhaps it was time to set his brothers free to explore the Federations dominion.

"How would you like to take some of your Wasps on a tour of the Federations dominion?" He asked.

Tamu looked straight into Wolf's eyes and responded. "Why?"

"Because, I think it's time for you to expand your knowledge base and travel a bit."

Tamu considered the suggestion weighing up the pros and cons and decided to take Wolf up on his offer provided Ridmon, Naya and Ki accompanied him.

"Deal. Naya, Ridmon and Ki will join me. We leave in a few days." Smiled Tamu.

Wolf merely nodded acceptance, finished his beer and teleported to his chambers and family. Zakrose and Gnee followed suit. Tamu told his partners about the deal. Both jumped at the chance to go off world for a while on new adventures. Tamu telepathically contacted Echo the following day.

"We have been given permission to go off world to tour the Federations dominion. It also means some of your Wasps will be coming with us. So, who do you suggest accompany us?"

Echo was silent for a few seconds then responded.

"Sierra and Zulu."

"Any reason for you three?"

"Yes, because we have had extensive battle experience under your Father's command."

"I Accept. We move in two days."

"Affirmative."

Tamu joined Naya and began their preparations. The next day Tamu asked both Ridmon and Ki.

"Do both of you have a girlfriend who would possibly like to keep you company on our journey?"

Ki looked perplexed for a moment then his fangs showed indicating his consent. Tamu smiled telling him they would pick her up from Reptilia on the way out. For the rest of the day Ridmon went in search of a close girlfriend willing to accompany him. She agreed so brought her back to the Crystal City. She was a lovely girl with long black hair and brown eyes, nice figure and a genuine smile. Ridmon introduced her.

"Hi Guys, this is Qing Fe, she is Chinese as you can see and will be joining us on our little trip."

Everyone smiled and welcomed her to take a seat and join in with the family. That evening they teleported into Echo then three Wasps jumped through a portal onto Reptilia. Zi welcomed the five and sat listening to their reason for being there. Standing up he approached his son and exchanged points of view and suggestions till finally consensus was met and Zi hissed a command. A short while later, a Reptilian female arrived on the scene and bowed to Zi. He hissed something at her and she responded by bowing then moved to stand next to Ki. A few more words from Zi and he turned to Tamu and wished them bon voyage, got up and entered his dwelling place.

"What was that all about? Naya queried.

"Oh, just gave those two the riot act about marriage and such and would be a wedding when they got back. She is from an important family and carries a lot of weight in their community and a marriage would be very beneficial for Ki and his father."

"He doesn't seem too pleased about it does Ki?"

"You bet."

Teleporting back into the Wasp Echo, Tamu and Ridmon sat figuring out where to go first. Thanu was out of the question so it was just Karagan. The other consideration would be Ki and his girl's exposure in environments where they would be considered as hostile and possibly killed. Karagan was a good place to start as there were Reptiles living and functioning as part of the Reptilian delegation. That being the case they had to come up with a reason for being there, get their stories right, place of origin and function.

"Echo, do you know the Reptilian delegation on Karagan's pass card configuration and could you duplicate two sets, in addition, four sets from Thanu?"

"Affirmative." Awhile later six sets of perfect pass cards appeared on the console table.

"Thanks Echo. We will be going down onto Karagan so I want you to be on standby in case we run into trouble, but be careful, you know how touchy Karagan's are of their air space."

"Chicken feed." Remarked Echo

Tamu smiled to himself wondering where Echo had picked up that remark then realized Echo was after all his fathers and Uncle Moti's Wasp at one time. This could turn out to be a very interesting trip after all. For twenty four hours the Wasps scanned Karagan checking for patterns and movements of the various delegations there. Where they lived, how they moved between places and what were their security protocols. Having super computers on steroids and the ability to zoom in with magnification right down to a speck of dust from outer space or eves drop on conversations, even hack into computers on the planet and cause all sorts of mischief. The Wasps were a genius of creation and with their new modifications made them even more to be respected. Popping in and out of portals gave them an overwhelming edge in combat scenarios, now you see them, now you don't and bang, you're dead. They had more than proved their capabilities in the past and were completely reliable and fiercely loyal, and would without hesitation sacrifice themselves for their masters. Tamu had no intention of having to make that call as he valued the Wasps greatly. Naya crept into his lap and snuggled in for closeness resting her head on his chest.

"Do you think Ki is alright, he's just sitting there stiff as a board?" She commented.

"I imagine the thought of marriage has frightened the hell out of him poor thing and she looks in the same predicament. They will have to work things out between themselves and a trip down onto the planet should loosen them up a bit." Remarked Tamu, who stretched out his legs and promptly fell asleep. The events of the last few days had worn him out a bit and sleep was a good refresher.

The sun rose on Karagan and four humans and a pair of Reptiles were beamed down onto the planet outside the principle Delegation Commission building. The six knew the exact routine and so waited for the delegations to start arriving for their weekly joint sittings of the Federation. The wait was short and so Tamu's team split to their respective delegation groups and onto hovering platforms which ferried them into a massive circular chamber reaching down at least five stories in depth lined around its inner walls, levels of open cubicles. The huge dome above was decorated by artistic murals depicting bygone Federations history. Hundreds of persons and entities looked down from their cubicles onto a center podium where the Speaker of the House stood. Minutes ticked by as more delegates took to their seats. Finally the Speaker raised his arms as a signal for silence. The chamber went quiet, all waited then the President of the Federation walked on to the podium.

"Friends, members of our Federation, today we have decided to expand our area of interest and shift its focus further outward in a circular pattern outside the circumference of the Federation's present protocol. In short, this means long range exploration by vessels manned by personnel who may never see their home base again in their lifetimes. We have taken this step to align ourselves to any potential threats, new worlds and or new technological discoveries beneficial to our societies. Our main objective will be to refurbish four of our Star Battleships and man them with contingents of volunteer staff covering every aspect required to run those ships effectively and efficiently. For defense purposes we will be re-arming these vessels with the latest up to date weaponry and be supported by our new generation of fighter cruisers with their crews and pilots. We need not emphasize the importance of these expeditions for the Federation. Therefore, delegates here in this chamber kindly convey our message to your leaders and we shall wait for their recommendations, suggestions and solutions for this proposed task force in due course. All the fundamental issues are recorded in the foyers consoles for your scrutiny and download. That will be all, Thank you."

The chamber remained silent until the podium was empty, and then there erupted a buzz of conversation as delegates exited the chamber on hover platforms into the large foyer. Tamu telepathically instructed Echo to access the consoles and upload the data. Making for the sunny exterior through the throngs of bodies he and Naya, Ridmon and Qing Fe waited seated on a convenient bench with a backdrop of lovely flower gardens and lawns. It did not take long before Ki emerged surrounded by a whole bunch of Reptilians. Everyone on Reptilia knew each other by sight or by name and Ki the son of Zi was a special surprise for them right here on Karagan. None bothered to ask what exactly he was doing there as such a distinguished quest accompanied by the daughter of one of the most prominent Reptiles on Reptilia, the feared warrior Mis could only collate to some form of behind the scenes participation with the Federation. The group walked passed Tamu and Naya and on towards the Reptilian delegations quarters.

"That should sort the big oaf out being with his own kind for a while and besides hear all the latest news and gossip of what's going on around here. We will pick up on them later. In the meantime my darling Naya why don't we take a tour of this city the easy relaxing way in an open air shuttle with a tour guide I see buzzing about around here." He suggested.

The others agreed then Naya being a very practical person asked a very simple question.

"Ok wise guy, how do we pay for this and other entertainments we might feel the urge to try?"

"Have faith my love and observe." So saying communicated with Echo and sure enough after a pause a bunch of Credits as the same used on Karagan was beamed down to Tamu whose eyes gleamed mischievously. Naya just stuck her nose up in the air saying,

"Cheeky"

"Come on then let's get with the program."

So saying, for the rest of the day entertained themselves lavishly at all the high spots where delegation members gathered, all the while Tamu was on listening watch telepathically for any snippets of information of significance he could channel back to planet Ridmon. His aim was to find out who was who in the Federation and who ultimately pulled the strings. Meantime Echo and the other two Wasps were not idle and had hacked into the Federations data banks and extracted all the plans of the Cruisers, the Star Battleships plus deployment agendas and above all, stumbled upon something of greater intrinsic value. Someone in the Federation was articulating a plan to use the expeditions as a cover up for their actual intensions of wealth and power and to turn rogue against the Federation if successful. The Wasps sifted through trillions of pieces of data and found what they were looking for, the identities of the perpetrators. At the close of day Tamu teleported his team into Echo where the Wasp debriefed him as to what was about to transpire once the Federations overall plan kicked into effect and the Star Battleships were out of Federation range. One particular ship was targeted as the ideal vessel for their plan to take effect; the Battleship Karas whose voyage plan as fate would have it, passed close to Ridmon and was an ideal choice for what Tamu was considering proposing to Ridmon's committee. He had time. Refurbishing would take months, training of Cruiser pilots, their maintenance crews and complete ships contingent to a level as prescribed. Armed with all the information Tamu and his team headed back to planet Ridmon and called for an emergency meeting of the committee.

The war room as it was aptly called, was a dull affair with monitors decorating the walls, terminals everywhere and in the center a huge table which had everything from communications, video, holograms for simulated battle procedures, holograms of all the galaxies in the Federation and beyond, trillions of data bits and three thousand Wasps with their phenomenal collective computing power. In effect planet Ridmon was a super power of unprecedented technological knowhow.

"Gentlemen, Ladies. Tamu has called for this meeting with information gathered on Karagan which he maintains is of utmost importance." Bordred announced.

Seated around the table were Wolf, Zakrose, Gnee, and representatives from the other two cities, Djnu from Bruni and Trisha from Dagor. Tamu with Ridmon stood to the one side with Ki standing behind them.

"The floor is yours Tamu."

"Thank you, I took three Wasps to Karagan to eves drop on their delegation meetings and stumbled across a situation which could have negative consequences if left to realization for the Federation and perhaps ourselves. Four names came up, four Federation leaders, two from Trafodj and two from Vimusi. They are, Gozim, Dagna, Wavzi and Byen. We keep this knowledge to ourselves for the time being and follow along with their plan and watch what transpires. On your consoles are the projected plans for the Federations intended expeditions out into deep space and we are talking very, very deep space. Now if you will observe these are the hologram depictions of both the Star battleships and the new fighter Cruisers."

On the table top three dimension copies of the ships rotated while their physical characteristics paged down on each person's console. The figures were eyebrow raisers. After a few more minutes Tamu continued.

"As you can see the Federation has excelled itself with these latest additions to their arsenal. The capability for those battleships to exist indefinitely in outer space must be applauded, so must the array of newer weapons at their disposal. The Ship Karas has a voyage plan passing within a short distance of Ridmon and it is this ship which will be operating on its own agenda once out of reach of the

Federation. On board the other three ships will be the persons whose names I have already informed you about."

A moments silence as the committee reflected on the names with grim faces. Tamu continued.

"My proposal therefore is to insert spy's onto the vessel on its outward journey to infiltrate and observe and report back to Ridmon. One or two Wasps to shadow the vessel acting as protection for the spy's, and if needed, destroy the vessel. Their main objective would be to hack into its data banks and monitor communication traffic both within and outward secret transmissions to Karagan or elsewhere."

"Just how do you propose to do that?" Queried Bordred.

"There is time to submit names of possible candidates for these expeditions into the Federation's recruitment program and as all know, the Wasps can manipulate information to ensure our candidates end up on Karas without raising suspicion. It is imperative for complete initiation and integration with the candidates originating out of Thanu or Reptilia as a front cover. Thedarians still exist scattered about the universe so will not raise suspicion."

The committee sat digesting the information for a long while then Zakrose spoke out.

"In our Matabele Regiment we have an outstanding few possibilities for candidate nomination. They are without reproach and loyal to Planet Ridmon and can't be bought off. Tough, resilient, battle hardened and highly trained with exceptional IQ's. They were some of my Father's best students when he was still alive and I for one know them personally from my academy days."

Bordred nodded acknowledgement and pressed his communication console.

"Send Ezos and Samre to the war room."

The committee sat in silence engrossed in their own thoughts whist waiting for the two summoned men to arrive. Thirty minutes later the two men strode into the room and halted to attention, saluting.

"Stand at ease men." Prompted Bordred to which the men obliged.

Zakrose stood up and walked around the table to the two men and shook hands. Smiling she asked them to approach the table where the holograms were still active.

"I don't have to tell you what these are as you both already know by past experience. We have called you here to offer you a task which we feel you are more than capable of dealing with. It means that you both will have to operate independently on your own and integrate yourselves into the mainstream of the Federations upcoming expeditionary force on the vessel Karas. You have also been chosen for the simplicity of being Thedarian survivors relocated to Karagan years ago for all intents and purposes. Your mission will be to monitor and work your way up the command line by whatever means at your disposal and have full authority to kill, to use deception, manipulate and be completely ruthless to achieve results. We need you to be in the high echelon group of officers on board. From the onset we will fabricate a fool proof military record with ranks of Majors for each of you. We will implant into your minds a history of Federation activity on the outer reaches and the so called role you both played in that occupation. Complete with identifications and personnel files, records of military academy, records of promotions etc. You will have two Wasps shadowing the vessel tuned into you thought waves and are your escape ticket should things go wrong. If you accept you will undergo a week of intense memory acceleration of names, dates, recollections, places and events you will need to know for this mission then you will be sent to Karagan to the recruitment office for these expeditions. Kara's schematics and those of the Cruisers will be implanted into your subconscious. Are you two willing to consider this mission? Take time to think it over and report to your commander tomorrow with your response."

The two came to attention, saluted and exited the room. Wolf stood up saying,

"We have our work cut out for us now so let's create the perfect cover story for those two men. Their lives and our mission depend upon it. The rest is up to them and I am sure they are going to use every trick in the book to achieve it."

The committee closed their meeting and went separate ways to do what was expected of them. Naya and Qing Fe waited for Tamu and Ridmon at a kiosk on the walkway and when he arrived studied his face.

"Well, did they buy it? "She demanded.

Tamu smiled, "Hook line and sinker and even selected two Matabele for the mission."

"Don't tell me it was Ezos and Samre?"

Tamu nodded confirmation.

"Oh, Madre Mia, now the preverbal is going to hit the fan with those two unleashed. Heaven help those on board." She exclaimed

"Yup! That's the whole point because there is no love lost between those two and the Federation and some are going to be in for a Shyte load of pain and suffering. We are in for some very interesting times ahead. At least it will keep the boredom away and besides, we still have the authority to go adventuring which translates as follow up on Karas from time to time giving Ezos and Samre moral support and if needed letting Ki loose to help them."

"Oh my word! That threesome combination is absolutely deadly." Naya said in awe.

Planet Ridmon did honor its dead and every year a day was set aside as a memorial day for those who passed away. On the heights was a commemorative plaque for all those poor souls who lost their lives on Thedrah when the Nirques destroyed their planet and with it many Ridmonians. This year was no different and the solemn ceremony conducted across Ridmon brought every single person and entity out into the open to lay flowers at designated places and stand in silence in remembrance. For Zakrose, Gnee and their brothers were particularly painful and the loss of their parents had impacted on them very harshly. They laid fresh flowers on the graves in the cemetery and stood with linked arms, joined their minds as one to re-encounter visions of their parents' lives imprinted deep within their sub-conscious. On these occasions Protector Friend would manifest into their circle offering comfort and hope. Tamu never knew his mother Tara and could only affiliate to Jane his Aunt who had brought him up as her own. Gnee was the one who recounted stories about Tara and their father. Tamu was able to construct a picture of his mother in his mind. Known as Mikes shadows, Tara gave Tamu his life at the cost of her own.

Ezos and Samre stood to attention in front of Bordred who paged Wolf and Zakrose, they intern advised Tamu and Ridmon who teleported into Bordred's Office.

"We volunteer for this mission and will be honored to serve." Stated Ezos.

Tamu circled the two sizing them up. Physically they were ordinarily looking Thedarians but everyone knew these two were Mike's star pupils and had a whole list of accomplishments to their credit. They were in essence the ultimate Ninja having mastered the art of translocation, a form of basic teleportation across short distances which was a very impressive achievement. Tamu was satisfied so addressed the two men,

"We will be monitoring this mission and I have a lot of respect for whom and what you are. But, I need to know if you two will work as a team with others in the field if need be?"

Ezos nodded his head in agreement to which Tamu asked again.

"Are you sure?"

Bordred butted in with a protest.

"What's your game Tamu?"

"This."

Ki appeared in the room to stand next to Tamu. Ezos and Samre smiled inwardly and sighed with relief. Samre spoke out loud.

"It will be a privilege and an honor to have Ki with us."

"Not so fast, Ki comes in when things get too hot on board and you both know what I mean."

Tamu was very explicit in his expectation. The Reptile had a tendency to switch to attack mode when under pressure and was unstoppable. His lightning speed combined with immense strength and deadly purpose impressed even Ezos and Samre. What the two didn't know was Ki had been in accelerated training with Tamu and Ridmon for the past two years following a prescribed training schedule found in a cupboard in their father's training ground. So advanced was the method that the three almost overnight achieved amazing results. Bordred was irritated and wanted to put an end to this interference and declared.

"Tamu you are wasting time damn you, get on with it."

Turning to face Bordred Tamu smiled, stepped forward and smashed his hand onto the top of the large crystal desk shattering it in to thousands of fragments.

"When I am good and ready." He growled.

Ezos watched and knew without a shadow of a doubt his mentor Mike was alive in Tamu and his heart rejoiced. Samre stepped forward and bowed.

"Master."

Bordred realized then he was facing a re-incarnation and for the first time in his life knew fear. Just then, the girls with Wolf teleported into the room and stood between Tamu and Bordred.

"Tamu." Cautioned Zakrose. "This is neither the time nor place."

Wolf looked from Tamu to Ki to Ridmon and the two Matabele and the air was heavy with vibrations emanating out of the five. He understood then this was another higher breed of his Father's legacy and one far beyond his comprehension.

"Bordred, get out of the room, now." Advised Gnee. He took no further convincing and fled.

Tamu linked arms with Ridmon the two Matabele and Ki then teleported out leaving Wolf and the two girls highly perplexed.

"What's come over Tamu?" Gnee questioned.

"Come, let's go and don't worry so much. Tamu has to work it out and come to an understanding with his inner self."

"Wolf I am afraid, he and Ki with those two Matabele and Ridmon, they are going to be up to something no good, I feel it." Pleaded Gnee.

"Easy, they can look after themselves." Wolf declared.

Eco reported in to Zakrose.

"Subjects on board, destination Karagan. Mission Karas mobilized. Persons present, Tamu, Naya, Ridmon, Qing Fe, Ki, unidentified Reptile female, Ezos, Samre and one more, Mis."

Zakrose sat down weak at the knees.

"Mis, this was developing into a thriller and had the makings of a suspense mystery. Wolf, Gnee get in here."

The two arrived.

"Mis is active again and he has Tamu, Ki, Ridmon, Qing Fe, Ezos, Samre with him and the two girls Naya and a Reptilian with no name."

"We have been duped." Gnee exclaimed.

"Son of a b......!" cursed Wolf, "They are onto something big if Mis is involved."

"Nothing we can do right now so let's all take it easy and wait." Suggested Zakrose.

Echo deposited his cargo on Reptilia and waited with Sierra and Zulu in the upper atmosphere.

Down below Mis sat next to Zi in debate while Ki was off somewhere with his companion and Tamu sat with Naya on his lap nibbling his ear and whispering sweet nothings. Ridmon and Qing Fe sat back to back making small talk. The two Matabele sat crossed legged in meditation seemingly oblivious of their surroundings. Finally, Zi rose and summoned his son. Ki stood before his father with Mis to one side and the female reptile. Tamu sat up and got to his feet, Naya following.

"What's up?" She asked.

"Shhhh! Ki is getting married."

"Oh crap." She exclaimed.

"Come, this is important so don't screw it up."

More Reptiles started to gather and formed a circle around Zi and Mis. One Reptile who appeared to be the local medicine man stepped into the circle and began to recite some ritual then an aged female stepped in with a helper. They carried a basket and other implements unidentified. The hissing grew in crescendo and as it did so bodies began to jerk to and fro. The tempo accelerated to a higher pitch and the encircling Reptiles dropped to their knees, linked arms and swayed from side to side. Ki was ushered into the center of the ring and knelt down and given something to drink from a gourd. Next the female was brought up and made to kneel in front of him then repositioned herself right up against him with her back touching his stomach and chest and in like manner was made to drink. Next Zi and Mis joined them, one on either side kneeling at right angles to the two. The old female reptile then extracted a shaft of wood from her basket and kneeling in front of the young female prized the girl's knees apart then rammed the shaft up the girl's vagina hard. Naya almost feinted at the sight of it and instinctively cupped her privates. The reptile female convulsed and collapsed forward at the same time the wooden shaft was withdrawn against a rush of blood. With the hissing at fever pitch Ki mounted his female from behind and rammed hard in to her. Tamu teleported his team into Echo not wanting to intrude any further on his friends strange and somewhat weird wedding rights.

"Ouch! How embarrassing to get done like that in public. What kind of ritual is that?" Naya fretted.

"From what I could understand, young Reptile females have extra strong virginity membranes which prevent normal copulation so as you saw it requires a little helping hand. As for the ceremony, well can't say that turns me on but different strokes for different cultures. Now Ki is married and has the whole community as a witness to the couple's marriage consummation."

"Another thing, when and why did you bring Mis into this?" She queried.

"I kind of figured it was a wise move in case we are over our heads he will be brought in with his most experienced troops who know the layout of Star Battleships from time past."

Their stay on Reptilia lasted four days in which time all falsified documentation, identities past backgrounds and activities were firmly entrenched in their minds and would withstand interrogation if push came to shove. They were ready. The plan was to separate and make their applications at different time intervals, Tamu and Naya would apply as a married couple together with Ridmon and Qing Fe followed by Ki and his new wife Nah then Ezos and Samre individually. Echo beamed the group down under cover of darkness and relocated itself to outer orbit hacking into the Federations database and downloaded all relevant information regarding the infiltrators, their identities, palm prints and retina scans together with fabricated life histories.

"Good luck everyone, stay safe."

So saying Tamu walked away with Naya hanging on to his arm. They would not meet again until on board Battleship Karas, but Tamu would be in constant communication with each of them telepathically. Bright and early the next morning Tamu and Naya stood in a queue outside the Federations Expeditionary recruitment offices Ridmon and Qing Fe behind them. Slowly the line shortened until at last, the couple stood in front of a desk behind which was seated a non-descript elderly man with greying hair. On top of the desk facing them was a console and a hand print recognition monitor.

"Are you a couple?" Tamu nodded. The man entered something on his console then said.

"Place your right hand on the monitor please."

Tamu placed his right hand onto the monitor and a second later a monotone voice confirmed identification. Naya followed with equal recognition.

"Go through the entrance behind me to the next stage." The man told them.

Into the next entrance they went and walked along a ten meter corridor with both side walls glowing with a blue neon light. Emerging out of the corridor they found themselves in a small room. At the end of the room a door with a box type contraption at eye level containing a reflective convex mirror at its center. Another monotone voice gave instructions.

"Kindly approach the door and place your open left eye close to the mirror and do not to blink."

Tamu did what he was told and waited. There was a flash of light blinding his eye for a second. The monotone voice confirmed recognition and the door opened to let him through into a large well-lit hall. Tamu waited for Naya and together they approached a long counter behind which stood black uniformed men and women. All along the line new applicants were receiving items of clothing, bedding and toiletries. An overweight woman with cold unemotional brown eyes pressed a button on her console muttering.

"Couple Layette, you will move down this line and collect all the items you are required to have and at the end you will be told where your quarters are to be."

Tamu and Naya walked down the line each collecting items of clothing, foot wear, bedding and toiletries.

"How do they know our sizes?" She whispered.

"Remember the room with the blue light, a scanner." Tamu answered.

At the end of the line laden with bundles and packages the couple was ushered into an elevator and descended into the bowels of the planet. Sixty stories down the elevator came to a stop, doors opened and the couple stepped out into a concrete corridor lined with doorways. A monotone voice instructed them to proceed to room 13a and both were to place their right hands on the monitor in the door simultaneously then wait, which they did. Seconds later the door clicked open and the couple entered a sparsely furnished room with an adjourning bathroom. On one wall was a large monitor screen, below it a console. Up against the opposite wall was a double bed. Next to the bathroom entrance was another door leading somewhere. One wall was equipped with a wall closet so the couple busied themselves stacking items of clothing which were basic black overalls, socks, boots, baseball type caps, underwear, belts and parkas. Sheets and blankets for the bed but no pillow. The bathroom was minimal consisting of only a shower, toilet and wash basin with a wall mirror. An intercom squawked and instructions.

"You are to dress in uniform and in fifteen minutes the door next to the bathroom will open, you will then follow alone the blue line to your right."

The couple hastily donned their uniforms and stood by the door. On queue the door opened outwards into a corridor and on the floor were two marked lines, one blue the other yellow. So following instructions the couple followed the blue line to the right, the corridor turned sharply to the left and they found themselves confronted by another double door which opened at their approach leading into a large dining hall full of people busy eating breakfast. Tamu spoke to Naya telepathically saying to her only to eat recognizable foods. Thirty minutes later their name was called and told to report to a desk at the exit of the hall. So began their integration into the Federations Expeditionary Force and the four were assigned to gunnery positions where they became expert gunners. Ki and Nah were assigned to maintenance and both Ezos and Samre were assigned to the Cruiser launch pads as controllers. Ridmon and Qi assigned to fighter cruisers. For the next six months their training covered related aspects of function within the realms of their duties. Both Ridmon and Tamu continually trained their bodies and mind s in the secret methods their father left to them. In all this time no one was allowed on to the surface. Like a typical military establishment surprise call outs in the dead of night, all night exercises happened regularly. Physical fitness was compulsory and each month everyone was evaluated. The final battery of tests came after their sixth months of training and all the planet Ridmon's infiltrators passed with high distinctions which paved the way for them to be reassigned on to Star Battleship Karas.

EUREKA

NINE

Karas hung in Karagan's orbit, poised and ready for her maiden flight undergoing last minute ship chandelling with commodity stores, maintenance parts, and completion of her self-sufficiency agricultural gardens, where water is extracted from the humid air within the ships lower levels and sprayed over the gardens in a continuous cycle on given time intervals in addition, the conversion process of water to oxygen to compensate for the plants inability to produce sufficient oxygen to support life. Refuge recycling of whatever was possible for reuse which included human excrement. Oxygen manufacturing systems were incorporated on all levels as was pressurization. Crew orientation and emergency reaction for all gunnery crews, fire crews, hospital personnel and so the list went on. For Karas to be able to exist indefinitely in space she had to be self-generating which meant completely self-reliant from

506

the smallest to the largest part or piece within her interior and exterior. Safety came first and all were very well aware that loss of life was a drain on resources. The ship would operate with two shifts around the clock with exception of battle conditions where it was a case of all hands on deck. In the outer fringes of known space it was imperative to protect life as there were no replacements. Mini factories were found everywhere on the ship manufacturing a wide range of products. Karas even boasted a highly sophisticated foundry to smelt down and remanufacture any metal part in her machine shops. She consisted of 200 primary levels at her highest point over a two kilometers and a half which tapered from bottom to top to fifty aft of the vessel and twenty in the bow. Most of these levels were sub-divided into lesser levels numbering fifty thousand in all and those in turn sub-divided into smaller cubicles and compartments. Her length overall stretched for three kilometers and at her widest point measured one and a half kilometers. Perched on top at amidships was the ships control center where the helmsman, navigator, Battle coordinators, officers of the bridge dealing with communications, engine room and various auxiliaries and ship's admiralty. Above that was a dual gunnery emplacement bristling with canons complete with crew quarters where Tamu and Naya lived. Oddly enough so did Ridmon and Qing Fe though their function was fighters, due to space constraints were billeted together. With Naya, Tamu operated the huge multiple computer guided laser gun placements. They were completely self-contained and were not required to move about the maze of corridors in case of emergency.

Off duty hours offered a variety of activities and entertainments, but most crew gravitated towards the various lounges where alcohol was available for low prices and music blared non- stop twenty four hours a day. Although Tamu was in contact with his group telepathically they never crossed paths.

A loud speaker shrieked followed by a voice barking commands.

"All personnel, man your stations. Karas will be departing Karagan air space in fifty minutes so prepare for warp jump."

On occasions like these when all hands were on deck, Tamu and Naya doubled up on the guns in one gunnery station. Seconds ticked by then the slight feeling of vertigo and Karas jumped into warp drive. Ten minutes later the order came through to stand down. So both couples retired to their separate bedrooms. Echo opened channels with Tamu.

"We are as one." Then broke off the connection

Ki and Nah relegated to a machine shop on the lowest levels of the ship where other Reptiles were deliberately placed and used for muscle work and whose existence shamefully Spartan and humid, angered Ki. For the sake of their mission he tolerated his situation and waited patiently having already selected some sons of bitches who abused their authority to the extreme for pay back. If it had not been for Tamu communicating with him telepathically he might have lost it and gone into attack mode. Nah watched Ki and realized her husband was no normal every day Reptile, there was a lot more she knew nothing about concerning him and the human Tamu. She found it strange how the two of them were such great friends more so when Mis her father had recounted his story of Tamu's father and Zi. In the beginning when first introduced to Tamu she was amazed at the power this human demonstrated sparring against Ki in their training sessions back on Reptilia. Watching them now she understood the uniqueness of their partnership and how cohesive they worked as a single unit with lightning speed and crushing power. One, a bulldozer, the other an acrobatic aerialist and Ridmon a Tran's locator expert, basically defined as someone who could visually disappear from one's sight only to reappear within split seconds and seriously deliver lethal killing blow, a dangerous martial artist.

Ezos and Samre played their part to perfection and began to target their choices and play on weaknesses by manipulation and deception. They played it so well by turning one against the other in such subtle ways those targets took each other out. Of course it was inevitable that command began to investigate the disturbances in the cruiser sector of operations where at least three crew members were reported killed and this is where the Ridmonians capitalized on their success by planting evidence where it would be found in the right place to convict those who murdered their crew mates. Some crew just simply vanished without trace including officers. Those, Ezos and Samre were responsible for. As things go command was short of flight deck officers on the Cruiser decks and that is what propelled the two infiltrators up the ladder of promotion where they ran a very tight and extremely disciplined operation until their next planed strategy moved them once again up the ladder to flight command. So well-orchestrated and in true Ninja style using untraceable poison ingeniously killed one flight commander on his weekly inspection of the outer shell of the flight deck which necessitated the wearing of a space suit. Now each flight commander had his own issue suit with his name embossed on it so there could be no mistake when tampering with it. Ezos was next in line according to the promotion schedule from command and Samre bided his time allowing for distance between the two killings so as to avoid suspicion. The next "accident" came later using a mind altering drug disguised as XR-one, a popular drug used by addicts to induce behavioral alterations and caused one crew member to openly pulverize his flight commander's head, in front of many witnesses. Make way for Samre to take his new seat of office. Once again the two performed their duties to the letter with more than satisfactory results and command was impressed. Carefully, methodically the two ran a tight command and built up a reputation for being strict yet fair. What better way to camouflage their set goals.

Karas was now eight months into her outbound journey and so far from Karagan on the outer reaches of the Federations range that command began to prepare for the unknown. They stepped up security and imposed a round the clock duty watch. Here things would begin to change and Tamu prepared for it with a timely rendezvous on Echo with his team.

"Well done you guys. Ki, did you manage to secure a place where we can hide Mis and his soldiers?

"Yes, and I am sure we will have support when the time comes from a lot of my people on board who are being badly mistreated." Ki confirmed.

"Ezos, you and Samre are now in position to do a great deal of damage, but remember, we want this ship intact with as many of its crews as possible and I am confident in a short while we are going to see how the proposed takeover will unfold.

"Just remember, keep a low profile until we are ready to spring our trap."

With that they returned to the ship and waited. The Wasps monitoring every signal the ship made and eves dropped everywhere, tapped into private consoles and calculated possibilities. A further uneventful three months passed by and Karas was now out of reach of the Federation. She travelled outward for another entire year then entered onto the fringes of a massive spiraling galaxy system where Command halted and commenced systematic scanning to chart their find and named it for navigation purposes "G48 Major" and fired exploratory probes out. Galaxies such as these were home to thousands of solar systems with Suns and their own planetary structures and life forms if any. But in space other life forms are a guarantee and one is best to remember it. The probes penetrated deeper and deeper sending back data and gradually Karas was able to begin filling its charts with factual references. Each secondary solar system within G48 major was given its identification and co-ordinates from Kara's stationary position. These changed in the data banks automatically as the ship moved deeper and deeper into the terrestrial body of G48 Major cross referencing its position in relation to its original fixed point.

Echo relayed those same co-ordinates to Ridmon's data banks in real time enabling the Wasps to home in on them via the portals. Sierra and Zulu made long range scouting forays ahead of Karas. Fore warned is pre-warned. So far nothing seemed amiss. The probes were doing what they were designed for and Karas long range scans detected no threats or life matter on vessels of any kind. If by definition one would use earths Milky Way as an example, then the sheer magnitude of what a complete Galaxy entailed is mind boggling. G48 Major is defined as a spiral Galaxy and its parsec [one parsec equivalent to 3.26 light years] measured in kilometers would be 3 x times The Milky Way 1,000,000,000,000,000,000 Km about 100,000 light years so G48 Major was triple that measurement across a total of 300,000 light years. Karas would be there forever just exploring this one galaxy alone. It was phenomenal and the impact of it said one thing, no going home.

Wolf picked up a transmission from Echo and whistled.

"Jeepers! This is big, no…massive in fact. Do you girls realize what Karas has stumbled upon? Now we know the answer to the riddle of Karas. How the hell they found out about G48 Major is anybody's guess and you know what? They actually travelled exactly in a straight line directly to G48 Major. Is that coincidental or not. Tamu was right, breaking from the Federation based on what they have now found and what all this entailed, means whatever is there Karas doesn't want the Federation to get its greedy hands on. Obviously we were misled so now the question is what we do about It.?"

Zakrose digested what she had seen and heard then answered.

"We would be well advised to deploy our Wasps to check on where the other three Star battleships are at this moment. I have a sneaky feeling they are following on the heels of Karas."

Wolf called Delta.

"Take a thousand Wasps and head out through portals to the co-ordinates I give you and be aware there are three Star Battleships heading for G48 Major and they are to be considered extremely hostile and if there is a confrontation, destroy them.

The vessel Karas you don't engage, is that understood?"

"Acknowledged."

Tamu shook his head, how wrong had they been in assuming the negative and the info relayed to him by Wolf was disturbing enough. The news changed everything so he called in his team and explained to them the gravity of their situation.

"It doesn't change anything." Ki protested. "I still want to fix a few heads that have it coming to them."

Ezos agreed and all looked to Tamu for a leadership decision.

"OK guys here are the deals. We have three battleships on our tail that are for sure going to take negative action against this ship when she refuses to comply with their persuasive recommendations. But, good news, so relax, Delta is here with a thousand of his brothers. Mis will be on his way shortly. Ki get down there and be the welcoming party and deal with your little problem quickly."

Ki's fangs protruded which basically meant he was beside himself with joy. Whether or not emotion registered in his reptile brain was doubtful but getting even with someone definitely was prime priority. Echo opened communication, confirming Mis was through the portal and in Karas with three thousand Reptiles fully armed and itching for a fight.

"Ezos and Samre, you know what you have to do. Take this ship into the first space nebula of ultra violet radiation you find and hide inside it with all shields up then wait for further instruction."

Tamu teleported into Echo with Ridmon and streaked out to intercept three Star battleships of the Karagan Federation with the full contingent of one thousand and two Wasps. In the meantime all hell broke loose on Karas when the Reptiles went on the rampage. It did not take long before Samre was sitting in the Admirals chair shouting orders like a true professional and Karas warped into a nebula hidden and undetectable. Three Federation battleships in formation approached G48 Major and took up defensive positions.

Chief Admiral Jares called a meeting with all heads of command from the three ships that convened into his board room and sat around a conference table with its consoles and refreshments.

"Gentlemen, welcome. You all know why we are here. The Federation has directed us to proceed with our mission into this sector and to obliterate any or all opposition in our way and that includes Karas. We know Karas came here for alternate motives and although she has the best crews on board her, against three of us she is out gunned and will be destroyed with all hands and nobody will grieve for her."

"Excuse me Sir." One deck officer entered the board room. "There is no trace of Karas at all and she does not respond to our signals. We have conducted an extensive scan and came up with nothing."

"This means she is on to us and is hiding. Check the Nebulae around here, she is possibly hidden in one of them, so instruct gunnery crews to fire high incendiary into any nebula they suspect and if Karas is in one of them they will come out like a dog with its tail between its legs when the gases explode."

Laughter echoed in the board room as everyone congratulated themselves on a job well done. But laughter was short lived when Tamu and Ridmon teleported into the room with a few Reptilians.

"So the mighty Jares sits here and gloats like a stuffed pig thinking he has the upper hand, well gentlemen, sorry to disappoint you. Right now your three ships are in extreme peril and are about to be annihilated."

"You can't frighten me, who the hell do you think you are?"

"My name is Tamu, son of Mike of Ridmon and this is my brother Ridmon. These others are my friends and out there are my other friends, all one thousands of them who no doubt you have heard rumors about, but never had the privilege of being introduced. Well here and now that privilege has been granted because three Federation ships are about to be blown to hell. But, we are reasonable people so this is what we are going to do. We are going to send all of you here in this room and your ship back to Karagan with you tail between your legs with a warning, G48 Major is out of bounds and is not part nor will ever be, of the Federation. Just so that you think we don't have the balls or the power, think again. Kindly observe Gentlemen your two Star battleships on you monitor and tell me I am a liar."

On the monitor two battleships disintegrated and were no more. No dramatic explosions no burning just simply transformed into fragmented debris.

"Murderer." Screamed Jares.

"No Sir, all crews are safely on board this ship and if it's any consolation you bastard, you were willing to kill an entire crew aboard the Karas so frag you. By the way, you are trespassing on Planet Ridmon's territory and are in breach of terrestrial law. My advice to you is get the hell away from here while you still have the chance before my patience runs out. One more thing, your data banks have been formatted, every last byte every last storage disk and no records exist of G48 Major on this ship or on Karagan. G48 Major is officially under the protection of Thanu."

With that Tamu and his team teleported out and activated a huge portal sending Jares and his overladen ship back to Karagan. On Karas the scene was one of mixed feelings. Some were jubilant will others loyal to the Federation attempted to put up resistance to their detriment. Mis was merciless. Reports filtered to Planet Ridmon's committee who agreed that Thanu should be informed she had officially inherited G48 Major as part of her jurisdiction and that the Federation had been kicked out for not observing diplomatic etiquette. As there was no direct communication between Thanu and Ridmon for obvious reasons it was decided to use a third party to do the job. The choice was a small planetary system called Xrano, one group on Thanu's defensive radar who suddenly received a message from unknown sources requesting Thanu be informed giving all co-ordinates and relevant information required. Thanu on receiving the message acted with speed knowing the Federation was about to react to being crucified out there in deep space and called an emergency meeting with Karagan. On Karagan the Federation was in a state of shock. A lot of time and money had gone into this expedition and was not about to see the loss of three Star Battleships go un-avenged. Jares was the first of many who was brought before a disciplinary committee and publically humiliated. To add insult to injury the authorities on Karagan placed the Federation on notice.

Thanu was intrigued, this smelled too much like a past history suddenly rearing its ugly head and repeating itself.

"What do you make of this? Think someone is trying to undermine us by causing a rift between us and the Federation." Queried Frux, Thanu's chief negotiator.

"Don't know, but all considering, what do we care if the Federation got its butt kicked by a Good Samaritan who obviously has our interests at heart." answered Uzin.

"Can't help it, this sounds all too familiar of you know who, ex Planet Ridmon individual called Mike."

"No ways Mike was killed a long time ago." Stated Frux.

"Has anyone heard of Planet Ridmon since then?" Queried Uzin.

"No, and don't even try to go there, that place is off the grid and as far as everyone is concerned it does not exist.

"Aren't you at least a little curious?" Questioned Uzin.

"For what it's worth I couldn't care less, because what we have been given, without any effort, is a whole Galaxy G48 Major and that's good enough for me. If there are life forms there then it's our benefit to promote diplomatic co-operation and of course economical and mineral trade beneficial to all." Exclaimed Frux.

Back on Karas, Ki was delivering pay back and together with his machine room colleagues showed some individuals the error of their ways in no uncertain terms. The ship was finally brought back to order and the Admiral paraded in front of Tamu and Ridmon in the control deck's conference room.

"Be seated Sir." Tamu addressed the man who complied.

"Please accept our apologies for the disruption to your ship and sadly, the needless deaths. We are the Matabele Regiment of Planet Ridmon who unfortunately made a small blunder by misinterpreted information, yet have since rectified our error and saved almost your entire crew from being blown out of the universe by Jares of whom you know personally I believe." Exclaimed Ridmon.

The Admiral was no coward, a man of many years of intergalactic travel and skirmishes for the Federation. Yet a man of honor who detested the way the Federation had become a political hornet's nest. When news of a Galaxy way out in deep space of enormous proportions became known by a passing trader ship, certain Federation members developed more than an interest in its procurement for their own agendas not aligned with policy. The Admiral by chance picked up on the agenda from the Captain of the Trader ship after some high ranking members of the

Federation interrogated him. And so the Admiral construed his own agenda going along with everyone and even playing the part of the faithful and loyal soldier he was. However, even the best laid plans sometimes have flaws and his agenda was uncovered leading to his current predicament at the hands of the notorious Matabele Regiment, who until this moment was only heard of in rumors and fables. Standing, the medium sized elderly man with a rugged bearing of so many years in the service stood straight and ridged to attention then asked.

"May I know the nature of our fate?"

Tamu walked around the man and smiled. Was a pleasure to find someone who still maintained perspective on life in spite of the temptation to follow the sheep on Karagan's so called Federation?

"Admiral, I find you to be a man of character and a tribute to your station. So we of planet Ridmon will put forward to you a proposal. But first, I imagine it's time for you to address your crew and give them reassurances that all is well aboard."

Tamu ushered the man to his console and left him to his duty. It was time to bring Wolf and sisters on to the ship to lay the foundations for Kara's future as a Thanu vessel under Thanu's protection. The details of which would be transmitted to Thanu on an accept it or leave it basis. Ridmon's delegation arrived and together with the ship's contingent of officers loyal to their admiral sat in the conference room and thrashed out an agreement conducive to all parties. This type of negotiating was best left to Wolf and Zakrose so he regrouped his team in one of the lounges for a stand down drink. The Reptilian contingent under the command of Mis and a few new recruits were relocated back on Reptilia pleased with themselves for a job well down.

"Well admiral, allow me to make introductions. I am Wolf and these two lovely ladies are my sisters Zakrose and Gnee. My brothers Tamu and Ridmon you have already met. We are here to put forward to you a proposition which we feel will be fair and offer you and your ship's crew a new future, if not a more rewarding one."

Zakrose continued with the narration.

"Don't assume anything gentlemen by our youth, we are after all the leaders of a planet the Federation has been for years trying to undermine on the grounds of its radical disobedience to Federal protocol. The truth of the matter is they are very much afraid of Ridmon's military might and the ever dominant Thanu."

Pacing alongside the large center table she stood behind the admiral. Tamu exited the room.

"Gentlemen, there will be a slight delay unfortunately while we wait for the Thanu delegation to arrive. We have our security to consider firstly and the situation is a little complicated between us."

Silence fell on the room and no one spoke. Gnee studied the faces of the Karas officers and sensed the tension in the air. All were upstanding gentlemen academically trained and disciplined. She hoped that Thanu would at least offer them something worthwhile seeing as they could never return to Karagan. An inter-leading door opened and Tamu returned with the Thanu delegation. Wolf stood up saying.

"Welcome members of Thanu, your presence here is most fortunate for this ship and its crew. Let me enlighten you as to what exactly you have here. G48 Major is a fairly newly formed Galaxy uncluttered by known civilization and an extremely important one at that. We don't know at this stage if there are life forms here and this is the purpose of Karas to ascertain. We may find civilized nations or not,

it does really not matter. What matters to Ridmon and
likewise to Thanu that this pristine galaxy does not become
a wasteland by unscrupulous mineral mongers?"

One female delegate from Thanu spoke up.

"My name is Thena, a member of Thanu's supreme
council and these are my aids" pointing to the three other
Thanuians. "I have been given explicit authority to offer
Karas a new role in its mandate and that is one of allegiance
to Thanu and to operate as her eyes and ears in G48 Major
together with a fleet of Thanuian Warships which you no
doubt are familiar with. My role in this picture is that, as
of this moment, please be advised my position here will
be permanent on this ship as Thanu's representative in
G48 Major. The fleet of which I spoke about is already
here thanks to our most esteemed friends the Ridmonians.
My engineers will be coming aboard to make some major
structural and required changes to bring this vessel up to
standard with the rest of the fleet out here."

Turning to face the Admiral she asked.

"Are you in agreement Sir?"

The Admiral stood up, bowed and declared.

"We are now in the capable hands of Thanu and sworn
to allegiance and to obedience and welcome you Madam
Thena on board."

All Kara's officers in the room stood to attention
and saluted. Tamu Teleported out to where his team still
sat drinking. They all looked at him with curiosity and
questioning eyes.

"Well, what's the news?" Asked Naya.

"Done deal, it's agreed. Karas is now a Thanuian fleet
ship and her crews are under new management who by the
way, is on board by the name of Thena. Matter closed for
us though. We return home to a quiet and demur life style

not suited to our talents. Would you guys be interested in tagging along with this bunch of Thanuians and do some adventure of our own in G48major as official representatives of planet Ridmon?"

As one, the team answered.

"Affirmative."

"There is just one small problem to overcome. Wolf and my two sisters. Ezos do you and Samre have wives, children or girlfriends?"

"We have girlfriends who are in the Regiment and very good soldiers." Ezos answered.

"Good, what are their names?"

"Utan and Visni."

Tamu opened a portal into the Matabele barracks and said.

"Fetch them."

The two men jumped and ran down a corridor like the wind, appearing moments later hand in hand with their girls and returned aboard Karas.

"Thank you, thank you." Visni blurted out and hugged Samre.

"Touching." It was Wolf with Zakrose and Gnee.

"What a lovely scene. What are you up to Tamu?" He demanded.

"Oh, just a little rearranging of priorities for myself and my team here." He answered knowing Gnee was trying to read his mind and shut her out.

"Rearranging priorities, perhaps dear brother, you might explain as your family seems to be a little confused by those words." Zakrose asked.

"Sit down Sis and listen to what we have decided here, please."

Zakrose, Gnee and a bemused Wolf sat down and listened to Tamu's whatever, they were so used to his ranting and raving only sometimes taking him seriously as often times were just one of his pranks.

"We, that's the team and I, have decided to stay here on Karas and pursue a life of adventure and exploration in G48 Major as the official representatives of Planet Ridmon and have a small favor to ask, I am sure you will agree, Echo, Sierra and Zulu be our, how would you call it, protection."

It was Gnee who came to his rescue.

"You know, he has a point and think about it, we will not have to put up with his antics for a while which will be a relief, trust me. It also solves the problem of planet Ridmon's representation on board."

Wolf just grinned even broader thinking what a wonderful opportunity to see the rascal bugging someone else for a change, thus planet Ridmon could return to normalization once again.

"Settled and yes, Echo and his two sidekicks will be your constant companions and will be reporting back to us." With that he teleported out with the two sisters leaving Tamu and his team ecstatic.

Time to inform the Thanu delegation Ridmon had representatives on board. Dressing in their black body stocking battle fatigues complete with white death rods and crystal helmets strapped to their backs they found Madam Thena down on the flight deck trailed by her aids and the Admiral with his officers. The Admirals eyebrows rose when Tamu and his team marched up to them in perfect synchronization and came to a flawlessly executed halt without a single command given. Tamu stepped forward and declared.

"Madam Thena, may we present ourselves. We are the delegation from planet Ridmon as was agreed by our Committee to be present on board and let me assure you we come highly recommended."

Thena eyed Tamu from head to toe and asked,

"I take it Mr. Tamu you will participate in a positive and responsible manner understanding that Thanu and not Ridmon are in control here and you will do as you are told."

"Begging your pardon dear Madam, but I think you are missing the point. We are independents and operate according to our own agendas with our own people and military safe guards for whom we are most famous or infamous for. Just to advise you so that there are no hidden secrets, we are accompanied by our own Fleet of war craft more capable and out gunning Thanu's mighty battleships here in G48 Major."

"Ah, young man you seem to be well informed." She smiled. "I hope at least we can work together for mutual benefit, don't you agree?"

Tamu laughed out loud.

"Madam if it was not for Planet Ridmon, Thanu would not exist so do not presume anything and keep to your station and perform your duties as is required of you. On this ship everyone carries their weight. You are not on Thanu in some plush apartment pampered by aids. You are reminded you are on a battle ship therefore expected at act accordingly with the rest of us."

"Young man, I shall lodge a formal complaint against you and have you withdrawn from this ship" she fumed.

"Sorry babe, of that there is no chance to get rid of us, so we Ridmonians are here to make sure you keep within the boundaries of protocol."

The admiral stepped forward and taking Thena by the elbow ushered her away saying.

"Come my dear, let us retire to my lounge to cool off with a refreshing drink. Planet Ridmon is here and believe me, they are not to be trifled with, and I have witnessed their effectiveness on my very ship. Besides, we have much to discuss."

Strike one for Planet Ridmon. It was time now for a much deserved bit of rest and recreation. A job well done meant loosening the hair a bit. Question was where and what, so Tamu put it to the vote.

"Are we a team or not?" He shouted.

"Matabele." Roared the response.

"Right, hair down time. Where and what?" Asked Tamu.

In unison the vote was unanimous. "Matabele Ridmon."

For the next year Karas underwent major transformation to her outer and inner infrastructures. Gradually she was transformed into one of Thanu's super Battleships. Additional crews were brought in from Thanu and trained Kara's original crews in the function of the various new technologically advanced components of Karas. She was ready to fulfill her duties. There was no hurry, G48 Major was going nowhere and the estimation of exploration amounted to centuries, so it was imperative to establish settlements where communities could be developed as replacement crews when age and usefulness failed those on board. Colonizing G48 Major was not the prime objective. If and when it came to the point of withdrawal, all delegations, their communities and complete infrastructures would be returned to Thanu and planet Ridmon respectively. However, protection of G48 major was up to both Thanu and planet Ridmon to enforce and maintain.

During the year of Kara's refurbishment Tamu and his team went into extensive training in a secret camp deep in the dark forests of the valley well away from the crystal city and Tamu blocked all his teams' minds to intrusion of any scan by either his family or Wasps and Drones. He already had achieved a high level of proficiency almost equaling that of his deceased father and those of his team were of a standard none of the Matabele had thus far achieved. Ki for once in his life understood so many things and became elevated from primitive Reptile to a highly intelligent and capable representative of Reptilia. At the end of that year the team returned on board the Karas with a renewed commitment to each other and what they stood for.

During that year planet Ridmon communicated with Echo who for the first time since his creation lied openly. The question put to him was where was Tamu? He without hesitation confirmed on Karas. No one doubted his word and was none the wiser. Three thousand Wasps knew different though yet remained silent in support. An air of anticipation buzzed around planet Ridmon, the wasps were on a high, and Tamu they believed would summon them soon. Zakrose being highly sensitive and intuitive picked up on the vibrations of the Wasps. She called Wolfe and Gnee together and told them what she was feeling.

"Something is going on with the Wasps, there is an air of anticipation among them I can't interpret. When I questioned Echo he said Tamu was on Karas, but Karas denied Tamu was there. If I have to make a calculated guess I would say those brothers of ours are up to something and the Wasps are poised to go. They are like guitar strings under tension and the slightest excuse and they will be off. Another thing, Tamu has blocked his mind and those of his team so we have no way of knowing where he is and what he is up too."

"This thing with the Wasps worries me. We are in the soup should they leave Planet Ridmon. It is apparent Tamu has far more control than we gave him credit for and perhaps all his monkeying around was a guise for what was really going on in his mind." Commented Wolf.

"I think we had better ask that brother of ours exactly what's going on and bring him here for a heart to heart talk." Advised Gnee to which Zakrose agreed.

Wolf channeled a message to Echo requesting Tamu's presence on Planet Ridmon. Echo in turn relayed the message to which Tamu agreed and teleported into the great hall with his team. When Zakrose saw her brother she was shocked. Tamu looked and bore the air of her father right down to the posture, the small insignificant gestures and facial expressions. Her legs refused to function so sat down. Gnee sat down next to her and swore under her breath. Wolf walked into the hall and seeing the team sitting at the bar was primarily filled with anger thus blinding his judgment and perceptions then seeing his sisters with tears running down their cheeks, hurtled at Tamu. He never reached his target and felt a terrible force clamping down on his body. Ki had grabbed him in both hands. There was no way he could free himself and no matter what telepathic influences he might have, could not wrench him free. Tamu stepped forward and asked.

"Still want to take me on bro?"

Wolf was for the first time in his life at a loss of words and knew then Tamu had showed his hand.

"Ok, that's enough, put me down already."

Tamu shrugged his shoulders and looked at Ki.

"You think we should do that, after all we have always been the naughty boys around here and it really pisses me off thinking my own family treats us like freaks. Perhaps we should teach this brother of mine a lesson. No! That would make us lower than him and you know what that means for us, public disgrace and we can't have that can we, so Ki, let him go."

Ki dropped Wolf unceremoniously onto the floor. Wolf was an expert martial artist and immediately retaliated only to find darkness and unconsciousness at the end of Ki's fist. Zakrose was beside herself on seeing Wolf hit the floor and pleaded with Tamu to stop. Tamu hefted Wolf on to his shoulders and going to the bar, asked the barman to splash water on the unconscious man's face who complied. Wolf coughed and sputtered back to reality and a beer shoved into his hand. Still reeling from the impact he looked at Tamu and muttered two words.

"Matabele Ridmon." Then sank to his knees still groggy from Ki's punch.

Gnee went up to Tamu and stood in front of him with hands on hips and scolded.

"Tamu, that's enough from you and your thugs. Shame on you, how could you do such a thing to your brother?"

"Easy Sis. Wolf has always walked around like he is someone special and above everyone else because of Dad. Well actions speak louder than words and it is time he climbed off his high horse and joined us siblings here in the world of reality and that goes for you two as well."

"How can you talk like that?" Protested Zakrose.

"Yeah, well no fine girls, but excuse me, as long as I am the half-brother there will always be a division between us and don't deny it."

"You are wrong. We love you very much and sorry, but you haven't given us reason to think otherwise."

"Well here is news for you, this Tamu is different and will not put up with your nonsense anymore and from now on you three will treat me as an equal or else it's your loss and the loss of a whole lot more."

Turning to the team, he asked Ridmon.

"You staying or coming with Brother?"

"With you Brother."

They teleported out leaving the three-family members wondering what on earth happened to Tamu.

With her refit complete, Karas maneuvered into formation with the Thanu fleet and together they journeyed deeper into the depths of G48 Major searching for a possible inhabitable planet to set up a base from which crews could enjoy time off from the rigors of Ship life. Unknown to the fleet Echo and the two Wasps were themselves engaged in the same activity only they had a distinct advantage over the fleet, the ability to use the portal to hop scotch from point to point and so cover greater areas of space. It was not long before they found what appeared to be an ideal inhabitable planet for humans in one of the thousands of solar systems within G48Major. Echo reported to Tamu on Karas of their find. So he instructed echo to scan the entire planet and make sure everything was documented clearly and any life forms no matter what form, microbes to any upright two legged creatures. Run diagnostics of diseases on the planet's surface, in its waters if any and below ground. To analyze what impact human habitation would have on the environment and whether or not it was in all fairness the right thing to do even for a short period of time. Additionally construct a geological break down and atmospheric chart, and weather patterns to make sure no surprises waited on its surface and if they did, what measures it would take to neutralize same.

On Karas Tamu and his team waited for Echo's final diagnostic report busying themselves with refining their skills and adapting new ones to fit into their own personal abilities. Activity for them on board was limited to diplomatic duties only. Excluded from participation in the ships affairs left little to keep them occupied so the days past slowly. They had to keep up appearances and attend the weekly briefings on progress otherwise Tamu would have been compelled to return to Ridmon. The news Echo reported in was very encouraging, but caution was needed before any decisions to relocate were made. If the news was positive then a fully functional settlement had to be setup as a base of operations for planet Ridmon's usage only and bring in air support, ground support and technical knowhow. Question being whether planet Ridmon would agree to the establishment of a secondary base of operations and what would the benefits be to them. Two months passed until Echo presented his findings. Leaving his team on the Karas, Tamu went to Ridmon armed with a fully comprehensive report and a feasibility study on human habitation. He was met in the war room by Ridmon's committee.

Wolf studied his brother closely. The man had changed. There was an air of authority on him and a look of determined purpose. Zakrose and Gnee still smarting from Tamu's last visit were somewhat skeptical.

"I did not come here to repeat the events of my last visit. I came here to put a proposition to you. We have discovered an inhabitable planet within the constellations of inner G48 Major which is off the record as far as Karas is concerned who know nothing about this. I have here a fully comprehensive report from Echo and his two partners which is so promising it would be a shame to pass this opportunity to establish a base of operations in that sector. Before you scrutinize these reports be advised whether or not you decide to either accept or reject this opportunity, I will not."

He instructed Echo to download the information then continued.

"Ridmon's role on Karas is best suited to a more diplomatic orientated team and not Matabele soldiers, so my team and I are handing in our resignations from that obligation as of now. So while you study the information downloaded into you data banks I will take my leave and retire to my Mother's old home and wait for your response."

The committee began to analyze the reports and realized at once due to the sheer volume they would have to call in a technical team and to come to some point of positive acceptance or rejection which would take a few days at least. Gnee exited the War room deep in thought. What Tamu had brought back was in itself a small wonder and a feeling deep inside began to take shape, a feeling of anticipation. She took off into the forest in search of Tamu and found him sitting on the outside platform of the house drinking Ridmon beer.

"Got any more?" She asked

Tamu reached under the chair and handed her a bottle.

"Amazing don't you think that in all the time we have lived on this planet and our parents before us, Ridmon beer is still fermented in Black Nut gum bottles. Kind of neat don't you think?"

"Sit down Sis and out with it."

Gnee sat down on a spare chair, cracked the cork on her beer and took her time to answer.

"Take me with you."

Tamu studied her face seeing the sincerity in her eyes.

"You do realize we are walking into the unknown."

"So did our parents and look what they achieved in their life time on Ridmon. I feel this is what I want to do for me."

"Exciting isn't it"

Tamu hit the soft spot and his sister suddenly projected into an excited young girl bubbling with ideas, he let her rave on, but his mind was elsewhere until she kicked him on the shin.

"Hey, knock! Knock! Anybody home?" She asked.

"Sorry. In principle I would love to have you with us but you are going to have to pass a test we will set for you so that we can be confident of your basic abilities out there in outer space and you will have to agree to continue training to meet our standards of approval."

"I'll buy that and am willing to go the whole hog."

"Good, that's settled then. Now we wait for management's decision."

The two sat in silence for a while sipping their beers when Echo interrupted Tamu's thoughts.

"Karas are looking for you and say they will not discuss matters with anyone but you."

Tamu looked at Gnee and asked. "Want to go on a trip right now?"

Her eyes sparkled. "Yes."

With that he teleported into Echo with Gnee and dived through a portal for Karas. Instinct told him to materialize into the conference room which he did and sitting like a Prima Dona was Thena. His arrival frightened the hell out of her especially materializing like he did with Gnee.

"What's the problem now?" She demanded.

One of her aids opened his mouth to speak, but no words came out. Tamu telepathically shut him down then put pressure on Thena who stammered.

"I want you to control that monster Reptile of yours. It is rude ill-mannered and damn right disobedient."

Tamu was amused because her statement meant she had been pushing her weight around when she realized he was not on the ship and picked on Nah who just like KI, put her in her place.

"Madam Thena, serves you right for exceeding your authority once again and interfered with one of my staff which you have no jurisdiction over nor authority to do so. Now for your edification this delegation has been withdrawn from Karas and filled a letter of complaint against you on Thanu."

Echo was one step ahead and made the communique to Thanu who acknowledged receipt ordering the immediate repatriation of Thena and her aids. The Wasp downloaded the message into Kara's communications center. Next moment a runner came into the conference room with a digital electronic tablet and handed it to the Admiral.

"Madam it seems you have been relieved of your post and summoned back to Thanu."

Without a word she stood up and exited the room with her aids. The Admiral looked at Tamu and asked.

"What game are you playing at young fellow? I can smell a set up when I see it?"

"I like you admiral, but that woman is a pain in the butt and not a good candidate to represent Thanu on Karas. If, and I am saying if, there was a real threat which escalated into full confrontation and lasers being fired left right and center, she would only be a liability. You need personnel on this ship who under those circumstances are an asset not a hindrance."

"Tamu, you surprise me and I must say your team really is expert in espionage. I don't condone what some of your men did to my staff, but I have to acknowledge the courage and bravado of your mission and the way you went about it with such meticulous and patient application. Any chance you and your team would work for me?"

"Sorry Sir, we are Ridmonians and do not change loyalties at any price. I hope you understand."

"It's quite alright son, just promise me Planet Ridmon will stay close, real close because I am sure the Federation will come snooping."

"It will be a pleasure Sir."

With that Tamu exited the room with Gnee and found his team in the usual lounge.

"Attention on deck." He shouted.

This resulted in an immediate reaction with the team jumping to attention. Gnee folded in half with laughter at the look on their faces. Ki glared at Tamu and hissed his disapproval while Naya screamed with glee and jumped into his arms smothering him with kisses. Gnee was still bowed over with a stitch in her side caused by the laughing. Ezos flopped down on a chair and smiled to himself. Samre shook his head and sat down. Their girls followed suit. Extracting himself from Naya's embrace he addressed his team.

"Guys, we are off the hook and Diplomatic games are over so we are going home. Where is Ridmon and Qing Fe?"

The reaction was spontaneous. "Don't ask."

Tamu just smiled realizing the two were being overly intimate somewhere.

"Collect your gear and meet back here." He ordered. With that he fetched his and Naya's gear and returned to the lounge where Gnee was deep in conversation with Utan and Visni. A short moments later the rest of the group arrived including Ridmon and a sheepish looking Qing Fe.

"Echo, beam us aboard, we are going home."

With that the Ridmonians left Karas and jumped a portal for Planet Ridmon and the forest. Gnee walked up to Wolf and hugged him.

"What's that for?" He asked pushing her out at arm's length.

"No special reason dear brother, can't a girl express her affection sometimes?"

Wolf laughed. "Gnee, if I didn't know better I would say you are up to something, out with it girl."

"You will have to wait for Tamu for an answer to that." So saying skipped off leaving Wolf shaking his head.

An hour later Tamu walked into the great Hall with his team, sat down near the bar and ordered drinks. The mood was jovial and light hearted. Internal security however advised Zakrose on her console of Tamu's presence to which she made her way down to the Hall. Standing at the entrance of the elevator she watched the ten people having a good time so slowly walked up to them and announced herself.

"Hello you lot. I was wondering when I would see you again. We have a meeting in an hours' time so don't get too inhibited. For what it's worth, welcome back."

"Hi to you Sis, and yes, thanks this is after all our home and we will be ready in an hours' time as you request. Why not sit down and join us, we have lots to tell you."

"No thanks, too busy." So walked off.

"Ooops! She's pissed." Exclaimed Naya.

An hour later the team convened in a conference room attached to the Great Hall and waited. Committee members and technical personnel began to file in and take seats around the large oval table. Moments later Zakrose and Wolf entered the room and took their respective seats. A large console lowered from the ceiling and rested on the table top.

"Gentlemen and ladies, this meeting is called to order and will be recorded. We have called this meeting to discuss the possibility of opening a new settlement in G48 Major and for those of you who are not aware of this it is a newly discovered spiral Galaxy three hundred thousand light years across out in very deep space. In front of you on your table consoles you will find all relevant facts and figures relating to this planet we have named Eureka, an ancient Greek word for "I have found [it]. As far as we have been able to ascertain the planet is very habitual, does contain what could be defined as wild life, but no sign of intelligent life forms. Our delegation that were on the Federation battleship Karas at the time of a takeover by Thanu are the ones who discovered Eureka by their own means using the Wasps. G48 Major is a massive constellation and will take centuries to discover and to be able to do that in conjunction with Thanu we need a forward base of operations in the area."

Zakrose paused briefly to check the console then continued.

"What we propose therefore is to split our resources and send a team of Ridmonians to Eureka to establish a secure base together with one Drone and one hundred wasps as protection. My brothers Tamu and Ridmon have been nominated by the committee to oversee this mission and later manage operations from there. This base is to be a semi-permanent base easy to assemble and break down and relocate somewhere else if need be. We have no way of knowing who's out there and what's out there so security is priority. You all have you facts and figures which you will scrutinize and in two days report back here with a workable simple plan of execution. A contingent of one thousand Matabele soldiers will be barracked on Eureka under Tamu's command as ground strike force and base security. There you have it.

This is the first of several meetings so suggest you study all aspects well. Any questions please? If no questions we will reconvene in two days and discuss in detail all aspects of the base of operations on Eureka." Zakrose concluded.

Tamu and his team moved out of the conference room to the Bar and sat down.

"I am a little surprised I have to admit." Declared Ezos.

"I think all of us are." Echoed Visni.

"OK, this is what we have courtesy of the committee. One Drone. One hundred Wasps, a thousand Matabele and a support team of techs, medical and maintenance crews. Not bad for starters. Ezos and Samre will you go and start making a selection of men and women who are couples in the Matabele Regiment from officers to ranks and put our proposal to them. Explain Eureka is a permanent position and return to Ridmon will only happen on retirement if they so choose. We don't want singles if we can help it, but if no choice make your selection as equal men and women in numbers."

Ezos and Samre headed off with their girlfriends to the main Matabele Regiment barracks housed in the third crystal city of Dagor by inter-city shuttle service. Twenty thousand personnel were not going to be an easy task to sort out and interview potential candidates. Zakrose nominated a diplomatic team to be established on Karas initially then once Eureka was functional would be stationed at the base. A day later she called in Ridmon and gave him the task of taking the Diplomatic team to board the Karas. A group of six individuals gathered on the platform outside the Crystal city and were beamed into Echo and jumped through a portal into G48 Major Space alongside Karas. One of the group was an intelligence expert while the others function was as negotiators and translators. Echo beamed them down into the conference room where they were joined by the Admiral and some of his officers.

"Ah! Welcome Ridmon. I see you have delivered your diplomatic colleagues."

"Yes Sir and if you don't mind I will have to leave you as I have pressing matters to attend to. Please excuse my haste, but we shall meet at another more appropriate time."

Echo beamed him out leaving the group to make their introductions. Once inside Echo Ridmon asked.

"I hope all this beaming up and down is untraceable to Karas?"

"We are untraceable."

"That eases my mind a great deal, thanks."

"What are your orders?" Asked Echo.

"We have been given one hundred Wasps to be stationed here in G48 Major and we are going to leave their selection up to you. I know all the Wasps would like to come, but be fair by explaining to them what we could do is have a rotational system in effect where all Wasps will be given a chance to operate here for a period of three months each rotation. We would like very much if you would consider yourself as appointed spokesperson between the Wasps and us."

Echo realized he had been elevated in position and standing, responded.

"Affirmative, Echo will consult the others."

"Home James." Laughed Ridmon and Echo jumped through a portal into Planet Ridmon's air space. The following day Zakrose once again opened the meeting of Ridmon's dignitaries and those of the two outer cities.

"Ladies and gentlemen you have had to chance to review all aspects of our intended settlement of Planet Eureka and now we would like your recommendations and plans of engagement."

For sixteen hours the debates, agreements, recommendations, disagreements until finally a consensus was reached in principle so Zakrose closed the session until the next day when the actual planning phase had to be worked in detail. Feeling exhausted she made her way to the Bar for a well-deserved drink. Gnee sensing her sister's thought patterns came down from her room and joined Zakrose.

"Hi!" And sat down.

Zakrose starred into her drink lost in thought oblivious of Gnee's presence. The younger girl waited a moment then touched her sister on the arm saying.

"Hello, anybody home?"

"Sorry, I was day dreaming, my apologies."

"Long day for you and will be tomorrow as well from what Wolf mentioned to me earlier on. Anyway that is not what's bothering you so out with it." Gnee demanded.

"I don't know, I guess it has to do with Tamu and Ridmon. While Tamu is around we hate him, when he is gone we miss him and now he will be going and we may never see them again and that's what worries me."

"Well I am sure they will visit, but you must tell Tamu because he thinks you are mad at him, so mad you want nothing to do with him. I too have made a decision and that is one you are also going to be upset about." Gnee advised.

"What decision?"

"I will be going with Tamu to Eureka."

Zakrose sat silent for a few moments then responded.

"Are you sure you want to do this? There will be no life like we have here and it will be hard living with unexpected dangers we know nothing about yet. What will you do there anyway?"

"Doing what Aunty Jane trained me to do, animal and plant species studies. I am so excited you can't believe it. A whole new world to explore and document, besides, didn't Uncle Jack teach me so many things when he was here and didn't he make sure his son Ronnie did the same? Between the two of us we could be very productive."

"Yeah, just how productive? Work or you know what."

"Hey, what are you implying? Gnee protested.

"Nothing, forget it. I'll miss you very much and you're happy smiley face around here."

With that Gnee hugged her sister.

In the dark forest Tamu sat with Naya on his lap discussing the up and coming settlement on Eureka when Echo advised him that a Federation Destroyer Class One was tracking after Karas. This type of ship was smaller than Karas but carried a lethal bite called a Neuron canon which unlike a proton canon which needed time to charge up to full potential, the Neuron canon was instantaneous and fired in rapid session with devastating results. The other advantage of the neuron canon was once fired the oncoming projectile was untraceable as it gathered momentum until the last moment. Evasive action was useless at that point and goodbye target. Tamu came aboard the Karas and sounded the alarm. The crews of the Karas were well aware of the dangers posed by this type of weapon. Karas was an ex federation battleship whose capacity to raise shields was not strong enough to withstand a Neuron barrage in spite of Thanu modifications. Tamu teleported the Ridmon delegation aboard Zulu and gave it instructions to jump a portal into planet Ridmon. He then sent Echo and Sierra through a portal to engage and kill the Destroyer. He ordered Karas to warp to where the Thanu fleet was and advise them of the situation as where there is one might be others. Tamu opened a portal and stepped into the Great Hall where the returned delegates from Karas were standing talking to Wolf. He walked over and gave Wolf a situation report and the group waited. Echo reported in.

"Target destroyed. Second target illuminated by Thanu fleet, but Karas went down with all hands."

This was a blow. After all she had been through, it was not a fitting way to go especially by a back stabber like a Federation destroyer. Tamu felt anger well up inside of him and for a moment let down his mental guard.

"Easy Tamu, easy. We will pay them a visit in our own time and reciprocate with interest." Sounded Wolf's voice in his brain.

He turned and went out onto the platform to one of the kiosks and celebrated his own form of Irish Wake for those lost souls aboard the Karas. The news of the tragedy reached Naya who contacted Ezos and Samre. They found Tamu and joined in the faire.

Tamu's group was not present at the next morning's meetings and after a long complicated day the settlement of Eureka was finalized. Planet Ridmon gave its go ahead and a time line for preparation. A week later Ezos and Samre completed their assessment of the one thousand Matabele and Samre ensured all logistical and tactical equipment, spares and support commodities were packed and ready for dispatch. A month after that the Eureka project was ready to go with its full contingent.

Twenty Drones and one hundred Wasps beamed up a thousand Matabele and the five thousand support personnel needed for the construction of the settlement plus all the equipment, stores and building materials plus military hardware and sensitive computing parts and spares. Finally, Tamu and his team stood on the platform with Gnee and bade farewell to Zakrose and Echo then beamed them up.

"OK Echo let's get this show on the road."

Portals opened and the Ridmonians jumped into Eureka's space. Echo and the one hundred Wasps scouted along the Planets equator searching for the most suitable location to establish a base camp offering relative protection and camouflage with a water source, accessibility from the air and all round defense. Echo was quick to find an ideal spot with overhead jungle foliage from a large cluster a high trees to the rear side forming a natural barrier, a large section of flat ground shaped like a boomerang roughly four hundred meters long and one hundred and fifty meters wide then the ground dropped sharply for forty meters to a fast flowing river. Behind the line of trees at the rear a steep wooded granite hill and as luck would have it, a cave complex offering all kinds of potential possibilities. Echo hovered above the location for Tamu to make a visual assessment. One significant aspect taken into consideration was the hill and its geological structure, water runoff from rain and falling rock damage. It was an ideal spot so Tamu gave the go ahead to beam down the construction teams and materials to commence immediate work.

The plan was simple, the whole section of trees the length and breadth of the site was to be excavated carefully and raised off the ground into the air by the Wasps tractor beams. The construction teams would then construct the whole accommodation complex with its supporting facilities made of extremely strong materials able to withstand tremendous pressures. The whole complex was modular easy to construct and easy to deconstruct. Once the buildings were in place the gaps between modules would be filled with soil and rock and leveled then the whole tree line hanging in the air would be lowered on top of the complex roots and all, cosmetically adjusted to look as natural as possible as its surroundings. Water, power and communication were just a plug in system throughout the complex with a separate unit for waste recycling and water purification. Twenty four hours later the work was completed and fully functional and to become the home of the Matabele Regiment and the Eureka command. On the opposite bank of the river an almost identical layout was found and there the support crew's accommodations were erected in similar fashion. Both complexes were screened from the air and undetectable to scans, probes or other search devises. The caves became the command center for operations and housed one of the most sophisticated computer systems in the known universe. On completion of their task the construction crews were beamed out and twenty Drones returned to Ridmon.

The next few days were spent finalizing all facilities and setting up security parameters. The Wasps made a three hundred and sixty degree scan out to a range of a thousand kilometers and detected nothing. Everything was set, now all that remained was to synchronize everyone's movements to a set schedule and function. Tamu checked the complex from the air and was amazed at the almost perfect job done to make it blend into the surroundings without any trace of tampering. He hoped the uprooted Vegetation was going to survive after being uprooted, roots soil and all. Hopefully all the growth hormones applied would do their work. Tamu telepathically contacted Zakrose.

"We are on site, everything is in place. You can send our one Drone back to us with the last load of Power modules and additional supplies, and Zakrose, love you."

The Drone jumped into Eureka space and beamed down the last of the supplies then moved into orbit with the wasps. Ground crews quickly dispensed with the goods and moved the power modules into the caves. Each module had a life span of six months and the stock level stood at two years of power for the base replenished by the support relief units coming in. All was set to go. Ezos was appointed commander of the Matabele unit and immediately began sending out patrols in all directions to familiarize them with the terrain. Eureka's climate was tropical on the equator with polar caps at the poles. Small land masses concentrated along the equator line at intervals and three large continents, two on the Tropic of Capricorn line and one on the Tropic of Cancer line in opposing orientation around the Planet's surface. The land masses were somewhat strange in their orientation and formation over eons of time and Nature does have her mysteries. Scattered around the lines of Capricorn and Cancer were numerous small Islands the circumference of the globe. Eureka was a far cry from planet Ridmon and more to the likeness to Earth.

At 13.30 hours each day without fail the skies opened up and for thirty minutes the rain pelted down. When the sun re-emerged from behind the clouds and started to bake the ground clouds of steam rose into the air giving the site an eerie ghost like appearance. Early mornings were shrouded in mist just before the sun rose into its zenith. It took a while, but gradually the jungle began to come alive with sounds mainly from birds. Gnee was in her element, this is what she dreamed of and now it lay right at her fingertips. However her wondering about was curtailed by Tamu who insisted she take with her at least two Matabele. She and Robbie began to create a complete documented library of life on Eureka which included Ornithology, Entomology, Zoology, ichthyology [study of fish] and Botany. The purpose was to find alternate food sources which could be cultivated and harvested without impacting on the natural ecology. Tamu's mission was not to set up population settlements on Eureka but rather to limit to the minimum any human activity on the pristine Planet for the time being. His Wasps ventured deeper and deeper into G48 Major charting solar systems and likely planets where life may be found even at its base level of cell structure. This function would take decades just to discover a fraction of the solar systems present. Thanu's Fleet continually patrolled the outer limits of the Galaxy watching for Federation infiltration.

Over the course of the next few months Tamu's activities were confined to the base ensuring most of the bugs in the systems were worked out and running smoothly. The caves became a Fortress where every scrap of data relayed in from the Wasps was analyzed, catalogued and stored then re-transmitted to Ridmon. All were aware that Thanu might eventually send in their teams of scientists, technicians and the like so it was imperative to establish ground rules in much the same way done on earth decades prior on the solar caps between nations for research purposes only. Thanu did not know planet Ridmon was already very active in G48 Major so when a Delegation met with Thanu representatives on one of the fleet ships and advised them that planet Ridmon had established bases on various solar systems [blatant lie] out of bounds to Thanu by pre-agreement; they were shocked realizing the speed at which planet Ridmon had executed her strategy. So Thanu was left with no alternative but to do catch up and didn't waste time either by bringing in her re-enforcement fleets to cover more space. Ridmon was content however, based upon the data from the Wasps there was more than enough room for everyone and the big question looming like a thunder cloud was the fact that there might be more than one advanced society in G48 Major who would stop at nothing to protect their own environments against any intrusion. The other side of the coin was equally problematic and one all participating players had to adhere to. Primitive societies were to be left alone and only observed from outer space and in no way interfere with or attempt to change any or everything pertaining to evolutionary process. Ridmon and Thanu were in effect "Gods from the skies".

The Federation was making waves on Karagan protesting Thanu's role in G48 Major. They were not aware of planet Ridmon's participation nor to what extent was Thanu involved in the Galaxy. The protest involved a share in the find coming mainly from delegates from Trafodj and Vimusi. Thanu was not impressed by their rhetoric and reminded them emphatically their past and although members of the Council of Planets, they were in the minority and held the least seats therefore the majority vote won the day. Thanu further went on to rebuke the Federation for allowing itself to become part of a involvement resulting in the destruction of Karas and two Destroyers of the Federation fleet in G48 Major who by rights should not have been there in the first place and the Federation equally were responsible for their loss of two Star Battleships, illuminated by unknown forces when the federation ships attacked Karas without provocation.

"Speaker of the House, there has been mischief afoot here by members of the Federation and it appears misappropriation of Federation assets. Two Battleships and two Destroyers amount to a substantial loss and a needless sacrifice of manpower. We of Thanu make strong protest and declare that any, and we mean any, Federation ships found in or near G48 Major will be destroyed. We further declare and announce a partnership for maintaining the integrity of G48 Major. Someone you all know, some more so than others. Speaker of the House, fellow delegates, allow me to introduce you to the Ridmonian delegation from the Planet Ridmon."

Planet Ridmon's delegation stood up and bowed. A sudden hush fell in the Great Chamber, a pin drop would have been more audible. Both the Thanu and Ridmon delegations then exited the chamber without excusing themselves, a symbol of protest leaving behind an uneasy silence. The Federation States knew not to mess with Ridmon even in the absence of Mike, no one wanted to lock horns with her. The Speaker of the House dismissed the session and delegates filed out quietly. The news that Thanu had aligned itself with Ridmon came as a heavy blow to the Federation who began to purge from within their ranks negative elements.

On planet Ridmon, Wolf was recounting the events of the Federations general meeting on Karagan they had attended on invite from Thanu who explained the reason to which the Ridmonian delegation was more than willing to participate in.

"Thanu made a speech kicking the butts of the Federation and lodging official protest then hit them with a bomb shell, our participation in G48 Major. I tell you that Chamber must have had a heart attack because they just went dead quiet."

"What do you expect? Since Dads death we have been keeping such a low profile I suppose most people thought we had dropped off the map. Even when there were a few alterations with Trafodj, we kept out of it. So I can well imagine their dismay to find out Ridmon was still alive and kicking. The other matter they will realize is who took out their ships in G48 Major. Actually I am more than pleased

Ridmon and Thanu work together seeing as we are related to each other as planets so to speak." Answered Zakrose.

"I suppose the time had to come. Anyway, now we have access to Thanu the conventional way and that could be a friendship builder." Wolf reflected.

Back on Eureka systems worked like clockwork with a two shift rotation program of support crews which included the Matabele Regiment on security details. A lot of grunts and groans emanating from their quarter due the hum drum daily boring stuff. Tamu satisfied his base camp met all the criteria decided to use the Matabele with Wasp support to explore other land masses on Eureka. It was not too wise of him to spread too thin on the ground so kept half the troops in base. Around the circumference of the planet on the equator were hundreds of small continents and a variety of sizes of Islands. It would take a long time to explore them all so a cross pattern scan with the Wasps cut out a lot of the Islands bearing no significance and enabled them to concentrate on the larger ones. The Reptiles he would bring in for the large continents as he felt that there might be some nasty surprises in store. Initial scans did not reveal much, but that was not to say there was nothing on them. So, charting and naming the inner land masses was priority number one, documenting their wild life if any was the task of Gnee and Robbie to whom were allocated Zulu the Wasp as their watch dog. Thus the major continents and smaller ones were categorized into eight parts and named accordingly for security purposes and served as evacuation destinations in case of an overwhelming attack force, these locations served as regroup areas. The idea was to split forces into small groups and spread the groups throughout the land masses and ensure survival of at least a few resistance pockets. No matter how powerful one might be there is always someone or something more powerful. So bearing in mind this sobering aspect nothing was to be taken for granted. The division was set as such.

The three main continents, five smaller continents and the balance made up the islands. Each one was named by code Parnos, Vatnu, and Goras. The smaller continents, named Zazmi, Hamya, Rasanj, Dwarsu and Eftiri. The smaller islands were allocated numerical codes. If one made a study of earth and followed evolution on that planet one would see how nature evolved over time to produce some really amazing life both above and under the sea. So it was on Eureka. Sierra found on Vatnu a predatory plant that fed on small what looked like birds of Paradise. These birds were colorful, beautiful yet dangerous. Gnee summed it up one day with her explanation of a documentary in the Ridmon library. One predator would prey on another with tact cunning and disguise only to have the prey turn into the predator and consume the attacker. The plants themselves looked innocent by any standards with overly bright red large flower buds and grew in twisted thorny vines roughly fifty centimeters in height. A bird would perch on the stems of the plant and that was the last thing it knew. The birds of paradise on the other hand had the advantage of very thick plumage and razor sharp teeth in their beaks. These plants posed no threat to people yet were an object of interest because of their ability to feed on some really strange insects inhabiting the jungle floor.

"Tamu, what is this part of Eureka are we exactly on if I may ask?"

"We have named it Eftiri, which in Thanu means new home."

"I am glad I made the choice to come with you to this place, it's so full of new things, wonderful things we do not have on Ridmon."

"Just be careful sister, small things have bigger bites so I don't want to see you end up as dead toast. Besides, a lot of things here may be highly poisonous and that's what you are to find out." Smiled Tamu.

"You think Zakrose and Wolf will come here for a visit sometime?" She asked.

"I am sure they will. And Gnee, do me a favor, never go out of this complex without your combat suit on, you with me on this one please?"

"Yes brother dear."

The combat suit, a marvel of invention and a predecessor of the ones used on Ridmon at the time of Mike and Moti. This suit was amazing, made from a light weight combination of crystal fiber mixed with black gum and the sap of a plant found on Ridmon. To the layman the ingredients were unimpressive yet when the finished suits were heated to three thousand degrees centigrade their molecular structure changed. Elastic, flexible and impervious to almost anything and kept the wearer alive in adverse climatically conditions. A soldier was so much more efficient. No need for bed roles. No need for clothing, No sun stroke, frost bite, completely water proof and breathable. The suit could take direct hits from any light arms fire, projectiles and grenades and the wearer suffered no ill effects because impact energy was dispersed into the ground.

"Gnee I am serious, wear it. I know it has one disadvantage, getting it open to pee or you know what."

"I know."

"And Gnee, keep the face masks on, no cheating. I don't want to have to tell Zakrose you are blind, or that half your face is missing." Instructed Tamu.

"Hey, Tamu! I am a big girl, so what's with the third degree here?"

"Just do as I ask sweetheart."

"Got yah!"

Gnee was no fool, walking around the jungle out there were some really strange plants, insects and the like. In spite of Zulu hovering about like an overzealous protector it could not stop a sudden attack by some venomous plant or creature within the time frame it needed to react. Because of the suit, Zulu learned to recognize the different dangers and became grease lightning in identification and irradiation if the situation warranted it. Whatever one Wasp learned the rest of the Wasps picked up on it collectively and became that much more proficient. Brilliant would be the word to describe the Wasps.

The systematic exploration of the Planets land masses proved to be a little more complex than anticipated. Much of the inner continents and Islands were rugged jungle terrains full of swamps, quick sands and weird plants and insects. The proverbial food chain syndrome and Ridmonians just happened to island on the equator, called J16, a Wasp reported life forms found. This immediately sparked a reaction and Tamu with his team went to investigate and what they found was amazing. Hovering unseen the Wasps scanned what could be described in two words, Cat people. A whole community of primitive yet intelligent beings almost human in form except the bodies were covered in a very fine layer of hair, facial make up was human like, they walked upright and physically looked like humans with the exception of a tail. The hair color varied from creature to creature but did not in any way distract from the perfect physical forms. It was obvious they were hunter gatherers and sported various weapons such as spears, clubs and rock axes. Equally obvious was their diet. This consisted of plant and meat.

Tamu was puzzled a bit wondering how his Wasps missed this in the first initial scans. It soon became apparent as darkness shrouded the skies why. The cat creatures withdrew into cave like shelters which were made up of a combination of granite and lead ore, perfect habitats to avoid detection. Scanners could not see through lead. Gnee was beside herself with excitement and Tamu had to remind her of planet Ridmon, policy of not interfering with indigenous life forms, only observe. All focus now rested on this new discovery and a round the clock surveillance was posted to record very facet of the creatures existence, their social behavior and structure, eating habits, hunting techniques and how they dealt with crisis both medically and by threat whether from natural causes or by predators. Males of the species were between five and six foot tall and females ranged between four foot nine and five foot seven. Female's sported long flowing auburn colored hair while the males was short cropped. Scant clothing in the form of skins covering midsections and the women's breasts indicated some form of moral conscious. Children ran about naked like most children from poor developing countries.

On one occasion while Tamu was watching from Echo the comings and goings of the community a young woman emerged from a dwelling and gazed up into the shy. She was strikingly beautiful with amazing colored eyes. A coppery bronze color. She stood starring for a long while then shouted a warning and everyone dashed for cover. Echo scanned above him, around, below, but detected nothing.

"No hostile elements detected." Echo declared.

Tamu's curiosity made him replay the scene in his mind and realized without a doubt she was looking straight at the Wasp. It took her awhile to figure out there was a distortion in the sky above her and the more she looked the more pronounced the distortion became until she could identify the Wasp's outline and a light of understanding and caution flashed across her face.

"Geez, that beats all. A simple creature spotted a cloaked Wasp. Not even scanners could do that, this is amazing." Tamu laughed.

This raised a problem for him because now observation would have to be conducted from a greater distance. The woman intrigued him though. She was obviously more intuitive than most of her clan and more intelligent than most. He started to concentrate on her and probed her mind seeing through her eyes thinking she would not realize it. The wealth of information gathered in this way was indispensable and in real time, on the ground, living the life with the cat people. For weeks Tamu lived with them through the woman's eyes until one day when by herself on the banks of a river did she speak, not to anybody near her, not to herself, but Tamu.

"I know you hear me. I have felt you inside of my mind a long time and perhaps you don't know it, but I have been studying you as well Tamu of Ridmon."

It was like a ballistic missile hitting Tamu, she was telepathic. All the while he had observed through her eyes she was doing the same to him.

"I would like very much to meet you if I may?" He asked.

"As long as you do not attempt anything to harm me otherwise you will be sorry believe me." She responded.

Tamu materialized next to her and she slowly stood up to face him. Being this close he was dumb struck, she was lovely and very captivating. They both gazed into each other's eyes and Tamu smiled.

"May I know your name?" He asked.

"I am called Svanis."

"There are a lot of questions both you and I have of each other and I want to just say I am not here to hurt your people, but as we come here from a very far place in another world we did not want to interfere with any living things or people on this world of yours only to observe and protect from others who would come here and destroy without hesitation through greed."

"Tamu, you know my people and the way they live and any change would not be good for them and perhaps you bring with you diseases we know not of or some of your people might want to do us harm. How do I know what you speak is truth and not just to confuse me."

"Svanis, I am going to ask you to trust me and also to meet me here each day and we can sit and discuss everything you wish to know and perhaps you might consider coming with me to where I live here on this planet. No one will know it's you because this black suit I am wearing also comes with a mask and I will make sure when you wear it everyone will think you are one of them."

"I agree to meet with you every day until I am happy and can fully trust you before I go on any place other than around here."

And so for the following weeks Tamu secretly sat with Svanis and told her about his parents and how they came to be on Ridmon. About his mother, his half-brothers and sisters, but mainly how a community had flourished against all odds and even ended up being a super race of sorts yet still maintained a simple life style on home planet. She asked many questions, about how other families lived, about children and what did the people eat and what games they played. Tamu allowed her to look into his mind and see for herself in real time what was going on in planet Ridmon. These journeys seeing another civilization through his eyes was for her an adventure of gigantic proportions. Tamu explained to her about the Reptiles, all the how's and whys of the relationship between humans and those creatures and gradually it dawned on her what Tamu and his people were attempting to do and realized from out of nowhere had come this man and by fate were brought together. She started to regard Tamu with different eyes. And he was careful not to do anything that might be of an affront to her. He marveled at her naïve innocence yet she was extremely intelligent. A few weeks later Svanis asked Tamu if he would take her to visit his base camp.

"I will take you, but you must promise me you will stay by my side no matter what. The reason for that is we have a security system and should you get lost or go where you should not even by accident there will be problems for you. As long as you are with me you will be alright. Now I am going to take you up there. Pointing to the sky, so please don't be alarmed. Hold my hand."

Svanis held onto his hand and Tamu teleported into Echo. Once inside and the full realization of where she was completely overwhelmed her and she clung to Tamu like glue her fearful eyes darting around taking everything in.

When Echo's voice sounded she almost jumped out of her skin.

"Where to Boss?"

Tamu laughed out loud. "Echo, where you finding these words?"

"From the data base of languages and slang uses."

"Echo this is Svanis and the rest you know anyways." Tamu introduced the girl.

"Pleased to meet you Svanis." Greeted Echo.

The girl was really puzzled and asked Tamu who it was and where was that person and how did the person speak her language. This was going to be difficult to explain so he told her Echo was a kind of living thing who looked after him, his people and kept them safe. The explanation seemed to satisfy her, but sat with mouth agape watching the monitor screens flashing pictures of her people down below. Going to a storage compartment Tamu found a combat suit with mask for her and helped the girl put it on. Once on no one would know any better that inside that suit was a cat person except his broth and sister.

"OK Echo let's get back to base."

On the ground at first Svanis didn't notice the camp, so well was it concealed and camouflaged and it was only when Gnee skipped out of one of the lab modules did Svanis realize where she was.

Gnee came over full of smiles asking.

"Hey you, what you doing back so early."

"Well my dear sister, I missed you so much so decided to come and see what you were up to."

"Hah! Fat chance brother, what are you after?"

"Oh, nothing. Just showing this Matabele around who has just arrived from Ridmon, what's here in camp Eureka?"

Gnee eyed the female combat cladded figure with a mask on and raised an eyebrow.

"You being naughty Brother?"

"No, definitely not so get that out of your mind."

Svanis being telepathic herself smiled under her mask knowing exactly what the girl was about to ask and took an instant shine to Gnee. She then asked telepathically if Tamu would allow her to meet Gnee outside of the suit.

Now it was Gnee's turn to question.

"Tamu who is this and how come she's telepathic?"

"Gnee do as I say and go and put your suit on then come back here no questions please." He commanded.

The girl raced off her senses telling her there was something big about to happen.

Svanis spoke out loud." I like her, she is so bubbly and full of energy"

"Hmmm! don't get on her wrong side, she can be a little tiger."

Svanis looked at Tamu puzzled.

"What's a Tiger?"

So he projected into her mind a picture of a tiger from his memory banks.

Gnee came bounding up teeth flashing in a huge smile. Tamu grabbed both girls and teleported to one of the small islands. Standing on a beach the three figures faced each other.

"Right Gnee, what you are about to see remains with the three of us and goes no further are we clear on that?"

"Yes, absolutely." She began to fidget as she usually did when excited with expectation.

Tamu removed the mask to reveal Svanis face. Gnee sucked in her breath, hands coming up to cover her mouth and stood spellbound. It could not be, no ways. The scanners had not reported any life of this kind yet.

"Svanis this is Gnee and Gnee this Svanis." Introduced Tamu.

Both girls just embraced each other. Tamu was taken aback yet was more than pleased at the outcome. He had to take a back seat as the two girls exchanged conversation. One good thing about being telepathic was the ability to communicate and understand any language in the universe. After a while both girls approached Tamu with a request.

"Would it be alright if I see Svanis every day and I can make a study of her people at the same time without them knowing?" She pleaded.

Tamu studied their faces and the look of anticipation on them was too much to ignore.

"On one condition, nobody else is to know about this and you are going to have to come up with a story for Robbie that is totally convincing so I can send him out somewhere else, and you will be back in base before nightfall which Zulu will make sure."

Gnee dived into his arms thanking him profusely. Svanis watching this interaction was pleased as it showed these humans were capable of love and affection as were her own people. So from that day onwards Gnee and Svanis became inseparable. They learned so much from each other that Gnee built up volumes of information about the cat people. In the months that followed Svanis grew more and more attracted to the Ridmonian way of life she felt compelled to at least partake in it somehow. She knew exposure of herself would bring her people into focus and their lives as they knew it would be gone forever and she couldn't do that to them so she asked Gnee if she could speak to Tamu.

He found her the next day at the place where they usually met. Svanis came straight to the point.

"Tamu, I want to visit your planet and meet your people as a representative of my people."

"You mean as a diplomat representing the rights of your people and to get guarantees as to their ongoing existence without interference and influence in any way by anybody and would under treaty be afforded protection by the Ridmon committee to ensure such a treaty is honored."

Svanis squinted at Tamu and smiled." Something like that."

"Right, this is what we are going to do. I will take you to planet Ridmon and plead your case and in return you become my personal secretary. You will live in the next room to me, you will be on my tail the whole time and I will look after you. Anytime you want to visit your people I will send you in Echo or Sierra. We do this until you become so used to our ways and familiar with our procedures we can allow you to integrate without difficulty into the stream of things here with Gnee and friends."

"Agreed."

Echo beamed them up and Svanis changed into combat uniform. Tamu then telepathically advised brother Ridmon of his temporary absence and to take charge of operations. Informing Gnee what he was going to do and advised her to stay put and tell Naya he will be back shortly. Don't tell where I am just off base somewhere on the planet. Opening a portal Echo jumped through into Ridmon air space and beamed his two occupants into the Great Hall. Making their way into the conference room Tamu requested Zakrose and Wolf's presence there. They arrived with smiles and on seeing the dark clad figure of a woman before them and Tamu's arm around her shoulders immediately knew something was up.

"Hello, you two. I have brought with me a diplomatic representative from Eureka named Svanis. She is different from us, but also a telepath so I will caution you on that score."

With that he removed Svanis head gear. Wolf's eyes widened, this was totally unexpected. She was a lovely creature. Zakrose just smiled.

"Pleased to meet you Svanis." Welcomed Zakrose seeing her Brother Wolf's eyes just about to pop out of their sockets. "And welcome to Planet Ridmon. Please be seated and would you like something to drink?"

"No thank you." Sitting on one of the chairs feeling way out of place.

"Now tell us what we can do for you." Zakrose asked.

Svanis looked at Tamu who nodded and she began her request.

"My people are the cat people of the planet you call Eureka. We are a small community numbering around ten thousand persons. We know from legend there are more, but scattered on other islands or places we don't know where. I am the daughter of our leader and it was by chance I met with Tamu here who has been a very good friend to me. He also explained what your people were doing on our planet and why they did not want to interfere with any life there to enable them to proceed through the processes of evolution by themselves. It was not Tamu's fault he walked into me. If I had not been a telepath I would never have detected him seeing my world through my eyes. Anyway, I am here to request that Ridmon ensure the integrity and ongoing policy of non-interference of my people and afford us protection through treaty I will gladly sign. I have no knowledge of the whereabouts of other tribes of my peoples so this also includes them."

Wolf listened to her request and the news that there were other groups possibly on Eureka changed things in favor of the cat people. This was the first time a living creature was detected on the planet and here she was. Turning to Zakrose, he saw the look in her eye and spoke to Tamu.

"Well my brother you have just inherited a nation of Cat people and yes, we grant diplomatic ties and will remain true to our policy regarding protection. Tamu will be our official representative to whom you can refer. Therefore, there is nothing else to add except, we are pleased to make your acquaintance and look forward to a long and interesting relationship. Now if you will excuse me I have matters to attend to. Tamu see me before you go."

Wolf and Zakrose left the room leaving Svanis smiling and looking pleased.

"Thank you Tamu, I feel so much better now knowing my people will be safe and left alone."

"You realize of course we have to find the others if any, and bring them in to your community and in that way they will be contained on one continent and easier to protect."

"Yes I agree with you, but they will spread out again as before and I have to advise you off this potential outcome." She advised.

"By that time we will probably be gone to some other destination in your universe and do what we have done on Eureka." He stated adding,

"Come I will take you on a tour of the city, then of the forest and then back to Eureka."

Tamu gave her the full tour ending up on the forest floor at the cemetery where he placed fresh flowers on his father and mothers graves. Svanis was touched deep in her heart and before she could say anything Tamu grabbed her, swung her onto his back told her to hang on no matter what and hit the trees like an ape climbing up limb to limb with powerful arms then once into the canopy swung like a trapeze artist moving fast and furious to his mother's home where he jumped down onto the deck and released Svanis to the floor. She stood there visibly shaking at the knees not believing what had just happened.

"How! How can you do that? What are you?" She stammered.

Tamu laughed. "The same as all those people in the city only I am different because of my Father who insisted I climb trees, and as a result you see for yourself how good I am at it with years of practice."

Svanis settled down and stopped shaking saying.

"There is more to you than meets the eye isn't there Tamu. I felt it in your mind and body."

"I suppose you are right. I am a soldier, a fighting man who has developed a skill left to me by my Father that puts me over and above other men when it comes to battle. It is fearless, merciless, and fast and kills quickly. Now I am going to bring my best friend and partner here and he will be coming back to Eureka with us. I want you to be prepared for what you are about to see, it's not going to be easy. Stepping behind her he took her in his arms and teleported KI and Nah in. He felt her body stiffen like a rod on seeing Ki.

"Hiding behind a woman I see, what's wrong can't face me on your own?" Mocked Ki.

"Aw, shut up you mongrel and behave. Yes it's good to see you to. This is Svanis, the Cat people's representative of Eureka."

"Looks like you and she are more than representative's naughty boy." Growled Ki.

Tamu realized he was still holding Svanis in his arms and let go.

"One word of this to Naya and I'll brain you." Declared Tamu.

"You and whose army." Boasted KI knowing full well if Tamu put his mind to it Ki would be scrambled egg on the sidewalk.

"What the hell." Tamu embraced his friend.

Svanis couldn't believe her eyes. Tamu had explained to her about the Reptiles, but to meet one face to face was another matter. She breathed a sigh of relief, this was going to be interesting and one thing for sure an adventure of a life time with those two. Back on Eureka, Echo deposited Svanis on her home turf a happy and definitely a changed woman. She told her Father she was going to look for their other people as it was time for all cat people to be together. A lot of debating and argument until Svanis won the say and departed to her spot near the river and telepathically called Echo who beamed her up and delivered her to the base dressed in her uniform complete with head mask. Ezos, Samre with Utan and Visni arrived to greet Ki and Nah. It was Ezos who noticing a black clad figure standing next to Tamu and Naya asked.

"What's with the blimp?" Indicating to Svanis.

"The blimp as you put it is the official representative of the Cat peoples of Eureka. Gentlemen and ladies please meet Svanis." With that he took her hood off.

KI hissed and slapped his side. The rest of the team just blinked in surprise.

"Wow." Exclaimed Naya." She's lovely."

Tamu breathed a sigh of relief and stated.

"Guys and dolls this chicken is out of bounds to you all except Gnee and me. So where I go she comes with, she sleeps next door to me and if I catch any body, well you know what I mean. Understood?"

"Yeah, yeah, we get the message."

"Jokes aside guys, this girl is joining us on ops as liaison for her people."

Tamu decided to secure her position within the group by asking her telepathically to listen to their thoughts. She did as asked and told Tamu, Samre was thinking why now they have to be babysitters.

"Ask him." Tamu said.

"Samre why do you think I need babysitting?" she asked aloud.

You could have hit him with a sledge hammer.

"No, you are not one of those thought readers as well are you?"

Svanis merely nodded and Samre groaned.

Ezos chuckled, "Oh boy what next."

With the familiarities over Tamu escorted Svanis inside to her room, sat her down, took her hand and asked

"Are you sure you want to do this?"

"Yes, more than anything please do not send me away."

Tamu took her in his arms and whispered.

"I will look after you sweet Svanis."

She leaned her head against his chest and replied.

"I trust you Tamu. I trust my people's lives in your hands."

The next moment Gnee burst into the room and hugged Svanis which gave him leave to go. Naya was waiting for him and the stance was a classic one of defiance.

"So lover boy, I see you brought back a little toy to play with. Don't like me anymore?"

Tamu grabbed her and threw her bodily into the air and held her there telepathically.

"Well, well, the little vixen is jealous it seems of a Cat woman and a sexy one at that. Now what should I do with you, spank your bottom or make love to you."

Tamu forgot the team were still assembled in the yard and were now splitting their sides with laughter. Ki was hammering the ground with his fist and hissing so hard tears were cascading down his cheeks.

"Tamu." Screamed Naya. "Put me down."

"Not until you say you love me."

"That's blackmail and if I don't?"

"Let's just say I will dunk you in the river."

"You wouldn't dare." She shouted.

Instead of dunking her into the river he brought some of the river to her and dowsed her good and solid then teleported her into his room. Tamu with as much dignity as possible about turned and headed for his room and a very irate Naya leaving his crew still in stitches of laughter. Svanis over the course of the next few months drew closer and closer to Tamu and his team and one day asked Gnee if Tamu would teach her to defend herself. Gnee studied Svanis face and replied.

"Sweet Svanis, Tamu and his team are the most dangerous people on Planet Ridmon and I don't think your beautiful nature would stand to see what those men are capable of. I am frightened of them myself and I have seen what they can do and it's not for gentle people."

"What about their girls, are they also like that?"

"I am afraid so. "She replied.

"It's hard to believe Tamu being like that, he is so gentle and understanding." Declared Svanis.

"That he is when he is not fighting. Come, we have to fix something for you to eat."

Tamu intensified his search for possible other cat people in and around J16 Island and eventually found three communities on another nearby group of islands. Now the question remained what to do about it. So Wolf and Zakrose were called into Base Eureka for the first time. Zakrose was more than impressed with the setup and once she had seen the Cat people in their natural habitat was hooked. She moved into the room with Gnee and Svanis. Wolf preferred to be on his own and spent his time in the cave deciphering data about the cat people. It was agreed then that the only way to move all three communities at once was with a Drone and the Wasps. Whole communities had to be put to sleep, their entire villages, places of abode and personal effects moved with them and re-established on J16. Then Svanis would have to do her thing and ease the surprise of re-location. Tamu, Wolfe and Zakrose reached consensus and brought in the Matabele armed with console pictures of exact locations of every piece of basket, hut, and fire place, Urns and anything else significant to the location. At the dead of night the Ridmonians struck spraying a harmless sleeping gas into the communities. An hour later destiny changed the community's future and deposited them on J16 within close distance of each other but not enough to create friction and deposited complete replications of their habitats right down to pebbles. Svanis beamed down just before dawn and entered her room in a cave she shared with a couple of orphaned kids. Dawn broke and light streaked across the morning sky and slowly the sun rose over the horizon to pandemonium. Three communities woke to find themselves in familiar surroundings but in different locations and freaked. Svanis made her appearance and for the next few days Ridmon kept their distance, but recorded everything taking place. Svanis was beside herself and the reunions with her people were a spectacle to behold, charged with emotion. After a week Svanis called Tamu. He teleported her into Echo and she threw herself into his arms hugging him tightly.

"Thank you, thank you, this means so much to me."

Tamu lifted her chin up with one hand and kissed her on the mouth.

"Be seeing you Svanis, remember we are just a call away, and beamed her down to her people.

What he didn't know was that kiss impacted on Svanis in a way he could not have imagined.

Zakrose sat down next to Wolf and took his hand in hers.

"I am sorry Wolf, but I have been denying myself all these years. I have to follow Tamu as I feel our Father wanted. I know Tamu is a rebel, but he has proved to me here on Eureka to be an inspiring leader and I want to share with him his and Ridmon's adventures."

Wolf contemplated her decision then answered.

"If things get too hot of which I am sure will happen sooner or later with Tamu and you want out just tell me and you come back to Ridmon."

"Remember once upon a time when we were still recruits and Dad gave us a chance to pass our final test and we went into a battleship and we killed in that furious battle and came out in one piece to earn our badges?"

"Yes I remember only too well. It's not for me Zakrose all this violence and bloodshed."

"I know, and I don't blame you dear brother, you just make sure planet Ridmon and us stay alive, promise me that we will have a home to come back too."

"Done deal Sis. Take care and I love you." He activated a portal and was gone.

Zakrose got up and called Gnee to her. When Gnee arrived looking a little surprised asked her.

"Aren't you supposed to be on Planet Ridmon?"

"Perhaps, but I would rather be here with you, Ridmon and Tamu."

Gnee whooped with glee and hugged her sister then taking her by the hand rushed to Tamu who was busy giving last minute orders to some troopers.

"Tamu, Tamu." She called excitedly. He turned to see Gnee and Zakrose running up.

"Guess what?" She declared.

"You discovered another creepy crawly?" He questioned.

"No dumbo, its Zakrose, she is going to stay with us."

Tamu said nothing just went up to Zakrose, took her in his arms and kissed her cheek, winked at her and turned to attend to other business.

"It's settled then, you move in with me and that's, that." Declared Gnee.

The following weeks were physical pain and suffering for Zakrose at the hands of her brother who insisted she get into shape again. He pushed her hard, determined to bring her back to her former self. Zakrose hung in there biting her bottom lip and slowly results began to show and she began to feel good again about herself. Tamu invited her to attend one of his training sessions with Ezos, Samre and Ki together with their girls. Zakrose had always watched her father in his training sessions and observed a lot, but was unable to reproduce due to the exercises being way out of her league.

Watching Tamu and his team shocked her into reality. They were beyond definition, beyond human even. Pure outright killing machines and it sent a shiver up her spine. But she knew in order to be with them she had to be like them and deep down something stirred within her, the spirit of her Father. Naya strutted alone humming to herself in between the shower room and Tamu's quarters when Gnee jumped out at her.

"Naya, can you help me?"

"What's up?"

"Please don't tell Tamu, but I have met a boy. I mean man, and I really like him. What should I do?"

"Geez dear girl, which century do you live in? If you like him, tell him. Is he nice, caring, understanding, affectionate and easy to manipulate?"

"Naya cut that out, my man is just fine and he is a man not a wimp thank you."

"Hold your horse's woman. Do you love him?"

"I don't know." She replied squirming uncomfortably.

"Well when you do find out, speak to me. Right now I am tired, hungry and mad. My husband is not home yet."

"But Naya you and Tamu are not married." Gnee exclaimed.

"I rest my case." With that Naya entered into Tamu's rooms leaving Gnee standing outside with a very puzzled look on her face.

Weeks passed into months and months into two years. In that time Eureka was completely charted and documented. It was time to move on. Tamu visited the Cat people's settlement for the last time and sat in Echo watching the comings and goings of the people. In his mind a voice spoke, meet me at the usual place. So Tamu teleported down and met Svanis. The two years had not changed her a bit and she still looked as lovely as ever.

"Hello Tamu. I see you have gained a little muscle since we last we met."

"Tools of the trade I suppose. We are leaving Eureka and relocating somewhere else. I just wanted to see you again to say goodbye and thank you, it has been a privilege to know you. Take care of yourself Svanis." He teleported out and Svanis wept deep throbbing tears.

Tamu returned to the base with a heavy heart. He had become very fond of Svanis. Walking to collect his gear together, Gnee met him with a young man from the Regiment. The young man saluted and stood stiffly to attention while Gnee confronted her brother.

"Tamu, this is Boram. We love each other and want to get married and stay here on Eureka as Ridmon's diplomatic representatives."

Tamu shook his head. The children of planet Ridmon are leaving their home one by one thinking to himself. He looked at Gnee then to the man and back to Gnee then took her in his arms saying.

"Ok sweet pee, but you get married before I leave, and this guy better be with the program."

Gnee jumped in his arms. "You're the greatest," then turned around and rushed to her man and linked arms.

Tamu felt tired suddenly and just wanted to be alone with silence so he teleported into Echo. Curling up on the floor of Echo's interior with hands behind his head lay in thought. Echo knew Tamu pretty well and seeing his kind of behavior ventured to say something.

"Boss, excuse me for saying, but why are you perturbed?"

Tamu responded. "You were with my Father back then in the days when you were different. Did he treat you right?"

A silence followed before Echo answered.

"Mike was our friend and he treated us as equals and we were loyal to him. When he sacrificed his life so that others may live we were devastated and knew then our duty was to honor his name and always show allegiance to his off spring and Planet Ridmon."

Tamu digested the words then said.

"We have come a long way since then and you guys have won your status as part of the family. We appreciate and respect all you do for us and salute you."

"Thanks Boss. Naya is looking for you."

With that he beamed Tamu down.

A few days later Gnee married Boram in a small ceremony attended by a few friends. An hour later Tamu and his troops, support groups lifted off from Eureka and jumped into another part of space leaving behind a handful of people from Planet Ridmon on Eureka who may never be seen again.

Ridmon, Qing Fe, Gnee and Boram with twenty men and women support crew, six Matabele and one doctor and Zulu the Wasp, constituted the Ridmonian delegation. Gnee was happy. She had her man and in the process met a very unusual friend named Svanis.

CARTONE

TEN

The Ridmonian Fleet hovered above an inhabitable planet called Cartone. This planet contrasted with Eureka in every way. It consisted of large land masses ranging from jungles to deserts spread over its surface in much the same way as Earths. The plan here was to establish a permanent base with a combined force of Ridmonians and Thanuians. In essence, Cartone was to become Thanu's sister planet in G48 major. Planet Ridmon was not too elated by the news as it deviated from the principle protocol slightly. Never the less, agreed to go along with the concept provided Thanu had no great expectations from Planet Ridmon in terms of military resources. As it was Planet Ridmon did not like reducing her own defenses and man power to the detriment of her people. Off world Ridmonians would be a limited source to Thanu as standalone independents. This was stretching

Tamu's forces a little and posed a problem in the long run for logistic re-supply of pockets of Ridmonians scattered about and tactically unwise. Planet Ridmon therefore insisted upon Thanu, with a population, one hundred times that of Ridmon to man any sub-bases with their own crews and equipment. It was agreed therefore that Eureka remained under Planet Ridmon supervision and Cartone would be a limited base for the Ridmonians. Gradually more and more Thanu Warships with full contingents of men and machinery began arriving. A city took shape, the city of Kotung.

Tamu would have none of it and re-located his forces a good distance away in a very craggy landscape of high rocky outcrops and deep gorges. The Ridmonians burrowed into the side of one of those gorges some measured over a kilometer in depth and as little as seventy meters across between faces. There was only one way in or out of this base and that was by Wasp. For the records the base was named Antrum, the Latin word for cave. Five hundred meters down one sheer walled side of a deep gorge they found in the area, a fifty meter long by twenty meter wide and fifty meter deep square hole was carved out of the rock face by a Wasp using its White death beams. This served as a staging area and could be sealed off from the outside by a force field. Leading off from there at one opposite end was the accommodations, mess hall, and ablution's, water purification and recycling. At the opposite end were storage, clinic and Command center. If one was to suspend oneself directly in front of the staging area one would see an array of windows either end of the of its entrance. From the top of the gorge or the bottom, the base was concealed. All personnel were either beamed out or into base by invisible Wasps. Tamu, satisfied by this arrangement could now concentrate his forces into doing their job. It also kept Thanu's prying eyes off his back. Tamu and his team were now three years in G48 major and time to give his forces a reward. Tamu sent a message to Zulu to pick up a consignment of Ridmon beer and Whiskey and deliver it to the Eureka base. He then recalled all his forces and assembled them in Antrum. Two thousand people stood waiting in the staging area wondering what was going on. Tamu, Ezos and Samre emerged from out of the Command Office and faced the assembled body of men and women.

"Fellow Ridmonians today marks the third year we have been in G48 Major and not once have we had a fall down which is customary practice of the Matabele Regiment. So we are going to break tradition to include our non-military comrades in our celebration. Now, everyone is to dress in combat fatigues, complete with weapons and helmets and you civilians in your special body stockings. You all know in these cloths you become invisible on any scan or radar. We will be paying a visit to Eureka for a few days as we can't ignore our friends there. Is everybody in agreement?"

The staging area erupted in a chant of Matabele voices. "Bayete Enkosi, Bayete Matabele" and dismissed to carry out orders. An hour later with the base on lock down, the entire Ridmonian force jumped through a portal and on to Eureka. Gnee was beside herself with excitement to have Tamu and Zakrose together with her. She quickly pulled Zakrose aside and the two disappeared into Gnee's laboratory where she kicked Robbie out saying he did not belong where it was woman's business. Boram presented himself to Ezos his commander and submitted his reports. With two thousand bodies milling around was problematic so Samre quickly organized some sort of order and portable tables and chairs were brought out of storage and placed in rows of thirty along the front of the base. The Quarter Master attended bar with Robbie and another civilian helper. A whole cow's carcass, compliments of one of the Wasps was on a spit over a fire roasting, salads and an assortment of food dishes on tables. When everything was in place, Tamu shouted on top of his voice.

"Matabele."

To which the response came in a roar,

"Matabele Ridmon."

Then Tamu shouted.

"Troops and civilians. Stand down."

All mayhem erupted. For two days the party raged, men and women slept where they fell or sat in drunken bliss. While all this was going on Svanis contacted Tamu telepathically and so he met with her in their usual place. Three more years of absence had not changed her in the least. She greeted him with a hug and smile.

"How are your people keeping?" He asked.

"We are well, although relocating the other groups did cause some problems and a struggle for chief of the combined clan did arise, but was resolved by appointing a representative from the two groups and my Father as a single committee. After all that, life returned to normal."

"And you, how are you?"

She took her time to answer then looked Tamu in the eye and said.

"I miss you people a lot, Gnee, that ugly Lizard man and you. It is hard for me now to live with my people knowing what I know and not being able to share it with them. My telepathic powers I believe were an accident and very glad for it. So I am having to make a choice and want to ask you if you would accept me into your group, if possible?"

Tamu considered her request weighing up pros and cons then made up his mind. Having another telepath in his group was an added advantage strengthening their overall efficiency. The other advantage was Svanis as a cat person which meant she was extremely agile and flexible with a light, but hard bone structure making her an ideal candidate for his brand of martial arts. If she proved herself he would use her talents on special assignments.

"Alright Svanis, you are in. Consider yourself as a member of my personal group, but you are going to have to prove yourself." He confirmed.

Svanis was beside herself and kissed Tamu on the cheek saying.

"Wait here I'll be back." She raced off to her settlement. It did not take long before she returned running and pleading with Tamu.

"Now Tamu, now."

He realized she was torn between her people and her wish to leave them so before she weakened her resolve he wasted no time and teleported into a storage room with her then retrieved a uniform from one of the shelves and waited until she was dressed then telepathically asked Zakrose to come by. Zakrose arrived with Gnee in tow and what a happy smile split her face on seeing Svanis.

"Svanis is here officially as one of our group. She is also here because she not only wanted it, but has some unusual talents one of which, she is telepathic. So I want you three to go up to the caves and wait for me, so go now please."

Zakrose teleported the girls in to the caves. Tamu checked on Ki, Ezos, his brother Ridmon and Samre and found then in a sober state which surprised him. Rounding them up they were teleported in to the cave to where Zakrose and the girls waited.

"Svanis, I am sorry to have to do this, but I must ask you to take the suit off. In this group there are no secrets between us."

She did his bidding and stood with scant underclothing on bear feet, arms to her sides her tail flicking from side to side. Ki was the first to react and hissed.

"Thank you, you are beautiful too Ki." Replied Svanis. Proving her telepathic abilities and seeing the reaction on Ki's face.

"OK Guys now you're seen, now you respect she is one of us in this group. The rest of you are extremely proficient now in martial arts so know what to do in training. Svanis here has the physical ability, but not the knowhow which is what I will be teaching her from now on until she reaches a level which I consider as an attribute to the rest of you. In other words, does not pull you down."

All nodded their heads in agreement and crowded around Svanis welcoming her to the group.

"Are you going to be doing what I think you are?" Zakrose asked Tamu.

"Yes and Zakrose you and Ridmon are in charge of operations during my absence and Ezos with Samre the Regiment. I will speak to Naya and explain and perhaps you can put a word in afterwards."

"Just don't break Svanis please, it's going to be tough enough on her as it is." She asked.

Tamu nodded and smiled then asked,

"Please issue Svanis with full battle equipment including pack."

Tamu found Naya passed out on a table and carried her to their room placing her on the bed and scribbled a note for her, collected his gear and teleported out to the cave.

"Gnee, I have put Naya to bed, she was passed out so be a sweetheart and check on her, thanks."

She nodded thinking all hell would break loose when Naya found out Tamu was off somewhere with Svanis. The Cat girl stood laden with equipment looking very out of place. Tamu went to Ki and gave him last minute instructions and told him he would bring him to his training place soon. Then holding Svanis activated a portal and stepped on to Karagan's isolated wilderness continent full of wild predator life. Where it was a place for the survival of the fittest, quickest and meanest. A huge number of animals brought in from Planet Earth when heavenly powers decreed it, had multiplied in number since then and so also animals of prey. Svanis was about to taste survival under these conditions and a training program that would change her into a lithe feline martial artist.

Two days later Naya woke with a slitting head ache and feeling terrible moved very carefully to the bathroom. Took a cold shower and slowly headed for the clinic to find something to ease the pain. Her foggy brain didn't register her whereabouts. Zakrose appeared in front of her shaking her head.

"Come, let me help you." Guiding her into the clinic where one of the doctors took a look at her and immediately shouted orders.

Naya was hospitalized, but died an hour later from a massive infection of the brain by something she contracted on Eureka. Doctors were at a loss as to what was the reason and performed an autopsy on her to attempt to ascertain the cause. They discovered that on Eureka was a vicious and fatal string of a type of Meningitis which Naya had contracted somehow. The rush was on to find a vaccine to deal with it and analytical computers went into over drive. Zakrose telepathically contacted Tamu who came in to Eureka with Svanis to take Naya's body back to Planet Ridmon for burial in the cemetery. The funeral was a solemn affair with Naya's family. After the funeral Tamu teleported out to Eureka, and disappeared back to Karagan. In all the time he never showed any emotion, but on Karagan he wept in Svanis arms.

Back on Eureka, Zakrose shut down the camp and moved everyone to Cartone. Tamu's training schedule progressed with surprising results. Svanis was a natural it seemed and picked up very quickly. After a year of living constantly training day and sometimes at night with Tamu pushing her to her limits she blossomed into a highly skilled and competent combatant. Now it was time to bring in Ki and Nah. There was no camp, no shelter, no sign people existed there, only thick bush, open patches of grass and more bush. Ki stepped out of the portal with Nah and looked around. The bush was alive with the sound of buzzing insects. Ki cautioned Nah with a hand and moved forward sweeping his eyes from side to side wary and alert. He had perhaps moved twenty meters when something hit him hard from the right side knocking him sideways with considerable force. Ki reacted spun and promptly received another strike on his buttocks. He stopped dead, placed his hands on his hips and hissed out loud. Sure enough Svanis sprang out of the long grass her lithe body coiling to land near Ki and Nah. From the bushes Tamu strolled out smiling.

"How do you like that little Mosquito?" He asked.

"Humph, one good swipe and goodbye Mosquito." Ki responded.

"OK big boy, try to swipe her." Challenged Tamu.

One powerful side swipe projected out with blinding speed right at Svanis whose body, as light as a feather was propelled away by the force of the strike. Ki tried again and again to no avail frustrating him even more until Tamu stepped up and stopped him.

"Svanis by chance, has been gifted with the lightness of air and with all the training combined with Chi, enables her to avoid being hit as you saw without any effort on her part. You actually moved her with the force of your strike which generates kinetic energy in front of your hand or fist even foot and this is the force that pushers her away without injury. Still think you can swat the Mosquito now?"

Ki just grumbled and looked at Svanis with new respect. For the next few days KI and Nah were in their element. Suddenly in the bush manifested another predator who hunted and killed any size animal and other predators with ease except when it came to the chase then Ki and Nah were out run every time. For those few days Tamu and Svanis relaxed, The Reptiles had a ball and everyone ate well on game meat. It was time to return to the fold so stepping out of a portal into the staging area at Antrum he reported to Zakrose. She sat at a desk entering information into a console.

"Hello Zakrose."

She looked up and blinked with shock, just for a second she thought it was her Father. Geez! She cursed under breath.

"Tamu do you always make a habit of sneaking up on someone, you almost gave me heart failure. You look more like Dad every day."

"I'll take that as a compliment. How are things here in your capable hands?"

"Some problems with Thanu, they want us to train some of their troops which I refused saying our training methods were classified therefore no go and they got a little rattled until Wolf put it to them in diplomatic ways. We have not heard any more on the topic, but keep vigilance in case."

"Svanis is ready and full of surprises believe me. I am happy. She will be a good asset to our team."

"How did she deal with the pressure?"

"You know, she took everything in her stride and not once complained feigned injury or anything else. I am sure you will agree with me when I say the choice to bring her in was a good one." He answered.

"And those two lizards had their kind of fun I suppose?"

"You bet, hunting African wild life on Karagan. Anyway, you need to brief me as to what has been happening in my absence."

For the next hour Zakrose filled in the blanks for Tamu who at the end had a look of disdain on his face. Excusing himself he went to his room and packed Naya's personal belongings and called in Echo to destroy them which he did. For a while he stood starring at the opposite side of the gorge and realized in all the time he had known Naya he could have asked her to be his wife, now it was too late and he for sure would not do the same again. Tamu walked into Svanis room unannounced and asked her.

"Will you live together with me, as lovers? As my wife?"

She looked at Tamu for long seconds then sprang into his arms.

"Yes, yes." kissing him hard on the lips. Her heart threatened to burst out of her chest because her prayers were finally answered. She fell in love with Tamu just after their first meeting and when he kissed her farewell before leaving for Cartone that was the decider she had to be with him whatever it took. The year on Karagan was the most difficult emotionally being so close to him like that, yet her perseverance paid off. She was sad about Naya, but then that's life, things happen. Tamu opened a portal into the Great Hall with his whole team, for a bit of R & R, inviting Officers of the Regiment for drinks and relaxation. After a while when the booze sank in someone shouted, Fall down fight, and the Matabele went wild.

Zakrose turned to Wolf and laughed then said.

"Tamu is in for it now."

"As supreme commander of the Matabele Regiment he is obliged to kick off the first game of the evening." Shouted one of the officers.

The hall echoed with shouts and laughter. Tamu striped to the waist, then stood in the middle of the floor waiting to see who had the balls to take him on. Two teams of six each divided and took up positions on their lines twenty meters apart. Zakrose herself placed two beers one on each end of the lines and slapped Ki on the thigh saying, "Get him big boy."

On the opposing team were Ezos and Samre with their team. A referee stepped into the center and recited the rules simply put. "Last man standing."

The Great Hall shook from the shout, Bayete Enkosi, Bayete Matabele. A whistle blew signaling the start and Planet Ridmon was given a taste of Matabele martial arts perfection. Tamu was devastating. It was the first time Wolf or Zakrose had seen their brother in action. Fifteen seconds later and twenty Matabele lay unconscious on the ground except KI who was kneeling stunned and breathing hard. Tamu walked up to him and slapped his shoulder.

"KI, my friend KI." Then hit KI knocking him unconscious. He calmly walked to each corner and opened the beer and drank its contents. The Hall shook with chanting,

"Enkosi Tamu, Enkosi."

Tamu had proved a very painful point to his Regiment even taking out Ezos and Samre was respect brother, wholly respect. Zakrose turned to Wolf saying.

"No ways, it's impossible. How did Tamu reach such development?"

"My dear sister, don't forget Tamu is our Fathers son and from appearances he now looks like our Father in all ways and dear girl, don't you think our Father didn't foresee this eventuality."

"What are you saying." Questioned Zakrose.

"Exactly this, we are the brains and Tamu with our brother Ridmon are the muscle. However, Tamu has also brains so there is no way to deceive him even if we tried and besides we are family and that man is first and foremost our greatest alley. Don't screw it up. But, dear sister, be careful. Tamu has an unforgiving nature and if I or you betray him he will be calling and either one of us will suffer the consequences. Consider the Wasps and where their allegiance lies, only with Tamu."

"Hey, I live with Tamu on Cartone, so what are you saying, I must now deceive him because you are afraid he will take the Wasps and Drones?" Questioned Zakrose.

"Something of that nature." Answered Wolf.

"Frag you Wolf. You have stepped over the line this time." So saying, she grabbed Gnee and Svanis and teleported into Echo.

Tamu felt the vibrations emanating out his brother and it saddened him yet he understood in a way being the half-brother had its bad side. Never the mind his fragen opinions it did not matter and he confronted Wolf head on.

"Right you, time to cut the bull and frag you and your opinions. Now I tell you what's going to happen. Firstly I am taking my Wasps, secondly I am taking the Matabele and thirdly, believe it or not, the Drones. What does that leave you? I will tell you, hanging on your privates and praying. Your choice."

Wolf looked at Tamu and realized Tamu had him dead to rights. Wolf the diplomat wanted to negotiate and Tamu turned to him and suggested he negotiate with Thanu and left the hall then teleporting every Matabele on planet Ridmon, every Drone and all the Wasps jumped through portals to Cartone. Later Svanis crept up to Tamu in bed and cuddled into him.

"Tamu, I know you are angry and you are right to be mad at Wolf, but consider this, without him you will be lost, I feel it. He is family, don't desert him please."

"No desertion my love only lesson time."

A few days later Protector Friend appeared in front of Tamu. His white shimmering form hovered in his room and Svanis clung to Tamu in sheer terror.

"Tamu, I will not allow you to strip Ridmon of its defenses, nor will I allow you to leave Ridmon exposed to retaliator attackers. So I am telling you to return the Drones, and all the Wasps.

Tamu stood up next to his bed and spoke to Protector Friend.

"I am tired of him treating me like a second class citizen and above all his attitude towards my girl. Sure she is different and perhaps scorned socially, doesn't mean he can ostracize her or me."

"Leave Planet Ridmon to herself, with her protection of Drones, the Matabele, and all the Wasps. I guarantee Echo, Sierra and Zulu will be by your side with the other ninety seven Wasps only a little more modified, you do this and I will personally speak to Wolf and free you from your commitment to Planet Ridmon."

"I agree."

The Drones, the Regiment and the Wasps returned to planet Ridmon. Tamu was irritated and decided to go back to Eureka for a while and relocated to the disbanded base and settled in. He was really angry and made no bones about it in spite of Protector Friend. Now began the difficult task of the cat people. He did not want for them to regard him as a god who disappears into the skies. So with the help of Svanis, Tamu dressed in a loin cloth and walked into the Cat village with Svanis. Well one can imagine seeing Svanis whom they knew with a non-cat person of intimidating physical physique. The community gathered around, curiosity drawing them in.

"You all know me, I am the daughter of Zud and this is my mate from a far place".

Tamu was an item they had never seen before and noticing he had no tail added to the mystery. Svanis father appeared and looked at Tamu, walked around him, felt his muscles, slapped his butt and moved to stand in front of Svanis saying.

"He will make strong sons and I want grandchildren before I die."

"Yes Father." She answered, turned to Tamu and hugged him whispering.

"Hold me tight and kiss me on the lips." She instructed.

He did as instructed and a whoop echoed in the community and that was that, Tamu was in, a member of the community. That evening was a celebration and Svanis with Tamu were the guests. Singing and dancing until fever pitch with drug inducing herbs, Svanis people collapsed in blissful slumber. Tamu and Svanis returned to base camp and their bedroom. Tamu gently took Svanis into his arms and kissed her. Her body arched in surrender to his hand on her breast manipulating her nipple until it stood on end then moving his hand down to her genitals stimulating her clitoris. She slowly began to convulse as he fingered and prodded and eventually she forced his head down to her genitals and told him to suck her. She thrust upwards in sheer erotic pleasure. Her hips were thumping, breathe short and ready when Tamu mounted her. She squealed in absolute passion and clutched at his buttocks forcing him deeper into her and heaved upwards pushing hungrily thrust for thrust. Tamu took her hard and long then climaxed together in an overpowering unison of body and soul. They both lay suspended sweat streaming off them and sighed. Ten minutes later Tamu made passionate love to her again. This time he took time to explore her body and discovered some interesting beautiful things.

On Cartone with Tamu out of the picture and not knowing where he was and had been gone for a considerable time, the Matabele contingent were less than enthusiastic, Ki and Nah requested transfer back to Reptilia which was authorized. Ezos and Samre returned to Planet Ridmon and promptly resigned from the Matabele sensing Tamu was devising a plan or something then relocated into the dark forest with their wives. Gnee was pulled back to Planet Ridmon with Robbie. The whole situation was falling apart and Zakrose was powerless to contain it. Thanu were making waves so Wolf made a major decision withdrawing support on Cartone and G48 Major as well as terminated all agreements with Thanu who retaliated by black listing the planet. With Tamu gone and his two best Captains resigned, Bordred faced a very unenthusiastic Regiment who became sullen and unresponsive. Many top ranking officers resigned and no matter the promises made to them by Bordred, just fell on deaf ears.

Within three years, Thanu's city on Cartone became a breeding ground for crime, prostitution and drugs. All the good intensions of G48 major fell away and in her weakened state the Federation ships moved in and took over bringing in their excavators and miners and began to decimate the landscape in search of valuable minerals. News of these events eventually filtered down to Tamu through the Wasps resulting in his anger finding focus and he mobilized. First port of call was Reptilia where he recruited five thousand Ridmonian trained fighters including Ki and Nah as well as Mis relocating them to Eureka base camp. Next he appeared in the dark forest on planet Ridmon and left again with four of his group, four Wasps and fifteen ex Matabele officers. Back on Eureka Svanis gathered together her twenty recruits from the cat people and briefed them on what to expect in the base camp, then called Zulu who beamed them up and relocated them to base. Tamu took stock. Seven Wasps, five thousand Reptiles, nineteen ex Matabele, twenty Cats.

For the next three months the troops were put through their paces rehearsing precise attack patterns and target illumination in preparation for a takeover of Cartone. Tamu reminded everyone this was no game, this was real and going to be a bloodbath when he released the Reptiles into the city. The Cats with all the ex-Matabele would be deployed jointly on the ground. Four Wasps directed to take out any and all Federation ships and when that was done, join the ground troops as air support. The other three Wasps were to take out mining installations, all of them. The small army stepped into Antrum, long deserted by the Matabele and set up operations. Tamu gave his troops a last minute instruction.

"Try to keep civilian casualties to a minimum and that's an order."

Echo received the go ahead to begin his attack.

The Federation fleet never knew what hit them, fifteen Destroyers and four battleships just disintegrated. Echo swooped down on the city and systematically destroyed installations, shuttles and military targets. It was done with such murderous precision. The City of Kotung's people were taken completely off guard and when Tamu released his army into the city all hell broke loose. With soldiers on the ground and Wasps in the air it did not take long to reduce the city to rubble. Many people fled into the open country and gathered together in groups for safety. One by one, Tamu teleported those groups out through a portal on to Karagan. It was a huge task gathering civilians up and relocating them and took him a few days with the help of the Wasps. Kotung was no more, but a pile of trash burying underneath her dead.

Back on Karagan the Federation was shocked and demanded to know who was responsible for this outrage. Both Thanu and Planet Ridmon emphatically denied any involvement yet did not venture to speculate either. Planet Ridmon knew there could only be one culprit and weren't offering any names, but rather reveled in the news Kotung had been taken out and with it a nest egg of filth. Once again the Federation was set to retaliate and that's when Karagan gave them notice to remove themselves off the planet and take everything with them. When the Federation objected Karagan took the initiative and threatened to use force if necessary. Whose force the Federation mocked to which Karagan cleverly deduced it was Tamu who took out Kotung so used that as a bargaining chip by answering, the same force that destroyed your forces on Cartone. Case closed, the Federation relocated to Vimusi.

Cartone was free for the time being of negative influences and cleanup operations were in the process to restore and landscape the surface to its original condition and nature would then do the rest. The Reptiles were sent home with trophies and high spirits for a good hunt. The Cats returned to their settlement changed men and women from what they experienced. The ex-Matabele officers with Ezos and Samre requested to remain with Tamu who insisted they have a woman with them as a mate if they didn't have one already. Quietly during the night on Ridmon fifteen women, some Matabele, some civilian with kids vanished along with crates of beers and whiskey. The next day on Planet Ridmon dawn broke as usual with people coming and going about their business. A school teacher caught up with Wolf in the Great Hall and told him some kids were missing and when she went to investigate found the parents were also gone as well as their belongings. Wolf assured her all was well and thanked her and sat back and laughed.

"You know who those kids are, don't you? They are the children of some of those Matabele officers who resigned and I will give you one guess where they are."

"Cartone"

"Yes my lovely Nina, Cartone and there is nothing we can do about it." He stated.

"So Tamu takes out Kotung cleaning up an undesirable nest of rouges, flattens the Federation fleet there, then Karagan gets balls and throws the Federation off their planet. Not bad for an exiled man like Tamu to achieve, makes Planet Ridmon look puny with no backbone especially with Thanu defaming Ridmon's character." Declared Nina.

"What are you suggesting, we align ourselves with Karagan and Tamu?" He questioned.

"Precisely, make us look better on the political front although we don't actually climb into bed with Tamu." she remarked adding, "Let Tamu have some more of the wasps, even some Matabele and my instinct tells me he will clean up where ever he is and we take the credit for it here on Planet Ridmon. A win, win situation don't you think?"

Wolf studied his wife's face, smart girl, nodded and said." It shall be done."

Sending a communique to Karagan, Wolf declared allegiance and congratulated the Committee for their action against the Federation and advised them Tamu was available should the need arise. Three days later five thousand Matabele stood in full battle dress before Wolf. Bordred marched up and saluted.

"All men and women named are present and correct and ready to board."

"Thank you that will be all." Wolf growled. He could not stand Bordred, but out of respect for his long service record tolerated him.

"Matabele, you will be joining Tamu on Planet Cartone and it is a permanent position. You will not see planet Ridmon again and I need not tell you it's because you are dissatisfied here and made no bones about mouthing off your opinions. I will not wish you good luck, but will say some of you will be missed."

With that the Matabele marched through a portal into Cartone base followed by twenty Wasps laden with stores and equipment. Tamu was no fool remembering the expression; "Beware of messengers bearing gifts." Wolf was up to something, yet he did not look a gift horse in the mouth either. The Regiment took up residence in the old base which was restructured to offer more room and another large opening became an entertainments hall, sports and training center as well as assembly hall for regimental business. Ezos and Samre his second in command introduced the Matabele to a new training method of scaling up the walls of the gorge using free climb and Ninja style climbing claws on each hand and feet. It was dangerous and initially climbing ropes were attached to climbers until they gained in confidence and learned how to use the claws efficiently. The base, built into both sides of the gorge walls was expanded once again when a group of new recruits came in from Karagan. Karagan had contacted Tamu via Ridmon and asked to speak personally with him on Karagan. Tamu with Svanis entered the huge Chamber where once the Federation had sat and presented themselves to Karagan's Committee.

"Gentlemen, Ladies of Karagan, we greet you from Cartone of the G48 Major Galaxy." Voiced Tamu.

Tamu and Svanis were dressed in their combat uniforms. The Committee members looked the two up and down then responded.

"Greetings to you Tamu and your partner. May we ask from which constellation she comes from?"

Svanis answered for herself, "I am from Planet Eureka and I am classified for your edification as a Jaqmuz and my name is Svanis, the mate of Tamu."

The Committee speaker's eyebrows raised in surprise then continued.

"We are very pleased to make your acquaintance. Now the reason we called you to this meeting is to say we are sorry for your dispute with Planet Ridmon and realize you must be a little short on man power so we suggest giving you five thousand men and women recruits who are waiting outside carefully screened and picked. You are able to review their personal files in the foyer as part of an agreement we would like to enter into between Karagan and Cartone something of mutual interest to both of our planets and a defense strategy. Would you consider such an offer?"

"You are most generous in your offer and we could use a few more men and women in our ranks. You do realize though every soldier of my Regiment has to swear an oath of non-disclosure and loyalty. They are bound to silence of any information pertaining to their training or anything else concerning the regiment." Tamu replied.

"We are well aware of that and respect the condition as a small price to pay for your guarantee of Military support. Is it agreed then?"

"Yes, you have my support in the defense of Karagan. We shall be on standby as of now."

Tamu walked out into the foyer and told Echo to upload the list of recruits and to screen them for acceptable candidates. While Eco was occupied Tamu saw the group standing outside and approached them. On seeing him with Svanis in their black uniforms the group became silent. Tamu projected his voice through Zulu's amplification module.

"I see you all volunteered to be recruits of the Matabele Regiment, however, there is just one criteria and that is age. Anyone aged over twenty four please leave the group and stand to one side on your right." He waited while bodies bumped and pushed into two separate groups.

"Those of you on my left are too old to endure the kind of combat training we have to put you through, but don't disappear there are other functions we will place you into and trained to become skilled in a number of functions within the Regiment. Those others in the group to my right are at this moment being screened and believe me only the best of you will be chosen. Those who don't make the grade will join the group on my right."

Echo contacted Tamu and the tally was surprising. Karagan had to be congratulated for initially screening all volunteers so well. Three thousand men and women qualified for combat training while the balance of two thousand would enter into another category of support personnel. The Regiment would be divided into Commando groups of a thousand recruits a piece and a new group, Support Group, was for the two thousand others. Tamu ordered Echo to instruct two of the Karagan Drones to beam up all the personnel standing in the square then to jump through a portal for Cartone. The next minute five thousand people just vanished into thin air. Some of the committee members watching the whole proceedings were very happy indeed. All the new recruits went through basic training which lasted four months. Irrespective of position all Matabele had to have the ability to take up arms as a unit and fight as a unit so all support members were expected to be combat prepared and fit. Route marches with full kit, distance running with weapons and crystal helmets on, unarmed combat training, weapons training, survival, general regiment discipline and basic tactical maneuvers. After the four months were up all five thousand recruits were appraised. Some of the men and women over the age of twenty four showed promise so Ezos moved them into the commando barracks to give them a chance to prove themselves. The intense training began with seventeen instructors dividing themselves into the three commando groups to instruct one hundred and eighty three recruits each. It was tough, really tough and a very intense program over the course of a year. In their passing out parade Tamu addressed the new commando members.

"Congratulations all of you, no drop outs, meant you learnt to work as a team making sure of each other's success. You now have the right to wear the uniforms of the Matabele Regiment so do so with pride because you have earned it. Some of you have been nominated for specialist training. Your names will appear on the monitors in you barracks. You will now be separated and relocated to the main regiment barracks newly constructed in the adjoining gorge where you will team up with the Regiment of five thousand Matabele as a single brigade of four commando units numbering two thousand troops each and an HQ consisting of Command personnel and a separate barracks for Support group. The specialist group will be located to another destination and will be under my personal instruction. Remember people do not think your training is over, it is not as there will be from time to time extended courses for self-improvement and evaluation for all concerned."

Ezos shouted, "Bayete Enkosi, Bayete Matabele."

The answering call thundered down the gorge.

"Matabele Cartone."

Tamu now had eight thousand fighting troops, twenty three Wasps, a two thousand and fifty support group which included medical staff. One hundred and thirty new members joined his specialist group on Eureka to add to Svanis twenty cats and two Reptiles, Ki and Nah. One day while involved with instruction Svanis telepathically contacted him and advised him that Gnee and her husband Boram had arrived with some important medical vaccines. Teleporting his students back to base where everyone was being inoculated against the virus that killed Naya. Gnee dispatched vaccine capsules to Cartone on a Wasp through a portal with an attached note of instruction. Tamu sat with

Gnee at an outside table while Svanis prepared something for them to eat.

"You happy Sis?" Asked Tamu.

"Yes and no, it's not the same on Planet Ridmon without you there and Wolf has changed, runs the place like a dictator and I don't like it. The Regiment is falling apart piece by piece with resignations and lots of grumbling. Bordred has no control anymore. I spoke to Boram and he is thinking of resigning and moving elsewhere. I know you and the Wolf are at each other's throats, but isn't there a way to patch things up between you?"

Tamu took her hands in his, "Sweet Gnee, why not come back with me to Cartone with Zakrose?"

He watched the glint in her eye and quickly added." I will take responsibility for "Abducting you" as it were."

Gnee burst out laughing.

"You would not like to see the look on Wolf's face. And while you are abducting, how about those poor Matabele who have resigned. My husband would be very appreciative."

It was Tamu's turn to laugh, "Remember the last time I abducted the Matabele, I got my head chewed off by Protector Friend."

"This is different, they resigned so there is no connection to the regiment any longer." Gnee pleaded.

"OK, I will pass on the order when Boram gives me a list of their names."

"Done." So saying Gnee jumped up and ran full tilt looking for Boram. Tamu watched her go and realized she was older than him yet her naïve innocence was so refreshing it seemed the other way around.

Svanis emerged with a tray laden with munchies and beer and placed it on the table.

"Where's Gnee." She enquired.

"Ran off to look for her husband to tell him very good news."

"What good news?"

"She is coming back to stay with her husband and a few more ex Matabele."

"Is she now? I wonder who put her up to that." She replied with sarcastic humor adding. "Want a beer?"

"Yeah, why not."

They sat in silence sipping beers waiting. Sure enough Gnee came bounding towards them with Boram in tow. Svanis giggled at the sight of those two. Panting Gnee excitedly thrust a list at Tamu.

"These are the names of the Matabele."

Tamu scrolled down the list transmitting the names to Echo. The Wasp didn't have to ask. His orders were clear, and families included if there were any. While Gnee was still fidgeting with anticipation watching Tamu, Svanis voice echoed in her mind telling her it was done.

"You staying or do you have to collect your things?" He asked her.

"No, they are here already." Smiling innocently.

"Why you little devil, good mind to beat your rear end." He playfully remarked.

Just then a group of men, women and children materialized in front of the base accommodation where Tamu was sitting. They looked completely bewildered until spotting Tamu. Then the expressions of relief flooded over them. Svanis went to introduce herself and spoke to them for a while explaining what had happened and that they should not be worried as everything would be taken care of. It suddenly dawned on Tamu he had missed out on a very crucial point, children and married quarters. He cursed under his breath and telepathically contacted Ezos telling him to make immediate arrangements in the old complex for married quarters and a school. Ezos himself swore and initiated construction as a top priority. It took three days to complete and another three days to fit out the rooms. In those six days Tamu and the Wasps had been very busy "borrowing" furnishings from Karagan and even Earth. There was no currency on either Eureka or Cartone to purchase with which posed another problem paying for imports out of planet Ridmon or elsewhere. Manufacturing facilities were nonexistent. So a plan had to be devised. Nah of all people came up with a solution.

"We know Federation Star battleships are equipped with just about every type of manufacturing equipment on board, so why don't we go and steal one and bring it back here, set it onto the land, hide it and we have a means to manufacture many things for trade or barter."

Svanis and Tamu stared at Nah for long moments while their brains digested what she had said.

"Echo, Jump into Vimusi's air space and see what Battleships are around, look for one that is sparsely manned or not at all and report back." Tamu spoke out allowed so all could hear.

"Wow! Nah you're a bright chicken." Joked Gnee to which Nah hissed in return.

"Learned from Mis."

Everyone burst out laughing knowing Mis was not too bright in the intelligence aspect and only knew one thing, fight to kill. Echo reported back. One ship fully equipped and ready, only standby crew on board.

"Grab it, beam the crew off."

Fifteen minutes later Echo reported again." We are in orbit above Cartone."

Tamu, Svanis and Gnee teleported into Echo.

"Right, what we are going to do first is dig a deep trench the length and breadth of the ship so it will sit half way down. Then we will put this monster down there into the trench in between that gorge to the right of the old base where the new barracks are situated. This needs precision so coordinate with the other Wasps your measurements and make the trench."

Echo relayed Tamu's message to all the other Wasps and within hours the trench was completed. By using their white lightning armament the Wasps blasted a huge trench out. There was dust everywhere and it took a whole day for it to settle. The following day back in Echo, Tamu planed the next move.

"We will need you all to beam the ship down and place it gently down and hold it while some of you beam huge rocks into place along its sides to support its weight so it does not tilt over." he instructed.

Echo relayed the message to the other Wasps and one could almost hear their brains racing, calculating and nominating who does what and how. The massive ship beamed out of orbit though the planets outer atmosphere protected from burn out and slowly she was lowered down into the trench and gently placed while other Wasps beamed in huge boulders and rocks to wedge around her. She rested solid and somewhat out of her element, but with a new purpose, a peaceful one. The Wasps scanned the ship for transmitters and tracking devices which ground crews destroyed. Matabele were all over the ship by this time making sure no crew were on board and shut down many non-essential operations except the gunnery turrets which would remain operational just in case. The next big problem was to disguise the massive ship of four kilometers in length and sticking up out of the ground by a kilometer and a further one and a half kilometers below ground level. From the air she had to be camouflaged in such a way it could not be detected and its drive systems signatures masked. This was indeed a marvelous idea and the first thing done was to recharge power pods, run power to the settlement and build a bridge connecting the ship to the gorges side wall. While that was being done the wasps were busy collecting huge boulders from all over the planet where they were placed in such a way to match the surroundings and completely walled in the ship. This was a mammoth task and took the Wasps a good month to complete working day and night. Next, enormous thin rock slices were bolted to the top of the Ship adding to the deception with false trees and shrubs identical to the surroundings. From a distance it looked like any other rocky mountain in the area. Tamu was more than pleased, so called in all the technical geeks and put it to them to come up with ideas for making something that could be used for trade and barter. Having completed that task Tamu returned to Eureka to continue his instruction of specialized students.

The community on Cartone was ecstatic; here they were, alive and kicking on another planet and out of Wolf's control. What's more fantastic were the living conditions. Who would have thought to borrow into the side of a vertical wall hundreds of meters off the ground and to top it all a Federation Battleship supplied the power and work for the nonmilitary community. Life was sweet, the kids attended school, medical services beyond reproach, everyone was fed and that was the winning factor. So they had to live in a Kibbutz type community, so what, everyone was safe and protected by the most powerful force around. Meanwhile back on Eureka, Svanis was recruiting other young Cats to initiate into her group and like Tamu drilled them hard without mercy until they emerged trained and combat ready. Her little army numbered seventy five individuals both male and female. All this training and no action in real life scenarios was not a measure of their abilities so Svanis confronted Tamu with a plan.

"Tamu my love are you busy? She asked.

He shook his head and grabbed her onto his lap.

"What is it my sexy little kitten?" He responded affectionately.

"You know I have seventy five Cats fully trained and willing to prove themselves?"

"Yes, so?"

"So the love of my life, I need to test their skills."

"Hang on a moment there Svanis, explain."

"I want to put them into a dangerous situation and see how they do; by the way, your Father did it with Wolf and Zakrose."

Tamu groaned, "Ok, we will think of something, alright?"

"Don't take too long to think my darling." She cautioned.

Tamu muttered under his breath, "Women, geez, who could understand them."

Planet Ridmon lay slumbering, comfortable in their beds oblivious of anything else but dreams. Crawling into the crystal city completely undetected, seventy five Jaqmuzians infiltrated in to the interior. Svanis followed their progress in her mind. There were Drones and Wasps out there also watching. Carefully, they crept into Zakrose's apartment and pounced. Zakrose did not know what hit her. She was gaged and bound and carted off into a Wasp and deposited on Eureka in front of the base.

Laying on a table with her body pinioned by straps she could not dislodge and looked around frantically. Something blocked her mind and could not teleport out. In short she was hog tied. They left her there for the rest of the night wondering what the hell was going on and she began to fume. Dawn broke and with it a group of creatures she realized were related to Svanis. They stood around laughing and joking pointing at Zakrose. For the first time in her life Zakrose knew defeat. She was laying there wondering what was to become of her when Svanis made her entrance and pushed her face into Zakrose's and smirked.

"So super lady, you are quite literally fragged. We have you hog tied and at our mercy."

Zakrose eyed Svanis and remained silent, waiting. Tamu's face appeared in her vision shaking his head.

"My, my Sis, getting sloppy babe. Looking good sweetheart all bound up and ready to be put on a spit and roasted to perfection."

"Frag you Tamu." She spat.

"Now Sis you listen to me, Eureka and Cartone are ours so unless you pull yourself together and come back here to be with us I am afraid Gnee and I will disown you."

"You would not dare, we are family."

"Sorry. But that's the deal and by the way, you were taken out of your bed and the Drones and Wasps didn't even blink. Now why do you suppose they did that?"

Zakrose kept silent and considered what Tamu had said. He was right and had her dead to rights and knew it.

"OK Tamu, I accept. Now let me go please."

"You know Sis, I kind of like you in this position, let's say because firstly you are at a disadvantage and it keeps you guessing and secondly, I am able to tickle your under soles until you bust from laughter."

Slowly Tamu moved his fingers down her thigh, to her calf then touching her ankle and down to her instep.

Zakrose convulsed her body in anticipation. Tamu blew hot air onto his fingers taking his time, and then tickled her instep. Zakrose was defeated, this was too much and she begged Tamu to stop. He continued until she screamed surrender. Tamu pushed his face into hers and kissed her cheek then teleported her back to Planet Ridmon. The humiliation drove home a message to Zakrose. Tamu was not to be messed with and his strength was far too great for Wolf and her to ignore. Most of all the realization shocked her most was that the Drones and Wasps showed reluctance to protect her. She marched into Wolf's quarters and found him tripping out on K 24, a potent mind bending drug. The impact shook her to her core to see her brother this way so immediately had him committed to detox. Zakrose considered her situation, Ridmon was in a mess, her brother Wolf was in a mess and she was losing control. She found Nina and her son Miteke hiding in the bathroom. Nina had been beaten and was in a bad way. Zakrose knew then what she had to do.

Svanis proud of herself and her team, confronted Tamu.

"So, did we or did we not prove a point?" She asked.

Tamu took his time to answer. After all, the Drones and Wasps on Ridmon did not raise any alarms conveniently and that made him wonder for what reason.

"Alright Svanis, you proved a point, but, you forgot in your haste the Wasps and Drones on Ridmon. For some reason they did not raise the alarm or take your group out as they are supposed to."

Svanis looked at Tamu and gulped as the truth dawned on her. She had made a huge tactical error and by chance came out of it intact. Echo beamed Tamu and Svanis up into himself.

"Sorry Boss, I have to explain."

"Go ahead Echo."

"It was me Boss, who gave the order not to do anything as it was a training test authorized by you."

Tamu shook his head and laughed.

"Well done Echo that was clever thinking. Svanis is still alive thanks to you. Do me a favor in future; inform me of any action you take so we all are in the same picture."

"Yes Boss."

Tamu teleported out of Echo with Svanis, through a portal onto Planet Ridmon. Immediately they landed Tamu received a telepathic message regarding Wolf from the Drones. Zakrose was found on the heights in tears. Tamu sat down next to her and took her hands in his.

"Zakrose, dear sister, enough is enough. We were told about Wolf by the Drones. Please, you need some rest and a change of scenery away from here for a while so come with us and bring Nina and her son. What do you say?"

"I am so sorry Tamu and so ashamed of myself I just want to hide away. How could I have not seen Wolf's problem. I knew he was going through some issues by the way he conducted himself, but drugs that blew me away. It made me realize just how low Ridmon has become and why we are being ostracized by our friends on Thanu and Karagan."

"Come Zakrose; come with us back to Cartone. You will be surprised at what we have achieved since your last visit. This planet can take care of itself. Another thing, the Matabele Regiment here is in a mess and with your permission we take them with us and give them an adjustment slap. But please, not Bordred."

Zakrose hugged Tamu tightly, what a fool she had been.

"OK you big jerk, I will come with you and you can have your precious Matabele along for the ride, but you are going to have to give me something to do otherwise I will go crazy."

"Don't worry about that, plenty to do believe me." Smiled Tamu.

"I'll just get some of my things then I am all yours."

Before she could move found herself on Cartone, personal effects and all. She was standing in the new complex docking bay when KI walked up and hissed.

"Hi sexy, I am at your service, may I take your things. Would the Madam like the left or right wing rooms or our tourist accommodation aboard our very own Federation Battleship here on the ground?"

"Cut the bull you big oaf, pleased to see you also." and hugged KI. That was a first and Ki was impressed, grabbed her things under one arm and Zakrose the other and bounded for a room in the interior where he gently let her go. The room was pleasant with a large window allowing one to see out across a wide panorama. The walls were a natural brick red and furnishings from planet earth and very tasteful Cape Dutch designs out of yellow wood. Yes, she could live with this. Turning to Ki she linked her arm in his saying.

"Show me around hot shot."

Ki hissed deep and loud.

On Eureka, there was confusion as twelve thousand Matabele found themselves suddenly in a strange place, in a very large grassy field surrounded by dense jungle. The next moment eight thousand hooded black clad men and women appeared and attacked. The scene was picturesque, a film makers dream of mass mayhem. After a twenty minutes of this mass mess a siren sounded and all motion ceased. People stood or lay where they had fallen and turned their gaze to an object hovering in the sky. A voice emanated from the object, a sleek Drone uncloaked.

"What an example of sheer stupidity, but I must admit very entertaining to watch twenty thousand people bash each other's heads in, especially fellow Matabele. Yes folks, look around, the whole Matabele Regiment stands here on this very field."

Heads turned from left to right and realization dawned, they had been duped. Ezos emerged out of the Jungle to stand firmly feet apart and using echo's voice amplification, shouted.

"Matabele, you bloody riff raff, atten.......tion!"

Twenty thousand troops abruptly stood to attention.

"Face off." Came the next command.

A lot of shuffling, bumping and finally ordered lines and files nicely spaced in military precision.

"Ah! So you do know how to obey orders. My eight thousand personal troops please return to base on the double."

Men and women broke ranks and doubled quick time back to base through the jungle. Ezos then bellowed.

"So, Gentlemen and ladies, I hear down the grape vine you have become lazy fragen mother fragers and complain too much. Well we brought you here to make some adjustments to that attitude and bring you back into the fold of our Brigade as worthy fragen soldiers once again."

Samre and fifteen officers emerged out of the jungle and stood next to Ezos. Then, Echo opened a portal onto Cartone saying.

"March."

All twelve thousand and seventeen Matabele passed onto Cartone and a rigorous re-training program. Zakrose walked about the base with Ki taking in all there was to see. She was impressed by the design of the base and how difficult it would be to penetrate it from the air as well as ground. The gorge walls were a mere thirty meters apart, sheer drops to the bottom below. From one side to the other was a bridge cleverly disguised as part on the rock formation into the opposite wall with a passage leading into the next set of large spacious accommodations and rooms for various purposes? These led once again to a large docking bay out from which overlooked another large rock formation and an interconnecting bridge fifty meters long to the interior of the opposite rock face. Zakrose thought to herself how things had changed. From tree apes, to rock rabbits. Ki guided her across the last bridge and to her utter disbelief found herself in a space ship. Stopping dead in her tracks she asked Ki.

"What's this?"

"Federation Star Battleship." He hissed with delight.

She was amazed, how in heavens name had Tamu managed that. From behind her a female's voice spoke,

"Simple really, send off a few Wasps and steal one right from under the noses of the Federation in Vimusi's air space, bring it back here and with a little ingenious maneuvering by the Wasps and there you have it, nicely snug in our back yard."

Zakrose spun around and flung herself into Gnee's arms. Ki wisely and quietly left leaving both girls crying on each other's shoulders. Another year passed. The Matabele were in top form and six thousand were returned to Planet Ridmon with Samre and Visni his wife as second in command. On the planet they marched into the Great Hall in full battle dress and announced their arrival. Bordred swaggered down and promptly barked commands. Seeing no response shouted even louder. Samre somersaulted up to him and dealt him a blow to the midriff which silenced the man, but did not put him out of action rather gave him a painful gut ache.

"Bordred, you are no longer Commander of the Matabele and have been retired from service by order of Zakrose and are to be relocated to Karagan where you will spend the rest of your life living comfortably. She thanks you for your loyal services and wishes you bon voyage."

Straightening himself the man about turned and walked off to his chambers. Zakrose's message was clear. He had failed in his duty and was to be sent packing. The pain was too much for him to bear and it spelt disgrace. They found him later hanging from a tree in the dark forest.

Gnee and Zakrose spent a lot of their time together both on Cartone and Eureka where Gnee introduced her to the Cat people. Zakrose was delighted. The cat people were so simple in their demands on life and so openly honest without candor, without manipulative conniving games of political intrigue or struggle for power within their ranks. Everyone knew their place and accepted it without question. For her this was refreshing and slowly her mind healed from Planet Ridmon and was, on top of it all, afforded the title of honoree member of the Jaqmuz people.

"Tamu." Questioned Svanis." How come you have not proceeded with G48 Major's exploration?"

"Simple my dear lovely Svanis, I prefer to be here with you romping in our bed and not out there in the dark cold world of the Universe."

"Cut that out you over sexed human beast. I am being serious." She replied.

"To be absolutely honest with you I have never stopped. The Wasps have been doing long range missions since we got here years ago. This is a gigantic galaxy and it takes time to explore every little corner there is, and we can't afford to be careless now can we?"

"No, I suppose not." Jumping into his arms.

"Want to have a little fun?"

"Hey what's this, you accuse me of being an over sexed beast and now you are soliciting me?"

"Yes my strong sexy man, take me, love me, and send me into passions heaven."

Back on Ridmon Wolf emerged from his haze to find himself lying on a bed constrained by shackles on his wrists and feet. Puzzled, he tried to think of what he was doing in this predicament, but his brain was too fuddled from the K24 drug after effects. Awhile later a woman came in and injected him with something and he passed out into oblivion. For almost a year Wolf drifted in and out of reality till the day he was brought out of it by doctors. No more the fuzzy feeling in his brain, the stupid lack of motor control of his body and loss of control over his bowels, embarrassing. Doctors confirmed he was clean and released him. Wolf headed for the conference room where he thought Zakrose to be, but on arrival found no one. He was sitting there trying to piece together the events of his life when Protector Friend materialized into the room.

"Well Wolf, what have you to say for yourself? Can't imagine very much."

Wolf stammered. "I don't know, it all became too much and I failed."

"That you certainly did and nearly killed yourself. Do you know what it did to Zakrose seeing you like that, it broke her heart. Your reputation outside of Ridmon is blemished almost to a point of no return. So now Mr. Good for nothing Wolf, you are going to go and heal the rift with Karagan and Thanu and bring this planet back into perspective and self-respect. Just so that you know, the Matabele Regiment on Ridmon has been rejuvenated by Tamu your brother. The Wasps and Drones will not listen to you anymore and take only command from Zakrose, Gnee or Tamu. You screwed it for yourself brother, time to make retribution and quickly. That's all I have to say on the matter, the rest is up to you."

With that he vanished leaving Wolf cradling his head in his hands. Wolf was sitting like that when he felt a presence in the room. Looking up, there standing quietly was Tamu.

"You look like shit." He remarked.

"Don't rub it in, I feel like it too." Slowly his mind opened and he saw feedback from his memory of Nina cleaning up after him when he tripped up on K24. His embracement was complete.

"Tamu, I am so sorry, what a fool I have been I must sincerely apologize to you, please forgive me."

Tamu came over and took Wolf's face in his hands and said,

"Wolf, you frag up one more time and I will personally see you go to hell, do you understand?"

The man shrank, what a blasted fool he had been.

"Understood."

Tamu returned to Cartone and a few days later Echo reported, "Wasps have jumped through a portal into Cartone air space with Wolf on board."

Tamu waited on top of the cliffs above the rock settlements with Svanis. Wolf beamed down and stood facing them.

"Tamu, firstly I have to apologize and ask forgiveness of me treating you like an imbecile. I know it's not going to be easy for you and the matter of trust raisers its head and I resign myself to your authority. Secondly, The Wasps are here to help you in your mission in G48 Major."

Tamu walked around Wolf prodding him with a finger and shaking his head.

"Wolf accepted. However, around here everyone has to carry their weight and you look like crap so need to toughen up or move out, your choice."

Wolf answered. "Toughen up."

Echo beamed him into the base where Zakrose and Gnee eagerly waited. When they saw Wolf, screeched with glee and showered him with kisses.

Tamu took Svanis in his arms and teleported through a portal to Eureka followed by Echo. On Eureka the Jaqmuz people's chieftains sat in debate around a fire. The topic of discussion was simple. No change in life style, the humans had to go. On Svanis next visit she received the bad news. Back on base she sadly walked to where Tamu sat chatting with some of his Matabele Officers and sat down leaning her head on Tamu's shoulder. They were quick to pick up something was wrong and quickly excused themselves. Tamu stared at Svanis for an explanation.

"We have been evicted from Eureka." She announced.

Tamu stood up, called in all personnel to the base, beamed them up into Wasps with their effects and then destroyed Eureka base. Seventy five Cats left their home land and never returned for the rest of their natural lives. Svanis was beside herself, but understood her father Zud's motives. What ailed her was her father did not say goodbye knowing she would follow her husband. Eureka was now a thing of the past and Tamu concentrated his energies to Cartone.

"We need material and the only material available is on Ridmon." Protested workers.

The manufacturing staff were seated in a room on the battleship stating their case before production supervisors.

"How are we supposed to produce with nothing?"

"Easy folks, we will take this up with management, in the meantime sit on your butts and wait."

The information travelled up the chain of command until it reached Tamu, who called in Zakrose and Gnee.

"Zakrose, we need your permission to mine crystal on Ridmon."

"For what reason." She asked.

"For the manufacture of protection suits, Crystal Helmet's, crystal weapons and a whole range of crystal crockery and trinkets and clothing for trade." He answered.

"Go for it. "She simply replied.

Nina proved herself to be a very useful merchandizer and was nominated to the task of distribution and trade with planets Ridmon, Karagan and Thanu in exchange for raw materials. One of their most successful products turned out to be special winter clothing made out of the processed crystal and black gum sap into woven fabrics which could be manipulated and dyed various colors or combination of colors and heated to a thousand degrees. The clothing offered protection from extreme elements and came in two parts, Jacket and trousers. The other most productive product hands down was Ridmon Beer and Whiskey which became a very good negotiating tool for trade with even Vimusi. Wolf got into the act and took charge of the actual deliveries making sure of fair trade. Karagan was the only planet known who employed a money system and unlike Earth who used gold as the basis of monitory evaluation, Karagan used diamonds, huge diamonds found only in one area of the planet and guarded with an army of security personnel. So the currency was hard Larinium, a very rare and precious ore found only on one of Karagan's moons and smelted into square disks the size of an American silver dollar and valued at a thousand Krans, smaller sizes representing metric equivalents. The Irony of it all was that gradually all planets preferred to trade and barter with Karagan's currency. This raised another problem and became very evident when closing purchases and having to deposit heavy cases of disks as payment. Cartone came up with a solution and thus was born the Cartone Bank, with an Office on Karagan run by Nina. Cartone came into a new commercial era and secured itself among the planets as a fair and upstanding dealer. Nina ran a very strict and efficient operation. Cartone's diamond reserves grew and ended up in special vaults on Planet Ridmon guarded by none other than the Drones.

It was during this boom of progress that Cartone found itself the object of curiosity from unidentified space craft out in space. The Wasps took up battle stations and Tamu sat in Echo watching and waiting. Down on the ground Cartone went into emergency lock down and shields were raised. Sixteen thousand troops on full standby ready to be teleported into that fleet if necessary. A tactic devised by Tamu to bypass electronic blocking and was fast, undetectable with deadly consequence.

"Can you tap into their communications?" Asked Tamu.

"I can, but a language I have not yet deciphered and in the process of doing just that."

The Wasps, poised and waiting slowly edged closer and closer to the intruders until they were in position to destroy quickly and effectively. Echo and his Wasps collectively deciphered the intruder's language with basic words sufficient to open communications and attempt to establish who and what they were. Echo indicated to Tamu which was the control vessel and he concentrated his energies to discover the identity. No known similarities. These were a new race from somewhere he identified as Wamzu who were from G48 Major. The ships of the Wamzu were inferior to those of anyone else, but did not detract from the point of being destructive to a community such as Cartone. Tamu projected his image into the Wamzu control ship and was surprised to see people of human likeness yet so much like the Vimusi with their red colored complexion and pitch black hair and eyes. His senses told him there was no threat yet history told him to be cautious so he instructed Echo to check for mind viruses and found none so teleported aboard the Wamzu ship. The effect was electric. They were in a flurry not knowing what to do. Tamu shouted in their language to calm down. One Wamuz male stepped forward identifying himself as their leader.

"I am Zoma of the Wamzu Federation, who might you be?"

"My name is Tamu of Cartone, be advised you are violating Cartone restricted space and are within millimeters of destruction."

"Tamu is it, well Tamu we are not here to be a threat, but merely to investigate and establish diplomatic relations with you. We are surprised to find a population on this planet never discovered before in our investigations. It is intriguing how suddenly we find you in our neighborhood."

"No surprise, let's just say we keep a low profile and up to now have maintained our silence and avoided detection by you in the past until now." Tamu stated.

"Impossible my friend, our scanners would have discovered you long ago. Who are you anyway?"

Tamu laughed. "Zoma, you have a very inflated opinion. Do you not know there are other civilizations out there who can take your planet apart without blinking? Ours on Cartone is one of those and right now you are sitting in a trap and will not escape at all so cut the bull and lets discuss your immediate situation diplomatically."

Zoma considered the alternative and could not be sure the man was bluffing or telling the truth so decided to play along for the time being and see what came out of it.

"Very well Tamu, what do you suggest then."

"Be careful Zoma, I can read your mind so no deception or I will kill you."

Zoma reeled backwards in disbelief when he felt a crushing pressure in his brain and understood all too well what Tamu had warned him about.

"I told you Zoma, play it straight or I will destroy your fleet here and now."

"We have to consult with our superiors on this matter before anything else and return with their answer."

"Zoma, I am not a trusting person so I will tell what I will do and that my friend, is this. You and your fleet will remain here and one of your ships will convey your message personally to your superiors and the answer will be relayed back to you here. If the message we perceive to be in any way devious, charged with ulterior motive we will destroy your fleet and will attack your planet. Just so we understand each other, at this moment on your planet are hovering a fleet of ships you can't see, can't detect and can't withstand the devastation they unleash nor the ground forces which we will land and take your planet apart with."

Zoma was frustrated and if what this Tamu was saying was true then he was in a fix and had to follow instruction. Tamu smiled and teleported Ki and Nah together with Svanis and a few of her cat people into the control bridge. There were mixed reactions from the crew of the Wamzu ship on seeing these different beings. Tamu waited while Zoma watched Ki with growing trepidation instinct telling him the beast was a killing machine and he shuddered.

"Well Zoma, are we in agreement?" Asked Tamu.

"Agreed." Confirmed Zoma and barked orders to his fleet, one of which broke off and warped out of Cartone's space.

Tamu sat down and indicated to Zoma to do the same. In the silence that followed Echo ran a scan of the entire ship and recorded every aspect of it into his data banks, analyzed, dissected and de-encoded. The weaknesses and strength of Wamzu technology became apparent. So echo contacted Tamu and stated.

"Boss, this is a two bit operation and bluffing. These ships are so inferior its amusing and a waste of time to bother with. However, one thing in their favor is the mineral composite of their ships manufacture which interests me. They may be primitive in construction but are able to withstand severe pounding and survive unscathed. We have a winner for trade purposes."

Svanis came over to Tamu and jumped into his lap nestling her head on his chest, Ki grabbed one sorry looking Wamzu and hefted him into the air screaming to which Tamu cautioned him to put him down. The classic good cop bad cop strategy. The poor man shrank and crawled away while Ki tried to sit in his chair and not able to fit ripped it out of its foundation and sat on the console instead. Zoma now knew without a shadow of doubt Tamu had cards up his sleeve that were beyond his comprehension and capability and so resigned himself to the outcome of his superiors. Tamu beamed Zoma onto Cartone and a warning, any attempt by any of his ships to warp will be destroyed. Zoma now a guest of Cartone was kept in Antrum where he came face to face with black clad troopers and became nervous. Tamu noticing his stiff posture said.

"Easy Zoma, no harm will come to you as long as you are with me." Then he walked Zoma around the docking station inspecting the assembled Matabele in full battle dress, with packs and helmets on.

"These are our ground forces, or should I say part of them, who are the most highly trained and efficient in the known universe and capable of turning your planet into rubble. Trust me when I tell you we have done it before and succeeded. There is one other aspect you must consider, our air support. You don't want to mess with them. They are indestructible and are the worst attack ships in any universe simply because they are beings with free minds and not constrained by dictate."

Zoma saw and marveled. Cartone was a hot bed of power to the likes he had never in all his days as Master in Chief of the Wamzu Federations forces witnessed and knew then he wanted part of it. Then he saw Zakrose and all melted away into a single determined direction. Tamu introduced him to Zakrose explaining to her who he was and where Zoma came from. Zakrose smiled and extended her hand out which Zoma took and kissed it. That simple gesture impacted on Zakrose in way she could not understand and in those slit seconds looked at Zoma though eyes of abject curiosity. Something inside of her stirred awakening dulled emotional feelings and urges and she knew then she was in love. Tamu read the scene and was a little taken aback by the speed of it and cursed under his breath. Geez, there is no accounting for taste. Anyway it was his sisters life so what had he to do with it.

Zakrose took Zoma's arm and guided him around. Svanis caught up with Tamu, linked her arm in his and commented,

"Zakrose has found a man she can relate too, don't deny her this chance to be happy, after all she deserves it don't you think?"

"OK wise guy, women's intuition and all that stuff is it?"

"Yes, my man and you should be glad, at least now you have an envoy on Wamzu."

A lone ship broke warp and returned into Cartone air space two weeks later with a message from Wamzu. The Message was relayed to Zoma who read it out aloud from the console before him.

"Greetings people of Cartone, we of Wamzu welcome you as friends and would very much like to establish relations and ties of economic interest between us. We understand you are a force of extreme power and persuasion and don't doubt your warnings, yet we believe there is room for co-operation and detente between us for mutual benefit. We invite a delegation from Cartone to visit our planet and see our intensions are honorable."

Tamu considered the message and turned to Zoma and slapped him on the back saying,

"Lucky you Zoma, you have your life back and that of your fleet. Now send them back to Wamzu with this message. We of Cartone open friendly relations with Wamzu in principle, and will deal with Zoma as go between. We trust this will be acceptable and through Zoma will proceed to send a delegation to Wamzu at an appointed time. Meantime Zoma stays in Cartone orbit waiting further instruction."

Tamu teleported Zoma back to his ship and told Echo to download all the information he had acquired into the central date banks from which an analysis of the composite breakdown of Wamzu ships could be studied and applied to Cartone in some way. In exchange for this raw material Cartone was willing to embark on a trade agreement that was beneficial to all. After a while, sitting and thinking about it. An agreement between Wamzu and Cartone was dully entered into and with it an exchange of delegations and the marriage of Zakrose to Zoma. It was a pompous affair on Wamzu with all the frills and excitement afforded to a Prince such as Zoma. Tamu was not impressed, but played along all the same to make sure his sister was safe. She entered the wedding hall clothed in the most divine dress any one had ever seen. Glistening with diamonds and precious stones, the peach colored full length dress, low cut showing her bare shoulders, tailored to her lovely form and gave herself to Zoma, body and soul. Tamu was impressed, how he could not be, it was a beautiful marriage and Zakrose's face was beaming with happiness he had never seen before. Gnee sniveling with joy hugged Tamu then went to congratulate her sister. Svanis smiled and taking Tamu by the arm walked with him onto a balcony and watched the Wamzu sun set. Later Zakrose found them and kissed his cheek.

"We will be alright, look after Gnee and planet Ridmon for me please Tamu and don't worry; I have found my place and am very happy. Take care, brother." Then she teleported out. Svanis hugged Tamu and whispered.

"Let's go home, it's done here and we have things to do back home my love."

He nodded his head and lifting Svanis in his arms teleporting though a portal to Cartone. With Zakrose on Wamzu and Wolf transferred to Karagan left planet Ridmon open for all sorts of problems so Tamu arrived in the Great Hall and made an announcement. From the war Room Tamu broadcast his message to the Ridmonians.

"You have three hours to gather your committees here in this hall so I suggest you do exactly that."

Everybody knew Tamu and his reputation preceded him so no one was arguing and complied. From the other two cities on Ridmon came committee members and assembled in the Great Hall. Tamu watched the members gather, be seated then he announced.

"People of Ridmon, we have sadly gone through a period of confusion and doubt and I know all of you have continued to put your trust in the system and for that I thank you. The news is that Wolf, Zakrose and Gnee have given me authority to take over command of Planet Ridmon. You of course all know I am a military man and as such am probably insensitive to your needs. Wrong, to the contrary. We are going to turn Planet Ridmon into a productive and self-supporting planet able to stand on its own two feet."

Tamu watched the faces of the gathered committee members before continuing,

"You have always relied on martial law to control this planet in the past, well folk's times are a changing and you are going to join the ranks of people who work for their living. So, as of now, teams of workers will be shuttled to Cartone and become workers of the Ridmon revival syndicate.

"What if we refuse?" Someone shouted.

KI entered the hall, walked up to the individual, grabbed him by the scruff of his neck and holding him off the ground stepped in front of Tamu and hissed loudly, Tamu translating.

"You get exiled to Reptilia."

No one said another word. So it was industry, economics and production. Planet Ridmon entered the age of workers and its community no longer sat on their rear ends and enjoyed life of the unemployed reaping benefits. Now they had to work, pay their own way in life. With Zakrose on Wamzu, Wolf on Karagan and on Cartone were Tamu and Gnee, law and order on planet Ridmon was left to Samre who applied himself well and soon had Ridmon back in shape and functioning as a productive community. Gone were the days of freebies, now one had to work to be able to afford to pay for living. It was a shock. But evolution is about change and change has to happen as it did on Planet Ridmon. On Cartone the situation was becoming critical. The manufacturing processes were running into problems trying to keep up with demand. As usual Gnee came up with a solution, steal another Federation battleship and place it on planet Ridmon. Tamu disagreed and commanded his technicians to pull their thumbs out of there, you know what, and get creative and come up with a solution on a mass scale on Cartone. With a huge redesign the Star battleship on Cartone turned into an Industrial complex second to none increasing output by a thousand percent.

With Zakrose's influence on Wamzu things began to change for the better and being married to a prince gave her much authority to make changes she saw fit which benefited the whole. Following Tamu's example created a marketing strategy for Wamzu's goods and traded between Cartone, Ridmon, Karagan and Thanu. Although Thanu maintained its policy of non-entry to her air space, did have a collection depot on Karagan. She looked at Wamzu's military capability and found it to be very inferior so made a selection of the finest soldiers around and put them through their paces out of which she selected the best of those and separated them to a new division. They numbered three thousands of tough hard core men. On Wamzu women did not participate in military matters at all. Contacting Tamu she requested he recruit these men into his forces, train them and use them as part of a multinational task force stationed on Cartone. Tamu accepted and took stock. Stationed on Ridmon there were six thousand Matabele troops under the command of Samre. On Cartone there were sixteen thousand Matabele, three thousand Wamuzians, seventy five Cat people and two Reptiles. On Reptilia a massive force of thirty thousand troops giving him a total of fifty five thousand and seventy seven troops, three thousand Wasps and a combined one hundred and Fifty Drones which he split in equal number between six planets giving each planet twenty five Drones a piece. From planet Ridmon he withdrew two thousand five hundred Wasps and relocated them to Cartone.

Based on feedback from Wamzu the G48 Major Galaxy housed a few populations spread far and wide some of who were primitive and some others advanced societies. One of which Wamzu had diplomatic ties with, the Planet Tatran. Tatranians were a highly telepathic nation who preferred to remain isolated yet traveled their universe telepathically frequently seeking out possible threats to their existence. As yet they had not stumbled on Cartone so before they did Tamu requested the Wamzu Counsel to arrange a meeting either on Wamzu or Tatran. The answer came back. Only on Wamzu. Tamu with Svanis, Gnee and Ki stepped through a portal in to Wamzu's council hall to be met by a smiling Zakrose and her husband Zoma. Zoma was petrified of Ki especially since his wife told him about the Reptile and his fighting skills so kept a healthy distance from him. There was a round table in the center of the Hall, well-lit with light streaming in through what looked like glass panes. Some of Wamzu's Council members were seated and so pleasantries were exchanged. Tamu and his strange group sat down and Zakrose made small talk with Gnee until the announcement that the Tatranians were on their way. A group of six persons dressed all in white robes, faces hooded and complexions as white as snow and their eyes had no pupils just white eyeballs. Zoma stood up indicating to them to be seated. He was about to introduce Tamu when one who obviously was their spokesperson spoke in a strange dialect. One of Wamzu's councilor's translated.

"His excellency, the minister of Foreign Affairs for Tatran says he knows about Cartone and has known for a while and does not approve of the large military force there. But, since they are there, were to be kept well away from Tatran."

Tamu smiled and replied.

"Minister it is not our intension to interfere in this Galaxy what so ever. However, our own history has been one of defending ourselves against some very nasty invaders and we have had to build up a sizable force to do just that."

Now it was the Ministers turn to smile "Your knowledge of portals and their usage puts you way ahead of most civilizations, yet using force never proved anything and I see your delegation are made up of different peoples from different worlds which we commend you on and the relationship you have with what you call Wasps."

Tamu blinked and stared at the Minister.

"We too are telepathic peoples and have learned to collectively channel our energies and so know all there is to know about Cartone and your home planet Ridmon."

From then onwards no words were spoken only thought transmittance to and from the Tatranians and Tamu, Zakrose and Svanis with Gnee listening in. The rest of the delegates were puzzled not knowing what was going on. Tamu was saying telepathically.

"We agree to stay away from Tatran and will only contact you through Wamzu if and only if there is some major crisis which we feel justifiable."

To everyone's surprise the Tatran delegation simply vanished and Tamu knew how. They used their own form of portal, an invisible one far more advanced. Zakrose looked at Tamu and raised her eye brows.

"We have been out matched by a superior race. This is humbling." Saying Zakrose stood up and kissed Gnee on the cheek and walked out of the Hall with the Wamzu delegation following behind.

"Guess that's all." Said Gnee.

"Guess so. Let's get out of here and back to Cartone." Svanis said and Tamu activated a portal onto the base and walked through to his office deep in thought.

What the Tatranians had told him about themselves started to add up. Collective channeling of thought. Performing or achieving a particular objective. His brains cells started working overtime and he called both Svanis and Gnee into his office. He sat them down on the floor facing each other, placed a cup in between them and linked hands. Telepathically he instructed then to concentrate on the cup and make it lift off the ground. All three collectively focused on the cup willing it to rise. Rise it did like a rocket shot up and lodged itself in the ceiling. For next few days the trio tried various other things in secret and gradually discovered collectively they could move really large objects and even explode them with mind power. Something clicked in their brains and opened for them other possibilities as well. They could see onto planet Ridmon, could see everything that was going on. All their extra sensory perceptions suddenly accelerated and the more they practiced together the stronger the trio became as a group and as individuals. Not a word was spoken about their new knowledge and was kept to themselves. For months they practiced trying to emulate the Tatranians portal activation and finally achieved a break through. Now the trio could monitor Wamzu or any other planet without being detected. This new found ability was awesome so had to be used with caution. The trio decided to visit Zakrose so first checked where she was and just appeared on her veranda. Zakrose jumped and starred wide eyed at them.

"What the hell! You gave me a damned fright you three. What are you doing here anyway?"

"Just thought to pay you a visit as we haven't seen each other for months." Gnee answered.

Zakrose was not stupid and realized they came for a reason. She was still trying to figure out what when the next instant found herself in the dark forest on Ridmon next to their parent's graves. She looked from one to the other in shocked amazement.

"How did you do that? She asked.

"Our little secret we share together, the three of us." Piped up Gnee.

"Let's just say we opened up a few abilities in our minds by months of practice and here we are to remember our parents. Just then Wolf appeared looking very perplexed followed by Ridmon their brother.

"Hey! What's the meaning of this?" Wolf demanded.

"Remembrance Day thick head, or have you forgotten." Growled Tamu.

Wolf fell silent as Tamu recited a pray.

"Lord, you commanded us to honor our Father and Mother, in your mercy grant that we might see them again in the joy of everlasting brightness. Amen."

No sooner had Tamu finished a split second later Zakrose, Ridmon and Wolf found themselves back where they had originally came from. A chill ran down Zakrose's back and mumbled.

"Now, that was scary."

Business was booming and everyone was benefitting from it. Planet Ridmon with its brewery industry was forced to develop agricultural fields for the beer and whiskey ingredients. Crystal mining stepped up under controlled conditions and the crystal ore shipped to Cartone via Drones through portals activated by Wasps. Cartone produced specialized clothing for military and nonmilitary purposes, a whole range of crystal fine wear and crockery, used her smelting facility to manufacture a wide range of mechanical parts mainly used on Karagan. The Regiment did not sit idle either, but were put to work building a new Town up on a high escarpment well away from strategic facilities using local materials and buildings kept at two levels only. The town blended in so well with its surroundings, gardens and a central park added to its attraction. The purpose of the small town was tourism. Cartone opened a new tourism agency on Karagan managed by Nina. This created job opportunities for Cartone residents as tour guides, caterers, entertainments, gyms and spa personnel.

By now Tamu had reached an extremely high degree of Martial arts proficiency, so high in fact he had equaled his Father. Svanis naturally trained with him and she too had aspired to a higher level as did Ki and Nah so it was Ki who suggested a month stay on Planet Ridmon and get back into Ape mode among the trees. Gnee was appointed boss lady in their absence. It was a month of joy for Tamu who relived his childhood days swinging about from tree to tree. This exercise did a few things. Not only did it strengthen the body, but also sharpened ones perceptions and judgment of distance at speed. Svanis adapted to it very quickly being quite comfortable romping around. Although Ki had a distinct weight and size disadvantage, soon learned which branches to dive for and those not to as it was a long way down to the forest floor, a whole one hundred meters down. Evenings were spent either at one of the Kiosks having supper and a few drinks or at Jane's old house or visit with the Ridmon branch of Matabele. Samre was pleased to know they were on Ridmon on a short training holiday. The month flew past very quickly and time came to return to Cartone. Tamu sent KI and Nah back to Cartone.

Sitting at a Kiosk with Svanis having a beer, Tamu reflected over the years. Jane and her love for him and her constant stories of his Father. She told him about his mother, and how fierce she was. He loved that woman so much. Her death was a tremendous blow and Tamu felt cheated. It took a long while to accept her parting. His half-brothers and sisters were for him a blessing in one way, but a problem in another. His birth to someone else other than their mother Penagee was a heavy pill to swallow for them and he always felt growing up there was a division between them. It was like he was overshadowed by their privilege. Yet his Father passed on to him a gift so precious, the gift of telepathy. A secret he kept to himself growing up. He became the courts joker deliberately fooling the girls and Wolf who regarded him as a prankster and it never occurred to them to see him in a more serious light. He grew up a lonely boy, not fitting in with the main stream, perhaps one or two friends. In general he spent a lot of time alone at Jane's old house brooding. Because of it, the other four family members considered him to be anti-social and basically ignored him. Svanis read his thoughts and put her arms around him.

"Tamu, it must have been painful for you growing up and I feel for you, but you must put it behind you and look forward. You have me now and you have so much more than all of them put together or could not have imagined of you. Let's go ahead together and show them who Tamu is."

"Woman, perhaps you are too clever, but one thing I do know, I love you with all my heart and I have to thank you Svanis of Eureka for making me feel whole again.

"Come, let's go home and leave this place to the ghosts that haunt it." She murmured.

"Yes I guess you are right. Cartone here we come. Echo, beam us up."

"At once Boss."

G58 MAJOR

ELEVEN

he Federation spurred on by Vimusi decided to pay G48 Major a visit only this time would go with Vimusi and Trafodj Battle Cruisers, a top of the range ships bristling with potent weapons and highly sophisticated on board electronics, a battery of fighter craft. Fast very nimble. Packing a nasty punch with their new and modified laser guns. These Cruisers were warp specialists and could go far into deep space very quickly. From Vimusi the ships would enter into G48 Major at the opposite end of the Galaxy to where Cartone was situated. Commanding the fleet of six ships was Admiral Atna, a Trafodjian battle hardened campaigner. It was to be a raiding mission and had orders to use maximum force if needed. On board, each ship carried a contingent of Marines from Vimusi and Trafodj backed by troop carriers and Tanks. This was a major strike force equipped to do serious battle. A week later the fleet received its orders and made for G48 Major. It took four months at max warp. The Fleet entered into G48 Major and went on full alert. A further two weeks to find a planet worth investigating and Atna unleashed his Fighters who swooped down on the planet meeting no resistance what so ever. Scanners worked hard, scanning the surface pin pointing targets down below then fired main canons in volleys of destruction. It was a massacre and any resistance crumbled. Then Atna sent in his ground forces. There was no resistance and if any was illuminated quickly and mercilessly. It was over before it began. Survivors were herded into enclosures and locked in. Then Atna beamed down to investigate and was surprised at what he saw. These were not people like he or anyone else he had met before, they were two legged creatures, which stood upright, hairy with almost ape like faces. Wore loin cloths, and grunted in a strange dialect. Obviously this was not what the federation was after so Atna ordered a withdrawal, relieved to be off the planet yet leaving behind chaos.

His next blunder came with Wamzu. The fleet had warped into Wamzu's air pace and immediately alarm bells rang. Wamzu's armada was no match for Atna's fleet and in the pursuing battle it became obvious to Zakrose she needed help from Tamu when Atna's salvos started to hit the planet. Tamu had just completed joint exercises on Reptilia and all personnel were boarded when Zakrose's call came in. His entire fleet of Wasps and Drones jumped into Wamzu's space right into the middle of the attacking fleet and simultaneously beamed thousands of Reptiles and Matabele into Atna's ships. While the infighting aboard the ships suppressed most of the gunnery salvos, some landed with destructive effect. The Wasps took out Atna's fighters like a knife through butter. Atna was shocked when hordes of Reptiles let loose in his ships killed everyone in sight. Sitting in his control console, striving to gain some form of control he knew the end was imminent when Svanis burst into the control deck with her Jaqmuz people and went ballistic. Atna died with a vision of Svanis burned into his brain. The fleet was crushed, its crews and Marines almost wiped out and only a handful of survivors from the six ships were teleported through portals to Vimusi bearing a message of terror and fear.

Wamzu took stock and shuddered. The speed and precision of Tamu's attack on the Fleet was their saving grace. Zakrose realized her brother was in a whole new category of war readiness and capable of mobilizing those Reptiles and Matabele almost at will and on top of it all, could bring the Wasps in with well-coordinated, devastating effect. There was something else she noticed. Gnee, her little sister was in there, in the thick of it with her husband. A still silence of the aftermath hung over Wamzu. Tamu called for a meeting with the Wamuz Council who assembled in a Hall. He teleported in to find Zakrose seated with Wamzu's Council.

"Greetings Wamzu, we need to discuss what to do with six battleships out there with Fighter cruiser's on board and a whole collection of military equipment. We suggest you take possession and use for your own defense now that you armada has been badly depleted. We will send in training officers to train your forces how to operate the ships and the equipment."

Zoma stood up and walked to a window saying.

"We respect you and your efforts, but don't want anything to do with that fleet and even if it is far advanced more so than ours, it will only attract too much attention here in our solar system and besides, our relationship with

Tatran must be maintained as is. So we want you to remove that entire war machine elsewhere."

Tamu responded angrily.

"Zoma, I think you are a fool and making a huge mistake. If it had not been for my sister you arse hole, your planet would probably be dead, so frag you. Next time we don't come and save your miserable butt, we leave you to your misery, and by the way, for what it's worth, Tatran will not help you."

Tamu stepped back, looked at Zakrose and shook his head saying.

"Sister." Then vanished.

Zakrose was shaken. Tamu came when called and responded in the most effective way he knew and saved her and her new adopted world from certain destruction she knew would have been the end result. They owed him big time, but what Zoma declared had freaked her out and she was not impressed with her husband. He was proving to be a weak personality and Zakrose had to step back and view her situation more clearly. That's it she decided and confronted Zoma.

"Listen you weak minded man, I've had it with you and I am leaving Wamzu and your stupidity. You have embarrassed me in front of my brother after he saved your life, then offered you a prize of immense worth to you and you like a fool, put your ego above all else including your people, so in the words of my brother, frag you, and goodbye."

Zakrose emerged onto Cartone in front of Gnee.

"Don't say anything Gnee, just hold me." And Zakrose wept great sobbing tears.

Out in Cartone space, six battleships orbited void of life waiting for an outcome guarded by Wasps who absorbed every facet of their construction and function nothing left to chance. The Reptiles back on Reptilia, were a very happy and contented lot. Tamu devised a plan with his Captains, a plan that involved the captured Federation Fleet. Time to teach the Federation a lesson they would not forget.

"What do you Gentlemen propose?" Asked Tamu.

"We have discussed it and although this idea may sound weird we think it will give all of us a chance to catch the Federation with their pants down using their own ships as decoys. Naturally, the Wasps could do the job very well by themselves, but we want a crack at them as a Regiment in a full combat assault using our combined forces with dual purpose. Knock out Federation facilities and deprive them of some of their Tanks." Remarked Ezos.

Tamu considered the proposal. The Tanks would be a great assist he could have modified to Planet Ridmon standards and put into active service.

"Agreed, but the Wasps will go and make a recce of the entire Federations set up down on the planet. We then formulate a battle plan that must be followed to the last detail. Timing is crucial. The Wasps will activate portals to the exact locations each group will be deployed to. As soon as the ground forces engage, the Wasps will take out all Federation ships in the area of the Way Station and the Station itself. The six captured Ships will then be jumped back into Cartone space and all ground forces retrieved from pre-determined RV points."

After two months a battalion of Matabele and Reptiles boarded onto the captured Federation ships and jumped them via portals into Vimusi's air space. Most Federation ships where in orbit docked around a Way Station where personnel shuttled to and from the planet. The Wasps activated portals at specific locations and the Regiments stormed onto Vimusi. The Wasps destroyed very Federation vessel at the Way Station and any others around it. All hell broke loose when the Reptiles attacked strategic installations housing Federation complexes. At the same time simultaneous attacks were carried out on Trafodj by Wasps knocking out any Federation assets. The Federation suffered critical casualties and damages, their fleet was destroyed and land based strategic Infrastructures demolished. Then just like that the attacking force was gone leaving behind total confusion and complete dismay at the speed at which the attack took place.

On Karagan the news of the attack was welcomed, perhaps now maybe the Federation would turn over a new leaf and return to the mandate originally entered into. Back on Cartone with six battleships and a horde of fighter Cruisers plus military equipment posed a problem. What to do with it. Svanis and Gnee solved part of that issue and Cartone inherited three space hotels after major refits. The fighter Cruisers were converted to Cadet Trainers, some were dismantled for spares and the balance recycled. From the remaining three ships Cartone constructed a Way Station above the city of Spes up in Space. All children from the age of fourteen began cadet training and learned to use various weapons, learned to pilot Cruisers and perform evacuation drills to various fortified bunkers armed with laser canons taken from the battleships.

The news of Cartone's activity in G48 Major by way of military successes did not go un-noticed to Tatran and Cartone's apparent abandonment of Wamzu after rescuing her from destruction somehow did not seem right. They were cautious; Tamu was dangerous, and posed a threat to Tatran's peaceful existence. Unless he deliberately crossed the line they had to allow him to continue to safe guard

G48 Major. They did not know Tamu so their Minister of Foreign Affairs approached him on one occasion at a conference of Planets held on Wamzu.

"Please, we are a simple nation, nonviolent and peaceful. We can't abide by brutality yet you come into this Galaxy with your negative vibrations and disrupt our peace."

"Don't make me laugh, did you for one moment consider this Galaxy to be paradise and your life style would never change other than by evolutionary process. I think not. This Galaxy became open the minute a Trader vessel passed by. Greed and deception caused much conflict here which we of planet Ridmon have been forced to act upon. Even you yourselves became involved by establishing relations with Wamzu. Did you think these actions would not have any effect on the events unfolding in this Universe? The laws of cause and effected stipulate for every action there is a reaction and it's happening here, right now. You are involved whether you like it or not so I suggest you get used to the idea. We will not interfere with your existence in any way, but our presence here will be a permanent one and to have good relations with our neighbors is important to us because of joint preservation."

"I shall convey what you have said to my Council and we shall deliberate." Answered the man.

Back on Cartone Tamu called Zakrose, Ridmon, Gnee and Svanis into his office.

"I have asked you here because I want to invite both Zakrose and Ridmon into our secret circle."

"Zakrose and Ridmon would you be willing to join us and be part of a unity of amazing things and to share in it with us as equals, as family, as the greatest thing you both will ever discover about yourselves?" Asked Gnee.

Zakrose studied their faces and saw the looks of anticipation so both she and Ridmon accepted. For the following days and weeks the pair experienced some strange and wonderful things and came to grips with their inner selves and joined with Tamu, Gnee and Svanis into a powerful force collectively. One day Tamu called the girls and Ridmon in and told them it was time to go to Thanu and breech their security to talk to their leaders and sort some issues out, some issues pertaining to Planet Ridmon and their Father. Five people emerged into Thanu's council chambers and sat calmly waiting. A security detail armed to the teeth burst into the room and demanded an explanation. Tamu simply teleported them out to the outside of the building and waited. Sure enough, a delegation approached with an armed guard detail and demanded clarification.

Tamu indicated to the empty chairs and the delegation took seats.

"Who are you? They asked.

"No one of importance, let's just say the children of a great man who gave his life that you might live. We are the children of Mike of Planet Ridmon and we come here to remind you of your commitment to this Universe. You withdrew your forces from G48 Major without explanation and left us to clean up a lot of mess by ourselves and this we do not appreciate particularly when there is a standing agreement between planets Thanu and Ridmon."

"Young man, the agreement between planets Ridmon and Thanu was considered not be in our interests any longer as a logistical and non-practical venture. We received no response from Ridmon of our intention so we assumed acceptance and withdrew." The speaker replied.

"To whom was your message addressed to?" Questioned Tamu.

A light flashed on the console and a monotone voice said, Wolf of Planet Ridmon.

Tamu looked at Zakrose. "We have to apologize to Thanu, and we were not aware of this and shall send a formal apology on returning to Ridmon."

"No need young man. No damage has been done here. Perhaps it would be wise to investigate planet Ridmon's communication receipts."

"This we shall do. Once again, we apologize for our intrusion." Zakrose said.

"Apologies accepted."

After decades of silence Mother spoke, her voice echoing in the room to everyone's surprise.

"Children of Planet Ridmon, after all this time you have finally arrived as I knew you would. I have a gift for you from your Father who passed this on to me before he died."

She told the four brothers and sisters to link hands and stand close to each other. No sooner had they done that when Mother passed into their brains eons of information once housed in their Fathers memory. Their bodies lifted off the ground by the intensity of the action until it ended and four people collapsed exhausted and unconscious on Cartone together with a much perplexed Svanis.

The four persons lying on the ground slowly regained clarity. Svanis was perturbed. Here in front of her were two brothers and two sisters, something was not right. Where was Wolf? Tamu opened his eyes and saw Svanis with a worried look on her face.

"Hello sweetheart, come here". He motioned.

She fell into his outstretched arms and breathed a sigh of relief. Tamu held her tight while his brain tried to absorb and digested what Mother had implanted into it. Gnee,

Zakrose and Ridmon sat up a little dizzy at first, but that soon dissipated when Tamu stood up and helped the others to their feet then, linked arms with them and suddenly their bodies spiraled upwards and a bright white light emanated out of them and in the center appeared Protector Friend. They hung like that for seconds then the light faded lowering them down to the ground. Something had happened and Svanis was not sure what, yet knew instinctively of a power and knowledge she never believed possible in living beings. Life on Cartone took on a new perspective for the four Ridmonians and Svanis who sat for hours honing their skills of extra sensory perception, telekinesis, telepathy, teleportation, psychometric reading. One other skill in their range was the ability to see in real time places very far away. Something still puzzled Svanis though. On Thanu, when Tamu, Ridmon and the girls were taken up by Mother, Wolf was not there and this became the nagging question for her, why. She could see the change in Tamu, Ridmon and the girls which Wolf did not display. Seems Mother figured he was excluded for some reason.

Wamzu found themselves wondering about Cartone's growing prosperity and intense tourism from seven planetary systems. So they sent a delegation to Cartone with a request to become participants in the Tourism trade. Cartone agreed in principle, but all operations would be controlled by planet Ridmon who operated the entry and exit of tour groups among the seven planetary systems. Eight Wasps were nominated to handle the work load on a rotary basis to shuttle groups through portals only after a full screening of the occupants was carried out.

Tamu rotated his ground troops between planets Ridmon and Cartone, gave them a fully comprehensive package of wages, leave and a pension scheme with option to purchase a retirement home on either planet Ridmon or Cartone. Married men received compensation for families in the event of death in action or death through accident. Planet Ridmon was the technical center and so all technical modifications to physical materials whether domestic or military were processed there.

Exploration of G48 Major continued through many solar systems, some new, some forming and some dying and it was one of those that the Wasps brought to Cartone's attention. A dying solar system is when its Sun swells into a red giant towards the end of its life; its outer layers are expelled via pulsations and winds. Ultraviolet radiation shining out from the stripped-down hot stellar core then lights up the ejected shells, resulting in intricate artworks the remnant of this evolutionary stage as a large, near-spherical shell of glowing material expanding out into space. This has the knock-on effect of accelerating the wind from the star to its present speed of 4,000 kilometres per second, over 14 million kilometres per hour. As this fast stellar wind catches up and interacts with the slower wind and clumps of previously ejected material, complex structures are formed, including the delicate comet-like tails which can be seen near the central star. The stellar wind bombarding dense clumps of material provides a chilling look at the possible fate of other solar systems and their fellow planets in Earths Solar System in a few billion years' time. When their Sun emits its final gasps of life at the heart of a planetary nebula, its strong stellar wind and harsh radiation will blast and evaporate any planets that may have survived the red giant phase of stellar evolution. If any distant civilisation watches, they might see the glowing embers of the planets light up in X-rays as they are engulfed in the stellar wind.

This one unfortunate solar system found by the Wasps had an inhabitable planet much the same as planet Karagan. Its peoples were very closely identifiable as possible cousins of the Thedarians in their likeness with only three million survivors. Wasps informed Tamu there was not much time to act as complete destruction was imminent. Fortunately for Tamu the people of that planet had brought themselves to one central point, all three million of them trying desperately to find a way out of their situation. All seemed hopeless. Then in a blink of an eye were teleported onto Cartone by the Tatran's. One could imagine the confusion of those poor people, not to mention Tamu's surprise and realization the Tatran's were monitoring his Wasps. However, there was no time to dwell on that subject as he had a whole major problem on his hands figuring out how to deal with so many people. Cartone set up aid posts, water and food points and brought in from planets Ridmon and Karagan specially designed space shelters to house these people. Gradually order was restored and a group of twenty elderly men and women dressed in long robes of varying colour approached the military command post set up to handle any problematic situations, requesting an audience with Cartone's leaders. Tamu with Zakrose teleported the group to the Tourist town's central hall, into the main reception area and seated them along a bank of chairs next to one wall.

"Gentlemen and ladies." He addressed them in their own language, seeing puzzled looks on their faces he expounded. "We are Telepaths." Then continued.

"We are going to have to split you up into smaller groups and re-locate you to other planets as part of their communities. Language is a problem so there is bound to be some friction caused by misunderstanding. We would like you to speak to your people and let them decide their groups, perhaps according to areas of habitation."

Twenty heads nodded in agreement, one man standing up presented himself.

"My name is Yu-mar, appointed leader of my people. Our planet was called Duras. On behalf of all the Durasians we thank you and will convey your message to our people."

The group was returned to the camp to deliberate.

"Tatran did a humane thing for those people. Talk about collective thought process that beats all." commented Zakrose.

"You are right. I don't think we would have been able to save so many on our own so we owe Tatran a favour I guess." Tamu responded.

It was time to approach Karagan and request assistance for the relocation of displaced persons. Gnee took charge of all processes entailed and arrived at a mutual solution with Karagan. On planet Ridmon, the circumstances were somewhat different and would take time to facilitate accommodation for the new comers in accordance with the planets building standards. Cartone faced a similar situation, so it was decided to contain the refugees in their camp whilst appropriate alternatives could be arranged.

Three weeks later the Durasian delegation presented Cartone with their decision. They divided themselves into three equal parts of one million people each, made up of families, the elderly, young men and women in a balanced and logical way. The Wasps scanned all of them looking for anomalies, finding none informed the coordinators all was clear to precede. Yu-mar enquired where each group was designated. One group would remain on Cartone; one group will be settled on Karagan and the other on planet Ridmon. Everyone would need to be tolerant whilst adequate arrangements were made for everyone. Yu-mar immediately recommended his group remain on Cartone as it contained more children than the others for the sake of minimizing stress. Tamu accepted that, instructed Yu-mar to separate the two groups who were to leave so they could be channelled through to Karagan and Ridmon. With help of the Wasps amplified voice hailers, the people were practically herded into their respective groups. A few hours later, the Durasians filed through portals to their new home planets. The whole procedure lasted three days and the strain was taking its toll. At last the portals closed and Zakrose breathed a sigh of relief. Gnee and Nina were appointed to act as liaison with Yu-mar. Svanis and Tamu with Ridmon scouted for a suitable area to build a city to accommodate the new arrivals and found a site on high ground not far from the tourist town with fresh water cascading down a waterfall into a natural lake. The city would be terraced and once again no building higher than two stories. Having selected the place Yu-mar was asked to provide any artisans, architects and engineers from his people to assist in the building of the city.

Many Durasians volunteered boosting the already large work force. Huge construction vehicles were brought in from Karagan which were exceptional. Apart from rippers excavating, massive stamping plates flattened the ground as the machine proceeded forward. Excess raw materials quarried were processed, converted into building blocks using a special quick drying bonding agent and formed into building blocks within the machines structure then deposited in large piles as the vehicle moved forward. Five of these machines at different levels on numerous hillside slopes cleared an impressive fifty square kilometres in thirty six hours. In just seventy two hours the job was completed and machines retuned to Karagan. Crews worked day and night in shifts laying sanitation, water lines, special power grids courtesy of recycled Vimusi Battleships, and erected two story housing, landscaping and features, parks, schools, shops and a host of other industrial buildings. Within one year the city was completed and formally named Spes, the city of hope. Yu-mar, thankful the Spes project offered hope for his people who contributed all their efforts into making Spes what it was and it did take their minds off of their cramped camp existence. Still a few cosmetic finishing touches to do, but all in all, the Durasians were finally housed and out of the camp.

It had been a hectic year for everybody, not only on Cartone. Planet Ridmon was the hardest hit by the Durasians arrival. Crystal manipulation was not something created in the spur of the moment, it took time to fashion the crystals into the shapes necessary for construction. Only Ridmonian technicians knew the secrets and were not willing to divulge them to anybody under any circumstances. Work was slow, painstaking yet precise across the three cities. On Karagan the situation was completely different. With all her heavy construction machinery, she was able to complete her task very quickly. With the Durasians settled it was time to incorporate them into the various societies, a function made more difficult by the language barriers. Like all good communities the desire to be part of the whole triumphs over solidarity and division. There will always be the odd drop outs and this is common throughout many societies with the best of intensions. It was those drop outs that Cartone recruited into its armed forces and gave them a reason to have self-esteem. One day Gnee was assessing the impact the new inhabitants made on the environment and its resources and came up with an agricultural proposal to create work to avoid the problems of complacency, idleness and the emergence of criminal influences, drug addiction and alcoholism among the people. Cartone became an example for the rest of the planets with her collective, but independent farm holdings cultivating a variety of crops and creating a whole industry around it.

Cartone was not happy to be a vegetarian society and investigated the possibility of raising both fish and livestock. To their amazement the conditions on Cartone were perfect for both, but animals like cattle carry ticks and undesirable other ailments so had to be thoroughly sanitized so as not to affect Cartone's pristine environment. They made a study of Karagan and found no adverse ill effects of game or domestic animals introduced to that planet from Earth years ago. The first Cartone Game and cattle ranches emerged which included wild animals in controlled closures and domestic animals for future slaughter. Zakrose was not amused being vegetarian, yet Tamu assured her it was a viable venture and exportable as a new industry for Cartone. Tamu was never the less concerned about the situation with Tatran and it played on his mind and so needed answers from those strange beings. Confronting Svanis he explained to her what he wanted to do.

"I need answers from those Tatrans, so we are going on a fact finding mission to their planet."

"You think that is wise?" She questioned.

"We need to set up diplomatic ties with them for obvious reasons whether they like it or not." He remarked.

"Just be careful, don't forget their collective telepathic strength." She cautioned.

Tamu was not a man to back down from a challenge and this was one of those occasions. Cross referencing any possible solar system in the vicinity of the Wasps initial sighting of the problem on Duras, Tamu with the help of the Wasps systematically found Tatrans location. With Zakrose, Gnee, Ridmon and Svanis they materialized into Tatran's world and understood the physical make up of these people in their freezing domain. Tamu's appearance caused a disturbance and seemed to echo around the population whose thought patterns were disrupted by the intruders. Tamu linked hands with the girls and Ridmon and concentrated. The five Cartonians spiralled into the cold air and hung there suspended. Tatran acutely aware of the power emanating from out of the five understood at once there was more than meets the eye to this delegation and settled for having dialog.

"We asked you explicitly not to interfere in our affairs to which you agreed so why now you come here?" asked one person.

"Fellow Tartans, we do not come here as aggressors, or to disturb the harmony of your existence, we come here to thank you for you unselfish act of humanity of the Duras peoples. We also come here to establish diplomatic relations as neighbours and respect your request of non-interference and will maintain that relationship. However, we only ask you advise us in due course of threats to your or our sovereignty or of those of our other neighbours." Tamu replied.

"Who is protecting you? We sense a strong presence not identified before." They asked.

"We are protected by higher order, far higher than yours so don't try to go in that direction, it will have dire consequences. Just do as we request and we will move on with our business and this meeting will be forgotten and you will carry on your lives as normal." Confirmed Tamu.

The Tatran's tried collectively to penetrate telepathically Tamu's hovering circle and the next minute Protector Friend appeared. His countenance became a livid florescent white and spoke to the Tatran's commanding them to abort otherwise he would bring untold destruction on them. Seeing this aspersion and hearing its warning they immediately understood these five Cartonians were special and protected by a force they could not oppose. Departing from Tatran, the five Cartonians left with the knowledge they had achieved a semblance of diplomatic success was in itself, a heartening thought.

Mis sat with Zi discussing matters in general when Tamu arrived. He hissed a welcome and beckoned everybody to sit down. Mis spoke.

"We have known each other for years and known your parents before you and we have an extraordinary relationship and mutual understanding, yet we feel somehow we are not receiving what is due to us. Our existence here on Reptilia is secluded and only in battle are we ever drawn out of our environment. You have acted beyond expectation with your friendship with Ki and Nah and we see that it is possible to co-exist with others than ourselves. We appreciate our physical make up is seen as frightening to some, but consider this, we want to be part of your world and reap the benefits of our services which is only fair. We have become tired of living on Reptilia, and yes, we did ask for it long ago. Times change, however we make our request formally, to be re-located to Cartone."

Tamu was taken aback by the request. This was a difficult problem, but not insurmountable and answered.

"Mis, Zi. I hear you and understand completely, yet I have to speak to my people and come up with an acceptable solution whereby all of us can co-exist side by side. Personally you are welcome, you know that."

Mis studied his face for signs of deception, finding none turned to Ki.

"Son of Zi, you have been with Tamu a long time and now your honest opinion. Would his people accept us on Cartone, yes or no?"

Ki answered truthfully.

"I believe on Planet Ridmon we are accepted. On Cartone we have a problem not with the Regiment or the Ridmonians, but with the other inhabitants who don't know us and regard us as blood thirsty killing machines and are fearful. Yet I believe given time, we could be accepted."

Mis and Zi looked at each other. Zi asked.

"Tamu my friend, would you accept us on Cartone?"

"Yes without any hesitation. Just say when and we will bring your people to Cartone to live alongside us." He answered.

"It is agreed then, contact us in a week and arrange for re-location to Cartone. In the meantime, you will be able to find a suitable place for us to live and we will do the rest."

Tamu returned to Cartone with a temporary plan. He evacuated the cliff dwellings of all personnel and relocated the Regiment to a camp not far from the city. It took two months for the Reptiles to organize themselves. The Wasps opened portals and the Reptiles left their planet for the last time taking up residence in the cliff dwellings of Antrum and on the gorge floor. Cartone was hit with a logistical nightmare to supply fresh meat on a weekly basis bringing in beef from Karagan and as far afield as Earth who were paid for cattle with diamonds and secured a very lucrative trade with cattle ranchers. One learns not to saturate a good thing and Cartone was cautious not to drain supply, but spread their beef purchases wisely while the herds on Cartone multiplied enough to warrant slaughter. Another industry rose in wake of this and an Abattoir complete with cold storage and packaging took shape. A central market came into being where all produce came in from out laying settlements and exported out to other planetary habitations.

Cartone was a large planet with an equally large sea surrounding it. Evolution produces strange creatures and under the oceans there existed all manner of life forms some of them predators, some intelligent life, but most existed on the preverbal food chain. On her continents vegetation ranged from dense forests to grass lands with massive ravines and rugged mountains. The climate was seasonal, with rain falls alternating in the different hemispheres. In remote mountainous regions, inaccessible to most people was a collection of wild life. One in particular similar to an averaged sized mountain goat only smaller and preyed upon by a predator resembling a large monitor lizard which in turn was preyed upon by a scaled wingless bird type of creature the size of a medium sized horse with a large eagle beak. Fortunately, these creatures all shied away from open spaces where the chance of being killed was so much more probable so kept themselves confined to rocky crags and caves offering better protection. This kept them out of areas inhabited by people. The Reptiles on the other hand found an alternate food source in the bird like creatures and lizards, yet were careful not to over hunt, but rather adopted a breeding program for domestic consumption by way of hatcheries. Some young birds were domesticated very early in their lives and trained as farm animals which could be ridden. The first time Tamu and Svanis saw this spectacle of a Reptile mounted on a scaled bird running full tilt down a gorge floor they packed up laughing. However, that scene was the beginning of a Reptilian cavalry. The birds were vicious and difficult to train yet once their pea brains got the message they adapted to their trainers very well, yet had to have their beaks bound as many a trainer bore testimony by the scars on their bodies from those vicious beaks.

The Durasians adapted well to their new home and soon proved their worth as farmers, technicians, and a multitude of small businesses emerged catering for the general public. Gradually small groups moved out of the city and established minor communities on the plains which were fertile and water readily available yet in light of a possible predatory reptile bird threat adequate settlement protection was installed in form of force fields. A breeding herd of African Eland, the largest of the antelopes was brought in. This animal's yield of milk rich in protein was much sort after by everybody. Yu-mar thanked the Supreme Being in the heavens for his people's good fortune. It took his people some time to get used to seeing Reptiles on Cartone so preferred to keep their distance. The community became overcrowded and strained inter-relations so something had to be done. In a general community meeting, the matter was put up for debate. It was unanimously decided the Regiment would be re-located elsewhere away from civilian communities, but close enough in case of emergency. The city and the Tourist village would remain as is; The Reptile community would also be relocated to a far more compatible area in the mountains more suited to their natural habitats. The Regiment occupied an area twenty kilometres from the city boarding onto the sea where the landscape perfectly suited their training requirements and the introduction of powerful mechanised vehicles bristling with armaments for troop transportation and deployment. Silent, highly mobile in all terrains, the ultra-fast across country vehicles powered by the same power packs as used on Star battleships, with a carrying capacity of a hundred combat troops. The aim was to free up the Wasps who could now be concentrated in air support offensively or defensively. Tranks as the vehicles were nicknamed were Multi-purpose able to deploy as auxiliary emergency services such as ambulances and civilian evacuation or field support. The one amazing thing about them was they could be beamed up into space, staked and interlocked to form a mini space station.

The Planet Reptilia suited the armed forces live weapons exercises, the ground consisted of all the various components making up for battle scenarios of conventional full out combined offensive assault or defence, alternatively, non-conventional guerrilla tactics and applications or specialised mission criteria. On one battle exercise, the Reptile cavalry were brought in to test the effectiveness of employing such a unit in a combat scenario. The results were promising yet hair raising requiring some much refinement to be efficient so provisionally was accepted as a part of the armed forces. While planets Ridmon, Karagan, Thanu and Wamzu were the peaceful planets preferring commerce over military involvement they did however, rely on Cartone for protection. Trafodj and Vimusi mustered their own armed forces selecting to handle matters themselves should the need arise. Where the Federation had failed, Cartone now became the silent inter-planetary Policeman. However, many young men and women from all planets enlisted into the military boosting the army by a further twenty thousand soldiers. To avoid the adage, don't put all your eggs in the same basket; Tamu split his forces evenly on planets Ridmon, Karagan, and Cartone with supporting logistics, air support and Generals he could trust. Knowing Earths history having had to study it as a boy, he was well aware of the reasons so many conquers lost their kingdoms. Mostly by collapse from within and or defeated in battle. Genghis Khan, Alexander the Great, the Roman Empire, Hannibal, were but a few examples. Although planet Ridmon's history was built on warfare, it had done so for reasons of survival and Tamu was fast becoming seriously close to a designation on Cartone as a warmonger.

Regular patrols went out across the planets in two Galaxies, new solar systems were charted and named with numerical values. This was an on-going exercise and not long before the Wasps bumped into a small fleet of out dated Warships accompanied by commercial vessels full of human looking people. Scanning the data banks the Wasps discovered they were third generation adults with families, survivors of a similar disaster which befell the Durasians. Only these people's planet was bombarded by massive meteors killing it and millions of life forms. They were desperately seeking a new home travelling in inferior space craft, slow and aged and on the verge of expiration. Something else disturbed the Wasps, so they scanned outwards and sure enough, shadowing the flotilla were unidentified battle Cruisers stalking the aged ships.

Tamu arrived inside of Echo and studied the Cruisers. They were huge and ultra-modern manned by an alien race never seen before and his senses became aware whoever they were somehow sensed his presence, but could not place him. Tamu cautioned the Wasps to be very careful. The aliens were probing trying to pin point what ever was out there besides the old Fleet. Tamu slowly re-positioned the Wasps in front of the aging fleet so as to distort his signature patterns. A game of cat and mouse ensued and Tamu projected his vision into one of the ships. What he saw amazed him. They were similar in stature to the Reptiles with a greyish skin tone, looking old and wrinkled, but not as large as the reptiles. Four fingered hands with short talons. Their faces gave the impression of being well aged, black eyes set back into their hairless skulls and a nose consisted of two slits. The mouth, a narrow slit displayed hard gums instead of teeth and no ears but a membrane covering the ear drums. Feet looked like they belonged to an Ostrich with three toes and knees bending backwards, clothed in some type of fabric overalls. He could see there was some sort of anticipation on board, and its then Tamu noticed the side arms, a sort of ray or laser gun. There were ten ships in total. Three Wasps were not comfortable odds against an enemy one knew nothing about so Tamu brought in twenty more just to be on the safe side. More scanning and the alien's fighter craft were discovered housed in concealed docking bays. The flotilla was completely unaware of the danger stalking them. Tamu monitored deciding the best course of action was to jump the aged fleet through portals into planet Ridmon's neighbourhood where the Wasps and Drones could protect them if things didn't go according to plan when they did so. The wasps targeted their subjects and on Tamu's command the fleet just disappeared.

Watching the Aliens reactions he could see utter surprise when they could not identify what had just happened. Most craft who engage warp drive leave behind a tell-tale signature. The Aliens seemed baffled yet tried every trick in their book to no avail. Echo calculated the direction the ships were heading towards and cross referenced Cartone, Eureka and Wamzu to that trajectory path and was relieved to find the enemy where way off course in those directions. None-the-less, Tamu conveyed the information to Tatran and warned his Wasps in all G48 Major to be weary and cautious and then teleported into the Command vessel at planet Ridmon joined by Zakrose and Gnee. In planet Ridmon's space a puzzled and perplexed group of people aboard antiquated craft were locked into retractor beams and held stationary.

Seeing Tamu and the two girls materialize in front of them was unnerving. Tamu raised his hand signifying a greeting and tapped into their brains telepathically.

Fifty thousand persons on eleven ships were all that remained of a nation. Incredible as it seemed, they had survived, out living two older generations and knew nothing of land existence. They originated from a planet outside of G48 Major in another close galaxy on a planet named Amakrin, voyaging nearly two hundred years to reach G48 Major. Their language was similar to that of Karagan, as Spanish is to Portuguese; both would be able basically to understand each other. There was only one solution, resettle them on Karagan where there was more than enough room.

"People of Amakrin, I am Tamu and these two ladies are my sisters Zakrose and Gnee. Let us explain why you are here and then discuss what to do about it. Firstly, we discovered your fleet in a Galaxy we call G48 Major. At the time of your discovery we also came across a fleet of ultra-modern Alien warships stalking you. Knowing you did not stand a chance, being completely out ranked, we decided to protect you and here you are in the Planet Ridmon's orbit. We realize none of you have ever been on land and it will be a completely new experience for you. We would like to welcome you and advise you your final destination will be on a planet called Karagan, who speak a language you will understand. Your ships are no longer capable of lasting much longer and it would be a shame, to see more of your people perish. So consider this offer please."

The Amakrin elders gathered exchanging words back and forth and came to a decision.

"We accept."

"Good, now we want your people to gather their personal effects and nothing else."

After living all their lives on board, some were sceptical and afraid of leaving the only home they ever knew. Yet there was an air of excitement as they dared to hope this was true and not a dream. True to his word, Tamu walked with those people onto Karagan soil through a portal. The reaction was phenomenal with hugs, weeping and singing. Planet Ridmon's Drones destroyed the eleven vessels turning them into vapour. Back on Cartone, after handing over the Amakrinians to Karagan authorities, Zakrose said to Tamu.

"You must be chuffed with yourself?"

"No more than necessary." He projected an image into her mind of the Aliens.

"Eeeek! Ugly. Those poor Amakrinians having travelled so far to be snuffed out would have been a catastrophe. Bet they are very happy people now."

"Just as well the Wasps found them in time." He remarked.

A second time populations where delivered out of extinction. G48 Major was earning a reputation for itself yet the knowledge those Aliens were skulking around was worrisome. Svanis teleported Zud, her father onto Cartone and explained to him Eureka's vulnerability now the stakes of some form of invasion force attacking was a possibility. She took him on a grand tour of Cartone ending with a meeting between him and the seventy five cat people stationed with the Regiment. Zud was a simple man, content to live his life with as little stress and strife as possible. All the modernization of Cartone was just too much for him and asked to be returned home. Svanis understood yet felt disappointed.

Karagan's capital city Belus became a bustling metropolis with such a variation in its citizens and cultures was in itself a major tourist attraction. Game parks, Oceanarium, theatres, sea side resorts with amusement parks, restaurants offering many types of cuisine, the list endless. Her Police force, an essential part of life sadly in any city, patrolled in shuttles equipped with the latest crime fighting technology available. The new arrivals from Amakrin and those from Duras hit it off immediately probably due to their similar circumstances which helped pave the way for Amakrin's to adjust more rapidly. On Ridmon and Cartone policing was carried out by the Regiment in their "Tranks". Life was great until the Wasps patrolling Wamzu sent a warning. The Aliens were in the vicinity. The Wasps on Wamzu formed a staggered defensive line in front of the approaching Alien ships. When Tamu received the message his reactions were lightning fast and jumped into Wamzu space in Echo accompanied by thirty Wasps.

A quick assessment revealed the Aliens taking up battle formation. Echo scanned one ship and acquired its structural schematics. The vessel was crewed by three thousand persons and five hundred fighter pilots. Multiplied by ten this hardly warranted an invasion force, but the fire power on those ships was enough to think otherwise. Tamu waited, watching for any sign of aggression ordering his Wasps to apply new tactics as practised. Then it came, the first salvos down onto the planet. The Wasps retaliated and opened portals right into the fleets docking bays then with merciless precision fired into the ships from the inside before the next salvos could rain down. The aliens did not know what hit them when their ships suddenly exploded. Down on Wamzu the situation was critical. Those salvos had inflicted major damage and many lives were lost including Zoma and most of the Royal family leaving only a young girl and her hand maiden in the ruins of the palace. The Regiment was then brought in to assist with clean-up and help remove the dead. News of the attack leaked to the other Planets who intensified their security vigilance.

Tamu and Svanis sat in Wamzu's committee hall with a few of the Committee members discussing what had happened and how to prevent a reoccurrence in the future. It was obvious the Aliens had somehow deviated from their course and knew exactly where to find Wamzu. Unless, and everyone looked at each other, unless someone like Tatran told them. The question remained, for what purpose they would do such a thing. Evaluate our defences and reaction times or deliberately offering the Aliens, a bargaining chip to leave Tatran alone. An investigation of Tatran's motives if any was due. Tamu left the Hall with Svanis and Joined Zakrose on Cartone. Linked arms and concentrated collectively channelling their minds to Tatran. What a shock they received to see the planet in total chaos, destruction everywhere. Very few survivors wondering around lost and confounded. Tamu mobilized his troops, instructed them to wear full battle dress and prepare for a lengthy stay if need be. Tranks were beamed up into Drones and the Wasps boarded troops and jumped through portals to Tatran. The place was in complete disarray, hardly any buildings were left standing replaced by huge craters, bits and pieces of bodies were strewn everywhere and the stench of phosphorous hung heavy in the air. This was total annihilation. Troops began rounding up any survivors and bringing them into first aid posts where they were treated for any wounds and shock. Gnee and Zakrose telepathically found out what happened by tapping into Tatranians collective memory. Other cities across the planet were devastated with very few survivors. The task was too colossal so re-enforcements were brought in, aid workers, construction crews and the massive Karagan excavators with additional troops. While all this was going on Zakrose told Tamu what she had found out.

"It appears Tatran did contact the Aliens after all, but not for the reasons we figured. They wanted assurances for their safety, but the Aliens had other plans and bombarded Tatran into the ground beaming up some of the people and subjecting them to mind torture until they gave up the name of Wamzu and in which quadrant the planet was situated. The Aliens killed those poor Tatranians on board then turned their attention to Wamzu."

"This is a mess here and will take time to sort out so let's concentrate our efforts in bringing all the survivors we can find to this one location, rebuild it then look outwards to see what will be the best plan of action." He suggested.

"Agreed"

Tamu teleported into Echo and made a survey of the entire planet from high grid by grid, relayed this information to the Drones who beamed up isolated groups of Tatranians and brought them into the control centres. It was a long and arduous task completely rebuilding a city to house a mere one and a half million people. With craters and rubble everywhere it took time for the excavators to flatten the ground to its original state. To top it all, Tatran winter was approaching and winters on this planet were severe to damn right unbelievable how temperatures could plummet to minus one hundred degrees centigrade. All personnel were advised to wear their Ridmonian full body stockings with special hoods insulating the whole face. Tranks played a huge role in the operation helping the Excavators clear rubble, troop transportation, any other number of tasks requiring muscle. Having a high centre of gravity balanced on eight articulated wheels could navigate through rough terrain very easily; the wheels were constructed from the hardest mineral

known, a mineral called S34. When mixed in its raw form
with another substance called B26 in a mould, a chemical
reaction occurred which bonded the two together to form a
slightly pliable substance resistant to canon and small arms
fire. The body of the Trank was fabricated with the same
substance which could be manipulated with crystal to form
transparent impregnable windows or a tough resilient skin
impervious to almost anything including re-entry heat.
Some Tranks were fitted with shuttle engines for specific
tasks. Light, extremely powerful and deadly with a full
assortment or armament. Other planets sent in relief aid,
by the tons. Soon buildings rose off the ground and a city
took shape. Enough shape to accommodate all the survivors
with enough rations to carry them through their winter. And
winter came in with vengeance compelling most ground
Crews to beat a hasty retreat for warmer climates on their
own worlds.

A contingent of troops remained snuggly inside their
Tranks where they lived for five months with blizzards and
snow howling around outside to a gloomy dark sky. Tamu
would often appear in those Tranks bearing gifts to keep
troop morale and even on occasions stayed for a couple
of days. The modified body suits, a throwback from early
planet Ridmon days were a genius of invention. A person
could survive out in the bitter cold without ill effect what
so ever or under the hottest sun and not suffer heat stroke
or dehydration. Resistant to Radiation, small arms fire,
breathable in the most putrid and deadly of stratospheres
and resistant to extreme pressure drops.

The incident with the Aliens puzzled Tamu no end.
How could an advanced nation of telepaths fall for the oldest
trick in the book? The answer sadly, blind trust. When fired
upon the collective reaction was one of panic resulting in no

telepathic resistance what so ever? The survivors on Tatran would now have to make some far reaching changes to their way of thinking. After the five months of winter ceased and a more workable environment presented itself, crews returned to continue where they left off.

It was at one of those outer camps that workers encountered a "Kayi" for the first time. A large white fur covered animal that walked on its hide legs resembling the Yeti or Sasquatch on Earth. It was scrounging around looking for something to eat not perturbed about the men at all as if he thought men were no threat to it. So used to it mingling with the gentle Tatranians it came up to the men sniffing around to find a morsel to eat. Everyone made no sudden moves and watched the creature. One worker had some sweets in his trouser pocket and the Kayi quite calmly ambled up, stuck its hand in the man's pants and took the sweets out, walked off as if nothing had happened. From that day onwards when Kayi came visiting sweets were on hand. Strange how sometimes nature pulls some unlikely creatures together as friends who tolerate each other when they most likely should be enemies. The crew named this creature "Dodge" on account of its swaying motion as it passed between the workers.

Finally, Tatran had its city. Crews said goodbye to Dodge who had become somewhat of a celebrity and Tatran was left to its own devices to regroup and rebuild. Tamu decided to follow up on the Aliens and starting from their last known location stalking the Amakrin, plotted a course along a possible trajectory with a one hundred and eighty degree search pattern out of G48Major. Jumping through portal after portal his wasps found the Aliens planet. Echo hung in their orbit and scanned. Tamu deliberately created vibration waves simulating cosmic winds so avoiding any detection. Three thousand Wasps and One hundred and fifty Drones hung poised unseen behind portals positioned at strategic points surrounding the Alien planet.

"Kill" Tamu commanded.

What a symphony of pure destruction and pay back Tamu meted out on that planet. Never in all his life had he become the ultimate slayer as he did then. Within hours it was over and as silently as they came so silently left behind a lesson the Aliens would not soon forget. The Wasps and Drones experienced a new force emanating out of Tamu which seemed to expand into them and magnify their capabilities beyond their expectations. Echo quietly asked,

"Boss, what did you do to us?"

"I made you more powerful, more capable." Silence followed then.

"That's fragen amazing."

Tamu rolled off his seat in stitches of laughter.

Back on Cartone, Svanis confronted him.

"We felt the telepathic vibrations from here and thought the Aliens were attacking, what did you do?"

"Just a little pay back." He replied.

"Pay back. No, don't tell me you found the Alien Planet?"

"Yes, and gave them a taste of their own medicine."

"Geez Tamu, take it easy, just now we will have the whole fragen Universe breathing down our necks."

"Not to worry my darling, the Universe will have to get past my revamped Drones and Wasps first."

Svanis stared at him for long moments then it sank in. He had modified the Wasps and Drones somehow and now they were omnipotent. Tamu took her into his arms and kissed her forehead gently holding her like that for long seconds.

"Svanis my darling, we have come a long way together you and I and I would not have it any other way. I love you crazy woman, love you very much."

"I know." She purred.

Wolf confronted Zakrose, Ridmon and Gnee a day later.

"Tamu's out of control and I am afraid he will ruin all the good relations we have achieved thus far."

"Ah! Shut up brother. Leave him alone." Quipped Gnee and both girls walked away leaving Ridmon with a huge grin on his face seeing Wolf cut short like that.

Tatran survived and the remnants of her people began to fit the pieces together and start life anew. This time they would do things a little differently. Strange how experience teaches us lessons from our failures and this was one time Tatran woke up with a jolt. So they requested a meeting with Cartone on Tatran because climatically conditions on Cartone were too uncomfortable for the Tatran people. Cartone's delegation arrived spear headed by Yu-mar, formally of Duras, an astute and fair mediator. Tatran's spokesperson, a woman, addressed the gathered delegation.

"Members of Cartone, we have requested your presence here to formally thank you for all your efforts in helping us rebuild after such a disastrous misjudgement of circumstances for which we, and we alone are to be held accountable. One of our regrets is Wamzu and their losses. Never the less, having said that, we put forward a proposal, which we consider to be a fitting indication on our parts as to joint co-operation between us. As our planets have such extreme climatically differing conditions, and the fact that we, as you well know by now, hibernate through our winter months leaves us vulnerable to problems. We would consider it an honour and privilege if Cartone could set up here a permanent watch dog."

"In exchange for our agreeing to support you, after all its manpower and resources we have to provide just to keep any military presence here, what do we get in return?"

"Our collective telepathic support which you, Yu-mar, are well aware of." The woman answered.

"No argument there." Agreed Yu-mar.

"Just because we hibernate does not mean we are fast asleep in our beds, no sir, that is when our powers of collective mental capabilities are at the highest peak and we are able to reach out into the universe. In this case, to warn Cartone if there are any threats to our parts of the world and those of yours."

"Madam, it seems we lack much understanding about your race of people, but after the disaster befallen you, I am sure you will agree, collective co-operation between friends for survival is after all a powerful motivating factor. Allow me to ask your name, please."

"Casjori." She answered.

"We will take this proposition to our principles and will inform you in due course. It has been a pleasure meeting you Casjori, and thank you."

A Wasp beamed Cartone's delegation out and jumped back onto Cartone where they presented themselves before Tamu and Zakrose with the Tatran's proposal Yu-mar finished his debrief. Tamu smiled at Zakrose saying.

"Well, let us consider this carefully and give benefit of the doubt to those people. This is a somewhat unusual request and having been on Tatran during winter, know how demoralizing it is. Any of our personnel there will be fighting the elements under extreme conditions. But, tactically, I feel a good opportunity to expose our forces to this type of situation which will make them much better trained operatives. Right, this leaves us with basically two alternatives. One being in their summer months our presence there will be to do an in-depth study of their planet, its environment, and any possible life other than Tatrans and in general give us as much data as possible. During the winter months, trust me nothing moves, we reduce our forces and leave a retaining group of Tranks with their crews to monitor and scan. All the Tatranians are in one single place now so it makes our lives simpler."

"Settled. Thank you everyone, we will deal with the formalities." Announced Zakrose dismissing the meeting.

Yu-mar and his team exited leaving her alone with Tamu.

"Why do I get the feeling you are up to something dear brother?" She asked.

"Oh, what makes you think that?" He responded.

"Let's just say woman's intuition."

Tamu laughed and teleported out to Svanis and into her warm soft embrace.

A team of specialists with military support were dispatched to Tatran together with two supporting Wasps where they constructed their own camp apart from the city. When winter approached the crews would change and the Tranks arrive with their crews of military personnel as was agreed. The data collected from Tatran was transmitted back to Cartone to be processed and evaluated. The Tatran Kayi affectionately named "Dodge" made his usual appearances and became quite a familiar face around the camp site. Then one day the strangest thing happened, Dodge walked into camp with his family, a female and small child. What an opportunity to study this creature and the news of it brought Gnee charging onto Tatran to investigate.

In the meantime, Wasps monitored the Alien planet from a distance recording every move the remnants of the planet did. Many battleships which had been out on long range patrols returned to find their world in shambles. None of them could elaborate on who and why their planet was attacked. What it did do though was to plant doubt into their hearts knowing someone out there was just as or more powerful and obviously the attack came as a reprisal for the Aliens blatant destruction of communities elsewhere. After a three month time elapse the Wasps withdrew and returned to Cartone. Svanis, Zakrose, Gnee, Wolf, Ridmon and Tamu gathered together on the Heights of the Planet Ridmon. It was a nice pleasant day. Below them lay the crystal city with its platform leading into the trees. The cascading waterfall fell into a steam, winding its way through the forest into the far distance. The crystal city had grown since the time of Mike and Penagee, expanding along the mighty cliff face away from the falls. Down on the platform people milled about or sat at kiosks.

"It's been awhile since we sat up here and much has happened during that time. We have changed. I have asked you all here to show you something. Let's look at what we have. Firstly, the ones we know of, Telepathy, Teleportation, Telekinesis, and Psychic sight. Secondly, we have in our repertoire, Bilocation, which is the ability to be in two places at the same time. Psychometry, here is something interesting so let me demonstrate."

Getting up, Tamu walked to another bench, placed his hand on it concentrated then returned and sat down. Within moments a young teenage couple appeared seated on the bench somewhat shocked, but seeing Zakrose relaxed.

"I am going to ask you a question and I want a true answer. There is no problem so don't worry. You were up here last night sitting on the same bench weren't you?"

The couple balked and nodded in response.

"Sorry about this you two now go and get on with your studies."

Tamu teleported the two back to their respective classes.

Svanis was the first to enquire, "And you got all of that by simply placing your hand on that bench?"\

"Yes and more as you saw. Now the other ability we have is conscious bilocation. Gnee, do us a favour and teleport down to a kiosk on the platform." He requested.

Gnee did what she was told and sat down. Tamu suddenly appeared sitting opposite her. Zakrose telepathically asked her.

"Do you see him?"

Gnee answered affirmative. Then Zakrose told her Tamu was up there with them and what she was seeing was a copy of Tamu, but not a true copy only an illusion that could speak, hear and see. Gnee stretched her hand out to touch Tamu, but her hand went right through. She teleported back up and shook her head.

"Now that's something. Who needs consoles, communicators or holograms?"

Things were getting interesting and Tamu added,

"There is also smell and hearing, but the best of all is our sixth sense, the sense of heightened awareness and intuition of psychic perception."

Wolf who had been silent throughout the whole thing stood up and teleported away without saying a word.

"What's his story?" Snapped Gnee.

"Leave him, he still has to answer for his action regarding Thanu." Zakrose answered.

Tamu challenged, "Anybody for a beer" and promptly disappeared reappearing on the platform seated at a Kiosk. The girls wasted no time in joining him. Ridmon went off to search for female company. They were sitting there when

Amnon and Michal with their five year old son Tomer came and sat down with them.

"It's hard to believe we have been here for five years already and extremely happy." Smiled Amnon.

"Time flies especially when one is busy. How are Ruth and Isaac?" Asked Gnee.

"They are fine. The boys really love it here and believe it or not miss that lizard thing." Replied Amnon.

The next hour the group chatted about this and that then parting company promising to tell Ki he was missed. Back on Cartone, things were running smoothly so Tamu visited the Reptilian settlements who were very engrossed in a new sport of mounted bird racing. Finding Ki he joined him seated at an amphitheatre where one could get a good view of proceedings. The scene was hilarious when riders attempting to get their birds on the start line were subject to painful pecks and a lot of jostling to bring the birds under control. As soon as the starters were satisfied a horn was sounded to begin the race. A mad house is all that could define the chaos as birds with their riders took off. The birds it seems were more interested in attacking each other than running down a track and this kind of disorganised mayhem is what appealed to the Reptiles preferring the more aggressive approach as opposed to controlled managed races. Not exciting enough. Riders got into the act as well and ended up in slugging matches spurred on by the roars of the crowds. It was a good laugh. Reptiles loved to have champions and to achieve recognition, so many would be free for all fighters jumped at the opportunity to take on the best and would train hard to do so. Like all contact sports there were weight divisions and each division had its champions. Ki always abstained from this reptilian tradition until this day when someone challenged him openly. He was in a pinch. Being the boss man's son and challenged from an arena or amphitheatre meant he could not refuse. The crowd went wild and started hissing louder and louder.

Ki got up and slowly ambled his way down to face his challenger. Just to look at his challenger told everyone this was a mean fighting machine all wrapped in a massive muscle bound and ferocious monster. Ki raised his arm as a signal of acceptance. Everyone held their breath as the two squared off then moved cautiously in a circle on opposite directions sizing each other up. Tamu cursed under his breath. This was going to end badly. The next moment Ki feinted to the right, his opponent was no fool and held his ground and that was his mistake a left back sweeping round house kick connected with such force it lifted the monster up into the air out for the count landing with a heavy thud. A stunned silence ensued then as one the crowd rose to its feet and roared. Ki was their new heavy weight champion and to top it all, Zi's son, which meant the future Reptilian leader. Tamu just smiled to himself. What a way to make a point. He had to hand it to Ki, very well executed with impeccable judgement. Then the smile left Tamu's face when some dumb frag challenged him. Looking down at his challenger he saw a large individual, nicely chiselled physique and the muscles on his legs meant he was one of the Regiment's troopers. Long muscles not short stocky ones, a martial arts fighter.

Tamu decided to have some fun with the guy, what the hell, and it was all in the fun anyway. Jumping down to his opponent he raised his arm into the air. A roar went up and immediately the Reptile attacked only his kick met fresh air. That day Tamu showed the Reptiles the meaning of bilocation confusing and frustrating his opponent so much the poor guy raised both arms in surrender. First Tamu was one, then all of a sudden two of him then back to one, but one that was kicked and punched harmlessly passing through the body as it were air. Then that same air became solid and Tamu would punch or kick just hard enough to drop the young challenger onto his rear end. After a few times of this happening is when the surrender came. Tamu bowed to him slightly as a gesture of respect, walked over to a huge boulder and shattered it with a finger strike. Bits of rock flew everywhere. The crowd just sat with mouths agape. This they had never seen before nor the trick played on the young challenger and began to whisper among themselves. Mis stood up and the crowd quietened down.

"Fellow friends and people, you have seen here today why Tamu is our Regiment Commander and believe me when I tell you this, I have fought side by side with his Father and later on with his son Tamu. None of you, not even Ki is any match for him in combat. Today we respect our leader." The crowd roared.

Tamu returned to the Regiment satisfied for pulling off the bilocation stunt so well. Seeing the expression on his face Svanis asked,

"You've been up to mischief again haven't you? I know that glint in your eye, come on out with it."

"First a kiss. Yes, I have been testing my bilocation out in a combat situation and I am impressed. Come here you adorable cat person, give me a hug."

Svanis was not prepared for what happened next. Jumping up and into the air at Tamu expecting him to catch her in his outstretched arms she went straight through and only on account of her feline abilities was able to land on her feet, with hands on hips shouted.

"That's not funny, not funny at all." And stormed out of the room.

Tamu realized his mistake so went in search of Gnee who was making entries onto a console. On his approach she looked up saying,

"Hi, what's up?"

"Want to have lunch with me on Karagan at one of those fancy restaurants?"

Gnee smelled a rat, "Where is Svanis?" She demanded.

"She's mad at me 'cause I played a trick on her which I shouldn't have done, so I thought we go to Karagan and I get her something nice as a piece offering and need your feminine intuition to help me." He replied.

"'I thought you grew out of that stage, anyway a break will be great and I can do some shopping as well."

Just then Zakrose butted in telepathically into their conversation, "Count me in."

"Hey girl, don't you know it's rude to listen in to others conversations." Protested Gnee.

Zakrose just laughed saying, "Well come on then you two."

Karagan's city Belus lived up to her name, she was beautiful as cities go. Lovely flower displays everywhere, shaded avenues, benches to sit on and low profile business and residential buildings. The trio decided to do their shopping first so with Tamu tagging along with much patience everyone eventually found what they wanted and a nice gift for Svanis then off to luncheon at a fancy and extremely popular Karagan restaurant. The place was packed so they had to wait for a table at the bar where drinks were ordered. An elderly man in his late sixties early seventies sat down at the bar, and ordered a drink. The trio were engaged in a conversation in English about trivial things when the old man apologetically asked.

"My apologies folks, but hearing you speak English surprised me. Are you from Karagan?"

"'No Sir, we are actually from Cartone, but originally Planet Ridmon."

There was an excited gleam in the man's eyes.

"Then you must have known my good friend Frank?"

The trio looked at the old man and Tamu broke the news to him.

"I am terribly sorry, but Uncle Frank passed away some time ago."

The man was silent then muttered, "So many of my friends gone, so many." Dropping his head downwards.

Now the trio were interested hearing who he was.

"Who are you Sir, if we may ask?"

The old man looked up at them and answered.

"I am Jack. I used to live on Ridmon, but was transferred back here to Karagan to deal with wild game problems years ago."

For a moment there was silence as the trio clicked. Then Zakrose got up and hugged him saying.

"Uncle Jack, we are Mike's children."

He looked from one to the other and smiled with tears in his eyes.

"I should have known it, you young man looks very much like your father, you two girls almost like your mother. Am I glad I bumped into you?"

A waiter came up and announced their table was ready.

"Uncle Jack, please join us?" Gnee asked.

"Don't mind if I do. I have so many questions I would like to ask."

The lunch was full of memories and laughter as Jack recounted stories about their Father, Mother and Jane. For the trio it was a blessing to find this man still alive who knew their Father way back when. When he told them about the incident in the Zambesi valley with the six poachers and how it was then how Jack came to be on Ridmon, they lifted their eyebrows. This was the first time they ever heard of that.

"Uncle Jack, what do you do now with yourself?" Tamu asked.

"I am retired, my wife died a few years ago and my children are all grown up living around. One I think is on Ridmon." He replied.

"Would you like to come back with us to our world, it's not as fancy as this place, but whenever you want you can visit." Tamu asked projecting an image into Jacks mind.

"Hey cut that out, your Dad used to do that to me just to piss me off. Yes, I would very much like that. I'll need to get some things first. Where can we meet?"

The question was never answered and Jack found himself in his lounge wide eyed and disbelieving.

"You kids as well?"

They nodded. Jack shook his head and went about his business collecting a few things then wrote a note and left it on the lounge table addressed to his daughter. With case in hand he simply said,

"Ready when you are."

Back on Cartone Tamu showed Jack to his quarters with quaint stylish furnishings and decor, offering a nice panoramic view of the seaside.

"Uncle Jack, we all eat together as a family here on Cartone. Get settled then come to the lounge. It is easy to find just follow the signs. There you will find a bar and comfortable chairs. We will join you a bit later. Tamu beat it out of there like grease lightning with Svanis gift in his hand. She was sitting on a bench outside in a small grassy enclave watching waves crash onto the sand.

"Svanis" he called.

"Yeah, what you want." She replied still starring at the waves.

"I have something for you."

"Another trick I suppose?" She pouted.

He came around the bench in front of her and knelt on one knee, took out a small package, opened it towards her and there, shining in the light were two rings. A beautiful engagement ring and a wedding band. Both with exquisite inlays mounted in platinum of her favourite precious stone, Rubies. She focused on the rings and slowly the anger in her eyes faded as realism hit home.

"Will you marry me Svanis of Jaqmuz from Planet Eureka?" He asked.

Svanis burst out sobbing, something Tamu had never seen her do before and it troubled him. She lifted her tear filled eyes and looked into his.

"Yes, yes, yes," Diving into his arms.

They would be married on Ridmon, a small affair with only close friends and relatives present then a reception would be held in the City of Spes on Cartone. The date of the wedding was set for two months hence to allow for preparations. The marriage would be officiated by non-other than, Protector Friend. Jack was enjoying his life, no longer alone and lonesome, he was with a bunch of young people who made him feel important again and Gnee finding out Jack was an excellent wild animal expert, told him she would take him to see something so very different on Tatran one of the days. The meal times were what he enjoyed the most, real family stuff. The Giving of Thanks, to the bantering between them, the jokes, the laughter and their serious side. I am an old fool he thought to himself, but at least in my old age life seems it's going to be very interesting. So Jake became part of the family. Gnee found her grandfather figure again and was happy. One day she grabbed him and teleported though a portal on to Tatran and down to the Regiments camp. Dodge was there with his family.

Sometimes in this life there are mysteries that can't be explained and best left to a higher order to figure out. When Jake saw Dodge he simply walked up to him then draped his arm across the creatures shoulders to which Dodge did the same and then two walked off. Gnee's eyeballs almost shot out of their sockets. How was it possible, this was a first? They found Jack two days later in a cave cradled in the arms of Dodge rocking to and fro grunting pathetic sounds of distress. Jack had died of a heart attack. Tamu gently released Jack from Dodge and sent his body to Ridmon where the wasps laid him to rest in the cemetery. Then Tamu lifted Dodge up, projected an image in his brain and Dodge shuffled quickly to a section of the cave and brought out his mate and child to stand in front of Tamu who took Dodge's hand and placed it on Gnee's shoulder. Then teleported the creature with its family onto Cartone into Gnee's personal lodgings with an outside large enclosed quart yard.

"Why did you put his arm on my shoulder "Gnee asked that night at supper?

"To show him you were his mother figure." He replied.

Humans on earth have their greatest friend, a dog, an intelligent canine and protector. Well on Cartone they had Dodge, who proved beyond a shadow of doubt to be one of the best tame animals the family had ever acquired and they loved him. All good things come to those who wait and Dodge was one of those things. This Kayi was an intelligent creature and learned fast. He loved Gnee so much he almost slept in the same bed. It was just because she was his mother and didn't want her in any danger. This caused other problems, Boram her husband. In the end things worked out and Dodge understood, but never let her out of his sight and would accompany her everywhere which did raise some eyebrows from time to time. Gnee advised everyone to not take Dodge for granted, he was formidably strong and would destroy anyone if he thought they posed a threat to Gnee.

One day Tamu took Dodge's wife and child to collect food supplements Kayi style on Tatran when Casjori contacted him. The Aliens are back in G48 Major and their fleet was huge heading for Trafodj. Tamu aborted the Kayi's food collection and sent both back to Cartone. He then sent out an emergency assembly call to every Drone and Wasp under his command. Assembled every Regiment fully armed and ready then called in the Reptiles and told them this was killing time. The Alien fleet was on its way oblivious to the fact Tamu was about to hit them with everything he had.

"Fleet forty strong battle ships accompanied by twenty very large troop transports. Warning, this is a major invasion fleet approximately one day away from Trafodj."

Cartone unleashed its forces into the Alien fleet attacking in well-co-ordinated and synchronized attack formations. Wasps pulled off their hat tricks by opening portals right inside the battleships and fired with everything they had withdrawing back inside their portal and reappearing somewhere else in the battle arena. Forty Battleships exploded almost simultaneously. Then Tamu changed the game plan and beamed his Regiments into ten of the troop transports and the Drones dispensed with the remainder. In side those troop transports was bedlam when Alien marine met Reptile and Matabele troopers dressed in full battle gear. This was hand to hand combat at its fiercest. The Aliens were no push over and fought every inch of the way.

But, the sheer ferocity of the attackers consumed, destroyed, killed and fraged everything living in sight clinically and mercilessly. Hideous was the word to best describe the carnage in those ten Transports. Mis turned to Tamu who had fought alongside him and hissed.

"It has been a long time since I have enjoyed myself like that."

"Mis, you always enjoy yourself in any fight, but I must admit, these guys made us work for our victory and yes Sir, respect." Replied Tamu.

"So let's do a body count of our side and see how effective they were." Grunted Mis.

"Ted, do helmets check please." Tamu asked one Drone.

A few moments later. "All present and correct."

"Thanks Ted."

"You know what amazes me, you give orders make last minute adjustments and all that and you never say a word, it's all through your mind?" Queried Mis.

"Yes, I will explain at another time in the meanwhile, we get our people off these transports." and the Drones beamed everyone aboard.

Ten Transports disintegrated and the Alien fleet was no more, not before a transmission was received on the alien planet. "Fleet destroyed by unseen craft and troop Transports taken out by overwhelming attack force from within.

"Tamu, you are a brother and in all the years both you and your Father have given us a place and trusted us like a family and we are honoured."

"Mis, you are an amazing person and I have so much respect for you. You are a link to my past and my Father and you are my extended family." Tamu answered.

Mis regarded Tamu quietly for a while then responded.

"Tamu, I am an old man and have seen so much. One day I will be gone, Zi will be gone and a lot many others. Promise me one thing son of Mike, you will keep my people safe and protected."

Tamu replied. "It will be done."

Time was passing and Svanis became anxious, would the marriage take place, what with all that was going on? She chose her wedding grown, organized the decorations and fittings, invites and all the other host of considerations. Tamu made sure the Great Hall on Ridmon was ready then on Karagan he demanded the best there was or the best that money could buy which ever fell into a successful end result. The day dawned and Tamu abiding by Christian tradition was not allowed to see Svanis until she appeared at the altar which was hastily erected that same day. Zakrose and Gnee as bride's maids pampered over her making sure everything was in place, the dress, a simple but tasteful white long sleeved, closed neck satin full length design. A charming ruby necklace with matching ear rings and her hair pulled back into a bun, a head band of diamond and ruby studded satin. White gloves and a white veil complete with bouquet of red and white flowers. They even slipped a garter up her leg

Meanwhile, Tamu refused to wear a traditional wear and opted out for an amazing refined Amakrin set of clothing consisting of a long sleeve thigh length jacket with high closed neck and matching slacks which he purposefully ordered in platinum colour. A broad red waist sash on top of which a wide platinum belt inlaid with gold tasteful designs wrapped around his waist. The hours ticked by with both bride and groom getting a little edgy. Zakrose brought in Zud, Svanis father to walk her down the aisle. Ki was Tamu's best man and the hour struck and so did planet Ridmon's band begin to play a rather catchy melody. Tamu walked up a carpeted staircase in the Great Hall to the Alter and turned to wait for Svanis, his bride. The invited guests were seated on either side of the carpet. The Great Hall filled with white light and Protector Friend emerged hovering next to Tamu. On queue the Ridmon Band changed its tempo and played a beautiful tear jerking piece of music just to get the assembled audience into the mood. The minutes ticked by and finally Svanis emerged in all her glory. She was radiant, lovely and shinning with joy. Her steps were deliberate, evenly paced. Tamu's heart jumped into his mouth, she was without words, beautiful.

At the steps the Father let her go and Svanis stepped up one at a time until reaching Tamu. Zakrose and Gnee stood to one side, and then Ki walked up the isle in his battle dress to stand next to Tamu. Protector Friend began his marriage speech.

"Friends, everyone gathered here, we are about to celebrate a wedding between Tamu and Svanis and there is just one thing I am able to do to make this wedding a true witness is to bring in Tamu's Father, his Mother and Jane his foster mother and Penagee."

Four ghostly figures appeared next to Protector Friend.

Silence. Tamu, Zakrose and Gnee almost fell over seeing their parents happy and smiling and right there with them and tears streaked down the girls cheeks. Protector Friend began.

"Do you Tamu, son of Mike and Tara, take this, Svanis daughter of Zud to be your lawful wedded wife, to love and to hold until death do you part?"

"I do."

Turning to Svanis he asked.

"Do you Svanis, daughter of Zud take Tamu, son of Mike and Tara as your lawful husband to love and to hold until death do you part?"

"I do."

"You may place the ring Tamu."

Ki thrust it into his Tamu's hand hissing broadly. The ring slid onto Svanis right hand ring finger next to her engagement ring.

"Therefore, with the powers invested in me by the Almighty, whom I serve, I pronounce you, Tamu and Svanis, husband and wife. Tamu you may kiss the bride."

Tamu wasted no time and kissed Svanis with such passion the spectators whistled with approval. Protector Friend faded slowly from the scene and with him the smiling waving ghostly figures. On Cartone, the City Spes was plunged into a celebration they would not soon forget. It raged for two days, continued on to Planet Ridmon. Casjori, the woman spokesperson from Tatran extended her congratulations and thanked Tamu for his timely intervention of the Aliens. Many more messages of congratulation were received. Zi asked Tamu to bring his wife to their settlement. So Tamu teleported in to the Reptilia settlement with Svanis. Ki greeted them grinning, his fangs certainly not demonstrating his inner feelings. In the amphitheatre a group of Reptilians were formed numbering fifty males and females.

"Svanis whatever happens; this is a symbolic wedding Reptile style."

Zi and Mis with KI took up their positions in a triangle around Tamu and Svanis. The female Witch doctor jumped into the ring and began her incantations, Tamu pulled Svanis to him her back and buttocks pressed against him firmly. The hissing grew louder, then Mis handed Tamu a cup and told him to give to Svanis to drink and to drink himself.

Tamu complied and suddenly his brain went crazy and his genitals erected with a force he had not known before. Svanis, her sexual cravings aroused to fever pitch backed harder into Tamu. Then Mis roared aloud and Tamu could not contain himself anymore, took Svanis and fraged her time and time again. The Reptiles were beside themselves and an orgy erupted into a mass sexual party. Spent and utterly tired Tamu teleported to his room with Svanis and slept for two days.

Dragging themselves bleary eyed and bedraggled into the dining room, Zakrose chuckled to herself. Two weddings in one day and the last in front of Reptiles and actually consummating their marriage visible of everyone, that was freaky.

"Feeling better?" Asked Zakrose innocently.

"Spare me your concerns sister dear, just be careful I don't introduce you to the Reptilians sex drug, it's deadly."

"No thanks,"

"Don't be too sure Iron lady." With that he kissed her hard on the lips.

"Tamu, behave yourself, she is your sister." scolded Gnee, walking into the room with Dodge trailing behind.

A month later the authority on Trafodj sent an urgent message to Cartone.

"Unknown forces invading need assistance desperately. Enemy ground forces large and well equipped and have deployed." Message ends.

Thirty thousand Reptiles and their "Cavalry" and twenty thousand Matabele troops poured onto Trafodj backed by one thousand Wasps, a hundred Drones and two thousand Tranks. Up in space Wasps took on the attacking armada of ships. On the ground the Reptiles washed over enemy forces identified only by their looks. The Aliens were back. While the Regiment secured strategic infrastructures and peoples of Trafodj clearing out small pockets of the enemy, the Reptiles dealt with the opposing ground forces in running pitched battles. This was one time the "Cavalry" proved their worth and what a terrible weapon they turned out to be. Those beaks and feet claws were devastating, tearing ripping and killing alongside their Reptilian hordes that decimated any opposition thanks to the body stockings casualties were minimal. Wasps swooped in laying air fire while Reptiles added the finishing touches to any fortifications, any enemy troops on the ground. It was a sheer blood bath to the likes of which had not been seen since taking out the Alien troop Transports in a previous encounter. Tamu not one to sit in some command post was in the front line fighting hand to hand using teleportation tactics to move his troops right into the heart of the enemy where they least expected it taking out command posts which resulted in confusion and misdirection. Up in space the situation was just as confusing and demoralizing to the attacking force who suffered blow after blow from a force they could not see or pin point. A few stray salvos hit the planet killing both Aliens and Tamu's forces before the Wasps were able to illuminate their opponents completely. The skies above Trafodj were littered with orange flashes as ships exploded. Air to air battles between the Wasps and Alien Fighter Cruisers. The Aliens were not giving up without a fight and stubbornly resisted. Days turned into weeks. Many unfortunate Trafordjians died in cross fires, used as shields or just murdered. Reptiles were not renowned for consideration on the battle field when driven by blood lust and contributed their share of carnage on local inhabitants which compelled Tamu to withhold the cavalry in populated areas knowing the birds didn't differentiate between Alien and Trafodjian.

Tranks became indispensable not only on the battle front, but as rescue and first aid support. Many questions were brought up concerning Trafodj defences and it's Military. In the past, they refused support from planet Ridmon and now were caught with their pants down and having to pay a high price. After a month and a half, all Alien's on the planet were defeated. No prisoners were taken. Counting their losses the regiment suffered three thousand dead and another five thousand injured. Trafodjian forces suffered a fifteen thousand dead in total before they were pulled out of the battle and used as construction crews to clean up behind the front lines. Civilian deaths amounted to three hundred thousand. Total figure of Alien casualties was not known yet clean-up crews counted in their thousands. Twenty battleships and their fighter contingents could not be estimated accurately, but loss of life approximated to seventy thousand.

Tamu withdrew his troops and Wasps to Cartone to regroup and debrief field commanders. The Reptiles incurred many losses especially the Cavalry unit. A mere one and a half thousand out of nearly four thousand riders and birds returned. Now was the time to reinvent the body stockings, or at least, improve on their design considerably. Most of the Regiments casualties came from heavy canon fire and no stockings could survive direct hits, only protected the wearer from flying debris generated by canon blasts except for large objects hurtling at speed would crush or brake limbs even kill. The scientists on Ridmon were assigned the task of coming up with a solution to improve or redesign a battle suit offering a greater protection without loss of mobility to the wearer. The attack on Trafodj also took Cartone by surprise so patrols of Wasps now had an additional duty on their roster, the solar system of Trafodj. One general after his debrief had some questions of his own to put to Tamu, Zakrose and Svanis.

"How is it the Wasps and Drones don't get blasted out of existence? Those Alien ships were equipped with awesome fire power. It just seems difficult to comprehend they suffer no casualties."

"On Earth, there are small birds in their thousands who fly about in flocks. Those flocks twist and turn and seem to orchestrate their own aerial dance in complete unison and hardly ever fly collectively in a straight line. I have seen this on Karagan. The reason for this is twofold. The larger the group the better the chances of spotting a predator and confuse and overwhelm a predator through mobbing and agile flight. The Wasps swarm in a similar manner and effectively confuse ships gunnery computers as the swarm darts in and out and between ships. When we say in and out we refer to their ability to open portals inside docking bays and fire killing salvos without actually being in the ship. The moment they fire they close the portal and emerge again in another position inside or outside the battle arena and pounce repeatedly from all directions without set patterns confusing the enemy who can't avoid hitting each other or their own fighters. Wasps are highly effective and work as a single minded unit in complete unison or individually, but know exactly where other Wasps are positioned and their game plans in fractions of a second." Tamu replied.

"I like that, opening a portal right inside the enemy ship and destroying it without even being near the ship at all. One more question. How do those creatures survive in Space? Amazing creatures and thank you for that, makes me more secure in my estimation of the players in any battle field on or above a planet."

"You're welcome General, and those creatures survive on all the gases which would kill us, but to explain more simply would be to say they feed on Ionized Hydrogen and Helium which is Plasma." Said Zakrose.

The man saluted and left the room. Svanis asked.

"Do those Generals get into the thick of the fighting or do they just set back somewhere safe and bark orders?"

"Not a chance, they are on the ground with their troops in combat directing as the battles pan out. You saw the crystal helmets the men wear, well those are no ordinary helmets just for head protection. They are the eyes and ears of the Regiment. No need for communication posts consoles and monitors the helmets channel info between the troops to the officers and back again across the entire regiment. Every single man or woman knows exactly in real time what is going on. We asked the question to our scientists about all that info coming in and going out, a soldier did not have time to concentrate on his job. That's when it gets interesting. All info is directed to a Wasp whose sole purpose is to relay, analyse, instruct different groups in different areas, and keep Command informed and relay orders from command back to ground forces all at once. Brilliant, absolutely brilliant. Those helmets are connected to the hand held crystal rods and continually charge them. The helmets receive their power source from Drones via power transmittance over the entire grid of land forces. It's a technological master piece."

"That means the helmets are constantly working even on their shelves when not in use?" She enquired.

"Definitely, otherwise how do we mobilize our troops simultaneously without sounding alarms or anything similar? Each soldier wears a chain around the neck fitted with a mini transponder tuned into the helmet. This devise can receive and send signals about the position and condition of the wearer such as alive, wounded or dead. It also emits a tiny pulse of energy into the soldier waking that person up or vibrates which tells the soldier its battle stations."

Svanis was impressed, such technology was mind boggling not to forget to mention the Rods as they were called. The soldier's standard weapon of combat. A blast from that and it was tickets, adjustable to different size and strength force for short to medium target size and ranges or long range up to two kilometres away with pin point accuracy by the helmet. The soldier for example would see an enemy behind a wall by thermal identification in the helmet and the Rod automatically adjusts itself and fires the appropriate blast to take out the enemy and part of the wall he or she was hiding behind. In the case of a non-combatant, a friendly as it were, details would be relayed giving position and condition to support vehicles to the rear.

Cartone cremated its dead with full honours in a solemn ceremony and inscribed the names of deceased personnel on a wall of remembrance in the Regiments barracks. These included the names of Reptiles. Three months later the first prototype battle suit was tested under laboratory conditions. A whole battery of tests, fire, water, freezing radiation, chemical, viral, blast, small arms fire all proved beyond expectation. The suit included a back pack which fitted snugly around the wearers back no thicker than five centimetres as part of the whole. Its function was to transfer high concentrate mineral compounds and liquids into the wearer's body through patch like membranes that adhered to the wearers back and conveyed intravenously directly into the blood stream. The soldier could survive and function for an entire month before requiring a refill by special valve sockets and a further one month then brought back in for two weeks rehabilitation. The hood was one with the whole suit without openings for eye, ear or mouth and seeing was done by the helmets. All body stockings were recalled and altered while newer ones sent out. It became mandatory to wear the body stockings at all times whilst on standby. The battle suits were housed in a small kidney pouch on the back of the wearer's body attached to the body stocking. They were activated by a transducer on the wearer's body on receipt of signals from Command. The transformation was instant enclosing a soldier in a cocoon of virtual indestructible synthetic armour. Command discovered a way to alter the body functions and speed up the process of digestion through chemicals in the food and subsequent bowel movement to coincide with set intervals. The Regiment rotated every two weeks with complete standby units on immediate call.

Zi and Mis met with Tamu and a team of planet Ridmon scientists to figure out a way to fix the birds brains so as to be more controllable and to see how to give them some body protection. His group headed down to the Bird pens and recorded video images on a small scientific console then securing a specimen bird on to a floating platform sending it through a portal into a laboratory on planet Ridmon. The Cavalry division having suffered many casualties were thinking of disbanding. Mis convinced them to wait and see what planet Ridmon could come up with. Tamu and the scientists inspected the Reptile soldiers on standby just to make sure their special body stockings were functional in the proper way. Because of their talons, each soldier was issued with a pair of hand and foot gloves which they wore only if warranted because the Reptiles liked to get in close and dirty using their talons as weapons with great dexterity and killing efficiency. Rods were issued to them, but this was considered as a secondary application and only used to breach walls and other obstacles to get at the enemy. Technology on planet Ridmon was of a highly advanced standard and did not take long for a crystal helmet made to fit for the birds to be tested so the bird's handler was brought in to assist with testing. Getting the helmet onto the birds head proved to be a mission so the creature was pinioned and clamped tight in a temporary stand. Once the helmet was on, the bird became submissive and responded well to the handlers heel and stick tapping commands on either side of its neck and chest. Tests were repeated and refined until perfected then with the Reptile in full battle dress the scientists calibrated the bird's helmet to the riders. A collar was fixed around the bird's neck and on it a pouch in which was its specially designed body stocking with almost the same activation method as the soldiers. The procedure was to activate the body stocking, lead the birds in Clamping stands, fix the helmet in place and from then, saddle up and both bird and rider were ready to be deployed. As with the Reptiles, the foot talons and beak remained exposed and covers applied as warranted. Further tests in attack mode proved the value of the new combination between bird and rider. The cavalry was now certain of minimal casualties and practised and practised refining their activation times down to the absolute minimum. Standby birds were secured in their clamping stands, with body stockings activated free to shift body weight even to lie down, but with the necks clamped to prevent their beaks from causing any damage.

Spes City like all cities expanded with demand and city planners were careful to keep its sky line as low as prescribed. Moving people around soon posed a problem and so a system of transport was introduced which both was aesthetically pleasing as functional and above all, silent. Controlled by a computer system, the streamlined carriages suspended beneath a rail configuration with a capacity of one hundred passengers equipped with voice recognition consoles at five doors on either side of the carriages. The propulsion was governed by an electromagnetic system powered by rechargeable power packs. A passenger just spoke into the console the destination and the computer did the rest delivering passengers to the nearest stop closest to their destinations. Carriages operated on twin rail systems both incoming and outgoing. Restaurants, shops, and hair dressing salons, Gyms, various small businesses, and hotels, side walk cafés, Museum, a Library and a much needed Laundry. The city bustled from morning to night with evening entertainment in form of Shows, dance and the side walk cafés with their own live musicians. Soldiers off duty frequented these places with their wives or girlfriends while the single ones just hoping to dance with a pretty girl or in the case of the girls with a handsome man.

Cartone was coming into its own and the services of someone of Tamu's calibre, was a little over qualified now that the Regiment was in excellent shape with highly trained officers in charge? Wasps and Drones were more than capable of commanding the Regiments forces in battle scenarios. So Tamu called in Zakrose, Ridmon and Gnee, sat them down and told them what he was going to do.

"Listen you guys, I have decided to spend some time off world with Svanis."

He watched their faces for reactions and saw none.

"Ok, what's the problem?" He asked.

"We are family and since we have been here on Cartone we have become closer than we have ever been. So I guess we feel where you go we go. Where exactly are you going by the way?" Enquired Gnee.

She had him there, he didn't really know or hadn't figured it out yet, but it entailed an adventure.

"Well don't really know right now, however what I can tell you it's about going out there and seeing if another world or other worlds exist. That's the size of it." He answered.

Zakrose smiled." Admit, you're bored, not enough adrenalin rush."

"You got me, now what?" He asked.

"Well Brother didn't it occur to you we might also be feeling a little adventurous and need some time out." Muttered Gnee.

"So you want to come with and bring your husband, Dodge with his family and Zakrose with whoever and Ridmon with someone. Perhaps Wolf and family too?"

"Yeah, and you bring that gorilla thing Ki and his wife." Pouted Gnee.

"Break it up you two. Tamu, we come without Dodge and without Wolf, but with Ki and Nah and a Regiment commando of one hundred men and women, one Drone, thirteen Wasps and four Tranks. That should cover it." Suggested Zakrose.

"You're serious aren't you?" Asked Gnee.

"She's dead serious, trust me." Answered Ridmon.

There was one thing they had to do and that was to release Dodge and his family back on Tatran. Gnee was distressed about it yet knew it was for the best so she altered the Kayi family memory's and teleported them into their cave. A month later a Drone accompanied by thirteen Wasps jumped out of G48 Major for destinations unknown. On board a group of people full of anticipation for what they might find hoping it would not be the last thing they did. In the Drones lower levels were the four Tranks with spare parts and a large supply of power modules along with a good stock of Ridmon Beer and Whiskey and quarters for the troops. Quick assembly survival cabins, support equipment including an ingenious fold out medical clinic, water purifiers and oxygen machines. They were ready as ready could be. The Drone chartered their portal jumps meticulously making sure of a return path in case of retreat and or return. Three weeks into repeated jumps brought them into a spiral Galaxy. They needed to find a suitable place to rest up and give the Drone some breathing space of its own. Wasps darted out jumping through portals and came across one planet likely to support life but on closer inspection decided against it. A hot, humid and densely vegetated planet on which grew many weird looking plants. The type that feed on you. So the search continued for another month until they found the ideal place in a small solar system with a fairly new sun. Caution is the better part of valour so Tamu went on Battle stations and beamed down the four Tranks, divided his team equally into them while the sisters remained on the Drone.

Four Wasps hovered above scanning as the Tranks made their way along a ridge in formation. The terrain was similar to Earths which could mean a whole lot of things like a Jurassic environment judging by the type of vegetation. Or it could mean a whole different ball game, something even worse. A few days later came to an ideal place. Well protected, on high ground with water nearby offering a three hundred and sixty degree clear view. The knoll was vegetated suggesting limited cover, but enough to hide the Tranks from view and camouflage the men's movements. Tamu did not set up camp, careful to wait it out a few days and be sure nothing was lurking around on the ground or underneath it and commanded the Wasps to do just that. A week passed and nothing. Still Tamu's sixth sense itched at his brain. The Tranks were positioned in all round defence and at night everyone slept in full battle dress inside the Tranks providing a round the clock parameter watch from up down and around. Wasps hung suspended above the Tranks also in all round defence scanning. Tamu's intuition paid off, two days later they appeared. A group of fur clad full length animal skinned individuals, hooded and walking upright with primitive spears and clubs. The Tranks cameras zoomed in and on monitors close ups appeared. Tamu whistled. Cave men. So he was right, this was similar to a period of Earths evolution sixty five million years after the Cretaceous period when the Neanderthal man appeared, but these people were humans, grubby and dirty yet humans all the same. This was an amazing piece of luck. They watched as the group wound its way past them down in the shallow valley and headed off out of site. One Wasp followed. Tamu telepathically contacted the girls.

"Did you see that?" He asked.

Gnee's excited voice jumped in first.

"Geez Tamu, do you know what we have walked into, the beginnings of a period of evolution of man."

"Isn't it great? But, you know we can't interfere don't you." Zakrose butted in.

"How can we interfere, making friends with some of them, dressed like them, will not change anything if we live with them and be part of their lives surely." Gnee protested.

"Gnee, you forget one thing, what about Ki, Nah and Svanis. How do you think those simple people will react to them?" Tamu elaborated.

"Oooh! You are right."

"Tell you what. When the Wasp who's following them reports back I will let you study those people from inside the Wasp and no way must you interfere even in a life and death situation. Are we in agreement?"Tamu asked.

"Yes, I agree and thanks."

The Wasp returned and downloaded image data into a Trank where Tamu and Ki watched. Sure enough they headed down a section of a rocky ravine and into a cave about ten meters from the ravine floor by hauling themselves up a platted leather thong ladder.

"Interesting." Tamu nodded to which Ki hissed.

"Yum, yum."

"Hey, easy big boy. They probably taste crappie you know, never wash or wipe their arse."

"Yuagh!" Ki hissed.

"OK you guy's what about us up here, boring?" Zakrose protested.

"Come on down, we will set up a temp base here for tonight then look for a more inaccessible location tomorrow. It will still be full battle dress. OK?"

The next moment the girls arrived clothed to the teeth in battle gear carrying their Rods and stood before Tamu like soldiers at attention. Tamu gave them a few moments them burst out laughing bending at the waist and dropping to his knees clutching at his side.

"What's the joke Tamu?" demanded Svanis stamping her foot.

"Leave him Svanis Honey, who knows what tickles a man." Proclaimed Zakrose.

Walking off to one of the Tranks followed by the rest of the women.

The Matabele were puzzled, but didn't flinch a muscle. After a while Tamu composed himself and got to his feet, teleported into the Drone and uploaded the caveman images.

"Ted could you reproduce replicas of those cloths down to the last detail?"

"Yes Boss no problemo."

"You've been chatting with Echo?" Tamu asked.

"Yes Boss. He teaches me new words to use when you are aboard."

"OK Ted, send those cloths down when they are ready, and thanks."

"Anytime Boss"

Tamu teleported down to camp really amused, thinking how human Echo was becoming. Actually he enjoyed that Wasp and his use of expressions. Gathering some of the troops together he advised them of the cloths coming in shortly and to tell him when they did. Svanis had her helmet and battle suit off. Tamu grabbed her in a vice grip and kissed the nape of her neck which always made her knees weak.

"So my little kitten did you miss me?"

"Let go Tamu, I warn you."

"Hmmmm! That sounds threatening and my knees are shaking, sweet thing,"

"If you don't let me go then there will be no more you know what." She purred.

"Aw shucks Babe." He mocked and let her go.

Svanis attacked full on going for the soft spot and hit fresh air. She spun around, no Tamu.

"Not fair." She screamed and went to join the other girls.

A while later the caveman clothes and ancient weapons were beamed down. Tamu inspected them, perfect. Calling the Matabele group he had chosen earlier on, he addressed them.

"Gentlemen, you see those cloths on the ground I want each and every one of you to put those cloths on over your body stockings with your rods and when you have done that call me."

There was no rush, each individual stood clothed in caveman furs over their battle suits. Tamu walked up and down checking, all appeared authentic. Then he dressed up and stood there transformed and joined his men. Next moment Zakrose walked over.

"What the hell is this?" She commanded.

Tamu changed his voice and answered, "Tamu's orders Madam."

She walked off looking for her brother and Tamu smiling from ear to ear teleported the group out quickly before she realized she had been duped. Down in the valley he started to pick up the pace to a jog, and thirty figures ran down a path like a bunch of untrained and careless cavemen. Back in the camp Zakrose made a mental count of the Matabele and hello, something was wrong. Thirty were missing. How convenient she thought, Tamu was up to his old tricks again. She had her own tricks and commanded a Wasp to seek out and follow Tamu. Of course the Wasp obeyed, he was Echo and it was his job to look after his "Boss". Meanwhile, down on the ground a marathon was in progress and Tamu telepathically advised his men to be on the lookout, dinner might be around somewhere.

Sure enough, they rounded a bend into a ravine and there it was. A huge ugly grey fury creature looking like a shaggy mammoth without a trunk or tusks, equipped with fangs like a sabre tooth tiger. It roared and charged. Bad luck, these were the Matabele and they never backed down from a fight and attacked. Tamu leaned back and watched. His men swarmed over the creature killing it instantly. Teleporting the remains of the carcass which was substantial to the base of the cave where the cave dwellers lived, they made their way back to camp carrying choice pieces of off cuts and entered the camp in triumph. That night the Matabele dinned well and drank their fill to contentment around a nice warm bon fire. Tamu was in the dog box with Svanis, but he didn't care, he was having fun for a change. One of the advantages of the battle suits is that a person could sleep on the open ground without fear of being eaten, bitten or the weather. So Tamu curled up on the ground under one of the Tranks and went to sleep. During the night Svanis curled in next to him,

"Husband, you don't sleep without me you understand even when I am mad at you."

"Yes the love of my life, come here."

The next day Tamu and Svanis uncoiled themselves from each other to the rising sun and stood up. It was a glorious sun rise. Zakrose strolled over and stood silently next to Svanis admiring the view. It didn't take long for Gnee and Ridmon to join them.

"I suppose you have a plan brother dear?" Asked Zakrose.

"Simple really, we keep moving looking for an ideal base from where we can operate under disguise."

The Matabele commander ran up and saluted.

"Your order's Sir?"

"Relax Boram. Discipline will be maintained on a more relaxed level, however obedience is without question and your bunch will maintain standards which means you guys are not on Karagan's hot spots, but on a planet which may have some nasty surprises an it does not pay to get too confident just because you have the suits on. You get it?"

Boram confirmed. "Yes Sir." About turned, and left to join his men.

"Why do you treat him like one of your Reptiles?" Gnee asked hotly.

"Because my dear sister, proof is in the pudding and until he proves to me he is what I expect him to be, I will continue to treat him how I please."

"He is my husband for frag sake." Her voice raised in anger.

"All the more reason to stand up, and be a man."

"Be a man? He is my man so lay off Tamu." She declared.

"Suit yourself sweetheart. He frags up, he is out, get me." Gnee walked off in a huff.

"A bit hard on the girl aren't you?" Questioned Zakrose.

"Dear sister, we are different. It does not mean we are a class apart, it simply means who ever we have as partners may not be like us with special gifts and therefore are under tremendous pressure to fit in. Confidence, in knowing our partners, whoever they might be, and seeing them excel themselves to their limits will make us respect and admire them. Ultimately, accept them into our fold."

"You are a hard bastard Tamu, but completely right" remarked Zakrose.

"Thank you sister and just for the record, Dad married Tara so I am no bastard." He walked away before an argument escalated into a mini war.

The Drone Ted beamed up the Tranks and left thirty two Matabele down on the planet dressed like cavemen.

"Ok Boram, let's get this show on the road, move them out and remember, we are cavemen so act like it."

They took off at a slow jog winding their way along game trails Tamu in the lead. The pace settled and continued hour after hour across open grassy planes down to rocky ravines and out to thick vegetation and back out to savannah type surroundings. All the while everyone and everything was searching, scanning and watching. Then the runners hit dense jungle then everything changed. Tamu and his team took up into the trees and waited. Wasps scanned ahead and sure enough located some nasties. Unbelievable, survivors of a Cretaceous past here were Velociraptor dinosaurs and these were fast intelligent calculating predators with good eye sight. Tamu was amused, here he was on a planet in the process of evolutionary changes and by all rights the dinosaurs down in the jungle were supposed to be extinct if one followed Earths evolution patterns. Predators such as these were well worth a study and should make Gnee very happy.

Velociraptor were smart with an unmistakeable basic logic. Geared to one thing and one thing only, kill to eat. One can't imagine how anything really works in reality along the food chain and how it was possible to tap into resources such as these primitive creatures and find a way to control them. Use them for advantage at the same time allow them their natural instinct. Perhaps a change in diet might entice them. Tamu selected one possible candidate and deliberately stood in front of it. A morsel right there, too much to ignore and the creature lunged only to find itself flat on its side with a throbbing head. The creature got up, shook its head, focused on its target and lunged again only to be smashed to the ground again. Its brain worked, calculated and realized a new tactic was needed to get that tasty piece of whatever it was. So it circled, bearing its rows of vicious teeth, flexed its leg and arm talons ready to strike again.

Tamu played another trick and KI found himself facing an ancestor full on. Food was all the Dino was concerned about and there it was, blinked, a shape change, but food all the same. Dino meet Lizard, Dino loses. The creature lay on its side knocked into oblivion with Ki standing over it, hands on hips hissing with pleasure. Dino became an experimental genie pig. It was furious to find itself clamped and secured and effectively hog tied. Even its jaws were taped tight hanging high up in the trees. Ki enjoyed the moment and slapped the Dino across its face, staring into its furious eyes and hissing. Something in that Dino's brain registered and it almost purred. The sound was low and guttural. Ki had found a friend, a really unpredictable friend. Tamu tried something and lowered the Dino to the ground, released its shackles except its jaws and Ki stood in front of it ready to react. The Dino wobbled to its feet, sniffed the air and came up to Ki and rubbed its head against his body. You could have slapped Tamu's face with a sledge hammer. Ki stroked the Dino's head and hissed something then took the restraining bands from the Dino's jaws. It just stood there waiting. Ki hissed and it scampered off. Gnee was impressed. That Dino was a mean creature by all rights yet was putty in Ki's hands and she had to find out how come.

"Ok KI out with it, what's with you and your Dino friend?"

KI roared shaking with laughter." The Dino was a she and I told her if she didn't behave I would frag the shYte out of her."

"Come off it Ki, tell the truth now, please."

"It's hard to say, but you had better get back up into the trees because Dino will be coming back with her brothers and sisters."

No sooner had he said that when Dino bounded back with her family, all ten of them. Gnee was gone, teleporting up into the trees leaving Ki to face the music. Nature is really strange sometimes how she brings together bed fellows like these vicious carnivores and a Reptile from another planet. Nah was beamed down to stand beside Ki as the Dino's circled and sniffed the air both Ki and Nah hissed loudly and a transformation seemed to come over the ten Dino's who became docile, responsive and affectionately rubbed themselves against Ki and Nah and playfully bumped them. Ki and Nah seemed to be enjoying themselves and when the Dino's got bored ran off Ki and Nah followed.

"Well I'll be fraged. That beats all and some." Burst out Gnee still not quite assimilating the info which just passed her eyes.

"Well, well, now I have seen it all. Reptilian power of persuasion." Remarked Ridmon.

Tamu dropped to the ground and smiled. Strike one to Ki and Nah. This was a truly enlightening experience. Svanis joined him holding Tamu around his waist.

"Something tells me we won't be seeing either Ki or Nah for a while." She stated.

"I think you are right somehow." He agreed

"What do we do now?" She asked.

"We set up camp here and wait to see what transpires."

Tamu gave his orders and a camp quickly took shape, only this time a little surprise would be in store for any intruders who came sniffing around. A force field was activated around the camp in a spherical dome. Nothing could penetrate that security wall. Days past, Wasps tracked Ki and Nah following every move, every action and recorded the same on monitors then relayed it back to Gnee. Tamu meantime took his troops on exploration sorties on foot joined by the girls. They explored, checked plants, geological structures and the lesser seen creatures of the smaller world, insects, birds and grubs. It was an exciting phase of exploration for Gnee. The troops on the other hand were bored so Tamu dressed them in caveman cloths and took them without their Rods only primitive weapons and introduced them into the old world of existence and hunting as the cavemen did. This was a new experience and Tamu insisted the girls joined in. To be reduced to such primitive levels after living in sheltered environments with all facilities on hand kind of brought one down to reality and realise just how spoilt one had become. They hunted, gathered and built shelters, moved on and did it again, always in different locations. One day they stumbled on a large community of cave men in some form of celebration. Tamu called in a Wasp and instructed it to find a large edible creature they could use as a peace offering. An hour later the Wasp asked where to deliver it and Tamu told it just outside the gathering.

Ridmon raced into the crowd shouting and pointing at his stomach and indicating with a hand to his mouth, food. The reaction was electric. The whole crowd followed and sure enough there it was, a huge dead sabre toothed mammal and on top of it some troopers jumping up and down shouting excitedly. Language did not matter, stomach was more important and it did not take long for the carcass to be stripped to its bones and fires roaring roasting the meat. What an experience for the visitors from outer space this reverting down to base primal existence. Up in the Drone Svanis watched and her heart went out to her man. This was for him an adventure of a life time without violence or war something the man was not used to and it showed in his outward reactions to these simple primitive people whose life revolved around day to day survival and constant struggle. She saw Tamu as he was, a happy laughing man full of heart and sensitivity and she smiled though her tears of joy. The iron façade he put up was only to hide the man within and Svanis loved him like never before.

Back in camp the Matabele formed up and Boram took a gamble.

"Sir, we have come to an agreement among ourselves and request you to allow us to live with these people without all our modern weapons or suits. We are highly trained Matabele and will always be and our allegiance is to you, yet we feel we have to live like they do to understand what it's like to be in their shoes. We ask you to please consider our appeal for what it's worth, in the spirit of the Regiment."

Tamu walked between his men and women of the Regiment studying their faces and saw a determination written there.

"OK guys, granted, but on one proviso, when it comes time to move we move, no regrets and no problems. If any of you singles attach yourselves you will have to make a choice, bring your partners and family with or stay behind. The choice will be yours. I ask only one thing, you keep your battle gear close and hidden so if we call to arms you will be ready."

He walked to Gnee and placed an arm around her shoulder, took Zakrose's hand in his and shouted. "Bayete Matabele."

The response was unanimous, "Bayete Enkosi."

It was settled, cavemen they would be until Tamu decided otherwise. And so Ridmon with the Commando, Gnee and Zakrose joined a family of cave persons to live a life of hunter gatherer. Tamu took his Wasps and Drone and left leaving behind his family, the troops and the Reptiles. Svanis held him in her arms feeling his pain.

"I love you Tamu, and this experience has shown me something, you are an amazing man, a warrior yes, but a wonderful husband."

So began a journey into the vastness of space, a Drone with its escort of thirteen Wasps and two people. On the planet with no name Zakrose telepathically contacted Ki and told him what was happening. The Reptile simply answered.

"We will meet again"

Samre and Visni were summoned before Wolf in the Great Hall. They stood before the man with feelings of trepidation in light of the goings on around Planet Ridmon of late. The man seemed to have lost his senses by destroying everything related to his Father. Now what had the evil man conjured up this time?

"So, here stands the famous Samre and his wife, commanders of the Regiment. The last Matabele Regiment of my Father's legacy. Well, unashamedly I have to be the bearer of bad news and therefore must insist on both of your resignations as I am disbanding the Regiment once and for all."

Wolf stood up and walked around the couple smiling enjoying the moment and the final nail in his Father's memory.

"Do I have your resignations or not?" He shouted.

"No ways. We will not be party to your vengeful destruction of your Father's memory and besides, who gives you the right to take the law into your own hands when this action has to be censored by your brothers and sisters before any major changes occur here on this planet." Replied Samre.

Wolf burst out laughing and took to his throne, flopped down regarding the two before him. His patience was running thin so did the unexpected. He telepathically destroyed Visni where she stood. The woman uttered no sound, just collapsed in a heap at Samre's feet. Samre looked down into Visni's blank dead stare and anger welled up in him, real deep festering anger. Wolf's hysterical laughter echoing in his ears Samre went into attack mode and lunged. He never reached Wolf, but was suspended above the ground in a telekinetic grip.

"Ha! Do you think for one moment I would be caught off guard? Knowing your reputation I was prepared and now my dear Samre you are going to rue the day you attempted to attack me. Let me see what I will do with you to make your life a terrible second by second nightmare until I see fit to end it." Mocked Wolf.

Samre was powerless to move so did the only thing he could. Began his meditation and braced himself projecting his Chi, pulsating it around his body. Wolf took his time and Samre was subjected to hideous mind torture over and over again. It took a long while before Wolf got bored and ended Samre's suffering with a slow gradual crushing of the man's brain. The pain was beyond human endurance yet somehow Samre uttered no murmur, but passed on as a true Matabele soldier. Wolf screamed in disgust, frustrated by his failure to make Samre scream or beg for mercy. He sat on his throne for long minutes gazing at the two bodies on the floor and was about to stand when he was wrenched up into the air and held paralyzed. Protector Friend emerged into the room descended to the floor next the two bodies and teleported them to the cemetery in the dark forest where a Wasp buried them in the ground. Proctor Friend turned his attention to Wolf suspended in the air.

"You, I take from you all your powers, all the good things your beloved Father bestowed upon you and leave you to your fate, to your drug induced world with a warning, you will pay by your brothers hand for what you did this day."

Wolf fell to the floor with a thump, his brain fuzzy and confused. He needed a fix and quick. Just then Nina and Miteke walked in and stood confounded by Protector Friend's presence.

"Nina, your husband has committed a double murder of two special people for no reason other than out of spite and vindictiveness. I have taken from him all his powers and now leave him to destroy himself and my advice to you is to remove yourself from Planet Ridmon with your son and put this evil man out of your life." He advised.

Nina turned about and fled in tears while Protector Friend returned to his own domain leaving Wolf still sprawled on the floor giggling like a crazy person. Miteke silently observed his Father and cursed the man vowing to one day to pay him back for the times he had beaten Nina and himself in his drug crazed state of mind. He too exited the Great Hall in search of his mother and felt a deep sense of loss for Samre who had been his mentor for so many of his growing years. Miteke found his mother sobbing her eyes out and gently took her into his arms.

"We must get out of here, let's take Protector Friends advice and go." He suggested.

Nina took his face in her hands and smiled through her tears and answered.

"I can't my dear son, I know your father is a monster now and I am his wife and will always be and can't change that. I have to stay by his side no matter what."

"Mom, I think you are making a mistake but, as my mother I will stay by your side to protect you from that monster and if he hurts you again I will kill him."

"Hush my son, that is foolish talk, you know your Father is far too strong for you and in his anger will kill you just as easily as he killed Samre." She warned.

Miteke remained silent but, in his mind he made a mental note and knew the one person who would stand by him with more than a fighting chance and that was Uncle Ridmon. There was also Uncle Tamu. Miteke walked out of the crystal city up to the heights and sat on one of the benches there and wept.

FINALE

TWELVE

Tamu left his brother and sisters on a planet with no name and voyaged into empty space going nowhere, just going. They jumped from Galaxy to Galaxy neither searching nor settling, charting many solar systems with life and peoples all preserved in the data base with in the Drone and Wasps. Time passed and Svanis longed to see her people once again. So Tamu set course back to Eureka. It took many years to reach Eureka and both Tamu and Svanis had aged over those years. Hovering above the Jaqmuz people's settlement. Svanis beamed down and was greeted with great remorse. Zud had passed on long ago. She did not linger so asked Tamu to take her away. He instructed Echo to return to Ridmon. Their entry into Ridmon's space was greeted with joy by Drones and Wasps alike. It had been a long and lonely voyage and both Svanis and Tamu were weary so teleported down to the platform and a kiosk. Tamu already in his fifties ordered Ridmon beer for two and sat sipping when a small contingent of non-Regiment uniformed men approached

"Identification." One demanded.

Tamu looked at Svanis then stood up.

"Why do you ask for identification?" Asked Tamu.

"Just give me your Identities and stop fragin around."

"This is my identification shit head." Tamu teleported the individual up onto the heights.

The rest of his crew backed off sending a signal to somewhere and all of a sudden a mob of armed men appeared. Tamu took Svanis by the elbow and stood her up holding her close creating a force field.

"Be careful men your lives are hanging on a thin thread so I advise you to stand down."

"Frag you man, you are under arrest, come peacefully or we will kill you." Ordered their man in charge.

"Young man, you are a fool and very stupid one at that and I would like to teach you a lesson in manners, but I will leave that to one of my commanding officers."

"What the frag do you know about any commanding officer?" The man questioned.

The next moment the man was smashed to the ground unconscious. Tamu teleported the rest of those men deep into the dark forest. Ezos walked forward and embraced Tamu.

"Good to see you, after all this time Boss."

"Ezos my old friend, it's been too long and many travels and my wife and I are tired. We are only looking for a place to live out the rest of our lives quietly."

"Not here Boss, Wolf is crazy, his brain is screwed and he controls everything around here with spies and mercenary thugs."

Tamu placed a hand on his shoulder. "Ezos, you have been a good solid soldier and I want you and Samre to come with me and I will take you to somewhere amazing to finish out your lives in peace."

Ezos bowed his head. "Samre and Visni were killed by Wolf for refusing to hand in their resignations."

Tamu was shocked and took a few moments to digest the sad news then asking Ezos to sit tight and wait for him. He entered the Great Hall shielding Svanis and himself in a force field. There sitting on a throne of all things was Wolf dressed like a prima Dona. On seeing them he giggled like a little girl.

"So the prodigal son has returned with his creature wife, how fitting."

"Hello arsehole, I see you have been misbehaving yourself here on Ridmon. What is it? Taking drugs again?"

"Frag you Tamu. What do you want here?"

Holding Svanis hand Tamu generated a massive power field between them then said.

"Wolf, you have stepped over the line here on Ridmon, to everything our parents stood for."

"Frag you, what do you know, you mother fragin half cast. I have destroyed my Father's legacy, his Matabele Regiment, all his tree dwellings and training camps. You think I did not know I was left out of Thanu's little surprise gift it gave you four and there would not be a reaction from me. So I waited until you left Cartone on one of your voyages and personally executed your General Samre and his wife, but before I did, I made them suffer. Must say, the man was a tough son of a bitch. The biggest joke of it all,

Protector Friend took away all my powers." The man burst into hysterical uncontrollable laughter his drug crazed mind withdrawing into a world of its own.

Wolf never knew what hit him. He simply disappeared onto a distant planet and became food for some really nasty plants not before his fuzzy brain woke up to where he was and powerless to do anything about it.

Somewhere out in the universe both Gnee and Zakrose felt the passing of Wolf and they cried knowing it was Tamu who put the man out of his drug crazed existence. The girls were happy with kids of their own. Zakrose married one of the troop's officers and bore three children. Ki and Nah lived in the forests and only occasionally met Zakrose. On Cartone Mis and Zi had long passed away and so many others of that era. Tamu and Svanis rejoined Ezos at a kiosk.

"Boss, it's not the same here anymore. The Regiment is finished everywhere and does not exist thanks to Wolf. The one thing he could not do was to control the Wasps and Drones."

"How is Utah your wife?" Asked Tamu.

"She is great, we have four sons and three grandchildren." He smiled.

"Congratulations."

Tamu stood in thought then gave Ezos a task to do.

"I want you to recall your Generals and any Matabele who want to rejoin the force here on Ridmon and I have as of now, declared martial law. Those that do come do so in full uniform and assemble in my Father's old training camp and wait."

Tamu teleported into the great hall and took Wolf's throne and sent it smashing down to the forest floor below. Just then Nina entered the great hall. She looked terrible and bore the marks of physical abuse on her face, skinny with dark rings under her eyes. Tamu's heart went out to her knowing how she must have suffered. She walked in a daze not recognizing Tamu until he took her in his arms, gently lifted her up and teleported to the heights. Sitting there with her she broke down and sobbed her heart out. Svanis appeared and Tamu asked her to look after Nina while he made things right on Ridmon. Next he entered the War Room, switched on every console there and broadcast a message across the planet.

"People of Ridmon this is to advise you that your planet is under martial law as of now. Your former leader has been deposed and disposed of. I want to see official representatives from the three cities in the Great Hall within the next hour and don't be under any illusions."

Contacting Echo he asked. "Would you mind going to Cartone and take Ted with you and check on the status of the Regiment there and the Reptiles. If there are troops still active as we left them, bring them in to Ridmon, but hold them in Ted till I give the word."

The Wasp wasted no time and jumped through a portal with Ted to Cartone. Ezos was busy. He contacted known members of the Matabele he could trust and the response he received was unanimous. Word spread like wild fire and they came in from everywhere on Planet Ridmon in full Battle dress secretly to the pre-arranged place in the forest not far from the city and waited. In the meantime, delegates from the three cities had already arrived and sat facing Tamu in the Great Hall. Svanis teleported in with Nina and stood behind Tamu.

"Gentlemen, Ladies. I return to Planet Ridmon to find a nest of hooligans and thugs running the show here and on top of it all, my drug crazed brother, who by his own admittance has ruined this planets reputation, her morale and her armed forces and personally killing two of my top generals. This kind of behavior is not acceptable and nor will it be tolerated. From today, things change."

One of the delegates jumped up and shouted,

"Who are you to play god, you and those creatures out there in space?"

Tamu telepathically read the man's mind, and then sent a message to Ezos to move in.

"So Mr. Vuz, I take it you run a very lucrative import and export business here on Ridmon courtesy of Wolf Enterprises for the sole purpose of drug trafficking and prostitution. You also have a band of thugs to protect your interests here on planet Ridmon now there is no Regiment to stop you. How convenient I must say and how bad for you especially seeing what damage you have done to so many lives throughout the collective planets."

"Frag you, without your so called army you are nothing, and so as you know, my thugs are on their way now and should be here at this moment." Vuz gloated.

A bunch of heavily armed mercenaries strolled into the great Hall and ambled up to Vuz who laughed saying,

"What now fragen shit head?"

Tamu smiled.

"You must be a real dumb frager to think this little show of force will prove anything and to think I am so stupid to be intimidated by these thugs. I suggest you look behind you." Tamu cautioned.

"Ha, Ha, come off it, that's an old trick. What do you take me for?" Smirked Vuz.

Tamu clamped the man in a telekinetic grip, raised him off the ground and swirled him around so he could see over the heads of his thugs. Standing there were over a thousand Matabele in full battle dress. From the shock on Vuz's face the thugs spun around and came face to face with their worst nightmare. The next moment Ted beamed in a Commando of three hundred mixed Matabele and Reptiles to stand behind Svanis. The remainder of the delegates froze in their seats.

"Now Mr. Vuz, I am going to play god and pass judgment on you and your thugs here who are responsible for, beatings, extortion, rape and murder all on your orders. So, I am going to be sporting. I am going to allow you your weapons because where you're going you will need them. To keep you company, your counterparts on Karagan, Wamzu and Cartone. The beauty of being telepathic is you can't hide any secrets from me."

With that Tamu sent the entire syndicate through portals onto the very same planet Wolf was deposited on. Just before the portals closed gunfire could be heard. Turning to the rest of the delegation he said.

"Now my friends let's see who else. Svanis you may do the honors."

She read each and every members mind and found two persons, a woman and a male.

"Pedophiles and child abusers." Was all she said? They too disappeared.

"Ezos." Commanded Tamu, "Form them up."

Ezos shouted a command and all Matabele formed up in ranks. Tamu walked up and down between the ranks then came to stand in front of them with hands to his sides and bowed.

"Friends, it has been awhile and arriving here to see and hear the news angered me. What displeased me most of all was the person behind all this, my brother. I can't tell you all how happy I am to see there is still some left who hold true. Probably most of you have families and are quite settled out of Regimental life and for me it is an honor to see you standing here today. Thank you."

He paused for a moment then addressed the Reptiles directly.

"Who is your leader at this moment?"

"We have no leader, we wait for Ki son of Zi." Came the reply.

Tamu formed the reptiles in the front line told them to take their helmets off. Opened a portal onto the planet with no name and their standing looking very surprised was Ki with Nah and two teenage children. When the Reptile troops saw him they hissed loudly and saluted.

"Ki son of Zi, we have been waiting for your return to take your father's seat as leader of our race. Our people need your leadership and if you don't return you know what will happen, there will be a blood bath and many will die until a champion is found and we have come very far since Reptilia to revert back to barbaric ways."

Tamu stepped through and confronted Ki with the Reptiles close on his heels.

"Hello old friend, it's been too many years."

Ki just stood there staring his mind working. "OK human, only because my people need me."

He turned to the teenagers, hissed some orders. The two scampered off and reappeared minutes later with Ki and Nah's battle uniforms. The Reptiles walked back into the Great Hall accompanied by their Leader and his family. Tamu did not give them time to think before they found themselves back on Cartone. What a triumphant welcome Ki received from his people.

Back on Planet Ridmon, Tamu began a massive routing out campaign in all the cities and weeded out the most undesirables and for the first time in the planets history was a penal colony established on Reptilia for criminal incarceration. A Police force made up of ex Regiment members supported by a judicial system came into being on planet Ridmon. By the time all these arrangements were completed all the surrounding planets knew Tamu was back and dishing out retribution. Echo was sent on a fact finding mission on the planet with no name to make an assessment of the planets condition. He reported back two months later and advised Tamu there were some massive pressures building up underground all over the place and he recommended getting everyone out of there within a year. A year later he and Svanis stepped through a portal into Zakrose's village bringing with them Nina and her grown up son Miteke.

Zakrose and Gnee were on their knees grinding wild wheat kernels to flour and chatting between themselves and completely unaware of four black clad figures behind until a child screamed. Zakrose was on her feet in a flash and turned around, Gnee following on her heels. One can imagine the reaction of the people on seeing those figures in their village. Spears and rocks rained down on the figures only to bounce off harmlessly. Zakrose shouted and raised her arms calling for control. Then stepped closer, hands on hips saying.

"Well, well, if it's not brother Tamu. What brings you to this part of the world?"

"Nice to see you to, keeping busy I see. Hello Gnee!" He acknowledged.

"What did you do to Wolf?" She angrily protested.

"Dear Gnee, I won't blame you for being angry, but please hear me out and let me explain."

"This better be good otherwise you are persona non grata forever." She blurted out.

The villagers had gathered around curious to see who these four strangely dressed people were.

"When we were on Thanu and mother gave to us that amazing information and technology, we did not know Wolf was excluded. Mother knew something we did not and apparently foresaw what Wolf would become and refused to pass that privilege on to him. He figured it out anyway and started to go bad, really bad and got into drugs again. He destroyed anything Dad had built up, the Matabele were disbanded not before he first killed Samre and Visni, destroyed the whole tree top villages and walkways, started to allow crime to operate on Ridmon with vicious thugs who killed, raped and brutally bullied the citizens of Ridmon. He was getting so bad he was having delusions of grandeur, dressing like some Roman Caesar and even had a throne erected in the Great Hall. His mind was fried by the drugs and no way to fix it this time. It was so bad even his powers were taken from him, by Protector Friend. He then began to abuse Nina and beat her up many times and even Miteke here who was trying to protect Nina. When I confronted him he was already half dead and one or two more K24's would have killed him. There was no chance for him so I sent him off Ridmon to another planet where he died, followed by all his nasty followers."

"Couldn't you have just locked him up somewhere and let him die from his drugs?" Asked Gnee.

Tamu shook his head. "No my sweet Gnee, his time was up."

Zakrose looked at him and enquired. "Where have you been all this time if not on Ridmon or Cartone?"

"We have been so far into this universe, seen so many Galaxies with solar systems inhabited with intelligent life forms, some so far advanced it's unbelievable. We travelled for years and years with our one Drone and thirteen Wasps collecting data, making new friends and discovering things too fantastic to explain here. We visited Protector Friend's realm and believe me that's way, way surreal. So we did not know what was going on with Ridmon or Cartone." Svanis answered.

Just then a hunting party arrived back laden with spoils from a hunt, Ridmon with all one hundred troopers with a number of locals. Seeing Tamu and Svanis they froze. Tamu turned to face them.

"Relax guys, carry on." With that the men rushed forward to deposit their burdens and returned to listen.

"Well everyone, I guess there is no need to mention agreements. But I will say I want all of you to bring your families forward. I would love to see how this village has developed since my last visit. So please, don't be shy."

Slowly with a deep sense of foreboding they did what Tamu had requested and brought their families forward. Young men and women, teenagers, young children and babies. The Troopers themselves showed their age and Zakrose stood there with three young teenage kids next to her husband. Gnee with Boram and two teenage daughters. He walked among them smiling recognizing how these people had managed to survive in this post Cretaceous era against some formidable odds with sheer primitive ingenuity and collective co-operation.

"I think I have to congratulate all of you and bow in respect. We did not intend to be away for so long, time just seemed to get away from us. I am really filled with admiration for you lot and have to say, amazing guys. But sadly there is a catch. I can't in all honesty leave you here when I know this planet is in for a major structural change and none of you will survive. Therefore I am taking you all out and this includes the locals in this village. By the way, Ki and Nah and their two kids are on Cartone already." He advised.

"Where will you take us Tamu? We have lived here for years and adapted to a life style of hunter gatherer and I don't think our local family will be able to adjust to Cartone or Ridmon." Asked Zakrose.

Tamu was silent for a while understanding the essence of what Zakrose was implying. He needed time to think about it so replied.

"OK Sis, lets sleep on it and I will give you an answer soon. In the meantime, come we are here so what about a bit of fresh roasted game meat and I bring the Beer, what do you say?"

"You're on, and by the way my husband's name is Danwas."

A portal opened and Echo shot through and beamed down crates of Ridmon beer.

"Hang around Echo and get Ted in here. I want to beam these people up and out of here by morning."

"Yes Boss 10/4."

Tamu shook his head and smiled. Echo was something else and he knew one day he would give him his freedom, but until that day he would enjoy interacting with this amazing creature. Darkness set in and with it the bon fires, the smell of roasting meat and the beers. Laughter echoed all around. Tamu felt the tremors deep down in the planet and cautioned Echo and Ted. People were up and dancing, clapping hands and having a ball when Ted beamed them up into its self and jumped with Echo through a portal just as the ground under the village erupted in molten rock and belching smoke. All the people of the village including Zakrose and Gnee were in a state of induced sleep and did not know what was going down. Ted scanned their new home on a planet called Tarnag, satisfied beamed his package down complete with all shelters and their contents and deposited them exactly as originally placed then shielded everything under a domed force field. Ted hung in the sky just above the sleeping people and continued scanning, checking and analyzing. Zakrose was the first to awake and sitting up was a bit stumped to find herself on bear ground. She jumped up and looked around, everyone was there, but something definitely had changed. She shook Gnee awake and others slowly stood up and knew straight away, they definitely were in another environment.

"Geez Sis, Tamu did it. He put us somewhere. That somewhere is any bodies guess. Something else, there's a force field sheltering us and I wonder why." Commented Gnee.

"Means there are some nasty things here and until we figure it out, the force field will remain. It also means we can come and go through it, but nothing else. Now that's a cool piece of technology. Three cheers for Tamu. Right' let's get with the program and organize ourselves."

Echo checked on the settlement then jumped with Ted to Cartone where Tamu and Svanis waited.

"Transfer successful Boss"

"Thanks you two, appreciated."

Turning to Svanis he stated. "Nina and her Son are in good hands now and will be well looked after."

Cartone was completely changed. The city of Spes was a tribute to a well-designed and innovative planning scheme. In short, she was beautiful and romantic well laid out with thought and perspective. Someone had the foresight to enlarge the river flowing through her ending in a large lake at its end which then cascaded down a waterfall and continued on its journey. Lit at night with lights over the surrounding board walks, Tamu walked with Svanis holding her hand and found a bench to sit on watching the flickering patterns from the lights reflecting across the darkened water.

"My husband, has it ever concerned you we have never had children." Asked Svanis snuggling into him.

"The thought had crossed my mind many times sweet Svanis. Yet our life has been so full of many things and to bring a child into that situation would not have been fair." He commented.

"It is not too late Husband if you want, we can still have a little Tamu or a little Svanis." She remarked.

"Would you like that, would you stop the wondering to bear a child after all we have seen and been through in our life. Could you find peace and tranquility settled in one place?"

"Yes my husband, my body tells me it is time to produce off spring and it yearns for it. I am much younger than you so there are no unforeseen complications."

Tamu was silent for long moments then answered.

"On one condition, you bear our child on Tarnag."

"It is agreed." She replied.

A delegation of a combined theological assembly from planets Vimusi, Trafodj, Karagan, Cartone and Wamzu gathered at a symposium on Karagan in the Great Chamber. The subject of deliberation was centered on the moral principles of scientific recreation and manipulation as opposed to conscientious sacred belief. Many representatives of various denominations were present each with their own interpretations of philosophies regarding spiritual matters. All however, were in unison with one dominating factor. The right of any one person or persons to not interfere in the natural processes of evolution and progression of life and how such an interference went against the natural cosmic order of things. The consensus reached was unanimous. A single appointed representative was nominated to take up their case in the annual United Federation of Planets congress to be officiated on Cartone at the end of the month.

Invitations were sent out to representative high ranking government officials. The Tourist Town much enlarged over the years now boasted a large conference center which would be the venue for the symposium. An all in one complex, ideal with accommodation and catering requirements for visiting delegates and their support staff. Cartone mounted a major cleanup operation throughout the city and surrounding areas in preparation. Shops, restaurants and Cafés stocked up ready to cater for the extra demand. The Regiment geared itself for the task of policing and protection for duties assigning specific tasks to different groups from up in the Way Station, to shuttle transfer, down to VIP body guards on the ground and security personnel at every point of the Town's commercial areas. An air of anticipation hung in the air. These type of conferences brought big bucks into the municipal coffers for ongoing project financing.

On the appointed day, by unified planetary calendar scale, the second day of the third month of Itra, 75 years post Mundus, and delegations began arriving at the Way Station and shuttled directly down to the Conference Center. All day shuttles came and went until all invited guests had arrived and accommodated. Huge Monitors flashed bulletins across their screens of announcements, schedules and time tables in various languages. That evening a full banquette was held to welcome all participants and afterwards treated to a show put on by a local Cartone Theater group followed by music and dancing. The subsequent few days were dedicated to formulating unilateral co-operation through trade agreements, development financing and military expenditure. The proposed redrafting of planetary policy, pertaining to legal matters, and to the introduction of proposed legislation covering a number of issues affecting the group of planets as a whole. Having concluded major agendas the floor was given to issues pertaining to individual planets and agendas. For two days delegates put forward recommendations of various topics, one was Tourism. Then the Theological Assembly had the floor and immediately launched into rhetoric of religious ethics and morals till eventually the Speaker of the Conference politely told them to get to the point.

"The point is that Thanu and Ridmon play god with everybody here and defile the sacredness of our Spiritual temples with their Reptiles and those devilish creations used for destruction and war. We would like to see this assembly gathered here to impose restrictions on those two planets and prohibit them from entry anywhere." Demanded the delegate.

There was a mixture of laughter and verbal mobbing and one delegate jumped up and shouted,

"Are you fragen stupid? Who has saved your butt on more than one occasion from total extinction? Planet Ridmon. Whose creatures of war, as you put it, protect our planets? Planet Ridmon. How many times have you asked for assistance in matters none related to war and it has been given, free of charge I might add."

A delegate from Trafodj stood up.

"We still bear the scars from those Reptiles the last time they were on our planet. Every time they are deployed they are a menace and kill innocent people."

Suddenly hovering in the center of the Conference Hall hung the figure of Tamu. Silence fell on the assembled delegations.

"It's amazing, the dogs that bite the hands that feed them. So the theologians will have me banned from everywhere, remove my protection that has been operating since my Father's time until now without a single thank you, not to me, but those entities out there who scan day in and day out weary of any danger. You, Trafodj, rejected our offer of help thinking you were strong enough to withstand an attack. Shame on you, it cost the lives of fifteen thousand troops and an untold number of civilians before we arrived to save your miserable souls. You, Vimusi, sent Federation Battleships into G48 Major for one purpose only, to plunder and destroy. Well you paid dearly for that assumption didn't you. As for the rest of you ungrateful blow hards I have just one thing to say, from now on you fight your own battles. I withdraw my protection from all planets with exception of Karagan, with whom we have a standing agreement, Cartone for the time being and Planet Ridmon. From now on people, protection will cost you a fee, no more freebies and I get to dictate terms. You want protection, pay."

"That's extortion." Someone shouted.

"Suit yourselves. But I tell you this. Out there in space some really aggressive life forms exist who would find you delicious morsels and believe me, your technology is primitive compared to theirs. I rest my case quoting one recent example, the Aliens."

Tamu's image vanished leaving the Assembly silent and contemplating the extent of what Tamu's words implicated. The Speaker adjourned proceedings and left the Hall making straight for the Cartone Security Council offices and broke the news. Almost immediately the Council dispatched a shuttle to the Regimental Barracks with their chief negotiator on board. Tamu met him in the main lounge. Gur-ug studied Tamu for a moment, and then spoke.

"We have not had the pleasure of meeting before, but I have heard all about you and what you have done for this planet and for the lives of many of our peoples here. We have always assumed, and I guess that was our mistake, protection would continue to be in place. Coming back here after a long absence surprised us. Our dealings with your brother were tantamount to tyranny and he imposed heavy taxes on us for a protection he could not command. He threatened to disband the Regiment here, but they told him to go to hell. We on Cartone are concerned you will carry on where he left off and we are very uncomfortable with that thought."

"The Regiment and the Reptilians have been here for nearly thirty years and in all that time financed themselves not taking a single Credit from Cartone which has become a very wealthy planet built off the backs of the Regiment and Reptiles. If my brother taxed you heavily then all I can say is I did not know about it. You have your own system of taxation here, whereby all business, the sale of goods is liable for payment of taxes. We are not living thirty five years ago and I still have to feed my troops, cloth and equip them, pay their wages and pensions. Give them medical aid and compensate them for loss of income due to an arm or a leg, missing for example. I have to support the families of the deceased and all this takes finance. Where am I supposed to obtain this finance when all the time you and the other planets have been receiving free protection? We can't do this anymore, so are obliged to charge you just like any other business for services rendered. Operation with a Regiment divided across planets places a heavier burden on us financially and not worth the logistic headaches any more. We can't function as in the past, so it's now a case of take it or leave it, your choice."

"I will take the matter up with my council and refer back to you." Confirmed the man.

"Don't take too long about it, we are preparing to evacuate Cartone with the Reptiles soon if our needs are not met satisfactorily." Declared Tamu.

Gur-ug boarded his shuttle and reported to his council. After hearing his account of the discussion with Tamu, excused him saying they would deliberate and have an answer in the morning of the next day. The Council still smarting from Wolf's abusive actions influenced their decision by five votes to three against Tamu's continued protection. Gur-ug was shocked at the news and personally apologized to Tamu who shook his hand and smiled wishing him well.

Tamu walked up to Ki, bowed as was the custom to a Reptile leader and told him the facts in no uncertain terms. Ki sat listening and made up his mind. Going back to Reptilia was no option, returning to the Planet with no name was out of the question and that left only one alternative, Tamu.

"What do you suggest?" He asked Tamu.

"There is a planet, a wild place, the kind your people like, which I believe will more than meet their needs with many edible species of plants and animal, some very large ones. There is just one condition, some of us humans are already there and more will follow from the Regiment who are volunteers, the others will be sent back to Ridmon."

"Who is on the planet now?" KI questioned.

"Zakrose, Ridmon and Gnee and the people from their village on the planet with no name." Tamu answered.

Ki smiled thinking back over the years how the girls had always kept in touch with him telepathically. Yes, this would be a good thing for his people to live like he had lived for many years as a hunter gatherer.

"It is agreed we will relocate to this new world." Ki answered.

"Be ready in a two weeks' time with the birds, any and all their eggs and food for at least a few days and battle dress, everything."

Ki nodded and Tamu teleported out to base and assembled his troops.

"Friends, we have been given our marching orders by the Cartone Security Council so we have to evacuate as soon as possible our entire base. However, you have two options so decide on. First one is to relocate to Ridmon where Ezos waits for you and the second is on a voluntary basis only, to the Planet Tarnag where some of your fellow Matabele live, have families and are hunter gatherers now. I would prefer it if those who volunteer do so with a mate because on the planet there are no available single men or women. Take your time and discuss it between yourselves"

Two hours later the Regiment formed up together for the last time and an officer marched into Tamu's office informing him they were ready to report their decision. He walked out and stood to attention while two Officers came forward.

The first officer, a young man in his twenties saluted and stated.

"We are two thousand troops who have decided to volunteer. We are all young and have mates and also young families. We will look forward to a new life's adventure with you Sir."

Tamu thanked him and turned to the other elderly officer and smiled.

"Three thousands of us who have families and many due for retirement opt out for Ridmon. We trust you will understand and we take this opportunity to thank you and it has been a pleasure to serve with you here on Cartone and in battle." Remarked the officer.

"No Sir, the pleasure is mine and I wish you all the best in the world. Ezos will be your commanding officer and will be responsible for any financial matters relating to pay, retirement and compensations. He will even assist in securing for you homes and those of you who wish to resign may do so and all benefits apply. Now before we close this gathering I would like everyone to assist in packing this place up lock stock and barrel. Once we have done that, it will be fall down time on planet Ridmon."

The regiment roared so loud it could be heard in Cartone. It took a mere four days to pack up, crate up and ship out onto Planet Ridmon. Ezos was waiting to receive the new arrivals and opened the barracks to them with a weeklong fall down. Tamu stayed behind on Cartone to completely destroy the barracks, all infrastructures around it and the cave base with its abandoned space ship no longer used for manufacturing, then jumped through a portal for Tarnag with Svanis. Tarnag was at its equivalent Cro-Magnon age on earth roughly fifty thousand years behind Karagan. Wild life was abundant and more than enough room to accommodate the reptiles and Tamu's people on so many continents of choice to locate to and never come across each other for hundreds of years based on primitive migration patterns. Echo and all the other Wasps scouted for a suitable settlement for the Reptiles and found the most ideal place on a small continent in the middle of an ocean breaming with wild life and offering an abundant edible plant species. At the end of the week the Drone's beamed the Reptiles up with everything they owned and jumped into Tarnag depositing the Reptiles on their new home. Ki was impressed, this time Tamu had come through for his people and was grateful indeed.

Tamu and Svanis with two thousand volunteers landed next to Zakrose's village with all their equipment and a good supply of Ridmon beer and whiskey. The force field was still activated so Tamu extended it outwards and so began a new life for a people who pioneered into space and found settlement. Svanis became pregnant and both Zakrose and Gnee were hovering around her making sure all was well. There was still one critical aspect facing Tamu and that was the Drone's and Wasps. They had more than earned their freedom. The question was where would they find a place to go? Tamu consulted Protector Friend on the matter who advised him to send them to him when he was good and ready. With that knowledge he felt relieved, but he was going to regret losing Echo. Community life settled down and hunting groups would go out while armed gathering parties would roam the forests and hills for berries, wild wheat and fruits. Zakrose, Gnee and Tamu, like their father before them had to learn which plants were edible and which were not. Unlike their father they had one huge advantage, their phenomenal psychic abilities.

One day when Tamu was scouting a far distant range of mountains on foot he came across a stone dwelling so well concealed he almost missed it. The construction was simple enough; rocks piled one on top of the other staggered to form a double wall with an arched doorway and a wooden door partially open and one closed wooden window. His instinct warned him someone or something was inside so he sat on a rock and waited. He could have easily have used his psychic sight, but this was more of a challenge and who knows what would emerge. He did not have to wait long when a man and a child emerged out of the house. They looked like the Aliens with distinct differences. These had a nose and a mouth and hair, no talons on their fingers, but dressed in skins. Something else he noticed, primitives didn't walk around with elaborate finely crafted swords and daggers. It was the child that first spotted Tamu sitting there and almost jumped out of its skin. The older one reacted immediately and drew his sword at the same time pushing the child behind him. At almost the same moment the door of the house slammed shut and secured from the inside.

Tamu smiled and showed his upturned palms indicating no weapons. The creature watched his every move and Tamu probed his mind. In the house was a female and a young female child and he sensed the fear there. Tamu spoke.

"Hello, I hope I didn't frighten you. My name is Tamu and I come from another planet with my friends and family and we live way over there in our village. I was walking past here when I saw your home and it made me wonder who you were as this continent is not supposed to have any intelligent life forms on it. Then I got to put the pieces together and realized you have been stranded here."

"How do you know my speech?" The man creature asked.

"That's difficult to explain so let's just say I can read your mind. I mean you no harm honestly." He replied.

"I don't believe you."

"OK then how about this. Your name is Xiyo and come from the planet Xivzan. You were in a battleship when attacked by your arch enemies the Phinaski. You, lucky fellow escaped simply because you are a prince and your crew got you out in the only survival module available down to here in time before their ship was destroyed. You have a woman in the house called Viya and a little daughter."

Xiyo lowered his sword and stood boggling at Tamu in disbelief. What a terrible experience it was for him losing his ship like that. Viya was the daughter of the ship's captain and he had begged him to take her with. One thing led to another and two children. Later, here sits this creature telling him information only someone with great skill could do.

"Where are you from?" He asked.

"I am from a planet called Ridmon many, many light years away. My father was from planet Earth so I am a half human being." Tamu answered.

"I have never heard of those planets or of human being before." He stated.

"Viya, why don't you come out here with your daughter, I won't hurt you." He called.

Gingerly the door opened and a timid female emerged with the daughter to stand next to Xiyo. This prince had to come way down the ladder to survive here and it must have been a struggle for the female who seems was used to rough times whereas he lived like a king on his planet. Tamu had to take his hat off to her with respect. The kids were curious now an apparent danger had turned out to be a friendly creature.

"Would you kids like to meet other kids your own age just over there in my village?" Asked Tamu.

Both looked at their parents who looked at Tamu with suspicion so Tamu telepathically sent an image into their brains in real time in motion. There in the village kids were dancing around and playing games, chasing each other and laughter, excited laughter. Xiyo blinked, how was it possible? Tamu teleported pregnant Svanis in to him and that really startled the creatures. She smiled and asked in her sweetest voice sitting down on Tamu's lap and resting her head on his chest.

"Who are your friends Tamu?"

"This is Xiyo and she is Viya, the boy is Duga and the little one is Yimi." He answered.

Svanis shifted herself to a more comfortable position saying.

"Pregnant, you know how it is."

That seemed to strike a chord in Viya's brain because her face split into a big smile. White teeth, not fangs, but regular teeth. She cautiously came forward and touched Svanis stomach feeling the baby move inside and her eyes sparkled. That was it, Tamu was in. After exchanging more words Tamu convinced the family to come back with them to the settlement. He asked them to hold hands and close their eyes. Next thing they were inside the village standing holding hands with eyes closed.

"Xiyo, you can open your eyes now." Whispered Svanis.

Slowly they all opened their eyes to a gathered curious people.

"Folks this is Xiyo and his mate Viya and kids Duga and little Yimi." Everyone waved and smiled. Tamu continued.

"They were stranded here when their enemies destroyed the ship they were on and a survival pod landed them here. Xiyo is a prince by the way, too bad, because down here everyone's equal."

Zakrose stepped forward and took Viya's hand and led her to a fire place and handed her a piece of cooked meat which was devoured without touching sides. Zakrose turned to Tamu and telepathically said,

"They are starving, living on a diet of plants is not their body's form of sustenance and they are meat eaters like us."

So Tamu ushered the group to the fire, sat them down and fed the adults with meat and the young ones the only thing they knew, berries and plants and something they did not in all their lives imagine, delicious flour and berry patties. It took time, but eventually Xiyo brought his family into the village to live. Tamu took Xiyo under his wing and showed him how to survive, how to hunt with a bow and arrows. This really impressed Xiyo and went on every hunt there was eager to test himself and in the process became really proficient. One day Tamu and Xiyo were on a hunt tracking a set of prints of a large carnivore when the message came through to him.

"Come now, Svanis went into labor."

Tamu grabbed Xiyo and teleported into the village and to his hut, but Gnee blocked the doorway shaking her finger. Tamu started pacing up and down like a typical expectant father. Viya emerged carrying a large bowl to fetch hot water and said to him.

"It's a boy and a girl and another girl."

Tamu's knees went weak, triplets. He sat down sweating until Viya emerged once again and told him it was alright to go in. The man bounded through the doorway and there on the bed was Svanis cradling two babies in both arms and Gnee with the third. He was beside himself and kissed her forehead. Gnee handed him the third baby and everyone left leaving this new family to themselves. For days Tamu hovered around a little out of place not knowing exactly what to do so Zakrose kicked him out and told him to go hunting or something. The babies needed milk and Svanis was not producing enough. Then Gnee remembered on Cartone there were Eland antelopes whose milk was rich in protein. Before she could say anything Echo butted in.

"We will bring a few cows and a bull Eland here. Just prepare a place for them."

Gnee blinked uttering, "Well I never, go for it Echo, bring the whole heard."

"10/4 Gnee."

Zakrose wasted no time. She had a coral built with a makeshift lean too and lots of grass she ordered the men to gather. Echo satisfied all was ready jumped onto Cartone with Ted the Drone and stole a whole herd returning to the village and deposited his charge into their coral. Gnee dashed in with a bowl and milked one of the females then filtered the milk through a cloth, poured the milk into beer bottles with makeshift teats on each and success, babies were fed at regular intervals. The women in the community took turns feeding them. Tamu returned a few days later with the hunters laden with spoils of game, furs for processing and edible plants. You can imagine Tamu's face when he spotted the Eland, then it hit him, milk for the babies. Handing the food over to the women he went to see Svanis. She was beaming. Mother Hood had made such a positive impact on her she was a changed woman and when Tamu came into the room her eyes said it all.

Weeks elapsed into months and a year passed. Xiyo and Viya were part of the family now, accepted and functioned as one. One day Tamu while watching Xiyo's kids had a brain wave. Why not take them to their home. He discussed it with Zakrose and Gnee and they agreed. So Tamu tapped into Xiyo's brain and extracted all the information lodged inside and found the answer to where Xivzan was. He relayed the information to the Wasps who took off leap frogging portals until arriving and relaying a message.

"Occupation by forces other than type recognized."

Tamu received the Message. He relayed back,

"Keep position, will bring in the full forces."

He mobilized the entire Wasp and Drone force, pulled out of Planet Ridmon all the Regiment, called Ki and asked him if he was up to it, he agreed and Tamu passed recognition images into the Reptiles and birds, bordered his own troops and from everywhere came in the most amazing army ever assembled together on route to a planet to free it from a tyrant oppressive invader. Xiyo sat with Tamu in Echo and his brain reeled, this he had never in all his born days imagined was possible. This man Tamu was a terrible avenger yet a man of unexpected sensitivity.

Tamu's force broke into Xivzan air space and dived into an attack of well-orchestrated and with deadly precision of destruction clearing out all enemy air targets everywhere across the planet. This time the Wasps and Drones were given full license to kill. Ground troops swarmed onto the planet at different locations across the globe and went ballistic. The speed and massive strike capability smashed the opposition crushing them into oblivion. Xiyo watched this dance of death and shuddered. Never before had Wasps and ground forces worked in such operational unity with brutal effectiveness using the portals to maximum devastating consequence. The Reptiles cavalry screamed into opposition strongholds and stomach churning results were left behind. This was Armageddon and an occupation force was completely and totally exterminated. On the fourteenth day Xiyo was beamed down with Viya and their kids to an awaiting Royal greeting. The King and his wife greeted their son with open arms, some small talk then Xiyo introduced Tamu.

"This human has been a friend and taught me so many things and looked after me and Viya and our two children as part as their own family. We owe them more than we could ever repay and I as prince of Xivzan grant them the highest honor possible, the Brotherhood of Xivzan. Tamu pulled his troops out sending them back. Echo remained while Tamu said goodbye with promises to return to visit then raced back in Echo to Tarnag and his family. There were a lot of stories around the camp fires those next few weeks recounting the battles. Thus ended a period in their lives with rewarding consequence. The success of their mission spread on Planet Ridmon and many young men and women enlisted. The Reptilians rejoiced, it was a battle to beat all battles and they reveled in their success. Ki sat and brooded. Tamu did not forget his friends and expected his troops to give the same commitment as the Reptiles by fighting with them side by side. This last battle was a tribute to the unity of the Regiments forces and KI realized this was the secret of their success. Wasps, Humans and Reptiles as one. He sighed, one day he and Tamu would be no more and fall into legend only to be told in stories to children of a time past.

Svanis and the three kids now two years old were sitting in the late afternoon sun enjoying its warmth when Gnee came up to her and sat down. After a while she asked.

"Don't you miss your people at all?"

Svanis sat quietly for a moment then answered.

"Yes I do, but then I remind myself to look at what I have got and the transition from a little cat girl to the wife of Tamu, I have to say I have been a very lucky girl and now look at me, a mother of triplets."

Gnee laughed. "Svanis, I think Tamu is a very lucky man, give him hell babe."

"No Gnee, he is my husband and I will not be foolish enough to jeopardize that for nothing."

Gnee waited until Svanis was fast asleep then instructed Echo to take then to Eureka. Svanis awoke to find herself in Echo.

"Echo." She asked.

"Yes, Svanis."

"What are we doing here?"

"Boss wanted it." The reply.

Just then Tamu materialized into Echo.

Three little bodies decided to wake and start bellowing, food, we want food and please change our nappies, because we pissed ourselves. Tamu did his thing and changed nappies, plugged the kids into bottles and Echo incinerated the offending smelly nappies. Svanis sat watching her husband performing his duties and smiled. Tamu beamed Svanis down with the kids for the last time, allowing Svanis to see her people again. A few months later Nature took them all out and changed the evolution of Eureka forever. Svanis became the sole survivor of her Jaqmuz race.

It was one thing to play god in a godless universe and not suffer the consequences of ones actions somewhere along the line. Trafodj fell foul once again to the Aliens who invaded in force to crush an enemy who continually undermined their integrity. They came in with guns blazing and literally destroyed Trafodj then returned back to their planet satisfied for a job well done. Trafodj was completely and utterly broken with remnants of survivors all over the planet trying to make out some understanding of the whole thing. The Great Trafodj Empire had fallen with its tail between its legs and no one came to help. Karagan was the first to hear of the news and she mustered relief teams and sent them to Trafodj to give whatever assistance she could. Thanu who had been silent for a long time finally came out of her shell and did what she should have done years ago, mobilized herself on an impressive scale. Battle Ships from Thanu arrived in Trafodj and beamed down masses of relief workers all over the planet. This was Thanu at its best, saving lives. Thanu's Drones hung in Trafodj orbits protecting and deploying ground teams in search and rescue. It took two years to bring some form of stability to Trafodj.

Far away from it all, way out in deep space the Wasp Echo Jumped on to Planet Ridmon. Tamu, Zakrose, Ridmon and Gnee stood in the dark forest and paid homage to their parents buried there. The cemetery was overgrown with vegetation from neglect. The trio cleaned up and soon the cemetery looked respectable again. The girls collected flowers and placed them on the graves then stood back satisfied knowing one day they too would come to rest there. Planet Ridmon was bustling again with the dominating dictatorship of the Wolf era gone. Tamu and the girls entered the Great Hall in their skin clothing and caused quite a stir. Going to the center bar Tamu ordered three beers. The barman looked at him and said,

"You got money?"

Tamu smiled and answered, "I don't need money here, but since you insist." He reached into his skins and pulled out an uncut diamond small enough to have supplied beers for whoever was in the Hall at the time.

"Now frag face, line them up."

The barman gulped and did what he was told. The next moment an individual came over, sized Tamu and the girls up and down and asked.

"Excuse me Sir and Ladies, you are obviously tourists here on our planet. Are you looking for accommodation, a good time and something else? I can provide all your needs and wants."

"Sleaze bag." Is all Gnee said stepping forward and grabbing a handful of crutch and squeezing hard? The man almost feinted begging her to let him go.

"You listen you fragen frag, you don't know who you are messing with so I suggest you get the frag out of here like now." And she released her grip. The man bolted. She turned to Tamu saying.

"What's this world coming to?"

He hugged her to him and kissed her forehead and answered,

"Sweet Gnee, our time is fast passing and we are from another period in time. We can only visit, but never be part of this new world. Call it evolutionary change, but change must it be. Our children are the future and sadly not where we are going. When we see our children's children we will know our time has come and must bow out gracefully."

Gnee leaned her head on his chest and pulled Zakrose to her.

"We have known so much, done so much and achieved so much our children will never know about or reach the same heights in the future. Come lets go home, we don't belong here anymore."

Just then an aged man came up to them and extended his hand.

"Hello Boss."

Ezos stood there with a smile on his face, hand extended and Tamu shook it and embraced the man.

"My dear friend, it's good to see you again. Tell us what's happening with you and your family?"

"Things are not the same anymore here on Planet Ridmon, nobody is interested in the old ways and people like me and you are pushed aside and forgotten. Perhaps they are embarrassed, perhaps not, but one thing is for certain, they are not motivated by the same drive we have and that is what now more so that ever begins to ail me. My wife and I are ready to leave this place and go anywhere less advanced, less modern and less corrupting to the soul." Replied Ezos.

Tamu teleported Ezos wife into the Great Hall.

"Ezos, you are a man after my own heart and I am not going to leave you here, not with your talents and achievements to be ridiculed by modern thinking. Come with me, bring your kids whatever, but come with me to a place where you will find inner peace." Suggested Tamu.

Ezos studied Tamu's face and knew then what his answer would be so tuning to his wife to say something she silenced him with a finger to his lips and nodded her head. Tamu returned to the Tatran village with Ezos, Utah, four sons and their wives and six grandchildren to a warm and genuine greeting from everyone. Ezos became a hunter and what a hunter, keeping the community going with fresh meat as and when required. The years passed and gradually a legacy passed with it. Planet Ridmon was a bustling metropolis and so many changes to her peoples and cities. The old Matabele no longer existed and memories of them faded into the past. It was time and Protector Friend appeared to Tamu.

"You must release the Wasps and Drones to my keeping."

Tamu answered." Yes, but for one, Echo. I want him to carry us back to Ridmon, to the cemetery there and bury us with our parents."

"Agreed, it will be done."

So ended a part of History so profound that nobody in the modern world would ever believe it. Too farfetched and beyond comprehension. Yet on one planet way out in space, lived the remnants of a once great nation going through the throws of evolution just like everyone else, well not quite. Svanis had long passed away and so also Tamu's three children who had married with children of their own. On his death bed Ki called for Tamu who came to see his old friend and sit with him holding his hand until the light faded from his eyes. Tamu, a very old man nearly two hundred years of age sat with Zakrose, Ridmon and Gnee in silence. They had outlived their husbands and wife's and their children, and almost the children of their children who were now into their senior years.

"We are very close to our time brother and sisters, let us go to Planet Ridmon for the last time and prepare ourselves."

Echo beamed them up and jumped into Planet Ridmon. There the entire Drone and Wasp fleet were poised with Protector Friend. Tamu, Zakrose, Ridmon and Gnee knelt down next to their parents graves. Tamu kissed the girls and smiled.

"We have had a full life my sisters and achieved many things to be proud of, so our conscious cannot be faulted. I have only one regret, and that is Wolf. Come, let us link arms and give thanks to the Holy One for allowing us to live lives so full and so rich in diversity. Praises to the Lord and thanks."

They linked arms for the last time and moments later passed away into eternity. Echo buried their bodies with tender loving care. For the first time in his life, knew sadness. Hovering above, he said his farewells.

"You will be missed Boss, see you on the flip side."

"And around and about the throne were four beasts full of eyes before and behind. The first beast was like a lion, the second beast like a calf and the third beast had the face of a man, and the fourth beast was like a flying eagle. And the four beasts had each of them six wings above them full of eyes within, and day and night ceased not to praise Holy, Holy, Holy Lord God Almighty which was, and is, and is to come."

Revelations 4:7-8

The End

CPSIA information can be obtained
at www.ICGtesting.com
Printed in the USA
BVHW031750190819
556236BV00001B/4/P